MW01107431

THE POWER PACK

a novel by

ROSALAND A. REID

authorHOUSE™

1663 Liberty Drive, Suite 200
Bloomington, Indiana 47403
(800) 839-8640
www.AuthorHouse.com

This book is a work of fiction. People, places, events, and situations are the product of the author's imagination. Any resemblance to actual persons, living or dead, or historical events, is purely coincidental.

© 2006 Rosaland A. Reid. All rights reserved.

No part of this book may be reproduced, stored in a retrieval system, or transmitted by any means without the written permission of the author.

First published by AuthorHouse 4/18/2006

ISBN: 1-4259-0650-8 (sc)
ISBN: 1-4259-2751-3 (dj)

Printed in the United States of America
Bloomington, Indiana

This book is printed on acid-free paper.

Dedicated to those who dare to dream……

To the two loves in my life, Autumn Faith and Adam Garth. May God Bless your path with peace, love and soul….

one

A young Roberto Semione looks out the window of his dormitory. He has just finished making love to his girlfriend of the last nine years Diana. As Bobby gazes contently across the yard, he notices the long black limo as it pulls up. The sight of such an important looking vehicle catches his attention, as well as the attention of the other students, as they wonder who is arriving on campus in such an auspicious manner.

Bobby is standing in the window naked as the limo pulls to a stop in front of the building that is exactly across from his room. He reaches for his jeans and pulls them over his superb naked torso. Bobby is quite the Latin lover. As Bobby starred through the window he watched as the tall commanding figure of a Black man emerged from the car. He stood straight and tall with a very powerful and prominent appearance. He was dressed in all black and his clothes were very expensive. Demonstrating a great deal of taste.

As Bobby watched curiously it suddenly dawned on him exactly who this gentleman was. It was General Prescott A. Reid. What was he doing on the campus of the New York police academy? Why were his men scouring the dorm? Who or what were they looking for? Bobby was extremely intrigued at this point and wondered what was going on?

After determining that the room was safe, the team starts to unload and place the baggage in the room. Bobby is carefully watching everything that is happening across the street. The general is still standing outside of the vehicle barking orders as his men complete their assigned task of placing the luggage inside the room. Then she emerges. She is absolutely the most beautiful girl he has ever laid eyes on. Who is she? How is she connected to General Reid? Bobby is completely mesmerized by her beauty, her grace and her body. He notices her beautiful brown skin, her long flowing hair, her curvy legs, and her round supple ass as she stepped out of the vehicle. Wow!!

After totally emerging from the car, she turns her head and casually glances in his direction. She has the face of an angel. Deep commanding eyes. Who is this woman? She smiles in his direction, as though smiling at him, with a smile that lit up the world.

There was no way she could have seen him. He was up three stories in his window out of her immediate line of vision, yet her smile indicated to him that she knew he was there, watching, waiting and wanting to know her name.

She entered the dorm as the General followed. Bobby watched for couple of minutes hoping that she would come back out or that he might catch another glimpse of her. Whoever she was, she was certainly attractive and very provocative. No doubt about it, he would definitely find out who she was. "Hey what are you looking at?" Diana asked as she situated her body on the bed in a manner that invited him to come and please her, as only he could. "Some one just checked into the dorm across the street and get this; they came in a limo with a military escort to inspect the premises before hand". "You know who that is don't you?" Diana asked. "No who is it?" Bobby responded ignorantly. "Bobby, where is your head? That's the General's daughter. You know General Prescott Reid. His daughter is joining the academy; she is a candidate for officer training. They have been preparing for her all week; didn't you read the notice on the bulletin board?" "I guess I missed that." Bobby replied flippantly as he turned his attention away from the window and back to the invitingly naked woman that was waiting for him in his bed. The sight of the General's daughter had aroused his manly nature and fortunately for Diana she was about to capitalize on it in a big, hot and hard way.

Bobby made passionate love to Diana that afternoon that left her breathless and exhaustedly satisfied. All he could do was think about this mystery woman's beautiful smile. Who was she? What was her name? Why did she turn him on so much? Bobby couldn't believe it!! He was in love!! It struck him like lightening! How could he feel this way about a woman he didn't even know?

Tomorrow he would try to find out about this lovely exotic creature. He would ask around, get some scoop. Do a little digging; after all he was an officer in training and someday he planned to make detective. Somebody would tell him something. Little did he know that it would be five years before he would ever she her again!

two

Bobby had a good life. Too this point there had been nothing missing. Bobby's existence felt complete. There had always been plenty of money so his choices had basically been left up to him. Bobby followed a ethical path overshadowed by his love for hot women, fast cars and fine restaurants and dancing. Before deciding to join the police department, he bought a nice restaurant in the Spanish section of Brooklyn. The previous owner was a close friend of his grandfather's who took ill. The restaurant had a nice family atmosphere and Bobby was shocked one day to find that it was going to close.

He had discovered it on one of his late night rendezvous through the neighborhood and he always liked eating there. The food was down home and good. He asked his Grandfather what he could do to help when he found out the trouble the restaurant was facing. Papa instructed him to go and talk to the owner. After their meeting, Bobby came back to talk to his grandfather about the prospect of buying the place. Papa thought it was a good idea and offered to loan him the money. They certainly didn't want Internal Affairs sniffing around in their business. That wouldn't look right.

Shortly after Bobby moved the whole family into the restaurant facility in Brooklyn and they have been there ever since. Abuelita and Papa were very proud that Bobby had such community loyalty; a sense of commitment to his neighborhood, his Latin American roots and his heritage. Bobby had the kind of loyalty that brings constant rewards from family and friends, always giving back in some way.

After Bobby bought the restaurant he kept the establishment exactly as it was. This was his refuge. He could come here, clear his head, have a decent meal and get to know the people in his neighborhood. He kept a nice bachelor's pad on the top floor, with a terrace that overlooked the skyline. As a uniformed officer on the beat he looked after his district. He patrolled the streets in his neighborhood ever vigilant, always watchful and always there to protect and serve.

The community rallied around Bobby after his graduation from the academy. They were all very excited that he decided to keep the restaurant. Bobby knew that his establishment would provide jobs for the residents or provide meals when a family was experiencing hard times and he never made anyone feel unwelcome. If you needed him he was always there. Everyone in the community was extremely proud when he earned his gold shield.

Bobby moved up the ranks of his department because he truly loved his job and he had a great deal of dedication and respect for his fellow officers. After solving a series of burglaries, drug related crimes and murders that were plaguing the neighborhood, Bobby was promoted to detective. This is the move that placed him in homicide and moved him to the one five in Manhattan.

Bobby received his second promotion on a tip supplied to him from one of his around the way girls. This was a drug deal of unbelievable proportions going down on the border between the Brooklyn and the Manhattan docks. This bust established and ignited the connection between Bobby and the Calderon organization; a connection that would change his life forever.

This drug bust made Detective Semione and thrust him into the limelight. All the major newspapers, local, national and international carried the story of the far reaching impact of the seizure. It was phenomenal in proportions and propelled Bobby and his squad to the attention of General Prescott Reid, the man in charge of all the organized activities surrounding drugs, anti-terrorism, weapons or any threats to the national security.

The N.Y.P.D. at the time was under the leadership of a young up and coming detective, Lt. Arthur Yancy. A strong proud black man. The General had been familiar with the work of the N.Y.P.D. in the past. He was especially impressed with their endless pursuit of the illegal drugs and weapons that were continuously flooding the streets of Harlem, Brooklyn, the Bronx, and Manhattan.

Wall Street was becoming infected with the onslaught of narcotics, hallucinogens and controlled substance abuse. They were trading enormous amounts of both heroine and cocaine on the floor of the New York Stock Exchange along with other drug related commodities. The drugs were flooding the market in epidemic proportions.

The Calderon Cartel, one of the most powerful organizations dealing in the trafficking of narcotics was expanding its market into the U.S. and the General had to stop them. He had been waiting for a long time, gathering his troops and building his allies so he could fight the battle. The drug bust in

Manhattan gave him his in. Now he could install his covert team of highly trained operatives to work in conjunction with the N.Y.P.D. to draw the leader Mr. Calderon himself out into the open.

The General was now in position to supply the N.Y.P.D. with an intelligence specialist (his best kept secret) and to begin the initial groundwork to set up the O.N.S.I.: The Office of National Security Information. What better place than right inside the police department, working with highly skilled, trained and decorated officers and detectives. The General would carefully hand pick his team for this assignment. Only his best operatives would be considered for this extremely clandestine job. He would carefully recruit operatives and personnel that he knew he could trust under any circumstance, no matter what.

The General thought half to himself and half out loud "Of course he would enlist the services of his daughter!" This was the perfect assignment for her. The General had been waiting for years for an opportunity like this to present itself. Timing in his position was everything. He had hoped that he would be in position when the opportunity presented itself and he was. He and his crew were ready. He had been trying to get someone inside the Calderon operation for years, someone to go in undercover and send information out.

This was definitely going to be an extremely dangerous assignment and it would need to be handled in the most discreet manner. If any of his operatives including his own child were caught or killed he would have to disavow any knowledge of their actions and of the operation. He would implement Rosaland as his outside connection, but he definitely needed someone on the inside that could win the trust of Carlos Calderon. He needed someone feeding him enough misinformation so that could take him down.

The President had promised the General all the resources physical, financial and material that were within his power. Now the General would have to call in all favors to get his team inside the N.Y.P.D. He was on the threshold of fulfilling his dream. Imagine what could be accomplished with the joint cooperation between a federal enforcement agency and the talent of the local police department. Nothing like this had ever been done before. Ten years of watching and waiting had finally come to an end. The O.N.S.I.: Office of National Security Information was about to be born.

three

The General sat solemnly, focusing his full attention on the President of the United States. As the President spoke the words echoed in his head. "This man is becoming a growing concern. He is a threat to the national security of our nation. His drug cartel has taken over Central and South America and is threatening to expand into North America, as well as Eastern Europe and Asia. He has people everywhere, in the finance office, in the American legal system, you name it. It's rumored that he owns a couple of Supreme Court Justices, yet to be named. We don't even know who they are but we know that they are constantly supplying him with information about the outcome of our highest courts decisions. He knows just as much as we do, and he gets his information direct. Not through the traditional pipeline."

"He has eyes and ears in the Senate and in Congress keeping him abreast of new laws and legislation that we have passed under the R.I.C.O. statute concerning the penalty and incarceration of known traffickers of narcotics. He is in our banks, he is in our embassy and we have to get him out! By whatever means necessary. This man and his entire organization must be stopped! If he ever accesses our technology base, that is if he hasn't already, we are in deep trouble."

"According to all current information our technology base is still safe but for how long is the question." The President continued his train of thought. "Gentleman let's be perfectly honest this man is a threat with deep pockets. If information of his overwhelming influence would be made public, it would be very uncomfortable for the whole legislative and judicial systems. This man has the money, the power, and the influence, and that is why he is so dangerous. We need to turn up the heat, apply some pressure, press some buttons, and turn some of his friends into enemies, play them against him;

we need to shut down his entire operation and his organization! Now how can we do that? What can we do?" The President paused for effect looking over the rim of his glasses as the lights came on.

The President had just briefed the Joint Chiefs of Staff on the powerful Carlos Calderon. "Mr. Calderon is the most powerful drug lord in Central America. He manufactures and runs drugs on several of the small islands scattered throughout the country. He has old, powerful, and deep-rooted connections in Bolivia, Bogotá, Argentina, Colombia, Guatemala, Peru, Brazil and Belize. The exact location of his distribution centers is unknown but we know that they are somewhere close to the equator and his own personal residence is somewhere housed near Costa Rica..." The President continued flashing an old photograph.

Mr. Calderon was an extremely handsome man, the Latino equivalent of a wealthy American playboy with all the toys. The General starred grudgingly into his eyes, looking at the briefing board that contained hundreds of old pictures of the infamous drug lord. He was a very public figure for a man that deals in the business of drugs. Carlos was so gallant because of the respect that he had garnered in his part of the world and with the American business community. This was not going to be easy. The General contemplated the situation thoroughly. Carlos has ties everywhere.

The General turned his attention back to the President as he continued to speak. "Mr. Calderon has just made a new investment; he just purchased several weapons factories from the Israeli's. This report was just handed to me from the N.S.A., now he has weapons, munitions and explosives. According to this report that includes chemical weapons as well. This is far too much power for one individual to hold". The President shook his head and the Joint Chiefs all looked troubled with this new release of information.

"Mr. President does that include nuclear weapons as well?" The General listened carefully before he finally spoke. "According to this report that is a definite possibility. He has just purchased quite an arsenal". "Do we know the location of these factories?" "No, not as of yet, that information is forthcoming." "Gentlemen, this is a top priority directive. We need to get to work on this".

After the President dismissed the Joint Chiefs, he turned his focus directly to the General. "Pres, what do you have for me?" "Mr. President, our first order of business is to gather some intelligence. We need to answer some of these basic questions. There are far too many "ifs" in a situation of this magnitude. We need facts, and we need them now." The General was deep in thought. "Do you have an operation instituted at this time to accommodate that solution?" The President questioned expectantly.

"My team is being assembled as we speak; I'll have a confirmation in about three hours sir." "Why so long?" The President asked, showing some concern.

"I am hand picking this team, and there are still some candidates that need to be investigated as well as interviewed." The General nodded his head in acknowledgement. "Ok, I will meet you in the oval office in three hours for an update, Pres, this meeting is adjourned."

Three hours later, General Reid entered the inner sanctum of the oval office. The President was more relaxed than at the earlier briefing. He appeared deep in thought as he motioned for the General to sit down. The General took his seat and placed the file that he was carrying on the President's desk. The file was stamped top secret and only he and the President knew that it existed.

"The O.N.S.I. Office of National Security Information, a branch of the National Security Administration. "I have been developing this program for five years. The purpose of which is to gather intelligence on all peoples thought to be a threat to our national security. A special individual who has been specifically trained in intelligence, information systems development, communications, language analysis, personality profiles, psychological profiles, deviant sexual behavior, and information's systems analysis will head the O.N.S.I. This individual has also had academy as well as officer training supplied by the New York police department. She is currently an inspector fourth grade, working in national security systems here at the pentagon. This position I created just for her due to her unique skills and capability." The President listened closely.

"She has an undergraduate degree from Columbia University in business administration. Her Master's is in international trade from Harvard and her PhD. is from M.I.T. Sloan School of Management in computer information systems and economics. She also has a background in astral physics. She will institute and develop the first satellite office of the O.N.S.I.

"You seem to know a lot about this individual". The President looked intrigued. "Yes sir I do after all she is my daughter."

The President sat up in his chair and starred directly at the General, interested in where he was going with this spill. "You have been developing this plan for a while? How long did you say? Five years? It sounds to me more like twenty-five years. Isn't that how old your girls are now?"

"Yes sir." The General acknowledged the President's observation. "Where do you plan to set up the O.N.S.I.?"

"The first office will be contained within the New York City police department, Manhattan north, the one five. Manhattan north is a central location. We have plans to have our latest technology installed there, so it wouldn't look usual or raise suspicion for a federal operation to be conducted from a civilian facility."

"Manhattan north has one of the best detective squads. They deal directly with homicide, narcotics and weapons. Their arrest record is outstanding. Their lead detective just received his second promotion. Some hot shot homeboy. Spanish speaking, with an excellent track record, that always helps." Our experts will update their information systems and we can gain total access to all the world information satellites from there. The location is ideal for the type of operation we need to initiate. It is of the utmost importance that we maintain official government control. We must keep our hands on the operation at all times." The General carefully explained to the president in full detail.

"You know how those hot dogs in New York operate. As soon as the information is accessed those peons will start making all kinds of arrest and bust. We don't need that kind of activity. That would greatly jeopardize our position. Theoretically from this location, once we see and start to track our results we can establish other offices and tie all the information systems together.

All we need is to implement a successful operation in New York and the rest of the world of law enforcement will climb on board." This plan will take about five years to implement successfully. That will give us the time to gain a comparative advantage over Calderon. If he can't gain access to vital information he won't be able to move his product around so freely." Are you sure about this location?" The President second guessed." It's the best location for the set up." The General assured. "What about the rest of the team?" "We will move them in place one by one." "Let's do it." The President gave his final consent. "Consider it already done sir." The General commented as he left the room.

four

Rosaland awoke very early that morning. She was extremely excited about starting her new position. She had hours to spare as she entered the shower wondering what challenges might lay ahead for her today. She wondered if the department would be nice to her or if she would be given the blue code of silence. You can never tell when working with the police, but she was still looking forward to partnering with this unit.

The water was nice and warm as it cascaded down her full breast. For some strange reason she decided to wash her hair while taking her shower. Rosaland must have been very nervous because she never washed her hair on a work day, but she wanted everything to be perfect. What was she doing? Had she lost her mind? She immediately turned off the water and grabbed a towel to try and save what was left of her wet hair. After toweling off her body she grabbed the blow-dryer and began to work on her head. Rosaland's hair was long and thick and it hung past her shoulders. She looked at the bathroom clock to make sure she had enough time to accomplish this task. She wanted to make a good first impression. This was the first time she would be working with detectives and she was coming in the squad as their boss. She knew the detectives would not like that so she had to make a good start.

After taking an hour on her hair she decided to call Doris, her stylist. "Good morning Doris, this is Rosaland. How are you this morning?" Doris responded and Rosaland continued her conversation, pleading. "Doris I need a really big favor, but I will pay you for it!" Doris responded again and then Rosaland continued. "I accidentally wet my hair this morning in the shower and today I start my new job! Can you help me out? I need to be in the office by 9:00. It is now 7:00, what time do you want me in the shop? All I need is blow dry and curl, Doris nothing fancy just straight, but I must be at work on time. If you can't get me out in an hour I'm screwed and my hair looks a mess! Doris have pity on a sister and please help me out!" Rosaland stood quietly waiting for Doris to reply. "O.k. you will!" Rosaland screamed, "I'll meet you there in twenty minutes." Rosaland slammed down the phone and hastily finished dressing. It always took her so long to get dressed, no matter how much in advance she tried to prepare. The General always said she was as slow as molasses.

Being raised by a four star general, everything had its own time. The General never allowed his children to procrastinate or dawdle. Everything had to be done on time and in order, efficiently. When she finished dressing she looked into the mirror to see if she liked what she saw. She didn't. Something wasn't right. Her basic black suit was fine, what was missing? She decided to change her blouse for a white tailored shirt. Now that was better, she thought to herself, should she wear a tie? Why not! She proceeded to go through two or three choices before she finally decided on the right one. She checked the mirror again. This time she was pleased.

Now she needed some sexy stockings to set it off. She searched her stocking drawer until she found just the perfect pair. Shear black mesh with the seam up the back. Now she was right. She glanced at the clock and realized that she had about twenty minutes to get to the salon. She grabbed her briefcase and hurried out the door. She couldn't be late her first day at work. What would her co-workers think? She would never gain their respect. She locked the door behind her and headed to her car.

Rosaland pulled up in front of the salon just as Doris arrived. They greeted each other with their usual hug and kiss. Doris commented on how nice she looked. "I like those stockings; they make your legs look big and sexy. Nice choice! Now what is with that hair?" Doris scowled turning up her nose. "That's why I called you! Please Doris, work your magic. I can't go to work with my hair looking like this!" "Alright princess, calm down and sit here. I'm going to give you something quick and easy. That's all you like anyway." Doris said as she pressed Rosaland's excited body back into her chair.

Doris blow-dried Rosaland's hair and curled it loosely all over, afterwards brushing out the curls, which left her lustrous black hair shining with plenty of body. "Perfect! Doris you are the best!"Rosaland screamed as she jumped up from the chair looked in the mirror and applied her lipstick.

"Just remember me to your father the next time he needs a date." Doris snickered. "Your father is so sexy!" She smiled. "And much too old for you" Rosaland chimed in as she looked at her watch. She had less than twenty-five minutes to get downtown. She decided to take the subway. It would be quicker. "Doris, I'm going to take the train to work. I will pick up my car later." With that Rosaland handed Doris a hundred-dollar bill, gave her a kiss and off she went to the subway station.

The train arrived just as she entered the turnstile. She jumped on, and headed downtown to the station house. She noticed how the men were looking at her as she read her paper on the train. She was definitely paying attention. From all indications, today would be a good day. Rosaland departed from the train at Chambers Street and walked the half a block to Manhattan north. She stopped short in the street to marvel at the size of the old post war precinct. It was a huge building. It scoured the whole block. This was her new territory. It was on her shoulders to put the O.N.S.I. in full operation and she would not be intimidated and she would not fail.

She entered the "house" just as the roll sergeant finished instructing the morning shift of their tour. She waited patiently to get directions to the detective's squad. Once she received her directions she climbed the stairs to the second floor, after walking a little ways she finally saw the detective's unit. Just as she was about to enter, two hot young detectives approached. Rosaland stopped, standing at the top of the stairs, the two men buried deep in conversation started up the steps, when they saw her standing there looking perplexed, they both stopped. Bobby's eyes traveled up from the tip of her shoes to the top of her shapely legs. "I know those legs," he thought to himself as his vision continued to climb up midway to her thigh and then to the hem of her short skirt before focusing on her face.

Detectives' Bobby Semione and Danny Schmidt smiled as they noticed her. Bobby then realized surprisingly, after focusing in on her luscious attributes and trying to keep his voice down "I can't believe it!" He shouted softly "It's her! It's really her!" "Who?" Danny asked questioning Bobby. Bobby repeated, "It's her. Hot damn! That is the woman I am going to marry!" "What? Marry? You?" Danny was completely puzzled. "Yes, that's her. Wow, how time flies. It has been five years since I last saw her." "You know her?" Danny was curious "No, not really but I can tell you this, and this is strictly between you and me, I fell in love with that woman five years ago when I saw her at the academy, she didn't see me. She doesn't even know who I am, or that I'm alive, but that is my future ex- wife. I'm warning you Danny, stay away from her!!" Bobby threatened jokingly.

Danny laughed. "Sure, sure, Detective Semione anything you say, but know this, it's every man for himself. She is absolutely beautiful, and if she isn't married I will be asking her out." "Don't do it Danny boy, I would hate to have to hurt you". Bobby coughed. The two detectives laughed as they climbed the steps to finally meet this mystery woman face to face.

"Good morning gentlemen, can you tell me where Lt. Yancy's office is?" Rosaland smiled in their direction. Bobby's knees went weak as his heart skipped a beat. Actually it skipped a couple of beats. "This is really her!!!" He thought to himself. Remembering that splendid smile.

"Yes miss, Lt. Yancy's office is on the third floor. You can take the elevator." Bobby pointed in the direction of the elevator. "Thanks" Rosaland said as she walked toward the enclave. The two detectives joined her. When they got to the third floor they all walked to the lieutenant's office. Bobby knocked on the door. Lt. Yancy motioned them in as he finished his phone conversation.

When he hung up he smiled at the lovely lady. "Dr. Reid?" He asked "Yes" Rosaland answered extending her hand. Lt. Yancy stood up and walked over to shake it. "We are very excited to be a part of this new protocol. I was waiting until you and I had a chance to talk before I informed the staff. Actually now that you are here it would be a good idea if you briefed the staff." The Lt. concluded. "That sounds like a plan Lt. when do you want to get started?" Dr. Reid jumped right in. "I need to get all the pertinent information, I have blocked off the rest of the day so we can work."

"Gentleman, don't you have some work to do?" Arthur looked deep into their faces. The two detectives looked at each other after being unofficially dismissed and left the office. Lt. Yancy and Dr. Reid went to work. As the rest of the squad began to arrive they all noticed the Lt. with this beautiful woman busy in his office. "What's going on?" Diana asked as she settled at her desk. "Some new program." Bobby replied. Lt Yancy is going to brief us as soon as he gets all the pertinent information. What ever it is, it must be important. Lou never works with a smile on his face and also he hasn't mentioned it until now but he was definitely expecting Dr. Reid."

"She is a doctor? Why do we need a doctor in the police force?" Diana asked sarcastically. "Is somebody sick?" "She holds a doctorate degree in intelligence" Danny replied. "Oh really. How do you know so much about her?" Diana glanced in Danny's direction. "She looks kind of young to have that much education, don't you think?" "Well some of us do know how to read." Danny responded as he pointed to the memo that was attached to the bulletin board. We will all find out soon."

Dr. Reid and Lieutenant Yancy worked at a steady pace for the rest of the afternoon. After Dr. Reid outlined the O.N.S.I. in full detail. She provided the Lt. with a complete dossier on their target Carlos Calderon. The Lt. was astonished at the amount of information Dr. Reid had compiled on Calderon and the Cartel. After listening completely to her proposed approach Arthur was totally impressed with her knowledge, understanding and line of thinking on the nature of the beast. He knew she would implement the O.N.S.I. in a very detailed manner and he welcomed her aboard.

The next step was to brief his staff to the importance of their cooperation in this program. Everyone could benefit if this program was successful. It could mean a lot of promotions for his detectives as well as raise the visibility of his entire unit. The Lt. could see the long term benefit in becoming a partner with the O.N.S.I.

Also his city; the city of New York could gain some degree of control over the huge amount of narcotics and weapons that were bombarding his streets on a daily basis. The crime rate in his city could really use some adjusting and this just might be the vehicle that could facilitate that process.

Nine out of ten of his unsolved murders were drug related. A lot of crimes could be solved and a lot of bad guys could be put away for a very long time with the implementation of this key initiative. It was foolish to think that all the crimes could be solved but it was time that somebody tried to do something about the mayhem and the madness that defined the streets of New York. Arthur knew that this was his chance. Besides Carlos Calderon was a very powerful and extremely dangerous man who definitely needed to be stopped, shut down. The O.N.S.I. was destined to accomplish great strides in the preservation of the national security and he and his unit needed to be a part of it.

As the detectives returned from their evening cases, they noticed the two still hard at work. Bobby glanced over at Rosaland's legs and he smiled. "Don't even think about it" Danny warned noticing his partner's erratic behavior. "Too late" Bobby replied, "It has already been decided". Bobby settled in to start his final paper work. Usually he would wait until the morning, but this evening he wanted to hang around.

Arthur and Rosaland worked deep into the night. Around 10:00p.m. they finally decided to call it a day. As the two of them left the office Rosaland remembered that she had left her car uptown at Doris's salon. Bobby and Danny left shortly after and noticed the two of them standing in the parking lot talking. That was when Rosaland remembered that her car was not there. "Where is my head?" She questioned herself as Bobby and Danny walked over, listening intently to their conversation. "Is there a problem?" Bobby picked up on her forgetfulness. She had an extreme look of perplexity on her face. "Yes detective I left my car in upper Manhattan. Could you give me a lift uptown?" "Sure," Bobby replied offering his assistance.

Bobby drove her to pick up her car. They rode in complete silence, with him frequently glancing over at her lovely legs. The silence made them both a bit uncomfortable. Finally he commented casually, "You look tired?" giving her his alarming half smile "I am. I didn't think that we would be here so late." She sighed, rubbing her tired calves. Rosaland closed her eyes and rubbed her legs together while they proceeded through traffic. It took less than twenty minutes for them to arrive. "Well thanks detective." She said softly "There's my car," she pointed to the gold Mercedes that sat in Doris's parking lot. As she got into her car, Bobby said seriously

"Call me Bobby and I like those stockings. They make your legs look really sexy." He flashed his radiant smile and then he drove off.

Rosaland smiled to herself all the way home. She felt quite complimented by the detective's attention. Once inside the comfort of her Harlem brownstone, she kicked off her shoes and put her feet up. She had made some great inroads today on the installation of the O.N.S.I. but there was still so much work left to be done. After changing out of her work clothes into something more seductive she poured herself a nice stiff drink. She settled back with her Hennessey on the rocks and planned her next move.

She needed an architect, and an office designer to meet her tomorrow so together they could start to detail plans for a newly renovated office space to accommodate the computers and the satellite links for the O.N.S.I. Rosaland was deep into her planning mode when the phone rang. It was her father, the General.

"Hi Dad! How are you?" She started in. "Fine baby girl, what's going on with you? How was your first day?" The General waited with anticipation. "Everything went well today Dad. They have a very experienced team of detectives.Very impressive. You made a wise decision by choosing their squad." Rosaland forgot to mention how good looking they were.

"Lt. Yancy is an extremely knowledgeable man not bad looking either. Dad tomorrow I'm going to need you to be available to me. I'm preparing to move into the implementation phase of the O.N.S.I. and I'm going to need your assistance on some of my operational plans. Can you come to the city for a day? Also it would be very helpful if I could schedule a staff meeting. I would really like you to be there. Can you make it Dad?" Rosaland begged.

"Anything for you Babe. What time would you like to meet?" The General conceded. "Let's schedule for 1:00. That will give you time to get here" "Is that all princess?" The General was teasing "Yes sir" she pouted. "Well I'll see you tomorrow" he smiled. This is going to be interesting he thought to himself. "Goodnight Dad I love you". With that Rosaland hung up the phone and went to bed.

five

Rosaland worked around the clock for the next few months coordinating the activities necessary to install the O.N.S.I. She needed her father's help to secure a much needed communications contract with COM STAT. COM STAT is a quasi-government corporation, owned partly by the government and partly by private citizens; and of course the General had his hand in that. Some would think that there might be a slight conflict of interest, but he managed to cover it well.

The meeting with COM STAT was scheduled for the next week and Rosaland wanted to have all the necessary information before hand so that she would have time to review, preparing for her presentation. Arthur was amazed at her ability to organize and to accomplish a task of such great magnitude.

She constantly burned the midnight oil, sometimes working as late as 4:00a.m. in the morning from the day before. The O.N.S.I. was an important assignment and a top priority. The proper implementation was imperative. It had to be initiated just right. In areas that concern the national security of our nation nothing could be left to chance.

Carlos Calderon and his growing connections were posing a constant threat and he had to be eliminated. His presence in Central America presented a clear and present danger. It would be absolutely important to gather as much Intel and surveillance information on him as possible. Rosaland was going to ensure her team all the support she could garner. The contract with COM STAT was essential. It was a crucial decision at a highly vulnerable time. This contract could mean the difference in the whole investigation.

Bobby noticed how the unit was beginning to take shape under her direction. He marveled at how such a sexy young woman could be so diligent. Not that he was a male chauvinist but she kept him in a constant state of arousal. He wondered if she knew how stimulating she was. It was extremely difficult for him to work so close to her and remain professional. What kept him in line was that she had no idea he was having these kinds of lewd emotions or indecent thoughts about her.

He passed her in the corridors as she busily converted the third floor into her own personal command central. She and Arthur seemed to have certain chemistry and that made Bobby uncomfortable. He definitely couldn't storm into his boss's office and declare his feelings, or could he? His Lou was a friend as well as a colleague; maybe he could find some way to bring up a conversation about the enchanting Dr. Reid without causing suspicion, or jeopardizing his job.

Her presence on a daily basis was driving him crazy and there was nothing he could do about it. He always found some way to look at her legs or watch her ass as she walked down the hall or he would conveniently manage to get close enough to her to smell her hair without her really noticing. At times she could feel him starring but she was so preoccupied with the development of her division that she hardly noticed anything else, except the task at hand. She had a deadline to meet and she wanted to bring her project in on time and under budget. She wanted to make her father proud.

The President had as promised supplied the O.N.S.I. with a generous budget and even though she was going to spend the money wisely she definitely did not intend to spend it all. Before going to Washington Dr.Reid needed to have the blueprints and the architectural drawings of the new office facility. She determined that Arthur was someone she could count on, someone she could trust, so she decided to make him her new best friend.

"Lt. Yancy, I am going to be meeting with the architects and the office designer on this project before I go to Washington, are you pleased with your current office space?" Arthur was puzzled. "Dr. Reid my office is much too small, why do you ask?" "I ask because, I have a very generous budget and if you are unhappy with your current office space now is the time to speak up. I can write your renovation cost into my project budget."

"You can either have your office enlarged and redecorated or you can open up the third floor and have a new office custom designed to meet your specific needs, it's up to you". "Dr. Reid, that is an awfully generous offer, what do you get in return?" The Lt. inquired flinchingly waiting for her response. "A friend." She proposed sweetly.

"When is your meeting scheduled?" The Lt.was totally there. "In about twenty minutes, they should be arriving shortly." "Do you mind if I sit in?" "No it would be practical for you to talk to them for yourself that way you can make sure that everything will be done to your specifications. Your blue prints will need to be drawn up separately and they can give you a time frame for completion."

"Dr. Reid I don't know what to say" the Lt. shook his head. "Just say yes Lt." "Remember we are all in this together. You me and your sexy detectives." Rosaland made a slip. "Don't tell anybody I said this" Rosaland lowered her voice to a faint whisper "The government is paying!" She laughed as she walked away. Just at that exact moment Bobby was climbing the steps to the Lou's office.

He immediately noticed their laughter. He was beginning to sense that maybe there was something between them but the Lt. didn't give him the time to think. "Bobby what can I do for you?" He asked hurriedly. "Did I interrupt a meeting?" the detective barked back. "Actually Dr. Reid and I just finished. We have another meeting scheduled in about ten minutes. Is this really important or can I get back to you in an hour or so?" "Yes sir I can come back in a hour." and with that Bobby left the office.

Dr. Reid was standing in the door way waiting for the architect and the office designer who had just signed in. Bobby noticed that she was wearing a tight black skirt with sheer black stockings. Her ass was well defined and her legs were shapely and enticing to his eyes. "You look lovely today Dr. Reid". She smiled and tossed her hair "Thank you detective" she said as she moved by him in the hall. Bobby was going to make his move. If there was something going on between her and the Lt. he was going to find out now.

"You know" he looked down at her as if looking through her blouse at her full breast. "I like your ass" he said freshly hoping to get a rise out of her. Dr. Reid smiled as she walked over to meet her team. She tossed her head and said "I know". She wiggled her hips as if to tease him and then she looked back at him and winked.

She proceeded into Arthur's office. The meeting went well with the design team as they sketched out the proposed layout for the new facility. There were certain procedures they needed to investigate in terms of checking the building for any environmental problems or hazards before they could give an accurate time schedule for the renovations. They had to make sure that there would be no E.P.A. violations before they started to tear down walls.

That was always the concern when dealing with old post war buildings. If there were any violations it would delay them in getting the necessary permits to start the construction. Time is of the essence and they had to be accurate in their proposed time frame. They needed to get a copy of the original building plans before they could move forward.

The design team scheduled another meeting with Dr. Reid and Lt. Yancy. Dr. Reid told them of her meeting in Washington and asked if they could meet sooner, they assured her that as soon as they located the old building plans and had time to look them over they would get back to her a.s.a.p. This company had lots of experience with government contracts and they knew the ends and outs. It would make no sense for them to do anything else without knowing the restrictions of the plans. To make Dr. Reid feel better the architect told her that he would go to city planning as soon as he left the station and that he would study the plans overnight. With that the meeting was adjourned.

Lt. Yancy returned to his office and continued his work with his team of detectives. Rosaland decided to call Rachael to see if she was available for dinner. Both of the sisters had been very busy lately and had not spent that much time together. Rosaland wanted to have a drink and chitchat with her "big" sister even though the girls were identical twins. After confirming their dinner date Rosaland signed out and went to meet Rachael while it was still early in the evening.

Rachael Ann Reid was the District Attorney for the city of New York. It was a position that she had worked very hard to get. There had been several qualified candidates and this was the first time that an African American female held this office. After graduating from Harvard Law School with honors, Rachael went to work in the public defenders office. It was a trying job that came with long hours and little pay.

Rachael was constantly trying cases that put her in contact with the scum of the earth. The majority of her case load was drug dealing, petty theft, child support violators and child molesters. She hated the environment but she had to climb the ranks and work her way up.

After three years an opening came up in the prosecutor's office so she applied for that position, which would pay her a little more money but the hours would be just as long. In the prosecutors office she began to build her reputation as she successfully gained conviction after conviction on some of the city's most notorious drug dealers. Rachael was brilliant as a prosecutor and began to make headlines as her conviction rate soared.

The General decided to step in at this point and give her career a hand. She was promoted to head prosecutor for the state of New York. Quite a prestigious position for a twenty-five year old attorney. Rachael's conviction record earned her an invitation to join the all white male graduates from Harvard law at the Harvard Business Club. The fact that they would even conceive of a black female becoming a part of their exclusive family was indeed an honor. Rachael respectfully declined citing her Dad's position with the Pentagon as her reason. This way she would still remain a part of the inner circle without really being a part.

Everybody had a great deal of respect for the General and the powerful position within the government that he held so the invitation was left open.

They decided to offer Rachael an honorary membership. One that she in all good conscious could accept.

Rachael held the record for the most convictions in her office. She was fair and she never compromised her position also she rarely made deals. She was strict and adhered to the letter of the law. If she convicted you of a crime; she was going to put you away for a very long time. In this position she made a lot of enemies but she made just as many powerful and influential friends.

The Judges really had a great deal of respect for her and they enjoyed having her in their courtroom. Rachael was beautiful and very pleasant to look at. She had long thick black hair, a lovely body and long sensuous legs. She and Rosaland were identical twins. They were so much alike that often they would dress exactly the same without even talking to each other. They both dressed by their moods and it was amazing how often they were in the same mood.

They were very close sisters. They shared everything except their men. That was the line they never crossed. They truly loved each other and they were always there for each other. Rosaland was more of the explorer than Rachael. She always found the best restaurants or the new nightclubs. She occasionally drifted into uncharted waters. Tonight they would go scouting for a new place to have some fun. Rachael was a wine drinker. She liked fine wines and champagnes; Rosaland on the other hand liked hard liquor. She drank Hennessey, chocolate martinis and champagne only on special occasions.

The girls had been working hard lately and they needed a night out. It was time to let their hair down. They hadn't had time lately to talk and Rosaland was dying to tell her sister about all the wonderful men that worked for the N.Y.P.D. Rosaland thought Arthur was an extremely attractive man, but there was something about Detective Semione that really set her off.

The sisters met up at Rosaland's brownstone in Harlem. They started with a drink as they talked exceedingly about Rosaland's new position. "Do these detectives know that you are their boss?" "No, not yet. We haven't had the staff orientation and the unit isn't quite set up. I have to wait for the design team to complete their research of the building before we brief them. All they know is that the N.Y.P.D. is going to be a part of this pilot government project."

"How do you think they are going to react?" "Well, I hope they will give me full cooperation, the O.N.S.I. can be beneficial to everyone involved. But I doubt it. They are already giving me looks of "who the hell do you think you are? You know cops; they are not the friendliest people if you are on the other side of that blue wall. But if they work with me, I will work with them.

You know sis, I'm sure it's that way at your job too, one hand washes the other. Are you ready? Let's go have some fun!"

"Do you want to have dinner at the Harvard Club?" Rachael asked her sister. "I am an honorary member, they have really good food there and besides it will give me a chance to show off my "baby" sister. Also it would be a good political move; you will probably make some good connections. The fact that we will be there for dinner everybody will talk to us."

"First they will be fit to be tied that we are even there, second the northern good old boys will have to show their friends that they know a black person and third we are women and we will probably be the only ones there. They never bring their wife's to the club. So what do you say? Dinner at the Harvard Club?" Rachael coaxed "That sounds good to me. Let's go."

As the sisters drove up Eastside Drive Rosaland asked "Should we invite Matthew?" "Let's call him" Rachael replied. Rosaland dialed her brother on her cell phone and got his answering machine, she left him a message about dinner and told him to call her back on her cell phone.

"This is Wednesday night. I wonder where could he be?" just at that moment the phone rang. It was Matthew. He told his sister that he was on call this evening and that he would not be able to have dinner with them. He also asked what their plans for the rest of the evening were and told them that if they felt that they might not be able to make it home safely page him and he would make sure someone came to escort them home.

Matthew was a caring brother. He always looked out for his girls no matter what. They always came first. He knew that they could be wild; actually Rosaland had the wild side but that was because she was spoiled. He wanted his sisters to have a good time especially since the two of them had been working so hard lately. They told him of their plans for dinner and that they would call him again when they decided where they would have drinks. They hung up shortly after they arrived at the Harvard Club.

When they pulled up the valet was there to park the car. "Hello Ms. Reid. How are you this evening?" "I'm fine Michael thank you for asking." Rachael answered. Michael was a cutie and he did a double take as both of the sisters stepped out of the car. "This is my sister Dr. Reid". Michael smiled and extended his hand "It's certainly nice to meet you."

The two sisters entered the Harvard Club and were immediately seated at a really nice table. The word was out that the daughter of one of the Joint Chiefs of Staff was their new honorary member. After the ladies were comfortable the maitre'd took their drink order. Rachael was right. There was nothing but men in the bar and dining areas. Of course all eyes went immediately to them as their drinks were delivered.

Shortly after Andy their waiter came over with menus and recited the specials for the evening. He too did a double take. The ladies just smiled as they placed their orders. This was a nice place and a good choice on Rachael's part. The ladies enjoyed a delicious dinner. They both had a couple more drinks and then they left. Rosaland and Rachael laughed as they waited for Michael to bring their car around. The drinks had made them a little tipsy.

Rachael was still able to drive and they were off to their next destination. The next stop was One's a yuppie hangout in lower Manhattan. Rachael liked this spot. It was always live. The music was blaring and the club was packed. The sisters made their way to the bar and ordered a round of drinks. After looking around through the smoke filled room they finally spotted an empty table. The ladies made their way over to the table and sat down.

Rosaland had one bad habit she smoked. Both Rachael and Matthew hated the fact that Rosaland smoked. Rosaland's defense was that she only smoked when she drank. After tasting her Hennessey she pulled out her cigarettes. "Look Rachael I don't want to hear it let's just have a good time." "O.k. Sis I'll give you a break tonight. Now tell me about these detectives. You have talked about everything but them."

"Not now Rae let's dance." The music was jamming and the men were abundant. As soon as Rosaland finished her drink she headed for the dance floor. Within minutes male dancing bodies surrounded her. Rachael laughed heartily. She knew before the end of the evening that she would have to call Matthew. Matthew knew it as well and had already made arrangement to pick his sisters up.

Rosaland really needed to let her hair down she was under a tremendous amount of pressure and she was going to have fun this evening with Rachael. After a couple of tunes Rosaland went over to get her sister up on the dance floor. Again dancing bodies surrounded them both. They had a really good time. There were men all over them all around them and the sisters loved it. About an hour later the ladies made it back to their table. As soon as they were seated the waitress brought over another round of drinks. "These are from that gentleman at the end of the bar" as the ladies looked in that direction it was Bill Jones.

Bill had a thing for Rosaland for many years since high school.

Actually he intended to marry her. Bill walked over to the girls and gave them both a big hug. "What are you two doing here?" He smiled as he sipped his drink. "Partying!" they answered in unison. "Are you ladies having a nice time?" "Oh yes!" They both nodded their heads as their bodies bounced to the beats. "Rosaland would you like to dance?" "Yes" she answered as she guided him to the dance floor.

Rachael finished her wine spritzer and ordered another one. Rosaland and Bill danced up a storm. After they finished Bill danced with Rachael while Rosaland had another drink. She was definitely on her way to a hang over but for now she was going to enjoy her night out.

The bartender was calling last call when Bill and Rachael finally made it back to the table. The three of them laughed and talked of old times and then they decided to call it a night. "How are you two getting home? You know that you are not driving. Leave your car here and I will take you home you can come back for it in the morning." The ladies decided to go to Rachael's for the night, she lived closer and Bill drove them to midtown. He kissed Rosaland good night; a very passionate goodnight and the sisters went in the house. "Bill is still very much in love with you Roz, what are you going to do about that?" "Nothing" she responded as they undressed and went to bed.

six

The next morning Rosaland woke up with a bad headache. She had definitely had too much to drink. She rose slowly sitting on the side of the bed with her head buried in her hand as the tears rolled down her face. It was 7:00a.m. she walked down the hall to her sister's bedroom and looked in. Rachael was still asleep. Rosaland staggered to the kitchen and made some fresh coffee. Black coffee always helped to revive her after she had too much to drink. She had about an hour to pull herself together before she needed to be at work.

After two cups of hot black coffee she took a shower. Rachael was starting to stir as Rosaland went through her closet trying to find something to wear. She dressed in silence moving sluggishly. After she found a comfortable pair of her sister's shoes she left Rachael a note and off she went to work. Rosaland arrived at the station about fifteen minutes early and went up to Arthur's office to have another cup of coffee. Rosaland was suffering from a severe hangover but if you didn't know her you would never know it.

Detective Semione was the first to arrive for his shift. He came into the break room surprised to see her there so early. She looked really beautiful very professional and extremely sexy. Bobby's resistance was beginning to wear thin but he had to remain professional. "Dr. Reid I'm surprised to see you here so early. Did you sleep here?" He quipped. "No detective I took the train in this morning that is why I am here a few minutes early."

"You look nice this morning Dr. Reid." Bobby continued genuinely trying to show his interest. Rosaland just laughed and shook her head as she walked out the door. "If you only knew" she said half under her breath. "Well then tell me!" He added in a probing manner. "Maybe later Detective right now I have work to do". "I can wait." He called after her. Bobby watched her as she walked away smiling to himself at the way she unintentionally wiggled her ass. He didn't know how long he was going to be able to keep this deception up. He wanted to tell her honestly how sexy she was and how hot she made him; actually he wanted to show her but all she did was work or so he thought.

Little did he know that last night she was out until 4:00a.m partying with her sister and her ex- boyfriend? Bobby didn't even know she had a boyfriend. As a matter of fact he didn't know anything about her personal life at all and he decided that it was time to make some inquiries. Who could fill him in on the General's daughter? They all seemed to be so close and so secretive.

The one thing he had noticed from the months that she had been operating within the force was that her family was very close. Her father had already come to the station at her request. Her sister calls her a least twice a day. Her brother sent her flowers on her first day of work. Bobby wanted to meet them. He knew Rosaland had a sister and a brother and he wanted to get to know them. He still had no idea that she was a twin.

Her father had a very intimidating presence. Whenever the General was in the room he made his presence felt. One can feel the power, the authority and the integrity that he stands for. Bobby thought, after meeting him at the station, "That is definitely a man that I would want on my side. I would hate to go up against him." Everyone seemed to think that way about the General, including his own children.

Bobby decided to not let Dr. Reid off the hook so easily. All she did was work and she had no interaction with any of the detectives other than Lt. Yancy. He walked back to her make shift office to find her resting her head on her desk. She had no idea that he was standing in her doorway. Her eyes were closed. "Excuse me, Dr. Reid," Bobby interrupted as she slowly raised her head, looking him straight in the eyes.

This was the first time she noticed how beautiful his eyes were, she never noticed that they were so hazel and that they were so deep. Bobby had the kind of eyes that a girl could easily fall in love with. Actually she noticed a series of extremely attractive features that the hunky detective possessed. He was always well dressed at work very professional and he smelled incredible. He always wore the sexiest fragrances. She liked that a lot. Besides the fact that he had a banging body, he looked liked a well seasoned athlete. Bobby was very well built. There was nothing sexier than a well dressed man.

"Yes, detective, may I help you" she said as she lifted her head sluggishly. "Yes, you may" he smiled enticingly. Rosaland noticed that he always gave her that same smile. His smile was sexy and slightly sinister, as if he were up to something. She didn't know whether to trust him or to fear him. "You know detective, what is it with you?" She queried, "What do you mean?" He questioned innocently.

At that moment, a messenger entered her open office door "Are you Dr. Reid?" Rosaland nodded "Yes" in response to the question; "These flowers are for you, would you please sign here". Rosaland signed her name and handed him a tip, the messenger left. The flowers were beautiful. Very lush and exotic. Definitely expensive. She took great delight in receiving them.

Bobby noticed the joy she seemed to exude just from having received flowers, even before she looked at the card to see whom they were from. "Detective, would you excuse me?" Bobby felt like saying no. He didn't want to excuse her, he didn't want to leave. They had just started to talk. How was he ever going to get to know her if she kept putting him off? "Yes, I'll leave. That is certainly a beautiful bouquet, is it from someone special?" He was being nosey. "I don't know who they are from; I haven't had time to look at the card, that's why I would like you to excuse me, please".

Detective Semione stormed out of her office a little pissed off. But he had found out something about her, she liked receiving flowers. Expensive flowers. As he walked away, he thought that tomorrow he would have some flowers delivered to her. Maybe? He turned to notice her reading the card and smiling, she then picked up the phone and dialed a number; she waited awhile and then started her conversation with whoever had sent the flowers.

She laughed and tossed her hair as she talked on the phone. Detective Semione watched her for a long time. He liked looking at her. He observed that she twirled her hair around her finger when she talked on the phone. Bobby was so very much in love with her at this point that, it hurt. As he watched her his nature rose. He had to sit down at his desk so that no one else would notice.

What was he going to do about this woman who kept him in a constant state of arousal? Whenever he was near her his body was always on fire. Bobby knew lots of women, what was it about this one? How come Diana didn't turn him on this way? Why did he want her so badly? What was he going to do about getting her into his bed? That is where he wanted her, right smack in the middle of his bed stuffed to the hilt.

Bobby contemplated, as he poured over the pile of cases that were stacked high on his desk. His concentration was shot. He just couldn't stop thinking about her. He wanted to feel her under him; he wanted to feel himself buried deep inside of her. She was a luscious feminine being and he wanted to thoroughly enjoy her womanhood. The day was going by relatively slow and he was glad when the homicide calls started to roll in so that he could get out of the office.

Bobby was rolling with Wesley today. Both Diana and Danny were out. It was nice to work with someone new for a change. Maybe he could talk about his situation without really giving it up. The day went by in the usual manner. Bobby had several homicides and a drug dealer that he busted two months ago that he needed to finish the paper work on. He also was scheduled to be in court at about 1:00 to testify. This tight schedule would keep his mind off of the voluptuous Dr. Reid.

Suddenly he knew just what to do. After he finished his day he would go have dinner with his mentor, his grandfather Papa. When Wesley and Bobby pulled back into the house Bobby called Papa to make arrangements for the evening. Bobby looked in the direction of Dr. Reid's office to see if she was still around. The floral bouquet that had arrived earlier that morning from who knows who was still on her desk.

Bobby finished up the needed paperwork as he prepared for court. This trial was important. If the D.A. gets a conviction, this would raise his arrest record and he could be in line for another promotion. He would love to make captain before his thirty fifth birthday.

Rachael was in Washington D.C. delivering a lecture on the disparity of the criminal justice system in the United States so she wouldn't be handling this particular case. Her office was well aware of the importance of this conviction, so it was assigned to her protégé Matt Rosenblatt, an extremely capable attorney. Matt was talented and brilliant in the courtroom and the conviction was secured. Bobby emerged from the courtroom victorious. Another drug dealer was off the streets and behind bars. Another one bites the dust.

Bobby definitely wanted to celebrate and his grandfather was just the right person to share this moment with. When Bobby arrived at the restaurant the word was out and the community had arranged a celebration for him. Bobby was a very popular figure in Brooklyn. The neighbors as well as the rest of the community all ate drank and had a great time. After the cleanup Bobby sat down with Papa to talk.

"So, Roberto, what seems to be troubling you?" His grandfather always called him Roberto. That was always the clue when he was serious. "Well, Papa," Bobby smiled tenderly "I am not amazed that you would know that I wanted to talk to you. You can always feel me."

"There is this woman at work and her presence disturbs me." Bobby started in. "What do you mean Roberto, she disturbs you?" "You know, she makes me feel uneasy, nervous, I am always excited when I am near her. My Johnson is always hard whenever she is around." Bobby spoke to Papa very bluntly. "Papa I am deeply in love with her and I don't know why? I don't really even know her, yet I feel that I know her so well, why?" "Roberto, love has no why, love just is. Is it that Diana woman you've been seeing?" Papa quizzed in his broken English "That is what is so strange, Papa it's not her. It's a woman I saw for the first time about five years ago. I fell in love with her then; I am in love with her now. She is absolutely the most beautiful creation on this earth and now she is working in my unit".

"How does she feel about you?" The conversation continued. "She doesn't. She has no idea about me or how I feel about her, all she does is work. She is very professional, a real straight shooter and I know she has a gentleman friend that she sees. As a matter of fact he sent her flowers this morning so it might even be serious between them. I don't know. All I know is that seeing her everyday drives me crazy. She is lovely, smart, funny, very sexy, and the daughter of General Prescott Reid."

Papa was silent for a few minutes then he spoke "So when are you going to tell her how you feel?" Bobby looked at his grandfather and replied, "I don't know I need to get her out of the office but she is always so involved with her work. I am trying to find out about her and her family, you know Papa, so I can determine what the best way for me to approach her is. But I can tell you this, she is the one. Don't ask me how I know, I just know."

Bobby had a serious look on his face as he sipped his wine and Papa knew with no uncertainty that his grandson was in love. "Love takes time Roberto and if she is really the one it will happen naturally. Don't push. Just let it flow in its own time and at its own pace."

"I know you are a very passionate man Roberto. Sometimes that can be good and sometimes not so good. You must always follow your heart, but you cannot be responsible for her heart. You must win her love."

"And if I know you, you will probably do that by being yourself and continuing to do well at your work. If she is the right person, she will notice." Papa was silent for a moment and then he asked, "You really like this woman?" Bobby responded in the affirmative, "Yes, Papa I really do." With that Bobby's grandfather handed him a drink and the two of them toasted to Bobby's success. "Roberto, if you like her, go for her, don't let her get away." Bobby listened contently and stayed with his Papa for the rest of the evening.

seven

For the next six months Rosaland worked feverishly to complete the installation of the O.N.S.I. The construction was well under way and the third floor of the P.D. resembled a war zone. Lt. Yancy and his squad had to work around all the construction workers debris, with their crude remarks and innuendo's towards the female officers but they all seemed to manage.

Dr. Reid and her father had successfully negotiated the contract with COM STAT. The satellite links were being installed, as well as the network computer systems. Things were finally beginning to take shape. Now, she was ready for the final phase, it was time to let the squad know exactly what was going on.

Lt. Yancy called a full staff meeting officially introducing Dr. Reid to the N.Y.P.D. as the director of the newly formed O.N.S.I. All the detectives were present as they listened to the announcement. Bobby didn't know what it was about this woman, on the other hand, yes he did. She was beautiful, intelligent, charming and he felt a deep connection to her in his soul. It was if he had known her all of his life. Bobby knew at that moment, when she took the podium that they were meant to be together forever. She was definitely the one. He watched as her presence filled the room. He noticed how gracefully she took control. She was a chip off the old block. She must have inherited that trait from her father, he observed. It was a natural instinct to her. She had no problems converting the control of the one five into her own hands.

Bobby was happy for once that he had seated himself in the back of the squad room. Dr. Reid opened the meeting and explained the purpose of the O.N.S.I. and why they would be an active partner of the N.Y.P.D. She gave some brief background information on herself and her qualifications for the position, other than the fact that she was the general's daughter, which she made reference to.

She had heard them whispering in the office about her. She knew what they were thinking and now it was her turn to set the record straight. Rosaland handled the crowd of detectives quite expertly. Bobby on the other hand hadn't heard one word that she had said; he was so in awe of her physical attributes. He paid particular attention to her well shaped legs as she stood in front of the squad and how they grew out of her lovely ass that was shaped just right.

As Bobby thought about how it would feel to be inside of her his nature became excited and aroused. His manhood was hard and rigid as he slid down in his seat. Bobby removed his jacket and placed it over his lap; for fear that he would be discovered by the other detectives. He couldn't believe that the thought of some woman any woman could leave him in such a state especially a woman that he had never been with.

As Dr. Reid continued her briefing Bobby smiled to himself. She was doomed and she didn't even know it. There was no way that he would ever let her get away from him. No matter what he had to do she would be his. Bobby was so caught up in thoughts of her capture that he was completely unaware of what had happened.

"Are there any questions?"Dr. Reid asked the detectives as she made her final comments. Bobby was suddenly shocked back into reality. "Yes how will this change affect our chain of command?" The detective interjected. "That's a good question detective. I'll let the lieutenant explain the effects." Dr. Reid turned the podium over to Lt. Yancy. From his position in the back of the room the other detectives couldn't see that Bobby had all eyes on her; but Dr. Reid could feel it.

As the Lt. started his explanation of the change in command and what role Dr. Reid would play in it, all Bobby could do was smile at her. He was definitely flirting. When the meeting was over, Bobby waited to leave the room after her. He watched her movements as he listened to the other detectives discussing what they had just heard. Bobby wanted to watch her ass wiggle as she left the room. He liked the way her bottom fit into her almost too tight skirt. The skirt was tight enough to show the intriguing highlights of her well-shaped form and Bobby was completely smitten.

As she walked in front of him, he shook his head to himself. What was he going to do about her? At this point Bobby didn't know, but the one thing he knew for sure was that he was going to do something, and he was going to do something soon. Dr. Reid noticed his attentions towards her and she decided that she had better do something too.

"Detective, can I do something for you?" Bobby was caught off guard by the directness of her question. "Yes you can, but we can talk about that later." He smiled and walked back to his desk. Rosaland was slightly taken back by his response but strangely enough she was not offended. There was something about this man that left her curious as to exactly what was on his mind, even though in the back of her mind she already had an idea.

After a short coffee break Dr. Reid continued her briefing. She informed the unit that if the O.N.S.I. were successful how many promotions this would create. All the detectives were very enthusiastic about the prospects of the new promotions. Now they understood why there had been so much secrecy surrounding this project! Dr. Reid also announced the promotion of Lt. Arthur Yancy to lieutenant sergeant fourth class. This was the highest rank that an officer could achieve in his division. His next promotion would take him to captain.

Lt. Yancy's detectives had the most outstanding arrest and conviction record in their division. The next announcement was a shock. The Lt. made this announcement. He had known about it for quite some time, Dr. Reid was promoted to lieutenant 2nd grade and she was now their boss. The whole unit was under her control. All the detectives were speechless. How did she warrant such a promotion? Diana and Yvonne just looked at each other. Bobby didn't show any emotion one-way or the other; Danny made a comment to the effect that it must be nice to be the general's daughter.

Danny looked at Bobby who was looking down at the floor. Dr. Reid looked at Arthur in absolute shock. "Are you sure about that, Lt.?" "I have the order right here in my hand." He handed her the paper. "When did you receive that order?" She was quite puzzled. "It came in yesterday, and I decided to make the announcement today, do you have a problem with it?" "Yes sir, as a matter of fact I do". "Then you need to take it up with the inspector, the order was issued by him". "The inspector?" "Yes, the Inspector".

Dr. Reid stood in silence for a minute. The other detectives waited for her to respond. After a minute she composed her self and continued with her meeting. Bobby liked the way she handled what could have been an embarrassing situation.

Diana noticed how Bobby was looking at Dr. Reid. She and Bobby hadn't had much a relationship lately. He was always busy or tied up with something. He didn't call her as much, or stop by and their sex life was practically non-existent. Diana would call or stop by for dinner, but there was something wrong. All the passion seemed to be leaving. When Diana asked him about it, he told her that he was just going through some personal things and he would get back to her. Diana and Bobby had had problems in the past, so she was use to his wandering, but he always came back and she had no reason to believe that this time would be any different.

The meeting continued for approximately another hour. After making sure that everyone understood the brevity of the situation and the absolute importance of capturing Carlos Calderon and shutting down his entire operation Dr. Reid brought the meeting to a close.

There were a lot of questions that the detectives asked before they finally left the office. Bobby went over to congratulate the Lt. and the Dr. on their promotions. He would have hugged her, but remembering the words of his esteemed grandfather he just politely shook her hand.

Lt. Yancy was elated with his step up. He was ecstatic about such an opportunity. He would not let his team down. He was surprised that Dr. Reid wasn't happy about hers. She had worked very hard pulling this division together in the short amount of time that she had to do it. She had done a great job. Not only had the unit been pulled together, he now had a newly remodeled office. He was very grateful for her friendship. She deserved her promotion.

eight

Meanwhile Dr. Reid called the inspector's office. He accepted her call and told her he could talk to her sometime next week and hung up the phone. His reputation as a no non-sense individual still applied. He would get back to her when he had the time.

Rosaland's next call was to the Pentagon, after getting her father on the phone she told him of her promotion and asked him if he had anything to do with it. He assured her that he had not, and she believed him. He congratulated her and told her how proud he was. The General wanted to have dinner with his kids and he also wanted to personally congratulate his daughter on doing such an outstandingly fine job. The General told Rosaland to make her available and he would get back to her. Once Rosaland was convinced that her father had nothing to do with her promotion, she hung up the phone and jumped for joy.

Bobby was in his office when he saw her happily jumping up and down and he immediately came to see what she was so happy about. Rosaland was smiling when he entered her office. He loved her smile. She had a smile that could light up the world and did light up his world everyday. It melted him every time he saw it.

He returned the smile. "What's up?" He was being polite. "I've just received some great news. My Dad didn't have anything to do with my promotion. I earned it on my own! The inspector was impressed with my work! Now all I have to do is win over the rest of the unit!" Bobby watched her as he always did wondering when he was ever going to get her into his bed.

"This must be your lucky day" he smiled back at her. Just then the phone rang. It was Rachael. Dad had just called and they were all happy about her new promotion. He wanted to have dinner tonight. When the general gave an order they all jumped. They would wait until Matthew was off work and they would meet at Princess Carmella's for dinner and drinks.

Bobby remained in her office while she talked to her sister. He was listening to every little detail. He watched her full breast, her delicious legs and her wonderfully shaped ass as she walked around the desk to her fax machine. Again his nature was aroused as he thought about how she would be in bed. Bobby excused himself.

She had been around him for at least six months, probably longer and she never gave him more than a very professional conversation. It had never taken Bobby this long to accomplish anything, especially not a woman. This was absolutely unacceptable as far as he was concerned. Rosaland was head strong and she was not about to give up anything. Nothing. He had no idea if she thought about him or if he was just one of her many detectives. He couldn't figure her out or figure out what was he doing wrong?

He had made enough comments to let her know that he was interested. Every time he tried to talk to her, they were always interrupted or the topic suddenly concerned the business at hand. She was making it extremely difficult for him and all this delay was doing was making him want her more. For the next ten months the unit worked around the clock. Dr. Reid met with her detective's one on one to brief them on their specific duties. Everything appeared to falling into place. The O.N.S.I. would shortly be in full operation.

Dr. Reid planned to run her organization with an iron fist. The detectives all seemed to be letting go of the animosity they harbored because of her new promotion. Their first surveillance information on the Calderon Cartel had been transmitted from the satellite link-up. Dr. Reid carefully studied each document that came through her fax machine. She worked harder now than she did when she was implementing the unit. All her time was spent collecting, analyzing and deciphering data.

The input and output of her computer was her only companion. She constantly burned the midnight oil. This was becoming a very lonely job. She spent more time with her computer than she did with people. During the day she enjoyed the company of her unit. At night she was all alone with her system. Dr. Reid compiled psychological profiles on all the employees in the squad. She needed to know what made them tick. What set them off, and how they reacted under pressure? This information was strictly confidential. They had no idea that it even existed.

She needed to know exactly how these people worked. She needed to draw guidelines as to how these people would react in the field and under pressure. If she had to send them undercover or into the belly of the beast, what would be their tolerance level be? What would be their stress levels?

Their endurance levels? And under interrogation at what point would they crack? How much information would they divulge?

She thoroughly checked out each of the detective's pain ratio quota. They all seemed to have a high tolerance threshold ratio. Arthur had chosen his people well. Dr. Reid thought Detective Semione's profile was very interesting. He could go either way. "Bobby could very easily be a bad boy as well as a good boy" she commented to herself as she studied him intensely. "It was good that he was on their side; otherwise he would be a very formidable adversary." His profile displayed ruthless characteristics; on the other hand he had an enormous amount of loyalty. He could be a very good bad boy. He could be sexually deviant and that probably accounted for his constant innuendos regarding sex. Yes Dr. Reid had heard and noticed all his remarks she just never replied.

She did without a doubt think that the hot detective was the sexiest man she had ever met. That would be her secret. She would never confide that to anyone but she had to admit his profile intrigued her. She ran a complete background check on everyone for her own personal information. She knew as much about the detectives as they knew about themselves. She probably knew a great deal more.

Through her research, she learned of the interoffice relationships that went on in the squad and from the office gossip pool she found out about the long standing relationship that existed between Bobby and Diana. They seemed to have a great deal of history, a long and passionate history and it was all common knowledge. It was a good thing she had stayed away from him. If she got involved with this man he would certainly hurt her. It was all right there on paper. She had it in black and white. She was convinced that she had made a wise decision to ignore his advances.

Bobby was tall, handsome, muscular and exceedingly sexy. He was very physical and Rosaland found herself thinking about him probably just as much as he thought about her. She was terribly attracted to him but she did however have her standards. She would not get involved with anyone that she worked with. Her Father would never be able to understand if she did not complete her assignment and gather the necessary intelligence on Carlos Calderon and his infamous cartel.

She needed to stop thinking about Bobby and get a recent photo of the drug lord. The General hadn't been able to get one in many years. The photo's her father had received from the President were over ten years old. People can and do change a lot in ten years. When you have the type of money that Carlos has access to appearances can be bought. She needed to pinpoint his base of operations and send someone in undercover before he slipped through her fingers.

Dr. Reid still had so much to do; she shouldered a great deal of responsibility. Being the director of the O.N.S.I. was not an easy job, actually it was a whole lot more than she had anticipated, and these newly developing feelings for Detective Semione weren't helping. She had to remain emotionally detached. She couldn't afford to be involved or to get sidetracked, there was too much at stake. She glanced over Bobby's profile one more time before she called it a night. This man excited her in person and on paper. He was intriguing. He seemed so focused, so driven. Rosaland had no doubt believing that he could have anything or anyone he wanted.

On the way home Rosaland stopped to have a drink. She hadn't had a cigarette in about a week and she was dying for a smoke. She sat at the bar and ordered her favorite Hennessey on the rocks. She drank and smoked in silence. Her cigarette tasted really good. After her second drink she was beginning to relax a little. She crossed her legs as she sat comfortably on her bar stool, lost in thought playing with her hair; out of the corner of her eye she caught a glimpse of Bobby and Diana sitting at a booth in the rear of the bar.

They were very engrossed in what appeared to be an intimate conversation. Diana was smiling at something Bobby was whispering in her ear. They were so involved that they didn't even notice that she was there. She finished her drink and left the bar. Before she left she had the bartender take them both a round. As he delivered them, she was out the door. She watched as she left but for some reason that whole scene disturbed the hell out of her. She was really upset.

She hailed a taxi to Harlem. She knew that she had been right about him. She was happy that she had followed her first mind and not responded to any of his snide sexist remarks. Now she knew that whatever she thought she was feeling for this man, she would never give in to it. All that night she thought about the two of them in the bar and how close they appeared to be. All she could envision was the two of them making love all night, and she was right! Bobby and Diana did make love that night like never before. But what she didn't know was that for Bobby that would be the last time. Curiously, what had her more perplexed than anything else was why she cried all night?

nine

The next day it was work as usual. Dr. Reid called another staff meeting. This was to update her team on some new information that she had received on the possible where about of one of Carlos Calderon's' distribution centers. Late last night a surveillance satellite picked up this information and transmitted it to her computer. She filled the detectives in on the latest developments and asked for any questions, completely ignoring both Bobby and Diana.

The detectives working as a team carefully studied the material and started to map out the possibilities of where the camp might be. They came up with several scenarios, which they ran through the simulator. They worked well as a unit and investigated every possibility, leaving no stone uncovered. The team worked relentlessly and didn't stop until they had reached consensus.

Dr. Reid called her father with their results and the General instantly dispatched a fact finding mission to verify her hypothesis. They would have to wait a week or so for the outcome of the mission. Two weeks went by before they finally received a call from the general with a confirmation.

The surveillance paided off! It was confirmed that this location was one of the major distribution centers owned and operated by the Calderon cartel. It was a small operation but central to his South and Central American divisions'. The distribution center would be the first in a long list of assets taken down by the O.N.S.I.

The General dispatched O.N.S.I. Special Forces to handle this extremely difficult task. This would prove to be an enormous victory for the O.N.S.I. General Reid called the house to congratulate his girl. Dr. Reid was ecstatic! This was her first assignment and she had delivered a positive outcome. Even though this was a small operation, it was the first step in bringing the Calderon cartel to its knees.

Lt. Yancy was the first from the squad to congratulate her. She also received a call from the inspector on her perceptiveness. "Believe it or not Dr. Reid I do know what I'm doing" he commented as he hung up the phone. Since seeing Bobby and Diana at the bar Rosaland made sure to stay clear of both Detective Semione and Detective Rousseau. This was hard to do considering that she worked so closely with all of them. She always made sure not to be where he was and especially when there was no one else present.

Bobby noticed her evasiveness but he chalked it up to her being busy. He wanted to mention this to her but quite frankly he didn't know how to bring up the subject so he decided that he would find a way to address this issue with her in a more private setting and at a more appropriate time. All the detectives in the unit knew that if their productivity continued to climb in this in this manner a unit promotion would follow and they decided that a celebration was in order.

Lately Dr. Reid had been kind of standoffish and the detectives didn't quite know what to make of her new attitude. They wanted to include her in their plans but quite frankly didn't know how to invite her. She always appeared to be so preoccupied. As head of the O.N.S. I. they definitely wanted her to be a part of their plans.

Bobby noticed how excited she was about their findings being right whether she showed it or not. He knew that she must be extremely proud of her division's accomplishments. He actually caught a glimpse of her at her desk kicking her feet and musing her hair in victory. That's when he decided to ask her to join them at the party.

"Dr.Reid" she looked up at him smiling; wondering how long he had been there. "Yes detective" she looked straight into his eyes. "On Thursday night we are all going down to Natalie's for some drinks would you like to join us?" "No but thanks for asking" she was very blunt. "Why not? We are celebrating our first victory as the O.N.S.I. You are the head of this unit how are you going to just flat out say no! What's up with that?"

"I'm sorry; I have already made other plans for Thursday." Even though she knew she didn't have to give him a reason she found herself explaining. "My Dad is going to be in town and we are all having dinner that night." "Who are we all?" Bobby asked. "My family and probably a couple of my Dad's friends." "Well you and your family can stop by after dinner. We will wait for you" "I don't know my father can be kind of long winded especially after he's had a couple of drinks. I wouldn't want you all to wait. Maybe another time."

Bobby refused to take no for an answer so he changed his strategy. "O.k. we'll have a good time but we will miss you after all none of this would be happening if it weren't for you." "Have a drink for me detective" she cajoled.

"No Dr. Reid I would rather have a drink with you as a matter of fact we would all like to have a drink with you." "I'm sorry detective but I don't think I can change my plans. Like I said maybe another time. Now detective if you will excuse me I have some work to do." And with that she motioned him out of her office. "Please close the door behind you."

She smiled and turned her attention back to her computer. Bobby left her office very upset. "Who the hell does she thinks she is?" He thought to himself. "I have had just about enough of her and her damn attitude." He stormed out, slamming the door behind him. At that moment Lt. Yancy motioned to the detective, pulling him into his office. Bobby went in.

A few minutes later the Lt. was knocking on her office door. "Bobby tells me that you won't be able to join us on Thursday. You know this means a lot to the others. Isn't there any way you can make it?" Dr. Reid looking shocked looked up "What time are you all going to be there?" "Around 9ish" "I'll see what I can do". She shook her head and smiled. "That would be nice, you should be there" "O.k. I'll try to be there. I'll probably bring my sister." "Fine bring whoever you want. See you then." Rosaland shook her head as she continued her work. Rolling her eyes in the direction of Bobby's office.

All she could think about was Bobby and she definitely did not want to be thinking about him. How was she going to be in a social setting with this man? Even though it had been months since she spotted him in the bar with Diana she couldn't stop thinking about the two of them and how they looked at each other. Never mind she and Rachael would go have a nice time and leave. Maybe Matthew would join them as well. That would be fun.

Rosaland called her brother to see if it would be possible for him to join them. He told her he was on call that night but he would see if someone else could take his rotation. He would get back to her as soon as he knew for sure. Rosaland called Rachael and told her about the party. Rachael was delighted. She had been trying to get Rosaland to tell her about the men that she worked with, but Rosaland always for some reason avoided the subject. Rachael was very interested in why her sister always avoided the subject.

She had never been hesitant before to discuss work or men and Rachael always knew what was going on with her. This would be the perfect opportunity for her to find out. She generally could read her sister's moods, but lately she was confused. Rosaland seemed to be at odds with some aspect of her work, or her life, but Rachael couldn't pinpoint exactly what the problem was.

ten

Thursday seemed to roll around fast. After getting off work, Rosaland went home to get dressed for the evening. Rachael called her sister to see what see was going to wear. Tonight she didn't want to wear the same dress or even the same color. Rachael was feeling particularly sexy and she was going to dress to impress. Rosaland on the other hand wasn't sure how she was feeling. She narrowed it down to black.

"Don't forget Rae we're having dinner with Dad tonight as well" "I know" "And some of his Washington friends" "I know" "So just keep that in mind o.k.?" "Why?" "Do you want these drunken old men all over you?" "Rosaland are you serious? These men are scared to death of Dad. They might look but they definitely will not touch!" The girls laughed. Rosaland knew that Rachael was telling the truth. That helped her to decide what to wear.

She searched her closet for her skimpiest black dress. She chooses a strapless bustier that was short and tight with a deep split up the back. She topped it with a bolero jacket that was outlined with tiny black glass beads. Underneath she decided on a low cut strapless black teddy, one that would put a special emphasis on her cleavage, with shear to the waist French cut stockings with the seam up the back. She found a sexy pair of black sandals with a high heel that wrapped deliciously around her ankle.

She topped off her outfit with the diamond earrings and necklace that her father had given her for her graduation. Her make-up was a little heavier than normal. She put extra emphasis on her eyes. She wanted to look extremely sexy and very appealing. Rosaland liked her hair wild so she just brushed it out and let it flow. The less curls, the better. Her hair had grown since she started her new position and now it hung about five inches below her shoulders.

She grabbed her black Cartier evening bag and three hundred dollars. She added her diamond watch with the matching ring. She was dressed to the nines. None of her coworkers had ever seen her dressed like this before. She wondered if they would even recognize her. She didn't know what they were going to think seeing this side of her. But they had invited her out for a night on the town and she was certainly going to enjoy herself.

When Rachael arrived she was dressed equally as stunning. She wore a strapless red chiffon dress with a flared skirt. Her dress was also short and showed off her beautiful legs. Rachael sported gold glimmer stockings with red high heeled strappy ankle sandals. She too was wearing the diamond necklace and earrings that her father had given her for her graduation. No matter what these girls did they always thought alike. Rachael didn't need a jacket because her dress had long sleeves. Her hair was wrapped up in a very charming French roll with rhinestone accessories and a long bang that was combed to the side and hung sexy past her shoulders. Her make-up was impeccable and her red lipstick matched her nail polish.

The General would be very proud of his beautiful daughters. "You look beautiful Rachael!" Rosaland exclaimed. "So do you!" "If I didn't know you better I would say that you are trying to get a man." "No, sweetie I'm not trying to get a man, but I'm sure some man will try to get me!" They both laughed. This was going to be fun. Rosaland loved to party with her sister. Rachael was her favorite girl.

The two left for the restaurant. The General was already there with his friends when his daughters arrived. He was surprised and pleased to see his girls looking so seductive. He noticed immediately that they were wearing their diamonds. The General ordered champagne to celebrate Rosaland's success. After they toasted they ate a nice healthy dinner.

The General always let his children know how important they were to him. He never let anyone or anything not even his position come before them. His girls had done well. It was his honor to have dinner with them. After dessert and coffee the twins informed their Dad they had to leave. He invited them to stay a while longer and to have another drink or two but they declined. "Dad we have to go to Natalie's to a party for Rosaland. Her office will be really upset if she doesn't show up. After all she is the guest of honor and we are already late, we should have been there an hour ago."

The General excused himself from his other guest and walked the girls outside to hail a cab. Once the taxi pulled up he gave them both a big kiss and off they went. Rosaland and Rachael arrived at Natalie's around eleven. The doorman did a double take, as the ladies entered. The nightclub was jam packed with beautiful people.

Rosaland looked around to see if she could spot any of her co-workers. Rachael excused herself to go to the ladies room. Arthur spotted Rosaland and proceeded over to where she was standing. "Dr. Reid you look wonderful! We are so glad that you made it. We started without you but you can catch up" Rosaland smiled as she started to get into the music. "Lt. I'll be right back; I need to go to the little girl's room". Rosaland walked into the ladies room as Rachael walked into the club a few minutes later.

Arthur spotted her and was speechless. His mouth dropped wide open. This woman was gorgeous! How did she change her clothes so fast? Once the Lt. was able to regain his speech "Dr. Reid?" He questioned. Rachael laughed "No I'm her sister. Rosaland is in the ladies room." Arthur was amazed at the resemblance. "I knew that Dr. Reid had a sister. I didn't know that you were twins." "Identical twins" Rachael corrected him.

At that moment Rosaland came back into the club. "I see that you have met my sister." "Well we haven't been formally introduced." Arthur bowed his head. "Rachael this is my boss, Lt. Arthur Yancy. Lt. Yancy this is my sister, Rachael Anne Reid the District Attorney of our great state." Rosaland said politely making the introductions. Rachael extended her hand and the Lt. kissed it. "It is an extreme pleasure to meet you, Ms. Reid, please allow me to tell you how absolutely lovely you are this evening." Arthur added as he kissed her hand.

Rachael smiled and pulled her hand back. "Thank you, Lt. Arthur. It is indeed my pleasure." "Do you want to dance?" Arthur interjected "Yes I would love to dance." Rachael responded.

"Dr. Reid, the rest of the squad is over there." Arthur pointed to the back bar area. Rosaland saw the rest of the detectives having what appeared to be a great time and walked over to where they were. When she reached the bar she ordered a drink. As she waited for her drink she looked around really enjoying the music as her body bounced and gyrated to the pulsating beats.

Arthur and Rachael were already on the dance floor dancing up a storm. Arthur couldn't remember the last time he danced so much or had so much fun. The Lt. was very much taken with this woman. Bobby noticed them on the dance floor and his heart stopped. He knew that Arthur liked Dr. Reid and now he was convinced. That was the reason she had been avoiding him. She had a thing for the Lt. Bobby felt like punching him. He felt completely betrayed. "This motherfucker" he thought.

At that exact moment Bobby turned away mad only to spot another woman who looked like Dr. Reid at the back bar. He turned back again to the dance floor and then back again to the bar. The Lt. and Rachael were really enjoying each other. You could spot their attraction across the room. Bobby turned back again to the bar. What the hell was going on? At that moment he walked up to the bar. He would get to the bottom of this. As he approached Dr.Reid noticed him immediately. She started to smile as she sipped from her drink. Bobby knew that smile. He could spot that smile a mile away. "Rosaland?" He questioned. Bobby stepped back to admire her beauty. "You are breathtaking!"

"Hello Bobby." She cooed, "Who is that the Lt. is dancing with?" The detective inquired, "That's my sister." Rosaland answered. "You have a twin sister? I didn't know that." "An identical twin sister" she corrected him. "Now you know. There are lots of things you don't know about me". Rosaland smiled seductively, releasing some of her pent up hostility.

"Rosaland, I have been trying to get to know you for months, almost a year. You always put me off, you won't talk to me, and you won't look at me, what the hell do you want me to do? I know you like me, and you know I like you. Why do you have such a fucking attitude? What have I ever done to you?" Bobby already had a couple of drinks so he was speaking very freely. "We're not at work now, and you are going to talk to me, you can't shew me out of your office, because guess what? We are not in your office tonight." Bobby had decided that he could no longer resist her charms. She was here, she was beautiful and despite the advice of his grandfather tonight she was going to be his.

The rest of the squad started to gather in the same area. They had been waiting to toast her. Bobby ordered a round of drinks and he replaced Rosaland's empty glass with a fresh one. At this point Rosaland removed her jacket. Bobby went weak in the knees. This woman was outrageously fine. "Oh my God" he thought to himself. Bobby's convictions were set. He would make her understand the depth of the feelings he had for her.

"My, my, my" Danny said shaking his head "Who is this vision of beauty? Dr. Reid my heart hurts. Can I have this dance, please?" Rosaland laughed as Danny escorted her to the dance floor. Diana walked over to Bobby and gave him a big kiss. "Hey stranger, haven't seen you around lately, do you want to dance?" "Yes, I would love too" Bobby grabbed her hand and they went off to the dance floor. Everyone was having a great time. Arthur had not left Rachael's side since she walked into the club. She in turn gave him her undivided attention. They seemed to be made for each other. Rachael was delighted to meet such a fine gentleman.

"So you are the D.A." the Lt. remarked as they stepped. "I am" she responded sexily. "That's incredible" Arthur smiled as he supplied her with a fresh drink. He wanted to kiss her and he did. That kiss sent shock waves up and down his spine. Arthur was heads over heels in love. He couldn't believe it. He was forty years old and a pretty young woman had stolen his heart in a matter of minutes. This was a night that he would never forget.

The rest of the evening went very well for the squad. They all had the best time. They laughed, talked, drank, danced and really got to know each other as people not just co-workers. Rosaland noticed that she had danced with everyone except Bobby. Just as that thought entered her head he danced over and told her that there was a special record that he had requested. When this record came on he wanted her to dance with him. She agreed and had another drink. Rosaland couldn't help but to notice her sister and her lieutenant.

Rachael excused her self and came over to talk to her sister. "Rosaland this man is wonderful! How could you keep him such a secret?" "He's my boss" she shouted. "He is going to be your new brother-in-law" Rachael insisted shaking her head and smiling. "What!" "I'm telling you there is no way that he is getting away from me. No way!" The two of them hugged.

Rosaland couldn't believe her ears. She knew her sister and she also knew that Rachael was serious. Rosaland had never seen Rachael so attracted to any man. This was going to be interesting. Arthur came over to sit with the ladies as they continued to talk. The three of them had another drink and Rosaland noticed that Bobby was motioning for her to join him on the dance floor.

"Excuse me I'll be right back. I promised Bobby this dance." Bobby watched her as she walked towards him on the dance floor. As she approached the DJ started to play one of her favorite songs by the Dells. She fell into Bobby's arms and told him that this was one of her most favorite songs of all times. "It's my favorite song sweetie. All my life I have been waiting for this moment." Bobby whispered softly close to her ear. Rosaland looked into his eyes and she knew at that very moment that he meant it.

She immediately felt drawn to him. "What was she doing?" She thought to herself as she closed her eyes, and fell compliantly into his arms. In the background all that could be heard was "I can't do enough to show how much I love you…do enough to show how much I love you" the Dells crooned as she and the detective danced slow and sexy, their bodies melting into each others.

By this time the dance floor was full of couples holding each other tight. Bobby smelled her exotic perfume and pulled her closer. Arthur was whispering sweet words of longing into Rachael's ear as their bodies moved in harmony. Rosaland looked up at Bobby and started to kiss him but she pulled back. She placed her head against his chest as she felt his nature start to rise. She wrapped her arms gently around his neck and ran her fingernails down his back.

Bobby bent his head down to smell her hair. He loved the way her hair smelled. The two of them moved sensually together as Bobby ran his hands down her figure, feeling her soft smooth skin. Rosaland couldn't believe the emotion she was experiencing in this man's arms. She could stay here forever. He wanted her to stay here forever.

Soon the music stopped and she knew that it was time for her to leave. She wasn't going to be able to deal with being this close to Bobby. She excused herself from his embrace, to go to the ladies room. Rosaland was completely shaking as she exited the dance floor. Her body was trembling and her hear was pumping fast. Rachael joined her and they just hugged.

"Rosaland, are you alright?" Rachael noticed that her body was trembling. "I don't know." Rosaland responded honestly. "All this from one dance?" Rachael questioned. "Oh yeah, he is so fine and sexy, he takes my breath away. I need a drink." Rosaland's body was still shivering. She needed a minute to regain her composure.

"Arthur told me that Bobby is crazy about you. That he has been crazy about you for a long time". Rosaland looked at Rachael with a puzzled expression on her face. "How does Arthur know that? Has Bobby said something?" She was curious. "No he has never mentioned it but he knows Bobby and he knows. He said it's a man thing." "Rachael Arthur is trying to get me killed. Bobby already has a girlfriend and she has been his girl for a while. I can't get involved in a situation like that."

"I don't know Sis there is definitely something between the two of you." "Not yet but we'll see." When the sisters came out of the ladies room Rosaland ordered another drink. She felt like getting plastered. The feel of Bobby's hard muscle bound body next to hers had really disturbed her. She was really shook up and extremely turned on. He was strong, firm and powerful. She could feel the strength that surged through his veins. What the hell was she going to do! Rosaland could tell that Bobby was not a man used to hearing no.

Rachael walked over to tell Rosaland that she had called Matthew to take them home. The two sisters were under the influence and not in any condition to drive. Rosaland of course wasn't ready to leave, so she found her way back to the dance floor. Arthur offered to escort the ladies home safely, however Rachael explained the family rule to him. Whenever the girls are out, no matter what, it is Matthew's responsibility to make sure that they arrive home safely.

If either of the three of them violated that rule their Dad would have the heads. This was how he raised them and this is what he meant. There was no discussion when it came to the safety of his girls. "You're father is that strict?" Arthur insisted. "My father is a general, need I say more?" Rachael raised her eyebrow. "No, when I'm a dad, I'll probably be the same way. Can I have this last dance?" "Yes" Rachael cooed and the two of them hit the dance floor.

Rosaland was still on the dance floor. She looked around to see if Matthew had arrived. He always gets so pissed if they are not ready when he comes to take them home. The truth is they are never ready and he always has to wait. Rosaland was getting drunk and she had to go to the ladies room again. That was the one thing about drinking she didn't like, and that was how much time she spent in the ladies room.

Matthew arrived around three a.m. He took a seat at the far end of the bar and waited. He ordered himself a drink and watched all the pretty women as they walked by. Rachael spotted him first and walked over with Arthur to introduce them. "Arthur I would like for you to meet my brother Matthew, Matthew this is Lt. Arthur Yancy, he is Rosaland's boss at the N.Y.P.D." The two of them shook hands. "It's nice to meet you sir" Matthew responded. "Don't call me sir, that makes me sound so old, but it is a pleasure to meet you as well." Matthew had a lively personality. He was getting into the music and watching the ladies.

Matthew was tall and good looking like the general and had that same stern jaw line. He also possessed that famous Reid smile. He had just got off work so he was dressed pretty casual. The ladies didn't seem to mind. "Matthew what kind of work do you do?" Arthur asked trying to engage him in some conversation. "I'm a doctor. Chief of Staff at N.Y.U. Medical" "Oh really your parents must be extremely proud of all of you." Arthur nodded his head. "Have you met the General?" "Yes once" "Well he wouldn't have it any other way."

At this point Bobby walked over to where they were all standing. "Bobby I want you to meet my brother Matthew." Bobby shook Matthew's hand "Hey man what's up! You're the doctor from N.Y.U. do you remember me? We met at the forensics workshop about a year ago?" Bobby said recognizing Matthew instantly. Matthew thought a moment and then the workshop came back to mind. "Yes, what's up with you player? How the hell are you? Are you still with the P.D.?" "Yes as a matter of fact the information that I learned from that workshop helped me with one of my drug bust. I made detective from that case." "Way to go" the two of them slapped five. "Let me buy you a drink." Bobby and Matthew sat down at the bar.

"This is a small world" Matthew nodded. "Dr. Reid is your sister?" "Yes my big sister." "I work with her." "Yes I know. She is your new boss" Matthew joked. "She is always somebody's boss. She likes that bossing stuff." He made a joke. "I know that she is fine and finer" Bobby said half under his breath. "You sound like a fan" Matt observed. "Believe me I am. I could easily become her number one fan. Is that alright with you?" "You're a good man but that's between you and her. Where is the wild child anyway?" "You call her the wild child. She always seems so reserved." Bobby said noticing her as she walked up. "You just don't know." Matt laughed.

"Matthew!" Rosaland walked over and gave her brother a hug and a kiss. "How long have you been here?" She smiled as she continued to sip on her drink. "Twenty or thirty minutes. I arrived while you were dancing. Are you having a good time?" He asked smiling and sipping his drink. "Yes" she answered outwardly flirting with Bobby. Matthew looked first at his sister and then looked at Bobby. They were making eyes at each other.

Bobby used this opportunity to pull Rosaland to the side. "So why are you running from me?" He insisted "I'm not. What are you talking about?" She replied. "You dance with me one time and then you take off. I'm looking for you and you are out in the middle of floor dancing with Joe blow. What the hell is up with that?" He kind of raised his voice. "I didn't know you were looking for me." She answered smugly. Bobby had to catch himself "You know what it's all good. You look really hot tonight." Bobby escorted her back to the bar and then he walked off leaving Rosaland a little stunned.

"Are you ready to go?" Matthew asked after witnessing their display. "Yes Matthew I am tired, some what intoxicated and my feet hurt. I am ready to go. You need to ask your sister over there if she is ready to go." Rosaland glanced in Rachael's direction. She had never seen Rachael so responsive to any man. This was delightful. Rachael could use some excitement in her life.

Matthew walked over to Rachael and Arthur "I'm sorry to break up such a tender moment Rachael but are you ready to go?" Rachael smiled at Arthur and handed him her business card with her home number and cell number on the back. "Arthur will you call me?" Rachael suggested elusively. "Yes, I would love to. Is an hour too soon?" Arthur checked to make sure. "Yes, that is fine I should be home by then." Matthew gathered up his sisters and said his final goodbyes. With his arms around their waists he escorted them out of the club and to the car that their dad had provided for them.

The driver dropped Rachael off first and making sure that she was secure in the building they drove Rosaland uptown to Harlem. Again making sure that she was secure in the house the driver then dropped Matthew off at his boat that was docked at the midtown seaport and drove back to the garage. Matthew would pick his car up in the morning.

eleven

Rosaland prepared herself for bed. She was still very intoxicated as she finished her shower. She lotioned down her sensuous shapely brown body paying special attention to her feet. After dancing all night in 3 inch heels her feet hurt. She finally began to relax as she soaked them in Pretty Feet. The lotion felt cool and refreshing on her skin. As she sat on the side of her king size oval shaped bed she applied skin lotion to her legs, stomach and her full luscious breasts. She walked into her bathroom and dusted herself with glimmering powder. It made her body shine and shimmer and feel sexier than she was already feeling.

Now she needed to find something nice to cover her body. She searched her lingerie drawer and found a skimpy red lace teddy. She stepped into it and pulled it over her shapely figure. The thin straps at the top barely covered her full breasts. She stood in her mirror and brushed out her hair thinking of Bobby. Lately she always thought of Bobby. Even though he appeared to have quite a temper, she had a nice time with him this evening. For some reason she decided to put on the same perfume that she had worn earlier. She applied the perfume to her pulse points behind her ears, between her breasts, between her legs, down her thighs and on both of her wrists. Bobby complimented her on her choice of perfume while they were on the dance floor, which is why she probably put so much of it on. She turned out her bathroom light, clicked on the night light, and climbed into bed.

Bobby was at home wrestling with exactly what he was going to do. He couldn't sleep and he couldn't get her out of his head. He could still smell her very expensive perfume. She looked so incredible this evening. So desirable. It had taken every once of control he had in his power to resist her charms. All he could see was her wearing that short tight black dress that fit her body like a glove. The smell of her hair was still fresh in his mind. He remembered how soft her skin felt pressed up against his. The thought of her made him hard. He sat up in his bed and decided that he had to do something. He had had enough of this bullshit.

Bobby slipped into a pair of old jeans and his favorite N.Y.P.D. black tank. He grabbed his shield and his gun and decided that he would take a drive to clear his head. Bobby noticed that the moon was full and sultry and hung low in the sky. There was passion in the night air as he jumped behind the wheel of his 2003 black convertible Saab. The orange glow of the full moon only added to his excitement. Bobby was on the prowl and he had a certain Dr. in mind.

Soon he was heading up the East River drive to Harlem. He took the exit at Riverside Drive and drove the rest of the way on the backstreets cruising and enjoying his music. Bobby checked his watch, he was a little nervous. It was four in the morning. What was he doing in Harlem? Fifteen minutes later he pulled in front of her house. He sat in the car for another fifteen minutes getting his nerve up to ring the bell. How would he explain to her how he knew where she lived? He would have to admit to going through her personnel file and into her private records. That was definitely a departmental violation and he didn't quite know how she would interpret that.

All the lights at the brownstone were out so he assumed that she was sleeping. Rosaland was in bed but she was far from being asleep. She was tossing and turning and her mind was racing. Bobby noticed that there was a light on the second floor. This was the sign that he had been waiting for. Bobby locked his car and found himself at her front door. He rang the door bell and waited for her to answer. There was no answer so he tried it again. Still no answer. So he waited.

Rosaland was up and wondering who would be at her door at this time in the morning. She reached over to her night stand to take out her gun. Her door bell rang again. She left her bedroom and went down to the first floor where she turned on her outside lights. Bobby noticed the light and nervously waited for her to come to the door. "Who's there?" Rosaland asked as she carefully approached the door "Who's there?" She demanded in a loud voice. "It's me, Bobby." "Bobby?" She was shocked and amazed. "Yes, Bobby, come to the door." he ordered. "Show me something." She responded recognizing his voice. Bobby put his badge up to the window and waited. She knew the shield she carried one herself.

Rosaland unlocked the door to find Bobby standing on her front steps. She immediately focused on his bulging biceps that protruded from beneath his t-shirt. "Wow" she thought to herself, realizing just how turned on she was. Bobby looked deep into her eyes as he climbed to the top step of the brownstone. In all her haste Rosaland hadn't thought to cover herself so there she stood in the skimpiest red teddy with her cleavage completely exposed. Rosaland felt the closeness of his groin, but she held her hips slightly away, not trusting herself at all.

After gazing upon her half naked body Bobby noticed that she had her gun in her hand. He moved in close enough to kiss her never saying a word. Rosaland's resistance was a thing of the past as she fell deeply into his arms. Their lips meeting for the first time. Bobby gently pried the gun from her hand as he embraced her forcefully inserting his tongue down her throat.

Rosaland responded to his exciting embrace pressing her soft body closer to his. Bobby's hands moved along her curvy figure to firmly grasp her fully exposed breast. She jumped from the heat in his fingers. He delicately rubbed the tender mounds and tweaked her big nipples as he continued kissing her neck and the lobes of her ears. They were on the front steps of her brownstone locked deep in their illicit embrace for everyone to see.

Bobby released her quivering body picked her up in his arms and carried her in the door and up the steps. Slamming the door with his foot. The door crashed loudly behind them as he made his way up to her bedroom. Rosaland continued to kiss him wantonly as she wrapped her arms securely around his neck. She ran her nails through his hair as she nibbled on the lobes of his ears. When Bobby reached the top of the stairs he followed the light that led the way to Rosaland's quiet sanctuary. He was amazed at how large and elegant her boudoir was. It was something out of Harlem Nights. The only thing missing was the fire in the fireplace.

Bobby placed her feverishly on the bed as he pressed his muscular physique on top of hers. They remained lost in their luscious embrace, kissing and grinding as Bobby removed her teddy. Once he had her completely naked he surveyed and admired her beauty. "Damn" he thought to himself, realizing that he would finally discover what she was like in bed. Again he commented that she was "breathtakingly beautiful". Her body perfect in every detail.

Bobby began to tenderly kiss her breasts as he rubbed his hairy groin against hers. Rosaland was lost to his advances. There would be no turning back. Rosaland moaned in ecstasy as his hands and tongue roamed freely all over her.

Rosaland reached out and pulled the tank top that Bobby was wearing over his head exposing his bare muscular chest. He was a pure powerhouse. He pressed his naked chest into her breasts. It felt so good having her warm body lying under his. Bobby was horny and Rosaland was hot, all he wanted was to make her scream. (cum).

Bobby stood up to remove his jeans, of course he wasn't wearing any underwear, and his hard penis stood strong and proud. Rosaland was amazed at it's size, girth, and length. She had never seen one so big. He was huge!

She sat up in her bed and starred romantically in his direction. She couldn't believe she was doing this or she was going to do this. Her father would have her head if he ever found out.

Bobby looked longingly at her as he walked around the bed to turn the covers back parading his naked Johnson in full view as he rolled on the condom. He wanted her to see him in all his glory. Bobby slid hungrily between the sheets and motioned for his sweetie to join him.

Rosaland sexily slid across her bed and nestled herself comfortably next to him. She noticed how relaxed she felt in his presence as he again took her in his arms and pressing his body on top of hers kissed her erotically. As their naked bodies rubbed together rampantly Rosaland whispered softly "Bobby I've never done this before." Bobby lifted his body slightly and looked at her tenderly "Never?" He repeated shocked a look of disbelief on his face. Rosaland shook her head to indicate no. "Never" she replied innocently not knowing what he was going to do next.

"I'll be gentle" he assured her. Bobby strategically placing his strong naked body between her legs. "I'll be good to you" he promised as he kissed her passionately. She honestly believed him. Rosaland lay back on the bed and opened her legs wideinviting him to come inside. For some reason she just could not stop herself.

Bobby mounted her and began pressing his hard throbbing member between her thighs. Rosaland struggled faintly, but it was an unequal fight. Rosaland's eyes bulged out and her mouth opened but no scream came from it. Bobby was on fire and that added to both of their pleasure.

Rosaland anxiously prepared herself for his powerful penetration as he began to thrust the hot head of his formidable weapon inside of her. Rosaland winced and began to moan both in pain and in pleasure as she discovered his enormous manhood for the first time.

Bobby continued his deep thrust inside of her tight hot privacy. Bobby's belly pressed flatly against Rosaland's body, but instead of pain crossing her face, there was pure pleasure as Bobby's shadow fell upon her. "Oh my God!" Bobby moaned. This was too good to be true. He couldn't believe how sweet she was. Rosaland was a virgin. She had never been with a man in this way. He was her first. This would truly be a night that Bobby would always remember.

This excited Bobby even more as he pumped harder and deeper into her willing temple. Bobby groaned at the tightness he was experiencing as he thrust his enormous size into the very depths of her being. They both moaned and groaned and screamed out in ecstasy as they shared each others love. Bobby was generously endowed and he filled her cavity to capacity with his masculinity. Rosaland adjusted her body to accommodate his size and to relieve the pain as they writhed in pleasure.

Rosaland kissed Bobby excitedly and ran her fingers down his chest as he possessed her. She ground her body into his riding the wave of electric passion as he filled her with divine desire. Bobby pumped deeper and deeper causing her to cry out in ecstatically as she screamed out his name. "Ohh Bobby" she shouted over and over again as he cupped her ass and thrust himself as deep as he could go, giving her all that he had.

Rosaland dug her nails into his back as she received the full force of his hard erect ion. Bobby was in heaven. He had no idea that she was a virgin and that he would take her in this way. Bobby starred deep into her eyes and she into his as they continued to make passionate love. He kissed her longingly as he speared into her body with more and more intensity. Rosaland spread her legs as wide as she could, to allow Bobby full access to her inner charms.

Bobby had her wet and wide open and she was extremely sensitive to the stretching he was giving her. The intensity of their body heat was building as he buried his erect massive member deeper and deeper with each potent thrust. He pumped harder and deeper treating her to his full length as he pleased her.

Rosaland was swimming in a sea of sensual delight as she screamed out his name. Rosaland's body relished Bobby's attention. He was hungry and demanding taking total command of her heart and her soul. Bobby laced his fingers through her glossy mane of hair while he brought his mouth to her neck. He pumped and pressed and stroked her deeply as her first orgasm ever ripped through her wanton body.

Tears of pleasure rolled down her cheeks, as their excitement mounted. This was the most intense feeling she had ever experienced. She couldn't believe the feelings of raw lust and sensuality that came to life within her. Bobby was waiting for her to climax so he could bring her home. He rode her hard hot and long as his impending orgasm approached. About three hours later Bobby erupted deep inside her cavern, making her body explode in volcanic passion. She had never felt so good. So satisfied. So complete. Rosaland gave her body and her soul to him that night. As she secretly hoped this night would last forever.

twelve

Bobby loved the feeling of being buried to the hilt inside a woman when she climaxed around his huge machine. Bobby kissed Rosaland lovingly as he gyrated on top of her; their bodies completely covered in sweat. Bobby lay there holding her as they relaxed in each other's arms. She was incredible!! They both fell into a deep sleep.

Sometime during the night Bobby woke up to realize that he was in the bed of the woman he loved. He pulled her close, wrapped his arms tightly around her, and buried his face in her hair; he loved the smell of her hair. Bobby slowly drifted back to sleep holding her securely. He didn't quite know how to tell her, but she belonged to him from this day on. He knew it in his heart. Rosaland slept soundly, secure in the safety his arms.

The next morning Bobby awoke to find Rosaland already in the shower. He wasn't finished with her. She had been incredible last night and he wanted some more. He had no idea that she would be so sweet, so tender and so trusting. She was gentle, passionate and ultimately exciting. He remembered the tightness of her body as he penetrated her for the first time. As Bobby thought about what had happened between the two of them last night his huge Johnson began to harden.

He entered the bathroom to see the outline of her naked body through the glass shower door. Bobby slid the door open and stepped inside. The hot steam from the shower hit him in the face. Rosaland turned to look at him as he moved in close to her his chest pressed against her breasts. He bent down to kiss her as she wrapped her arms around his neck. Bobby kissed her longingly and wrapped his arms securely around her waist. "I love you," he whispered sincerely in her ear. Catching Rosaland completely off guard. "Thank you for waiting for me." The tears started rolling down her cheeks.

Bobby started kissing her breast and then he began to bite her nipples tenderiy. He kissed down her entire body leaving no spot unattended. The warm water ran over their bodies as Bobby fell to his knees and planted his mouth on the puffy lips of her honey spot. Rosaland moaned in delight as he eagerly began to lick her sweet tight love nest. He inserted the full length of his tongue between her wet mound and thrust in and out in a very sensual and appetizing manner.

Rosaland groaned out loud as he began to eat her like the sweet delicacy that she was. She grabbed his head and pulled his mouth deeper into her bracing herself against the wall as she opened her legs to receive his luscious attentions. Bobby allowed his hands to roam freely over her shapely figure as he continued to lick her enlarged clitoris. Rosaland began to tremble as Bobby thrust his tongue into her again and again deeper and deeper, kissing and groaning and eating away to his heart's delight.

Rosaland was still holding Bobby's head as she thrust her body roughly into his mouth, grinding deep into his face. He continued to nibble and suck and eat at a delicious pace. The orgasmic sounds of lovemaking filled the bathroom that morning.

Rosaland moaned, groaned, sighed and panted as Bobby brought her to another powerful orgasm her body shivering as she prepared for his emanate invasion. Bobby adjusted himself to fill her body with the complete length of his hard penis. Again she cried out as he began to thrust deeply inside her sweet slit and belly. Bobby immediately took possession of her most private place. A place that was known only to him. The steam in the shower appeared as a warm cloud around them as their bodies rhythmically pounded into each other.

Rosaland wrapped her legs around his waist locking him tightly inside. She screamed out in absolute delight as he pumped her with all the strength he could muster. Bobby securely held her in place as he fed her his full rod. Rosaland was helpless in his grasp. He pounded into her relentlessly, thoroughly impaling her with each powerful stroke.

Bobby ground himself tightly into her body as their orgasms exploded simultaneously filling her with his seed. Rosaland screaming out uncontrollably. The sensual pleasure of their lovemaking covered them like a warm blanket as they continued to be lost in each other's arms.

thirteen

Carlos Calderon was the man behind Natalie's. This was one of his most profitable investments. It was an information hub as well as a place for him to operate from when he was in New York City. Above the club he had an office full of the latest in high technology computer equipment. State of the art. The mirror behind the bar was two-way, thus allowing him and his staff to see all the activities that were going on even in the darkest recesses of the popular establishment.

Even though his business was narcotics he didn't allow them on the premises. He was very cautious to pay attention to the amateur drug dealers that used popular night clubs to solicit clients. Natalie's attracted an upscale clientele that could prove to be helpful to him in his various business endeavors.

Natalie's was also the chosen nightspot of the N.Y.P.D. It was an ideal way to keep track of the new cops that joined the force, as well as the old under covers. Carlos was surprised that with as much investigating that the cops did on his background and his cartel; they had yet to discover that he owned their favorite nightclub. Carlos thought all cops were stupid.

After the air strike that was conducted on his distribution plant, he made it his business to come to New York to see if he could gather any information on who was behind that discovery, and how they found out. He lost a lot of money in that raid as well as a lot of product. Losing money was something that never appealed to Carlos and someone was going to pay.

Lt. Yancy was the first to arrive that night and he sat at the bar waiting for the rest of his unit to join him. The bartender signaled Calderon when Arthur sat down. Calderon went to the two-way to observe. The Lt. came here a lot after work for a nightcap so the bartender was familiar with him.

"Lt. what would you like. Your usual?" The bartender asked. "Yes that would be fine." Arthur responded. The bartender poured his drink and served him. "Looking kind of spiffy there Lt. is this a special occasion?" "I'm meeting the rest of my squad for a celebration." That was Carlos's clue to watch and wait. He could find out tonight all at one time who were the detectives that he should be on the look out for.

Diana and Bobby were the next to arrive and when Bobby walked in a stunned Carlos dropped his drink. This man looked just like him! How was this possible? This could not be!! Carlos could feel Bobby all through his body. The stories he had heard in his youth; he knew at this moment were true. The only difference in their appearance was the hair. Bobby kept his hair cut short and his face clean shaven whereas Carlos sported a ponytail with a full beard.

They had the same height, weight, and build with the same hazel eyes. They also had the same bronze skin coloring and the same taste in women.

The bartender always wore an earpiece so that Carlos could tell him what he wanted him to find out from his customers. "Find out who that is," he ordered, even though deep down inside he already knew. There was an eerie feeling that crept over him. Could this be? The bartender nodded and walked over to serve the two new comers.

"What can I get for you two?" The bartender inquired. Bobby replied "The lady will have a white wine spritzer and I'll have Hennessey on the rocks". The bartender nodded and prepared their drinks. As he served them he commented "the Lt. is running a tab, would you like to run one too?" "Yes" Bobby replied, "I think we might be here for a while." "My name is Joe" the bartender extended his hand. "Bobby Semione and Diana Rousseau." They both reached over to shake Joe's hand.

Carlos turned to another member of his staff "find out everything you can on this Bobby Semione, I want to know where he lives, who his family is, everything!" "What about the girl?" "Find out about both of them. Is she his girlfriend, lady friend, partner or do they just fuck? It's obvious that there is some sort of a relationship there. Find out what it is. Before this night is over I want to know everything about all of them!" Carlos ordered as he filled his nose with the potent white powder.

This was going to prove to be a very interesting evening. Justin, Danny and Wesley arrived next and joined the rest of the crew at the bar. Carlos was photographing all the members of the squad. Antonio Martinez and Raul Gonzales came in a short time later and added to the group. "Who are the Latino boys? They look like men we might be able to do some business with." Carlos commented.

He had a great deal of faith in people from his own culture. He felt that he could always find a negotiating point when it came to them. Also once they were on your team, they were loyal, and that is what he valued most, loyalty. Carlos was on his third drink by now and decided to have some more blow. Cocaine changed his personality. It made him more aggressive than he was normally. Jorge had warned his young son before his death to never become a victim to his business. A young Carlos had no idea at the time what that meant. In his later years he would come to know all to well the message his father was trying to send.

A tray of cocaine was placed on Carlos's desk and he immediately pushed his face into it. Snorting up gobs of blow all at one time. Carlos continued to keep his focus on the cops that were gathering downstairs, listening intently to their conversations, while he amused himself.

Jillian and Yvonne were the last to arrive completing the group. The bartender waited for an order from Carlos on the two of them but he seemed to show no interest in these last two ladies. They had all been photographed and within twenty-four hours he would know everything that there was to know about all of them including what color panties the ladies were wearing.

He sat back and watched his entire guest as they had a good time. Rosaland and Rachael arrived approximately two hours later. Rosaland excused herself to go to the ladies room and Rachael entered the club alone. Carlos jumped to his feet when she walked in. He couldn't believe it! There she was! The last time he saw her she was fifteen years old. Their eyes met as she walked through the airport with her father. Her brother and her sister were also traveling with them. He would never forget the feeling that swept over him as he passed her.

He turned his head and followed her with his eyes as she disappeared through the airport doors. Carlos was twenty-two years old and he had thought about her everyday since that time.

That was eleven years ago, and now she was standing in his club. As soon as Rosaland walked into the bar he knew that was she. They were twins but he could tell them apart anywhere. He told the bartender to give the ladies anything they wanted. "Boss these ladies have drinks coming from everywhere." He had to step back away from the bar and turn around facing the liquor before he could respond. The club was full of cops and if they spotted him talking they would know that they were being watched.

Rachael did spot him talking; she just didn't say anything at the time. Carlos watched Rosaland all night. He took note of her every move including her dance with bobby. He couldn't take his eyes off of her in that short tight black dress.

At one point she leaned over the bar exposing her long legs in those sexy black stockings. She had grown into a shapely young woman. A fully developed, sexy, desirable female. Calderon had waited for her for eleven years and what was so ironic; she was the one that had been assigned to take him down.

"Boss" Joe said "this is the lady that the celebration is for. The cops just toasted her. She is connected to them in some way. I think she is a cop too." Carlos laughed, "Find out for sure and then get back to me," Carlos ordered. "So she's a cop, well I'll be damned! Check her and her sister out and get back to me in fifteen minutes. I want to know all about her before she leaves this club."

Carlos snorted an enormous amount of cocaine while he was waiting on the report never taking his eyes off of her, even when she went to the bathroom. Fifteen minutes later Carlos was handed the report. Dr. Rosaland Anne Reid: consultant for the N.Y.P.D. Rachael Anne Reid the District Attorney of New York State. Daughters of General Prescott Arthur Reid, Joint Chiefs of Staff. Brother Matthew Arthur Reid, doctor, chief of staff New York Medical Center. "Holy shit! General Prescott Reid. My my, how the plot thickens. Well at least she's not a cop." Carlos smiled to himself as he kept reading.

"Is this all you could find" Carlos asked feeling the influence of the drug. "That's it boss, that's all that came up". "Follow them when they leave, I want to know where she lives". That evening when Matthew picked up his sisters, Carlos's men followed them. They watched as Matthew dropped off Rachael, and then followed them as he dropped off Rosaland in Harlem. Carlos's men reported back that she lived in Harlem at 127th and Lennox. "Good job." "Carlos is there anything else?" "Yes, who's with her?" "Nobody her brother dropped her off and she went into the house alone." "Good" "Carlos what else do you want us to do?" "Nothing go home." They left.

fourteen

Carlos contemplated what he would do next but all he knew was that he loved her, and he would have her. There had to be some more information somewhere that they could access. Why would an information analyst be working with the police? What was she after? Or better yet who was she after? Carlos decided that he needed a contact in the N.Y.P.D. he needed someone on the inside who could keep him informed on what she was up to. If his operations were in jeopardy and obviously they were, he needed to prepare to move product from one location to the other. He would never let them catch him off guard like they did before.

Tomorrow he would have one of his associates to arrange a meeting with both of the Latino officers on the force. Perhaps one of them could be persuaded to join his organization. He would have to research his or her background to see if anyone had a problem that he might be able to help with. Carlos could be a very helpful man.

Carlos snorted some more cocaine and was beginning to feel sexy. He needed a woman. At this point, any woman as long as she knew how to please him. He thought about what Rosaland might be doing at this time in the morning. She was probably deep in sleep by now; little did he know that she was being possessed body and soul by Detective Semione. Carlos studied the report over and over trying to read more into it than was actually there. In a fit of rage he balled the report up and threw it across the room.

He needed a woman badly, so he called his associate from the bar to find him one. He would deal with the N.Y.P.D. tomorrow. He would enjoy himself tonight. Carlos walked into the bedroom of his office and waited. He continued to indulge in the use of the cocaine. About an hour later there was a knock on his bedroom door. He opened the door to find Joe the bartender standing there with a lovely young blonde. She appeared to be a little scared but she had been promised money and cocaine so she agreed to party with Mr. C. That's what everyone called him at the club Mr. C.

She had no idea that he was a notorious drug dealer and that her life was in danger. "Hi" she said sexily a little shy. I'm Joy". "That's a lovely name for a lovely girl. Come in". Carlos motioned waving his hand in the air. Joe waited silently as Carlos inspected her; looking over her like she was no more than a piece of meat.

"Take off your clothes!" Carlos demanded and Joy did as she was told. After undressing Carlos announced "She will do just fine Joe you may leave". With that Joe pulled the door behind him and went downstairs to close the bar. After cashing out for the evening Joe left.

Carlos put on some spicy Latin American jazz and invited Joy to sit down beside him. He offered her the tray filled with cocaine and a drink. Joy accepted and immediately snorted the cocaine up one of her nostrils. The strength of the product hit her like fire. She smiled as she snorted another line with the other nostril. Carlos watched the young girl as she continued to inhale line after line her face frozen from its potency. (Strength).

Carlos knew at this point she would pass out if he didn't stop her and she was not there to pass out. Carlos escorted her to the bed. "Strip" he ordered her in a stern voice. Joy did as she was told and soon found herself completely naked. "Now, dance for me" Carlos turned the music up loud and the lights down low as the naked girl swayed back and forth to the beat. Carlos watched as her naked ass danced around in a seductive manner. He started to undress as Joy continued to dance moving exotically to the tempo of the hot Cuban rhythms.

Carlos, now naked started to dance close to her pushing his body hard against hers. Joy laughed, high from the cocaine, and pressed her young body tightly into him. Carlos liked young women; they were always so helpless and so naïve. He was a cruel man and he liked overpowering them with his machismo. Carlos then pushed Joy down on her knees and inserted his soft penis into her mouth. Joy opened her mouth to accept him and begin sucking and licking his penis. "That's it baby, suck me harder. Joy obeyed and began to suck harder and harder. Soon Carlos's nature began to rise and fill her mouth with hard hot length.

As Joy worked her mouth back and forth on his weapon she began to choke with its size. This was exactly the condition that he wanted her in. Carlos grabbed the back of her head and shoved his full length down her throat, causing her to gag and choke. She sucked harder and harder as Carlos pumped in and out of her young stretched mouth. Carlos was lost in the music and had no regard for the young girl who was on her knees in front of him.

This is what cocaine did to him. It turned him into a beast, a living breathing monster. His only concern was for his own gratification. Carlos closed his eyes and pumped deeper and deeper in her mouth. Joy's jaws were hurting as Carlos stuffed his full length down her throat. He was stretching her beyond what she could take; soon tears began to roll down her cheeks as he continued his assault on her mouth.

"That's it you whore suck me. Suck my dick you bitch". Carlos shouted sadistically. Joy couldn't breathe as Carlos relentlessly pounded into her mouth. He pulled his huge weapon out almost to the tip and then shoved it back down her throat with the force of a bull. Just as she started to lose consciousness, Carlos filled her mouth with his hot semen. He grabbed her head and forced himself completely into her face causing Joy to swallow every bit of his cum.

A few minutes later Carlos released his grip and allowed the girl to fall to the floor. Carlos walked over to his bed unconcerned for her or her condition. He poured himself a drink and waited for her to stir, she didn't move. Carlos snorted another line sipped his drink and lost himself in the hot Cuban rhythms.

Carlos again found himself thinking about the sexy Dr. Reid. He couldn't get that black dress out of his head. He remembered her leaning over the bar and the shape of her ass in that tight dress and those beautiful luscious legs. He snorted another line and started to rub himself causing his dick to get hard. A shaken Joy began to revive. Carlos watched her offering no assistance. Joy sat up and began to cry. What was she doing here? Was this man going to kill her? Carlos watched her with no emotion. He was as cold as ice.

Joy looked around the room through her tear filled eyes to she if she could find her clothes. She noticed Carlos on the bed fully erect and she was scared. Carlos motioned for her to come to him and she hesitated. He then leaped off the bed to grab her by her hair and pull her over to him. He threw her on the bed and began to punch her ruthlessly in her face, the blood gushing down her mouth. "When I call you, you come!" he shouted! "Do you understand bitch?" Joy was hysterical by now and in fear of her life. Carlos shouted again "Do you understand me?" Joy nodded "Yes." Carlos released her and sat back on the bed rubbing his engorged member. He snorted another line of cocaine and finished his drink. Joy lay on the bed shaking. She was scared as hell and only wanted to escape with her life.

Carlos motioned for her to sit up and she responded immediately. Once she was sitting up he offered her the tray of cocaine. She accepted it knowing that the only way she was going to make it out of this situation alive was to do what he asked. She bent her head to snort a line of blow. "Do another line!" he commanded and she did. Carlos was starting to calm down. He took the tray of cocaine and ingested two more lines himself. He then passed it back to the frightened girl and motioned for her to do the same. She did just as he asked trying not to anger him.

Carlos was still erect and Joy knew what was going to happen next. Carlos pushed her down on the bed and mounted her. He spread her legs wide as he placed himself between them. Carlos pressed the head of his fully erect weapon hard into her body. Joy screamed as he planted himself deep inside her tender slit. Carlos pumped into her with the force of a raging bull. His penetration was deep and powerful. He stroked her over and over again unmindful of the pain or the tarring he was causing her.

Carlos grabbed her ass and rammed his full length up her, burying it to the hilt with each stroke. Soon their pubic hairs met as he continued to pound into her unwilling body. Carlos placed his hand over her mouth to stifle her screams. No one could hear her, no one was there and no one could help her. Carlos pummeled her body with each downward thrust. He grinded into her over and over again each stroke going deeper and harder.

Carlos continued his assault on the young girls' body for four hours before he felt his climax approaching. He then pulled his huge weapon out of her and shot his load all over her face. Carlos was satisfied. He left Joy battered, bruised and ripped. The next day Joy was found in a dumpster with her throat slit. Carlos Calderon was on his private jet headed back to Calderon Island.

fifteen

Detective Semione was called to the scene of the crime. When he arrived the uniformed patrolmen had covered the young girl, since she had been found completely naked. There was no identification found anywhere around the body. She was wearing no jewelry and had no identifying marks. Her throat had been completely slit from ear to ear. He approximated her age to be about seventeen. She was a baby. Whoever had done this was a cold blooded killer. As Bobby examined the body he could tell that there had been severe sexual abuse. She had been raped and sodomized.

There was residue around her nostrils that indicated excessive drug use. How would a girl this age get a hold of this much cocaine? Who had she been with? And where had she been? Bobby motioned for the officers to remove the body as he talked to the coroner. He gave them orders to take her to the morgue so forensics could do a complete examination and autopsy. This was a heinous crime and he would catch this creep. He hated to see this kind of crime scene first thing in the morning, but then again that was his job.

He would have to wait to see if anyone reported her missing before he could began to know who she was. They had no id on this victim. Danny assisted him at the scene and canvassed the area talking to anyone who might have any information at all about this crime. It was obvious that she had been killed somewhere else and dumped here, because she was wearing no clothes. As Danny walked through the neighborhood no one knew a thing. She was too young and too pretty to be dumped in this way. Someone would miss her and someone knew who had done this to her, but no one was talking. After thoroughly investigating the dumpster for clues and evidence, the two detectives headed back to the station. Joy had been found in lower Manhattan, which was blocks from where Carlos had raped her.

sixteen

Before Bobby got into the car, he made a phone call. He called the midtown florist to send two dozen long stemmed red roses to Rosaland. He remembered how excited she had been to receive flowers from whomever, so he knew that she would be very happy to receive flowers from him. He had not forgotten her.

He instructed the florist to include a card that read "Thank-you for waiting for me." He knew she would know exactly who they were from without alerting the other detectives. He also told them to put them in their most expensive crystal vase, so she could proudly display them on her desk. Bobby was in another world. Last night he had touched a dream.

Bobby was in heaven. He couldn't stop thinking about her. He wanted her right now in a bad way. As he and Danny rode back to the station, Danny mentioned what a nice party they had last night. All Bobby could do was display his cryptic smile. All he wanted to remember about last night was how good she felt. "Dr. Reid looked hot last night. That woman is on fire! And she has a twin. There are two of them and they both looked beautiful. The Lt. is a lucky man!"

"Why do you say that?" Bobby asked not thinking "Bobby where is your head? "How can you ask me why do I say that? Didn't you see the two of them? They were inseparable. What the hell are you thinking about?" Danny looked over at Bobby. "I'm thinking about that young girl we just found in the dumpster. I can't live with that." "Yeah I know what you mean. Don't worry we'll get the bastard. I don't know how long it will take but we will get him." Danny assured his partner.

Bobby's mind was on Rosaland. His mind was always on Rosaland and so was his heart. When Bobby and Danny arrived at the station Dr. Reid was hard at work. The flowers hadn't been delivered yet. As he approached her office she looked up and smiled at him. Once he entered her office the heat began to rise. "Hi" she said softly as she smiled again. "How are you?" He asked her caringly and she smiled again "I'm fine detective how are you?" "I'm in love..." Bobby winked displaying that half sinister smile and he left her office.

Bobby headed over to forensics to talk to the coroner about the autopsy of the young girl first. He wanted that report on his desk as soon as they finished. On these kinds of cases the more time lost in between, the less likely they would be able to find any important clues that could lead to an arrest.

This case was already beginning to trouble him. Bobby's instincts were very good. He could always trust his gut. He knew that there was more to this case than met the eye. Right now he just couldn't put his finger on it. There was something unnerving and it disturbed him. He hoped that someone would report this girl missing so that he could at least put a name to her.

About an hour later he returned to his office. He noticed that the flowers had been delivered to Dr. Reid. She had them proudly displayed on her desk in an exquisite crystal vase. Dr. Reid was on the phone as he walked by and tapped on the window of her office, she motioned for him to come in. He motioned back to her, pointing in the direction of the Lt.'s office. She watched him as he entered the office to talk with his boss. She turned her attention back to the phone. Bobby was reporting the facts about the D.O.A. they found this morning in the dumpster.

Danny entered the office about a minute later to add to the information that Bobby had given him. The three of them discussed the case for about an hour and the Lt. agreed that it should have priority. Bobby and Danny decided that they should canvass the area one more time. Before leaving the house Bobby poked his head into Dr. Reid's office and asked her to have lunch with him. "I'll be back in about an hour. Meet me at the Second Ave. Deli."

Rosaland nodded in agreement and the detectives left the building. Bobby suggested that they walk; on foot they might be able to talk to more people. "Danny I can't believe that nobody saw nothing? Who dumped her here? There are no traceable tire tracks. I'm certain that she was killed somewhere else."

Bobby stood at the scene and looked out in all directions. All he could see was abandoned warehouses, boarded up buildings, and no apparent signs of life. If the body had been dumped a day later, it wouldn't have been discovered for at least a week. They caught a break due to the fact that it was garbage day and the sanitation workers on this route found her while dumping the trash.

Whoever put her here definitely knew what they were doing. That is what disturbed Bobby the most. How many other murders had been committed or would be committed by this madman and how many would he get away with? Bobby and Danny thoroughly covered the neighborhood talking to all the small business owners, the residents, and the homeless but nobody knew anything.

Bobby suddenly remembering that he had asked Rosaland to meet him for lunch looked at his watch. He told her in about an hour, it was already two hours later. "Danny, I have to get back to the station" Bobby said urgently. Danny told him to go ahead, there was still a few more small shop owners that he wanted to talk to. Bobby proceeded on foot to the Second Ave. Deli. When he arrived she was still waiting. She knew that he was on a case and generally when you are conducting an investigation it is easy to lose track of time.

"I'm sorry I'm late" he apologized. "It's alright. How's the investigation going?" She asked trying to show some genuine concern. "I don't know. We just started but there is something about this case that disturbs me. I can't put my fingers on it yet but I've got this feeling." Bobby responded unable to shake the feeling.

"Thank-you for the flowers Bobby. They are beautiful." She said graciously. "You are beautiful. Beautiful flowers for a beautiful lady." Bobby took her hand and kissed it. Rosaland smiled and rubbed his face gently. "Bobby we need to talk." The detective sat up in his chair to give her his undivided attention. He continued to hold her hand as she proceeded. "How are we going to handle this? You know that it is against departmental regulations for us to be involved. We could both lose our jobs."

"Are you worried about your job sweetie?" He teased as he kissed her hand again. "You're the boss. How can you lose your job?" "All I'm trying to say is that at work we should remain professional. Bobby I don't want our relationship or our business to be office gossip and I don't want my personal life being discussed by my co- workers. What we share is no one's concern but ours. I want to keep it that way. We are going to be working closely together not only with each other but also with the rest of the detectives in the squad. I don't want them to be talking about us in public or in private. Also you have a history with Diana Rousseau and I don't want to play the other woman role which would be really bad for my image." She smiled sarcastically.

Bobby had wondered how long it was going to take Rosaland to mention Diana and it didn't take long. Bobby leaned over the table and kissed her tenderly. "Do you feel that?" He quizzed. "Yes" she responded "So do I!" He declared and he kissed her again. Rosaland reached her hand under the table and placed it on his lap. She began to stroke him gently.

"Baby I understand your concerns about Diana. She has been a part of my life for a long time. But that was in the past. We haven't been involved for over six months now. I know that is not a long time and you're probably not comfortable with it but it's the truth. All I can offer you is the truth and myself. I love you and I'm ready to be committed. This is not a one night stand. I'm the real McCoy and I'll take you however I can have you."

Rosaland was still rubbing him under the table and his nature was starting to rise. Bobby grabbed her hand "Stop that" he said softly "That's not fair." "As far as work is concerned you're right we don't need our business in the street or the topic of the office gossip pool. I agree. We should conduct ourselves in a professional manner especially in the presence of the other detectives. I can live with that. After work however is another story. After work it's you and me. Can you live with that?"

Bobby waited for Rosaland to answer. "I love you too Bobby. I just don't want to be hurt. We are moving kind of fast." "Did I hurt you last night?" "No well a little" she teased "But in a good way" she smiled. "I won't ever willingly hurt you. Can you trust me?" "Yes" "Then we are going to be just fine." Rosaland leaned across the table to place her lips gently on his; Bobby kissed her back lovingly. At that moment Bobby's pager went off.

Checking the number he said "It's Danny. Let me use your phone." Rosaland reached in her purse and handed Bobby her phone. He called Danny and listened intently to what he was saying. "Baby I've got to go. I'll see you this evening o.k.?" Bobby left the deli. Rosaland headed back to the office. She and Bobby had been so involved in their conversation that they didn't have any lunch. She was very hungry. She decided to order in.

Once back in her office another arrangement of flowers was delivered. This one was just as beautiful as the roses. It was filled with exotic wildflowers and birds of paradise. The card read, "These remind me of you". Rosaland assumed they were from Bobby and she placed them on the shelf next to the window.

seventeen

Bobby and Danny were away from the house for the rest of the day investigating their d.o.a. Dr. Reid used this opportunity to call her sister. Rachael was in court so she left a message and waited for her to call her back. She then placed a call to Washington D.C. The General was in conference and he too was unavailable. Again she left a very detailed message and waited for his return call.

The General was the first to call back. Rosaland gave him an update and requested some additional equipment. She needed a mainframe computer. Her information was pouring in and she needed to route it. A mainframe would give her operation that capacity. She knew that her request would be expensive; especially considering the money that had already been spent in developing the O.N.S.I. there was no way that she could achieve the necessary results without the new addition.

The General listened as she made her argument. She was prepared to continue when the General asked, "Have you prepared a budget?" "Yes sir" she replied hastily. "Can you fax it to me?" "Yes sir" she acknowledged "As soon as I receive it I'll call a meeting with the budget committee. Fax it on a secured line. I'll wait to receive it." Dr. Reid faxed the information to her father on the secured line just as he requested and waited for his answer.

Rachael finally returned her call. "We need to talk" she urged. "That's exactly what I was thinking. When?" Rachael said gleefully "After work I'll pick you up. Stay there at the station. No matter what Rosaland do not leave me!" "O.k. Rae. I'll be here." While Rosaland waited the General called back to inform his daughter that her request had been approved. The consultants would meet her in the morning.

"I hope you have your proposal ready." "Yes Dad I'm ready. Thank-you" the General hung up the phone smiling. He knew that she would be ready.

He was very proud of her. Dr. Reid finished her work and waited for her sister. Bobby hadn't made it back so she guessed that he would call her later. Rachael finally made it to her office. The first thing she did was look for Arthur. He was down at forensics checking on the results of Bobby's autopsy.

When she entered her sister's office she noticed the lovely flowers. "Rosaland those are lovely who sent them to you?" "That my dear sister is what we need to talk about, are you ready to go?" "Yes" the two sisters left the building and went around the corner to the same bar that Rosaland had spotted Bobby and Diana at several months back.

The ladies sat down at a corner table and ordered drinks. Rosaland pulled out her cigarettes. "I hate when you smoke" "Not today Rachael, not today." Rosaland inhaled her cigarette as she sipped her drink. "Now what is so important?" Rachael hesitated and then said "Rosaland I'm in love and I'm scared."Rosaland's eyes lit up "What's to be scared about Rachael? Arthur is a great man. The two of you seem perfect for each other. You make a great couple." "I know" Rachael agreed." So what's the problem?" Rosaland laughed at her sister. What kind of conversation was this?

Rosaland finished her first drink ordered another one and took a deep breath. She didn't know if she should tell her, but she really needed to talk to someone and when she felt like this Rachael was the only one she trusted.

"Rachael, last night...Rosaland hesitate then she continued... "Last night bobby and I made love." Rosaland confessed "What!" Rachael looked at her sister completely astonished. "How? When? How did you two even get to that point? The last thing you said was you weren't going to get involved. You can't get anymore involved than that! The two of you didn't even leave the club together. I didn't even know he knew where you lived." Rachael went on and on.

"I didn't either Rachael he just showed up at my door." "Showed up at your door and what time was this? We didn't even leave the club until 3:00?" "It was about 4:30 in the morning and I let him in."

"Oh, Rachael" Rosaland broke down. "It was wonderful. Bobby is awesome. Oh God he was so hot. It was so good. Really really good. I'm still thinking about it. My God is he big!!! He is huge!!!! I've thought about it all day."Rosaland exclaimed "Is he the one who sent the flowers?" "Yes. We had lunch today, actually we just talked. But we have decided to give us a chance." "Rosaland how are you going to do that? That's so against the rules. Dad will have your head if you screw up the O.N.S.I. I can't believe you had sex with him!"Racheal screamed. "You don't even know him." She scowled "Rachael I know I love him. I love him. I really love him." The tears were rolling down Rosaland's face. She knew she had messed up.

Her sister reached over to console her. "It's all right Sis" Rachael handed her a Kleenex. Rosaland composed herself "Rachael you can't tell Dad. Bobby and I will figure this out. You can't tell Arthur. You have to keep this a secret. But I had to tell you."Rosaland sobbed "Rosaland what about work? How are you going to work with this man having this much feeling for him? You get too emotional. I don't see how you can remain objective."

Rachael was right about her sister. She was already heads over heels in love with Bobby. "Rachael I can handle this. Bobby and I will keep this underwraps."Rosaland said not believing a word that came out of her own mouth. .

"You'd better. Isn't this interesting? You and Bobby, me and Arthur. What a combination." Rachael had some other concerns on her mind. "Rosaland please tell me that you used protection. Did you use protection?" Rosaland looked nervous "Yes and no."

"Yes and no! What kind of answer is that? Have you lost your mind? How are you going to have sex with a man that you know has been with another woman in the not so distant past and not use protection? What if you're pregnant? Rosaland you are not a child experimenting with sex for the first time. You are an intelligent woman experimenting with sex for the first time with a good head on your shoulders. What were you thinking?"

Rachael couldn't believe it. "I was thinking about Bobby!" "Well you should have been thinking about you. What about H.I.V? What about sexually transmitted disease? What if this guy doesn't marry you? What are you going to do then? Are you going to keep on having unprotected sex with him? Are you trying to get pregnant?" Rachael was preaching.

Rosaland knew that everything her sister was saying was right. She also knew that she had no excuse for her irrational behavior. She would never be so foolish again. What was she thinking? Rachael continued "Bill has been after you for years. You never broke down with him. Here this guy comes to your door in the middle of the night, and you give it up!" Rachael was shaking her head in disbelief.

"Rachael you are making it sound so cheap. It wasn't like that! He's not like that! It meant just as much to him as it meant to me." "How do you know that?" Rachael snapped back. "I know what I did was stupid but I won't allow you to turn this into a sleazy one night stand. It wasn't like that!" "Me?" "You're right I don't have any guarantee that Bobby will marry me but I know he loves me. I know Rachael because I felt it last night and I feel it now."

Rosaland pulled the two cards from her purse and handed them to her sister. Rachael read the cards and looking at her sister said "I'm sorry. These cards are beautiful. I just want you to be careful that's all. You can't afford to lose your head not now. Finish the business with the O.N.S.I. Don't let Dad down." Rachael advised her. "I won't." Rosaland replied weakly but it was much too late. Rachael knew that Rosaland had already lost her heart along with her virginity. As she looked at her she knew that her sister was deeply in love with Detective Semione.

The two sisters had another drink before deciding to call it a night. "Well if it isn't the D.A and her lovely sister." Rachael recognized the voice. Turning around in her chair it was Bill. He was starring intensely at Rosaland. "You never return my calls" Bill shook his head indicating that was not acceptable. "How the hell are you?" Bill leaned over to kiss her softly. Rachael watched her sister wondering what she was going to do. Rosaland allowed him to kiss her again.

"Bill I have been so busy. How the hell are you?" She smiled. "I'm on my way to Washington. I'll be leaving first thing in the morning. I called your office and they said you had already left for the evening. I just took a chance stopping in here and here you are. I really need to talk to you. Can I take you home?" He offered. "Yes I have a meeting in the morning and I probably need to get prepared. Rachael are you ready?"Rosaland addressed her sister. "Actually Rosaland Arthur just called. He's going to meet me here in a few minutes. The two of you go on. I'll call you when I get home."

Bill and Rosaland left and drove uptown. As he drove they talked "I'm going back into the service" Bill started "I'll be working for your father. I'll be gone for a while and I want to know if you will marry me when I come back?" Rosaland was shocked. She looked at Bill and knew that he was quite serious.

"Bill are you serious? How can you propose to somebody like that? I can't make you a promise like that. I work for my Dad and right now I'm on an extremely important assignment. I'm pleased that you would ask me..." her voice trailed off.

"Alright you're right maybe that was a bit rough. Do me a favor and just don't marry anyone else. Give me that chance." Bill was negotiating. Rosaland's cell phone was ringing "Excuse me. Hello?" Rosaland listened as Bobby talked "I'll meet you in about an hour. Are you home" "Yes" she said sweetly "O.k. I'll see you then" Bobby hung up.

"Bill give me some time to think this over. I have always cared about you but you're springing this on me at the last minute and at a bad time." Bill understood. As Rosaland leaned over to kiss him goodnight, Bill grabbed her and hugged her tight "Take care of yourself sexy. It will be a minute but I'll be back."

Bill handed her a box as Rosaland got out of the car and stood on the steps of her brownstone. She stuffed the box in her purse as she entered her house. Once inside she opened the box. Bill knew that she would like this gift. She had picked it out herself. She placed it on her finger and poured herself a drink admiring the shape of the large glistening stone.

After taking her shower and putting on a very sexy black nightgown she sat waiting for Bobby. As she looked at her finger she wondered what Bill would be doing for her father. Rosaland was working on her proposal when Bobby finally arrived. She had papers spread all over the living room floor arranging them in the order that she would to present them in.

She made some notes so could remember the important points. Bobby rang her bell. She went downstairs to open the door for him. He greeted her with a very passionate kiss holding her tightly in his powerful arms. He missed her. Rosaland melted as he held her. She could feel his emotion. As they walked upstairs Rosaland warned him about her paperwork and he stepped over the mess to sit on the couch.

Rosaland poured them both a short drink and sat on the couch next to him her luscious cleavage dangling in his face. "What are you working on?" He asked her as he sipped his drink and looked over the papers trying to take his eyes off her breasts. "I've requested a mainframe. Tomorrow the board of directors has scheduled a meeting and I have to make a presentation. My proposal is complete. I've already faxed my budget to D.C. now I just have to sell the idea." She was still looking over her notes as she spoke.

"It sounds like you've already sold the idea" Bobby observed. "No not yet but I will sell it tomorrow morning. We need this computer network. It's really imperative to my work." she concluded. "But you already have an office full of new computers." Bobby noted "Yes but the mainframe will allow me to route and store the information as it comes in. I didn't realize that the satellite would provide so much useless information. I spend most of my day sorting through junk. This will alleviate that problem. I know I've got vital information important stuff that I'm overlooking."

Bobby looked longingly at her. He liked the way her nightgown clung to her curvaceous body "How much longer are you going to be?" He asked. "I'm almost finished." "Good I want to take a shower. I've been sorting through garbage all day." Bobby took his drink into the bathroom where he undressed and took his shower. He was very much at home at her place. Rosaland continued to work on her presentation. Just as she finished compiling her paperwork and putting it into a folder Bobby walked back into the living room wet from his shower.

"That's better." He sighed as he wrapped the towel around his waist. Usually he air dried. She looked up at him. Her hair falling lazily in her face. "Would you like another drink?" Bobby asked "Yes" she nodded. She motioned to where the bottle was and held out her glass. He poured hers first and then his suddenly realizing how late it was.

"Baby are you ready for bed?" Bobby was anxious. "Not yet. I need another couple of hours." "A couple of hours that's not going to happen, it's already 1:30. You can finish in the morning." Rosaland stood up and walked towards the bedroom. Bobby followed her closing the door behind them. As Rosaland lay back on the bed he reached over and turned down the lights.

The feel of his wet body excited her beyond belief. Bobby ran his fingers through her hair as he kissed her; releasing the clamp so her hair flowed freely into her face. He slowly slid his hands down to her soft full breasts touching them tenderly. Rosaland moaned delighted in his touch. His fingers were so gentling yet so forceful.

Rosaland wrapped her arms around his shoulders and began to rub his back as she softly nibbled on his ear lobes. Bobby loved that, the feel of her hot breathe on his ears and neck. Bobby deliberately removed her nightgown and told her to relax. "Just relax" he ordered as he opened the scented body oil that he placed on her night stand after he finished showering.

Bobby poured some oil in his hands and rubbed them together the friction of his palms adding heat to the oil. He then began to gently massage her naked body starting at her shoulders and working his hands down her smooth chocolate torso. He massaged her slowly and sensuously moving down to the small of her lower back. Rosaland groaned as she felt some of her pent up stress start to leave.

He kneaded her body firmly working his fingers delicately on her shoulders. Bobby was kissing her down her neck and on her back. She relaxed completely under his tender touch. She was so caught in his web. He massaged her legs rubbing her cramped calf muscles working down to her tired feet. Bobby was fully erect by now and she could feel his hard schlong as it pressed into the arch of her back. "Turn over" he whispered soothingly smiling at her. At this point he was applying the nice warm oil up and down his swollen member.

She turned over spread eagle taking his full length deep inside her body. They both moaned out loud as he penetrated her. The warm oil allowing him to slide right in. Bobby began to press himself into the very depths of her wet privacy stretching her completely. She sighed "Bobby" as she opened herself wide to him. He speared into her tight honey pot steadily with each powerful stroke.

Rosaland relished his attentions as she thrust her wet cavern up to meet his downstrokes.Their bodies moved in a hypnotic rhythm as Bobby made delicious love to her for the second time. He possessed her completely as she called out his name over and over again and again.

Bobby whispered lustfully in her hear, promising her all the pleasure he could provide. "Is it good baby?" He whispered softly as he pumped into her hot love spot. "Yes Bobby its so good." she murmured in between strokes. The two of them rode a wave of exotic ecstasy as they totally enjoyed each other's charms.

Bobby loved the way she felt. She was so tight and so warm inside. He adjusted his body so she could take more of him. He wanted her to take all of him. She grunted in pure delight. Bobby began to ride her harder and deeper. Her sexy sounds exciting him, making him hotter than he already was. Completely turning him on. "Ohh Baby I'm Cumming!" he screamed out hours later still pumping relentlessly. "Are you ready?" he shouted as he speeded up his tempo "Yes ohh yes" she cried out seductively. "I can't stop I can't stop ohh Bobby I'm Cumming!!!" And with that last thrust their bodies exploded in orgasmic pleasure.

Bobby kissed her deeply inserting his tongue down her throat as her filled her wet cavern with his creamy flood. Rosaland was flying through the stars. She prayed this night would last forever. The two of them languished in each other's arms as they slowly drifted off into a comatose sleep.

eighteen

When Rosaland awoke the next morning, Bobby was gone. He left a note on his pillow telling her that he had gone home to dress for work. She smiled, remembering last night. Last night she heard the angels sing as the room filled with light. Glancing over at the clock, she jumped out of bed and ran to the shower. She dressed in a hurry, careful not to forget her perfume. This was a very important meeting and she could not be late.

She rushed to the train brief case in hand. Whenever she was running late she always took the train. She arrived at work approximately ten minutes before her scheduled meeting. Dr. Reid had just enough time to compose herself and fix her hair before the Boards of Directors were announced. She greeted the Chairman and escorted the members to the conference room. After making sure that everyone had coffee she presented her information.

Dr. Reid carefully outlined the need for the mainframe. She presented her cost projections for purchase and installation. She provided a blueprint for the proposed location and she requested additional funds for an administrator. She needed someone to monitor the output of the system at all times. She had made copies of her proforma and presented each member of the board with a packet that enabled them to read along as she spoke.

Her presentation was detailed, precise and right to the point. She spoke in a clear voice and exhibited an extreme amount of confidence. She had made a very impressive case. Her argument was exceptionally strong. The Board approved her request upon the completion of the meeting. She would have her mainframe. The need was clear. The Chairman of the Board asked if he could speak to her in private after the meeting was adjourned.

Dr. S.D. Rowe was Chairman of the Board. He was a tall handsome black man and very refined. He outlined the details of the funding. The

O.N.S.I. would receive the proposed funding in three increments. The first check would be for the initial purchase of the network. The second increment would be for installation and the third increment would be for completion of the project. Dr. Reid agreed to the terms and signed the necessary papers to facilitate the loan. Dr. Rowe handed her the first increment before he left her office.

Smiling, she thanked the Board for their confidence and their support. Dr. Rowe shook her hand and wished her the best of luck on the completion of this task. "This is certainly an important undertaking." Dr. Rowe continued, "I wish you much success. I'll definitely sleep easier at night knowing that you are on the job." "Thank-you Dr. Rowe, I will do my very best." "I'm sure you will. Your father has every confidence in your abilities" Dr. Rowe shook her hand again and left.

Dr. Reid emerged from the conference room victorious. She smiled broadly from ear to ear as she entered Lt. Yancy's office with the first installment on the network. "I heard you did one hell of a job on the Board" the Lt. smiled. Dr. Reid proudly displayed the check "Yes we got it!" She screamed as she waved the check in the air. The first thing Bobby noticed when he entered the Lt.'s office was the tight black skirt. He needed to remain focused but the sight of her always distracted him. His eyes wondered down to the long stocking legs.

She always wore thin black silk stockings when she wanted to be impressive. His senses picked up her fragrance. This fragrance drove him crazy. Dr. Reid turned as the detective entered the office. Her hair swung around as she turned her head. She flashed her beautiful smile as she held up the check. It took all the strength he could muster to not grab her and take her in his arms. She excited him beyond words.

"Dr. Reid" the detective asked, "How did your meeting go?" "We received the funding!"Rosaland replied still holding on to the check. "Way to go!" Bobby congratulated her. Dr. Reid excused herself. "I know you gentlemen have work to do, Lt. I'll talk to you later." She left the office. Once back in her office she watched Bobby through the window.

She had to make the arrangements to purchase the mainframe so she started making her phone calls to get the ball rolling. She set up several interviews with perspective firms that handled this type of hardware. She also put in a call to her Dad whom she knew could provide her with more resources. Also she wanted to thank him. He had definitely made it happen.

The General faxed a list of companies that the government did business with on a regular basis. She studied the list carefully and eventually narrowed down her selections. She placed phone calls to these firms to set up interviews.

Between her list and the list that the General had furnished her with she knew that she would find the right dealer at the right price.

Dr. Reid turned her attention back to her computer. She had information pouring in from all over the place. The Intel satellite was transmitting intelligence information on Calderon. Another one of his distribution centers had been discovered. This one was in Bolivia. The O.N.S.I. would have to use Interpol to participate in this bust. Interpol is the Organization of International Police. Bolivia was out of the jurisdiction of the N.Y.P.D. The O.N.S.I. however had international jurisdiction. There was no way Dr. Reid was going to turn over her operation to another jurisdiction. She worked much too hard for that.

She contemplated her next move as the rest of the information poured in. She was ecstatic. Dr. Reid fed the coordinates into her processor; within minutes her computer screen outlined the center. She had a precise location. She jumped up and down in joy. She immediately called all the detectives to an emergency session. Every one in the field was pulled in. While she waited for her team to assemble she placed a call to the General on his secured line.

"Dad we've got another location on a Calderon distribution center. This one is in Bolivia. I've got a complete outline of the whole operation. I haven't briefed my team yet but it looks like we might have to bring Interpol into play on this one. Is there any way I can get around that?" She listened as her Dad spoke and then continued "With a bust of this magnitude I don't want to leave my unit out. Dad if we bring down this center this would be a major blow to the Calderon Cartel. I can't leave my unit out. If I bring in Interpol will they take jurisdiction? Dad I'm faxing you this information. I really need your help."

The General listened intently as his daughter spoke. He waited by his fax machine for the documents to come through. Once he received them he told her to hold off on her meeting with the detectives until he had time to look over the material. In the meantime she should alert her Lt. to her discovery and discuss any and all possibilities with him. "Dad" Dr. Reid continued… "Find me a way."

Lt. Yancy was waiting for Dr. Reid to update him on why she called an emergency meeting. He wanted to know what was so important that he had to call all of his detectives out of the field. He needed them on the street. That is where the real crimes were committed. The streets were the pulse of the city. That is where the information flowed and that was how they solved their cases.

Dr. Reid briefed him on the recent particulars that she had received on the Cartel. She had downloaded the location on to an USB key and she loaded it into his system to pull it up. Arthur was amazed at how she did that. "What's your call?" He asked after reviewing the Intel. "Lt. I need some time to confer with my Dad; I'll get back to you." She responded in what she hoped was an acceptable manner. "In the meantime I need the team." Arthur barked. "I need them back on the streets as soon as possible. We have unsolved cases coming out of the woodwork. "

"Maybe you could give me Bobby, Danny and Diana" Arthur was pleasantly surprised that she would request Diana. Even though he didn't have anything definite he knew that there had been a relationship between Bobby and Diana and he had a sneaky suspicion that there was something between her and Bobby. "Let me think about it." He thought trying to spin doctor what could possibly turn into a nasty situation.

"The sooner you make your decision the sooner I can put your people back where you need them." She added trying desperately to convince him of the necessity. "Good work, Dr. Reid" he nodded as he went back into his office to contemplate her request. "Thank-you Lt." Rosaland went back to her office to await her father's call.

Once the General had time to study the information he designed a plan of action for her. The O.N.S.I. is a federal organization, so they could retain jurisdiction. Dr. Reid could enlist the aid of Interpol or any other federal agency on the raid under the R.I.C.O. statute. Narcotics destined to be distributed for a profit is a federal offense. The O.N.S.I. had complete jurisdiction under the R.I.C.O. statute to make the appropriate arrests.

The general offered this solution to his daughter, the final call was hers to make. Dr.Reid hung up the phone and formulated her plan. As the detectives started to arrive they all wondered what constituted emergency status. They had never been called off the streets before. Dr. Reid was exerting her power and she wanted to use the whole squad. She had developed a close-working relationship with the dicks from the N.Y.D.P.and if anyone was going to get the credit she would make sure her unit received the commendations.

Dr. Reid convened the meeting in the same conference room she used this morning for the Board of Directors. After everyone was seated she told the squad "This briefing has top secret priority status. If any information that is disclosed today is leaked it will be an issue of national security and any violator will be prosecuted to the full extent of the federal government." She playfully wielded her finger in a warning gesture.

Bobby watched her as she moved gracefully in front of the unit. He smiled to himself as he thought about last night. "We have just received pertinent information on the Calderon Cartel. We have located another major distribution center, only this one is outside of the jurisdiction of the N.Y.P.D. However it does falls completely under the jurisdiction of the O.N.S.I. and as Director of the O.N.S.I. it is up to my discretion to use whatever law enforcement agency or agencies that are at my disposal. This bust could lead to many arrests and convictions; it could also lead us directly to Calderon himself if we act swiftly. Time is of the essence."

Dr. Reid walked over to turn out the lights as she continued. "Here is the location of our latest discovery." She pointed to the screen. "It is buried deep in the jungles of Bolivia. It is the major international distribution center supplying Colombia, Bolivia, Argentina, Paraguay, Brazil and Chile. These countries are important to the drug trade. If we can shut it down there we can stop some of the trade that ends up here in our streets."

"We are going to enlist the aid of Interpol to get our warrants and to get our feet in the door. The F.B.I and the D.E.A. will assist in the seizure of the center. What I need for you all to do is pinpoint exactly where we need to hit. We have more information than any of the other agencies. I will fill them in once we know that we have covered all our bases. This way the O.N.S.I. along with the N.Y.P.D. will be credited with the bust and the impending arrests."

Dr. Reid turned the lights back on and asked "Are there any questions?" She had made copies of the report for her detectives and handed them out as she waited for questions. "When do you want us to start?" The question came from Detective Rousseau "As soon as possible right now I promised the Lt. that as soon as we get this done, you all can go back on the streets. The crime in this city will get out of hand if we spend too much time on this. The sooner we get busy, the sooner we'll be finished." "Are we pulling over time?" Dr. Reid looked in the direction of the Lt. "I'll authorized overtime" Arthur agreed "O.k. people let's get to work."

nineteen

Dr. Reid issued the orders and the team went to work. Dr. Reid excused herself back to her office; she needed to call Rachael to fill her in. If any of the arrests were expedited back to New York Rosaland wanted Rachael to handle the indictments. She wanted to talk to her sister because a case like this could create a lot of powerful enemies from within the drug trade. Drug lords have long arms and their reach seems to extend everywhere.

Rachael listened "Bring me the evidence, I'll get the convictions." Lt. Yancy knocked on her door. Dr. Reid motioned for him to come in, "Yes Lt." She put her hand over the phone. "I've decided to approve your request." She nodded appreciatively as the Lt. left her office. The unit worked most of the night mapping out possibilities. Dr. Reid called it quits at about 3:00 a.m.

Diana asked Bobby for a ride home. Bobby agreed. "I want to talk to you Bobby" she was sincere. The two of them left the house. Dr. Reid watched as all the detectives left. Forgetting herself that she needed a ride home, she had taken the train this morning. She called Matthew to drive her home to Harlem where she waited for him to call.

As Bobby drove Diana she started in "Bobby what's going on with you?" "What do you mean?" Knowing very well what she meant. "Maybe I should rephrase my question, what's going on with us?" Bobby was silent for a while and then answered "Diana right now I have some other things on my mind." He was trying to be as honest as he could be under the circumstances. "What kind of an answer is that?" she screamed. "What kind of things and what do they have to do with us?"

"Bobby I haven't seen you other than work. You don't call, you don't come for dinner and we haven't made love in months. Tell me something. Is it over between us? If I'm being dumped you should at least have the guts to tell me to my face. Or have I already been dumped and you just forgot to mention it to me? Is there someone else?" Diana demanded some answers. "Diana I've got some other things on my mind and yes there is someone else." Diana sat silent knowing that he was telling her the truth. "How long has this been going on?" She was starting to cry. "For a while. A couple of months" "Is it serious?" "Yes" "Is it anybody that I know?" "Yes" "Well are you going to tell me or do I have to play twenty questions?" "No Diana I'm not going to tell you. Not now it's not the time. Diana I will always care about you that comes with our history. You can always call me if you need anything. I'll be there but for now let it go."

"Bobby weren't you ever going to tell me?" She asked stunned. "Yes when I felt that the time was right." Diana was in tears. She really loved this prick. She couldn't believe that he would end their relationship like this. What the hell was wrong with him? Bobby was silent as he drove the rest of the way home.

He never meant to hurt her, but he was hopelessly in love with Rosaland. It was hard enough for him to work with her all day and not be able to touch her or tell anyone about her. The last time Bobby made love to Diana she could tell that his mind was somewhere else; she had no idea that his heart was there too. Now she knew.

"Bobby you owe me this, who is she?" Diana screamed as the tears rolled freely down her face. "Diana I can't tell you. I'm sorry" "You're damn right you're sorry. I would never have expected this from you!" At this point all Bobby could do was try to console her. Diana reached over and slapped him as she ran from his car to her apartment building. Bobby got out of the car and ran after her but she slammed the door in his face.

Diana was his friend; he didn't want it to be like this between them. One day he would explain and make her understand. Once Bobby arrived home he poured himself a drink. He handled the situation with Diana poorly and he didn't feel good about it. She deserved better, much better. Also he didn't feel good about not being in a nice warm bed with Rosaland.

Bobby was lost in thought when his phone rang. "Bobby" he heard her soft voice "Hi Baby" he answered half heartily. She could immediately tell that something was wrong. "Bobby I can't sleep" she whined trying to entice him. "Try. I'm at home tonight sweetie; I'll see you in the morning. Oh by the way you were great today. Remember that." With that Bobby hung up the phone. Rosaland hung up and went to bed. She didn't sleep at all that night, tossing and turning, thinking about what was wrong with her man.

Bobby knew Diana. She was probably outside right now. He was right. A few minutes later Diana was knocking at his door. She was right. He did owe her more than that. Diana was a good detective and she would find out.

Bobby promised Rosaland that he would keep their relationship discreet and he would keep his word to her. Bobby opened the door to let Diana in. As soon as she entered he closed the door behind her. "Bobby I don't know why I'm here but I'm here. I want to talk. I want to clear the air. We have to work together, sometimes on the same cases. Bobby please tell me something."

Diana was crying again. He knew that he had hurt her. He held her close in his arms to comfort her. They talked for a couple of hours; Bobby trying to explain as well as he could without telling her who his new love interest was. "So how come you can't tell me who she is?" Diana was becoming more furious as the time went on. "Because you don't need to know who she is. The fact that you know that she is, is more than enough. Diana I'm sorry." As Diana left his apartment she commented "You'll be back. You always come back." she proudly threw up her head, kissed him softly and closed the door behind her. By the end of the night Bobby felt like shit and both of his women were mad as hell.

twenty

Rosaland started her day with a hot bath. She tossed and turned all night thinking about Bobby. Rachael was right; he was beginning to affect her objectivity. She couldn't allow herself to become distracted. She had a major bust to facilitate. Rosaland finished her bath and got dressed for work. She decided to wear her blue pinstripe suit today. She fumbled through her closet looking for a tailored shirt. She found a sheer white chiffon blouse that was low cut. She liked this one. Rosaland proceeded to get dressed. Her lingerie was exquisite. She choose her skimpiest silver lace bra and panty set.

The bra barely contained her full luscious breasts and the panties were barely there. They were the tiniest thongs that tied on both sides. She found the matching garter belt and comfortably wrapped it around her waist. She attached her silk stockings and admired herself in the mirror.

She dabbed perfume in her pulse points. She applied her makeup carefully. She put more emphasis than usual on her eyes and in outlining her full sensual lips. She brushed her hair, shook it out and fluffed it up with her hands as she left for work. She would drive in to work today so she opened her garage to start her car. Dr. Reid was so preoccupied she forgot the jacket to her suit. She ran back into the brownstone to grab it. Where was her mind? It was on the fact that Bobby didn't come to her last night. She slept alone.

When she arrived at work she put her briefcase on her desk and went into the break room for coffee. Dr. Reid never went into the break room. As she entered she over heard Diana talking to her partner Yvonne… "I don't know what's going with him. But I know that he is seeing someone else." Rosaland froze in horror as she continued to listen. "How do you know that Diana?" Yvonne questioned. "He told me." "He told you?" Yvonne was confused. "Bobby has never been good at lying. It's not his style."

"He told me that he was seeing someone else and that it was serious. He wouldn't tell me who it is. But he said it was someone that I knew. I tried to talk to him, reason with him but you know Bobby. He is always right to the point. That's one of the reasons that I love him so much. When he loves a woman she knows it. What am I going to do? How did I lose my man so easy? And to whom?"

Diana was in tears again her body shaking. Yvonne held her as she cried. Dr. Reid dropped her cup as she listened to the detectives talk. The two of them looked up when her cup hit the floor. "I'm sorry ladies I didn't mean to eavesdrop. I just came in for coffee." Dr. Reid bent down to pick up the broken cup. Diana was still sobbing. Dr. Reid cleaned up the spilled coffee and left the break room. She walked back to her office and sat behind her desk. "So that's were he was last night" she said to herself. He was officially breaking up with Diana. Rosaland couldn't help but to notice how broken up the detective was. Why did she have to see that? She was the other woman. This whole thing was becoming so complicated. How did she get involved with this mess?

"Excuse me Dr. Reid" Detective Rousseau said interrupting her thoughts. Rosaland turned her chair facing the detective "Yes?" "It's about this morning…" Dr. Reid stopped her not letting her finish her sentence. "That was personal. I'm sorry that I didn't leave." At that moment Dr. Reid spotted her father as he came off the elevator. "Saved by the bell" she thought. "Detective is there anything else?" She stood up. "No" "Then if you will excuse me."

Diana left the office as the General entered. She looked back to see the General hug his daughter. Dr. Reid walked over to her file cabinet and produced the Calderon folder. She and the General carefully discussed its contents. She pointed out to her father all the possible strategic locations that the center could be in and how much area it encompassed. Dr. Reid sent out for coffee.

Once their coffee was delivered Dr. Reid turned off the lights in her office to show the General the aerial map. She used the pointer to indicate where her team thought it would be effective to hit the center and why. The General listened intently. He was making mental notes as she spoke.

Dr. Reid shared all the information that she had gathered with her father. They talked for hours. The General was impressed with her comprehension of the situation. Detective Semione entered his office to notice the lights off in Rosaland's office. He wanted to see her. He needed to talk to her about last night.

"What's going on in there?" He asked the Lt. "The General is here. They've been talking for hours." Arthur informed the interested detective.

Bobby nodded his head and went to his desk. He looked through his files for the folder on the D.O.A. he found last month in the dumpster. This case still bothered him. She was still unidentified. He had made no progress what so ever on this case. He studied the folder, looking for some clue that he over looked. He was still coming up blank.

At that point Dr. Reid left her office with the General. She had a folder in her hand as they headed for the basement. This was the area she had selected for the installation of the mainframe. The basement was clean, cool and spacious. It would accommodate the mainframe just perfectly. She provided the General with a tour of the basement facility to see if it met his approval.

She put the folder down that she was carrying as they measured the space. "Dad, this room is in line with my office. This is where I want the coaxial feed. It can be connected directly to my system. We can secure the line and apply a security code that no one would have access to. I could have all the surveillance information routed directly to your office in Washington." The General smiled with approval.

He had taught his daughter well. She was planning to install a completely secured line right to his office from her mainframe. Smart girl, she knew how to handle the hand that feeds her. They exited the basement. When they were back in her office, the General mentioned Officer Jones. Rosaland appeared to be listening. "He's a fine officer and a good man. I'm using him as lead on my surveillance team. He'll be in training for another 6 months before I send him into the field. You know he has a real thing for you."

"Dad, that's personal. That's between him and me." Rosaland was uncomfortable. "I like him; he would make a good husband." The General kept talking. "Well Dad, you should marry him." Dr. Reid snapped as she rolled her eyes in her father's direction.

The time was getting late and the General needed to head back to D.C. He planned to drop in on Rachael and Matthew as well before he left town. Dr. Reid was pleased with their meeting but happy to see him go. She really didn't want to discuss Bill. She settled back in her office and went back to work.

She looked for the folder that contained the measurements for her mainframe. She searched all the papers on her desk but she couldn't find it. She needed that information. What had she done with it? Backtracking her steps she realized that she must have left it in the basement.

Bobby noticed her heading toward the elevator. He left his office and headed down the back steps. He reached the lobby before she did. Bobby stood quietly under the steps waiting for her to descend. Once in the lobby Rosaland started down the steps. When she reached the bottom she looked around for her folder.

Bobby grabbed her hair from the back and forced her against the wall .She fought back starting to scream until she recognized his smile. He pressed his lips fully on hers and kissed her erotically as he began to roughly remove her jacket.

He let her jacket fall to the floor as he starred at the sheer blouse she was wearing. He opened the buttons and placed his hands under her blouse to feel her soft breasts. Rosaland moaned as he touched her nipples. He rubbed her gently. "Bobby what?" He kissed her again pulling her blouse over her arms, exposing her slightly covered breasts. Bobby began to kiss her passionately along her cleavage, opening her bra and sucking her nipples.

Dr. Reid responded to his advances, grinding her body firmly against his. She reached down to touch his engorged penis that was hot, hard and fully erect. She stroked him up and down squeezing his enormous weapon in her hand. "I missed you last night" he whispered in her ear kissing her earlobes and then inserting his tongue deep into her mouth.

Rosaland opened her mouth to receive his tongue; kissing him passionately as she ran her fingers through his hair. Her body was on fire. Bobby reached down and ran his hands up her thighs. The feel of her silk stockings excited him as he fingered her tender slit. He inserted two fingers into her vagina and started rubbing back and forth on her clitoris. Shock waves coursed through her body as she became wet and aroused.

Bobby ripped the thong from her body as he loosened his belt and unzipped his pants. He hiked up her shirt and picked her up. Rosaland opened her legs wide as Bobby inserted his pulsating rod deep into her hot wet private part. They both moaned out simultaneously. Rosaland wrapped her legs around his waist locking him in place. He ground himself deep and deeper into her moist hairy mound. Bobby pumped her harder and stronger burying his full length deep with each powerful stroke.

Rosaland groaned in ecstasy as Bobby stuffed her body with the full length of his hot throbbing weapon. Bobby cramming every inch of his pulsating penis deep into her. Bobby had her impaled on his weapon as he enjoyed the pure essence of her hot wanton body.

Rosaland gasped loudly from the pressure he was applying taking him to the hilt with each steady thrust. Rosaland wanted all of him. She never wanted him to leave her temple. She pumped him harder and stronger giving herself to him completely.

Bobby had to cover her mouth to stifle her cries. Bobby continued to feed her body with his. "Oh Bobby… Bobby." She repeated over and over. The sound of her voice increased his fire as he speared deeper and harder with each delicious stroke. Bobby felt her body trembling in his arms. She was so tantalizing. So absolutely desirable. He could never get enough of her. Bobby pummeled her body relentlessly showering her with his raw passion.

He rubbed her innermost parts with his huge intrusion. She nibbled his ears and held him tightly in her arms as she allowed him to ride her with all his force and persuasion. Bobby's thrusts were hard and deep. He buried himself stroke after stroke, jab after jab. Bobby was whispering in her ear how good she was and how good it felt to be inside of her as she stifled her screams.

Rosaland rode him up and down thoroughly surrendering to his powerful loving. She melted in his arms. Bobby could feel her body tingling, building up to explode. Bobby pounded in and out back and forth until he felt her violently climax around his throbbing intruder. His eruption came next filling her body with his juice. Rosaland was shaking from the power of their orgasm. Bobby held her tight as she whimpered breathlessly in his embrace.

He kissed her quietly trying to calm her down wiping the sweat from her forehead with his hand. Her makeup was running profusely leaving a tear trail down her face. Rosaland's legs were shaking and her stockings torn as he lowered her dangling feet to the floor. It was hard for her to stand or keep her balance and Bobby offered his support.

Rosaland looked down at her clothes. Her blouse was off, her breasts exposed and her hair disshelved. When she was finally able to catch her breathe she spoke "Bobby what are we doing?" "They call that love" he said coolly. Bobby leaned over and kissed her putting on her blouse and pulling her back together. He ran his fingers through her hair musing it the way she liked.

"Can I have my panties back?" She asked holding out her hand. "No, I'm going to keep these in my pocket." He smelled the crotch and put them in his pants. "Bobby I can't walk around all day with no panties" she insisted reaching out her hand for them. "Who's going to know?" He asked teasingly holding them over her head. "You are bad, you are really bad!" She said shaking her head. Bobby grabbed her again and kissed her deeply.

"You had better get back upstairs, I'll come up after you." He handed her the folder. Dr. Reid went back to her office. She couldn't believe what had just happened. They fucked in the basement of the N.Y.P.D. What if some one had discovered them? Dr. Reid went to the ladies room to clean herself up. She combed her hair and applied fresh makeup. She looked at her watch. She and Bobby had been in the basement for over an hour. As she pulled herself back together Detective Rousseau entered the bathroom.

"That's a really pretty blouse." Diana said kindly. Dr. Reid turned around not realizing that anyone was there. "Oh, thank-you. It was the only one I could find this morning." Dr. Reid hastily put her jacket back on. "Dr. Reid I really want to talk to you about this morning."

"Detective if you don't mind I'd rather not get involved in your personal life. I should have left when I noticed that you were upset. Are you alright now?" "Yes, I'll be fine." Dr. Reid nodded and left the bathroom. This was the second time today Detective Rousseau had tried to befriend her.

twenty-one

Dr. Reid needed a drink. She was terribly shaken up. As she switched pass his office Detective Semione smiled. When she got back to her office she had flowers. She smiled and looked in his direction. He smiled back and continued his paper work. The card read "You are so exciting!" she shook her head. Bobby was encourageable. What was she going to do with him besides love him? And she did love him. She loved him very much.

The relationship between Arthur and Rachael wasn't progressing nearly as fast as the whirlwind sexual affair that Rosaland was caught up in with Bobby. Rachael and Arthur was taking it slow and easy, getting to know each other and enjoying each other's company. They spent all of their time off together and Rachael even invited him to dinner with her father. The General liked Arthur and that made Rachael happy. She wanted Arthur but she wasn't going to be caught up like her sister.

Rosaland and Bobby were out of control and Rachael knew it. She was afraid for her sister and she prayed that she wouldn't end up hurt. Rachael knew that they were sleeping together every night. If Bobby wasn't at the brownstone then Rosaland was at his place in Brooklyn. This situation was going to explode and Rachael didn't know what she could do about it.

Arthur decided that it was time to ask Rachael to marry him. They had been dating for months and he wanted to share the rest of his life with her. He also wanted her family to know how much he loved her and that he was serious. Arthur was raised a southern gentleman. He knew before he could ask Rachael, he first had to ask her father. Arthur took a deep breath and called Washington to schedule a meeting. The General was receptive to the Lt. and gladly accepted his meeting.

Arthur left the house early that morning to catch the red eye to D.C. The General had a car pick him up once he arrived and transport him to his office at the Pentagon. The General thought very highly of Arthur for his initiative. The two of them had a nice breakfast and Arthur gingerly announced his intentions towards his daughter. The General was pleased, approved and gave his blessings.

"I wish that my other daughter would come to her senses" Arthur looked puzzled "What do you mean sir?" The General shook his head. "I've got a fine young officer that has been in love with her for years, and she won't give him the time of day, nice young man. This year she claims to be too involved with her work."

"She is dedicated to the O.N.S.I. She spends a lot of time at work. She arrives early and leaves late everyday. She is really concentrating on this Calderon case." Arthur backed her up. He didn't know for sure but he had his suspicions about her and Bobby.

"That's a good report Arthur. Do you know if she is seeing anyone?" "Not to my knowledge, but I'm not really into her social life. Rachael would know. The two of them are inseparable. I'm sorry sir, that I couldn't be more helpful." Arthur did have his suspicions but he had no facts. So he decided to stay completely out of it.

Arthur finished his meeting with the General and the two men spent the rest of the day together, getting to know each other. Arthur left late that night to catch the last train back to New York.

When Arthur arrived back in town he immediately called Rachael. "I know that it's late Rachael but can you meet me for a drink? I just got back in town and I really need to see you." He asked wishfully. "Where do you want to meet?" "What about Natalie's is that easy?" "Ok Arthur I'll meet you there in about an hour."

Rachael arrived at Natalie's before Arthur. When she entered she looked around for him and then sat down at the back bar. Rachael noticed again for the second time that the bartender was talking to himself. Upon further inspection she caught a glimpse of his earphone. She hadn't mentioned it the last time she was there but she would mention it to Arthur this evening.

Rachael sat non-chantlantly waiting for her man. The bartender approached her recognizing her from before "What can I get for you this evening?" He asked kindly. "I'll have a glass of white wine. I'm meeting someone so I'll wait until he arrives." At that moment Arthur walked into the joint. He looked around and spotted his girl waiting at the bar. He walked over and sat down next to her.

"Arthur let's move away from the bar" Rachael requested. "That sounds good." Arthur motioned for the bartender and ordered a bottle of champagne. "Put it on ice" he instructed as he escorted Rachael to a booth in the back. Arthur tenderly kissed her hand. The bartender brought over the bucket with the champagne and two glasses as Arthur continued "Rachael I love you and I have loved you from the first moment I laid eyes on you…" He stopped short to catch his breath. "I want to spend to spend the rest of my life with you. Will you marry me?" Arthur got down on one knee and placed the large diamond engagement ring on her finger. Rachael looking down at the large brilliant stone started to cry; Arthur had caught her completely by surprise.

"Yes Arthur yes!" she reached over and kissed him passionately. Arthur poured the champagne and they toasted. Rachael whispered to Arthur after they finished their bottle "Baby let's leave. I'll explain later." Arthur put the money on the table and escorted Rachael out of the club. Once outside Arthur asked Rachael why she was in such a hurry to leave.

"I think you had better have your detectives check out that place. We were being watched." Rachael explained. Arthur and Rachael went back to Rachael's place to continue their celebration. The two of them danced the night away in the comfort of Rachael's lavish living room. Arthur was ecstatic that Rachael had accepted his proposal of marriage. Arthur was much older than Rachael and he was surprised that such a young beautiful woman would even consider his proposal let alone accept it. The two of them would make a powerful couple.

"You know Rachael the General asked me about Rosaland tonight" Arthur was feeling the bubbly "Oh really what did he say?" "He wanted to know if she is seeing anyone socially." "What brought that up?" "Me asking for your hand in marriage. He said that there is some officer that wants to marry her but she won't give him the time of day and he wanted to know why?"

Rachael was dumbfounded. "Why would he ask you that?" "Because we work together is the only reason that I could come up with. I don't know about your sister's life outside the office but I know for sure that one of my detectives has the real hots for her." Arthur concluded "She is always so professional at work she never gives any indication of anything else but she does receive flowers everyday from somebody." Rachael laughed "That's my sister!"

"Baby I've got to go it's getting late." As Arthur made his apologies the champagne was going to his head. "Seems like I've been up all day." Rachael excitedly kissed Arthur goodnight. As soon as he left she called her wayward sister to share her good news and of course Rosaland wasn't home.

When Arthur arrived at the station the next day he called Detective Semione to his office. Bobby immediately noticed his pleasant attitude. "Bobby that club Natalie's I want you and Diana to check it out. Find out who owns it and what goes on there besides what we see." Bobby was curious "What's up boss?" "I'm not sure just check it out and get back to me." "Am

I looking for anything in particular?" "You're looking for anything you can find." Bobby nodded. "Do you want us on this right away?" "Yes whenever you get around to it but it is important." Arthur confirmed as he finished up some paperwork. "O.k. Boss" Bobby nodded accepting the assignment.

As Bobby passed Dr. Reid's office he noticed that she was on the phone. He tapped on the glass and kept on walking. Rosaland was talking to Rachael. Rachael was telling her about her engagement. At that precise moment Dr. Reid was receiving some information from her fax machine. She scanned over the material and told Rachael that she would call her back.

twenty-two

Rosaland watched in amazement as the information poured in, the paperwork flooding her fax machine. The Calderon bust was in place. Interpol had just faxed confirmation. They would have her warrants when she arrived in the country. She was ready to make the trip. Dr. Reid ran into Lt. Yancy's office with the confirmation. "We are ready to move Lt." She shouted trying to remain calm. She really didn't want Arthur to know just how nervous she really was.

"Who are you going to pull in on this besides Interpol?" He questioned her intensely. "Well on the agency side, we will coordinate with the D.E.A. and the F.B.I. From the squad I want to use Bobby, Danny, Wesley, Justin and you Lt. a five-man team that I can trust. This is going to be an extremely dangerous mission and we have to move now. In approximately ten hours we can be in Bolivia. We can fly in just under the radar. But we have to move now. Oh by the way congratulations Brother in law." Rosaland hugged him and left a fat juicy kiss on his cheek.

The General had made provisions for the lodging and the transportation of the team. Rosaland placed a call to her father to update him on their status and the fact that they were ready to go. "Dad we're ready. We need lodging and transportation to the airport immediately. We have just received our confirmation from Interpol; our warrants are on the way."

"The car will be there for you in two hours; I'll call ahead and have the plane waiting. Interpol will pick you up at the airfield. I'll meet you in Bolivia." The General barked as he hung up the phone. He and his men were on the move. Arthur called Bobby, Danny and the rest of the team into his office. Once he briefed them to the facts of what was going down Dr. Reid and her crew prepared to leave for the airfield. They had little less than an hour before the plane would arrive.

Once on the plane Dr. Reid filled them in on the entire mission. "My father will facilitate the raid. He is here to lend air support if needed. The D.E.A. and Interpol will conduct the raid. The F.B.I. will offer backup. Detectives Semione and Schmidt will assist in the tactical assault. Lt. Yancy will provide back up with the sharpshooters. I'll be coordinating my efforts with Intel from Interpol headquarters to scrutinize and decipher information." Rosaland looked directly at Bobby who was pleased with her decision to stay out of it.

As Dr. Reid spoke she handed her team the top secret folders that her office had compiled of the location. "Are there any questions?" She asked repeatedly. "This is going to be a precision exercise down to the last minute. Time is of the essence and our timing on this is everything. If we are off even by a half of a second a lot of some bodies will die. Calderon is a very dangerous man and his cartel is ruthless. He's not expecting us not that we know anyway. That will be our advantage our element of surprise, but if we are remotely successful there will be extreme repercussions. Calderon will strike back."

"My father and I have agreed that we don't want to endanger the lives of the whole team. In the event that something goes wrong the whole unit won't be in jeopardy. That is why we have chosen just a few select men for this operation. Are there any questions? I need you guys to talk to me. Are there any questions?"

Bobby didn't want Rosaland in this situation. He understood that this was her job but now that they were facing danger he wanted her out. He wanted to protect her. There had to be something that he could do to keep her safe. "Lt." The anxious detective looked at his boss "Why does Dr. Reid have to be here? This is a drug raid; can't you keep her on the plane?" Bobby was wearing his feelings for Dr. Reid on his shirtsleeve.

"Detective Semione this is her operation. She is in control and she makes the calls" the Lt. spoke up. "Our role here is to assist." Rosaland looked at Bobby "I'll be alright detective. Thanks for the concern." She added sincerely. If Arthur had any doubts before he knew for sure that Bobby was in love with Dr. Reid. He could see it all over his face. He was deeply in love with her.

"Bobby you promised me..." she whispered under her breath "Not now..." she shook her head no. Bobby knew what she meant. "Did everyone have the opportunity to look over the location?" She tried to redirect. "The red arrows indicate where the insurgence team will strike. Detectives Semione and Schmidt will be a part of that team. The blue arrows indicate the backup shooters. Lt. Yancy, Detective Cole and Detective Schwartz you will be part of that team. You will all get your uniforms and your weapons when we arrive."

There was a great deal of anticipation as the plane headed towards Miami. The team had to fly from New York to Miami to make the connection from Costa Rica to Bolivia. They would have to land in La Paz which currently served as the capital of government and be transported to D.E.A. headquarters under heavy guard.

During flight time Dr. Reid briefed her team at least three more times constantly going over pertinent information and the entry and exit procedures again and again. She wanted the procedures drilled into their heads. Bobby wanted to put his arms around her. He wanted to hold her tight. He wanted to make to love to her but all that had to wait. He needed to keep his mind on the mission.

If he allowed himself to be distracted then he could jeopardize his life, her life as well as the lives of the members of his tactical unit. Bobby closed his eyes and tried to clear his mind. The team assembled when their plane started it's decent into the international airport at La Paz. Their pilot was instructed to fly below Bolivian air space so not to be detected by radar. If discovered they would be in violation of the international air treaty made between the United States and Bolivia.

Dr. Reid worked steadily on her laptop to make sure that there had been no changes in their position and to make sure that there would be no unexpected surprises. Calderon was a crafty adversary; he had eyes and ears everywhere.

Rosaland watched Bobby as he slept, running her fingers through his hair when no one was looking. Suddenly the plane hit some turbulence shaking up everyone on board. As they rapidly approached the airfield the General spoke over the radio supplying them with the correct landing coordinates. Once on the ground, the General was there with the insurgence team and the international drug enforcement agency.

Bobby and the boys were issued standard drug enforcement agency uniforms, vests and military side arms. The Detectives choose to use their own weapons. They felt more comfortable. It was too late in the game to toss in any new factors.

Dr. Reid was escorted to the base camp where she met with international police (Interpol) and the local Bolivian officials to present her warrants. After coordinating the Intel and other pertinent information the tactical unit was ready to strike.

In a military operation emotion only makes you sloppy. It interferes with good judgment. They had to hit fast, hard and effective. The General led black ops taking command of the insurgence team.

The demolition team was the first to strike. The distribution center was hit with c-4 followed by hand grenades and plastic explosives. Once the perimeter was secured the insurgence team went in with assault weapons, nine millimeters, m60's, m80's, Uzis, grenade guns, rocket launchers, and m16's. All hell broke loose as explosions followed and the bullets flew. Calderon's army fought back with as much precision as the insurgence team. They had an arsenal of weaponry that rivaled their nemesis. No way were they going down without a fight.

The siege lasted for days as the insurgence team fought to take the drug distribution center and Calderon's men fought to keep it secured. The General eventually had to call in backup air support as Calderon's men pinned them down. To launch the final attack would leave the land devastated. On his signal stinger missiles were deployed to completely destroy the processing lab and the surrounding area.

The facilitation of this operation would prove to be a major setback for the Calderon cartel. The casualties were high, the death toll rose, and many men were lost. The international D.E.A. confiscated an enormous amount of weapons and product and even more cash from the remains of the facility. This was the evidence the O.N.S.I.would need to convict Calderon of narcotics trafficking if they could ever capture him.

Back on the island of Calderon, Carlos was being advised on the destruction of his installation. He was furious! Who was behind this? How did they learn of his operation? Who was supplying them with the information? He wanted answers to all these questions and he wanted them now. How did they catch him so off guard? How many more of his centers would be targeted? This raid cost him millions. Someone was going to pay with his or her life.

Carlos prepared to return to New York. He would visit some old acquaintances from the United Nations to see if they could help lead him in the direction of some of his questions. He needed some inside information and he needed it now.

The raid on the facility was a success except it left one man down. The Lt. had been shot! Arthur was caught in the cross fire and took a bullet to the chest. He was severely injured and had lost a lot of blood. When Dr. Reid received the casualty list she was hysterical. Arthur was being airlifted to the military hospital in Bolivia. How was she going to explain this to her sister? They had just recently become engaged.

Rosaland had to make the phone call to Rachael. "Rachael, are you sitting down?" Rachael could hear the somberness in Rosaland's voice. "Rosaland what's wrong?" She asked suddenly realizing that she really didn't want to know. "Rachael its Arthur. He's been shot." Rosaland could hear her sister start to breath loudly and break down in tears as she continued to listen. "He has been airlifted to the military hospital in Sucre. He's been in surgery for about five hours. Rachael he's in the best of hands and we're waiting for the doctors to tell us something." At this point Rachael was sobbing hysterically.

"Is he dead?" She muttered through her tear choked voice. "No, sweetie, he's still in surgery. He has a good chance, but we just don't know yet. We're still waiting. Oh Rachael I'm so sorry!" At this point both of the sisters were in tears. "Dad is here Rachael stay by the phone I'll call you back. Arthur is going to be all right. We are all praying for him. Rae I'll call you back."

Dr. Reid hung up with her sister and went back to the waiting room. She felt responsible. She was responsible. She made the call and now her sister's fiancée' was fighting for his life. Bobby could feel her pain as he tried to comfort her. "This comes with the job Baby." That could have been anyone of us. We take this chance everyday. Every time we put on that badge and hit the streets, this is how it can end up." She knew Bobby was right, but it still hurt.

All she could hear in the back of her mind was Rachael's crying. Bobby held her tightly in his arms. She placed her head on his chest where she felt safe and secure. This was a very natural place for her to be. When the General returned to the waiting room he noticed their closeness. He stopped short looking at the both of them; they separated once they realized he was there. Dr. Reid turned her attention back to Arthur with tears rolling down her face.

The General knew at that moment that this detective was the man in his daughter's life. He would wait patiently to see how long it would take them to tell him or if he was right. The team waited in silence for some news on Arthur's condition. His surgery lasted for hours and hours. The doctors worked continuously all through the night in an effort to save his life.

If Arthur survived she would airlift him back to a hospital in New York. Dr. Reid prayed for the life of her future brother in law. Rachael would never forgive her if Arthur died. Rosaland would never be able to forgive herself if her judgment had been wrong. She needed Arthur on that wall. His presence was vital to the success of the mission.

Finally several days later Arthur was out of surgery. It had been touch and go. The doctors were able to remove the bullet but he had lost a great deal of blood and was still unconscious. They listed him in critical condition suffering from a severe chest wound. The next twenty-four hours would be crucial. All they could do was pray and wait. Rosaland immediately called her sister to give her the progress report. Rachael sighed in relief.

"Arthur is out of surgery Rae but he's not out of the woods yet. The doctors are going to watch him for another twenty-four hours. As soon as we know it is safe for him to travel, I'll arrange for him to be transported back to New York. In the meantime we still have to finish our business here." Rachael listened intently as her sister spoke.

"Is he going to be alright? I'm going crazy. I'm catching the next flight to Bolivia. It has already been days and I can't take this. I want to be with him. I need to be with him." Rosaland knew that there was nothing she could say that would change Rachael's mind and then again she didn't want to. Having Rachael here would also make her feel better.

"Ok sweetie have you already made your arrangements?" Rosaland inquired. "Dad's secretary has faxed me a copy of my complete itinerary. I'll be there tomorrow evening. I want to be there when he regains consciousness." Rachael's mind was made up.

"Rosaland, I know you and I know what you're feeling. There is no way you are responsible for this. It's all part of the job. It's unfortunate that it had to occur but Roz it could have been anybody and it can happen at any time. Thank God that he is still alive. Do you understand what I'm saying to you?" "Yes, Rachael, thank you." "How can you thank me I'm your sister? I love you. You know we girls have to stick together. I'll see you in the morning." Rachael hung up the phone and began to pack her bags for Bolivia.

Rachael was still quite shaken; she couldn't believe that Arthur was in Bolivia clinging to his s life. She had to go to him to be with him. She would never forgive herself if she didn't make it to see him. Shc had so much to tell him she couldn't lose him like this. The tears rolled down her face as she grabbed clothes from her closet and stuffed them into her bag.

Rachael called her office to let them know that she had an emergency and that she had to be out of the country for a while. She arranged for Matt Rosenberg to handle her case load until she returned.

twenty-three

The O.N.S.I's business with the Calderon Cartel was far from finished. During the raid several of Calderon's men had been captured. The General along with the international Interpol questioned them intensely. None of the men would talk. They would rather face death or imprisonment than to betray Carlos.

The men all shared a code of silence, and none of them would be disloyal. Loyalty was Carlos's number one rule and no one was willing to violate it. Nobody respects a rat. Dr. Reid made a very formidable enemy.

Carlos would show no mercy when he discovered who was ruining his organization and his day-to-day business. He had no idea that the federal government was hot on his trail. He thought the heat was coming from some rival faction of his cartel. He needed to know who was in charge and how they were able to strike so effectively without being detected. He would visit New York, and find his answers.

Carlos was too flamboyant; he had brought too much attention to himself. He had violated his father's first rule, never let the outside world know about the family business, and now he was paying the price.

Dr. Reid sat on the balcony of her hotel room overlooking the tropical lushness of Bolivia. She had a million things on her mind, foremost was the condition of the Lt. Dr Reid ordered a bottle of Hennessey with a tall glass of ice and was sipping on it. The events of the week had begun to wear on her and she was very tired. Tomorrow she would be in La Paz, which is the seat of government in Bolivia.

The night air was warm and the Hennessey was hot going straight to her head. She stripped out of her clothes and sat back in her scanty underwear on the balcony undetected. In the background she could hear the native music coming from the neighboring nightclubs. Dr. Reid listening from the distance decided to take a shower and go to one of the clubs.

It would be a good way for her to clear her head; also it would make her more familiar with the locals. Maybe she could learn a thing or two about the government before she had her meeting tomorrow. At any rate, she needed to get out of her room, especially since Bobby was still standing guard over Arthur.

She called the hospital to check with her detectives. There was no change in Arthur's condition. He was still unconscious and under constant watch. Rosaland talked with both Bobby and Danny making sure that they were all right. She suggested that the two of them should get some sleep, and she would send Wes and Justin as relief but they decided to stay with their Lt.

She told Bobby that she was going out to one of the local nightclubs and he should call her on her cell phone if there was any change in Arthur's condition. Bobby told her that he didn't think it was a good idea for her to be out alone. "I'm a big girl detective. I'll be alright." At that moment there was a knock at her door. She answered the door with the phone in her hand; Bobby could hear the General's voice in the background.

"Detective get back to me immediately if there is any change?" Bobby knew that she didn't want her father to know of their involvement so he hung up the phone. "How are you doing sweetie?" Her father was concerned. He knew how she felt about Arthur and about Arthur being shot. He wanted to make sure that she was all-right. "I'm fine, Dad. I just called the hospital to see if there was any word on Arthur. Nothing has changed. He is still unconscious. Rachael will be here tomorrow. I'll feel a lot better when she arrives."

The General hugged his daughter and kissed her on the forehead. "You did a wonderful job. I am very proud of you. Once this is over, I'm going to make sure that everyone involved gets rewarded for his or her fine work. You put together a great team, and the strike was very effective. The distribution center was completely destroyed and we confiscated a great deal of weapons, money and drugs. Unfortunately there was no sign of Calderon."

"We now have more than enough evidence against Calderon. Good work sweetheart. You need to get some sleep." "I was feeling tired earlier, but now I think I'm going to do some work on my computer. I need to check my mainframe to see if there have been any updates." Rosaland was lying. She had all intentions of being out in the club. "You need to get some rest. You have to meet with the Bolivian government officials tomorrow and you should be rested." The General ordered.

"I'll be fine dad, besides I can't sleep now," she complained. "Why, are you waiting for that detective?" Rosaland looked shocked and amazed. She was at a complete lost for words. "I saw the way he was holding you at the hospital, even if you don't care for him; he certainly cares a great deal for you. And I believe you care for him as well." The General spoke openly and honestly.

"We work together Dad. He is the lead detective in the unit. We were all shaken up over Arthur." "Whatever you say dear." The General shook his head as he proceeded to the door. After he left Rosaland started to laugh. She could never fool her Dad. Sooner or later she would have to come clean and tell him about Bobby.

As Rosaland stepped from the shower she heard the phone ringing. She ran to the bedroom to answer the phone before the caller hung up. She grabbed up the phone "Hello?" It was Bobby on the other end. "I was trying to catch you before you left. I'll be there in about an hour wait for me. You are not going out this late without me." Bobby hung up the phone.

Rosaland started to dress as she waited for Bobby to arrive. The night was very warm and the air was lusty so she decided on a slight sundress and a pair of strappy sandals. She put on a delicate black lace bra with the matching g-string and sat on her balcony with a drink as she waited for her man. She would have to tell him about the General's suspicions.

After Bobby hung up the phone he walked back into the waiting room where Danny was posting watch on Arthur. "Danny I have something to take care of. I'll be back in a couple of hours." Danny looked up and gave him a nod "Go ahead I'll stay here with the Lt. That something that you have to do wouldn't be the lovely Dr. Reid now would it?"

Bobby smiled that smile that men understand all too well "You know it every time I can." He replied completely serious. "Bobby you've got it bad for her. You need to go ahead and marry that girl. Her father is going to kill you when he finds out you have been shoplifting the poodie." "Danny you have been watching too many movies" Bobby laughed loudly shaking his head. "I saw him in action today" Danny continued "And believe me; I'd rather have him as a friend. He's too powerful to have as an enemy. What are you waiting for?" Bobby knew that Danny was right.

It was becoming harder and harder for the two of them to hide their feelings. Everyone was beginning to sense their involvement. Bobby wondered if he was ready for marriage. He loved Rosaland but marriage? He liked the relationship just as it was and he assumed that she did too. It was her idea that they remain a secret. They had a good thing going just the way it was.

Danny's question would haunt him for the rest of the evening. As Bobby walked toward the hotel he could hear the music in the air. Bolivia seemed to be coming alive. It would be nice to go and see how the natives partied. He entered the hotel and went to the second floor. He stopped in his room to shower and change his clothes. The night was tropical and there was a great deal of excitement in the air as he dressed for a night on the town with his favorite girl.

After getting dress Bobby took the steps up to Rosaland's room. "I hope you're planning to wear more than that?" Bobby said as he stood in the doorway of the terrace. Rosaland looked up at him and smiled. She pointed to her dress. "Yes" as she walked over to give him a kiss. Bobby took her in his arms as they kissed lustfully.

Bobby ran his hands along her well-formed full breasts and kissed her along the nape of her neck. At that point her phone rang. She slowly withdrew from their embrace as she walked over to answer the phone. "Hello?" She said breathlessly. The voice of her father came booming in "Rosaland?" "Yes Dad?" "What are you doing?" "I'm on my way out" "Are you going out alone?" "No sir Detective Semione is here with me. He and I are going out together for a drink."

Rosaland was motioning for Bobby to give her the dress she had hanging on the mirror. She quickly got dressed as her father continued "I'm glad that you found some one to escort you. Why don't the two of you stop by before you go out we can all have a drink"? "Ok Dad we'll be right there." Rosaland hung up the phone. She turned around to look at Bobby and they both started to laugh.

"He wants us to come up for a drink before we go out. Bobby I need to warn you my Dad has some suspicions about us." "What are you talking about?" "Yes he mentioned it to me this evening and I told him we were co-workers. He caught me off guard. We really need to be professional in his presence." "Ok we can do that. Let's go."

For some reason that disturbed Bobby. He really didn't like the fact that he had to remain discreet. When they arrived at the General's room they were surprised to see him in such a good mood. "Detective" he greeted Bobby extending his hand. Bobby shook the General's hand. "Sir?" "Your team did a good job." "Thank you sir." "So you're going to make sure my daughter is safe?" "Yes sir" "Would the two of you like a drink before you go?" "No sir we are going out for a couple of drinks." "Well Rosaland has an early morning meeting so I trust you won't keep her out too late?" "Dad I'm not sixteen" Rosaland spoke up. "No sir but I will make sure that she is safe." Bobby gave his word.

"Thank you. Ok I'll see you in the morning Rosaland. I would like to have breakfast to brief you before the meeting perhaps the detective can join us as well" The General offered. "Ok Dad I'll see you in the morning."

Bobby and Rosaland left the hotel and headed out for a night on the town. The two of them walked in silence hand in hand as they explored the town's demographics. They discovered a nice café' with live music. It was full of people dancing and drinking. They found an empty table and sat down surveying how live this whole in the wall was. Bobby immediately started swaying to the music. He motioned for the bartender and ordered their drinks.

At this point Rosaland spoke "Bobby what's wrong you haven't said a word since we left the hotel?" She picked up her drink and slowly started to sip it. "Have I told you how sexy you look?" Bobby looked at her. "Your father is making sure that I'm not going to sleep with you tonight. What are we doing?" "What kind of question is that?" "Rosaland you know what I mean, are you ever going to tell him what's happening between us?" "Tell him what? That we've been sleeping together out of wedlock for months? No Bobby I don't think so."

"No Rosaland. Are you ever going to tell him that we are in love and that we are going to get married?" Rosaland was speechless. She finished her drink and replied "Bobby you have never mentioned marriage" "I've never mentioned it because of your job." "What has my job got to do with marriage?" "Your job always comes first. I promised you that we would be discreet but we are not fooling anybody. We are just fooling ourselves. Come on we'll talk about this later. Let's dance and have some fun." Bobby was frustrated.

The Latin American rhythms that filled the room were intoxicating. Bodies swayed to and fro to the sultry beat of the drums. The night air was hot and exciting as the people pulsated and gyrated to the music. Bobby was in his glory. This music was native to his culture; he removed his shirt as the sweat poured over his muscular chest as he kept on dancing. Rosaland and Bobby danced close together gyrating seductively as the music carried them away.

The sweat poured profusely from their bodies. At some point Bobby opened the top buttons of Rosaland's sun dress to expose her gorgeous bosoms which had sweat running between them. The two were caught up in a magical mystical moment as the music filled their souls. Rosaland reached out and pulled Bobby even closer, wrapping her arms around his waist and burying her luscious breasts deep into his chest. Bobby grabbed her by the back of her hair and kissed her affectionately, while their bodies continued to undulate to the intense Latin rhythms.

Rosaland let her hands slide down to his well shaped ass and pulled him even closer, squeezing his buttocks between her fingers as they danced. Their momentum was building when Rosaland changed her position and now had her delicious posterior pressed into his groin as she rotated and wiggled her ass sensuously in front of him. Even though the club was full of dancing, sweating bodies, it was as if no one else was there but the two of them.

They danced erotically until the music stopped. Where had the time gone? Bobby grabbed her and picked her up in his arms, swinging her around in the air and then he hugged her tightly. She kissed him gently and he slowly lowered her body to the ground, sliding her down the bulge that was starting to grow in his pants. Bobby kissed her, this time applying a kiss that made time stand still.

They lingered there lost in their embrace. As their lips parted they both knew exactly what they wanted. Bobby starred at her amorously and then ordered another round of drinks. Rosaland wanted him badly. The sexual tension between them was overwhelming, as they sipped their last drink in silence and left the club.

Arm in arm they strolled through the crowd enjoying the sights and the exotic fragrance of Bolivia. As they walked Bobby picked some wildflowers from a bush and placed them in Rosaland's hair, which was damp from all the dancing. It hung limply around her face and over her shoulders. Bobby pushed the wet hair out of her face and began kissing her arousingly as they walked through the streets.

They walked a little further Rosaland spotting a secluded grotto and taking his hand pulled him toward the entrance. Once inside they looked around for a private area where they could be alone. Bobby pointed to a nice little niche and they proceeded over to where the small waterfall was forming.

The grotto was beautiful full of lush foliage and tall leafy trees. Rosaland sat down to remove her shoes and dangle her feet in the water. The water was warm and shallow and the night air was exuberating. It was the perfect setting for being with the one you loved. Rosaland removed her dress and her undergarments and slid into the warm water; she cupped her hands and applied the wetness to her face and hair. The warm water ran down her full breasts and over her flat belly to her private area.

Bobby was removing his clothes to join her; soon he stood naked in all his splendor and entered the water. Rosaland pulled Bobby under the small waterfall and wrapped her legs around him as the water cascaded over their naked and exposed bodies.

Rosaland kissed him hungrily; exhibiting a greed that he was not familiar with. Bobby was intrigued with her aggressiveness as he acquiesced to her tender touch. She began to kiss every inch of his body slowly going down to his strong Johnson which stood fully erect. She kissed the huge head of his weapon and inserted the shaft into her sweet mouth. She ran her tongue over the engorged member and sucked it deep into her throat.

Bobby was ecstatic and his body shuttered as she began to pull hard taking more of him in. She moved her head back and forth opening her mouth wide as Bobby pressed himself into her face. Rosaland continued her vacuum motions treating Bobby to an inordinate amount of pleasure. Bobby moaned, groaned, and spasmed under her lavish oral attentions.

Bobby reached down to cup her firm full breasts and began to rub them gently. Bobby was in ecstasy; he couldn't believe that she could possess him so completely. Bobby's body began to tremble and his knees became weak under him. It was hard to sustain his own weight while Rosaland continued to suck and nibble, to please her man. She was incredible. He had never felt like this before with anyone. Rosaland inhaled more and more of him, as Bobby thrust in the throes of his own excitement.

Rosaland grasp the shaft of his hardness so that she could have full control over the depth of his penetration into her mouth. She relaxed as she allowed Bobby to feed more of his massive intrusion down her throat. Bobby's moans grew louder as he whispered her name. The warm night air and the lushness of the grotto enhanced their excitement.

The lovely suction of her mouth was slowly beginning to build in his glans. At any moment he would explode right down her throat. Bobby withdrew his engorged manhood from her mouth. He lifted her from her knees, holding her tightly as he planted a deep soul-stirring kiss on her quivering lips. Rosaland responded to his embrace opening her mouth wide to receive his tongue, she wrapped her arms around his neck and climbed onto his body, her body trembling with desire.

Bobby positioned her as she enclosed her legs securely around his waist. He inserted the head of his monster erection between her legs. Rosaland groaned at the initial contact as he completely buried his entire length into her hot soaking privacy. The two were caught up in a lustful frenzy. Rosaland clinging to him as they released their pent up passion.

"That's my Baby" Bobby whispered amorously in her ear. "Ohh Bobby" she moaned breathlessly. Rosaland riding him like the fine sleek stallion that he was. That night the grotto was filled with the orgasmic sounds of erotica, as the two remained lost in love until the wee hours of the morning. The dawn was breaking when the lovers finally emerged from the mist.

They strolled arm in arm back to the hotel. All the events from the day seemed to be taking a toll. Suddenly they both felt very tired and extremely emotion filled. They appreciated the life that they had and the love that they shared. Bobby escorted Rosaland to her room and waited for her to open the door then he kissed her goodnight.

As Bobby turned to walk up the stairs Rosaland grabbed his arm pulling him back "Bobby stay with me." She pleaded deliberately trying to make her face look lonely. "No baby not tonight. Not with your Father watching. I'll see you in the morning before your meeting, and besides I need to talk to your old man. It's time." Rosaland handed him the key to her room before she locked the door behind her. Bobby waited until she was secure then he ascended the stairs and went to bed.

He tried to sleep but his thoughts were with her. He wanted to hold her in his arms to feel her warm exciting body in bed next to his and he wanted to smell her hair. Bobby loved the smell of her hair. He simply wanted her close to him where she belonged.

Bobby's instincts told him that they were being watched. He had done enough surveillance over the years to know the signs. The couple in the nightclub that was having a little too much fun or the stranger in the grotto that was a little too drunk and the mysterious van that appeared at the hotel entrance shortly after they arrived. He knew the trail would lead back to the General but what he hadn't figured out to this point was why?

The General was an exceptionally powerful man. Bobby knew that he could ruin his career as well as destroy his life with a single phone call. He would play it smart and give the General the respect that a man in his position deserved; on the other hand Bobby wanted the General to know that he loved his daughter and that she belonged to him. It would be he that would protect her and keep her safe from harm.

First thing in the morning he would clear the air. He would talk to the General about his feelings for Rosaland and ask for permission to marry her? In the meantime unable to sleep Bobby stood on his terrace and carefully observed the hotel comings and goings. It seemed to be inordinately busy for so early in the morning. There was constant movement as different teams of people shifted from here to there. Obviously there was something going on. Whatever it was the General was at the hub of all the activity.

twenty-four

The General's plate was full. He had at least a dozen phone calls to make before 0:600. He had several meetings scheduled including the one with his daughter who happened to be the head of the O.N.S.I. Rachael's flight was arriving this morning as well and he had to make sure that he had a strong military presence at the airport to meet her. It seemed that all hell was about to break loose. The word of the raid on the distribution center was out and the team was in eminent danger as long as they remained in Bolivia.

Carlos had a great deal of influence in this part of the world. He was playing on his home court where he definitely had the advantage. They had come into his backyard and shut down one of his major sources of income. There was no way that he was going to accept this slap in the face. There would be a great deal of retaliation to whatever American governmental agency that was responsible.

The General knew that it would be foolish to think that there would be no retribution.

The General had to worry about the safety of his children. They were in a country where it would be nothing but a matter of time, before Carlos would arrange for either a kidnapping or a murder. The General was not going to wait around for either one of these options.

Arthur was still lying in a deep coma and it was Rosaland's responsibility to make sure that he had adequate security. Danny had been on an all night watch while she and Bobby fraternized and now it was time for Bobby to take the next shift. Everything was happening too fast. There were too many decisions that needed to be made in a short period of time.

The General knew that he needed to get all the Americans on his daughter's team out of Bolivia. Also he was faced with another dilemma.

Was he going to open the manila envelope that was left on his desk? He knew what he would find if he looked inside at the contents but he didn't know if he wanted to invade his daughter's privacy on this level or if he would let her come to him on her own.

He picked up the envelope and then laid it back down. The General had invested a great deal into his family having lost his wife when the children were so young. He couldn't afford to allow anyone to dishonor the family unit that he had worked so hard to build. He sat down behind his desk to look over the file he had on Detective Roberto Semione.

Bobby's record reflected a fine officer and a hard working man. He had been highly decorated for his years of service with the N.Y.P.D. His academy record was impeccable and his personal background illustrated a good moral upbringing. He too was a family man being raised by his grandparents in a strong Catholic environment.

Bobby was highly trained in hand-to-hand combat, sharp shooting and he had an extensive background in forensics. The General was impressed with his outstanding credentials and his leadership abilities. It was very easy to understand why his daughter had fallen so hard and so deeply in love with this man.

As the General continued to study his profile he also noted that Bobby was dedicated to his community. Bobby had several drug busts to his credit and now the General had a real picture of why she had chosen him to come to Bolivia.

The General became distracted with the sudden knock at his door. It was very early in the morning and he wasn't expecting to get started until after breakfast. "Come in" the General answered still lost in the file. Bobby stepped in the room and stood waiting for the General to acknowledge his presence.

"Excuse me sir" Bobby said after a minute or two. The General looked up over his glasses and closed the file. "Yes Detective how can I help you?" "I want to talk to you sir, may I have a moment of your time?" "Yes as a matter of fact you can." The General turned his chair facing the Detective and motioned for him to sit down.

The General starred at him intently, waiting for him to speak. "Sir" Bobby was trying to find just the right words "I would like to assure you that my intentions are honorable and I do love your daughter. She is the best thing that has ever happened to me." Bobby was very nervous. "I apologize for not speaking to you before but due to our working situation we both decided that it would be best if we kept our relationship discreet." The word "relationship" perked the General's ears up. That was all that he heard.

"When we return to New York, I would like your permission to marry her." Bobby took a deep breath and continued, "I know that Rosaland has worked hard implementing the O.N.S.I. and I know that it is her first priority. As for my job with the N.Y.P.D. I love my work and I intend to stay with it. I know that my job is dangerous and no one wants to be married to a cop but I will protect her."

"You don't have to tell me about her hard work she has been bringing in the results since the inception. Her hard work is the reason why we are here today. The O.N.S.I. has a specific mission and that mission has yet to be accomplished. Detective nothing can interfere with this project which is important to our national security. We must stop this man and until now no one has ever been able to get this close or gather this much information."

"Rosaland needs to remain extremely levelheaded at this point. Emotions make you vulnerable to your enemies." It seemed as though the General was speaking more to himself than to Bobby. "Detective just how long has this been going on between the two of you?" Bobby looked surprised, "I'm sorry sir but did I miss something? I'm not here to discuss our relationship. I'm here to ask for your permission and most of all you're blessing to marry your child. That's it. What we share is ours."

Bobby's sense of loyalty and also his natural instinct to protect her took the General by surprise. But he would press him a little harder, to see how far he would go. "It's hard raising girls without their mother detective" the General continued "Please sir call me Bobby." "It's hard Bobby to raise female children without the guidance of a mother. I have always worried that my daughters would make good decisions when it came to the men they would marry. Their whole lives I have had to worry if they would be promiscuous or had I given them enough moral upbringing to know that their bodies were sacred and they should save themselves for marriage. No one wants used goods."

That last remark hit Bobby like a ton of bricks. Rosaland was a virgin until him and he definitely did not consider her to be used goods but he could not tell her Father that. All of a sudden it hit him. That's what she had been afraid of. What her Father would think of her if he knew about them.

"Sir you have done one hell of a job with all of your children. You should be very proud. I love Rosaland; I would give my life for her. All I have to offer her is my heart and she has had that for years. In you she has everything else. That is something that I could never compete with."

"I fell in love with her six years ago when she entered the academy. I saw you bring her to campus. I watched from my window as you pulled up and sent your officers through the dorm to make sure that it was safe that's when both you and she got out of the car. She was the prettiest woman I had ever seen. I remembered her smile and the way her hair was blowing in the breeze." Bobby reminiscenced, never ever having told this to anyone.

The General listened intently as Bobby continued his story, "I knew that day that she was the one for me. I waited five years for her to come back into my life and she did, you sent her back to me. I'll never forget the day she walked into the station, all I could do was smile. I bet I looked like a real idiot standing there smiling at her. I told my partner Danny that day that I was going to marry her."

Bobby smiled to himself as he thought back and then he remembered the first time they made love. Bobby turned to look the General straight in the eyes. "Sir she's mine and I am hers. She belongs to me. We belong to each other. I will protect her and I will love her, and I will make her happy you have my word on that." Bobby was finished. There was nothing else to be said.

The General knew exactly how he felt. Bobby extended his hand and the General shook it. "You're a good man Bobby. You have my blessings." The two gentlemen embraced and Bobby turned to leave, thanking the General for his time. "Bobby" the General handed him the manila envelope that had been lying on his desk unopened. Bobby looked puzzled. "I didn't open this envelope. I have a pretty good idea what it contains, you can either open it or destroy it, it's up to you. This is between you and me and as far as I am concerned, it never existed".

Bobby nodded, accepted the envelope and left the General's room. Once back in his room Bobby reluctantly opened the envelope. He poured the photos on his bed and sat down to look at them. As he browsed over the contents he noticed that they were of an extremely sensitive nature.

The photos were from the grotto the night before. They had been caught in the act and were fully exposed. There was no denying the content and the photos were very explicit. After carefully scrutinizing the contents of the envelope, Bobby decided to burn them. He didn't want Rosaland to see these sexually explicit photos of him and her. He knew that the General had ordered the surveillance to protect his daughter but he never wanted her to know that someone outside of himself had seen her displayed in such a manner.

Bobby would deal with this situation in time but for now he needed to destroy the evidence. Bobby was enraged that someone had seen Rosaland in this way. This was an extremely intimate moment shared by two lovers and only he had the privilege of knowing her in this most private sense of being.

What had the General intended to do with this intimate information? Would he blackmail his own daughter, or maybe he was trying to keep this information out of the hands of someone else who could blackmail him, or better yet, maybe they had been taking for the General's information only.

Bobby had a thousand questions; these pictures were very personal. As Bobby went to stand on the balcony he was just in time to witness the breath taking Bolivian sunrise. The horizon was picturesque as the heavens were filled with the colors of the rainbow while the sun moved into position in the sky. The tranquility was hypnotic.

Bobby stood there for what seemed to be hours, but in essence it was only a few minutes, lost in thought. Bobby was experiencing mixed emotions, on one hand he was grateful that the General turned over the photos, on the other hand he was very angry that their privacy had been invaded in such a manner.

He would find some way to show his appreciation to the General for the gesture of trust and consideration shown to him. He would also find a way to have his revenge for the invasion of their privacy. He decided to confide this to Rosaland. There would be no secrets between them. Bobby had good instincts and he was pleased with himself that he had followed them so early in the morning.

He stepped back into his room to call downstairs. He expected to hear a half-sleeping voice answer but the phone just rang. With his gun strapped to the inside of his jacket he casually strolled down the steps and used his key to enter Rosaland's room.

As he looked around the room he noticed her nightgown lying on the bed. Bobby could hear the sound of running water coming from the bathroom. Rosaland was safe. She was in the shower. She too was up early preparing for her breakfast meeting with the General. Bobby reclined back on the bed again focusing on the beautiful sky. He cupped his fingers together and placed his head in his hands as he concentrated on the amazing array of colors that permeated the early morning horizon.

Bobby must have dozed off because he didn't hear the water turn off when Rosaland finished her shower. Rosaland was slightly startled when she emerged from the bathroom, but she was very happy to see Bobby relaxing comfortably on the bed. Noticing that his eyes were closed, she tipped toed over to kiss him gently on the lips. "Wake-up sleepy head" she whispered softly, so not to disturb him.

She kissed him again and noticing how comfortable he looked, she decided to get dressed, and let him sleep. She unwrapped the large cotton bath towel, and began to lotion her naked body. The cool lotion felt nice on her skin. Bolivian summers were incredibly hot and could leave you feeling sticky by midday.

Bobby looked cool in his light beige linen shirt, so she decided that she would wear linen as well. She needed to present a professional appearance at her breakfast meeting with her Dad, so linen was the only logical choice. Rosaland had a busy day in front of her, after her meeting with the Bolivian officials, she had made arrangements to go to the airport to greet Rachael, and then they would be headed to the hospital to check on Arthur. She also had to finalize the paperwork to extradite the prisoners and the evidence back to New York.

Bobby watched Rosaland as she dressed. He noticed the way she applied the lotion to her beautiful breasts, he observed how she carefully encircled her large nipples, as she rubbed the creamy lotion into her skin. She gently rubbed more lotion over her firm flat belly in a circular motion and she then bent over to lotion down her lush thighs and shapely legs.

Rosaland straightened up; looking in the mirror at her shapely brown body as she applied the final handful of lotion to her firm well-shaped butt. Bobby loved how big her ass was and how it protruded from her lower back. She rubbed the lotion up and down her cheeks and into the small of her back. She then reached into her dresser to take a pair of cotton panties from the top drawer and slowly slid into them. She found the matching bra and clasps it in the front.

Bobby could no longer contain himself. "Come here Baby" he said, as she turned around, "I thought you were sleeping?" she responded coyly as she adjusted her bra over her large fleshy breasts. "Come here" Bobby was a little more demanding, but Rosaland ignored his commands as she continued to get dressed. Glancing at the clock, she noticed that the time to meet her dad was rapidly approaching and nobody keeps the General waiting.

"No" she shook her head as she reached for her body spray. Bobby remained on the bed watching and waiting for her to obey his command. He had all sorts of lewd thoughts racing through his mind, her body, her smell and the expressions of passion that was displayed on her face in the photos. He stared at her with intense emotion as she deliberately ignored his request.

Bobby liked her when she was defiant. He liked her when she was aggressive and her refusal to submit only added fuel to his fire. Soon he got up and walked over to where she was reaching for her dress. She could feel his heat as he stood behind her nibbling on her ear and rubbing his body against hers. "No Bobby we don't have time." She said softly as he placed his hands around her waist and grinded his erect manhood into her lower back.

"No Bobby" was the last words that escaped her lips before he placed his tongue deep into her mouth. Bobby's touch always melted her. Resistance was futile as he firmly kneaded her breasts through her wispy bra. She slowly wrapped her arms around his neck allowing him to carry her to the bed.

Bobby unbuckled his belt and his pants and let them drop to the floor. He reached down with his thumbs to remove her panties that were al ready wet in anticipation of his invasion into her most private place. Bobby unclasped the front of her bra, burying his face in the valley between her breasts. Rosaland moaned as he moved his mouth to her tender nipples and inhaled them deep into his mouth. He had never wanted her as badly as he wanted her right now. Bobby ran his hands slowly along her slender form before he grabbed her by her waist and positioned her to receive the full length of his hard erection deep into her love canal.

Rosaland opened wide to receive him as he plunged into her wet sweetness again and again. She responded to his down stroke as their bodies met in unbridled pleasure. She wrapped her legs securely around his waist affording him the deepest penetration as they satisfied their lust. Rosaland clung to him as he buried himself to the hilt with each thrust of his powerful member.

"Umm Bobby" she whispered in a soft voice as he pleasured her. She could feel his intensity growing as each stroke became more forceful. "I love you" Bobby moaned as he kissed her tenderly. "I love you so much. You belong to me." Bobby repeated suddenly overcome with emotion. He just couldn't get enough of her as he treated her to the full extent of his massive hot poker with each thrust into her tight love box. He wanted her to scream out his name; he wanted her body to shake and tremble in desire from his invasion. He wanted her to explode all over him while he was securely lodged inside.

He loved to feel her come. Bobby was on fire and he intended to appease his passion in her. Bobby could feel her body start to tremble beneath him and that's how he liked her. He knew that at any moment she would erupt like a volcano. Bobby pumped harder and deeper into her willing body. Each stroke carefully directed to hit its mark. Rosaland moaned and writhed in sensual satisfaction as he took possession of her soul.

The sweat rolled off their lustfully entwined bodies as Rosaland called out his name over and over. "Bobby Bobby" she cried out barely above a whisper. "Bobby Bobby Ohh Bobby!" Rosaland could no longer hold back nor did she have any control. The tears began flowing down her face as her body convulsed in a series of powerful orgasms.

She bucked and gyrated her hips up to meet her lovers powerful thrust as she came hard all over Bobby's engorged dick. Breathlessly she moaned out loud as her final explosion ripped through her body. Bobby excited by the force of her climax was in state of erotic frenzy. He rode her hard; plowing into her wet orifice extending the sublime pleasure his superior body was affording her. He wasn't ready to release her. "That's my Baby. Come for Daddy!" Rosaland spasmed underneath his sleek sweaty body as Bobby drove his massive weapon home.

twenty-five

The General was already at breakfast when Rosaland entered the restaurant; Bobby had gone to the hospital to relieve Danny. Arthur was still in critical condition and there was no sign of any improvement. The General wasn't sure what kind of reception that he was going to receive from his daughter but surprisingly enough she was in a great mood.

Apparently Bobby hadn't told her about the photos so there would be no need for him to explain why he had her followed. The General had good reasons for his actions but he was content to not have to discuss the why's and the how comes. Rosaland was ready for business as usual; she wanted to know how long the extradition proceedings would take. Also she wanted the General to help her to map out a plan to have Arthur safely returned to the states in his current medical condition.

Rosaland had a bad feeling about being in Bolivia for such a long time after the raid. She was responsible for the lives of her team and she wanted them out. She wanted them out now. They should have left days ago. "Dad what time is Rachael expected at the airport?" "Her flight is scheduled to arrive at 0:800. I already have her transportation arranged. Why?" "I was wondering would it be possible to coordinate Rachael's arrival with our departure." Rosaland looked as though a light bulb had just lit up inside her head. "What are you thinking?" The General was listening. "Dad I have a very bad feeling about still being here in this country. We have been here too long."

"Also Dad I need to know, what is the safest way we can fly Arthur back to New York?" "That's easy we can send in the med vac unit." The General replied off handedly. "Can you arrange that?" His daughter questioned. "Of course. I'll make the call right now." The General looked over his glasses at his daughter and asked, "Is there anything else that you want me to do?" "Yes

Dad I want you to get us the hell out of here." "Done. Oh by the way your detective friend, nice guy. Good choice." Rosaland was delighted.

Rosaland noticed during the course of her conversation with her father that she had forgotten to turn on her cell phone. She couldn't believe that it had been off for such a long time. At this point she placed a call to Danny for an update on Arthur's condition and she also wanted to know if Bobby had arrived yet. She instructed Danny to be ready to move at a moments notice and then she hung up.

Bobby noticed that there was a great deal of activity centered on the hotel as he was leaving. His instincts told him that something was wrong. There was too much hustle and bustle for all to be well. The roads were packed with Bolivian military vehicles all headed in the opposite direction. It seemed as though the Bolivian army was on the move. And where they were going is the question that troubled Bobby. Bobby felt extremely uneasy.

There were too many incidentals that just didn't seem right. Had Carlos discovered the temporary headquarters of the American insurgence team? That information was highly classified. How had it been leaked? And by whom? Bobby's thoughts immediately went to Rosaland and her father. For some reason he couldn't get them off of his mind. Whatever was going on had something to with them either directly or indirectly.

The General was the highest ranking official in charge of the Americans. It could be that Carlos had been informed of their whereabouts. Carlos had eyes and ears everywhere in this part of the world. The Americans were in enemy territory and their lives were at risk.

As Bobby approached the hospital he paid particular attention to the fact that the Bolivian soldiers were heavily armed and they were also carrying munitions and explosives. That was the last red flag. Again he put in a call to Rosaland this time she answered the phone.

"Yes?" Once she heard his voice she asked "Bobby where the hell are you?" "I just arrived at the hospital. There is some strange activity going on. Something is about to go down and I don't like it." "What are you talking about?" She too was feeling uneasy. "Listen to me I want you and your father to get up right now and leave the hotel. Rosaland don't argue with me just do as I say and get the hell out of there now! Rosaland right now!" Bobby was screaming at the top of his lungs.

"We're leaving!" Rosaland grabbed her Dad's arm as they made their way to the lobby. "Call me when you are out of that hotel." It was apparent at this point that a hit had been ordered and Bobby's gut told him that the General was the target.

"Dad that was Detective Semione on the phone. He wants us to leave the hotel right now." She said as she escorted him out. "Why?" The General followed "I don't know why Dad but he was pretty insistent that we leave right now. I've never known him to be wrong. Let's go!" Rosaland said giving Bobby the benefit of the doubt.

The General starred at his daughter and without uttering another word the two of them got up and proceeded toward the door. The General too noticed all the movement that seemed to evolve out of nowhere. The armed troops were scurrying to and fro taking position. His spider senses tingled as the General grabbed his daughter's arm and began running to make it to the entrance.

Suddenly out of nowhere there was a loud explosion. Rosaland could feel the building shaking as it started to collapse all around them. The General pushed her through the door as another explosion rocked the foundation and sent the hotel crashing down to the ground. The two of them had been blown out of the entrance and both landed face down on the dirt road that originally led to the pool.

The General lie there on top of his daughter shielding her body with his own as the debris fell down around them. They were both stunned from the force of the blast but quickly recovered when in the background they heard the sound of rifle shots and m16's. The General reached for his sidearm as he pulled his daughter to her feet as they fled to take cover.

Once regaining her senses Rosaland drew the police revolver that she had strapped to her thigh. Bobby had issued her strict orders that morning after they made love that she should wear her pistol at all times and was she glad that she had listened.

The two of them took cover in an old abandoned shack that was approximately one half mile from where the hotel used to stand. Once inside the General had time to access their situation. "What the hell happened?" He asked breathlessly once they reached what appeared to be a little bit of safety.

"Dad we need to get the hell out of here." Rosaland screamed trying her best to keep it together. "Take it easy honey; we'll get out of here." The General was looking around to get a handle on their location when he spotted an empty vehicle. "Let's move!" The General and his daughter made a hasty retreat as they commandeered the vehicle. "I need to get to the D.E.A or the F.B.I. but we need to know what the fuck is going on! I'm dropping you off at the hospital. You need to have Arthur prepared so we can move!" The General had given his orders and he expected his daughter to obey them unquestionably.

"Dad what about Rachael?" Rosaland was distraught. "Once I get to headquarters I'll make sure that she is secure at the airport. I already have her in place. You need to put your team in action and get your man out." "What time will the med vac unit be available?" "I'll have the unit on the roof of the hospital in one hour. The time is tight. Get to the hospital and get your team moving." These were the last words the General said before he dropped his daughter off in front of the hospital entrance.

Rosaland jumped out of the vehicle with her weapon drawn. She carefully surveyed her surroundings before she proceeded to enter the hospital keeping her weapon in full view she slowly approached the desk. When she felt that it was safe she placed her gun back inside the holster and took the elevator to the ICU.

Bobby and Danny were waiting outside of Arthur's room when she got off the elevator. Bobby immediately noticed that her dress was torn and her legs were bleeding. "What the hell happened?" Bobby screamed as she ran into his arms. Her body shaking from the trauma. At this point she didn't care who knew about them she just wanted Bobby to hold her. Bobby held her tightly trying to calm her down.

"Bobby they blew up the hotel! Dad and I barely made it out alive. We wouldn't have gotten out had it not been for you!" Rosaland was hysterical. Danny was standing there listening in disbelief. "We've got to move!" She continued trying to catch her breath. "The med vac unit will be on the roof in an hour; we've got to get Arthur out of here! Where is his doctor?"

"The doctor is with him right now. There hasn't been any change in his condition. Can we move him?" "We've got to we have no choice. Get the doctor." At this point Rosaland burst into the hospital room. The doctor was just finishing up his examination. He looked perplexed at the way she entered the room. "Excuse me Dr. Reid is there a problem?" "Yes doctor as a matter of fact there is. We need to move the lieutenant as soon as possible."

"You can't move him now. This man is in critical condition." "Is there any change in his condition?" Dr. Reid needed answers "Well yes, his vital signs have stabilized and his breathing is regular but I would not recommend moving this patient at this time."

"Doctor we have a med vac unit that will be landing on the roof of this hospital in exactly one half of an hour. Please have the Lt. ready to be transported at that time. This is a government operation and we are asking for your cooperation. Will you please help us? This might be the only way we can save his life."

Upon hearing the urgency in her voice the doctor knew that she was serious. "Ok Dr. Reid I'll get him ready but I would not advise this. His life is in your hands." "I'll take the responsibility but we need to get him to the roof a.s.a.p." With that the doctor prepared Arthur and had him moved to the roof for evacuation.

Rachael's plane had arrived in Bolivia on schedule. She was surprised to be greeted by heavily armed American soldiers rather than her sister as they had previously discussed. Upon disembarking she was immediately swooped up and taken directly to D.E.A. headquarters where her father was anxiously awaiting her.

"Dad what's all the cloak and dagger? Where's Arthur? How is he? When do I get to see him? What is going on?" Rachael would have fired a thousand more questions at the General except that for some reason she knew that if she remained quiet he would tell her.

"Rachael Rosaland is flying Arthur back to New York. They left twenty minutes ago. We are leaving now. I'll tell you on the plane home exactly what is going on. Rosaland needs you to sign these extradition papers. You have to be her. I'll explain later. Rachael did as she was instructed and after the final documentation was completed she and her father left for New York under heavy military guard.

On the plane home the General told Rachael of the events that had transpired in Bolivia. The Calderon Cartel claimed responsibility for the bombing of the hotel. They were also held responsible for the attempted murder of the General and his daughter.

The international Interpol in conjunction with the drug enforcement agency had gathered sufficient Intel to correctly place the blame of the hotel bombing on the doorsteps of the Calderon Cartel. Carlos was a proud man. How dare them come into his country and disturb his operations? Carlos wanted the American intruders to know that the bombing was his calling card. He wanted whoever was in charge of the operation to realize that the next time it wouldn't be that easy to catch him off guard.

Rachael listened without uttering a word as the General described the events of the last three days. "How did Detective Semione know about the bomb?" Rachael finally asked as her father finished his summary. "I don't know but he was certainly right. We made it out in the nick of time. I owe him one actually two; he saved both of our lives."

"Rosaland always said that he has the best instincts. I guess she was right." "She is always right about things like that. That's s why we pay her the big bucks and that is also why she was put in this position. She knows her shit." The General excused himself so that he could check on Rosaland and the other team.

Their e.t.a. (estimated time of arrival) was approximately 17 hours; New York University hospital had been put on alert and was on stand by awaiting the arrival of the lieutenant. Rosaland was still shaken up from the events earlier in the day but she was extremely happy to be heading home. Bobby knew that she was anxious and he remained by her side until the med vac unit touched down at N.Y.U. Arthur was immediately transferred to the ICU where his condition was stabilized. They had made it home alive and Dr. Reid was responsible for the transition.

twenty-six

A year later the N.Y.P.D. was still recovering from the Bolivian operation. The O.N.S.I. on the other hand was gaining in strength and reputation. Dr. Reid had been given more power and resources to run her thriving covert organization.

Carlos was growing stronger as well. After the raid he too had come to New York to gather information on who possibly could have been directly responsible for the destruction of his major distribution center. All roads led back to the N.Y.P.D but no one knew anything beyond that point.

Carlos decided that he needed someone inside the unit, now his problem was to discover whom he could approach. There had to be someone there who needed some extra money. He would make some inquires in the Latino community through sources he knew he could definitely trust.

Carlos was also able to get an active list of all the detectives in the one five. He did a thorough investigation on each of the names and everyone came up clean. He needed an inside connection. The name Roberto Semione troubled him and he didn't know why. Then it dawned on him that all these detectives frequented his club. He would just wait until the right moment presented itself, and then he would find the link that he needed.

He did know however that Detectives Semione, Schmidt and Lt.Yancy had been in Bolivia. But why the N.Y.P.D. was involved still remained a mystery. General Prescott A Reid headed the operation but there was no mention of anyone else. Carlos was furious. He was seeing red. He would try to find some weakness among these men something to break them down but he would destroy them by whatever means necessary.

As soon as Arthur returned to work he put Bobby and Diana back on the surveillance at Natalie's. It was given high priority. Arthur knew for some reason that there was a connection to Carlos, he just didn't know how or why.

The bond between Rosaland and Bobby had grown stronger than ever. They were still discreet but it was becoming apparent that there was something special between them. Rosaland talked privately to both Danny and Arthur and they promised that they would keep their secret. Rosaland knew that they could be trusted. Rosaland continued to track Carlos's movement through dedicated satellite and she knew that he was gaining in strength, power and position.

Everyday through satellite tracking she monitored the activities of the Cartel. Carlos was moving freely in and out of the country. It seemed as though he was expanding his current operations and his influence to other countries.

Rosaland kept the General informed on all the movement in and out of the country. They were trying to figure out what his next move was but he wasn't leaving anything to chance. They hit hard him before; but Carlos wasn't going to give whoever was out there the chance to hit him again.

Dr. Reid was on the phone with her father as Bobby walked into her office and took a seat. The General was discussing the promotions he intended to issue to her unit for the Bolivian operation. For all intensive purposes it had been a great success. The General was apologizing for the amount of time it had taken, "You know how slow the wheels of justice move in Washington. I'm just pleased that it looks like we will get this done this year."

"Thanks Dad my team earned those promotions. What is taking so long?" "Washington beauracy. What else can I say?" "You can say to get it done and it will happen." "I'll get back to you. Oh by the way how's your sister? I haven't heard from her in a couple of days. What's going on with her?" "She's making wedding plans Dad. I'm meeting her for drinks this evening. I'll make sure that she calls you from wherever we end up."

"You do that. I'll be expecting to hear from the two of you. Is your brother joining you two girls?" "No sir Matthew is in England, attending a toxicology seminar. Dad what is wrong with you? Where is your head?" "I've got so many things on my mind these days sweetie. Have a good time this evening and I'll be expecting to hear from you. Let me get back to these promotions."

With that the General hung up the phone. What the General wasn't saying, the reason that the promotions were taking so long was that he was making special arrangements to have Dr. Reid promoted as well. This was something that had never been done before having a federal employee promoted through the ranks of the state and federal governments simultaneously.

In the Generals eyes she deserved it. It would also increase her power, her authority and her jurisdiction. He had to go through several different channels to pull this off but he intended to get this done on behalf of his daughter. This promotion would give her departmental authority as well as federal jurisdiction.

"Good afternoon Detective" Rosaland smiled seductively. "How are you today?" "I'm fine Dr. Reid and you?" "I'm well thanks for asking" and with that Bobby walked behind her desk and gave her a tender kiss. Rosaland was happy to be in his arms and she was glad that the shades in her office had been drawn because otherwise they would have been exposed.

Rosaland pressed her body closely against Bobby's as he ran his hands along her curves. After a long embrace the two lovers composed themselves. "I've got to go under this evening; the Lt. has a bad feeling, that he wants us to check out. I'll be out late so I'll probably stay in Brooklyn tonight."

"Ok Baby. I'm having drinks with Rachael this evening anyway. We have wedding plans to discuss. I'm sure that we'll be drinking. So I'll probably be out just as late as you. It depends on where we end up if we are too far I'll probably stay with Rachael."

"I'll call you when I have a chance. Please have your phone on." Rosaland nodded "Bobby don't forget that tomorrow I have the World Affairs Conference. This year the focus is on the U.S. interest in Latin America. This conference could be important to our investigation. There might be someone here who can shed some light on the Cartel; you never know who attends these things."

"Are you going to be speaking?" "Yes and no I'm not sure? I might be just an invited guest." "Well Baby you shouldn't stay out too late and don't drink too much." "You know Bobby I didn't know that you had turned into my father." She answered sarcastically "But I won't drink too much." Bobby left the precinct while Rosaland called Rachael to confirm their plans for the evening.

The two sisters decided to meet right after work for a light dinner and then some drinks. It seemed liked ages since the girls had been out together. Over the past year their lives had become so complicated. Rachael was working harder than ever in the district attorney's office and Rosaland was absolutely obsessed with the O.N.S.I. It would be nice to have an evening of girl talk and laughter.

Rosaland wanted Rachael to plan her wedding so that she and Bobby could get started making plans of their own. It was kind of understood between them that Rachael would marry first sort of an unspoken agreement. Arthur had recovered quite nicely from his near death experience in Bolivia and was back to running the N.Y.P.D. in full force.

Rachael was going to be in court until about six so Rosaland decided that she would go to Bloomingdales. She wanted some new clothes. It was nice out so she hopped on the bus and went uptown to shop. She wanted something short tight and sexy. Her office clothes were becoming boring. She wanted to look different, she wanted to feel different and Bloomingdales was just the store. After browsing she decided to check the designer salon and found two absolutely wonderful outfits. The black dress was just what the doctor ordered.

It was an absolutely lovely little number. The plunging neckline carefully outlined her robust cleavage and it was cut very low in the back. It fit her ass to a tee. The hemline was just short enough to bare a small split which showed the right amount of her shapely legs when she walked. It was just barley long enough to cover the holster that held her gun. The matching jacket was an oversized double breast cut with rhinestone buttons. It described her mood perfectly.

She went downstairs to hosiery and found the exact pair of stockings that she needed to compliment her selection. She purchased the sheerest black pantyhose that featured one rhinestone tiger that climbed up her ankle to the middle of her calf. What the hell! She thought she also purchased new shoes.

Feeling just lovely she went back to her office to change and wait for her sister. Once Rachael reached her office they decided to have dinner at the Harvard Club. The ladies hadn't been there in a while and it would be nice to sit around drink and talk. They also decided that they would not talk about work this evening; they wanted to simply be sisters and discuss their family life, which of course meant they would talk about their men.

After ordering cocktails Rachael asked "Sis where did you get that dress? It's awesome!" "Bloomingdale's designer salon. Wait until you see the back." "When did you have time to go to Bloomingdale's?" Rachael sounded a little jealous. "I left a little early while I was waiting for you to finish up in court. I actually went because I needed a new suit for the World Affairs Conference tomorrow; this outfit was just a little something extra."

As Rachael sipped on her drink she became interested in the World Affairs Conference. "The World Affairs Conference? Who sponsors that?" she asked interestingly. "The World Affairs Council" replied her sister. "Why are you going there?" "The topic for discussion this year is the U.S. interest in Latin America. I'm sure that there will be some extremely valuable information that could possibly be useful in the future."

"It is very important that we keep our eyes on Latin America especially since Carlos practically controls most of that region. You know Rachael; I'm scare of this man. He is very dangerous. If it were not for Bobby I wouldn't be here. Dad wouldn't be here. We barely escaped that hotel with our lives. If Bobby had called a minute later none of us would have made it out alive."

"Our location there was classified top secret. Rachael, nobody knew we were there. Dad had the whole top floor turned into Intel headquarters. We were the one's that had the security. This man infiltrated our organization within a few hours after the initial raid and then proceeded to blow up the hotel before we even knew what hit us."

"We lost a large amount of important staff and equipment in that blast. He hit us back just as hard as we hit him and we prepared for the Bolivian operation damn near a year. Carlos hit us back in just a few days twice as hard and he caught us completely off guard. This Carlos Calderon and his Cartel are some bad boys."

Rosaland's hand was shaking as she finished her drink. This was the first time that she was really remembering the intensity of the situation. Rachael noticing that her sister was visibly shaken decided to change the subject. "Hey I thought we had agreed to not talk about work." Rachael reminded her.

"You know Rachael when Dad assigned me to this project; I had no idea that it would be this dangerous. And I wondered why he had chosen the N.Y.P.D. to implement and facilitate but after Bolivia I know why. Arthur has one hell of a team. They work well together. And speaking of Arthur how is he doing with his recovery? I know that he is back at work but I'm talking about his personal recovery. How are the two of you? And when are you getting married? I never have time at work to talk about personal issues with Arthur. Since he has been back he is playing catch-up. He's got everybody moving. They have so many investigations under way; he's looking at everybody for everything."

"You know Roz; he has been a different person since he got shot. He seems to be more cautious. But we have set a date which is what I want to talk to you about." At this point in the conversation the girls had ordered their dinner and the waiter was bringing their salads.

"We've decided on a June ceremony. Our date is June 19th and Sis I am really going to need your help to make this the most perfect day possible. Mom's no longer with us and I really want this to be a special day for both of our families. I really love him Rosaland and the fact that I almost lost him.... You know Sis we have been through some shit this year."

"Well June the 19th sounds wonderful. We need to get the invitations tomorrow. That only gives us about six weeks. But I promise you we will make Mom proud."

"So what the deal with you and Mr. Wonderful?" Rosaland smiled and shook her head. Whenever she thought about Bobby he brought a smile to her face. "He's still hot slut that I am." With that outburst the sister started laughing. "I don't know anything beyond that."

"Rosaland you and this guy. What are you doing?" "As much as we can!" Rachael looked perplexed. "Rachael Bobby has never mentioned marriage not to me. He mentioned it to Dad and that's the last I heard about it. He blames it on my job but come on is he marrying my job or is he marrying me? We are together. That's it. At work we are still attempting to keep a low profile but of course there are those who know Arthur, Danny and everyone else in the building.

I'm still not totally convinced that he is over his relationship with Rousseau. I don't know if there is necessarily anything going on between them. I do still feel uneasy about the whole situation. I love him and I trust him so I'm willing to wait until he's ready. But if I find out that he is still messing around with that broad I'm going to kill him. I couldn't take that."

"Rosaland how long is that going to be?" Rachael was acting just like her Dad. "Rachael I don't know? What I do know is that I can't leave him; I love him so much it hurts. I'll never be able to leave Bobby. Where are we going after dinner?"

"New club" Rachael said excitedly "This came through my office two days ago; a hot spot called the Oasis, located in Soho. Black and Latino yuppie haven. With extremely good drinks and music and from what I'm told you never know who might be in the house. Oh by the way where is the great detective this evening? And what would he say about that extremely small dress?" Rachael laughed as Rosaland choked on her dinner.

"Actually Rachael he's working. He is under cover this evening somewhere. He told me that Arthur had a bad feeling about some place and they were going to check it out." "Who is he partnering with?" "You know he didn't say I assumed it was Danny but I'm not certain. He told me as much as he could but that wasn't all that much." "Well let's go have some fun." "I'm right behind you."

Dinner was excellent. The girls had an after dinner cognac and a few more laughs about Rosaland's dress and off they went. The atmosphere at the Club Oasis was tropical. It was definitely a Latino hot spot. The bar was packed with the beautiful people and seating was limited. The music was loud, but surprisingly a DJ and not a live band was playing which is the tradition in most Latino clubs. The club had a sultry sensuous atmosphere and the music was hard hitting.

There were undulating bodies dancing to the hypnotic Afro Cuban rhythms all across the dance floor. Rachael had enough foresight to call ahead and make reservations so after standing in the line for only a minute or two the ladies were escorted to their table which was relatively close to the bar. Rosaland decided that now was the time to reveal the showstopper so she politely removed her jacket and exposed the back of her dress.

Rachael thought it was fabulous and so did several of the men that watched intensely as she took it off and slang the jacket over her arm. "Girl Bobby will hit the ceiling when he sees you in that dress without him." "Well Sis" Rosaland replied "Bobby isn't here and I'm going to have a nice time. This place is great."

Rosaland carefully surveyed the room and there was nothing but men everywhere she looked. They were all looking at her and her sister as well. Carlos Calderon looked through the two way mirror from his office upstairs. Yes this was his newest acquisition. He had the latest high technology security system. He could see in every nook and cranny of his club. He couldn't believe his eyes when he saw the two ladies being seated. There she was again.

By this time he felt that he knew her in his mind even though he had no idea that she was the head of the O.N.S.I. the new federal organization that everyone was whispering about. He smiled contently to himself. This time she would not escape his attentions. He would make sure that he made contact with her.

Rosaland and Rachael had no idea of the eminent danger that they were facing at that very moment. Carlos marveled at the fact that there were two of them but despite the fact that they were completely identical he could tell them apart without any problem.

He felt Rosaland immediately deep inside his heart. Carlos called down to the bar and ordered that the ladies be reseated in the V.I.P. section. He also had the bartender to bring them a round of drinks on the house. The ladies were delighted for the upgrade in their seating arrangements. They now had a clear view of the bar and the dance floor.

When the bartender returned with their drinks he informed the ladies that the owner of the club wanted to know if he could join them. Both Rosaland and Rachael were interested to see who was lavishing all this attention their way. Rachael is always precautious. She looks for the why in every situation.

"Rachael who told you about this place?" Rosaland asked "The legal team from the fourth floor. They come here all the time. Everyone in the office knows that I love to go to the newest nightspots so they told me to try the Club Oasis."

"Well I think this place is hot."Rosaland was suddenly interrupted by the emergence of a tall heavily bearded man with extremely long thick black hair that hung pass his broad shoulders. He was wearing very expensive clothing so she assumed that he must be the club owner.

He approached her in a manner that left her feeling that there was something familiar about him but she couldn't put her finger on it. "Good evening ladies. My name is Antonio Rivera and I am the owner of the Oasis."

"I would like to thank you for your patronage at my humble establishment this evening. It is my sincere desire that you have a nice time. If there is anything that you require I would consider it a personal honor, if you would allow me to serve you."

Carlos never took his eyes off of Rosaland the whole time as he made his obviously prescripted speech. At the conclusion he took her hand and applied a kiss starring deeply into her eyes. Rosaland was slightly taken by his gallant style. Carlos smiled as he excused himself from their table. "Do you treat all your guest in this manner?" Rosaland asked before he took his leave.

"Only the pretty ones" he readily replied "Or the ones that I want to return. You ladies fit in both categories. You look absolutely stunning in that dress. I hope that later in the evening you might allow me the pleasure of a dance." He winked as he graciously walked off.

Rosaland watched as Carlos moved smoothly through the crowd to greet some of his other guests. She took careful notice of the way he interacted with his club's patrons. He put everyone at ease and he made them all feel as though they were very important.

Rosaland also observed the other people that were seated in the V.I.P. section "Rachael isn't that your boss"? Rachael glanced around and noticed that the Mayor of New York was seated to the right of them. "Yes that's him. I wonder who else is here." This was turning out to be a very interesting evening.

"We need to go and say hello." Rachael accompanied by her sister walked over to greet the Mayor. Rosaland felt as though someone was staring deep into her soul. She turned slightly to catch Carlos eye to eye. Again he smiled at her and in return she smiled back. Then she turned her attention back to the Mayor.

Rachael introduced her sister as the director of the O.N.S.I. The Mayor in return stood to his feet to shake her hand. Now it was Carlos's turn to wonder who was this beautiful woman that had the Mayor of New York City standing on his feet to greet her? The Mayor made some off handed comment that caused both Rosaland and Rachael to laugh and then he invited them to join his table for a drink.

Carlos decided that it was time for him to return to his office to see if he might be able to catch some of their conversation on tape. Of course he was listening and recording every conversation that went on in his place.

Rosaland watched intently as he stood up to leave. Carlos changed his mind however and decided that he too would join the Mayor's table and find out for himself exactly who these lovely and apparently well-connected ladies were.

"Your honor I trust that you are having a good time tonight. I've had the pleasure of meeting these lovely ladies but I had no idea that they were with you or I would have made special arrangements for them." "Antonio this is Rachael Reid the illustrious district attorney of New York, and her twin sister Rosaland who is currently being contracted by the N.Y.P.D. as a consultant." The Mayor knew that the O.N.S.I. was top secret and was very careful not to make a slip.

"These ladies should be treated with the utmost respect at all times. It's my pleasure to have them at my table this evening." "Not only are they very beautiful women they are also extremely important." Carlos motioned to the bartender to bring the table another round of drinks.

"Ladies your money is no good here. Please enjoy my hospitality." "You have already been too kind." Rosaland said sweetly. Carlos didn't respond he just looked admiringly into her eyes and softly placed a kiss on her cheek and walked away. Carlos knew that Rachael was the DA but he had no idea that Rosaland was affiliated with the O.N.S.I. She could be very valuable to him in the long run. He had no idea that she was responsible for Bolivia.

Rosaland was mesmerized by his machismo. There was something about Antonio that reminded her of Bobby.The way he walked, his build and his raw sex appeal. They had a lot of similarities. Rosaland decided to keep those thoughts to herself for now. She watched as Carlos disappeared into the crowd. Carlos immediately had the files pulled on both Rachael and Rosaland. He knew exactly who they were and he also knew that they were the daughters of General Prescott A. Reid the man who earlier he had tried to assassinate. Rachael's profile was easy to access but Rosaland's was not available. "How interesting?" he thought.

This made Carlos wonder even more. She was a mystery to him. What kind of consulting did she do for the N.Y.P.D.? What kind of doctor was she? He looked down from the mirror and watched waiting for the right moment. There would be some body language or something that would indicate to him what his next move would be concerning her.

The sisters excused themselves to go to the ladies room. They both spoke at the same time. "Who is this Antonio Rivera? He is too smooth." "Rosaland what the hell is your problem? Bobby is going to kick your ass; you are lucky that he is not here. I can't believe you flirting with this man."

"Rachael calm down I'm not flirting well maybe just a little but I'll tell you this there is a lot more to him than just the owner of this club." "Just a little o.k. Ms. just a little. Well we both agree on that. I wonder who he really is?" "I'll tell you tomorrow. I'm definitely going to pull his profile first thing in the morning."

The evening was starting to really heat up. While the sisters were in the ladies room another interesting development was taking place. When Rosaland emerged Carlos was standing by the door talking to some of his other guest. He watched her as she climbed the steps. He came up shortly after her not wanting her to know that he had been waiting there for her. As she approached the dance floor he interceded and asked her to dance. The music was jumping as they began to follow the pulsing Latin beats. Suddenly without warning the music slowed to a sensual tango.

Carlos grabbed her up in his arms and began to rub his body close to hers. Rosaland tried to pull away from his tight embrace but her struggle only made him hold on tighter. "Relax I won't hurt you." He whispered softly in her ear. "Dance with me just let your body enjoy the closeness of mine."

Rosaland relaxed in his arms as he ran his hands along her shapely figure being very careful not to be insulting. They continued to dance in complete silence exchanging lustful glances between the two of them. After the music stopped Carlos whispered to her again this time complementing her perfume. And then he walked away.

Rosaland's mind was spinning; only one man had ever touched her like that. That was the same way that Bobby ran his hands over her curves. A chill went up her spine as she tried to shake it off. The same light touch using the same part of his fingers.

Rosaland's eyes followed Carlos as he crossed the room and disappeared into the elevator. Even though he had been extremely gentle there was something in his touch that let her know that he could be forceful if the need be. Rosaland went back to her table lost in thought and ordered another drink.

She sat thoughtfully nursing the cognac as her mind raced to Bobby and then back to Carlos. Carlos observing her from the two way knew that he had affected her but she had affected him as well. He would never forget how she felt in his arms and how firm her body was as he held her close. Carlos looked down at her plunging neckline and her shapely legs.

She would definitely find out who this man was! And why she was feeling this way about him. Rachael finally making her way back to the table said "Rosaland isn't that Bobby over there at the bar?" Rosaland glanced around nervously feeling quite guilty for having been attracted to this strange club owner. She wondered if Bobby was there how long he had been there and if he had seen her dance with this man.

"Where Rachael?" She was shaking. "Over there at the end of the bar. Isn't that Bobby?" Rosaland again focused her attention towards the bar where she spotted him standing comfortably drinking a beer. She noticed how he was dressed trying very much to blend in and not be noticed. Then she remembered that he was undercover which explained why he was wearing what he was wearing. A black leather hat, dark glasses, a black leather vest with a black shirt opened down the chest and his earring. Bobby would never wear his hoop earring when he was working his regular tour.

She looked around to see if she could spot his partner or who he was working with but she didn't see Danny or the Lt. anywhere in sight. Rosaland carefully observing the situation tried to figure out if she should approach him or if she would let him discover her.

"Rachael Bobby told me that he would be under cover this evening so obviously he must be checking out this place. I don't see who he is working with. I wonder should I go over there?" Rosaland was nervous. "Rosaland if Bobby is working you need to stay out of it. I'm sure that once he notices you he'll make some sort of acknowledgement of your presence. You need to follow his lead in this situation; he doesn't need you to blow his cover."

Rosaland watched Bobby as he mingled with the other guest and appeared to be sociable. He was swaying slightly to the music and casually sipping on his cerveza. She wanted him. She wanted to feel his arms around her especially in light of her experience with Antonio. She had to know that she was not losing her mind finding so many similarities between her man and this stranger.

Carlos at the same time was watching Rosaland from the two way mirror installed behind the bar. He had a clear picture of everything and everyone from this angle. He studied her body language and her feminine attributes. It amazed him that the pretty little girl the he had first observed in the airport so many years ago had grown into such a beautiful desirable and sensuous woman. Why did she have to be the daughter of the general the man who was out to destroy him?

twenty-seven

Diana Rousseau was leaving the ladies room as Rachael entered. They were not familiar with each other so Rachael walked right by. "Dr. Reid?" Diana commented in a low voice. Rachael looked at the detective and responded "Wrong one." "Excuse me?" Diana questioned "You have the wrong one. I'm not Dr. Reid I'm her sister." "I work with her. We've met before. About a year ago maybe even longer than that. You know how time flies." "Where did we meet miss…?" "I'm sorry I'm Diana Rousseau. Arthur is my boss." "Ok I'm with you now. What are you doing here?" "My partner and I are here on assignment." "Say no more." with that Rachael walked away.

Meanwhile Rosaland was upstairs very much into watching Bobby. Waiting for her chance to speak to him or catch his attention without blowing his cover. Rachael returning from the ladies room told her sister that she had met Bobby's partner a certain Diana Rousseau. Rosaland's attention then returned to the corner of the bar where the officer continued to sip his cerveza casually.

At that moment Diana walked up and struck up a conversation. Rosaland did not under any circumstance like the two of them together. She was very familiar with their age old history and the sight of the two of them very simply made her jealous.

"That's why he didn't tell me who he was partnering with?" she thought to herself. Apparently Diana must have told him about seeing Rachael because his eyes instantly started to roam the room looking for recognition.

It was at that moment that their eyes met. Bobby had found her. She would follow his lead as to how they would get together or if they would get together but she really needed him to hold her. This would be his call.

While Bobby was trying to figure out his next move Carlos took control. He had no idea of the connection between Bobby and Rosaland. He was also ignorant to the fact that there were undercover officers in his establishment and the officers had no idea that this was the infamous Carlos Calderon.

Once again Antonio presented himself at their table and asked Rosaland to dance. He wanted to feel her body again. Her perfume was exotic and he loved the smell of her hair. Bobby who hadn't taken his eyes off her since they made initial contact watched as Antonio escorted her onto the dance floor touching her very inappropriately. He deliberately made his way into the center of the crowded area and wrapping his arms around her slowly started to dance. He held her tight pressing his strong form indecently into hers.

Under the circumstances Bobby knew that he could show no emotion. He had to remain perfectly calm. The sight of another man touching his woman infuriated him even if it was just a dance. Bobby was very careful not to let Diana sense his anger. He moved in closer so that he could observe the situation and that's when he noticed Antonio whispering something in Rosaland's ear. She stepped back looking intently into his face and then he forcefully pulled her close again.

Bobby could sense her apprehension and that's when he decided to step in. At that moment the slow music stopped and Carlos released her from his embrace. Rosaland walked over to the bar and stood there not quite sure of what to do. Bobby took the lead and walked back to the bar and continued his conversation with Diana. All the time paying close attention to the enchanting design of her scanty dress.

"There's Dr. Reid" Diana commented "That's why her sister told me that she was the wrong one." "Where?" Bobby asked innocently. "Over there at the end of the bar." Bobby turned as if seeing her for the first time. Rosaland was talking to the bartender. A few minutes later the bartender sat a bottle of beer in front of the detective and said smiling "compliments of the lady." He pointed down to the end of the bar where she was standing slowly sipping on a new drink.

Diana turned away realizing that this must be the way that Dr. Reid could talk to the detective without causing any suspicion. Diana knew that for some reason Dr. Reid had never been that friendly towards her but she had to admit the she was a very smart cookie. She always seemed to know just how to handle any situation.

Bobby casually walked down to the end of the bar taking the bottle of beer with him. "What the hell are you doing here?" He asked in a soft voice with a smile on his face, just in case anyone was watching, and indeed Carlos was watching. Watching and listening. "Rachael and I came here for drinks. We had no idea that this was your assignment." She replied also with a smile.

"Who's dude that had his hands all over you?" Bobby asked still smiling but Rosaland knew that his smile was fake. "He's the owner of this fine establishment Antonio Rivera. But I don't think that's really his name. I'm going to run him through international tomorrow morning. Rachael and I both had the same feeling about him." "Yes but he doesn't have his hands all over her. Just you." Things were beginning to get heated. "How come you didn't tell me that you were working with Diana?" Now it was Rosaland's turn to issue her dirt. "You know who I work with is not my call." Bobby snapped back careful not to be too loud extremely heated under the collar. At this point they were at a stalemate.

Their conversation seemed natural for the setting but they both had issues with each other. Rosaland decided to walk away. She would talk to him later. Bobby followed a short distance really becoming excited by the way her dress fit her ass and the fact that her back was completely exposed. She turned to him gracefully and asked him to dance.

"What did he say to you?" Bobby whispered in her ear once they were on the dance floor. "He told me that he liked the smell of my hair." She replied quickly. But that was not what he had said as a matter of fact he had been very explicit as to what he wanted to do to her and how he would do it. Bobby looked deep into her eyes and held her close they were silent for the remainder of their embrace.

Bobby ran his hands along her curves and that motion sent a chill up her spine. How could both of these men know which of her buttons to push? Bobby walked her back to her table greeted Rachael and went back to his partner who was still waiting at the bar. "What did she have to say?" Diana asked half-heartedly, not really interested. For some reason she did not like the two of them together either.

It had been about two years since she and Bobby had been an item and to this day she still didn't know what happened to the love they had shared for so many years. Sometimes late at night she still wondered when they stopped being lovers and started being colleagues. Diana had yet to figure out what happened or who happened but she still longed for him now more than ever.

"She told me the name of the club owner Antonio Rivera and how she wants us to run him tomorrow through international Intel." "You know you have to give it to her she is always on top of things. You know Bobby Dr. Reid has never been friendly towards me. I remember when she first started at the station I tried to talk to her a few times she was always polite and professional but she would never give me the time of day. She didn't acknowledge me tonight either."

"Diana we are undercover. You know the rules. She can pass on pertinent information and that is as far as it goes." Bobby watched as Rachael and Rosaland left the club. Carlos also watched as Rachael and Rosaland left the club. This time for sure he knew he would see her again. He would find her if he had to but this time Carlos knew for certain that he would do whatever it took to make her his.

"Let's go. We can check out this guy tomorrow." Bobby walked out just in time to see the two sisters' enter her car. He and Diana walked to his Explorer and they left as well. Bobby dropped Diana off at the station so that she could get her car and once she was safely inside he drove off to find his woman.

His first stop was Rachael's place in mid town. On the way home Rachael commented "Rosaland I wouldn't want to be in your shoes." Rosaland completely baffled by that statement answered "What are you talking about?" Rachael looked at her sister as only a sister can and replied. "Somebody is going to get hurt."

Rosaland could no longer act naïve. She knew exactly what Rachael meant. What was going on? Was the question that she had to ask her self? What did this stranger mean to her that would make her lie to Bobby? When Bobby reached midtown it was about 4:00 in the morning. He had no idea that they had left the club so late.

His mind thought back to the first time that he made love to Rosaland. It was about this same time in the morning. This was actually his favorite time of the day. He thought about that night often. It was embedded into his memory; it was a night that he would never forget. As Bobby drove up in front of Rachael's building his first thought was to ask Rosaland what dude really said. He knew her too well. He knew she was lying. He thought it was to protect his cover but soon he would discover that there was more to it than he imagined.

Bobby double-parked and rang Rachael's bell. There was no answer. He rang it again thinking that maybe they had gone up to Harlem. As Bobby turned to leave he heard Rachael's faint voice. "Who is it?" She asked sleepily. "Rachael its Bobby. I need to talk to Rosaland." "Bobby she's sleep." "Wake her up. This is extremely important." "Hold on" Rachael went to Rosaland's bedroom where she was in a deep sleep. "Rosaland wake-up Bobby's here. He said it's important".

Rachael walked back to the intercom. "Bobby she's not waking up. Do you want to come up?" "Yes" he insisted. Rachael pressed the buzzer and Bobby took the elevator to the 19th floor. This was an interesting building.

There were only two apartments per floor and once you got past fifteen there was one apartment per floor. Rachael awaited him at the door "This had better be important" she warned. "Her room is at the end of the hall."

"Rachael the quality that I admire most about you is that you always mind your own business. Of course it is important otherwise I wouldn't be here." Bobby followed the direction of Rachael's finger and found Rosaland sound asleep. He entered her room and sat down on her bed. It amazed Bobby how Rosaland always managed to look so sexy no matter what she did.

He stroked her hair trying tenderly to awaken her. "Wake-up sleepy head" Bobby whispered giving her a nudge. Rosaland was starting to stir. "Wake-up we need to talk." Rosaland opened her eyes and still half asleep recognized her man. "Bobby what time is it? What are you doing here? You told me that you were going to stay in Brooklyn tonight?" Rosaland sat up in the bed allowing the covers to fall from her shoulders, exposing her voluptuous breasts.

Bobby reached down and stroked them tenderly burying his face between her cleavage. Rosaland reached up and held his head close to her body. "Get dressed Baby; let's go home we need to talk." "Bobby I've got a splitting headache can't this wait until the morning? Besides I've got to get up early for the World Affairs Conference. It will take us at least an hour to get to Harlem. Come on honey take off your clothes and get in bed." She urged.

"This is Rachael's house. I can't sleep here with you." "Why not? This is my room, my bed and you are my man. Please Bobby get in bed. We can talk about this in the morning." After much coaxing on Rosaland's part Bobby conceded and went to bed. Rosaland's body was warm and accommodating. They were both tired from the events of the day and the two fell into a deep sleep snuggly wrapped in the comfort of each other's arms.

twenty-eight

The next morning didn't bring much relief for either of them. Rosaland had a splitting headache. This happens every time she drinks Hennessey especially if she has more than one. Bobby on the other hand wanted her. He wanted to make love to her but felt very uncomfortable not being alone as he was accustomed to being with her. He couldn't make her scream knowing that Rachael was in the next room and they had never been able to be quiet. Their passion was always loud and thunderous.

He would have to wait until he had her alone but Bobby was still very upset about last evening. He felt that Rosaland was completely out of order with her flirting. Rosaland on the other hand was unsettled about the close relationships that still seemed to exist between Bobby and Diana. Both of them had unresolved issues with each other and that morning the shit hit the fan.

"How do you feel?" Bobby asked Rosaland as she emerged from the bathroom. "My head is killing me" she whined holding her head in her hands. "Well maybe you shouldn't have drunk so much last night." He said starting in with her. "What do you mean by that?" She hissed back even though she was well aware of where this conversation was going.

"Who was dude? And why did he have his hands all over you? What was going on with that?" Bobby was mad. "Bobby we were just dancing. What's the big deal?" Rosaland was mad. "Rosaland are you going to look me straight in my eyes and ask me what the big deal is. This motherfucker had his hands all over your body; he was feeling your ass, holding you as close to him as humanly possible, the two of you might as well have got a hotel!"

"What! How are you going to talk about anybody being close? That bitch Diana was on you all night! You didn't even have room to breath. She might as well have been your second skin. The looks, the hugs, the kisses yes Bobby

I saw you kiss her several times. I saw her kiss you several times. I watched to two of you be the most loving couple at the bar. Don't you dare talk to me about another man dancing with me when this chick was standing at the bar rubbing your ass! You were so busy with her that you didn't even notice me. You had no idea how long I was watching you and that pussycat."

Rosaland shot a scalding glance in his direction. Bobby knew how Rosaland felt about Diana. His only defense was to shift the focus away from Diana and back to Antonio whom they both would discover some years later was really the infamous Carlos Calderon. But Bobby didn't have a chance to make his shift he had started this argument and now the fire was turning into flames.

"You knew when you were going undercover who you were going to be working with. Don't you dare try to tell me that she was a surprise at the last minute? If the two of you were assigned to undercover duty then both of you were prepared for the assignment. Arthur is not going to let unprepared officers go undercover. Do you think that I am stupid Bobby? I work in the same precinct as you do .The same unit."

"I see how this woman oogles you. Last night was just her chance to do what she has been wanting to do with you for a while." "So what was your excuse? Yes Diana and I have a history we all know that. What the hell were your reasons for letting a complete stranger touch you in that manner?" Bobby was livid. "In what manner? All we were doing was dancing!" Rosaland screamed back. "Rosaland this man had his hand down the back of your dress. Your body was pressed so close to his that you couldn't move." At this point both Bobby and Rosaland were screaming at the top of their lungs. Their voices could be heard throughout the whole apartment.

Rachael who was about to leave for work came down the hall and asked them to lower their voices; the entire building could hear their shouting match. Bobby was angry and Rosaland was mad. "All Diana is waiting for is her chance to get you back into bed." Rosaland shouted "And dude wasn't trying to get you in bed? That's exactly what he was trying to do. You had his undivided attention the whole night. This motherfucker is whispering shit in your ear, playing with your hair, touching your face, rubbing your ass, and feeding you drinks. All he was trying to do was to get your ass drunk and take you to bed!" Bobby screamed back.

As Bobby remembered the expression on Carlos's face as he held Rosaland tight in his arms he became completely outraged. Rosaland was also thinking about the satisfaction that Diana displayed as Bobby leaned over to kiss her at the bar.

"You enjoyed being with her didn't you?" Rosaland asked Bobby in a sarcastic tone. "Did it make you think of old times back in the day? Do you miss her? Because if you do we can do something about that. Nobody knows about us anyway. We're a big secret!" She spat. "A secret! Whose idea was that anyway? That was your damned idea; this is how you wanted things. I would have told the whole world by now but no you're Miss strictly confidential. And you know what Rosaland; the joke is on us everybody knows about us. Arthur, Rachael and your Dad!"

"My Dad?" "Yes your father. He has known about us since Bolivia!" That statement took Rosaland back a little actually back a lot but somehow she knew that Bobby was right. "Diana doesn't seem to know now why is that?" Rosaland never knew when to shut up. At that point Bobby was ready to put an end to this scene. It was too early in the morning and this definitely was not the way to start the day. Besides they had been arguing for what seemed liked hours and it was going nowhere.

"I asked you a question. How come Diana doesn't know about us? She doesn't know because you didn't tell her!" "And when were you going to tell what's his name about us? After he fucked your brains out?" "What! Have you lost your mind? What makes you think that?" "I got you into bed so could he?" Rosaland reached up and slapped the shit out of Bobby.

"Get out!" She screamed "Leave!" Bobby stormed out of the apartment slamming the door hard behind him. Those last remarks crushed Rosaland and she fell sobbing on the bed. Arthur who always calls Rachael in the morning heard all the screaming through the phone. "What the hell is going on over there? Sounds like Beirut." He asked as he could hear all the shouting.

"Bobby and Rosaland are into it Baby" Rachael replied "They are both extremely pissed off about last night." "What happened last night?" Arthur inquired knowing that both of his officers were on the job. "Bobby was with Diana and Rosaland was getting attention from the owner of the club and neither one of them liked seeing the other with somebody else."

"Bobby and Diana were working. That's not like Rosaland; she never seemed to be bothered by them working together before." "Well sweetie I don't think it was the working that upset her. It was all the other attention that Bobby and Diana were lavishing on each other that set her off. And the owner of the club was lavishing the same amount of attention on her and that set Bobby off. If you ask me they were both off the hook and things got out of hand from there." "We're the officer's cover blown due to this situation?" "No they both handled it well last night but this morning is another story. They have been screaming at each other for hours. They started at the crack of dawn. I had to go and ask them to keep it down and they seemed to have gotten louder after that."

"Do I need to say something about this?" "No it's personal between them. We both need to stay out of it and let them work it out. I've never seen Bobby so upset. I thought he was going to put his fist through the wall." "O.k. would you like a ride to work?" "Yes" "I'll pick you up in about a half an hour."

The tension was so thick that you could cut it with a knife at the one five that morning. Bobby arrived at work first and was in a terrible mood. As the other detectives began to file in he didn't even acknowledge their presence. He busied himself typing reports and paid no attention to the signs of life that began to emerge as the officers started their daily work routine. He did however notice Diana when she reported in for duty. Bobby watched her as she went into the break room for coffee and decided to join her.

"Good morning Bobby" Diana said as she poured herself a cup of coffee "Would you like a cup?" "Yes that would be nice" he replied as she handed him the mug. "You did a good job last night Diana." He smiled as he accepted the cup. Diana smiling back questioned "What brought that on?" "You did a good job and I wanted to tell you that you did a good job." Bobby took his coffee and walked back to his desk.

Dr. Reid entered the station and immediately went into her office. Her mood just as bad. She noticed the Detective at his desk but refused to acknowledge his presence. She turned on her computer and began to search for the file on Antonio Rivera. As the computer was running the search program she went into the break room to get a cup of coffee passing directly in front of Bobby's desk and deliberately ignoring that he was there.

She noticed Diana as well and made a mental comment that she looked really nice today and that just made her more furious. She looked briefly at the two of them rolled her eyes in their direction and went back into her office to continue her work on Antonio before she left for the World Affairs Council.

Dr. Reid was looking devastatingly beautiful that morning even though she did not feel beautiful inside. She deliberately took time to adorn herself in the suit she had purchased from Bloomingdales especially for the conference. It was the smell of her perfume that caught Bobby's attention as she walked by his desk. He knew that he should say something to her but he was still hot under the collar so he just watched her ass as she went back into her office.

As the file on the mysterious Mr. Rivera appeared on her computer screen she picked up her phone and called Rachael to ask her to run him through the B.C.I. and Interpol so they could compare notes. She talked with Rachael very briefly as she sipped the hot coffee and waited for the file to completely download. "Are you alright sweetie?" her sister asked out of concern. "No I'm not but I'll be okay. Just see what you can come up with and call me back. If I'm not here leave me a message but don't discuss this file with anyone but me."

"What are you looking for?" "I don't know but I'll know it when I see it." "Where are you going to be later?" "Today is the World Affairs Conference and I'm scheduled to speak. I'll be leaving the office in about an hour, so if the information comes in after that we'll have to discuss it later." "O.k. I'll get back to you later." Rosaland was on the verge of tears and Rachael could hear it in her voice.

Dr. Reid continued to work on the file as Lt. Yancy entered her office. "Dr. Reid can I speak to you in my office for a moment?" Dr. Reid looked up from her computer, "Good morning Lt. I'm kind of busy right now." "This is important and it will only take a couple of minutes." "Give me a few minutes and I'll be right in." "The Lt. smiled and commented "You look really nice today special occasion?"

"Yes I'm speaking at the World Affairs Conference today at the Waldport." The Lt. left her office and called Bobby and Diana into his office so he could start the meeting. The two detectives were in the middle of their briefing when Dr. Reid entered. She nodded to all in attendance and quietly sat down as she listened to their report. At the conclusion Lt. Yancy handed her a manila folder and asked if she would look over the information and give them some direction on the accuracy.

As she reviewed the file she crossed her legs because she knew that she would get Bobby's attention without trying to get his attention. And she was right. She could immediately feel Bobby's eyes on her legs. "Can I use your computer?" "Sure" Dr. Reid walked around the desk so she could pull up the file. She deliberately brushed pass Bobby and sat down in the Lt.'s chair.

She fed the computer the information contained in the file and waited for the system to download the proper response. "This file contains a lot of red flags." She noted. "What do you mean by red flags?" She looked up at Bobby and continued "It contains a lot of planted information. The information that appears in the file has all been placed there in the event that someone would pull it like we did." Bobby could hear the attitude in her voice as she spoke.

"How can you tell?" "There are certain criteria that we look for. For example you all need to come around so you can see what I'm talking about." Diana, Bobby and the Lt. gathered around so she could point out the discrepancies presented in the document. Bobby intentionally placed his hand on her shoulder as she started her explanation of the various items that had been carefully placed in the file.

Bobby's touch set Rosaland's body on fire. She looked over her shoulder directly into his eyes and then she turned her attention back to the screen.

Bobby was teasing her. Under the circumstances he knew that she wouldn't react so he leaned in further and slid his arm around her waist. Bobby was intoxicated by the smell of her perfume and he was beginning to wish that he hadn't argued with her this morning.

He knew that he would certainly have to apologize to her before he could even think about any loving and Bobby was already thinking about making love to her and he wanted to make love to her soon. Dr. Reid proceeded with her explanation trying not to show her true emotions. The fact of the matter was that her body was on fire and it was a fire that only the stall worth detective could extinguish.

Dr. Reid looked at the time and reminded the Lt. that she had a previous commitment. Bobby was shocked. What was she talking about? What previous commitment? He had made plans to take her to lunch, so that they could resolve their issues. "I have done some research on this file. When I get all my findings I will be more than willing to share them with you." At that point Dr. Reid's pager went off. She checked the number and excused herself from the office.

Once back in her office she called Rachael. "Sis I wasn't sure where you would be that's why I paged you. I just got the information on Antonio Rivera. It's like he doesn't exist." Rachael shared her findings. Bobby noticed Dr. Reid on the phone and he was curious as to what had her undivided attention. Rachael continued "It's clear from the B.C.I. file that obviously Mr. Rivera is someone else."

"I suspected as much" Dr.Reid replied. "The file that I pulled up from the O.N.S.I. data base is full of red flags. It as though someone placed in there just for us. Everything in this file is bogus. Complete bullshit." Rosaland's mind was in an uproar because of the feelings that Antonio Rivera stirred up in her. Who was this mystery man? And what did he have to hide?

"Rachael see if you can pull up the charter for the club. That might give us some more information. Also check with the I.R.S. and see what is the club's tax status and whether it has been incorporated. I'll be leaving here in about ½ hour so page me if something worthwhile comes up." "O.k. I'll get back." Dr. Reid continued to study the documents. She really wanted to know who this man was.

At that moment Diana entered her office. She waited a moment hoping that Rosaland would stop to acknowledge her presence. When she didn't Diana spoke up. "Dr. Reid?" at that point Rosaland looked over her computer screen at the detective and snapped "Yes detective how can I help you?" Diana immediately noticed the sharpness in her voice.

"Is something wrong?" She recoiled. A bit offended by Rosaland's harshness. "What would make you ask me a question like that?"Dr. Reid was being mean. "Well you seem to be a little disturbed." "No Detective I'm not a little disturbed. I'm a lot disturbed. Actually I'm downright angry. Now what can I do for you?" She looked over her glasses.

"What has got you so angry?" Diana still trying to be nice. "That detective is personal. But since you seem so interested I had a bad fight with my boyfriend this morning." "I didn't know that you were seeing anyone." "I'm sure you didn't." That last remark struck a nerve with Diana and before she left Dr. Reid's office she commented "Well I'm sure that you can work it out."

"I already have. I no longer have a boyfriend. Please shut the door behind you." Diana realizing they never talked about her concerns. Rosaland was still extremely upset by Bobby's last remark. How could he cheapen her in such a manner? She had gone against all of her upbringing everything that her father had taught her and she was nothing more than another one of his conquest. That hurt. The first night that Bobby made love to her had meant so much. It was a precious and tender moment that should have been as special to him as it was for her. Right now she didn't have time to think about the situation. She had bigger fish to fry.

The O.N.S.I. had made special arrangements with hotel security at the Waldport to set up surveillance at the conference. This special detailed was assigned particularly to Carlos. If he showed up there, the O.N.S.I. was going to snag him. They had received outside information from a very credible source that he might be on the premises.

The General supplied to counter-intelligence unit. He delegated the responsibility of the organizing of the operation to Dr. Reid. She was put into the position of being the keynote speaker, so that she would be inside. It wouldn't be unusual for her to be present and it would also give her the carte blanche to move freely and gather information.

She needed to coordinate the security and make sure that her team was placed in strategic positions throughout the conference. It had taken several months of negotiations before the O.N.S.I. was able to reach a workable agreement with the hotel.

There was a great deal of compromise before they were able to reach a settlement. In the end the O.N.S.I. had made a valuable deal. They had access to all the surveillance including a satellite hook-up to record the attendance at the conference.

Bobby wasn't aware of the operation but his instincts told him that something more was a stake than just the conference. After Dr. Reid had left the office, Bobby asked the Lt. in an off the record conversation, what was going on? And did he have any knowledge of what was really behind this event? "We've been left out of this one. The O.N.S.I. wants the collar. We might have to go in as back-up, but the jurisdiction is all theirs. This is Dr. Reid's exclusive territory." "So is this an international incident?" The Detective was trying to put the pieces together. "No but it carries international weight. At any rate we're out of the loop."

"What's the danger element?" "Well with the amount of security that I understand will be present the odds are high." Bobby's first thought was that he hoped Rosaland had her gun. He knew that she didn't like to carry it but he always felt safer when he knew that she was strapped. Of course she would have her weapon. And of course she did.

"What are my chances of getting in on this?" Bobby was just about out of the door. "Bobby if you go in you can't go in as N.Y.P.D. We weren't invited and we have no jurisdiction. This is Dr. Reid's call. She wants us strictly in the event that the O.N.S.I. needs backup. That's the game." "Oh yeah well I'm going in." Bobby left the station and headed uptown.

Rosaland was already checked in at command central and was running her systems check. All of the operatives were in key positions and Lt. William Jones who was there on behalf of the General was coordinating the effort. It had been awhile since Bill and Rosaland had seen each other over a year and they had never worked together.

Now they were side by side working under the command of the General. Command central was quite an elaborate set-up occupying three floors of the distinguished hotel facility. The information equipment was aligned with the satellite so that transmissions could cut across time delays. Dr. Reid had the list of working operatives on disc and was running them for security clearance. Carlos was a very well connected man; his arms were long and his pockets were deep she could leave nothing to chance with him. Dr. Reid had to make sure that her team had not been infiltrated. Carlos was a powerbroker and anything and everything was possible.

Rosaland was being fitted with high-tech audio and visual equipment. She would be able to photograph everyone that was in her audience and get their complete dossier fed back to her within minutes of the information being processed. The O.N.S.I.'s intelligence capabilities were phenomenal; they were definitely an organization to be feared.

The stage was being set and soon there would be action. The O.N.S.I. was ready to go. The hotel security had a minimum role to play, but still a crucial one. They had to keep track of every visitor that came through their doors and that was a huge responsibility. As Bobby drove up Second Ave he wondered why Rosaland hadn't mentioned the intense ramifications that this conference presented.

Anytime she was working for or with the General she never discussed it. There was always this unspoken trust between them. Bobby could never penetrate that part of her life. Why was the N.Y.P.D. left out of the loop? This was their city and they should be involved. How could the O.N.S.I. get this kind of jurisdiction? There were more forces at work than even he realized, and Bobby was very astute.

twenty-nine

The lobby of the luxurious establishment had been transformed into the soul of Latin America. It was elegantly decorated and was like stepping into another world. The sights and the sounds echoed Brazil, Argentina and Peru. Hotel personnel and staff were treating the South American ambassadors and other dignitaries with the utmost respect. Bobby was very comfortable among the Latin American population. He was in his element. All Bobby could do was watch and wait. Meanwhile back at command central Dr. Reid was running her final surveillance check on the video equipment that was set up in each of the conference rooms.

She had to make absolutely sure that all systems were operable and functioning properly. She could leave nothing to chance. Carlos Calderon was a very influential man and he could infiltrate her organization at any time. She knew all too well of his capabilities to alter situations and circumstances to his favor. After all he was the head of the most powerful cartel in the free world. If the O.N.S.I. was not able to stop him his power and influence would spread to Eastern Europe and Asia as well. Dr. Reid conducted a final operative count to make sure that all personnel had reported in and was ready to work. Lt. Jones whom had never had the pleasure of working with her was impressed with her accuracy and control of command.

He observed as she delegated responsibilities to the O.N.S.I. team of professionally trained operatives. Her knowledge of the computer and information systems was second to none and her satellite surveillance was perfectly aligned with the digital camera interface so as to make sure that she could properly identify all the distinguished guest and visitors to the conference.

If Carlos was on the premises or in close proximity the O.N.S.I. would find him. "Lt. Jones I need you to run your diagnostic now please." Dr. Reid observed as the Lt. ran his program. She doubled checked his figures to verify their accuracy. She concluded with a last minute personnel check and now it was show time.

Bobby's instincts told him that things were about to jump off as the lobby of the luxurious hotel full of the excitement of Latin America began to come alive. The conference would offer the ambassadors and the other noted dignitaries an opportunity to let their hair down and enjoy the pleasure and the indulgences that only a city like New York could afford.

Dr. Reid had made special arrangements for some of the more private and powerful individuals to have services with which they would be forever in her debt. This accommodation could be the key to her securing the necessary information on the Calderon Cartel that the O.N.S.I. needed to stop him dead in his tracks. When you treat people with kindness and respect and put them at ease they might be willing to talk about subjects that normally might be off limits. Dr. Reid was counting on that.

Relationships, trust and loyalty mean everything in international negotiations. Dr. Reid would prove to be a woman of her word and in exchange she would hope that someone would supply her with the information that she needed. Somebody knew exactly what she needed and she hoped that they would share it with her of course for the right price or with the right incentives.

Either way Dr. Reid was prepared to facilitate her guest in the hospitality of the Big Apple. At that moment Dr. Reid thought about Bobby and for some reason her intuition told her that he was near. She could feel him inside of her and she knew from experience that her intuition about the detective was never wrong.

Bobby watched from the lobby as all the operatives slowly and inconspicuously slid into position. He was familiar with Dr. Reid's handiwork from the Bolivian insertion and he was absolutely amazed and astonished with the skill and the precision that she utilized to quietly secure the facility and place her key O.N.S.I operatives in strategic locations throughout the hotel.

Bobby watched the transition take place completely unnoticed and within a matter of moments the lobby was completely under her control. The World Affairs Conference was under way. It was at that point that Bobby spotted a familiar face. This was his in. His eyes followed his old friend to a place behind the front desk. Bobby also noted that he was wearing a hotel security badge and that badge was Bobby's thread to sew himself back into the loop.

Bobby waited while his friend prepared to start his shift. After getting settled into his job Bobby made his move. "Andy Martinez, how the hell are you?" Andy looked up from the desk into the face of his long time friend. "I thought I recognized that voice. Bobby Semione how the hell are you? It's been a long time." The old friends shook hands. "Yes it has man it's good to see you." "So what brings you here Bobby?" Andy was interested. "Actually Andy I need your help. Do you have somewhere we can go to talk?" "Yeah we can talk in my office or should I say my temporary office. I've been displaced for the next week."

Bobby and Andy went way back. They grew up together in the same neighborhood and attended the same schools. Bobby was about a year older than Andy and Andy always looked up to the detective as the brother he never had. It was Bobby that helped him to survive those means streets of the barrio and escape falling victim to the gangs.

Bobby entered the academy straight out of high school and Andy followed a year later. As Andy and Bobby entered the elevator Bobby's attention was directed towards the reception that was gathering in the lobby area. "What's going on here?" "This week we are hosting the World Affairs Council and the conference on Latin America."

At that point they had reached Andy's office. Bobby noticed that they had traveled at least six floors before they came to a stop. "Why is security so far from what is going on?" Bobby questioned. "I told you that our offices have been temporarily relocated. In the event of a hotel emergency we are to contact the head office and they will handle the situation." "Who are they?" "Some special unit that the hotel brought in especially for this conference."

Bobby knew that he was on the right track. "So Bobby what can I do for you?" Andy finally got around to asking. "I'm looking for someone. Her life could be in danger, this is extremely important." "Her?" "Yes" "Is this official police business?" "No this is personal. The N.Y.P.D. is not involved with this operation, so I'm here unofficially, but the department needs to ensure her safety. The information that she gathers here could help us with a couple of unsolved murders."

"O.k. what do you need?" "I need access to the special security detail. I need to know where they are located. I'm sure that I'll find her there." "Bobby if I didn't know you so well I might be inclined to think that something more was going on here. Is there something more going on here?" "No Andy this is purely professional strictly business." "If you say so command central is on the third floor and it's completely off limits." "How can I get in?" "I don't know hotel security is not even allowed in." "Andy give me your badge." Andy obliged the detective and Bobby left his office. Bobby knew that Dr. Reid would be at command central and he was going to find her.

Bobby was detained immediately as soon as the elevator stopped on the third floor. The O.N.S.I. agents were on full alert and they questioned the detective as to why he was on this secured floor. "I need to speak to Dr. Reid." That fact that he knew her name alerted her team. "Did you not hear me; I need to speak to Dr. Reid. I'm on orders from the General." The detective had said the magic words and he was instantly taken to command central.

Lt. Jones opened the door and this was the first time that the two of them met. For some reason Bobby knew that this was the man that her father had hoped she would marry. Bill was a tall dark and very handsome black man. He was dressed in military attire and appeared to be in command. "Yes what can I do for you? Are you hotel security?" Bill asked noticing the badge that the detective was wearing on his lapel.

"I need to speak with Dr. Reid; we have an emergency situation in the lobby with one of our guest." Bill immediately became alarmed and using his communications device ordered the surveillance team to bring up the lobby on the screen. Bobby at this point had adequate time to scan the office and again he was absolutely amazed at the state of the art computer and surveillance equipment that the O.N.S.I. had in place.

Only Rosaland could have set up an operation this advanced, this office was her calling card. Dr. Reid was in her office being fitted with her audio and visual apparatus as she prepared to walk the lobby before she began her speech. "Dr. Reid, I believe we have a problem." Lt. Jones said as he entered her office unannounced. He noticed that her blouse was still slightly opened and he couldn't help but to notice her full voluptuous breasts.

Bill had wanted her for years but he had never had the pleasure. After the brief glimpse he caught of her exposed breasts he wanted her even more. He had no idea that she had grown up to be so lovely. "What is it Lt.? What seems to be the problem?" "We have a gentleman here from hotel security who is reporting a problem in the lobby; we can't get it on the surveillance camera, so we might need to send someone down to the lobby for verification."

At that moment Rosaland walked out of her office to look Bobby directly in his eyes. "Is this the gentleman Lt. Jones? I'll speak to him in my office." She said as she calmly led him away. "Bobby what are you doing here?" Dr. Reid screamed once they were behind closed door. Bobby simply starred at her before he answered.

"This is quite an impressive operation you've got going on here. When were you going to tell me what was going on? Or where you going to tell me what was going on?" "Bobby please this has nothing to do with you. Have you lost your mind? This is O.N.S.I. business. Your presence here could completely jeopardize this mission. That is why the N.Y.P.D. was deliberately left out of the loop."

"Your department is too high profile. That's all we need is a bunch of very easily recognizable officers running around the hotel and all our work is down the drain. Bobby I'm here because I have a job to do. What are you doing here? I know Arthur explained to the unit why you all are backup."

"I'm here because you are here." Bill could tell that there was something more going on between the two of them other than hotel security even though he was not quite sure what. The exchange was interesting and Dr. Reid had turned off the audio so he couldn't hear what they were saying to each other.

"Bobby you can't be here because I'm here not this time. You have got to work with me on this. I've got this. I have been working on this for months." At that point Bill had all he could take and he bust in the door. "We checked the lobby. There is no emergency."

"Lt. Jones this is Detective Roberto Semione of the N.Y.P.D. Bill felt a little more at ease knowing that this could possibly be official business even though he didn't like how Bobby got in the door. Rosaland continued "This is one of the detectives from the anti- crime division work in conjunction with the O.N.S.I. Detective Semione this is Lt. William Jones from the Pentagon. He is here on special orders from the General. Lt. Jones is my second in command coordinating security for the World Affairs Conference."

The two officers grudgingly shook hands. "I work in the same unit with Detective Semione. He is here to coordinate the backup effort on behalf of the N.Y.P.D. now Lt. I need to talk to the detective alone. We will bring you up to speed after we confer." Bill knew that was his cue to leave, so he reluctantly left her office.

"Bobby" Rosaland looked at him. Bobby slowly walked over to her window and closed the blinds. He then grabbed her in his arms and kissed her deeply and tenderly. Rosaland responded to his advances and wrapped her arms securely around his neck pressing her body close to his.

"I'm not leaving" he whispered in her ear as their lips parted. "Please Bobby you can't stay. You have no right to be here." "You are my right to be here. I'm not leaving." "Bobby you have to let me work you can not stay." "I'm staying so you need to find something for me to do. I'm not leaving you here alone. This could turn into an extremely volatile situation."

"Remember I was in Bolivia and I know that this whole charade is all about Carlos Calderon. I'm not leaving." They had both forgotten the terrible fight they had earlier that morning. If there was any chance of danger Bobby was not leaving her side and Rosaland knew it. "Please Bobby; you have got to let me work. I've worked on this too long for any last minute changes my team is in place and we are ready to move."

"Rosaland I'm staying. What do you want me to do? Leave you here well I'm not. Now where are your weapons and what is the reaction time of your team? If something goes down how long will it take your back-up to arrive?

I know that the one five is on stand-by but they are about ten blocks away. What kind of plan is that? You need a team of shooters at your disposal right now."

"Bobby the O.N.S.I. has a team of shooters who are on the premises right now. We have all the exits covered with both surveillance and agents. Bobby we are not expecting any trouble but we are prepared in the event that it comes to that." Bobby took of his jacket and walked over to the surveillance cameras. He noticed how all the agents were in strategic positions ready to strike.

"Where's the conference room?" Rosaland pointed to the main camera. "Will you be highly visible from there? Where is the blind spot? How long will it take for me to get to the main conference room from here?" "Bobby why are you asking me all these questions?" "Rosaland in an operation of this size you always need to make sure that all your bases are covered. I'm just making sure that they are that's all. You need to check your weapon; you do have your gun right?"

"Yes Bobby." Rosaland realized then that she was wrong to keep him out of the loop. She should have told him about the conference but he was here with her now and that was all that mattered. Rosaland pulled her gun from the holster and released the safety. Bobby was checking both of his guns when he noticed that the conference was starting to fill up with the Latin American ambassadors and all the other invited guest.

"Looks like its time to get this show on the road." he smiled at Rosaland. Lt. Jones came back to the office and Dr. Reid instructed him to take Detective Semione to command central. "Dr. Reid, you didn't answer me" "I beg your pardon?" "How long will it take me to get to the conference room from here?" Lt. Jones answered for her. "It will take about a minute. The conference room is located right under us. There are two ways in and two ways out detective.

The stairwell lies directly to the north on both ends of the building and the elevator faces east on the first five floors. We have shooters posted at each exit as well as at both ends of the building. The fire exits are in between the elevators and the stairwells and we have shooters posted there also. That's the complete layout of the first five floors detective."

Bill walked over to get the floor plans and laid them out on the desk for Bobby to look at. "If you are going to be a part of this team, then you will need to know what's happening." "Thanks" Bobby said looking at Rosaland with one eyebrow raised. He checked out the floors plans carefully committing them to memory. He had a very uneasy feeling about this setup. Something about it just wasn't right. Bobby always trusted his gut and they were completely buzzing now.

After he surveyed the floor plans he went back to watch the monitor as the conference room continued to fill up. The Ambassadors and the other select dignitaries were seated first. The media took their positions in the section that had been reserved for them, and now the General population was being seated.

The security in the conference room was very tight. Lt. Jones motioned to Dr. Reid that it was time for her to open the conference. "Lt. Jones check Dr. Reid's audio visual before she goes down to the lobby." Bill requested. Her system checked out. It was fully operational. From where she would be standing on the podium, Bobby would be able to see the faces of everyone in her audience; he would also be able to photograph all the participants.

Bill noticed how efficient Bobby was operating in this new environment. He was very comfortable taking control and he was leaving nothing to question. Bill admired that; he knew that he was a good officer. "Detective I'm sorry about all the attitude. It's nice working with you. We could use a few more good men." Bobby nodded in his direction. "The N.Y.P.D.. is on stand-by. Take care of her!" Bobby gave his final command as Bill nodded back in his direction and escorted Dr. Reid to the lobby of the hotel. Bobby watched her as she made her way through the lobby to the conference area. He observed how casual she was despite that fact that she was under a great deal of pressure.

She had pulled a lot of strings to assure her guest that they would be safe and she needed them to supply her with information on Carlos. She knew that somebody here could furnish the necessary information on what Carlos had up his sleeve and she also knew that for the right price somebody would tell her. She counted on that fact.

Bobby pulled out his cell phone to call Arthur. "Lt. I'm in." He reported "Bobby you know I can't hear this you are not supposed to be there. How's it looking?" "It's not right. I don't know why but it's not right. How long will it take back-up to move in?" "Just a phone call" "I'll get back to you." After carefully observing the audience. Bobby decided to go down for a closer look.

thirty

Dr. Reid smiled as she donned the podium. She was very happy to have been chosen for such an honor. She greeted the Ambassadors and the other visiting dignitaries and thanked them for their patience and their participation in the conference. Dr. Reid noticed Detective Semione moving through the crowd as she continued her opening remarks; she followed him with her eyes while trying to remain focused on the contents of her speech.

"What was he up too?" Was the first thought that flashed through her mind as she watched him cruise the crowd. She noticed him reaching for his weapon when a hail of gunfire filled the room. Bobby looked toward the podium at the exact moment that Rosaland hit the floor.

"Rosaland!" Bobby shouted and took cover trying to get to her as the sound of assault weapons filled the air on top of the loud shouts and shrill screams of the people in the room. It was complete pandemonium as everyone was scrambling trying to escape death. The Latin American Ambassadors were going down one by one. The shooters seemed to be everywhere. Bobby returned fire in the direction that it was coming from moving his way toward the stage. The ambassadors, their wives and all the other invited dignitaries were dropping like flies all around him.

In all the confusion it was hard to tell who was who. The death toll was adding up as media reporters, cameramen and innocent people were all caught in the crossfire. From his kneeling position Bobby noticed that both of the exits had been completely blocked so he knew that the attackers had no intention of letting anyone escape alive. His only thoughts were of her. He had to get to her to see if she was still alive.

The O.N.S.I. agents were rapidly returning fire as the battle erupted. Again, Carlos Calderon had hit them off guard. He had shooters on the roof firing into the crowd. Carlos wanted everyone in this room dead, there was no doubt about that and Bobby wasn't going to let that happen. Bobby fired back again in the direction that a hail of bullets that hit two other ambassadors had just been fired from.

He had to get these people out of this room; it would be certain death if he didn't. At that moment Bill came up behind him returning fire. "What the fuck!"Bill shouted. "Man these motherfuckers are everywhere! Who the fuck is who?" "Shoot now ask questions later" Bobby responded. The two men were embroiled in the heat of battle. "Where's the back-up?" Bill shouted. "On the way!!" Bobby shouted back. Bobby moved to a clearing to reload. He motioned for Bill to follow him, as he made his way to the podium.

When Bobby arrived he found Rosaland crotched on the ground holding her gun in her hand, she looked up at him with a fear in her face that was very recognizable. Bobby stood up and fired directly at the shooters that were blocking the door. They went down. Bobby had created an exit. "Get her out of here" He commanded. "I'll cover you!"

Bill stood up to fire and was hit by a spray of bullets. He went down. As Bobby ran toward Rosaland a bullet hit him in the chest and he went down as well. Rosaland stood up and fired in the direction the bullet that hit Bobby had come from. She had shot and killed one of her own agents. Bobby struggled to get to his feet and taking her hand ran to the exit.

"Stay here!" He screamed, as he ran back in to drag Bill out of the line of fire. It seemed like an eternity before the N.Y.P.D. bust through the doors. Arthur had received the call over the low ban radio of reports of shots being fired at the Waldport Astoria, and remembering Bobby's last words, had dispatched the back-up immediately. The shooters all started to fall one after the other as the N.Y.P.D. backup unit returned fire.

Once Bobby had made sure that Bill was safe he collapsed. Rosaland was in complete hysterics as she held the fallen detective in her arms. There was so much blood; she had no idea where all of it was coming from. "Bobby! Bobby!" She screamed but the detective was losing consciousness. The General had got the report of the gunplay and was on his way by helicopter to rescue his daughter.

The General barked the orders for a car to be dispersed to the scene and to retrieve his daughter. The General had no idea that Bobby would be with her. The N.Y.P.D. had been ordered to stay out of this. This was a mess. How was he going to explain this fuck up to the President?

The streets were full of the sounds of sirens, with the N.Y.P.D. everywhere. Now they were coming out of the woodwork. When the ambulances arrived the paramedics were like madmen scurrying around trying to help the fallen officers as well as the other wounded. Bill was bleeding profusely from the chest and was rushed away to N.Y.U. Medical. Rosaland was screaming for someone to attend to Bobby. The General arrived to find his daughter slumped over the bleeding detective. "Take them to D.C." the General ordered as the military escort tried desperately to separate her from him.

"No, I'm going with him!" She fought the aide as he tried to place Bobby in the ambulance. The General grabbed her to let his aide move Bobby to safety. "No Dad I'm going with him." She pulled away from her father staying close to Bobby. "I'm going with him!" The General nodded and the aide let her enter the ambulance as it hastily left the scene.

Once inside the medics started the I.V. and tried to stop the bleeding. They administered oxygen and that helped to regulate his breathing. "He's going to make it." The medic assured her once they had him stabilized. Rosaland rode the rest of the way in silence, holding Bobby's hand in hers. She was covered in his blood. "Where are you taking us?" She asked when she noticed that they were going in the opposite direction of the hospital.

"The General wants the both of you in Washington. The detective is going to the Memorial Hospital in the district." "Why?"Rosaland was concerned. "General's orders" the driver answered as he kept on moving. Rosaland was tired and nervous and completely shaken up as she tried to relaxed for the ride to the district. She knew no matter what she did or said she couldn't fight with the General. They were on the way to Washington D.C.

Before she drifted off she wanted a phone so she could call the hospital to check on Lt. Jones. "Can someone please get me a phone?" She growled as they sped towards Washington. "I need to talk to my father." She was handed a small military issue cell phone. "This is a direct line to the General."

"Dad" Rosaland was in tears. "Baby how are you?" The General asked in a very concerned voice. "Dad it was a bloodbath! A complete slaughter! Who did this?" She screamed as the hot tears rolled down her face. "I only made it out of there because of Bobby he and Lt. Jones saved my life. How is Bill? Did he make it?"

"Lt. Jones is in surgery right now. I have the nurses on staff monitoring his progress. I'll let you know if there is any change when you get here. Let me speak to the medic." The General talked to the medic about Bobby's condition which he assured him was stable. "Get my daughter and that detective here A.S.A.P. Drive 100 m.p.h, exceed the speed limit but I want them here now! Did you hear me? I said now!" The General hung up. Rosaland closed her eyes and sat back numbly as the ambulance sped on. Ultimately she tried to drift off to sleep.

Four hours later Rosaland was awakening as the ambulance pulled up to the back of her father's estate. A full medical team evacuated Bobby and took him to a wing that the General had especially prepared for him. In the event of an emergency there wasn't anything that the General couldn't make happen. He didn't want Bobby at the hospital. He wanted him right here where he could monitor his progress and ensure his safety.

He had also placed armed guards at N.Y.U. Medical to guard Lt. Jones. The World Affairs Conference had been infiltrated nobody was safe. The General rushed out upon their arrival and grabbed his daughter to his heart. Her father hugged her tightly as she cried in his arms. Her face and legs covered in blood.

Rosaland was nervous, shaking, covered in blood and in her stocking feet. She lost her shoes running out of the conference room, her heels were too high and she had to get rid of them if she was going to make it out. Her clothes were torn, dirty and bloody from being on the ground with Bobby.

She sobbed uncontrollably fearing that she was losing Bobby. The General escorted her into the house. She immediately wanted to find Bobby. Her father assured her that Bobby was being treated for his gun shot wounds by the best doctors that the military had to offer; as soon as he was out of surgery she would be able to see him. "In the meantime you need to get cleaned up. We'll talk in the morning."

The General motioned for Esmeralda to accompany her upstairs and help her to bathe. "Esmeralda where's Bobby?" Rosaland pleaded with her once they were alone. "I don't know Ms. Rosaland." Esmeralda shook her head. "Esmeralda please help me find out where he is. Please." Rosaland begged. Esmeralda nodded as she ran her a tub full of nice hot water. She placed some scented bath oil beads in the water and handed her a drink.

"You need some rest Ms. Rosaland, drink this; it will help you to relax while I go find your detective." Rosaland stripped down and sat in the nice tub of hot scented water. At one point her body started to shake uncontrollably as she broke down again in tears. She had killed one of her own agents. She had never shot anyone. This was the agent that shot Bobby. That bullet could have been meant for her and with everything happening so fast, it was hard to tell. The one thing that she did know for sure is that the O.N.S.I. had been infiltrated.

Rosaland ducked her head under the water; she needed to wash the smell of death out of her hair and Bobby's blood off of her body. She wished she could wash the memory of the blood bath from her mind. Bobby was the only thought that crossed her mind. She needed to see him, she wanted him to hold her and comfort her and she was in dire need.

Rosaland washed the crusted blood from her body and the smell from her hair. After she finished bathing she poured herself another drink and applied lotion to her body to soften her skin. She closed her eyes as she rubbed the cool lotion on her skin and thought of Bobby.

She applied more lotion to the flat of her stomach and down her smooth shapely legs. She found a nice pair of white silk panties and gently slid into them. She sat at the vanity and brushed her wet hair. She decided to let it dry naturally as she went over to relax on her bed to wait for Esmeralda to return with news of her wounded lover.

Rosaland waited for what must have been hours before Esmeralda came back with her report. The doctors had removed the bullets and Bobby was resting in the west wing. He had made it through the surgery the bullet narrowly missing his heart. The general had placed a guard in the west wing more out of habit than anything else.

Growing up in this house had always been fun. Rachael and Rosaland had discovered all the secrets of the house when they were small girls. Rosaland would rely on the information gathered from her fun filled childhood to guide her to her future. She quickly grabbed the white silk robe that was lying at the bottom of the bed and went to find her man.

She took the back steps that led over the top of the house through the attic tunnels and down to the west wing. There was a guard standing at the door and she really didn't feel like any games. She wanted to see Bobby and she wanted to see him now. As Rosaland approached the door she looked at the guard turned the knob and went inside.

One of the army doctors was still attending to him when she walked in. She sat quietly in the corner waiting in silence for him to finish. "Doctor. How is he?" She asked in a soft voice so not to disturb his sleep. "He's going to be just fine. He's a strong man. He's a little weak from the surgery and I've given him a mild sedative with a couple of weeks of rest he'll be as good as new. The bullets barely pierced his chest; he is a very lucky man."

"How are you? I understand that you were also there. Do you need something to settle your nerves? I could prescribe something." "No I'm still a little shaken but otherwise I'm fine. Besides I've been drinking. I just want to make sure that he's alright." "Well with some rest he will be fine." "Thanks doctor." "No you should thank you father. He was very adamant about this young man. Are you going to stay?" He looked over already knowing the answer. "Yes" "Make sure when he wakes up that he takes two of these. This is to help fight off any infection." "O.k. does he need anything else?" "Just some rest but he will probably have a voracious appetite when he wakes up."

Rosaland laughed as she made an off handed comment to herself. "I'm counting on it." Rosaland walked over to the bed and sat at the top by Bobby's head. She placed his head in her lap as she lightly stroked his hair. She ran her hands over his chest with her fingertips as the tears slowly started down her cheeks. Rosaland fell asleep cradling Bobby's head in her lap.

Sometime during the night Bobby woke up. He looked around the barely lit room to try to get a bearing as to where he was. He lifted his head slightly from her lap to feel a sharp pain shoot through his chest. He looked up to find Rosaland asleep holding his head. He relaxed a little as he felt her hands around his neck. She was awakening when she felt his movement in her lap. The room was dim but he recognized her instantly.

"How do you feel?" She asked gently softly stroking his hair." I've been better, where are we?" Bobby was in severe pain and confused. "At my father's house. He brought us here after the conference. The doctor said that you should take two of these; they will help to prevent any infection. Rosaland reached for the bottle of pills and handed him a glass of water to wash them down.

"You smell good" he said as she reached across him to place the glass back on the nightstand. Rosaland's robe opened slightly revealing her voluptuous breasts. Bobby reached his hand up to stroke her large nipples sending a wave of electric shocks through her body. "Come here" Bobby whispered pulling her close to him. Rosaland leaned down to place a kiss on his lips. Bobby opened her robe and let it fall softly around her waist.

Bobby tried to get up but again a sharp pain shot through his chest and he was deflated. "Don't move Baby" she said tenderly "Let me" Bobby placed her hand on his enlarged erection and she stroked it softly. Bobby hungrily placed his tongue deep in her mouth as she fingered his massive member. Rosaland lowered her body on to his as they continued their passionate embrace. Bobby kissed her along her neck and nibbled at her ears, she sighed sensuously as he passed his hands over her body.

Bobby held her tightly in his arms as he sucked her delicious nipples and sumptuous breasts. Rosaland moaned as he continued his lavish attentions to her soft fleshy mounds. Bobby began to rotate his body under hers rubbing his huge penis between her legs. Bobby used his thumbs to remove her tiny silk panties.

"Bobby please…" she murmured in between his lengthy kisses. Rosaland reached down to slide his briefs over his hips allowing his fully extended member to spring free from its restraints. She grinded her pubic hairs into his crotch and he could feel the moisture from her deep cave as it invited him in.

Rosaland mounted Bobby and carefully guided his enormous weapon to her waiting orifice. She placed her body on the tip and pressed down taking his full length in one stroke. "Oh Bobby" she groaned as she adjusted her body to take more of him on her next down stroke. Bobby moaned weakly as he completely filled her tight cave with his hot meat.

Rosaland rode him as he pumped forcefully up into her body. She bit her lip as she took more and more of his powerful thrusts. Rosaland opened her legs adjusting her hips as she straddled him.

Bobby pounded furiously up into her body feeding her all she could take of him. Rosaland cried out as he bucked under her. Bobby sat up despite the pain and pressed her luscious breasts into his sore chest. He held her tight crushing her nipples into his freshly bandaged wound. He kissed her mouth passionately as he pumped lustfully in and out of her.

"Ooh Bobby ooh!" Were the only words that were audible. Bobby grunted and groaned at the pleasure she was giving him. She could feel him all through her being and Bobby absolutely delighted in her sweetness. "Ooh Rosaland ohh Baby!" He responded much to her enjoyment as he pumped pleasingly. "Bobby I can't stop…" she sighed as she rode his weapon hard "I can't stop!" "Don't stop Baby don't ever stop." He hissed.

Rosaland extended her legs and locked them around Bobby's waist as she took his length repeatedly over and over again deep into her inner sanctum. Bobby could feel her body start to tremble and he knew that was her signal. Her climax was approaching. But he didn't want her to come yet. He wanted some more. Rosaland's cave was hot and Bobby loved her when she was like this. Her excitement only added to his enjoyment.

"Come Baby, Come for Daddy" Bobby coaxed her sexily. "Ooh Bobby" she whimpered as the intensity of their bodies increased. "Bobby Bobby ooh!" Bobby refusing to let her go. He held her in place on his lap applying his huge smoothness between her legs. "Come on Baby. Come for Daddy. Show Daddy how good it feels." That last comment sent Rosaland over the top. Her body convulsed in orgasm as Bobby stuffed her with his luscious intentions. Rosaland bounced up and down trembling and crying as Bobby filled her completely with the power of his love.

Bobby wanted more but his body had other thoughts. He was totally exhausted as his sweat covered body collapsed back on the bed. His freshly bandaged chest wound starting to bleed. He held Rosaland in place on top of him, kissing her wantonly and seductively. "I love you Bobby" she murmured quietly. "I know Baby. I know. I love you too." Bobby's chest in total agony. "Thanks for saving my life." She whispered sweetly. Bobby kissed her on her forehead and held her tight.

thirty-one

The next morning, the general found the two lovers in the exact same position. He was shocked to find them in such a compromising situation. He nudged his daughter who was sound asleep in the detective's arms. Rosaland awoke; surprised to see her father starring her straight in the face.

The General excused himself as she released herself from Bobby's arms and slid out of bed. Once she found her robe, she covered her naked body and looking over at Bobby lovingly; she kissed him on his forehead and left the room. Her father was standing outside the door as she passed him to head for her room. She hadn't meant to stay there all night. She didn't want her father to see her with Bobby but it was too late. They had been discovered.

As she got dressed she had no idea what to expect at breakfast but she knew that it wouldn't be pleasant. Her father was going to kill her but last night she had to be in the arms of the man she loved. She could have lost him yesterday he could have lost her yesterday and last night was just for them. They both realized that. She would face whatever she had to face but she would stand by Bobby no matter what.

Even though the General was shocked to see the two of them in bed together it wasn't unexpected. The General knew exactly what was going on between them and he knew exactly how long it had been going on. The General had the evidence on Bobby since Bolivia.

The General was a smart man; he would use this situation to accomplish a goal. He wanted his daughter out of this game. He knew when he gave her the assignment that it would be serious but he never anticipated that it would blow this much out of proportion. This game was dangerous and eventually somebody was going to get hurt. The General just didn't want it to be his child.

The blood bath at the Waldport had left 140 people dead and another 200 wounded including Lt. Jones who was still fighting for his life. Detective Semione was currently recovering from a gun shot wound to the chest. The General would make his play. He wanted Bobby to take Rosaland out of this game and he wanted him to keep her out for good.

Sooner or later Carlos was going to realize that she was the brains behind the O.N.S.I. and he was going to come after her. He might even come after their whole family. The general knew that there would be a price to pay. The General went back to the detective's room, to still find him sleeping. After all he had neglected to take into account the hours of passionate lovemaking that he had shared with his daughter and in his weakened condition the detective was exhausted.

thirty-two

The General woke him up. "Bobby I want to talk to you." Bobby having no idea that they had been discovered. "What's up sir" Bobby stirred and tried to sit up in bed his chest in extreme pain. "Do you mind if I get dressed?" "No detective don't get dressed. You need to rest but I would like to talk to you before breakfast." "Yes sir. It will only take me a couple of minutes to get dressed. Where are my clothes?" "You can dress in anything that's here. I believe you'll find something in your size." "Thank-you sir" "No Bobby thank-you for saving my daughter's life. You will always have my deepest gratitude." Bobby smelled like raw sex. He smelled of her. His wound was still to new to shower so he had to take a quick sponge bath to wash her scent off of his body.

Bobby was still experiencing a great deal of pain but he knew he had to get back to New York. The Lt. had already estimated the extent of the damage. This had happened in his city so his department would be all over it. Before his sponge bath Bobby scoured the bed. There they were, he found her panties. After his bath Bobby went to tell the guard who was still standing at the door that he was ready to talk to the General. The General entered Bobby's room a short time late where he found the detective laying flat on the bed.

"Bobby this is none of my business but what is going on between you and my daughter?" Bobby was at a lost for words realizing that some kind of way the General knew what had happened last night. "I love her sir." Bobby started "O.k. and?" "And what sir?" "Detective do you think that I'm going to let you screw my daughter's brains out right under my roof and not say anything about it. I don't know what kind of father you think that I am but know that I'm not the one." The General was completely outraged. "No sir I never thought that you were." Bobby having no idea where this conversation was going. Was the General going to kick his ass? He had heard stories to this effect. How back in the day the General had no mercy on his daughters' suitors.

"Well you need to do something about it. I want you to take her out of this game. It's getting too dangerous and I want her out." The General starred at Bobby with a look of total sincerity on his face. "And how do you suppose I do that?" "Marry her? Get her pregnant? But get her out of this shit. I want her out."

"You can always reassign her. You hand picked her for this assignment." Bobby reminded him. "She won't go for being reassigned not now. You know her better than that. She's in too deep and she won't quit. It's going to have to be something more personal with her. It's going to have to be you." And with that the General left the room dumping the weight of his decision on Bobby's shoulders.

The General was already seated when Rosaland came down for breakfast. She didn't know what to say, and she was absolutely surprised that he didn't say anything to her. "Good morning Dad" she tried to sound cheerful. "Good morning. How are you feeling this morning?" The General asked lightheartedly. "I'm feeling fine Dad. Thank-you for asking." Rosaland got up and went over to hug her father. He embraced her wholeheartedly. Bobby entered the room shortly after their embrace. "Good morning Bobby" she was cheerful after seeing him walk in. "Good morning sweetheart" Bobby walked over and placed a tender kiss on her lips "Thanks for watching over me last night."

"It was my pleasure. How do you feel? Are you still experiencing a lot of pain?" She replied. "Yes but I'll live." Bobby took a seat at the table next to Rosaland as Esmeralda served their breakfast. Esmeralda looked at the two of them together and she knew she had done the right thing. The look of love in Rosaland's face was undeniable.

They ate in silence occasionally glancing at each other. After breakfast the General escorted both of them into his private study. "What the hell happened yesterday?" He asked after they were seated. "We have 140 dead Latin American Ambassadors and dignitaries not to mention the women and the innocent bystanders.

The media caught the whole thing on tape. That is the one's that survived. We have a massacre on our hands which has developed into an international incident and I need to know right now who is responsible for this? The President is on my ass and he wants some answers. Right now he is holding off the Latin American government from taking action but that will be short lived if we can't find somebody to point the finger at."

"Dad it was Carlos Calderon." Rosaland spoke up immediately. "Some kind of way he has infiltrated the O.N.S.I. and I have to find out just how deep the security has been breeched. I know for sure that one of my agents was a traitor because she was the one that shot Bobby. I know this because I shot her." All this information was news to Bobby.

"I'm sure that one person could not have been responsible for the extent of the damage that we sustained. It has to be more people involved for Carlos to know exactly when to hit after I kept the security as tight as it was. Dad I checked out those agents myself. I ran every security protocol known to man and a few more that I made up myself and we were still breeched. It was definitely an inside job but I need to know who else was involved."

"The involvement has got to be bigger than the O.N.S.I. Rosaland continued. Her dad could see that she was far from taking this matter lightly. "You need to check out the hotel, the owners, the corporations and the investors" Bobby added. "Somebody had to spread a lot of money around for an operation like that. You need to follow the money and that will give you a lot of information on your possibilities. And there is going to be more than one possibility so you need to be prepared for that."

"You can start by seeing if there are any new projects or developments that involve the hotel? What are their current expansion plans? Who inside could be susceptible for black mail or extortion? If you know for sure that Calderon is responsible than you know he will do whatever and you know that his pockets are deep?"

"He can buy anything or anybody at anytime. I don't know. You might not like what you come up with. It smells of a cover-up. There is too much money and too many high level officials." Bobby was shaking his head as he continued to talk. "I knew yesterday that it wasn't right. I was just following my instincts. I like Carlos for this but I'm sure that there are others that are just as involved. Many others."

At that point Esmeralda entered the study, interrupting their conversation. "There is an emergency call for Mr. Bobby." She announced. "He can take the call here in the study." The General replied. Bobby walked over to the table and picked up the phone. "This is Detective Semione" "Bobby?" "Yeah boss" "We have a situation here Bobby and its bad. It's real bad. How long will it take you to get here?" "What's going down Lt. Talk to me?" "Bobby it's your grandmother. You need to get here now!"

"I have to go something has happened to my grandmother. I have to leave now!" Bobby explained. The General called for his pilot "Get the detective to New York right now!" Bobby kissed Rosaland and told her that he would call her as soon as he hit the city and he was off. Rosaland watched tearfully from the window as the chopper lifted from the ground and Bobby sped away.

Rosaland immediately ran to the phone. She called the N.Y.P.D. and asked for the Lt. "Arthur this is Rosaland. What is going on?" She inquired completely alarmed. "Is Bobby on his way?" The Lt. was insistent. "Yes Arthur he just left but you didn't answer my question what is going on?" "Rosaland it's his grandmother and that's all I can tell you right now. As soon as Bobby arrives he can call you and tell you the rest. How are you?"

"I'm still shaken up but I'll be alright. Right now I'm worried about Bobby and I can't believe that you won't tell me what's happening up there." "Rosaland trust me on this one when Bobby get's here he can fill you in. Don't ask me anymore. Rosaland you know if I'm not telling you that means I can't tell you. Be patient and stay available." And with those words Arthur hung up the phone.

Rosaland stood in the study of her father's house holding the phone wondering what could have happened to Abuelita. At that moment a chill passed through her body and all her instincts told her that whatever had happened it wouldn't be good.

thirty-three

The atmosphere inside the station was somber when Bobby arrived he could tell from the looks the other officers were directing his way that what ever had happened was bad. When he reached Arthur's office he was surprised to see his grandfather sitting there. Bobby still standing in the door first glanced at his Grandfather and then at Arthur without saying a word.

"Bobby we have been waiting for you. I'm sorry but we have some very bad news. Your grandmother has been murdered. She was the victim of a drive by shooting that occurred shortly after 10:00a.m. this morning." This was one of the hardest things Arthur had ever had to do.

"Apparently she was on her way home from the market when an unidentified vehicle sped up and fired three shots, all of them hitting her in the chest. The detectives from Brooklyn South are handling the investigation but so far from we have been able to determine we think the shooters are from a rival gang and that your grandmother was in the wrong place at the wrong timc."

"There is no evidence that the shooters were aiming at her; we think she was caught in the middle of a turf war. This particular area is known for its high prevalence of gang related activities." A very emotional Bobby was speechless as he listened to his lieutenant. Bobby's first reaction was one of disbelief but when he focused in on the saddened expression on his grandfather's face he knew that it was true.

Bobby sank down slowly in the chair next to his grandfather and placed his head between his hands as the tears slowly began to fall from his eyes. The rest of the detectives in the squad had started to gather outside the office door to offer Bobby their condolences. Arthur motioned that they should leave to allow Bobby to compose himself and they did. They would give him a few minutes and then they would come back to offer their help. The two units Brooklyn south and the one five would work together on this one; they would find justice for Abuelita they would find her killer.

Papa put his arms around his shaken grandson and held him tightly. At that point Arthur's phone rang "Listen I can't talk now. I'll have to get back with you." Arthur stood there quietly listening to the voice on the other end of the phone and he calmly repeated "I'll have to get back to you" and he hung up the phone. Of course it was Rosaland.

It took a moment for Bobby to regain his composure "Papa where was Abuelita when the shooting happened?" "She was on her way home from the market. You know your grandmother Roberto; she always has to be the first one in the morning. No matter how many times I have asked her to let one of the others go and buy the vegetables she always has to go herself."

Papa spoke of his beloved Abuelita as if any minute she would return from the market with the fresh produce for the restaurant. "Now she is gone from us forever." A grief stricken Papa could contain himself no longer and he began to shake and sob uncontrollably. Now it was Bobby that was holding him. Bobby looked up at Arthur and Arthur knew the signal.

"Detective why don't I leave the two of you alone so that you can look after your grandfather? Besides I need to make a couple of phone calls. I'll be in interview room three if you need me." Bobby nodded as Arthur made his exit. "How's he doing boss?" Diana asked very much wanting to run to him. "They are both taking it pretty hard." The Lt. replied. "Is there anything we can do?" The rest of the squad asked. "I'm sure he will let us know. Right now all we can do is help the detectives in Brooklyn solve this crime."

"Who is heading up the investigation?" Diana asked curiously. "Justin Sanchez. He has been working with the gang related homicides in Brooklyn. I'm told he is pretty good. Excuse me detective I need to make some calls but hold that thought let me get back to you." Diana and the rest of the unit watched Bobby and his grandfather through the window as they shared their moment of grief.

"Arthur what is going on over there?"Racheal was screaming in the phone. "Rachael please calm down. We've got a bad situation here. Bobby's grandmother was murdered this morning in Brooklyn." "What!" She shouted excitedly. "Honey am I talking to you or am I talking to the DA?" "Arthur how can you ask me something like that. You are talking to me and I want to know what happened?" "Sweetie calm down! I have to ask you this because if I'm talking to you then what I say to you is between you and me. But if I'm talking to the DA then what I say to you is on the record and right now we are not prepared to release any information or make any statements without the permission on the next of kin. Do you understand what I'm saying?"

Rachael did understand. She knew exactly what he was saying. "Has Bobby arrived yet?" "Yes he just got here and he is not taking this well. His Grandfather has been here most of the morning and he refused to talk to anyone until his grandson arrived. They are together right now." Rachael was completely stunned by this news. "Is that why he left D.C. in such a hurry?" "Yes I had to call him at your father's house when the report came in."

"Rosaland and my father are both really worried." "Is she on the other line?" "No but I'm going to call her. She really needs to know this. She's a mental case right about now. Now I am speaking as the DA. When do we get this?" "Brooklyn south has it. A detective by the name of Justin Sanchez is heading up the investigation." "Justin Sanchez I'm familiar with him. He does good work." "So I've been told. We'll see what type of cooperation he'll give us." "You won't have any trouble with Justin. He is one of the good guys. He'll work with us." "Good. I'm glad to hear that because you know a certain detective is going to be out for blood. Bobby might lose his badge over this. He is really taking this hard Rachael. My heart goes out to his family."

"I'm calling my sister." "Rachael look I need to go to Brooklyn to talk to this Justin. Why don't you meet me for dinner at about 7:30? No, make it eight. Meet me at my place. Is that o.k.? "That's just fine; I'll see you at eight. Arthur be careful out there." "I'll be just fine." Arthur smiled as he hung up the phone.

"Rosaland I've got some terrible news to tell you. Are you sitting down?" Rachael waited. "I am now what wrong?" Rosaland was scared. "Bobby's grandmother was murdered this morning." "What!" "She was shot this morning in Brooklyn." "No Rachael not Abuelita! Where's Bobby? I've got to get there!" Rosaland hung up the phone and ran to her father.

"Dad I've got to get to New York. Bobby's grandmother was shot this morning. She's dead! Please Dad get me there!" The General lost no time in ordering the helicopter and a military escort to take his daughter to New York.

"Arthur I need to take my grandfather home. He is not good. Do you need him for anything else this afternoon?" "No Bobby take him home we can talk to him later if we need him." "Who's heading up the investigation in Brooklyn?" "Justin Sanchez. Are you familiar with him?" "I've heard of him. I need to talk to him. Do you mind if I go there after I make sure my grandfather is ok? I need to know what happened."

"Well as a matter of fact I was just about to head over the bridge to talk to him. Do you want to go with me? I can have a uniform to take you grandfather home." "No I'd better take him but I can meet you there if you give me about an hour to get Papa settled." "I can do that. I'll meet you at

Brooklyn south in about an hour. Bobby are you sure you are up to this?" "I've got to be. I'll see you in an hour."

"Bobby how's that chest wound?" The Lt. asked remembering yesterday. "Actually it hurts like hell and i need to change my shirt and my bandage but I'll live." "That's good to know. Now go take care of your family." Bobby's mind was reflecting back over the events of the last three days. He really needed to sit down and take an assessment of his life but today was not the day.

"Boss I need to call my girl. She is probably going crazy." "Don't worry. Her sister has already called her; I'm sure you will be hearing from her very soon. Now go and take care of your business. I'll see you in an hour." As Bobby escorted his grandfather out of the station all the detectives took the opportunity to show their concerns.

Bobby thanked them all for their kindness and told them that he would see them later. "Bobby are you alright?" Diana had been waiting by the elevator in the hopes that she might be able to have a private word with him. It had been what seemed like an eternity since they had been together and she missed him terribly.

"Thanks I'll be alright." He replied sadly. "Call me later. Papa I'm so terribly sorry about your Abuelita. She was a wonderful woman. If there is anything I can do please let me know." Diana kissed Papa lightly on the cheek as he entered the elevator. Papa hugged her tightly. "Call me" she said again as the door slowly closed.

The ride home was solemn. It was the first time in fifty years that Papa had been without his beloved Abuelita. When they arrived home the restaurant was crowded with neighbors, well wishers and friends. They had been waiting there all morning for Papa and Bobby to return home with some news of their fallen angel.

The neighborhood was still pretty much in shock with the tragedy. It was hard to believe that someone as kind and loving as Abuelita would have such a tragic end. As Bobby pulled up in front of the restaurant he asked his grandfather "Papa are you sure you are up to this?" "Roberto what can i do? These are our neighbors and friends. How can I turn them away?" Bobby knew that his grandfather was right; there would be no way that any of the neighbors would leave Papa to face his grief alone.

Once inside the restaurant Bobby escorted his Grandfather upstairs so that he might lie down. Papa was exhausted and a little rest would do him good. After putting his grandfather to bed Bobby spoke to Maria one of their long time waitresses. "Maria I need you to look in on Papa until I return. I have some business that I need to take care of."

"You go ahead Roberto; we will take good care of him." Bobby gave her a half nod as if to ask if it was really o.k. for him to leave. "Go Roberto. Do what you need to do. I will take good care of your grandfather now go." Maria coaxed him out of the door. Bobby's first stop was the scene of the crime. The area was cordoned off and a couple of uniform patrolmen were still on guard. It took a great deal of strength for Bobby to exit his vehicle and walk over to the street that was still splattered with his grandmother's blood.

Bobby was overwhelmed with emotion as he approached. He didn't know if he could do this but he knew that he had too. His grandfather would be counting on him to find the answers. There were still uniform officers at the scene. Bobby acknowledged their presence as he bent over to survey the sight.

For a brief moment it seemed that he could hear Abuelita calling to him. At that second Bobby started to experience flashbacks of his Grandmother and all the special memories that they had shared. After all she was the only mother figure that he had known in his life.

Bobby carefully surveyed the scene. First looking at the bloody sidewalk and then looking around to see who could have possibly seen exactly what had happened. Bobby's attention became focused on a row of buildings in the background that seem to be partially inhabited. For some reason his keen instincts was leading him to believe that those buildings would be a good place to start his own investigation.

In his gut he knew that he would find some answers some clues that would lead him to the truth. "Excuse me sir this is a crime scene." The officer had spoken before he noticed the detective's badge on Bobby's jacket. Bobby stood up from his crouching position and identified himself to the officer. "Roberto Semione Manhattan north. Who is the lead on this case?" "That would be Detective Justin Sanchez." "Where can I find him?" "Brooklyn south. Detective Sanchez has placed priority status on this case. All the neighbors that we spoke to said she was a very nice lady." "I know she was a wonderful lady. She was my grandmother."

The officer looked shocked and then offered his hand and his condolences. "I'm sorry if I was rude detective. I'm sorry about your grandmother." Bobby nodded his appreciation to the officer as he turned to stare in the direction of those dilapidated buildings. Bobby was lost in thought when his cell phone rang. "Semione" "Bobby where are you?" "I'm at the crime scene boss. I had to come."

"We are waiting for you. How's your grandfather?" "I left him in the care of some friends. I'm on my way." Once Bobby was in the safety of his vehicle he realized that all his strength seemed to have been drained from his body.

Suddenly he was very tired and the pain in his chest was throbbing. At that point he remembered that he had forgotten to change his shirt and the blood from his wounds was everywhere. Somehow he managed to get his bearings and fifteen minutes later he arrived at Brooklyn south.

Arthur was in a deep conversation with Detective Sanchez when Bobby entered his office. Bobby noticed immediately that the detective had a very pleasing manner. Arthur made the introductions "Justin Sanchez, Bobby Semione" the two detectives shook hands as Bobby took a seat. "I'm sorry for your lost; I promise you that we will give this case our first priority."

"Thanks can you tell me what happened?" Bobby was very interested. "I have to tell my grandfather." "According to our witnesses a sleek black sedan pulled up and opened fire. Your grandmother was hit in the chest by three of the bullets." "Was anyone else hit?" "Yes a sixteen year old girl and her mother. They were both rushed to Brooklyn Medical. The girl is in critical condition and her mother was treated for a shoulder wound. We are thinking that maybe it was a boyfriend or a husband but right now this is all we have. Apparently your Grandmother was just in the wrong place at the wrong time." "Did anyone get a plate number or the make and model of the vehicle?" "Yes we are running the plate now through the D.M.V. but they haven't got back to us yet." "What was uncovered through canvass did anybody see anything? Does anybody know anything about the other two victims? Are they from the neighborhood?" "Yes the girl is Juanita Fuentes a student at P.S.16 and her mother is Theresa Fuentes she works in the cafeteria at the same school. Apparently they were on their way to school.

The mother has no priors nothing she's clean. We are working on locating the father, and checking to see if there is a boyfriend or a lover who could have been responsible for this. I told your Lt. that we will give you full cooperation and anything that we come up with will be shared as soon as we get it you got it. And if there is anything else that you need here's my card."

Bobby took the card and promptly gave him his. "Here are all my numbers. I would appreciate a call anytime when you hear or know anything." "You got it." For some reason Bobby couldn't shake the feeling about that set of buildings. He would investigate them on his own. If he came up with something he would let Detective Sanchez know. For right now he would keep that information to himself.

"Your guys didn't uncover anything in canvass?" Bobby was still trying to put together the pieces. "We have plenty of eye witnesses to the shooting and their stories collaborate. They saw what they saw. Everyone that was present on the street was more than cooperative; we didn't have any problems getting people to talk to us."

"Excuse me; can I interrupt for a moment?" Wesley interjected. "This is my partner Detective Wesley Cole. This is Detective Bobby Semione and Lt. Arthur Yancy." Detective Cole entered the room and shook hands with the two detectives. "We just got back the information from the D.M.V. The black sedan is a rental and it was reported stolen three days ago. It was taken from LaGuardia airport from the aviation lot."

"We were able to locate the father. He is an engineer for the city and he reported to work this morning at 7:00a.m. and he was there all morning. I spoke with his boss before we notified him of the shooting. He's at the hospital now with his family. The girl is still listed in critical condition."

"Bobby Wesley and I will go over to the airport to see if we can come up with anything we'll give you a call. Is there anything else we can do?" Justin offered. "Just call me." "You got it; again I am terribly sorry for your lost. It's a shame that we had to meet under such circumstances." Bobby and Arthur shook the detective's hands and all four of them left the station.

Justin and Wes were headed for the airport while Arthur and Bobby headed for Manhattan. "Bobby why don't you take the rest of the week to handle your business. I'll give you comp time. If anything comes up I'll call. Right now you need to be with your Grandfather." "Thanks Lou. Thanks a lot."

When Rosaland and the General arrived in Manhattan they rushed to the precinct. Rosaland was hysterical and her thoughts were only of Bobby. She was slightly alarmed when she failed to find either he or Arthur there. The squad room was buzzing with the news of the shooting so it was very easy for her to get the story of what had happened.

"Danny where is he?" She asked "Where's Bobby?" "He and the Lt. went to Brooklyn. He is probably at home with his grandfather now." "No he's not there; I have tried several times to reach him, that's why I thought he was here." "No. They left a couple of hours ago; they have been gone for a while. Page him?" "I did. He's not answering his pager." "Just sit tight Dr. Reid he is with the Lt. They'll be back."

"No I can't just sit tight detective. I'm going to find him. I'm going to Brooklyn." It was at that moment that Danny discovered how much she loved his partner. Bobby never talked about the relationship they shared even though Danny knew that they had been seeing each other. Both Bobby and Rosaland always remained so professional at work but their secret was out now.

Danny could see the love in her face and he could feel the love in her heart without her saying a word. Danny recognized that look because he had seen it so often on Bobby's face. He saw it whenever Bobby mentioned her name. Bobby told him two years ago that she was off limits and now he knew it for sure.

Danny had been there in Bolivia. They shared a strong bond then. A bond that was even stronger now. It was so obvious, how could so many people have overlooked it.

Diana Rousseau passed Rosaland and her father as she rushed out of the building. The look on Rosaland's face was the same look she had seen on Bobby's face the day he rushed out of the precinct. The day of the massacre. When Diana reached the squad room she mentioned to Danny that she had just passed Dr. Reid in the hall.

"Where is she going in such a hurry? She hardly even noticed me; she damn near knocked me down." "I don't know" was Danny's reply as he went back to work. "Has anyone heard from Bobby?" "No I was just about to ask you. I'm going over to his house after I finish my shift; as a matter of fact we are all going. Do you want to come?" "Yes I'll go Bobby is my partner."

The neighbors had already started to gather. The restaurant and the house were full of neighbors and friends there to offer the last respects and their condolences for their fallen angel. All the women in the community brought dishes of covered food to make sure that Papa would eat. Everyone was very worried about his state of mind. They knew how close he was to his wife and wondered what he would do without her. They would look out for him. Father Peter had been called to come and sit with Papa. He offered prayer and tried to shed some understanding of God's plan for his sweet dear Abuelita.

Father Peter had known Abuelita every since she and Papa moved to Brooklyn. She was one of his most faithful parishioners. Always busy doing God's work. They shared a special relationship. He had been saddened to hear of her death and wanted to be as helpful and as comforting to the family as possible during their time of grief. Father Peter had often chided Bobby about his absence from Sunday mass. Bobby had been raised with strong catholic values. Bobby always promised that he would attend but he never seemed to make it.

Bobby arrived to find his Grandfather and Father Peter deep in prayer. His first instinct was to turn away and leave the room but the next moment he decided to join them and found himself immersed in a state of deep meditation. As he began to grow still and peaceful the tears that he had been holding back started to fall freely from his eyes. The reality had finally begun to take a hold of him. His Grandmother Abuelita was dead.

It would have been a much easier pill to swallow had she died from natural causes or even from a prolonged illness, but abuelita had been murdered. Shot down by a stranger who had nothing to do with her life. Bobby emerged from his meditation to find Papa and Father Peter comforting him. He had completely broken down. His Grandfather held him tightly to his chest and let Bobby cry in his arms.

"Rosaland, I would like to pick up Rachael and Matthew before we go to Brooklyn." The General said in a calm soothing voice. "I'm sure that they would like to pay their respects to your detective and I would like to have my family with me."

"Ok Dad but we really need to hurry. I have to find Bobby. I can't let him go through this alone." "I know, this will only take us a little out of our way. We will be there soon." The General was worried about his daughter. He had never seen her so effected before. "Call your sister and let her know that we will be there shortly. I'll call Matt." In less than an hour the General had retrieved his family and they were on their way to Brooklyn.

When the General's car pulled up in front of the restaurant the first thing that Rosaland noticed was the large crowd that was gathered outside. They had placed a picture of Abuelita on the sidewalk and were lighting candles in her honor. There were flowers everywhere. The crowd inside seemed to be just as large. A feeling of relief swept over her as soon as she spotted Bobby's car. Bobby and Papa were seated together in the restaurant when the General escorted his family inside. Rosaland immediately went to him. "I've been trying to call you all day Bobby. Why didn't you answer your pager? How come you didn't call me back?

Bobby silenced her with a kiss and held her tightly in his arms. He was very happy to see her. He squeezed her tightly in his embrace, an embrace that seemed to last forever. Rosaland wrapped her arms tightly around his waist as she clung to him. Her face wet from her tears. "It's alright, it's alright…" He whispered softly in her ear as he dried her tears. He led her to the table where his Grandfather was sitting.

The General approached the table and Bobby politely introduced the family to Papa. "Papa this is General Prescott Reid. This is Rosaland's father. Her sister Rachael who happens to the district attorney of New York state and her brother Matthew the Chief of Staff at New York University Medical. Papa greeted them with as much warmth as he could muster up under the circumstances.

"Bobby Arthur and the rest of the squad will be here after they finish their shift." Rachael informed him. "I talked to him right before I left my office. I'm so sorry about your Grandmother. We all are."

"Thanks Rachael. I'm glad you all came." "I'm sorry Bobby; I know how you must be feeling." Matthew knew exactly how Bobby was feeling because he remembered how he felt when he lost his mother at such an early age.

Bobby hugged Matthew and then led him to the bar where Bobby poured drinks for the four of them.

"What does your father drink Matt?" "He drinks Hennessey what else?" Bobby smiled to himself. That's why she drinks Hennessey. Bobby looked over to check on his grandfather and he was happy to see that he and the General seemed to getting along so well. Bobby placed the drinks on a tray and walked back over to where the rest of the family was seated. He then sat next to Rosaland and put his arms around her.

Rosaland was very comfortable in Bobby's arms; this was the place where she belonged. "Bobby did you eat anything today?" "No. I'm good." "How's your wound?" "It was bleeding earlier, still hurts like hell but I'll make it." "Baby you need to eat something. Why don't you let me fix you something? You've got all this food here you really need to eat." "Ok just a little." Bobby gave in noticing at that moment that his stomach was growling.

thirty-four

"Bobby I would like to talk to your grandfather in private. Is there somewhere we can go?" "Yes General you can go upstairs." "Papa the General would like to speak to you in private. Why don't you take him upstairs?" Papa led the General upstairs to his living room so that they could talk. Rosaland handed Bobby a plate as she sat down next to him while he attempted to eat. "Come closer" he instructed her as she nestled her body in his arms. The two of them sat together as Rosaland sipped her drink and Bobby played with her hair.

"You are supposed to be eating." She gently reminded him. "I would really like to take you upstairs" he whispered. Rosaland smiled and shook her head. When Bobby got up to make her another drink Matthew asked Rachael "How long has this been going on?" Carefully observing the two lovers. Rachael laughed "Since they met." Matthew looked at his sister with surprise "No way?" Rachael nodded her head "Yes way" "Well I'll be damned. I knew that he liked her. Does Dad know about this?"

"He does now. Bobby was in Washington when Arthur called him this morning. Rosaland has been hysterical all day." Matthew glanced in their direction and there was no denying the look of love on both of their faces. Rosaland was right by his side and this is where she intended to stay.

Rachael had been looking at her watch since they arrived. "What time do you have to be there?" Matt teased. "What?" "Rachael you have been looking at your watch since we got here." "I'm waiting for Arthur. He said he would be here when he finished his shift. He should be here soon."

"Arthur is checking into Abuelita's murder. He might have some news. I feel sorry for Bobby's grandfather. I know how I felt when Arthur got shot and this poor woman has been murdered." Matthew shook his head; he knew exactly what she was saying. About twenty minutes later Arthur walked in the door. He looked around for Bobby who was lost in admiration for the woman that was sitting by his side.

Rachael strolled over to Arthur and gave him a kiss. "Bobby how are you doing?" The Lt. asked. "I'm good" Bobby replied looking at Rosaland. Rosaland ran her fingers through his hair. "Hello Matthew long time no see. How are you?" Arthur reached over and shook Matthew's hand. "Bobby the rest of the squad is on their way over. Everybody is concerned. They all want to help." "They can help me find the bastard that did this. Believe me I am going to find him." Arthur and everyone else in the room knew that Bobby would not rest until he found the person or persons responsible for Abuelita's death.

"Arthur would you like something to eat? They have so much food here." Rachael was taking care. "Yes I could eat a little something." Rachael led Arthur over to the table where they talked while she made his plate.

Matthew was engaged in conversation with a pretty Puerto Rican nurse that worked in the emergency room at the hospital. He was pleasantly surprised to see her there and that she knew Bobby. "Rachael I've been thinking. We have been engaged for damn near two years. Are you ever going to marry me?" Arthur's bluntness shocked Rachael and she had to laugh. "Yes" she choked. "Ok when?" "When do you want to do it?" "Now" "Today right now?" "Rachael we have waited long enough. Look around you. Look where we are and look why we are here. This is a memorial. Life is not guaranteed to anyone and what life I have left I want to spend it with you."

"I asked you to marry me once. Now I'm asking you again. Will you marry me?" "Yes Arthur I love you." replied a tearful Rachael. "Will you marry me soon?" "Yes arthur I will" "Thank-you. I'm glad we got that straight. Now let's eat." Rachael pressed her body close to Arthur as she kissed him passionately.

There were so many people in and out of the restaurant that night that Bobby hadn't notice exactly when the rest of his squad arrived. The atmosphere in the restaurant was quiet when the detectives filed in. The crowd has started to thin out but there were still plenty of neighbors who had just got the news of Abuelita bringing in food.

"Hey Bobby" Bobby immediately recognized Danny's voice. "I see you found him." Rosaland smiled and nodded her head. Bobby looked puzzled. Bobby got up from his seat and hugged Danny. "Thanks for coming partner." "You knew that I would be here. Sorry it took so long but it seemed like today everybody in New York was committing a crime. Man I need a drink. Bobby walked with Danny over to the bar and poured him a nice big one. "Make it a double. I really need a drink."

Bobby poured some more liquor into the glass and handed it to his partner. At that moment Diana and Yvonne walked in and went over to the bar where Bobby and Danny were standing. Diana hugged Bobby and after she released him from her embrace Yvonne did the same. "Bobby I'm sorry about your grandmother" Yvonne said. "Would you ladies like something to eat or drink?" Bobby offered kindly. "Yes both." They answered at the same time. "What a day. Its days like this that make me wonder why I choose to be in this line of work." Yvonne commented as she sipped her drink. "I know what you mean" Diana chimed in.

"What was going on today? This had to have been the worst day I've had on the job in years. I can't remember a day with so many arrests." "Don't forget all the paper work." Danny joined in the conversation "That's why we are all so late." Rosaland was talking to Arthur and Rachael and then she walked over and sat down with her brother at the bar. "How long have you been seeing Detective Semione?"

Matthew asked her in private. "For a minute" "Were you ever going to tell me?" "Yes Matt when the time was right. I was going to tell everybody. We work together and for us to be seeing each other is against the rules. That's why we kept it quiet." "Rosaland I don't work with you. I knew that guy had the hots for you. You should have told me."

"I'm sorry Matt. I apologize." "You are lucky that I like him. Otherwise I might have made a scene." Matt joked threateningly. "So the wild child is in love." Matthew started laughing as he kissed his sister on the cheek.

Bobby was surprised when Justin Sanchez and Wesley Cole walked in. They both walked over to shake his hand. Diana noticed Justin immediately. He was tall and dark and very handsome. He reminded her instantly of Bobby; the slender yet extremely muscular body, the dark hair, the golden skin and the sexy eyes. Wesley was very attracted to Yvonne. She was short and stacked and really pretty.

"Bobby who are these pretty ladies?" Wes asked in a friendly manner. "Detectives Rousseau and Easley these are detectives Sanchez and Cole." "Please to meet you detectives Yvonne extended her hand. Yvonne had an extremely flirtatious nature when it came to men. "Where do you guys work?" "Brooklyn south" Yvonne was asking all the questions Diana was being friendly but she kept her eye on Bobby.

"How do you know Bobby?" Yvonne still running off at the mouth. "We met him today at the precinct and since we are working on his Grandmother's murder we thought it would be in good taste if we came to pay our respects. Our captain at Brooklyn south likes Bobby. He has known him since the academy; Lt. Yancy has a lot of friends at Brooklyn south so we are all working over time to solve this case."

Bobby walked over to where Matt and Rosaland were sitting and out of habit ran his hand down her waist and across her thighs. Diana noticed this immediately. Bobby was talking to Matt when he positioned himself in back of her chair and bent over to kiss her on her cheek. Rosaland looked over and smiled invitingly at him and that's when Diana knew. Dr. Reid was the reason why Bobby had stopped seeing her.

She felt so stupid. How could it have taken her this long to figure this out? "Excuse me for a moment; she said softly. There is somebody that I need to talk to." Yvonne continued her conversation with Wesley not even noticing that Diana had walked away. Justin had spotted Arthur and was talking to him and Rachael. As a matter of fact he did a double take looking from Rachael to Rosaland. "That's my sister" Rachael decided that she would help him out.

"Aren't you the DA?" "Yes." "I've been in your office. Actually we've met." "Yes I remember detective. How are you?" "I'm working on this case. I hope we come up with some leads soon. I really want to help solve this one." Bobby had walked around to the other side of the bar and started serving another round of drinks. "Would you like another drink Baby? You Matt?" Bobby poured three drinks and sat two in front of Rosaland. "One is mine. I'll join you as soon as I take care of the rest of my guest." Bobby made the rounds taking drink orders and serving his friends. He was very happy that they all came out.

"Bobby can I speak to you for a moment?" Diana had finally got up her nerve. "Sure give me a minute. I'll be right back." "No. Bobby now! How long have you been fucking Dr. Reid?" Diana shouted almost hysterically. She was really mad. "I'm not fucking Dr. Reid. I'm in love with Dr. Reid and I have been in love with her for a very long time.

The look of hurt on Diana's face was undeniable as the tears slowly started to descend from her eyes. "Just when were you going to tell me? Or were you ever going to tell me? Were you just going to let me guess? How could you do me like this?" The more Diana thought about it the more enraged she became.

She and Bobby had been an item most of her adult life. The fact that she hadn't seen him for a while was par for the course as far as their relationship goes. Because they see each other at work their bond had always remained strong. Tonight watching him with her Diana knew that it was over and that it had been over for a long time.

Papa called Bobby from the top of the stairs and motioned for him to come up. Rosaland noticing how long Bobby had been gone looked around to see if she could locate him. She saw him going upstairs. She turned her attention back to Matt and the two of them walked over to where Arthur and Rachael were just about to leave.

All of a sudden Diana approached Rosaland and hauled off and smacked her across the face. Rosaland was in shock and her first reaction was to strike back. Without thinking she hit Diana hard in the face with her fist. Arthur was outraged that one of his detectives would strike a superior officer. Yvonne shouted "Oh my God!" And ran over to grab her friend who was staggering from the blow.

Diana's nose had started to bleed. Matthew ran over to grab his sister who still had no idea why she had been attacked. She turned around to look at her brother with a complete look of shock on her face. "What the hell is going on?" "Rosaland it's time to go." "No Matt I'm fine. I'll wait for Bobby. I'm sure he knows what this is all about."

Yvonne gathered her partner up in her arms; she grabbed some napkins from the bar for Diana's nose. "Come on honey it's time for us to leave. I believe we have overstayed our welcome." Yvonne hustled Diana out of the door and into the car. Once seated behind the wheel Yvonne gave Diana time to calm down before she asked her "What the hell was that all about? Diana do you know how much trouble you are in girl? You hit a superior officer in front of a room full of witnesses one of which is your boss!"

"It's not work related. He can't file charges against me for that." "You want to bet! You should have seen the look on his face. He was horrified. What was that all about anyway?" "Bobby!" "What!" "She has been seeing Bobby. Bobby has been seeing her. However that goes but I know now that she is the reason he stopped seeing me. When I confronted him about her he told me that he is in love with her and that he has been in love with her for a long time."

At that point Diana broke down in tears. Yvonne's heart went out to her partner because she knew how much Bobby meant to her. She was sorry to see it end this way for the two of them. When Yvonne pulled up in front of Diana's apartment she asked her if she was going to be all right. "I think my nose is broken." Diana responded, still holding the bloody napkin next to her bleeding nostrils." I can take you to the hospital to have it checked out or I can stay with you. I would hate to leave you this way."

"I'll be o.k. Later on if it still hurts I can drive myself to the emergency room. Let's just pray that I still have a job tomorrow." "That certainly is going to take a lot of prayer." Yvonne joked. "You'll be all right. See you tomorrow." Yvonne hastily sped away with thoughts of Wesley Cole on her mind. Diana did in fact end up in the emergency room that night her nose was broken in two places.

When Bobby came back downstairs all the commotion had died down. Arthur Rachael and Matthew were surrounding Rosaland trying to calm her down. Her face had started to bruise from the force of the blow she had received at the hands of her subordinate. Rosaland was fighting mad. Diana wasn't going to get away with this. "What is going on down here?" Bobby shouted as he made his way down the steps. Arthur motioned for him to come over to where they all stood.

There had already been enough of a public scene for one night; now Arthur was desperately trying to bring some kind of order to the chaotic atmosphere that Diana had created. Fortunately the crowd had dispersed and only police personnel remained. Detective's Cole and Sanchez left right after Yvonne escorted Diana out to her car. The people who remained were family members and the General was still upstairs with Papa.

Danny had managed to hang around and was at the bar pouring himself another drink. He didn't quite know what to make of this situation even though he knew something like this might happen. This had been a bad day for everyone involved. Emotions were running high and tempers had been flaring at work all day. Danny was not at all surprised that the day would end in this manner.

"Bobby we have another problem." Arthur spoke calmly once Bobby approached. "What happened?" He asked looking at Rosaland's face. "Your girlfriend slapped me in my face!" Rosaland hissed. Bobby reached for Rosaland and she pulled away. "Don't touch me! Don't you dare touch me!" Bobby grabbed her anyway and held her in his arms trying to get her to talk to him. Rosaland struggled and tried to break away from him but he held on to her.

Arthur and the others decided that it would be best to let the two of them work this out alone so he motioned for everyone to step outside. Soon they were alone in the restaurant. Rosaland had tears of anger streaming down her face. She felt completely outraged and very insulted. She struggled against Bobby's strong body but he refused to let her go. "Bobby let me go!" "No not until you calm down." "Let me go!" Bobby added more strength to the grasp he had on her and didn't say another word.

She knew then that he was not going to let her go until she calmed down. Finally she leaned against his body exhausted from her struggle for freedom. He some how had managed to calm her down enough so that they could talk. Bobby lifted her face in his hands and gently kissed her lips. He could taste the salt from her tears that formed on her lips. "Ouch" she whispered "That hurts!" Bobby lifted her face again this time looking at her bruise.

He walked over to the bar and put some ice in a towel and gently laid it on her cheek. "I'm sorry." Rosaland looked deeply into his eyes and she knew that he meant it. "She asked me about us tonight and I was honest. I told her that I was in love with you and had been in love with you for a very long time." Bobby looked soulfully at Rosaland as she sat nursing her bruise. "I think your father is going to be here for a while. Why don't you let me take you home? Besides I'm tired Baby I need some sleep and my chest hurts. Not unless you want to join me?" "I would love to but another time."

Just then the General started his way down the steps. He was surprised to see that everyone had left; he had lost complete track of the time. "Where is everyone?" He asked surprised. "They have all gone home Dad." "Are you ready to go?" The General asked looking first at his daughter and then to Bobby. "Yes Dad I am very tired." "You should be. You've had a long day. Good night detective." "Good night sir thanks for coming." Bobby kissed Rosaland softly on her cheek as she left. It was a long and silent drive home. Rosaland very much lost in thought. That night Bobby didn't sleep well he tossed and turned and thought about Rosaland all night.

thirty-five

The next day was business as usual. Dr. Reid reported to the office. Her face red and bruised. Detective Rousseau was out that day but she had disciplinary actions that would be taken against her when she returned. Everyone at the precinct was quiet that morning. Dr. Reid was sure that they all knew about the events of the preceding evening. But at this point there was nothing she could do about it other than her job.

Dr. Reid still had the Latin American situation knocking at her door and she needed to provide some answers and some good answers soon. She decided to take Bobby's suggestions and start a paper trace. She placed some calls to the Pentagon so that she could get clearance and gain access to sensitive files. She knew that this would be very confidential information and the O.N.S.I. had to be careful as to who besides herself would have privy to this. After the infiltration of her organization she had to be very discreet.

She decided that she would use outside sources for reasons of national security. She had to locate the moles within her organization. A mole hunt always turned out to be very dangerous for everyone concerned. Dr. Reid had to wait for her security status to be granted before she could proceed. Once the clearance was secured she immediately began to carefully select a team of coverts who would help her to collect the necessary documentation.

She wanted to enlist the aid of the O.N.S.I. staff so that the Pentagon could monitor them during this fact finding mission. With the all too recent infiltration she dare not. She knew that she needed some top security help. Her current dilemma was how to attract the help she needed without drawing attention. Some how some where some one was monitoring her organization. It was imperative that she find out if this person or organization was on the outside buying in or were they on the inside selling out. Dr. Reid worked diligently at her computer all morning scrutinizing files and looking for possible red flags only to come up empty handed.

After running into dead end after dead end it was time to call the General. The General always had a way. “Hi Dad. I’m having a little bit of a problem.” “Are you calling from a secured line?” “Yes.” “Then proceed” “Dad I need a team to gather some information for me. I’m following up on that paper trail we discussed and I need some highly sensitive documents to help me pinpoint who infiltrated the O.N.S.I. I also need to know for sure if these infiltrators might be responsible for the Latin American situation.”

“I have a sneaky suspicion that they might be one in the same but I need some real evidence. I can’t use my usual resources because they might be tainted. The walls might have ears so I would like to utilize some fresh eyes and ears. Do you have any suggestions?” “When would you like to get started?” “As soon as possible I’ve been working online all morning and all I have managed to come up with is road blocks. Mr. Wizard I need a little help.”

The General had to laugh. “Alright I’ll see what I can do. It might take a minute but we will come up with something. Anything else?” “No not right off hand.” “How are the detective and his family coming along?” “I’m sure they are hanging in there. I know that’s it has got to be hard on both of them right now.”

“They are strong men they’ll survive. I had a really long conversation with Papa last night. He is a very interesting man with a more interesting background; I’m looking forward to having the opportunity to talk with him again. Give them both my regards.” “Thanks Dad.”

It had taken a conversation from her father to remind her to call Bobby. It’s not that she hadn’t been thinking about him because she always thought of him but the fact that she was still slightly irritated about the events of last night was probably why she choose to bury herself in her work rather than to call and check on her man and his family.

At this point she had bigger fish to fry. The O.N.S.I. could be in danger. She could be in danger and matters of national security were at stake. Dr. Reid took a moment to think and then she realized that she was being unreasonable Bobby would need her now more than ever and she should be there for him.

She would never have escaped the Latin American ordeal had it not been for him. Without hesitation she picked up the phone and dialed his number. She was hoping that he would answer when he didn’t she decided to page him and to wait for his reply. She continued to work expecting at any moment that he would call and he did. “Hey what’s up?” She smiled when she heard his voice.

"I'm just checking in. How is your grandfather? My father sends his regards and he wants to know if there is anything that we can do?" "Right now we are in the middle of making her arrangements let me call you back. Are you alright?" "Yes I'm fine." "Ok let me get back to you later. I love you." "I love you too call me if you need me." "Rosaland I will always need you. Don't you know that by now?" Bobby hung up the phone.

The seriousness of his tone completely caught her off guard and the irritation that she been experiencing slowly dissolved. "How does he do that?" Dr. Reid thought out loud as she smiled amorously to herself.

Bobby had been wondering if she was going to call. He knew that she was upset about last night and he had hoped that she wouldn't make it into an issue even though he was prepared to go there with her if she insisted. But she didn't and that was one of the many reasons why he loved her so much she never disappointed him. Bobby smiled amorously to himself as he returned to his task.

Meanwhile Dr. Reid continued arduously at her project. She had to find the missing piece of this extremely complex puzzle. Just knowing that the O.N.S.I. was no longer secure was driving her crazy. Dr. Reid was so engrossed in her work that she completely lost track of time; it took a phone call from her sister to break her concentration.

"Hi sweetie." Rachael pleasantly greeted her "Are you busy?" "Yes but I'm never to busy to talk to my sister what's up?" "I need to talk to you. What about dinner?" "Sounds good where and when?" "What about the Harvard Club this evening? Let's say around 8:00." "That will work will anyone be joining us?" "Well I really want to talk to you so how about making it just us tonight?"

"That's fine with me. Sounds important." "It is" "Ok so I'll see you then." As soon as she hung up from Rachael the call from the General she had been expecting came in. "Hi honey I've got that information that you requested. But I don't want to do this over the phone. When can you come to Washington?" "I can be there first thing in the morning." "Well I suggest that you get here as soon as you can. I'll have a car for you in the morning that will take you to the airport." "O.K Dad I'll see you in the morning."

Dr. Reid sat back mentally exhausted in her chair and stared out into space. If the General was instructing her to come to Washington she knew that this information was for her eyes only. She could only surmise how deep it would go and how intense it would be. Glancing over at the clock she realized that she had been lost in her own world all day.

It was almost five o'clock and she hadn't even stopped to eat. She needed to get out of this office and since she had a couple of hours before she was to meet her sister she decided to do the girl thing. She was going shopping.

Bloomingdale's was full of wonderful surprises. She found all sorts of items to attract her attention. Her first stop was the designer's salon where she found a nice black suit for Abuelita's funeral. Because of the time element she really didn't want to leave town so close to the funeral but she knew that she had no choice. As she gathered the rest of her accessories she thought about Bobby and wondered if he had everything that he was going to need.

Without thinking she journeyed to the men's department and dedicated some time into choosing just the right shirt and tie combination for him as well. Bobby was always so immaculately dressed that when she found herself having a difficult time in making her decision. She relied on the superb taste of the salesman to help her make her final selections.

Papa would also need to look his very best so she chose something for him as well. Buying clothing for a man is such a personal thing and she hoped they would not be offended that she took this liberty on their behalf. Latin American men are such proud creatures and she truly only wanted to be of some help. She wouldn't have any trouble explaining her impulses to Bobby, and she would make sure that he explained to Papa.

When Rosaland arrived at the Harvard Club Rachael was already seated at the bar sipping some white wine. "I know you want a drink" her sister smiled as she took her seat next to her. "Actually Rachael I need a couple of drinks. I haven't eaten a thing all day so I had better wait until I have some food on my stomach."

"Why didn't you eat today?" "Oh Rachael I am so sick that I took this job. I feel like James Bond or some damn body." Rosaland looked around to see who might be within hearing distance. "Give me a Hennessey on the rocks" Rachael ordered the bar tender. "We would like to be seated at our table please." The bar tender motioned to the maitre'd and the ladies were escorted to their table.

"Drink this" Rachael said once they were seated. "One drink is not going to hurt before dinner and you need it. Now what the hell is going on?" "Well as you know the O.N.S.I. is a top secret organization and we have been infiltrated. We are not even supposed to exist officially so how could we be infiltrated? The massacre of the Latin American ambassadors was an inside job. Somebody sold us out and it's my job to find out whom and how far up this goes."

Rosaland sipped her drink as she talked quietly with her sister. The Pentagon is putting an enormous amount of pressure on Dad. The United States is being held responsible. Now I have to initiate a mole hunt. Do you know how dangerous that can be? One hundred and forty people are already dead. Bobby took a bullet. Bill took a bullet and if it weren't for the two of them I would have taken a bullet as well. Rachael I actually had to shoot one of my own agents. I have never had to use my gun. I have been carrying a gun since we left Bolivia." Rosaland hands were shaking as she finished her drink. Rachael put her own hand over her sisters and slowly lowered her glass to the table.

Rachael had no idea what had happened and she was absolutely horrified as her sister filled her in on the intricate details. "Now Bobby's Grandmother has been murdered. I might be wrong but somehow I think these incidents are connected. I haven't had the time or the opportunity to talk to Bobby about my suspicions and of course I have no proof whatsoever. There is too much coincidence involved, the timing." Rosaland shook her head "I just don't like it."

"Dad wants me in Washington ASAP and if I'm going to find any connection I have to go." "Rosaland we had better order I can see we have a lot to talk about." "Rachael I am starving. Can we just eat now? Besides you wanted to talk to me and you haven't mentioned one time what you wanted to talk about." Rosaland started to eat on the salad that had placed in front of her while Rachael continued to talk.

"Rosaland when were you going to tell me what has been happening? Why are you so secretive all of a sudden?" "Rachael it's this assignment. Things are occurring so fast all around me. Just when I think I have a good handle on things there is some new stew thrown into the pot. What is so strange, some kind of way this is all connected to Carlos Calderon who still seems to elude us."

Rachael was listening intently. Her sister always seemed to be involved in so much excitement and so much danger. The sisters paused from conversation so that they could enjoy their meal. Rachael loved dining at the Harvard club because the food was delectable. She also liked to take advantage of her membership. It was a privilege that she had earned.

The sisters were just about finished with dinner when rosaland's cell phone rang. After retrieving it from her purse she immediately recognized the number. "Hi, I was just thinking about you." "Where are you?" "Rachael and I are at dinner, I was waiting for you to call." "I did call; your phone was off. Where have you been?" "After I left the office I went shopping. I thought we both could use some new things for the funeral. Did you finalize the arrangements?" "Yes I'm really worried about my Grandfather. He is taking this very hard." "I'm sure. Is there anything that I can do?" "Yes you can. Just be here." "Bobby I need to talk to you. Can I see you this evening?" "There is nothing that I would like better but I have to stay with my Grandfather can we talk tomorrow?" "I'm going to be in Washington tomorrow morning. It's urgent business that's what I wanted to discuss. I'll be back in the evening. Maybe we can get together then."

"What are you going to Washington for? We just left Washington." "No Bobby we left unfinished business in Washington. Business that I have to finish tomorrow. Business that would make me feel a lot better if you were with me. But I know you can't go so I have to go without you." "I don't really like the sound of that but there is nothing I can do about it. When are you coming back?" "I'll be back tomorrow evening."

"I guess I will see you then. I'll pick you up from the airport. Call me from the plane." "Ok" "Rosaland I mean it call me from the plane." "Ok." "Bobby take care. I'll see you tomorrow night." "I love you Baby." "I love you too."

"Let me guess Mr. Wonderful." Rosaland rolled her eyes at her sister and then they both started to laugh. "Rosaland my dear sweet sister I need your help." "What is it that you need Rae?" "I need you to help me plan my wedding. Arthur doesn't want to wait any longer and neither do I. So last night we set another date two weeks from now." "Two weeks from now Rachael is that enough time?" It's going to have to be. That's all the time we have to do this. Two weeks and if anyone can pulled this off you can."

"Please Rosaland I love him and I don't want to wait any longer. We have waited long enough." Rosaland got up from the table and walked around to hug her sister. "I'm very happy for you and of course it would be my pleasure to help you. We will start as soon as I get back."

At that moment a bottle of Moet Crystal as delivered to their table. It was presented to the ladies on ice. They both looked at each other with surprise and then to the waiter who had placed it at their table. "This is compliments of the gentleman at the corner table. He wants to know if you ladies will accept his hospitality."

When the sisters looked in the direction of the corner there was no one there. "Should we accept it?" "Well we are celebrating. Why not?" "Yes tell the gentleman that we are very grateful for his kindness and we thank him for his hospitality." The waiter popped the cork and served the twins. They proposed a toast to Rachael's upcoming nuptials and they tipped their glass to their anonymous benefactor. The ladies were on their second glass of bubbly when out of nowhere Mr. Antonio Rivera appeared.

"Dr. Reid" He called her name as he came closer "You are looking beautiful as always." Rosaland looked up in complete surprise. She hadn't seen him since the nightclub. He took her hand and placed it softly to his lips. Rachael was totally speechless. She was remembering the huge fight that Bobby and her sister had concerning him. She did not feel at all at ease with this new development. She looked nervously at her sister who was still trying to get a handle on this situation. "Mr. Rivera how nice to see you again.

What are you doing here?" "The same as you and your lovely sister, having dinner. The food here is really quite good."

At this point Antonio turned his attention to Rachael. "And how is our illustrious D.A. this evening?" "I'm well. Thank you for asking and thank you for the champagne." Rachael noticed that all the time he was talking to her he never took his eyes off of Rosaland. It was very obvious that he was quite smitten with her and he was doing nothing to hide his feelings.

"Perhaps you ladies would care to join me for some dessert? They have a truly wonderful selection here." "You eat here?" "Yes such as yourself on a regular basis." Rosaland had alarms going off everywhere. The red flags were out. She had just talked to Rachael about timing and now here he was. There were just too many coincidences. Yet at the same time her body was tingling from excitement. His presence set her off, just as Bobby's presence set her off.

The attraction was undeniable and unexplainable and very hard for her to ignore. Rachael watched the non-verbal communication that was going on between the two of them with interest as well as with reservation. Rachael knew that it was up to her to make the first move. "Thank you for the invitation, but we were just about to leave as soon as we finish our drinks." Rosaland don't you have an early day tomorrow?" "Yes as a matter of fact I do. Thank you anyway."

"Dr. Reid perhaps you will do me the honor of dining with me at some other time. Maybe tomorrow night?" Antonio was insistent. "I'm sorry; I'll be out of town." "Well if I could call you maybe we could arrange a more mutual time." "I'm sure."Rosaland complied and handed him her business card. "Well i'll call sometimes this week." He replied smiling to himself. "That will be fine." "Don't worry about your bill it has already been taken care of." "You didn't have to do that." "No, I insist besides it is my pleasure." "Thank-you." "Rosaland we need to go." Rachael was pulling her away. Both Rosaland and Rachael were feeling anxious and they were happy to leave.

Once outside Rachael couldn't hold back any longer. "Rosaland are you out of your mind? Don't you remember the last time you saw this man it was world war two! Bobby will kill you if he knew you were even considering spending time with this man. Dinner? You have got to be kidding." "Rachael please calm down. I'm not going to see him but I had to tell him something." "Well then you should have told him no." Rachael looked at her sister earnestly. In all the haste to leave Rosaland forgot her packages. The gentleman in the coat check area was about to deliver the packages outside where he saw that the two sisters were engaged in a serious conversation. Antonio Rivera took the packages from his hand and walked outside. "Excuse me; do these belong to one of you?"

Rosaland looked directly into his eyes and for a brief moment time stood still. He and Bobby had the same eyes deep soul stirring and elusive. "Yes they belong to me." Antonio handed her the packages smiled and in that instant he was gone.

Carlos went back to his club to contemplate his next move. Dr. Reid stirred his soul and he wanted her. The kind alter ego that he had created for himself Antonio Rivera was moving to slow. Carlos was used to getting what he wanted when he wanted it. In all his life he had never had to wait for anything but he was willing to wait for her. How long of course was another issue?

The rest of the evening all he could do was think about her. He remembered the smell of her perfume the sway of her hips and the feel of her skin. He loved the smell of her hair. He would try one more time as Antonio Rivera to get her attention. If it didn't work he would take her like Carlos Calderon.

Carlos had to carefully formulate his plan. He knew that any violation of her person would cause a war that he couldn't possibly win. After all she was the daughter of General Prescott Reid and messing with her would be equivalent to messing with death.

Carlos had to be careful. He knew that the General was closing in on him. He just didn't know how close he was. He also didn't know that the General's daughter was the source of the information. The Latin American project had gone quite well for him. Now it was time for him to lay low and there was still that small matter of the unsolved murders including the latest one in Brooklyn.

thirty-six

"Hi Baby I just wanted to hear your voice before I left." "What time is it?" "It's about 7:00a.m." "What time are you leaving?" "In about an hour" "When will you be back?" "This evening around six." "Ok you know Abuelita's services are tomorrow. I want you to ride with me and my grandfather." "Ok" "Call me from the plane. I'll pick you up from the airport." "Ok" Dr. Reid finished dressing and waited for the car to drive her to the airport.

The General as always was very happy to see her. After breakfast they talked about the different avenues she could take to find her information. As they talked the General regretted now more than ever that he had gotten his daughter involved in this situation. He knew that no matter what he said she would see it through.

"Dad the first thing I need is someone who can trace the hotel records. I really need to know if they have received any large deposits of money either before or after the massacre. I need to know who was the first and last hired and what connections they might have to the Cartel."

Even though I have no evidence I know that the Calderon Cartel was responsible for the incident. Dad if we are ever going to capture this man we have to be able to track his moves and he is so slippery he always eludes us. Who is covering his tracks? What connections does he have? Somebody higher up the chain is helping him and if we are going to stop him we have to know who his affiliations are."

"This is so frustrating and so many people are dying. I have got to stop him; I just don't know how I'm going to do it." The General listened intently to his daughter. She definitely was on the right track and she was absolutely correct about another thing, Carlos had to have somebody in a powerful position helping him. The General decided then he would make it a top priority to find out whom.

"Rosaland I have taken the liberty of inviting someone over this afternoon that can help you to secure information. She is an information specialist; all she does all day long is gather intelligence. I think you will like her and you can trust her. I've picked her personally just to aid you in this crisis. She already has an organization on the streets so all you need to do is use her."

"Availability is the name of the information game. A game that she plays very well." "Dad Bobby's grandmother's funeral services are tomorrow. Are you going to attend?" "Of course. We will all be there. Did you remember to send the arrangement?" Rosaland eyes widened she hadn't remembered. It had totally slipped her mind. She rushed to the phone to place the order. "Thanks Dad I had completely forgot. I have been so preoccupied lately."

"Rosaland don't ever become so involved that you forget about the ones you love. When it is all said and done family is the only thing you have. I assume that Detective Semione has a special place in your heart, you have certainly violated all my rules for him."

Rosaland looked at her father both sincerely and regretfully "Dad I haven't violated your rules for him. I do love him. I love him with all my heart. Please try to understand."

"I do. We don't have to talk about this anymore. It's almost time for your guest to arrive. You should take a minute before she gets here to make sure that you have a list of all the things that you might need." The General left the room to give his daughter some time to reflect.

When Diana Rousseau reported to work the next day her nose was bandaged. Both of her eyes were black from the pressure due to the fact that her nose had been broken in two places. Everyone was quiet when she entered the squad room. As soon as she sat down at her desk Lt. Yancy called her into his office.

"Detective Rousseau we need to talk about the incident from two days ago. I don't know if you realize how much trouble you could be in, including a possible suspension for striking a superior officer. There were too many witnesses for me to over look this even though it occurred after working hours."

"Lt. the incident wasn't job related and it happened after office hours. It doesn't seem within department policy that you could suspend me for my actions." "On the contrary detective. You struck a superior officer. There is no regulation that makes an exception to that rule. No officer is allowed to strike another officer especially a superior officer with the rank that Dr. Reid holds."

"That rank outweighs anything else in this case. Now formally she has not pressed charges and she is out of the office today so I can't bring her in. Officially this is going on the record and if she swears out a formal complaint I will have to take action. You will be suspended pending a full investigation. That's all Detective." When Diana left the office she felt like she had been chewed up and spat out.

Sonia Blackwell arrived at the General's estate shortly after noon. She was a tall slender light complected woman with a really beautiful face surrounded by a halo of golden blonde hair. Sonia had the most amazing green eyes that sparkled like diamonds when she laughed. She was the kind of woman who could blend in to any situation. Rosaland could see why the General had picked her for this assignment. She was very much a spook.

Sonia's mannerisms were casual and polite even though Rosaland knew that had she met her under different circumstances Sonia probably would have been extremely standoffish. That was the nature of her business.

"Sonia I'm so glad that you could make it." The General extended his hand. "This is my daughter Dr. Rosaland Reid she is the head of the O.N.S.I." "I'm very pleased to meet you." Rosaland was still trying to figure this person out and she hadn't decided if she liked her or not.

The two went into the dining room where Esmeralda was waiting to serve lunch. "Dad aren't you joining us?" Rosaland glanced expectantly towards her father. "No I think the two of you can use this time alone." With that last statement the General left the room. After Esmeralda served lunch she also left the room.

"So you are the sister that is screwing the detective correct?" "How do you know this?"Rosaland was highly irritated. "This is just an example of what kind of business I do. It's my job to know everything. That is why your father pays so well." Rosaland's mind had just been made up she didn't like this woman she didn't like her at all.

"I'm sorry about his grandmother; I understand that they were very close." That was the last straw; Rosaland had to say something, "What can you tell me about that seeing that you know so much?" "I know that it was a drive by shooting. I'm not so sure if it was an accident. I think that it was made to look like a drive by. I'll know more in a couple of days."

"This is not why I'm here. You want to know about the O.N.S.I. and who could have infiltrated your top secret organization. That's that real reason why I'm here. Detectives Sanchez and Cole will solve the murder of Abuelita; I believe that was her name. That's a matter of simple police work; you have a much bigger problem and a problem that is going to take some time."

"I've already got some people on the paper trail of the hotel and I'll even take it one step further and investigate the connection of the O.N.S.I. agents at the conference with the hotel." I'll find your missing link. It will take a couple of weeks, but you will have your answers."

"Ok if my Father trusts you so do I." Sonia smiled and finished her lunch. "Esmeralda is such a wonderful cook." Rosaland was slowly beginning to warm up to Sonia even though she did not like her she found her quite interesting.

"Sonia tell me how I can get around the red flags that come up on my computer when I'm trying to access sensitive material. I know you know how to do that." Sonia smiled; Rosaland was smarter than she thought. "So I take it that you have already begun to figure out how you can get around the flags other than that you would not be mentioning them to me."

"No Sonia I'm mentioning it because I want complete access. I want to be able to get in and out at my leisure without being detected can you help me?" Sonia wrote something on a piece of paper and handed it to her "Here are the codes to all the pentagon mainframes. With these you can slip easily in and out."

"Also Sonia how can I secure my e-mail?" "Only the feds can do that." "Are you telling me that there is not a line I can use to secure my e-mail?" "What I'm telling you is that only the feds can do that and if I'm not mistaken the O.N.S.I. is a federal agency. You need to ask your father about that. The General thought I could help you. It seems to me that you could show me a thing or two."

"I'll consider that a compliment." "It is a compliment." Rosaland and Sonia spent the rest of the afternoon sharing secrets and pertinent information; the two were so involved in their work that they lost track of the time. The General knocked on the door of his study at about 6:00. "Rosaland it's six. Your plane will be leaving in about 45 minutes."

After the time Rosaland spent with Sonia she would be very careful as to her phone calls and her e-mails. She would also be more precise in her job. She thanked her for her time and her efforts. As Rosaland was preparing to leave Sonia handed her a card "Here are my numbers. Take them and use them if you need too".

"Sonia I do want you to help my friend find the person responsible for the murder of his grandmother. If you get your hands on anything concerning this matter I would really appreciate a call." "You got it; I'll keep my ears open." Rosaland nodded thanks as she made her way toward to car. "Your daughter is a very smart lady." Sonia commented. "I know. She's too smart that's why I want her out of this business."

thirty-seven

On the plane home Rosaland again found herself wondering how she could be so involved with all this cloak and dagger information. Everything was so hush hush. Sonia Blackwell was a very interesting character and someone whom she knew she would be happy to know. Maybe she had been wrong about her. She looked over the codes that Sonia had given her and decided that it might be best to memorize them. She devised a system that would help her commit the codes to memory and then she folded up the paper.

She placed her call to Bobby to let him know that she was on her way home and the rest of the flight she relaxed. "Excuse me Ms. would you like something to drink?" Rosaland opened her eyes to see the flight attendant standing over her. "Yes. I believe I would like a cognac." As the attendant handed her the drink she informed her that it was complimentary. "Why?" "One of our pilots asked me to serve you. He would like to come out and talk to you."

"Why?" "He'll be out in a minute." As Rosaland sipped her drink, she thought of Bobby. Her thoughts were interrupted when the handsome pilot sat down beside her. She looked in his direction and smiled. "Hello how are you this evening. Are you enjoying the flight?" "Yes I'm fine. How can I help you?" "Well I was wondering why such a beautiful lady was traveling alone?" "Business." "Do you travel a lot on business?" "Yes as a matter of fact I do." "Please excuse my lack of manners. My name is Captain Gregory Frederick's and you are?" "Dr. Rosaland Reid" "You are a doctor? What kind of medicine do you practice?" "No I'm not a MD. I'm a PhD." "Smart and beautiful I'm impressed."

"Do you think we could possibly get together for dinner sometime?" "No I'm seeing someone." "Well take my card just in case you change your mind." "Thanks but I won't." Captain Frederick's got up and went back into the cockpit. Rosaland wanted this flight to end. She was tired and she wanted to see Bobby. About twenty minutes later the pilot announced the descent into J.F.K. International Airport and the fasten the seat belt light was turned on.

In another fifteen minutes they were safely on the ground. Bobby was standing by the door when she exited. "Hey beautiful!" Bobby smiled as she fell into his arms. Captain Frederick's was watching as the two engaged in a passionate embrace. "I've missed you" Bobby whispered as he wrapped his arms around her and escorted her out the airport. When they reached the car Bobby asked "How was your trip?" "It was interesting. My father knows so many colorful characters." "Did you eat?" "Just lunch. We were working so hard that we lost track of time." "Are you hungry?" "Yes Bobby I could eat something" "Good. We'll stop by the restaurant and grab a bite to eat then I'll take you home." "Sounds good to me."

"What were you working on?" "Well I'm trying to follow up on that paper trail. My Dad is taking a lot of heat about that Latin American incident. We need to come up with some answers. He's not going to be able to keep stalling. We are taking a real beating on this one." Rosaland moved closer to Bobby and relaxed her head on his shoulder as they drove to Brooklyn.

Papa was waiting when they arrived. Bobby had asked him to prepare a special meal for her. He hoped that she would be hungry and he wanted to sit down with her and Papa for dinner like a real family. Bobby still had to tell her about the funeral arrangements and he wanted to know if the rest of her family would be attending.

"Yes my entire family will be there." "Good Papa would like them to sit with us." "I'm sure that will be fine. We would feel honored to sit with you Papa." Papa went in the back to the kitchen and Rosaland leaned across the table to kiss Bobby. "I'm sorry I wasn't here earlier but I'm here now."

Rosaland's body was burning with passion. Bobby reached across the table and softly fondled her breasts. She always experienced such delight in his touch. "Roberto come and help me in the kitchen." Bobby got up and went into the kitchen "Hold that thought" he whispered as he left. Rosaland contemplated whether or not she would share the information that Sonia had given her about Abuelita's death. She decided against it until she had more facts. While Bobby was in the kitchen with Papa he too was lost in thought. He wanted to ask her more about her trip to Washington but whenever she was with the General for any length of time she was always so secretive.

He hoped that she would share whatever was so important that she had to leave town but he knew that was asking for too much. He decided that he would get her to talk to him in another way. He wanted to know what she knew and his instincts told him that she knew more than she was revealing.

Dinner that night was wonderful. The three of them ate and drank and generally had a good time. It was so nice to find Papa in such a relaxed mood. Sometime during the course of the meal Bobby reached under the table to feel her legs. As he ran his hand along her inner thighs he was stopped short by her gun. She looked at him and smiled making that funny face with her eyes and he in turn smiled back.

"I'm glad you remembered that" he said in a low voice. "Since the South American incident I will never leave home without it trust me on this." They both laughed and finished their dinner. The hour was drawing late and Bobby was ready to take her home. They would have an early day tomorrow and she needed some sleep.

"Are you about ready?" He asked. "Yes I'm really tired." "Papa I'm going to take Rosaland home. Do you need anything before we go?" "No Roberto I'm fine. Maybe I'll ride with you. That is if you don't mind." Bobby was stunned that his Grandfather would want to leave the house so late but he couldn't refuse him.

"That will do some good; the night air might help you to sleep." Bobby glanced at Rosaland with a look on his face that translated into "oh shit" but there was nothing either of them could do. Bobby really wanted to make love to her this evening but that would have to wait.

The church began to fill up as early as seven in the morning with friends and neighbors there to pay their last respects. The viewing would start at eight and the service was scheduled to commence at ten. Bobby sent the limo for Rosaland at about 7:30. He wanted her to be by his side today. He had a feeling that he would need her strength.

Papa was having a slow start as well. This was the day the he would bury the one love of his life. He and Abuelita met as teenagers back in the old country and they had been together ever since. Fifty years of their lives they had spent together and now it was over. The reality was finally beginning to set in for him. He wept openly for his dear sweet angel.

Bobby came into the bedroom to try and comfort him and to offer him some consolation. This was the first time that Papa had really broken down. Bobby held him in his arms and allowed him to experience his grief. When Rosaland arrived she found the two of them in this position.

Bobby looked over his shoulder and nodded his acknowledgement of her presence. She placed her packages down on the bed as she silently stood there waiting for Bobby to give her a visual cue as to her next move. After a moment Bobby whispered to Papa that it was time for him to get dressed. Papa sullenly straightened up and went back to his bedroom to dress.

Rosaland looked sorrowfully in his direction as he left the room. "I know this is so hard for him. I feel so bad. I wish there was more that I could do." Bobby wrapped his arms around her and held her tight. He held on to her as if there would be no tomorrow. Rosaland relaxed in his deep embrace and wrapped her arms tightly around his neck. She lifted her head so that she could kiss him. When their lips met her body became wet and his body became excited.

Bobby tenderly returned her kiss and started fingering her breasts through her blouse. She pressed her body close to his lost in the feel of him. Bobby started to lift her skirt wanting to feel her warm flesh. At that moment Papa entered the room. If he had come in a second later he would have caught them in the act.

Bobby slowly released his powerful embrace and Rosaland straighten her clothes. It took a minute for Rosaland to catch her breathe. When she did she picked up the package from the bed and handed it to him. "I bought these for the two of you. Abuelita would want her men to look very special today." Bobby took the garments from the bag and smiled. "You always think of everything."

"I'll just wait downstairs while the two of you get dressed." Rosaland left the bedroom and went down to the restaurant to wait. Papa was having a real problem. Nothing was right. Abuelita always made sure that he had the right clothes without her he felt lost. He didn't like his suit and his shirt wasn't right. Papa just didn't see how he was ever going to make it through this day. When Bobby was half dressed he noticed his Grandfather fumbling around and decided to dress him. He opened the package and handed Papa the new shirt. "How did she know his size?" He thought to himself as he placed the shirt on his grandfather.

He laid the four ties she had purchased on the bed and chose one for himself and one for his Grandfather. "She has real nice taste" he mused as he tied his Grandfather's tie. Bobby marveled at her thoughtfulness. In another twenty minutes they both were dressed. Just as they were about to descend the stairs Papa said "Roberto, what are you going to do about that one? She loves you very much and her father is a very powerful man." "I know Papa don't worry. I'll do the right thing."

Rosaland was gazing out of the window when they came down the stairs. "Don't you two look nice? Abuelita would be very proud." It was a solemn day and Papa wanted to walk, so they walked to church. Once they were on the street others who were walking as well joined them. Father Peter waited for Bobby and his Grandfather to be seated and then he started the service. Rosaland looked around to see if her family had made it. When she spotted the General she gave her full attention to Father Peter.

The service was extremely emotional. All throughout the eulogy you could hear the sobs that overwhelmed the audience. Bobby lowered his head and put his hands over his eyes as his tears flowed for his Abuelita. Rosaland placed her arm around his neck to offer her support. When Bobby raised his eyes he noticed that she too was crying. He reached into his pocket and handed her his handkerchief that she politely accepted.

Father Peter wanted the family to say some words on Abuelita's behalf. Papa was so struck with grief that he was not able to speak. Bobby stepped up and spoke on behalf of the family. The emotions were so high after Bobby remembered his Grandmother that the crowd began sobbing out loud. Abuelita would really be missed by everyone who knew her and who loved her.

At the conclusion of the services Bobby and the other pallbearers took Abuelita's casket from the church and placed it in the hearse. Rosaland escorted Papa outside to take his last ride with his lovely wife. At the gravesite the final interment was simple and touching. It all proved to be more than Papa could bear. He completely broke down in tears.

As the crowd dispersed Papa wanted to stay behind to have a final word with his wife. Bobby asked the General if he would escort Rosaland home. "Baby I would like to spend some time alone with my grandfather. He is a little emotional and I think that he might need me. Your father is going to take you home. I'll call you later."

Rosaland nodded her approval and kissed him gently on his cheek before she left. The neighbors would be gathering at the restaurant after the burial and Bobby told her that he would come for her when they left the cemetery.

Papa had so many things he had to say to Abuelita that he didn't know where to begin. He had promised her that he would tell Bobby of his heritage. How he had come to live with them and the secret of his past. Abuelita always felt that Bobby deserved to know who his real family was and that he had a brother a twin brother who neither one knew that the other existed.

Everything was happening so fast and Papa didn't know exactly where to begin. He would need Abuelita's strengths now more than ever even in her death. He couldn't afford to lose his grandson; they were the only family they had left. Even though he had promised now was not the time. He would wait for the right moment, if there ever were a right moment for a thing like this. For now it would remain his secret.

Papa looked up at his unsuspecting grandson and motioned to him that he was ready to leave. Rosaland waited for Bobby to call. When the hour got late she decided that maybe he wouldn't make it tonight. Her feelings were a little hurt that he would leave her out but then again she knew him and she knew that there was probably some other reason for his lack of response.

Her first instinct was to call him just to check on him but then she decided against it. She knew that she would hear from him when he was ready. Rosaland had experienced a very a long day. It was nice to be at home and to have a chance to relax; she decided that what she needed was a tall drink and a hot soothing bath. Finally realizing that Bobby wasn't coming she undressed and went upstairs to prepare her bath.

thirty-eight

Rosaland had dozens of scented candles that she placed all around the tub. She was feeling exotic so she pulled some petals from her fresh floral arrangement; she always had fresh flowers in her bathroom and her kitchen. This is one of the habits that she inherited from her mother. As a child they always had fresh flowers in their house. After all her mother kept a rose garden.

She placed the petals in the tub along with her bath milk and turned the facet to fill the tub with hot water. While her water was running she slipped out of her underwear letting them fall freely to the floor. She put on a short satin robe and went downstairs to make a drink. While in her study she looked out on her deck and thought about the last time that she was out there, she placed an Al Jarreau c.d. on her sound system and went outside to enjoy the night.

The melodic sounds of al jarreau filled the study. She opened the sliding glass doors so that the sounds could seep out onto the deck. It was then that she remembered her bath and ran upstairs to stop the water before the tub ran over. She returned to the deck and made herself comfortable in her hammock while letting the melodious voice of Al Jarreau take her away. She decided at that point that she would remind herself to start enjoying some of the simple pleasures in life. The niceties that she could experience right here at home.

The sun was beginning to set and it cast a beautiful array of oranges, yellows and gold's all across the sky. The night air was warm and enticing and the effects of the cognac were starting to make her body feel all tingly inside. She let the robe slip quietly from her shoulders as she lay there allowing the sultry night air to engulf her naked flesh.

She ran her hands along the contours of her firm breasts as she thought of him. She lay back in the snug fit of the hammock and gently ran her fingers from her breasts to her pubic hairs and finally she placed them between her legs. Only Bobby could fill this cavity. It was his and she was in need. Rosaland relaxed lost in the music and absorbed by the thoughts of her man.

"Umm" she moaned as she continued to please herself. But she wanted more she wanted him. Rosaland put her robe back on her shoulders and got up to make another drink. It was at that moment she discovered that he had been standing there watching her. "How long have you been standing there?" She asked him a little shocked but not in the least embarrassed.

"Long enough. How long have you been out here?" "Long enough" "Are you expecting someone?" He joked softly "Not expecting just hoping." She replied. Bobby came out into the night and looked over the deck. "It's nice out here. You know I've been here a thousand times and I have never been out here." "Come; join me would you like a drink?" Rosaland brushed past him deliberately pressing her body next to his as she made his drink. She handed it to him and then poured another one for herself.

"I was expecting you to call me earlier." "I'm sorry but my Grandfather was in a real bad way. I had to stay with him." Bobby sipped his drink as he loosened his tie and sat down on the chaise. "What is this music?" He asked after a few minutes of silence. "It's Al Jarreau. Do you like it?" "It's nice" Bobby motioned to her to come sit on his lap; she tied the belt from her wrap loosely around her waist and sat on his lap crossing her legs.

As they sat there together enjoying their drinks Rosaland leaned over and kissed him. Bobby put his hands in the opening of her wrap and softly squeezed her breasts. He let his hands roam all over her body completely taking advantage of her naked form. When their lips parted he whispered in her ear "Come dance with me." Rosaland placed her glass on the table and stood up. Bobby grabbed her up in his arms as their bodies began to sway in time with the crooning of Mr. Al Jarreau.

Bobby pulled her close as he wrapped his arms tightly around her waist. Rosaland closed her eyes as Bobby led her across the deck moving in harmony to the slow gyrating melody of the music. Bobby leaned over to kiss her running his fingers through her thick long black hair. Rosaland began to sigh as she eagerly returned his hot embrace.

They were so caught up in the rapture of their passion that neither one noticed that the music had stopped. "The music?" "What?" "The music has stopped." Rosaland slowly withdrew from his arms very much affected by his brute sensuality. "Is there something else that you want to hear?" she asked coyly "Or do you want to go upstairs?" "No not just yet play something nice." Rosaland went through her collection and found the master of love Mr. Marvin Gaye. This was one of her favorite compilations. It was perfect for her seduction.

When Rosaland returned Bobby was more comfortable. He had taken off his jacket, his shirt and his tie; he was in a white tank that carefully outlined his muscular chest. Rosaland loved to look at Bobby's body and to feel his muscles. She handed him a fresh drink and sat down on the chaise waiting for the maestro to begin. They sat close to each other Bobby playing in her hair. She put her head on his shoulders and ran her finger tips up and down his chest being extremely careful not to disturb his wound.

She enticingly squeezed his muscles causing him to become aroused. Bobby leaned over and kissed her again. This time planting his tongue deeply down her throat. As Marvin filled the air they became entangled in a passionate embrace. Bobby slowly rose from the chaise and took her in his arms. The night was filled with the magic of their love and the music of Marvin Gaye.

Bobby removed her robe exposing her naked body to his touch. She was so beautiful in his eyes; the brown coffee colored skin, the firm full breasts, the long shapely legs, and his favorite her luscious ass. He loved to see her naked. Rosaland fell into his arms as they began to move in time to the music. Bobby reached up to remove his tank but Rosaland intervened "Let me" she whispered as she removed his shirt. "Does this still hurt?" She questioned gently rubbing his chest. "Yes. It hurts like hell." "Why don't you let me kiss it and make it feel better?" Rosaland placed her lips on the very spot where the bullet had penetrated his flesh and began to kiss his chest. She then moved her hot mouth over to his nipples and encircled them with her tongue.

She moved from one to the other in a titillating motion; slowly, sensuously, deliciously mouthing his hard nipples. She let her hand drop to his crotch and teasingly ran the balls of her fingers up and down his excited manhood. Bobby let his hands slide along her curves delicately outlining her form. He cupped her ass and pulled her even closer.

He bent down to kiss her neck and her shoulders and back to her full lips. Bobby picked her up and carried her over to the hammock. He laid her gently inside and then removed his pants letting them cascade nonchalantly to the ground. Rosaland watched breathlessly as he prepared to take her. Rosaland's body was burning with desire and Bobby was her delicious ice.

He mounted her opening her legs wide as he placed himself deep inside her cavern. His initial contact sent shocks of electricity through her body and she moaned loudly as he lodged himself to the hilt within her inner core. Bobby slowly began to pump his muscular form deep into her wanting cavity allowing her to accommodate his girth. Bobby sucked delectable kisses from her quivering lips as he pounded incessantly into her very being. "Ohhh Bobby" she sobbed as his hard erection continued to explore her private interior.

"Ohhh Baby you feel so good." He murmured in her ear. Her sobs increased his ardor as he released his unbridled passion. Rosaland wrapped her legs tightly around the waist of her stallion affording him the deepest penetration possible. She needed to feel every inch of him. She dug her fingernails into his back as he continually pumped his hot weapon into the very depths of her soul. Bobby's purpose in life at this moment was to love her and to please her and to afford her the ultimate pleasure.

Rosaland gyrated beneath him conscious only of the immense pleasure he was so generously bestowing upon her glorious body. She held him tightly in her embrace as Bobby made love to her leisurely and so very affectionately. The warm night air was filled with the sounds of their amour and Marvin playing oh so sweetly in the background.

The two lovers were so oblivious to their environment that neither one of them realized that it had started to rain. The rain fell gently on their sweaty bodies and as the first clap of thunder pierced the sky Bobby filled her body with his seed relinquishing her fire.

Rosaland lay there panting breathlessly as the terrestrial downpour drenched the deck. The air had started to cool and when a bolt of lightening lit up the Harlem sky; Bobby knew that it was time to take her inside. He gathered her shivering body up in his arms and carried her into the brownstone.

After making sure that she was secure Bobby went back for his clothes. While Bobby retrieved his soaked garments Rosaland went upstairs to start a new bath. She drained most of the contents and filled the tub with fresh hot water. She took time to light the candles that she had placed in the bathroom. She lowered her spent body into the tub and waited for him to return.

Upon entering the bathroom Bobby was amazed by her sense of sensuality. She was so tempestuous. Everything she did turned him on. He smiled as he placed his drenched pants on the towel rack to dry. Rosaland was soaking and dunked herself fully before he got in. Her head emerged from the water with her wet hair hanging down her back. She wiped the water from her face and ran her hands along her hair to smooth it. "This water feels really good" Bobby said as he settled himself in back of her. The two of them lounged leisurely in the bath with their eyes closed and her head resting on his chest.

Bobby tightened his arms around her and serenely fondled her breasts. "I like these" he said in a familiar tone. "Is that all you like?" "No just one of the many things." "Bobby my whole being belongs to you." Rosaland kissed him longingly; it was so nice just to be in his arms. She turned her body slightly pressing her breasts into his wet naked chest.

They shifted their positions so that Rosaland was now facing him. She could feel him becoming aroused again as she reached down to finger his enormous penis under the water. She let her slippery hands glide across the hard erection as she inserted her tongue deep into his throat. She kissed him lustfully her own fire starting to ignite. Rosaland raised her torso slightly as she lowered herself on to his throbbing manhood. Her slightest touch set him off.

She gasps as she felt him enter her body for the second time that evening. The warm water made his insertion easy as she began to rise and fall on him. Bobby moaned loudly as she rode his hungry weapon up and down. The water began to swish as the intensity of their bodies came together as one. Bobby whimpered at the ultimate pleasure he was experiencing being buried so deeply inside her. "Ooh Baby ooh Baby" she cried inaudibly as he filled her more and more. The water splashed out of the tub as their ferocity amassed extinguishing the flames of the dimly lit candles that lined the floor around the tub.

Rosaland and Bobby clung to each other as if there would be no tomorrow totally engrossed in the essence of their love. The volcanic force of the orgasm that exploded in them caused them both to collapse in exhausted satisfaction. Rosaland held on to him with urgency as their ecstasy ebbed.

Later that evening as they lay in bed Bobby had a lot of things on his mind. "Baby I want to thank you for all the support that you have given me during this situation. This has been a very emotional time for both me and my Grandfather. I thank you for being here and I thank you for caring. I don't know if I could have made it if it weren't for you and your family."

"Bobby you have a lot of friends, co-workers and neighbors who were there for you and Papa." "Yes but you were there for me. I know how important it has been for you to keep our relationship under wraps and I haven't always agreed with it. Actually I didn't like it at all but as the work became more complicated I understood."

"When my Grandmother was murdered you stepped forward and let it be known. I will always love you for that." Rosaland listened intently as Bobby continued his train of thought. "You know I was thinking about my Grandmother and about how much she used to do for Papa from buying his clothes to telling him off when he needed it. I used to hate when they argued and afterwards Papa would always say that's because she loves me. I never understood what he meant by that. I never even equated that to love until I met you."

"I couldn't believe that you took the time to buy shirts and ties for us. That was something Abuelita would have done. Yesterday after the funeral once I had Papa settled I decided that I wanted to do something for you. I wanted to show you how much you mean to me. I walked around Fifth Avenue until I found the perfect gift. I passed this small specialty shop. Their advertisement said they carried rare and exquisite items. I thought about you and started laughing. How perfect."

"When I entered the store and started to look around. There they were. All I saw was you" Bobby reached under his pillow and handed her a black velvet box. Rosaland sat up in bed with a look of pure delight on her face. Bobby loved to see her face when she received gifts; she had the same look of pleasure as when she received flowers.

"You are rare and exquisite. You bring pure joy to my life" Rosaland opened the box to find the most exquisite set of black pearls. They were lovely, black and luxurious. The clasp was solid gold and contained a small diamond along with her initials. "Ohh Bobby, these are beautiful!" Rosaland exclaimed as she fought back the tears.

"Here let me help you" Bobby took the box from her shaking hands and removed the pearls. She thought he was going to place them around her neck, but instead he moved to the bottom of the bed and placed them around her ankle. "These black pearls are for my Black Pearl." All she could do was cry.

thirty-nine

Rosaland had two weeks to help Rachael prepare for her wedding. Even though she was right in the middle of solving the Latin American situation it was her obligation to dedicate this time to her sister. She knew that she would have to work furiously between the two projects so she set a time table to allocate the time she needed for each.

Bobby was expected to return to work this week and she needed to have a meeting with the eccentric Sonia Blackwell. She was going to introduce Bobby to Sonia, this way she knew for sure that Bobby would get the information that he was seeking concerning his Grandmother's murder.

She wanted to schedule another meeting with her Father to confirm what she and Sonia had discussed. She was developing a trust for Sonia and her instincts told her that it would be a wise decision to form a permanent alliance with this woman; Sonia's hands could reach to high places and her ears could go even higher.

While Rosaland was sitting at her desk checking her messages she looked down at her ankle and smiled. Rosaland worked feverishly over the week trying to balance her responsibilities to Rachael and to her job. Because of time restrictions Rosaland and Rachael decided to use the internet to send the invitations. They started to receive r.s.v.p's immediately. After all she was the General's daughter and anybody who was anybody knew that if they were invited they needed to attend.

Arthur was one of four brothers but he was the only brother who had yet to be married. His family lived in New Orleans so arrangements and accommodations for their travel needed to be made. There was a whirl wind of excitement at the one five and in Washington. Rosaland and Rachael went to spend a day in D.C. with the General so they could coordinate the activities in Virginia. Rachael's wedding would be held on the estate in the rose garden.

Anna kept a rose garden filled with the most exquisite cross breeds of exotic roses, American roses and hybrids. After her tragic death her garden was one of the parts of the estate that the General made sure remained unchanged. It was always well cared for. He hired a full time gardener just to nurture this area. It would the perfect setting for Rachael's nuptials.

Once they convinced the General to prepare the estate "Dad," Rosaland pleaded, "These are the instructions that I want you to follow. I won't be able to come to Washington until next week so you have to have this all set up for me when I return." "Rosaland I am not going to be in town this week." "Dad you have to do this before you leave. Please give us a day. This has to be just right for Rachael. Once you make all the calls Esmeralda can make sure everything is set up according to plan."

The General knew there would be no reasoning with his daughters when they made up their minds to do something. He agreed to postpone his business for two days just in case. The General had a real soft spot for his children. He knew they would have anything they wanted. And besides he had to arrange for security to cover his estate and only he could do that. The girls had to get back to Manhattan for a dress fitting so the General flew them back to the city.

Rosaland had to stop by the one five before the fitting only to find Arthur waiting for her. "Dr. Reid could I have a few minutes?" he said as she rushed in. "Lt. I'm right in the middle of something, could we make it another day or another time maybe in about an hour?" "Actually I know that you are very busy it won't take long." "Rachael is waiting downstairs Arthur we have a very important appointment."

Arthur was caught in a dilemma. On the one hand he had departmental business that he needed to conduct and on the other hand he knew that they were preparing for his wedding. "I promise this will only take a minute." "Ok can you send someone to tell her that I will meet her at the dress shop in about an hour?" "Yes I'll send a uniform down right away and then I'll make sure that you get there in an hour. Will that work?" "Yes. That will be fine. Let me freshen up and I'll be right there."

As Rosaland walked into the ladies room she noticed Diana and Bobby talking. After washing her hands and brushing her hair she went into Arthur's office. "Dr. Reid I know that you are very busy and I thank you for taking the time out of your schedule to meet with me. I want to know what you intend to do about Detective Rousseau?" "I don't understand. What I intend to do about Detective Rousseau?"

"It is my duty to inform you that you have the right to file a formal complaint against the detective for striking a superior officer. If you do intend to file a formal complaint disciplinary action will be taken against the detective." "Why would I file a complaint against her? As far as I am concerned that was personal and it doesn't have anything to do with the job or her performance on the job. No I don't intend to file any complaint. Detective Rousseau is one of our best and to take disciplinary action would be totally inappropriate."

Arthur was relieved. Even though he knew that she would be fair he had to do his job. "Is that all?" "Yes." "I really have to go." Rosaland looked around for Bobby who was nowhere in sight. As she left she noticed that the Lt. had Detective Rousseau in his office.

Rosaland paged Bobby and waited for him to call back. She hailed a taxi to meet her sister. When Bobby returned her call she was heading over the bridge to Brooklyn. "Hey where are you?" "I'm on my way to Brooklyn." "What's in Brooklyn?" "We have to be fitted for our dresses. Where are you?" "At a crime scene let me call you back." "Ok call me when you're free." Rosaland had a thousand things to do and the time was slipping away. She needed to let Bobby know that at the end of the week she was going to Washington and that she would have to stay there until after the wedding.

Rosaland was the last to arrive for the fitting. Rachael was beginning to get a little anxious. When Rosaland bust in the door, Rachael smiled and insisted that she get measured right away. "Rosaland they are going to give us priority service, so you have to pick a dress." After the measurements had been taken and the color scheme decided on Rosaland found that she had a million choices. She wanted something really sexy. She begged Rachael not to be so traditional but it was Rachael's wedding and whatever she wanted was what was going to happen.

On the other hand Rachael knew her sister's taste and she wanted her to be comfortable as well so the twins were able to reach a compromise. Rosaland found a beautiful red gown that would blend in perfectly with the pink and chrimsom choices of the other two attendants. Rachael had chosen two of her best friends from undergraduate and law school to stand with her.

Rosaland cried when her sister came out in the most beautiful gown that she had ever seen. "Oh Rachael that is definitely the one. You look so beautiful." The two hugged in delight as they all made their final selections. After the fitting all the ladies went to have drinks and a light meal with Papa at the restaurant.

When Bobby finally got back to her she informed him that they were at the restaurant and he should come through when he finished his shift. While they were eating Rachael asked "Rosaland I noticed that lovely ankle bracelet. Are those black pearls?" Rosaland smiled "Yes aren't they wonderful?" "Yes. They are lovely. Where did you find something like that?" "Bobby gave them to me last week" "Where did he find something like that. That is a very unique gift?" "At a shop in Manhattan."

"Who's Bobby?" Annette asked "The King!" Rachael answered sarcastically. Rosaland rolled her eyes at her sister and they both started to laugh. "You know Rachael Arthur asked me if I wanted to file a complaint against Diana today." "Really? I'm not surprised he was pretty angry about the whole incident. He didn't like it at all." "I told him no. Let's just let lying dogs lay dead plus we have a wedding to choreograph. I don't have time for that."

Rachael loved her sister; she knew that Rosaland wouldn't let anything interfere with her happiness. Papa came over to make sure that his guests were comfortable and being treated well by his staff. "Is everything alright Rosalinda?" "Everything is fine Papa, thank you." Papa had developed quite a fondness for Rosaland and Rachael. He marveled at how much they looked alike and how different they were.

The bond these sisters shared was incredibly strong. Papa was then reminded of the dilemma he was facing. If Bobby was ever going to marry he deserved to know his family background. Annette whispered under her breath "Girls don't look now but the most gorgeous man I have ever seen just came in. Heart be still he is so fine." Annette was fanning herself.

Everyone looked around to see whom she was talking about. Rachael said calmly "Annette if you want to live you will take that back. My sister will kill you!" Everyone bust into laughter. Rosaland shook her head as she got up to kiss Bobby as he approached their table.

"Oh shit is that Bobby?" "The one and only" "I could just die." Bobby was close to the table now and kissed Rosaland sweetly on her lips. "Hey ladies! Rachael are you having a good time?" He flashed that gorgeous sexy smile. "Absolutely" Rachael responded. "We decided to spend some of the General's money and what better place than here?" They all laughed again.

"Ladies this is Detective Bobby Semione N.Y.P.D." "Bobby this is Annette Hawkins and Bridgette Evans my best friends from college. "Ladies pleased to meet you." Bobby smiled as he shook their hands. "You come with me!" He pointed his finger as Rosaland walked over to the bar for a minute.

Annette watched very much interested "Does he have a brother, uncle, nephew?" Rachael laughed "Annette you are still the same crazy as ever." "Bobby don't be mad" Rosaland said sexily "but I'm going to have to leave town at the end of this week. I have to put Rachael's wedding together and the rest of what I have to do is in Washington."

"Do you have to be there the whole week?" "Yes" "so when do I get to see you?" "When you get there and please bring Papa." "Ok. I want to talk to you about what you did this afternoon." "What I did this afternoon? What did I do this afternoon?" Rosaland was puzzled and Bobby could see the bewilderment on her face.

"What you did for Diana. That was very noble." "You know when I started seeing you I knew that there was history between the two of you. I'm just sorry that things went down the way they did. She bruised my face, I broke her nose; I should have had more control. So now we are both the talk of the station, that's enough punishment right there. Everybody knows our business."

"Go back to your party. I'm going back in the kitchen to help Papa." Bobby smiled at her as she walked back to the table. After he took off his jacket he disappeared into the kitchen. Arthur came in shortly after Bobby. Rachael noticed him right away and said gleefully "If any body says one thing about this man, I will have to shoot you." They ladies looked around as Arthur walked up.

"Hi I'm Arthur. How is everybody?" "Hey handsome come join us." Arthur took a seat next to Rachael. "Arthur this is Annette Hawkins and Bridgette Evans my best friends from college." Arthur shook both of their hands "It's a pleasure to finally meet you." "Arthur have you heard from your family? Do you know when they will be arriving?" "Yes they all plan to be here first thing next week and they will all be here." "Good we'll all be at the General's."

Arthur ordered a drink "Where's Bobby?" "He was here?" Rachael replied looking around. "He's in the kitchen with his Grandfather" Rosaland chimed in. "How is his Grandfather?" "He's hanging in there; you know these things take time." "I'm going in the kitchen to talk to the guys; I'll leave you ladies here to finish your party."

Arthur took his drink and went over to the opening of the kitchen. Bridgette finally spoke "Rachael I hate you rich girls. You always get the best men. Where did you find him?" "My sister. She works with him; she introduced us at a party." "Where do you work and are there anymore like them?" Bridgette asked Rosaland teasingly.

"As a matter of fact there is a whole squad room full of them." "Are you a cop?" "No but they are." "I head an agency that is temporarily stationed in the N.Y.P.D. but hopefully we will be moving to another location soon. We have outgrown our current facility. Besides they will all be at the wedding. So you will have plenty of opportunity.

Doesn't Arthur have four brothers?" "Yes but they are all married" "It doesn't matter; there will be plenty of single men there to meet." It was getting late and the ladies needed to call it a night. Rosaland went in the kitchen to retrieve her love and Arthur came out to escort Rachael home.

"Bobby we need our bill?" "What bill? I'll take care of it." "No Baby we'll pay. This is the General's treat. He would be very upset if we didn't pay." "Papa would be truly offended if you did pay."

forty

The General had a much harder job ahead of him. After looking over Rachael's guest list he knew that he had to secure his estate. Everyone from the Attorney General to the President of the United States would be attending as well as his immediate family. He knew that if his enemy's would decide to retaliate this would be the prime opportunity. He decided that along with the department of the Secret Service he would also use the Black Wolverines as well as the O.N.S.I. select forces.

Lt. William Jones had recovered successfully from the injuries he received at the Latin American shoot out and he would assign him to head the security detail. With the Latin American incident unsolved he could not afford to be caught off guard and he would do anything to make sure that no harm came to his children. The General would use selected military personnel for the catering, the photography and any other incidentals that might arise.

Everyone that would be on the estate that day would be accounted for. This was his daughter's wedding and he would leave nothing to chance. He would call on his old friend the Reverend Louis Vaughn to conduct the ceremony. He and the Reverend were friends from the old neighborhood and he knew that he could be trusted. Besides it would be nice to see him again. It had been about twenty five years since they were together.

Rachael's wedding was coming along very nicely and the General would make sure that it stayed that way. He would invite Sonia Blackwell himself. He wanted her ears there more than he wanted her there but since they were inseparable he would have to settle for her presence. The General would have all his players in the house and the deck stacked against anyone who might have a different agenda.

When Rachael woke up that morning she was very excited. The day of her wedding had finally arrived. On this day she and Arthur would be united as one. They had waited two years and today they would become man and wife. She ran down the hall to wake her sister. Rosaland was feeling a little sluggish, but she could make it through one more day. After this she would certainly need a vacation.

She had organized Rachael's wedding in two weeks; a wedding that should have taken a year to plan. "Wake up sleepy head!" Her sister said as she stood at the top of her bed. "Rachael what time is it?" Rosaland felt as though she had just gone to bed and now it was time for her to get up. "It's 7:30. I can't sleep. I'm so excited." "Rachael please let me sleep until 9:00. I promise I'll get up then. The ceremony isn't until 6:00 this evening. Here come lay down with me. Come on get in." "No. I'm too excited. You go back to sleep. I'll be back a little later." Rachael strolled down the hall looking for somebody anybody to share in her excitement. The General's estate was so massive and with as many people that were in the house this weekend the halls were so isolated.

Mrs. Yancy was an early riser. She was leaving her room at the very moment that Rachael was about to go downstairs. "Rachael what are you doing up so early? The bride needs her beauty sleep." "Good morning Mrs. Yancy. How did you sleep?" "Just fine my dear" "Would you care to join me for a cup of coffee?" "Yes I would love to." The soon to be in laws went down to the dining room where Esmeralda had just begun to set up for breakfast.

"Miss Rachael what are you doing up so early? I'm not ready for breakfast yet. I just started to set up." "It's ok Esmeralda we just want coffee. We can wait for breakfast." As Rachael spoke she looked at Mrs. Yancy for confirmation. Mrs. Yancy shook her head in acknowledgement. Esmeralda went into the kitchen and came back with two china cups and a nice pot of hot coffee.

Rachael and Mrs. Yancy served themselves and sat down to talk. "Rachael I haven't had much of a chance to talk to you or to get to know you. I want you to know how very honored we are to be guest here this weekend. I was worried that Arthur would never find anyone. You know my other three sons have been married for years. You are certainly a blessing to him and he loves you very much."

Rachael smiled as she sipped her coffee. Esmeralda was in the background continuing her work. "I love him too. Arthur is a wonderful man. I am the lucky one." "How did the two of you meet?" "We were introduced by my sister. She works in his unit." "That pretty girl is a police officer?" "No actually she's not. Her agency is located in the precinct." "The two of you look so much alike. Do you have a hard time with that? I've never met identical twins before."

"We could get away with it if we tried but we are so different otherwise. I love my sister. She is my best friend and I can always count on her. She put my wedding together for me." A sleepy Rosaland entered the dining room at that moment. She was dressed in her pajamas and her robe. "I felt so guilty that I couldn't go back to sleep." Rosaland walked over to give her sister a big hug. "Good morning Mrs. Yancy."

"This is your day sweetie." Esmeralda poured Rosaland a cup of coffee and handed it to her. "Thanks Esmeralda" Rosaland sat down to join the conversation. "Mrs. Yancy are you enjoying yourself?" She asked sleepily. "Oh everything has been so wonderful; I was just telling your sister." "The best is yet to come" Rosaland promised. "Rachael tells me that you work with Arthur?" "Yes we work in the same unit." "But you are not a police officer?" "No my agency is partnering there." "Are you married?" "No Rachael beat me to it."

Rosaland and Rachael both laughed. Mrs. Yancy was a little confused but she didn't comment. "Esmeralda what time are you serving breakfast?" "If you are hungry Miss Rosaland I can make you something now." "Would you? I am starving and I have a lot of work to do this morning. I need to be ready before the florist and the caterer arrive." "Ok I'll have your breakfast in a minute."

"Rachael where are the boys? You know Arthur can't see you before the ceremony its bad luck." "They won't be here until about two. What time is Bobby and his Grandfather arriving?" "Probably around the same time" "Good that means you can get some work done" Rachael looked at Esmeralda and they both started laughing. Rosaland smiled and shook her head "I hate both of you" and all three of them burst into laughter.

At this point with all the laughter going on Mrs. Yancy had to ask "Who is Bobby?" "He is one of the detectives in the unit." "Yes Bobby Semione I've met him. He has been working with Arthur for years. He has been to my home on a number of occasions. He is a very nice man. Is that your special friend?" Mrs. Yancy looked at Rosaland with one of those motherly expressions on her face.

"We are friends Mrs. Yancy." Rachael and Esmeralda started to laugh again. "Don't pay them any attention" Rosaland started to laugh "I've got to go. Esmeralda could you please bring my breakfast upstairs? See you ladies later. Enjoy your breakfast." Rosaland sashayed out of the room.

As Rosaland stood on her balcony overlooking the estate the hustle and the bustle of the wedding preparations had started. Rosaland watched as the grounds crew erected the tent in the rose garden. Rachael could not have been blessed with a more perfect day. The catering trucks had started to arrive and the driveway was full of vendors and suppliers as they set about the task of the finalizing their duties.

Rosaland also noticed the select collection of secret service agents that had started to assemble. The estate was slowly but surely being turned into a fortress, where only a chosen group of individuals would be allowed to penetrate. Rachael's guest list included politicians, international dignitaries and law enforcement officials. The General could leave nothing to chance with this many important and influential people all being housed under his roof.

He wanted his daughter's guest to have the best security that money could buy and he paid for it dearly. Everyone and their mother owed the General a favor and he was calling in all his cards. The special forces of the O.N.S.I. under the leadership of Lt. William Jones were the next to arrive. Rosaland hadn't seen Bill since the Latin American incident so she was pleased when he pulled up with his associates and started placing them in strategic locations where they would go undetected.

Rosaland took note at how nice he looked and how well he had healed from his injuries. The General greeted him warmly and escorted him inside. The rest of the agents started to blend in naturally with the workers as they prepared the grounds for the upcoming festivities. Rosaland knew that they would be in the General's private study so after she dressed she headed down to talk with Bill. Her dress was a delicate float of material that hung loosely from her body. She knew that later she would be in the garden so she found one of Rachael's hats and went to the study.

It was just as she had imagined. The General was sitting behind his desk with the full layout of the estate on the computer. Bill was standing over his shoulder watching as the General pointed out the various areas of the estate that would be vulnerable in the event of trouble. Rosaland walked over quietly and listened as the General detailed his plan. She watched silently and listened intently to the security measures that the General was implementing on behalf of his daughter and her guest.

Rosaland pulled up a chair and as she crossed her legs her garment opened slightly exposing her well-developed calves. Bill would always hold the memory of her nearly nude body in her underwear deeply in his heart. So often he wished he hadn't been called away that night. The one night that she might have been his. When the General had finished his briefing with the Lt. they both acknowledged her presence.

"Rosaland" Bill said smiling "You look well. It's nice to see you." Rosaland walked over and hugged him "It's nice to see you too Bill. I haven't seen you since your release from the hospital. How are you?" "Much better now. You look beautiful." "Thanks. So are you here to protect us?" "Absolutely." The General always wished that the two of them would have gotten married. He always liked Bill and he hoped that she did too.

"Good morning Sunshine. Don't you look lovely?" The General hugged his daughter tightly. "Thanks Dad. That's quite a plan you've outlined there." "Do you like it? Do you think it will be effective?" He looked over his glasses wishfully. "Are you kidding? You'll have this place tighter than Fort Knox." The General laughed heartily.

"I'm sure you remember what happened the last time the two of you were together." "Do I. I still have nightmares." "My entire family which consist of your sister, your brother and yourself will be on this estate today and I would rather be safe than sorry. Not to mention the hundreds or so of invited guest including the President of the United States that I personally will responsible for."

Rosaland understood completely. She knew how seriously her Dad took his responsibilities. "Rosaland from this point on I would like you all to stay close to the estate. Lt. Jones will send a car for everyone that will need to be transportation from either the airport or the train stations. I need the list and times of arrivals e so that we can coordinate the transportation from here. I'm going to pick up Matthew in just a few minutes and after that the rest of the transportation will be handled by select O.N.S.I."

"This is your new team. You will meet them formally after all this is over." "It would take the General to turn Rachael's wedding into a military operation. Then again he turns everything into a military operation." Rosaland thought secretly to herself. "Ok let me get the information. I need to go the garden anyway. I'll do them both at once." Rosaland walked out of the room.

"You know sir may I speak freely?" "Yes, of course soldier what's on your mind?" "I love your daughter sir." "I know son but you might be a little late. Right now you need to keep your mind on your assignment." "Yes sir." Rosaland walked back into the study with her list and handed it to her father. "Dad are you going to have Bill working all day?" "Unfortunately yes. The Lt. is the only one that I can trust with such an assignment." "Well I'll see you guys later." Rosaland walked across the estate to the rose garden and was very pleasantly surprised at how lovely everything was shaping up.

She walked into the tent that had been situated adjacent to the garden and observed the caterers working diligently to make sure that everything was in the proper place. After building the trellis and placing the red, white and pink candles that Rachael had requested for the ceremony the florist started to decorate the house with a variety of roses and orchids. Rosaland was so busy coordinating the event that she lost track of the time. She was expecting Bobby and Papa at about two o'clock and she wanted to make sure that everything was done by then so she could spend some time with him.

She hadn't seen him for a week and she missed him. Once she was satisfied with the work that was being done on the grounds and in the garden, she returned to the house. Rachael, Annette and Bridgette were relaxing comfortably in an upstairs bedroom that had been turned into a beauty salon.

Rosaland had her favorite hair stylist Doris flown in from New York especially for this occasion. Doris had brought her manicurist, make up artist and her top hair designers to take care of the wedding party. Mrs. Yancy was having a massage in the dressing area of the bathroom. "Is everyone alright?" Rosaland asked as she peaked her head into the room. Rachael was having a pedicure and totally absorbed in her beauty treatment. "Yes" Bridgette answered from across the room "This is so wonderful!" "Good. I'm glad you are enjoying yourself." "Rosaland you need to get in here. You know how long it takes your hair to dry."

"I'm coming Rachael. I just want to make sure that the guys get here before I disappear. Matthew is going to host Arthur and his brothers and he isn't here yet. Dad went to pick him up from the airport and they are not back. Give me a few more minutes. I'll be right back." Just as Rosaland turned a pair of strong hands covered her eyes. Matthew put his finger to his mouth motioning to Rachael and the other ladies to be quiet. Rosaland started smiling recognizing the antiseptic smell of Matthews's hands.

"Guess who?" "It had better be my brother or I'm going to kill him!" Matthew kissed his sister lovingly on the cheek. "It's me!" "Hi honey!" Rosaland said exuberantly as she hugged her brother. "This ladies is my favorite brother!" "Actually I'm her only brother. Her's too."

Matthew stepped fully into the room full of women. They were all astonished at how fine this man was. He made his way around the room greeting and shaking all of their hands. When he came to Rachael he bent down and placed a big kiss on her forehead. Rachael smiled broadly happy to see him.

"I was just about to send a search party after you Matt. What took you so long to get here?" "It's called the emergency room sweetheart. Don't worry I'm here now. So I'm finally going to lose you to another man." "No you will never lose me; you are stuck with me for life." Everyone in the room laughed. "And me too! Don't forget about me!" "How could we forget about you? You would kill us if we did!" "That's right and don't either of you forget it."

Annette, Bridgette and Doris were still in shock over Matthew. "You ladies have a regular operation going on here; can a brother get a hook-up?" "You sure can" Doris was the first one to speak. "Maybe later. I know right now Rosaland has some orders for me. She is so good with the orders." "As a matter of fact Matthew I need you to go and check to see if your sister's future husband and his family are anywhere on the premises." "I told you she would have some orders. Let me go. I'll see all you lovely ladies later. By the way where am I putting these guys?"

"You guys can have the complete run of the third floor. The rooms are already prepared. Bridgett had caught Matthew's eye, he glanced in her direction as he left the room. As soon as they thought that he was out of hearing range the whole room burst into hysteria.

"Where have the two of you been hiding him?" Doris was the first to comment. "No where." "What does he do?" Annette asked. "He's a doctor. He runs N.Y.U. Medical. You ladies don't remember Matthew?" "I don't remember him being that fine." "Neither do I" Bridgette finally spoke up. "Well ladies that's Matthew and he is single." A few minutes later Matthew knocked on the door again. "Rachael, Arthur and his family just arrived." He closed the door behind him and went to take care of them.

Arthur was accompanied by his father Arthur senior, and his three brothers Jonathan, Demetrius and Keith. The General greeted them at the door and Matthew escorted them to their rooms. Once Matt had everyone settled in he took them downstairs for lunch. Esmeralda had prepared a wonderful lunch and the General supplied the liquor. "How was your trip, sir?" The General addressed Arthur's father.

"It was fine, a little long. But we made it in one piece. Where is my wife?" "She's upstairs with the rest of the ladies getting beautiful. She's in good hands." The General ate a light lunch with the guys out of hospitality. He knew that Rachael would kill him if he didn't spend some time with them. Rosaland came downstairs to meet everybody.

Jonathan went blank when he saw her smiling face. He gazed at her as if a bolt of lightening had hit him. All the men stood up when she entered the room. "At ease guys it is lunch time." She teased "Hi I'm Rachael's sister Rosaland. We are so pleased that you all could make it. Are your rooms alright?" "Yes Miss Rosaland thank-you." "Just Rosaland please. Is there anything that you need?"

Arthur walked over and kissed her softly on her cheek. "Rosaland. That sounds so strange; I'm so accustomed to calling you Dr. Reid." "We not at work and you are family now." "Guys this is the famous Dr. Reid" "So I guess you are going to play this Dr. Reid thing Arthur." "No it's just that I have told them about you. Now they have met you." "Don't worry its all been good" Jonathan chimed in. I'm Jonathan. It's a pleasure to finally meet you."

"The pleasure is ours. We are very happy to have you here." "I'm Demetrius" she shook his hand. "I'm Keith" she shook his hand. "Rosaland this is my father, Arthur Yancy." "It's an extreme pleasure to meet you."

Arthur's father shook her hand. "What a lovely young lady." The General spoke up "Thank-you" "Well I'll leave you now to your lunch. I'll see you all later." Rosaland walked over to kiss her Dad. "I love you Dad."

The General smiled as Rosaland floated out of the room. Jonathan was still in shock. He had to remember that her father and her brother were in the room so he kept his lewd comments to himself. He would find out about her later. Rosaland went back upstairs to report to the ladies. "Mrs. Yancy your family is downstairs. They are having lunch. Would you like to go down?"

"No I can see them later. Just as long as I know they are all here." "You have a nice looking family."Rosaland commented. The hour was rapidly approaching and there was still no sign of Bobby and Papa. Rosaland was beginning to worry. She made a final check of the garden to assure that everything was perfect.

The seating was completed and the tent had been transformed into a tropical paradise. The fresh flowers were fragrant and intoxicating. Rachael would have a wonderful wedding. One that they would talk about for years to come. Before entering the house she checked with the transportation coordinator and Bobby had not called or arrived.

forty-one

Rosaland was standing on the second floor landing looking out the window when Bobby's car pulled up. He was the first to step out expectantly looking around hoping that she would be there to greet him. She was. She stepped out of the door and smiled. She ran graciously over to the car and gave him a deep soul stirring kiss. He smiled not saying a word and turned to help Papa.

Papa was amazed at the size of the estate; he had no idea of the world that he was about to become a part of. He knew that the General was a powerful man but he really had no idea how powerful until now. "Papa" Rosaland greeted him with a tender kiss. "I'm so happy that you are here. I was beginning to get a little worried. The General is waiting for you. How was the trip?" Rosaland looked to Bobby to answer. "We had a small problem that's why we are a little late." Rosaland looked concerned and Bobby assured her that it was nothing to be alarmed about. As they walked toward the house Bobby looked at her salaciously "nice hat." He said. She winked at him as they entered the residence.

"Wow look at this place. It looks great!" Bobby noticed. Papa was even more astonished and impressed at the elegant but practical décor of the General's home. The general was very hospitable and generous with his guest. He was happy to be part of such a nice family event. The General was told of the arrival of Bobby and Papa and he excused himself from his other guest to go and welcome them.

He was extremely interested in Papa. He knew that there was some secret that Papa held. A man that has a secret can always recognize another man with a secret. When he entered the foyer Rosaland and her guests were inside the house. "Dad looked who finally arrived" The two men greeted each other in a warm manner as Bobby stood next to his grandfather.

"Papa thank you for coming. It's nice to see you again sir. Welcome to my home." Both the General and Papa knew exactly what that meant. The driver placed their luggage in the foyer. "Detective Semione it's nice to see you again." The General shook Bobby's hand in a friendly manner though he remained a little distant. He General did not like the fact that the Detective was sleeping with his daughter. That was the one line that no man could cross with his daughters.

Rachael was getting married today. Rosaland wasn't. He didn't like it. The General knew what this man meant to his daughter. He knew how deep her feelings flowed. He couldn't treat Bobby in any other way accept with the respect that he had earned. The General wanted the sex stopped or he wanted it done in the right way. This was a decision that Bobby would make over this weekend. Bobby and Rosaland were becoming too public with their relationship.

"The Yancy's are in the dining room. Come this way. The General lead Papa into the dining room. Bobby on the other hand lingered in the foyer. Bobby walked over to Rosaland and embraced her deeply; from the moment he saw her he wanted to kiss her. And now that they were finally alone he wanted to hold her in his arms. Bobby held her firmly against his body. He squeezed her close to him. He wanted to feel her he wanted to touch her and he wanted to smell her hair. Rosaland could feel his need and Bobby could feel her desire.

"I need you. Is there somewhere we can go?" Bobby whispered tugging at her waist. Rosaland quietly escorted him up the steps. She knew exactly where they would go. Bobby followed as they slipped into the first available bedroom. Once inside she locked the door and placed the key on the night table. She kissed him tenderly pulling him toward her wanton body. Bobby's arms fit gently around her caressing the firm contours of her form. His lips relaxed on hers his hands releasing her heaving breasts.

Bobby opened her dress and exposed her luscious heavy breasts to his nibble. Rosaland purred as she felt the contact of his warm mouth on her fleshy mounds. "Ohh" she moaned out loud. Bobby kissed her breasts deliciously savoring the feel of her large nipples in his mouth. Rosaland melted feverishly in his arms. Bobby released her slightly and walked over to the bed.

He sat down and opened his arms to indicate that she should be in them. When she walked over to meet him Bobby began to disrobe her. Rosaland unbuttoned Bobby's shirt exposing his muscular chest and stomach to the touch of her lips. Bobby's body weakened from the sensations of her wet mouth on his hard chest and nipples. "I know what you like" he whispered in her ear as he slid back on the bed and pulled her on top of him. His strong arms pressed her body into his. He ran his hands over her hot naked flesh totally exploring her exposed warmth.

Bobby rolled her onto her back; the soft down comforter cushioned her body as he slid her panties off with his thumbs. "Take this off" he murmured as he removed her dress. Bobby lost no time in taking full and complete possession of her being. Rosaland watched as he slowly disrobed in front of her. She reclined upon the bed in anxious expectation. The black pearls sexily encircled her ankle.

Bobby placed his hard frame on top of hers. He kissed her passionately as he inserted his hard pulsating erection into her tight wet privacy. Rosaland could feel him throbbing inside of her as he stretched her and pumped himself into position. She gasps with desire as he pushed himself deeper and stronger with each powerful thrust. Bobby moaned and groaned as he rode in and out of her hot gyrating cavern.

Rosaland met his strokes with a fire of her own. She pressed her body into his offering him complete and total access to her sweet essence. She squeezed the tight muscles inside her honey spot to hold him captive with each stroke. She needed all of him; she wanted him to fill that void. Rosaland wrapped her legs tightly around Bobby's waist and held him securely inside her accommodating orifice.

"Umm, I've missed you Bobby" she whined breathlessly as Bobby's fever increased. Bobby buried his massive hot throbbing length to the hilt in her body with each powerful stroke. He strove to reach her deepest emotions. Rosaland screamed and groaned in ecstasy as Bobby rode her furiously. Rosaland was weak from passion and desire. She clung to his muscular physique experiencing ultimate pleasure in his powerful embrace.

"Ooh Bobby Bobby!" Bobby muffled her cries with his lips. He pressed his mouth hotly on hers as she cried out in delight. He moved his mouth away allowing her to catch her breath and then he inserted his tongue sucking throaty kisses from her lips. He nibbled sweet kisses from her quivering lips and he continued to plunge aggressively into her soul.

Rosaland's body trembled in hunger and delight as she opened herself to him. Bobby craved her. Only he could satisfy her appetite. Bobby was captivated by the feel of her. He wanted nothing more than her. "Baby I love you" Bobby whispered tenderly as the rhythm of his body harmonized with hers. "Ooh I love you. I love you." She responded sexily as their passion increased.

Rosaland pumped her body lustfully and greedily into his as her final orgasm exploded deep inside her inner sanctum. Bobby could feel the powerful reaction in her body and was swept up in her crest. His torrid orgasm burst through his soul as his seed left his body filling her completely with his potency. Rosaland's body spasmed from the force of his deluge. "I wish I had more time…" Bobby moaned as the two lovers lay satiated, their sweaty bodies still entwined totally entrenched in their ardor.

It was about an hour and a half later when a relaxed Bobby made it to lunch. The Yancy's and Papa were just finishing up. The General had left to go attend to other matters. "Hey Bobby" Arthur was the first to notice his entrance. Arthur walked over and shook his hand. "I'm glad to see you." "Are you ready to tie the knot?" Bobby asked smiling. "I'm as ready as I'm ever going to be. It's now or never." Arthur introduced Bobby to the rest of his family.

Esmeralda had started to clear the table when she noticed that Bobby had just taken a seat. "Mr. Bobby. What would you like for lunch?" "Something light Esmeralda thank you. Have you met my grandfather?" "Yes. The General introduced us earlier" Esmeralda replied as she continued her duties. Bobby ate quietly as the rest of the guys talked and exchanged wedding day stories with Arthur. Bobby listened just as intently as Arthur did.

"Hey Detective" Matthew shouted from across the room. Bobby wiped his mouth with his napkin and got up to go shake his hand. "What's up brother in law?" "Hey Matt. How's it going?" "Rosaland was worried sick about you. Have you seen her? She is somewhere around here giving orders." They both laughed.

"Its time guys." Matthew escorted everyone up to the third floor dressing area. Everything had been prepared so that the guys could take their time while getting dressed. They were all excited and commented on what great lengths that had been taken on their behalf. When they were finally all together Jonathan couldn't hold back any longer "Arthur how come you didn't tell us that you were marrying royalty? Look at this spread. And how come you didn't tell me that your royalty had a twin sister? A beautiful twin sister."

"Jonathan you are a married man. What are you going to do?" "Anything that she will let me." They all laughed and Arthur shook his head. Jonathan was standing by the window when he noticed her standing on the lawn below. He stood and watched as she finalized the details of her sister's wedding. At that moment Bobby walked across the lawn to where she was standing and whispered something in her ear. She turned and looked lusciously at him then he whispered something else this time moving even closer to her than he was before. "Bro?" Jonathan turned to look in Arthur's direction and then back to the lawn. "Is there something between Bobby and my fairy princess?" Arthur laughed "Big time!"

The General was in his private study reviewing the security measures that Lt. Jones and his team had put in place. As the General pulled up the various blind spots on his estate he had a visual on each and every one of the remote locations. “Good job son. Lt. I would feel more comfortable if you were on the grounds. Have Matthew find you something to wear.”

“Yes sir.” The General wanted Lt. Jones on the premises for two reasons. He wanted him to be among the guest and also he wanted him to be around Rosaland. Bobby would be challenged tonight and he wouldn’t even know it. The General deliberately set them up and may the best man win. The General had made his decision. His daughter was too precious to him and if in fact Bobby loved her then he would have to do the right thing.

Rosaland relaxed leisurely in the bathtub her mind adrift lost in her thoughts. Rachael entered the bathroom to check on her sister’s progress. Doris was waiting for her in the bedroom turned salon to freshen her hair and apply her make-up. “Come on sis. Hurry up. You have to get your hair done, everybody else is ready.”

Rosaland stepped out of the tub and put on her robe. She walked over to the sink and cleansed and moisturized her skin “Rachael wait for me before you get dressed. We should get dressed together ok?” “Well then you need to hurry up.” “Ok, I’m done.” Doris was waiting when Rosaland entered. “With all that hair that you have how are you going to come so late? Sit down.” “Doris please just put my hair up and do my make-up I’m fine.” Rosaland sat quietly as Doris completed her services. She liked what she had done.

“Thanks Doris, a great job as always.” Rosaland found Rachael in her bedroom with Esmeralda. “Miss Rosaland I put your things in your bedroom.” “I’m going to get dressed in here with Rachael. Would you mind getting them for me please?” When Esmeralda left the room Rosaland said “Rachael come I would like to talk to you.” Rachael sat down next to her sister; Rosaland could see the excitement in her face.

“Rachael we have both been so busy lately and I haven’t had the opportunity to tell you how very proud I am of you. If Mom were here she would be as happy and as proud as I am. Rachael you always do things right. You have made Dad very happy. At least one of his daughters made it to the alter.”

“You talk like you are an old woman. You’ll make it to the alter. I see the way Bobby looks at you everybody does. Your relationship with Bobby started in secret but your secret is in the open now. There is no way that the two of you won’t stay together.” “I know but you know what I mean. Marriage is a sacred relationship; it’s more than what I have with Bobby. It’s much more.”

“Rosaland you’re not going to believe this but I disagree. There is no way that any two people could have more than what the two of you share. You are his destiny. I can’t envision Bobby with any other woman or you with any other man. It wasn't written that way for the two of you. The one thing I know about you is that you love him and I would know that even if you hadn't told me."

Esmeralda returned with Rosaland's clothes and laid them out on the bed. Rachael was deeply touched that Rosaland would remember their mother today. They never really talked about her anymore but she would remain forever in their hearts. "Mom would be pleased that your ceremony is going to be held in her rose garden."

"Mom put a lot of love and care into her garden. I know that Dad was deeply touched by the fact that you wanted to hold your ceremony here. Today will be the first time in years that we will all be together as a family. Mom is here in spirit Rachael; her presence can be felt all through the house, especially in the rose garden."

Rosaland walked over to the window and noticed that the guests were starting to arrive. "We had better get dressed. Your guests are starting to arrive. Rachael I love you!" "Rosaland I want to tell you something. I want to thank you for everything you have done for me."

"I don't know anybody that could put a wedding together in two weeks but you did. You came through for me like you always do. I couldn't believe that you would leave work for a week to make sure that all the details were correct. You are incredible and the best sister a girl could have. If Bobby is so blind that he doesn't see that then it's his lost."

Rachael held her sister in her arms as they dried their tears. "Come on stop crying. We are ruining our make-up and we need to get dressed." Rosaland removed her robe and started moisturizing her body. "Rachael look in the closet on the top shelf. There are some presents in there for you." Rachael reached on the top shelf and removed her gifts. "All of these are for me?" "Yes. Open the big one first and tell me how you like it."

Rachael squealed in delight when she opened the package "It's beautiful." "That's for tonight" Rosaland grinned. "Now open the rest of them." Rachael exclaimed "This is exactly the fragrance that I wanted. I just didn't have time to shop. How did you know?" "Because it is the same fragrance that I would wear on my wedding day." Rachael opened the box and began to spray her pulse points with the perfume. At that time Esmeralda came back into the bedroom.

"You ladies had better hurry up. The General sent me up here to check on the two of you. Now stop your foolishness and get dressed!" When Rachael stepped into her gown both Rosaland and Esmeralda became speechless. She was beautiful. The form fitting delicate white lace of the bodice accentuated her bust line perfectly leaving her cleavage slightly exposed. The bodice flowed into a graceful chiffon skirt with a satin train.

Rosaland fitted her veil on her head and Rachael stood ready to become Mrs. Arthur Yancy. Rosaland sat at the vanity carefully placing the fresh roses from her mother's garden in her hair. The roses were a perfect match and complimented her beauty. Her red chiffon dress flowed softly off of one shoulder into a full skirt. Her delicate red strappy sandals finished off her ensemble and she too was ready. "Oh, Rachael I forgot something?"

"What everything is perfect? Where are your gloves? Where are my gloves" Rosaland handed Rachael her white lace gloves and she placed her gloves on top of her bouquet. She left the room for a minute and returned with a black jewelry box. "Rachael Mom left me the necklace and the earrings she left you the bracelet and the ring. You should wear all of them today." Rosaland placed the diamond necklace on Rachael's neck and Rachael put the lovely diamond earrings in. Now she was ready.

The General knocked on the door; he was there to escort his daughters to the rose garden. Rosaland opened the door and the General's heart stopped. Rachael was beautiful and he recognized her jewelry immediately. He had bought that set for his dear Anna on their fifth anniversary. This was the first time since her death that he had seen them again and he was happy to see them on Rachael's neck.

"You girls are so lovely" the General was a little teary eyed and his girls could hear the emotion in his voice. "Rachael I want you to know that this will always be your home. My home is open to you and arthur always." Rachael kissed her Dad on the cheek. "Rosaland you did a wonderful job for your sister. Well done" Rosaland kissed her Dad on his cheek. "The garden is full of our family and friends. It's time." The General escorted his daughters down the grand staircase into the rose garden.

Father Louis Vaughn was standing at the alter when the wedding procession formed at the back of the garden. Arthur stood at the altar with his father waiting for his bride. Jonathan was busy making sure that he would have the opportunity to walk down the aisle with Rosaland. The bridal party flowed into the garden and took their places in front of the alter.

The pink, red and chrimsom floats of their gowns blended in very naturally with the assorted array of roses in the garden. Once they were stationary the alter boy lite the candles on the trellis. Bobby was mesmerized by Rosaland as she walked down the aisle. He couldn't take his eyes off of her. He had never seen her look so beautiful or so sexy. She was absolutely tantalizing. Papa turned to look at his grandson and carefully observed the expression of love on Bobby's face.

Bobby didn't see anyone but her. On Father Vaughn's signal the organist began the hymnal and the General escorted Rachael down the aisle to take her place by Arthur's side. The ceremony was intimate and emotional with

Arthur and Rachael pledging their love to each other for life. The couple requested that their families join them in a silent prayer. They kneeled at the alter and prayed for the blessings of God to nourish and strengthen this union.

The ceremony was concluded with a kiss as Father Vaughn announced "Ladies and gentlemen I present to you Mr. and Mrs. Arthur Yancy." The General beamed with joy as Arthur and Rachael made their way up the aisle united in holy matrimony.

The reception was a joyous occasion. The music was softly playing as the crowd enjoyed the General's hospitality. Rachael and her new husband were introduced to the President of the United States and the many other distinguished dignitaries that were in attendance. Bobby joined Rosaland on the Diaz for dinner.

"Remind me later to tell you how delectable you look." He whispered in her ear as they ate. Rosaland smiled at his attention. At that moment Jonathan stood up to offer a toast to the bride and groom. Everyone lifted their champagne flutes and toasted the newly weds. Rachael was the next person to stand and speak to her guests.

"I would like to offer a toast to my father General Prescott Reid, my sister Rosaland and my brother Matthew for making this the most unforgettable day of my life. Also I would like to thank my mother Anna may she rest in peace for planting and nurturing this wonderful rose garden." The crowd lifted their glasses again in recognition of Rachael's family.

Bobby stood up and applauded and the rest of the guests followed suit. Rosaland looked up at him and smiled. Lately she was always smiling at him. After dinner the venue shifted and the dance floor was packed. The entire guests mixed mingled and had a good time. The General was hobnobbing with all his political friends but he was careful to watch his estate.

Rosaland excused herself from Bobby for a moment so she could network and mingle among the guests. "Bobby there is somebody that I want you to meet" "Who?" "Her name is Sonia Blackwell and you might find her interesting to talk to." "Really. Ok? Where is she? Better still who is she? There's Danny and the rest of the squad. Let me go speak to them and I'll find you later."

Bobby kissed her cheek and went to mingle with his fellow detectives. Bill noticed Rosaland talking to her father as he walked up. "You look lovely as usual" he marveled. "Thanks Bill. So do you." "Would you care to dance?" "Sure. I would love to dance." Rosaland and Bill headed towards the dance floor. Rosaland couldn't help but notice how debonair the Lt. looked this evening. She allowed him to lead her to the dance floor and pull her close as they danced.

"You smell wonderful" Bill whispered in her ear once he had her in his arms. "You know I still think about you." Bobby noticed immediately that another man had his arms around his girl but there was nothing that he could do. He starred in heir direction for a while before he recognized the Lt.

Bobby had mixed feelings about Bill. He liked him and he knew that he was a good man but on the other hand he didn't like anyone who had eyes for his girl. He knew that Bill did and later that evening he would find out that Jonathan did as well. There were so many people on the estate that evening and it was hard for Bobby to keep track of Rosaland's movements. He watched her as closely as possible out of love and out of safety.

After talking to his grandfather to make sure that he was all right Bobby walked over to the edge of the dance floor. He was standing there when Annette walked up "Hey detective, do you want to dance?" Bobby turned around to find Annette standing directly in back of him "sure" he answered.

As they hit the dance floor the music changed from the slow song that Bill was holding Rosaland so close on to a fast song. Bobby danced with Annette as he watched Rosaland leave the floor. Sonia Blackwell was talking to the General and Rosaland wanted to join in their conversation. She knew that whatever they were talking about was something that she would want to know. "Hey you two" she said as she walked up "Are you having a good time?" The General nodded in the affirmative and as the waiter walked by Rosaland grabbed two glasses from the tray and handed one to Sonia.

"Sonia there is someone that I want you to talk to." She said casually sipping her champagne. "It wouldn't be that handsome stud of yours would it?" Rosaland looked at her and shook her head yes. "Ok where is he?" Rosaland looked around and spotted him on the dance floor with Annette. She walked over to where they were dancing and politely interrupted. "Excuse me Annette but I need to borrow him for a minute." Bobby looked curiously at her and allowed her to lead him away.

Rosaland handed him a glass of champagne as she introduced him to the infamous Sonia Blackwell. "I'm trusting you with him but I want him back." "She's just kidding." Bobby quipped. "No she's not." Sonia responded. Sonia and Bobby walked away from the crowd as they talked.

Matthew was sitting at the table talking to Bridgette and they seemed to be deeply involved in their conversation. "So what have you been doing since you graduated from law school?" Matthew inquired. "I'm the A.D.A in Boston." "Really?" "Yes" "I'm impressed. Would you care to dance?" "Yes I would love too" Matthew and Bridgette made a nice couple. Matthew escorted her to the dance floor only to be intercepted by Annette who was feeling a little tipsy. "Where are you going handsome?" she said in a flirtatious manner. "We are going to dance" Matthew responded as he pulled Bridgette by Annette and onto the dance floor.

Rosaland was with Arthur and Rachael which was very natural because the three of them spent a great deal of time together. "Arthur wasn't Rachael a beautiful bride?" Her sister gleamed. Arthur kissed Rosaland on her cheek and thanked her for everything she had done. "Yes. When Rachael entered the garden my heart stopped." Arthur kissed Rachael deeply and tenderly in front of her sister. Rosaland was so happy for them. This was good. This was very good.

Jonathan noticed Rosaland standing with his brother and came over to join them. "I just wanted to tell you how pretty you look. Doesn't she look pretty Arthur?" "Yes she always does." "Do you want to dance?" "Maybe a little later Jonathan. I really want to talk to my sister." "You have your whole life to talk to your sister. Why don't you dance with me right now?" Rosaland was slightly offended but to avoid any confusion she consented to dance with him after all he was Arthur's brother. He was family now.

Jonathan smiled and took her hand as they made their way to the dance floor. Matthew was dancing with Bridgette and they seemed to be having a lovely time together. Jonathan was a little bit aggressive with her; they had all been drinking so she overlooked it. As the music changed from fast to slow Rosaland started to leave the dance floor and Jonathan grabbed her arm roughly pulling her back. Matthew noticed his actions and immediately spoke up. "Don't do that. Don't pull on my sister. Let her go."

Jonathan let her arm go and Rosaland walked away. Bobby and Sonia were still deeply engrossed in their conversation but Bobby was watching. Jonathan approached her and apologized. "I'm sorry. I didn't mean any harm." "Its ok no harm done but please don't pull on me." Rosaland walked away. There was so much activity going on and everyone was having such a marvelous time there was no need to create a scene. Jonathan's eyes followed her as she sat down at the table with Danny.

"Danny how come you aren't dancing?" "I just sat down. Man what a shindig!" "Where is the rest of the squad?" "Out there having fun. They're all over the place." Rosaland laughed as she sipped her champagne. "Where's Bobby?" Rosaland pointed in the direction where sonic and Bobby were talking. Danny wanted to go and talk to his partner but Rosaland interceded. "Come on and dance with me Danny" Rosaland led him to the dance floor.

Jonathan noticed her having fun with Danny and caught an attitude. Bobby had concluded his conversation with Sonia and was making his way back to the party. Bobby noticed that Rosaland was on the dance floor with Danny and walked over to where they were. "I'll take over from here" Bobby teased Danny. "Partner partner" Danny shouted. "Please take over. I see another femme fatale who needs my attention." Danny moved across the floor and started dancing with a very seductive woman who had given him the eye earlier.

Bobby moved Rosaland from the dance floor to a more secluded area. "Why did you want me to talk to Sonia?" He asked her after he had gotten them a fresh drink. "She is an information specialist Bobby; she has eyes and ears everywhere." Bobby shook his head "Did you know what she was going to say to me?" "No. What did she say to you?" "She shared a couple of her theories, a few of her thoughts, and later she said she might have some more definite details." Bobby looked at her suspiciously.

"Bobby I was just trying to help. I know that you are all tied up in knots about Abuelita and I know you want some answers. You deserve some answers. Maybe she can supply some answers or some leads to some answers. I don't know but if my father trusts her so can we."

Bobby reached out and pulled her to him "That's why I love you so much. Come on let's go back to the party. I want to check on Papa." Rosaland and Bobby made their way arm in arm across the lawn and back to the crowd. "Bobby!" Bobby recognized the voice and turned around. Lt. Jones was walking towards him. "I was wondering when we get a chance to catch up with each other."

"Bill how are you!" They embraced "I haven't seen you since the hospital. I see you made it." "Yes I'm still here" Rosaland smiled as they two of them talked "Would you guys care for a drink. After all it is a party." Rosaland left for a minute to get the drinks." What can I say? When she's right she's right" "Nothing for me. I'm on duty." "Duty. You're working? What's going on?" "Nothing and I intend to keep it that way. But I will get back to you later for that drink. Oh by the way. I'm still mad at you." "Mad at me for what?" "For stealing my girl." Bill walked away but he was very serious about his last remark.

"Where's he going?" Rosaland asked when she returned with the drinks. "He's working or did you already know that?" Rosaland sat down and crossed her legs. Below the hem of her dress Bobby could see the black pearls around her delicate ankle. Those pearls around her ankle absolutely turned him on. Bobby looked at her seriously and she was quite puzzled.

"Are you ready for me?" She was even more puzzled "What are you talking about. I was born ready for you." she answered flippantly. "So you are ready to do this?" "Do what?" Bobby reached into his pocket and handed her a small box. She looked at him never even opening the box as the tears ran down her face. Bobby reached over and kissed her tenderly. Rosaland wrapped her arms around his neck as she kissed him again. As soon as their lips parted he reached up to wipe her tears away. "Since you are not going to open the box then I guess I'll have to do this the right way."

Bobby took the box from her hands and got down on bended knee. Rosaland was at a lost for words. She couldn't believe this was happening. Bobby continued "Rosaland?" "Yes. Yes I will" she sobbed nervously. Bobby placed the four-carat diamond solitaire on her finger and that was the first time that she actually saw it.

Rosaland sobbed helplessly in his arms kissing his lips ecstatically through her tears. Bobby gave her a few minutes to compose herself drying her eyes with his handkerchief and then he whispered "Now let's go check on Papa."

The reception had been going on for hours and all types of relationships and new friendships were being formed. Matthew and Bridgette were enjoying each other's company and Jonathan seemed determined to have some sort of contact with Rosaland, no matter what. When Rosaland and Bobby returned to the table Rachael asked her "Where have you been? Dad has been looking all over for you."

Rosaland held out her hand and showed Rachael her ring finger. Rachael could see that she had been crying. "Where's dad?" "He's with Papa. They are walking toward the house and if you hurry you can catch them." Rosaland grabbed Bobby's hand and headed toward the house. "Dad!" She called "Dad!" The General heard her voice and stopped. She and Bobby walked hastily to where her father and his grandfather were standing.

"Sir" Bobby took a deep breath. "I have asked your daughter for her hand in marriage. I love her and I will continue to take good care of her. All we need is your blessings." Rosaland held out her hand and showed her father and his grandfather her ring. "Dad you know that I love him. Please give us your blessing." The General hugged the detective and nodded his approval.

"It's about time that you made an honest woman out of her. Of course you have my blessings." Rosaland threw her arms around her father's neck and Papa hugged his grandson. He was very proud of him. Papa kissed Rosaland and gently squeezed her hand. "Welcome to our family."

"Do your sister and your brother know?" "I just told Rachael" "Well looks like a family toast might be in order. If you all can wait a couple of minutes Papa and I have something to discuss. I would like to have the pleasure of making the announcement." Both Bobby and Rosaland agreed to the General's request and they strolled back to the reception area hand in hand to enjoy the rest of the party.

Rosaland requisitioned the band to spice up the music. "You know detective" she said as she held Bobby by his tie "I have danced with all most everyone here tonight but you." At that moment the sounds of Latin America filled he air "And if my ears aren't deceiving me I think they are playing our song."

Rosaland stepped out of her shoes and motioned for Bobby to come and join her on the dance floor. She shimmied enticingly, shaking her voluptuous breasts sensuously in time to the beat. The hot pulsating rhythms filled the night air as all the remaining guests crowed on to the dance floor. Bobby stood there sipping his drink and watching her hips gyrate seductively as she tried to persuade him to join her.

Bobby decided that she looked too sexy to be dancing alone so he opened his shirt and removed his tie to join her on the dance floor. Rosaland rubbed her body sensuously close to his sending electric shocks straight through him. Bobby ran his hands down her curves as he moved his body in time with hers. Bobby grabbed her arms and flung her away from him causing the full skirt on her gown to cascade out in a swirling motion in the air. Bobby could see the shape of her well defined legs as she twirled in front of him. The crowd was starting to gather around them as he lifted her in the air. She slid erotically down his body as he lowered her back to the ground planting a kiss lightly on his lips.

Bobby held her tightly as he waltzed her around the floor their bodies swaying rhythmically to the vibrant sounds of Latin America. As the music died down they could hear the applause from the crowd that had encircled them. As they walked over to the table Rosaland commented "You see how good we are together." "Yes Baby I know. We have been good together since day one." "Bobby I have to go to the ladies room." Rosaland was starting to feel a little tipsy from the champagne. As she made her way through the crowd Jonathan grabbed her arm again catching her off guard. She jerked away from him violently and went into the bathroom. She tried to remain calm but she was upset that this man would grab t her in that way.

Earlier this evening Matthew had spoken to him about her. Did he think that they were kidding? When she emerged from the ladies room Jonathan was standing by the door, smiling drunkenly. As she tried to brush pass him he grabbed her to stop her.

"Have you lost your mind? She screamed nervously. "What is wrong with you?" Bobby looked towards the door and noticed that Jonathan had her blocked in. Bobby rushed over and grabbed Jonathan in a head lock "Man what is your problem?" As Jonathan tried to struggle to get away Bobby tightened his grip "Lay down Jonathan. I don't want to have to hurt you. I know that you have been drinking but you need to get yourself under control."

Bobby relaxed the hold on Jonathan's neck and Jonathan tried to swing on him. Bobby immediately body slammed him and placed his foot on his chest pinning him to the ground. "Stay down Jonathan. I mean it. If you move I'm going to split you. The choice is yours." Bobby left Jonathan on the ground and as they walked away Bobby back kicked him in the face leaving him unconscious in the grass. "He needs some time to cool off."

When they were back with the rest of the family Bobby pulled Arthur to the side and told him what had just happened. Arthur had a look of disgust on his face but he knew how Jonathan could be when he was drinking. Bobby and Arthur discussed the problem for a few more minutes and decided that they would go and revive him. Just as they were about to make their exit the General called the crowd to attention. He instructed the band to lower the volume as he called Bobby and Rosaland to the stage in front of the crowd.

"This is indeed the proudest day of my life. First it was my honor to host the wedding of my daughter Rachael to Lt. Arthur Yancy and now it is my pleasure to announce the engagement of my daughter Rosaland to Detective Roberto Semione." The crowd roared. "I would like to propose a toast to Bobby and Rosaland!" The crowd lifted their glasses and toasted the newly engaged couple. Rachael hugged and kissed her sister whispering "I told you. Bobby is no fool." Bill heard the announcement through his headset and smiled half heartily.

One of the local reporters who had been chosen to attend snapped a picture of the couple as they were being toasted. He thought the follow up story would be a great addition to his paper. This engagement was an exclusive and he had it first. The General signaled for the music to come back up as the party continued well into the wee hours of the morning.

forty-two

When Rosaland arrived back at work her fax machine was overflowing with transmissions. Arthur and Rachael were still on their honeymoon and Bobby had temporary command of the one five. The atmosphere at the precinct was relaxed as the detectives settled back into their regular routines. Rosaland was completely overwhelmed with the amount of backlog as she sorted desperately through the faxes and other memorandum trying to prioritize them.

It would take her all morning to get this mess figured out; she had hours of work ahead of her and the best strategy would be for her to get busy. As Bobby passed her office with the assignment roster he noticed the look of confusion on her face. "Hey beautiful need some help?" A very flustered Rosaland responded "Do I? Yes do you have anyone you can spare today?" "I can probably get you a P.A. would that help?" "Yes that would be a lifesaver. Can you do that?" "I'll see what I can do." Rosaland was comforted by the fact that help was on the way.

She would need to hire an assistant and that would be the first project she would undertake as soon as she got this mess straightened out. She worked feverishly through lunch and slowly but surely the mass of paperwork in front of her started decreasing. Rosaland was so caught up in her own circumstances that she never even noticed that detectives Justin Sanchez and Wesley Cole had come to pay Bobby a visit.

The three detectives had been in Bobby's office for at least an hour before she paid any attention to their presence. Bobby stood gazing out of the window with his hands in his pockets as he listened intensely as the two detectives brought him up to speed on the results of their investigation. They were finally making some headway. The forensics showed the caliber of the bullet that had struck down Abuelita and they had caught a break through the canvass of those abandoned buildings that sat in the background. The very same buildings that Bobby had insisted they recanvass.

They found a witness. Right now they had her and her daughter tucked away in a safe house and they wanted Bobby along for the interview. "Can you keep her on ice for another twenty-four hours? My Lou is out and I can't leave right now. I'm filling in. I can get my Captain down here tomorrow. My boss will be back in two days and then I can hang out in Brooklyn until we get some real answers."

"What's this witness's status? Is she homeless? Married? Was she living in those abandoned buildings? Because if she was two more days in the safe house with three meals a day ought to sound like a pretty good deal to her. I know it would sound like a good deal to me if I were in her shoes? Can we hold her a couple more days?"

Bobby looked to the detectives for help. This was the first real lead they had come up with. There had to be something that they could do to hold her. "Well I'm sure we can work out something. She seems comfortable and her daughter is being fed. We'll hold her." "Has she said anything?" "She has a description of the car and the plate number you can't ask for more than that." "Is her kid dirty or clean? Does she need some clothes?"

Detective Sanchez knew exactly where Bobby was going with this. "She could use some things." "Good. Tell her that if she would consider staying at the safe house for a couple more days the department will get her daughter some new things. A coat some shoes, some dresses. We will clean her up." "Ok. We'll get back to you." Detective Cole was trying to see if he could spot Detective Easley while he was at the station but he was unsuccessful; Detective Semione had all the available detectives out on assignment.

After the detectives from Brooklyn south left Dr. Reid entered his office. "What was that about?" She inquired innocently "They have come up with a lead on Abuelita's case. They found a witness and they are holding her in a safe house for another twenty-four hours until I can get there to talk to her. I need you to do me a favor; can you go and buy me some kids' clothes. A coat, some shoes and some dresses things like that?"

"What do you need that for?" "This witness has a young daughter. One good turn deserves another. You know how it goes. You have to give something to get something. This is life on the streets. I know that you are swamped but if you could do this for me I would be very appreciative."

"Sure you got it. What size clothes?" Detective Semione looked stumped. He had no idea. He picked up the phone and paged detective Sanchez and waited for him to call back. Dr. Reid could see the anticipation on the Detectives face she knew how much this meant to him and she had to help him.

"Semione" Bobby answered when the phone rang. "Yes. How old is this little girl? What size would that make her? Is she big for her age? Is she small? Undernourished? I need some details." Bobby listened and made some notes as Justin filled him in. "Good. Thanks." Detective Semione turned to Dr. Reid with his notes. "She's five years old and small for her age. Can you work with that?"

"Sure I can. When do you need these things?" "ASAP" "Why did I even bother to ask you that? I knew that was the answer. I'm gone. You could work on getting that PA while I'm out. Oh detective, what about the mother?" Bobby looked stumped again. "I'm cleaning up her kid; do I have to clean up the whole family?" "It couldn't hurt. Think about it. Women love to receive presents and especially something that will make them feel pretty. It's strange the kind of details that might come to mind."

Bobby could see where she was going with that train of thought. "Ok I'll do that. Thanks Baby." She blew him a kiss as she left the office. Rosaland hailed a cab and made her way uptown wondering where she could find children's clothing. This was a new area for her after all no one in her family had any children yet. She watched the stores as she rode up Seventh Avenue and stopped at Alexander's once she was in familiar territory.

She had so much work of her own to do. What was she doing here? This witness was important to Bobby so she was important to her. She carefully selected a nice assortment of things for the girl and e went into the women's department and found some one-size fits all outfits for the mother. If this lady could be of some help to Bobby in any way she wanted to make sure that she would help him.

When she returned to the precinct Diana, Yvonne and Danny were all reporting back to Bobby filling him in on the various details of their assignments. Rosaland watched from her office as the detectives talked among themselves. Her first thoughts were to go in and make her presence known but she knew better so she tried to pick up where she left off with her own work.

Rosaland didn't like Diana anywhere around Bobby. She didn't even want the two of them in the same vicinity let alone the same office. But what could she do? She had her chance to have Diana transferred but she wouldn't act on it so now she was stuck with the two of them working together again.

Dr. Reid pretended to be absorbed in her work as their meeting broke up. Diana hung back and as soon as they were alone she sat on Bobby's desk and crossed her legs. Bobby was a little taken back by Diana's aggressive behavior and he found himself at a lost for words. "Would you mind getting off of my desk? What's this all about?" "I just want to talk to you." "You can't talk to me now and you need to get off my desk." "I'll get off your desk if you agree to talk to me after work it will only take a minute and after all the time we've spent together you owe me this."

Bobby agreed to meet her at Oscar's for a drink after work and Diana got down from his desk. When she left Rosaland stormed into his office and threw the bags at him hitting him in the face. She slammed the door behind her. The O.N.S.I. would find a new home immediately if not sooner. After gathering up the garments that had hit the floor Bobby went to her office and closed the door behind him.

"What was that all about?" "You tell me. What was she doing sitting on your desk like that?" "We were just talking." "I could see that much. What were you talking about?" "It was just business." Even though Dr. Reid accepted his explanation she didn't buy it for one minute. She couldn't make herself believe that Bobby would deliberately lie to her so rolled her eyes at him and kept working. "Rosaland?" "What!" She looked at him "Ok!" Bobby walked behind her desk and placed a kiss on her forehead. She jerked her head away from him and he left her office.

From the time Diana sat on his desk Rosaland hadn't gotten a thing done. "What are we doing for dinner?" Bobby asked her after his shift was done. Rosaland looked up from her computer and shook her head "I'm not hungry besides I'm not finished."

"What do you want to do?" "Nothing tonight. I'll see you in the morning." Bobby starred at her in disbelief and then he left. Rosaland worked for another hour and then she left. Her cell phone rang as she headed up Harlem River Drive "Yes?" She answered shortly "Are you going to act like a mad woman all night?" His sexy voice commanded "Yes!" She snapped and she clicked off her phone.

As Bobby headed toward Brooklyn he called Diana. He waited patiently for her to answer and then he blasted her. "Diana I have some other business to handle this evening so we will have to have that talk another time. And tomorrow if you decide to pull another stunt like you did today I'll have your ass suspended." Bobby didn't wait for her to reply before he hung up.

He'd had his feel of temperamental females today. He was going to have a nice dinner with Papa a couple of drinks and then he was going to bed.

Carlos Calderon was sitting on his terrace overlooking Calderon Island when his servant brought him his daily stack of newspapers. Like all businessmen of his caliber he often read the London Times, the New York Times, the Wall Street Journal and his local paper. He glanced through the papers leisurely paying careful attention to the international business sections and the stock market.

For some reason he didn't follow his usual pattern. He continued to leaf through the New York Times as though he was searching for something in particular. When he reached the society page he stopped dead in his tracks. There she was smiling and looking as beautiful as ever. As he read the article he became enraged. So enraged that he balled up the paper and threw it into the trash.

As he charged around cussing and swearing he turned over the table and let it crash violently to the ground. The glass top shattering into a thousand pieces. "I need to get to New York!" He shouted "Make the arrangements now!" Carlos's servant had never seen him like this before. He hastily left the terrace and started to prepare for his boss's trip to the United States.

Carlos got dressed ranting and raving in his native tongue. The only word that his servant could understand with any clarity was something about engagement and the New York police. Carlos grabbed his weapon and proceeded to his private airstrip where he boarded his jet. Once on board he phoned New York "Find her!" He screamed violently.

Bobby was relieved to see Arthur nestled securely at his desk deep in conversation when he reported to work. This would be the perfect time for him to go to Brooklyn south and interview the witness. Bobby waited until Arthur was off the phone and then informed him as to what was going on with the investigation. Arthur gave him permission to go but suggested that Bobby remain available.

"Detective is this going to take all day?" "I don't know. I can cut it short if you need me on something else." "I might later this evening. I'll page you if this tip comes through. We're working on it now." The detective nodded and was gone. Dr. Reid was unaware that Arthur would be returning to work today. If Arthur was back then Rachael was back and she desperately needed to talk to her sister.

"I just don't like the two of them together!" Dr. Reid spoke softly into the phone. "I'm not going to apologize. I didn't do anything wrong. She was sitting on his desk... You should have seen her... No he's not in yet... But I'll talk to him. Doesn't she realize that we are engaged? Are we still on for dinner? Ok I'll see you then. Love you. Bye."

Rosaland always felt better when she talked to Rachael. Rachael could always make her see the other side of the story. There was no other side to this story Diana was off the hook and Rosaland didn't like it.

"Lt. Did Detective Semione call off today?" The Lt. looked perplexed. "No he's in Brooklyn working with the guys at Brooklyn south." Dr. Reid shook her head in remembrance and noticed the aura of wedded bliss that surrounded Arthur. "Are we still on for dinner tonight?" "As far as I know" she nodded as she left the office and went back to her desk.

Dr. Reid continued to work on her backlog hoping that Bobby would get back to the precinct before her shift ended. She worked diligently and around lunchtime she paged him. She was walking up Second Ave when he returned her call. "Yes?" "You paged me?" "I did" "Well?" "How's it going?" "So far so good" "Did she like the things?" "Yes. That was a good call on your part." "Are we still on for dinner?" "I don't know I might have to work late. I'll let you know"

"Bobby I'm sorry. I lost my head. Can we talk about this?" "We can but not now. I'll get back to you." Bobby was gone. As Rosaland strolled along Second Ave she was so adrift in her thoughts that she neglected to realize that she was being followed. The car moved slowly behind her watching her every move. "We've found her boss. What do you want us to do?" "Nothing just stay with her." "She's headed back to the police station." "Wait outside and keep an eye on her. I should be landing this evening." Carlos had her in his sights. Now he had to figure out what he was going to do with her.

forty-three

Once on the ground Carlos paid a visit to State Chemical. State Chemical was a pharmaceutical company that he had a major investment in. Dr. Roget greeted him at the door having been alerted of his visit. "Mr. Calderon. What a pleasure to see you again sir." Dr. Roget escorted Carlos into the building and his private office. "If you don't mind me asking sir what can I do for you today?"

Carlos smiled sinisterly "How is that project coming along that I have invested so much money into?" Carlos asked without a smile on his face. Dr. Roget was starting to feel uneasy and said calmly "We have made some major break throughs sir." "And your research?" "Our research is inconclusive at this point." Carlos thought a moment and then continued.

"I need a mind altering substance. Something that will distort the perception maybe something with a strong sexual side effect." "Mr. Calderon I can't give you anything like that. It's too dangerous." "Do you have something like that?" "Yes we have been formulating a product that sounds like what you have described. It hasn't been tested yet and we don't have F.D.A. approval. I can't in good conscious give you something so inconclusive."

Carlos listened as the good doctor expounded on the reasons why he couldn't deliver. When he finished Carlos walked over and stuck his gun in his mouth. "You can and you will give me what I came for." Carlos pulled back on the trigger as he pushed the gun further down the throat of Dr. Roget. "You've got two more seconds"

Dr. Roget nodded as he opened the refrigerator in the lab and stepped inside with Carlos and the gun stuffed down his throat. Carlos removed the weapon so the doctor could find what he was looking for. Dr. Roget finally found a vile of a clear solution marked rd25. He handed it to Carlos who smiled gratefully and thanked him. "Please Mr. Calderon" Dr. Roget pleaded. "This drug is very unstable. It is still in its experimental form. To this point we don't know the true affects. It could prove to very lethal." Carlos allowed him to lock the refrigerator and then shot him twice in the head leaving him in a massive pool of blood. His brains splattered all across the wall. Carlos slipped out of State Chemical undetected as he preceded to his New York headquarters.

Carlos didn't have a plan he was just angry and when he became angry all hell broke loose. The one thing he knew for sure was that he was not going to allow her to marry this detective or anyone else for that matter. He had played Mr. Nice guy with her long enough. She never returned any of Antonio's calls or accepted any of his dinner invitations. It was obvious that he was going to have to show her who was in charge. Carlos always got what he wanted and why should she be any different.

She had spurned his attentions for a cop. A lousy cop! One whom she intended to marry. There would be no way he was ever going to allow this union to happen. Carlos was so consumed with jealousy that he couldn't see straight.

When Carlos entered the Club Oasis Arthur's pager went off. This was the call that he had been expecting all day. Bobby was finally finished to his satisfaction in Brooklyn and reported back to the station to check with his lt. "Detective that tip that I was waiting for came through. I need you and Rousseau to go undercover this evening."

Bobby didn't like the sound of partnering with Diana this evening not after yesterdays events but he listened carefully. "One of my sources had reported that our friend Carlos Calderon might be in the city tonight. He will probably hold up at the Club Oasis. I want the two of you on this because you have already been there and you know the layout. Just go observe and report directly back to me. Are you going to have a problem with this?" "No what are we looking for?" "Any suspicious activity." "Are you going to bring Dr. Reid in on this?" "Yes. After all the O.N.S.I. has reason to suspect narcotics trafficking. If he's there they can arrest him."

But if he is in the city then we need to know." "Have you contacted Detective Rousseau yet?" "Yes she is on her way." "I need to change. I can't go in looking like this; they would make me right away as a cop." "You're right. How long will it take you?" "Give me thirty minutes. Hold Rousseau here until I come back. We should go in together. This could get dangerous and I don't want her in there alone."

"Ok do what you have to do." "What about back-up?" "Your old friends from Brooklyn will back you up. They are new faces so they can move around unnoticed." Bobby didn't like this but this was his job and he had to do what he had to do. As he drove to Brooklyn he called Rosaland on her cell phone.

"Yes?" she answered, "Where are you?" "I have to work. Arthur will fill you in on the details. He's on his way to the restaurant." "Bobby what's going on?" "I want you to stay with Arthur and Rachael tonight. I will call you first thing in the morning. I love you." "I love you too. Please tell me what's going on?" "Arthur will fill you in. Just do what I ask." "Ok."

Rosaland was deeply disturbed by their conversation and she looked at Rachael for support. "Something is going down and I don't like it." "Arthur just called me. He wants us to wait here until he arrives. He sounded nervous. I don't like it either." The two sisters were on edge as they waited for Arthur in the restaurant. Carlos's men had followed her from work and were watching her and her sister from an adjacent table. "They look just alike. How can he tell which one is which?" "I don't know, but he's got it bad for her, real bad, this is going to get ugly."

"Rosaland we have reason to believe that Carlos Calderon will be in the city this evening." Arthur spoke calmly as he sat down at the table. Rosaland's eyes became big as he tried to fill her in on the details. "When did you find this out?" She asked curiously "Does the General know?" "I received a tip from an informant this morning; he confirmed it just a few minutes ago right before I got here."

"Is that what Bobby is working on this evening?" "Yes he is going under." Rosaland started to hyperventilate at the thought of Bobby undercover. "I've got to call my team; we need to go in with you."

"This is my call. I'm sending in two of my best. You can't jeopardize their positions and you definitely can't go in. You'll be spotted a mile away. He definitely knows who you are." "And he doesn't know who Bobby is? Bobby has been with me every time we have come up against him. He'll recognize him immediately. He'll kill him!"

"Rosaland calm down. This is Bobby's job and he is very good at it. You ought to know that by now. Look I'm taking the two of you home. Rosaland you should stay with Rachael tonight. I've got to get back to the precinct."

Arthur motioned for the check and escorted the ladies home. As they were driving towards Arthur's house Arthur noticed that they were being followed. He didn't want to alarm them, but he had to lose the tail. Arthur picked up his radio and called for a black and white to intercept. "This is Lt. Arthur Yancy and I've got unwanted eyes on me. My location is third ave at Fifty Ninth Street intercept and detain."

Arthur drove leisurely up Third ave waiting for the black and white to apprehend the suspects. As the two units swooped down and surrounded the vehicle Arthur sped safely home. Rachael and Rosaland were shaking like a leaf when Arthur escorted them into the apartment. "You're safe now. Stay here. I have to get back to the station." Arthur was gone in a flash.

"Dad, the .Y.P.D. has reason to believe that Carlos Calderon is in town." "What! How come I wasn't informed of this?" "I'm telling you now. What are we going to do?" "Where are you?" "I'm at Arthur's with Rachael." "I'm sending a car for the both of you. Get some things together." "We don't have any things to get together; we're at Arthur's apartment not Rachael's house." "I know where you are and I want the both of you here with me. I'm sending a car so be ready. Rosaland I told you that I was going to introduce you to your new team, seems like this is as good a time as any."

"You need to be here. I'll have them all here when you arrive. Where's Bobby?" "He's working undercover with Arthur." "Where's Arthur?" "He's at the precinct." "I'll try and make contact but in the meantime you girls be ready to move." "Ok Dad." "Rosaland I'm staying here with my husband."

"Rachael your husband is not here you're going with me." "No I'm not and you shouldn't be going either. Arthur told us to stay here and I'm going to wait until he comes back. You all might be making a mountain out of a molehill; nothing may even happen this evening. I'm going to stay here until he returns."

"Rachael this man is dangerous. He's very dangerous please just come with me. Besides I need to go Dad is calling the O.N.S.I. Special Forces together and I need to be there." "Well you go. That's your job but I'm staying here." There was no reasoning with Rachael when she was like this. She could be just as stubborn as Rosaland when she wanted to be. Rosaland called her Dad back and told him of Rachael's decision.

"Ok I'm sending a man to stay with her but you need to get here." "Ok Dad as soon as your men arrive I'm on my way." Thirty minutes later the General's men stormed the building. They safely escorted Rosaland to the car and the other two stood guard at the door.

The atmosphere at the Club Oasis was tense when Bobby and Diana entered. The walked in arm in arm pretending to be lovers and took a seat by the bar. Bobby looked really hot in his all black attire and it was hard for Diana to remember they were undercover. She wanted to talk to him so now seemed just as good a time as any.

Carlos was perched in his office and noticed their entrance immediately from behind the two way mirror. The God's were smiling on him; this couldn't be more perfect than if he had planned it himself. Diana sat close to the detective and rubbed her hands through his hair.

"Pay attention Diana we are probably being watched. Arthur doesn't want us to draw any unnecessary attention." "The boss wants us to be realistic and this is very realistic to me." Diana leaned over and planted a kiss on the detective's lips. "Just in case anyone is watching" she smiled as moved even closer to him.

She rubbed her hands along his muscular chest feeling his muscles through his shirt. Bobby relaxed and put his arms around her shoulders as he ran his fingers up and down her arms. Carlos observed their behavior from behind the mirror and noticed how intimate they appeared to be with each other. There was still some chemistry between them and it was starting to show. "Let's go mingle with the crowd put some feelers out and see what we catch."

Carlos eyed the couple as they moved to the dance floor. He wanted to see if they were going to make contact with anyone. He would use them to draw out the other under covers. Carlos watched as Bobby's hands roamed all over Diana's body as they danced. He was insulted that Rosaland would choose this womanizer over him but when the opportunity presented itself he would remedy that situation.

Carlos relaxed and snorted another line of cocaine never taking his eyes off his uninvited guests. As Bobby moved around the dance floor he noticed Wesley sitting at the edge of the bar and Justin was lounging by the jukebox. After making eye contact Wesley turned his back to the detective and pulled his hat down over his eyes.

Wes was really a smooth operator. Bobby liked his style. Justin was finding it hard to take his eyes off of Diana. She was very sensual this evening. Carlos talked to the bartender through his headset and instructed him to put the rd25 into their drinks when they finally ordered. He would use them as his experiment. The bartender nodded and continued serving the rest of the guest at the bar. Justin went into the men's room and Bobby walked Diana back to the ladies room and he entered the men's.

After checking to make sure that were alone they finally spoke. "What's going on here? What are we looking for?" Justin inquired "Anything. Check the bar watch the D.J. any thing we can put our fingers on." "What's going on with you and the pretty detective?" "Nothing strictly undercover. That's all in the past." "Are you sure about that?" Bobby did a double take when Justin questioned him that directly.

"If you are interested man go for it." "I'm interested and I just might do that." Justin replied. Bobby threw up his hands as he left the men's room; Justin came out a few minutes later. Diana was standing by the door when Bobby emerged. She placed her arm around his waist as they walked back into the club. This act between them was very authentic.

At that moment a very pretty girl with a head full of long black hair passed right in front of them. Bobby followed her with his eyes to her place at the bar. If he didn't know better he could swear that Rosaland was here.

He stretched his neck trying to make a positive id the lady feeling his stares turned her head in his direction and that's when he concluded that it wasn't her.

"Are you seeing ghost?" Diana made a sarcastic remark. "Don't you think we should order a drink? It would look suspicious if we didn't. Nobody comes to a club to not drink." "Yes. What would you like?" "Something light. Some white wine. After all I am on duty." They laughed and proceeded to the bar where Bobby ordered for the both of them.

The bartender followed his orders and placed a generous amount of the rd25 in both of their drinks undetected. Bobby carried the drinks as Diana led him back to their table. As they sipped their cocktails Diana commented "I see our back-up team is here. Have they noticed anything?" "No. It seems pretty routine." "How long do we have to stay?" "Maybe another hour or so if nothing happens" Diana nodded as they continued to drink ingesting an enormous amount of the rd25.

Bobby and Diana had been made. Carlos had informed his men of the presence of the officers so the rest of the evening went on pretty uneventful. At about 1:00 a.m. Bobby was ready to call it a night. His head was starting to feel a little funny. "Did it get hot in here all of a sudden or is it just me?" "You're always hot" Diana responded fondling his manhood under the table. Diana's fingers on his Johnson sent sparks surging through his torso.

"Don't start something you can't finish" he jokingly warned pushing her hands away. "Oh I can finish it" she said enticingly as she leaned over and placed her tongue in his mouth. Bobby responded to her attention as his hand lightly cupped her breasts. He could not believe that he was being so fresh with her. The drug was already starting to take effect.

"Let's get out of here" he whispered in her ear. As they started to leave Diana stumbled suddenly being overcome by the rd25. "Are you alright?" He asked her as he caught her in his arms, he himself suddenly becoming lightheaded. "Yes but it is awfully hot in here. I need some air."

Bobby noticed at that moment that he too needed some air. When they were outside Bobby noticed that Diana had broken out in a heavy perspiration. "Are you sure that you are alright?" "No Bobby I'm not. Something isn't right." "Here get in the car. I'll take you home." Bobby called Arthur at the precinct to check in and told him that he was going to take Diana home because she was not feeling well.

"Call me at home later. I need to check on Rosaland." "Rosaland is fine. She's with Rachael." Arthur assured him. As Bobby drove up First Ave he too began to perspire heavily. His driving became erratic as he darted in and out of traffic. At one point almost losing total control of his vehicle. He definitely knew that something was wrong. It seemed like it took forever before he was finally in front of Diana's building.

Diana appeared to be passed out on the front seat her head slumped over leaning on his chest. Bobby was being overcome by drowsiness so he opened the door to get some fresh air. The fresh air seemed to revive him temporarily as he pulled Diana from the vehicle.

"Diana you're home. Where is your key?" Diana fumbled around in her purse and produced her key. She placed it in his hand. Bobby grabbed her up in his arms and carried her to the door. "Can you stand up?" He mumbled "Yes" she answered in her semi conscious state as Bobby unlocked the door to her building.

Bobby stumbled and tried to shake it off as they made their way into the elevator. Diana pressed the button leading to her floor as Bobby desperately tugged at the buttons on his shirt trying to release the heat. By the time they had arrived at her door Bobby's shirt was in his hands and his muscular frame was covered with sweat.

The leather of his shoulder holster was sticking to his body as he continued to sweat profusely. Diana had regained her senses enough to pull Bobby into the apartment and slam the door behind them.

Bobby's pants were the next item of clothing to hit the ground. Diana stripped bare to the buff and ran into the bathroom to start a cold shower. Diana jumped under the cold water and stood in the shower gasping for air. She allowed the cold water to run down her body cooling her off.

After a few minutes she noticed that she didn't hear Bobby. She returned to the living room to find him passed out on the floor. She pulled his strong limp body across the floor and into the bathroom. "Bobby Bobby wake up!" She tried slapping his face frantically. She lifted him barely and stuffed him into the tub letting the cold water run freely down his limp body.

As she noticed his breathing returning to normal a relieved Diana sat down next to Bobby's limp body and placed her head on his chest as the cold water lowered their body temperatures. As Bobby's life force was returning he took comfort in the cool droplets from the shower that covered his muscular physique.

In his mind he imagined that he was in Jamaica under the mineral falls with the cool water splashing down his naked form. Bobby opened his eyes not really remembering exactly where he was or how he got there.

He wiped the water from his face with his hands and pushed his hair back from his eyes. Bobby's abrupt movements caused Diana to regain consciousness and she raised her head from his chest. "What happened?" Bobby asked incoherently "How did we get here?" "I'm not sure?" Diana answered just as perplexed as he was. Diana tried to stand up but her legs gave out and she fell back into the tub.

"Take it easy" Bobby said as he guided her with his arms. Once she was on her feet then he was able to stand. Diana stepped out of the tub and wrapped a towel around her wet body. When Bobby stepped out of the tub she handed him a towel and he wrapped it around his waist. Diana walked to her bedroom and Bobby groggily followed her.

Bobby fell back on the bed still not sure of what was going on. Diana balled up at the top of the bed feeling just as dazed and confused; both of the detectives heavily influenced by the rd25 in their systems. Bobby turned over on his stomach and looked for her "Diana come here" he ordered her in a gruff voice very uncharacteristic of him.

Diana scooted over to where he was on the bed and placed a kiss on his lips. Bobby unwrapped the towel from her body and placed his lips on her breasts sucking her delicate nipples. Diana responded to his touch. It had been two years since she had felt him and now she wanted him more than ever.

Bobby licked Diana's body in between her breasts kissing her seductively down to her navel and then inserted his tongue firmly between her thighs. Diana cried out "oh god!" as Bobby nibbled harshly at her tender love spot. Bobby ate her like she was a delicate sweet dessert; licking, nibbling and sucking her into total submission.

Diana moaned as Bobby applied pressure with his tongue to her erogenous zone. She writhed as she pumped her torso up to meet his mouth as he tasted her love juice. This was just the condition he wanted her in; as Bobby removed his mouth from her leaking opening he slid her body down to meet his as he entered her.

Diana screamed in ecstasy at the force of his entry as Bobby plunged deeply into her cave. Diana couldn't believe how good he was making her feel as he moved in and out of her hot body. Diana thrust back to meet his powerful strokes as Bobby rode her steadily. Diana opened her willing core as Bobby crammed his massive length deep into her unmindful of the stretching he was affording her.

"Ohh Bobby! Oh I've missed you! Ohhh Bobby!" she screamed as she bucked under him. Bobby smiled sexily as he planted himself deeper within her with each stroke; Bobby pummeled Diana's privacy pumping her wet orifice harder and harder. Diana sighed as he took her completely overpowered by his brute masculinity. Diana's lithe form quivered under his amorous administrations as she felt her orgasm approaching.

Bobby buried his length to the hilt in her body as his seed shot out. "Ohh Rosaland! Rosaland!" Bobby screamed loudly in ecstasy as he collapsed fatigued on top of her body. Diana froze in horror as the tears welled up in her eyes and ran down her face. The effects of the rd25 were becoming more overwhelming as they both feel into a deep coma like sleep.

Bobby's pager must have been going off for hours before it awoke him. As he arose sluggishly his head felt like a ton of bricks had hit him. He looked around to get his bearings and he didn't recognize his surroundings. The sound of the pager led him to the living room where he noticed his clothes were all over the floor in disarray.

Bobby sat on the couch holding his head in his hands and trying to remember how he got here. The odor of sex was on him and in the room and he definitely didn't like that. He was completely disoriented and sat there trying to put two and two together but the four he was coming up with wasn't what he wanted. Bobby hoped that he had been honorable but for some reason he knew that he hadn't.

Bobby walked back into the bedroom and noticed that Diana was sound asleep; he carefully scanned her naked body and placed the blanket over her. As Bobby dressed his pager went off again as he looked at the number he realized that it was Arthur. Anytime Arthur calls him at this time of morning it can't be good.

Bobby grabbed the phone to return the call expecting bad news but he was not prepared for what the news would be. "Yeah what's up boss?" Bobby said still feeling the effects of the drug in his system. "Detective where have you been? I've been paging you for hours. Bobby we've got another homicide."

"Arthur what time is it?" "Its 4:30a.m. Where are you?" "I'm on my way. Who's partnering?" "Danny is up we can't seem to locate Rousseau. She hasn't answered her pager." Bobby looked across the room and he knew that Diana would be out for hours. Bobby knew that whatever had happened between them was wrong but it was over now. How could he ever explain this?

"Bobby you might not want to take this call." "Why not?" "Its up in Harlem, 135 East Lennox Ave. Bobby who had been getting dressed while he talked to his boss was out of the apartment like lightening all he kept saying to himself was no! No! As he drove up Harlem River Drive impetuously. 135 East Lennox Ave was his second home when he wasn't in Brooklyn, he was in Harlem.

Rosaland lived at 135 East Lennox Ave. He had just buried his Grandmother. He couldn't even entertain the thought of burying Rosaland. A thousand questioned passed through his mind. Why hadn't he married her? He asked the General two years ago for her hand and tonight he had made love to another woman? Or at least he thought he did. What was he doing? Where was he heading? Bobby would answer these questions later. Right now he had to face the possibility of another murder of someone close to him; someone that he loved.

When he pulled in front of the brownstone the police already had the crime scene marked off. The traffic division wasn't letting anyone through. Bobby flashed his badge and was given the go ahead. As he parked his car he noticed Danny talking to a uniform officer whom he found out was the first officer on the scene.

The uniforms were still questioning the neighbors about what they might have seen or heard. There was a lifeless corpse that had been partially covered on the front steps leading up to the door. As Bobby got out of his car he remembered the first time he went up those steps. That was the first time that he made love to Rosaland and that was the first time that she had ever made love.

All these thoughts flashed through his head as he made his way over to where his partner was standing to find out what was going on.

The look on Bobby's face couldn't be disguised; he was visibly shaken and extremely anxious as he approached the corpse. "Bobby!" Danny called motioning for him. Bobby cautiously approached his partner still feeling the effects of the drug in his system.

"What do we have here?" Bobby asked taking a deep breath. "We have an African American female in her late twenties, early thirties…" as Bobby walked over he noticed the long thick black hair that was in disarray. The next thing that caught his attention was what appeared to be a black pearl ankle bracelet that was around the victims left ankle.

Bobby stumbled back against the building gasping for air. The sweat was running heavily down his face and over his brow. He was going to be sick. The tears immediately welled up in his eyes as he bent over and lost the entire contents of his stomach. It looked like the ankle bracelet he had given her a couple of weeks ago; the last time that they were together at the brownstone.

He had called her his "Black Pearl" when he placed the pearls around her delicate ankle, before entering her body again for the third time that night. "Bobby are you alright?" Danny had no idea of what was going on. He was totally in the dark about who lived at this address; he was waiting for the uniforms to deliver that information.

When the police found the D.O.A. there was no identification, no jewelry except the anklet, and her body had been stripped completely naked. Her throat had been slit. It was the same M.O. as the other unsolved murders starting with Joy. Forensics would have to match the fingerprints in order to identify the corpse.

They didn't know at this point if the victim lived here or if she was dumped here after the murder. "Danny" Bobby whispered pulling his partner to the side after he had regained his composure. "Rosaland lives here. This is Dr. Reid's house!"

"What! What did you say?" Danny looked at him questioningly. "Did I hear you right?" Danny was astonished. All it took was one look at Bobby's face for Danny to realize that he had heard him right. Danny looked at Bobby and placed his body in between the victim and his partner.

"Bobby leave. You need to leave right now. I'll handle this." "No I need to see her." "No you need to leave. This is going straight by the books." Danny motioned to the uniform officers "Get this detective out of here now!" He ordered. The two officers tried to remove the detective and Bobby struggled with them pushing them out of his way. The two of them finally overpowered him and held him back from the scene.

"Bobby get in your car and leave. I'll page you later. Just be available. Now get out of here!" Bobby tore away from the officers and kicked the door of their cruiser several times leaving it dented and the windshield smashed before he got in his own vehicle and sped away.

He told her to stay with Rachael tonight! What was she doing in Harlem? How come she just didn't do what he had asked her? As Bobby drove towards the George Washington Bridge he knew that he was going to be sick again so he pulled over. Once outside his vehicle he slumped over the hood of the car and cried.

forty-four

Once Bobby was gone Danny had a chance to get the situation back under control. After several minutes He looked at the D.O.A. If this was Dr. Reid he didn't want his partner to see her like this. He knew how much Bobby loved that woman. He can still remember the look on Bobby's face that day she walked into the precinct for the first time. He told Danny then that he loved her and in the last two years their bond had only grown stronger.

Danny pulled the sheet back and starred at the D.O.A.'s face. There wasn't anything recognizable about this corpse. He didn't know who this person used to be but he knew for sure that it wasn't Dr. Reid. He grabbed his cell phone and paged his partner. When Bobby didn't call back he called his phone and left a message for him to meet him back at the station.

Bobby was still standing in front of his car when a black and white pulled up behind him. "Sir is everything alright?" As the officer got closer he recognized the detective. "Detective Semione what are you doing here? They're looking for you all over the city. The Lou wants you back at the station."

When Bobby arrived at the station the morning shift was still on. He looked for Danny but he didn't see him anywhere around. "Has anybody heard from Detective Schmidt?" "Yes. He's still up in Harlem working on some case. A black hooker or something?" Bobby turned around to see who would say something that stupid.

"A what?" "Some hooker. They found her naked on Lennox Ave." Bobby lost his head and ran over to the detective. Before he knew it he had hit the detective in the face sending him flying across the desk. The detective jumped up "What the hell is the matter with you?" as he charged at Bobby. Bobby side stepped the attack and swung again landing another blow straight to the

Detectives head. The whole unit was in an uproar as the cops tried to separate the two struggling men.

Danny hearing the commotion came running in and jumped over the desk shouting "Bobby it's not her! It's not her!" Danny finally lodged his body in between the two battling giants and said softly "Bobby it's not her." Bobby held back and sank weakly into the chair as the tears rolled freely down his face.

forty-five

When Rosaland arrived in Washington the General was alarmed. He wanted to know how the N.Y.P.D. got wind of Carlos's visit to New York before the O.N.S.I. had the news. "Arthur has informants on the street and one of them came through for him. He felt that the tip had enough validity to a least check it out."

"Do we know what the results were?" "No not yet." "Who's working this?" "Bobby and his partner." "Detective Semione is on this?" "Yes" "So I guess we'll have to wait until he reports in" "Dad he'll be reporting to Arthur. Arthur will report to me."

"Sounds good to me as long as we get the word. In the meantime you need to meet your new O.N.S.I. team. These agents have been hand picked by me. I have personally checked them out so thoroughly that I can tell you the color underwear they are wearing on any given day. If we are ever going to catch this desperado we need people that he can't buy."

"Dad for the right price anybody can be bought, especially when your pockets go as deep as Carlos Calderon's pockets go." "Well let's just hope that these agents have a sense of loyalty and a higher moral calling." Rosaland couldn't believe how naïve her father sounded but they had work to do and they needed to get down to it.

Rosaland walked into her father's private study and poured herself a drink from his choice selection of liqueurs and paged Bobby. She knew that when he went undercover his pager would be on vibrate and sooner or later he would call her back. She called Rachael to make sure that everything was all right with her and she wanted to make sure that Bobby was told that she had gone to Washington.

"Well I haven't heard from Arthur since he left but I'm sure that everything is all right. I'm going to bed. I'm prosecuting an early case tomorrow but

I'll leave Arthur a note telling him to make sure that he tells Bobby where you are." "Ok sweetie good night." Just as Rosaland hung up the phone the General summoned her from the study. "Your team has arrived." Rosaland left the study to meet her agents.

As they assembled in the outer office Rosaland was surprised to see so many familiar faces. Sonia Blackwell was the first to be seated. Lt. Jones of course was there along with a dozen or so new agents. She felt comfortable with the General's selection of both Bill and Sonia. The rest she would have to check out as they went along.

"This is Dr. Rosaland Reid the head of the O.N.S.I. and as you all know she is my daughter. Dr. Reid doesn't head the O.N.S.I. because she's my daughter; she heads the O.N.S.I. because she is the best at what she does. She has already uncovered and neutralized one of Carlos Calderon's biggest drug distribution centers in Bolivia."

"We know for sure that this bust hurt his operation and our intelligence tells us that he has been scrambling to relocate the remnants of that endeavor. Don't be misinformed that was one of many installations that is owned by this man and his Cartel.

Carlos has his hands in everything legal and illegal. His empire has grown vastly since the death of his father and he is still continuing to expand." "Also we have reason to suspect Carlos for the massacre of the 140 Latin American ambassadors that recently occurred at the Waldport."

Sonia chimed in, "I have been investigating this incident for the General for the last two months. We have traced the weapons back to a known Calderon associate but as of yet we haven't been able to produce enough evidence to make it stick."

Rosaland looked at Sonia with surprise as she continued. "There have been rumors circulated that the Calderon Cartel is trying to muscle in on the economies of several Latin American countries and this was the way he dealt with the resistance."

"With the ambassadors out of the way that clears a path for his expansion into their countries increasing his influence and his power base." "The O.N.S.I. was infiltrated by Calderon for the Latin American assassinations. That's why we had to clean house and start over again. Some of our top agents sold us out and we are still trying to see how deep the whole goes and if we can patch it up."

Lt. Jones added "This is a dangerous assignment and a lot of good men and women lost their lives at that hotel. So you need to know before you sign on what you are up against. We are dealing with a psychopath with an enormous amount of money and power. He'll do anything to get what he wants and he'll remove anyone that stands in his way and that includes us."

While Bill was briefing the agents on the character of their nemesis the General was called out of the room. When he returned he held a fax in his hands "This information just came in. This is information that we have been gathering for about two years. Through our friends in forensics we have been able to trace the cocaine that has been found on several murder victims in New York."

Rosaland's head was spinning with the wealth of information that she was being fed. "There have been at least four unsolved murders in New York city over the past two years including a murder that occurred in Harlem earlier this evening. All the victims have been left naked their throats slit and the nostrils filled with cocaine."

"Finally we have been able to trace the quality of the cocaine to a known drug dealer that works exclusively for Carlos Calderon. So we know exactly where the drugs came from. It's up to the detectives who have been working on this case to put the two of them together. This is a major break."

"I'll be faxing this information to the N.Y.P.D. in the morning. When I can make sure it goes directly into the hands of my son in law who will forward it to my future son in law who has been instrumental in solving this case. So now we have two ways that we can hold him if they catch him in New York."

"Excuse me Dad. Did you say that there was a murder in Harlem this evening?" "Yes" "where in Harlem?" "Somewhere on Lennox ave." "And this victim fit the same profile as the other three?" "Yes as far as we know." Rosaland dropped the glass that she was holding in her hand and began to shake profusely.

Lt. Jones rushed over to comfort her as she sat nervous visibly shaken by this information. "Dad I live in Harlem on Lennox Ave." "I know but this has nothing to do with you. It was just another random murder."

Rosaland wanted so desperately to believe him but her instincts were telling her different. "Excuse me" she said as she left the room. Once she was out of the site of the rest of her agents she paged Bobby with the 911 code. She needed to hear from him. Where the hell was he? And how come he wasn't returning her calls? She didn't like this but if he was still under then there was nothing she could do except wait.

Rosaland composed herself and returned to the room "Find out about this" the General whispered to Sonia and then she left the room. "Are you all right?" The Lt. asked "Yes I'm fine. General I would like to relocate the O.N.SI. We have currently outgrown our facility and we need a new home."

The General knew that anytime either of his children addressed him by his title that they were serious. Rosaland continued "In light of the information that has been discussed here this evening I feel that it's time we made a move. In order to expand our operations to keep up with the amount of work that we will be doing we need more space."

"Also I would like to staff my office with O.N.S.I. personnel. I feel that it will create a safer environment. I would also like to assign a liaison to the N.Y.P.D. so that we can keep our eyes and ears open in that direction. Foster more inter agency cooperation."

"Do you have anyone in mind?" "No I'll leave that up to you. But I feel that it should be a key appointment." "The cost? What is all this going to cost us? Just two years ago we did a major renovation to the N.Y.P.D. not the mention the mainframe we installed in the basement. Sounds costly and I don't know if we have the money."

"Dad in the interest of national security we need our own facility. Too many people have access to us in our present location. We need to be less visible if we are to continue to be effective and we need to increase our capabilities to gather information."

"Work up the cost factor and I'll consider presenting it to Congress." "Thanks Dad." This conversation between Rosaland and her father enlightened the new members of the team to just how much power and influence she had with the General.

Even though no one said anything they all knew she would get her new facility and they knew that they would be honored to be a part of her team. Because of the lateness of the hour the General called the briefing to a close.

Rosaland decided to page Bobby one more time before she went to bed. And when he neglected to return her call she retired for the evening. The General knew his daughter all too well so the next morning at breakfast asked her point blank "What is the real reason you want to move the O.N.S.I. out of the precinct?" Rosaland responded just as directly. "Bobby. It's becoming very difficult for me to work that closely with him. It seems that all eyes are on us every time we report to work. Our personal relationship is starting to interfere with our professional relationship and in the end that can only be counter productive."

The General was extremely proud of the fact that her perspective was that clear. "We have several government buildings in that area; I'll put out some feelers and see what we can come up with. I'm still going to need that preliminary cost factor. You know how tight Congress can be with the money. "Yes Dad but I also know that if anybody can loosen their grip its you."

"Rosaland I need to talk to you about your O.N.S.I. status" "Ok. What about it?" "I need to upgrade it." "Upgrade it to what?" "Well last night after you went to bed I was thinking about the best scenario to implement this move."

"If I upgrade your status to a federal officer I can supply you with more sophisticated intelligence equipment and I can open more doors to other resources that might prove to be helpful." "And do I get a raise in pay Dad? You know this job has a high risk factor that I should be compensated for." They both laughed. "Dad I need to get back to work. Did you fax that information to Arthur? "Yes. I faxed it to him first thing this morning." "Have you heard from your detective?" "No Dad I haven't and that's not like him. I paged him several times last night but he never returned any of my calls."

"I'm a little worried; I'm going to check on him. Can I take your private plane back to the city?" "Yes as a matter of fact I'll go in with you. I'd like to see for myself what's going on. Are you about ready to go?" "Yes."

When Rosaland and her father arrived in Manhattan her first stop was home. She wanted to see just how close the murder in Harlem was to her location. She was shocked to find her front steps cordoned off and even more surprised to find that Arthur had placed uniformed officers on guard at her front door.

She looked at her Dad in disbelief as they identified themselves to the officers so that they could gain entry to her residence. Rosaland had an eerie feeling as they entered her house. The General reached inside the door to turn on the light. Once inside he drew his side arm. Rosaland noticing that her Dad was armed followed suit and drew her weapon from her thigh holster.

After they had both secured the premises to their mutual satisfaction she screamed. "Dad am I going to have to walk around armed in my own house? How could you not know this? I refuse to believe that this is coincidental. I asked you last night just how close this was to my house and you told me that it happened somewhere else. Well it didn't occur somewhere else Dad it happened right on my doorstep!!"

Rosaland was visibly shaken and terribly upset. She couldn't believe that this had transpired and where the hell was Bobby? Why hadn't he called her back? She was slowly becoming infuriated with the whole situation. While the General went into the kitchen to make a pot of coffee Rosaland went upstairs to change her clothes. She desperately needed to get to the precinct. She wanted some answers and she wanted them now.

"Rosaland I don't know how safe it is for you to stay here?" her father said cautiously "Why don't you get some things together and come stay in D.C. for a while?" "Dad I am not going to D.C. or anywhere else for that matter. This is my home and no one is going to drive me out of it."

"If you feel that it is not safe then post some guards or get some men or do whatever it is that you do but I am not leaving my own home because they found a dead body! Look Dad I really need to get to work."

"Ok let's go." Before they left for the precinct the General did make a call and he did post some guards. The ride to the station was uneasy for both Father and daughter but what really had Rosaland upset was the fact that she hadn't heard from Bobby and short of death she couldn't imagine what could have happened or where he could be that he wouldn't return her calls.

As she rode to work in silence she looked down at her finger and nervously began playing with her ring. When the General finished his call he looked sincerely at his daughter and spoke sternly.

"Rosaland I had no idea that this incident had hit us so close to home but you can bet some bodies' ass that I will find out how come I didn't know that a murder was committed on your doorstep. Since you are being so stubborn about your own safety I have posted guards and they will remain there until I am satisfied that they need to leave."

"Furthermore I understand that you are upset but that gives you no right at all to raise your voice to me and under no circumstance will I accept that behavior from any one of my children. I don't care how old you think you are you are still my daughter and I will not be disrespected."

Rosaland looked apologetically in her father's direction. "I'm sorry Dad." She was really sorry. I feel like I'm on a roller coaster ride and I'm scared. I'm really scared." The General leaned over and kissed his baby girl on her forehead. Rosaland put her arms around her Father's neck and squeezed him tight. "I really am sorry Dad." "I know." The General smiled tenderly.

forty-six

The atmosphere at the precinct was subdued as the rest of the staff was back to work as usual. There were no remnants of the excitement from the night before and strangely enough no one was talking. Dr. Reid reported to her desk and picked up where she had stopped the day before on the endless pile of paperwork still stacked high on her work area.

The General reported directly to Arthur and the two of them convened behind closed doors. As she worked Dr. Reid waited patiently for Detective Semione to report in and was surprised when he never arrived. Dr. Reid noticed how well the Lt. seemed to have adjusted to married life and how relaxed the relationship between Arthur and her father had become. She wondered to herself if her Father would ever be able to share that type of relationship with Bobby.

She had observed the strain between them lately and hoped that the fact that they were now formally engaged would bring the two men in her life closer. When the Lt. finally excused himself and entered the break area she too left her work and followed him.

"Lt. where's Detective Semione? Is he out on an assignment?" She looked hopefully at her brother in law and waited for him to answer. "Detective Semione called off for a couple of days. I assumed that he had spoken to you about it."

"No as a matter of fact I haven't heard from him. I have paged him several times and he hasn't returned any of my calls." "You haven't talked to him at all?" "No" "Then you don't know what happened here last night?" "No what happened?"

Dr. Reid was slowly but surely becoming alarmed. She tried to remain calm as she listened for the Lt.'s response. "Would you care for a cup of coffee?" "Yes thank you. Why are you stalling Arthur what happened?" As the lt. handed his sister in law her coffee he continued. "All hell broke lose last night or actually it was early this morning.

I paged Detective Semione for the Harlem call at about 5:00a.m. I tried to warn him before hand that he might not want to catch this case but before I could talk him out of it he was gone. When he got to Harlem, Danny was there doing the preliminary work up and Bobby obviously recognizing the address saw the D.O.A. and went to pieces."

"Danny had to ask the uniforms to escort him away from the crime scene. When he finally reported back to the station one of the detectives from the day shift made some off hand remark and Bobby started swinging. Danny had to break them up and send Bobby home. Before Bobby left he requested a couple of days off and of course I approved it. I know how I would feel if I had to answer a murder call at any address that had to do with my wife or anyone else that I loved."

Dr. Reid was horrified and at a lost for words. "What about the other detective? He is alright? Is he going to file charges?" "No Detective Schmidt explained to him what was going on and they agreed to let it drop." "What about you Arthur? Are you going to drop it?" "Bobby realized that he needs some time off. As far as I am concerned he is showing good judgment. I'm willing to let it drop."

"Did he say where he was going?" "No all he said was that he needed a couple of days to himself to get his head together that was good enough for me. Rosaland I have to get back to your father. We can finish this conversation later. Are you alright?"

"I've been better." before the Lt. left the break area Dr. Reid kissed him on the cheek. "Thanks Arthur." The Lt. smiled "That's what families do for each other. They look out. Keep your head up; I'm sure you'll hear from him soon. Oh by the way as soon as you get yourself together we need to have a meeting."

Arthur went back to his office with a nice cup of hot coffee for his father in law while Dr. Reid composed herself and prepared for the meeting. She entered the Lt.'s office and took the seat opposite of her father.

"Lt. did the undercover operation last night turn up any information on the whereabouts of Carlos Calderon?" Dr. Reid was direct and came right to the point.

"Unfortunately the detectives weren't able to come up with anything. According to their report there was nothing out of the ordinary that we were able to put our fingers on. Plus this information was supplied to me through one of my informants and sometimes they are not reliable, this seems to be one of those times."

"Do you think Carlos could have gotten wind of the fact that they might have company last night?" "Very easily we can't underestimate this man; he is connected to everything and everybody.

"Carlos could have been watching from the time the unit entered. We used a backup team from Brooklyn South, in the event that our officers were made, but they didn't come up with anything either. We drew a blank on this one."

"What time is Detective Semione due in?" The General interrupted. "I would love to hear his take on this to see what those keen instincts of his came up with." "The detective is out on personal leave for a couple of days but I will arrange a meeting as soon as he returns." The General was stunned to say the least but knowing Bobby and how passionate he was about Rosaland he wasn't at all surprised. "I know that this is department business and slightly off the record but who answered the Harlem call?" "Detective Semione and his partner Detective Schmidt caught the case." The General knew Bobby and he just wanted to make sure that he was right about him and he was.

"Well Arthur I won't take up any more of your time. Tell my daughter that she needs to keep in touch and the two of you should come to D.C. for the weekend." The General stood up and shook Arthur's hand. "Rosaland I need to speak to you in private before I leave." The General escorted his daughter to her office and closed the door behind them.

As Arthur watched the two of them engage in deep conversation he wished he could be a fly on the wall. He would love to know just what that conversation was all about.

forty-seven

It was about two o'clock in the afternoon the first time Bobby opened his eyes. He head was pounding as if he had been drinking all night. His body was soaked in sweat and his heart was racing furiously. As he headed for the bathroom he bent over the commode for what seemed like hours. The room was spinning around him and he felt like his body couldn't support his weight.

He sank slowly to the floor weak and dehydrated, regurgitating profusely gasping and wheezing for air. He mustered up the last bit of strength he had to try to make it back to the bed. As the room became engulfed in total darkness he blacked out at the foot of his bed.

As the Lt. checked his assignment roster he paid particular attention to the fact that both Semione and Rousseau were out. Semione had requested his time off after leaving the precinct in a shambles. No one had heard from Rousseau and this wasn't like her.

Arthur was beginning to get an uneasy feeling. There was too much work to be done and he had to get about the business of making sure that the work was completed. Arthur made a mental note to himself. After his shift was over he would go check on his both detectives. The day seemed to go by pretty much uneventful. Dr. Reid called Detective Semione still no answer. If he wanted some space she would let him have it. This would be hard for her because she really needed to talk to him. She desperately wanted to know what happened last night and she wanted to hear it from him.

She knew that he could shed some light on the whole Harlem situation but until she had a chance to talk to him all she could do was speculate. For some reason she had a bad feeling about last night. Something deep in her soul told her that all was not well but she had no evidence to back up her suspicions.

Arthur left the precinct headed for Brooklyn. When he arrived he noticed that detective Semione's Saab was parked outside the restaurant so a least he knew that he was home. Papa greeted him as he entered the restaurant. "Arthur it's nice to see you. What brings you here?" "I need to talk to Bobby is he around?" "Yes he's upstairs sleeping. He's been here all day. Is something wrong? Bobby never sleeps all day."

"No Papa everything is alright. He had the day off. I just need to speak to him. Do you mind if I go up?" "No go ahead. I'm sure he won't mind." Arthur climbed the steps that led to the second floor and called out for Bobby. When he didn't get an answer he walked over to the door of his bedroom and knocked lightly. "Bobby!" Arthur noticed that the detective's door was slightly ajar so he slowly pushed it open.

Arthur's eyes adjusted to the darkness in the room as he looked around to locate his detective. Bobby was nowhere in sight. Arthur walked over to flip on the light and that's when he discovered Bobby still unconscious at the foot of the bed his naked body covered in sweat.

Arthur ran over and immediately began to check his pulse which was faint but steady. Arthur went into the bathroom and wet a face cloth and placed it on Bobby's forehead trying desperately to revive him. Arthur gently slapped the detective in his face calling out his name. "Bobby! Bobby! Are you still with me?"

Arthur continued to try and arouse the detective changing the compress that he had applied to his head frequently. Soon Arthur heard Bobby start to moan as he gradually regained his consciousness. "Ooh my head!" Bobby groaned faintly as Arthur continued his efforts to revive him.

"Can you sit up?" Arthur was concerned. Bobby sat up slowly holding his head in his hands trying to get a feel of his surroundings. Arthur handed him another compress and Bobby applied it directly to his splitting head. "Where's Diana?" he asked in a raspy voice noticing how dry his throat was. He reached for the glass of water that Arthur had in his hand. "Where's Rousseau? She might be in trouble. We need to check on her."

"Bobby what happened?" Arthur asked seriously. "I don't know but I believe we were drugged. I think the bartender put something in our drinks." Bobby's body was starting to convulse. "Rousseau didn't report to work today and she didn't call in. That's not like her." "She's probably out of it just like I was or would still be if you hadn't stopped by. Why did you stop by anyway?" "I wanted to talk to you and I find you like this." "We need to go!" Bobby said as he dressed quickly.

The two detectives rushed uptown to Rousseau's building. They rang all the bells until someone buzzed them in. They ran up the steps to the fifth floor where Diana lived. Bobby knocked on the door and when he got no answer he forcibly kicked the door down to gain entry.

They found Diana spread out on the bed unconscious. Bobby placed his fingers to her neck to feel for her pulse. Her pulse just like his had been faint but steady. "We need to get her to the hospital." Bobby wrapped Diana in a blanket. He and Arthur rushed the drugged detective to Sinai emergency. Her body too starting to go into convulsions.

Once they had her admitted Arthur ordered Bobby to be admitted as well. "Both of these detectives need treatment!" he told the emergency room staff as he flashed his badge. Both Bobby and a still unconscious Diana were taken in for testing.

Arthur sat patiently in the waiting room for hours while the doctors at Sinai worked on his detectives. He called Rachael but he knew that if he told her anything about Bobby, Rachael would call Rosaland. This was department business and he would keep it under wraps.

"Hi Baby" he said when he heard Rachael's sweet voice on the other end of the phone. "I have to work late tonight and I don't know how long I'll be." "Is everything alright Arthur?" "Yes everything is fine. I just have to look out for two of my detectives. I'll call you later." Arthur hung up the phone and went to find the doctors that were with his team.

"What's going on here? What's the problem with my detectives?" Arthur demanded. "Well we have detected a foreign substance in their blood. We are running a toxicology screen right now but we won't have the results for a while." The emergency room doctor replied.

"Detective Rousseau has she regained consciousness?" "Yes she is barely conscious. We have her on a respirator to regulate her breathing. As soon as we know what's in her system and its effects we can treat her. She is still with us." That was a relief; at least Arthur knew they were receiving the best possible treatment under the circumstances.

Bobby was right. They had been drugged. That confirmed the fact that Carlos knew they were at his club. That was enough evidence for Arthur to get a warrant and search the club. Actually that was enough to close him down pending investigation. While he was waiting for the report on his staff he put in a call to the circuit judge to explain the circumstances and request a warrant.

The Judge listened attentively and the warrant was granted; they could pick it up first thing in the morning. Arthur wanted to make sure that Bobby was in tip top condition before he assigned him the job of shutting down the Club Oasis.

Bobby was the first to emerge from behind the doors. He found Arthur waiting reading the newspaper. Bobby walked over and took a seat next to his boss, still slightly shaken by this series of events. "Arthur how's Diana?" "We don't know yet. How are you?" "I'll live. Where's the doctor?" The toxicologist was walking toward them just as Bobby asked for him. "Detective?" "Yes" "The results of your drug screen just came back. Both you and the other detective had a large amount of an experimental drug in your system. It's something that we are not familiar with and from the signature it has no F.D.A. approval."

"This drug is new to us and we still need some time to analyze the contents of the construction. We know that it is a hallucinogen but that's all we know so far." "So am I going to be seeing things or hearing things?" "No we were able to flush it out of your system and all your vital signs have checked out positive so you'll be alright. Like I said we still need more time before we will completely know what it is. We know it's in the experimental stage because we can't find it in any of the current P.D.R's."

"The best prescription is to drink three glasses of milk a day for about a week. If there are any traces of the substance left in your system, the milk will neutralize it. Flush it out. We have still to determine its properties." "What about my partner?" "She seems to have ingested a slightly larger dose than you but the same goes for her. She'll be out in a minute. She needs some rest and I would suggest that you get some rest as well." "Thanks Doctor." Bobby stood up and shook the doctor's hand.

"Bobby I'm going to keep this information in house. I think that would be the best thing for everyone involved but as soon as you are ready we have received a warrant to shut the Club Oasis down pending investigation. This is your case and it's your call. I can assign it to someone else or you can take a day or two to rest up and take the club apart it's up to you."

"It would be my pleasure" Bobby said in a revengeful tone. "Arthur who was the girl in Harlem?" "A grad student from N.Y.U. I don't remember her name." "Is she still in the morgue?" "Yes for now." "Can you hold the body there for a couple of days?" "I can try why?" "I need to see her." "I'm sure her family will want to move her. I can probably only hold her body for another day or so." "That's enough time; I'll go see the body tomorrow." "Are you sure you are up to this?" Bobby nodded his head in the affirmative.

"Arthur when I arrived in Harlem early this morning I lost it. All I could think about was Rosaland lying in the street dead like she was nothing. I couldn't let her down like that; I couldn't let her Father down like that. I promised him that I would protect her. He is already upset with how intimate our relationship is. I know it and she knows it." Bobby continued. "We have violated his sacred rule. I'm probably lucky to still be alive. We have been like this from day one but Arthur I love that girl. She is my life. I don't want to know what it would be to be without her."

Bobby paused overcome with emotion. "For a moment in Harlem that life came to an end. Our love came to an end and I wasn't ready to give that up and I definitely wasn't able to face it." Arthur put his hand on Bobby's shoulder to console him, "I feel you. I know, I know. You need to call her. I would keep this episode under wraps."

Diana was wheeled out of the back at that very moment. She was drowsy and lethargic and barely covered in the hospital garments she was still wearing. Her body was listless and she was hot. The doctor who wheeled her over to join her team assured Arthur that she was fine. Her system had been flushed clean of the drug and she needed some rest.

"We'll take her home." Bobby stooped down and rubbed her face "Hey are you alright?" Diana nodded and whispered "Thank you Bobby." Bobby kissed her on the top of her head as they left the hospital with her. Diana slept all the way back to her apartment.

"Arthur can you get someone to come and stay with her? I really don't want to leave her like this?" Bobby was genuinely concerned. "Who can I call?" "Call Easley they have a good relationship. She needs somebody to be here with her until she sleeps this thing off."

"While I call Easley you need to do something about her door. We can't leave it open like this." "Bobby went down and banged on the super's door. When he opened the door Bobby flashed his badge and told him to bring his repair kit. "N.Y.P.D. We have an emergency in apartment 505 and we need some help." "That pretty detective lady lives there. What can I do?" The super said nervously.

"Bring your kit and some tools she needs her door repaired." The super cooperated fully and replaced the lock and the hinges before the night was over. "Bobby you need to go home. I don't want you here when Easley arrives. I'll wait with Diana." Bobby left the building and hailed a taxi back to Brooklyn.

When Arthur arrived home he was happy to see that his lovely wife had waited up for him. "Hey beautiful" he smiled lovingly as he placed a tender kiss on Rachael's lips. Rachael responded amorously and wrapped her arms around her husband's neck pressing her body close to his. "Umm" he said as their lips parted. "Did you miss me today?" "Rachael looked at him sexily and responded "I miss you everyday. All the time".

Arthur grabbed his wife and pulled her closer "Show me" he whispered softly as Rachael led him towards the bedroom. "We have a guest" she said as she pointed to the guest bedroom. "Dad wants Rosaland to stay here until he feels it's safe for her to return to the brownstone." "How does she feel about that?" "Not too good and she hasn't heard from Bobby so she doesn't know what to do. Believe me she would be somewhere with him right now if she knew where he was."

"Bobby's alright. Now where were we?" "We were just about to go to bed" "Let's go" Arthur said enticingly as he picked Rachael up and carried her to their bedroom. Rosaland was awakened sometimes during the night by the sweet sounds of lovemaking that filled the apartment.

forty-eight

Arthur was the first to arrive at work the next morning. He wanted to make sure that his warrants were issued and that he had adequate time for Detectives Semione and Schmidt to put their case together. "Bobby are you up to this?" Arthur was particularly interested in the detective's state of mind. The first matter that Detective Semione needed to attend to was visiting the morgue to view the body. The lt. handed him all the D.O.A's information.

Her name was Jennifer Walker; she was a twenty-seven year old graduate student from Fordham University who lived about two blocks from where her body was found. As Bobby reviewed the file he was alerted to the fact that he had seen this girl somewhere before.

"What time is Danny expected in?" Bobby asked. "I'm here" Danny replied as he came through the door "What's up?" "We need to go to the morgue and check out the D.O.A." "As soon as you two finish I need you back here? We have our warrant and we have the right to shut the Club Oasis down!" Arthur interjected into their conversation.

"I want to have a strategic planning session so that we make sure that this bust goes off without any problems." "O.k. we're on the move." Detective Semione passed Dr. Reid on the steps as he and detective Schmidt headed out of the station; "I'll be back ion an hour" he called to her as he and his partner hit the streets.

Dr. Reid noticed all the hustle and bustle around the Lt.'s office as she entered her own office. She watched with a great deal of curiosity as the Lt. rallied his forces preparing for the bust. "What's going on?" She asked as the Lt. brushed by her in a hurry.

"Dr. Reid this has something to do with you so you need to stay available. We will be having a meeting in about a hour and I'll bring you up to speed then. You might want to call your Father." Dr. Reid couldn't figure heads or tails of what was going on. She would definitely call her father but not until she had more clarity on the issues at hand.

All she knew was whatever was going on had to be big otherwise why would the Lt. need to go upstairs and consult with his captain? Everything was in an uproar. All around her uniforms and detectives were scurrying about and nobody knew why.

The forensics pathologist met the detectives in the morgue when they arrived. His report was conclusive as to the cause of death. Jennifer just like the others had her throat cut from ear to ear and her system was full of a controlled substance appearing to be cocaine. But the pathologist was able to go one step further. Arthur had supplied him with a sample of the high grade cocaine that had been gathered from the other victims. The cocaine traces found in her body matched the samples from the other victims. The connection had been made.

They finally found the common denominator; the drug could be traced back to the one dealer that worked for Carlos Calderon. Detective Semione would now be able to tie all the murders together. But there was something else as Bobby starred at the body; it hit him where he had seen her before. She had been in the Club Oasis the night she was murdered. He remembered her because of her close resemblance to Rosaland.

She had walked right by him headed towards the bar. He was sure that this was the same girl. No better still he was absolutely positive that this was the same girl. "Danny this girl was in the Club Oasis the night she was murdered. She walked right by me. I remember her because of her resemblance to Rosaland."

"That night in the club for a moment I thought she was Rosaland until she turned around and looked me directly in the face. But she was definitely there."

"Bobby are you sure? You were pretty shaken up that night?" "Yes after I left the club not before. This is the same girl I saw. We can place her whereabouts at the Club Oasis before she died."

"Well we've got our connection. This is definitely enough to take to the D.A. we've got a strong case here and plenty of supporting evidence." "We've got him; we've finally nailed that son of a bitch!" "Well let's not get ahead of ourselves. We have enough to shut him down but we can't touch him on these murders."

"No but we can arrest the dealer and with enough pressure maybe he will give him up. You know there is no honor among thieves, murderers or drug dealers." The forensics pathologist had another surprise for the detectives. "Your boy got sloppy. We found semen in the vaginal area and from this we can obtain the D.N.A. of her rapist." "When will you have that information?" "We're working on it now; all we need is someone to compare it to."

"That sounds like where we come in. We'll get back to you." The two detectives had about twenty minutes to get back to the precinct before the Lt. started his planning session for the demise of Club Oasis. Once Bobby could connect the death of Jennifer Walker to the night club they could shut it down permanently pending the outcome of the investigation.

This information would sound like music to Arthur's ears. The precinct had been tracking these murders for approximately two years and now they finally had a break. It is rare that a murder case that is older than two months gets solved especially without the help of an informant or someone on the streets. The detectives had a good handle on this one all the results of hard knocks and even harder work.

When the detectives arrived back at the precinct Bobby burst into the Lt.'s office "Boss got a minute?" Arthur was on the phone and signaled for the detectives to wait. As soon as he hung up Bobby told him what they had discovered "This time the rapist got sloppy. He left semen. Now we have D.N.A. all we need is a match."

The Lt. was elated at this breakthrough and congratulated the detectives on a job well done. "It's a little too early to celebrate. We still need to arrest the dealer and hope that he will give him up. That is if it's not him. We could already have our man." "That's closer than we have been for years. Let's go with it."

"Now we have other business to conduct. We need to close this club down." "Who's our back-up?" Detective Schmidt asked "We will be using the swat team, the narcotics division and O.N.S.I Special Forces. Both of you have worked with them before on various operations. I understand that Lt. Jones is highly effective." "Yes he's a good man and he's a good man to work with. I like him."

"I have to make a personal request. We're not taking Dr. Reid on this bust. She stays out. Not this time. This is too dangerous." "Well I think you had better talk to her because I know for a fact that she plans on going in." "She's not going in! Not this time." Bobby was adamant.

At that point Dr. Reid casually strolled into the Lt.'s office. In her eyes it was obvious that she was very happy to see Detective Semione. "Who's not going in?" She asked overhearing the end of their conversation. Bobby turned around to face her marveling at how beautiful she looked this morning. "You are not going in. This is going to be dangerous and you are going to sit this one out." He remarked starring at her point blankly.

"No I'm not. This is my job. If this has anything to do with Carlos Calderon then I'm in. I'm going with you." Rosaland defended her position.

Detective Semione grabbed her by the arm and stormed out of the Lt.'s office. He jerked her into her office and slammed the door behind them. "For once could you just do what I ask you?" He screamed. "What is wrong with you? Don't you know when someone is trying to help you? You don't need to be in this mess."

"The O.N.S.I. will get Carlos if we apprehend him. But you don't need to be in the middle of a gun fight. Can't you get that through that pretty head of yours? As smart as you are you can't understand this?" Bobby threw up his hands in frustration as Rosaland listened in disbelief at the outrage in his voice.

"Please just one time listen to what I'm telling you. I don't want to go through again what I went through three nights ago thinking that you were dead or better yet watching you die." Bobby grabbed Rosaland and held her tightly. She could feel his heart beating rapidly as he planted a long deep kiss on her lips. "Please not this time." He said softly as their lips parted. Rosaland was at a complete lost for words as she sank slowly into her chair as he rushed out of her office. Dr. Reid sat in her chair starring out of the window trying to get a handle on the moment.

It was definitely time for the O.N.S.I. to relocate. They were much too personally involved and their personal involvement was affecting both of their jobs.

It took a while for Dr. Reid to recover from the detective's shocking display of emotion but she had to compose herself. She appeared again in the Lt.'s office.

"Detective Semione I appreciate your concern but the O.N.S.I. has jurisdiction over this or any other operation that involves Carlos Calderon. I am just as qualified as any detective in this unit. I have had the appropriate training and I am going on this bust."

` "Please don't make me pull rank. It would be in bad taste especially due to the relationship that our agencies have worked so hard to cultivate over the years. We all want the same thing here. We want Carlos, so I would suggest that we continue to work together on this."

"Dr. Reid" Arthur interrupted "We have no intention of moving in on the O.N.S.I. but our detectives have uncovered some crucial evidence that ties Mr. Calderon to a series of unsolved murders that have happened in this city over the past two years. So in terms of jurisdiction that does make him ours, and we know that the families of these victims would like some closure as to what happened to their loved ones."

"Lt. you don't have a problem with me on that. As we all know these murders are hitting close to home. The O.N.S.I. would like to help in any way we can but if I am forced I can file a federal injunction right now that would stop this whole scenario and put it directly in the hands of the O.N.S.I.

"But I have no intention of doing that and violating a perfectly good working relationship as well as a professional trust. All I want is to be included. I have dedicated two years of my life chasing this man. How can you ask me to give up now that we are so close?"

"I'm not asking you to give up" Detective Semione interjected "I'm just asking that you stay out of the line of fire. You can stay in the van or here in your office. We can patch in a satellite link so that you can observe. You have all this high technology surveillance equipment; for God's sake use it."

"You are a communications analyst and you don't need to be there. I know that this is going to get ugly and I'm going to have enough to worry about. I don't want to have to worry about you as well. If you are there, there is no way that I won't worry. I don't need that kind of distraction. Rosaland I am asking you please try to understand. I don't want you there."

"Lt. Jones is a good man. He will do the dirty work for the O.N.S.I." Detective semione was remembering the conversation that he had with the general some months ago. The General said that she would never give up or quit and now Bobby knew exactly what he meant.

"Have the two of you worked this out yet? Because we need to move on. Time is of the essence." The Lt. waited for Detective Semione and Dr. Reid to come to some sort of an agreement or some sort of a truce. "Yes" Dr. Reid conceded "I won't go in but I do want to be there. Will that work?" "Yes that's fine. You can coordinate the surveillance from the Intel van and I promise to keep you in the loop." Dr. Reid nodded her head in agreement.

"Dr. Reid we need you to set up the Intel link with COM STAT and we need your O.N.S.I. Special Forces to secure the outer perimeters with c-4 and any other non detectable explosive that we know you can get your hands on. We need them to go in the night before and have everything in place before SWAT arrives."

I want you to monitor any unexpected movements from the club; we need documentation on all the comings and goings of the employees, delivery men prostitutes, dealers and the cleaning crew or anyone else that is seen in the vicinity of The Club Oasis."

"I want names, faces, social security numbers and plates on anything that moves. Also I would like for you personally to coordinate the communications from D.C to the N.Y.P.D. during the actual event. Make sure that O.N.S.I. forces have been carefully screened. Partner your people with my people so that we have two or three man teams at every entrance or exit of the building."

"Ok you got it." "Detectives I need you to go through that club with a fine tuned comb and gather enough evidence to prove drug dealing, illegal gambling, prostitution, money laundering, anything. Gentlemen so before you start busting up the place make sure that we have what we need to substantiate our case. We need evidence; we need arrests, if everybody is dead then we have no witnesses."

"No witnesses, no testimony. We want this bust to stick and we want to capture Mr. Calderon and company. Is that understood? You can use whatever force you deem necessary but try to remember the objective and that objective is to catch Carlos Calderon shut him down and put him away. Dr. Reid you can jump in here at any time."

"As the Lt. has stated we have been conducting a joint operation on the whereabouts and the nefarious dealings of Carlos Calderon for years. Every time we have even come close to apprehending him, just when we think we have him pinned down, he eludes us and he always strikes back. He takes great pride in striking back."

"If we don't stop him he will hit us and he will hit us hard especially if this attempt fails. He never leaves any identifying marks, any signature or calling card but we always know that it was he and he never tries to hide that fact."

As the detectives of the N.Y.P.D and the agents of the O.N.S.I. coordinated their efforts they had no idea of how extensive this operation would be. Little did they know that Carlos ran his entire east coast drug operation from this nightclub? They had no idea to the wealth of information that they would uncover as well as another processing and distribution plant hidden deep within its bowels. Dr. Reid, Lt. Yancy, Detective Semione and the rest of their dedicated detectives and agents worked deep into the night outlining their plan of attack.

The General made arrangements to have Lt. Jones flown in from Washington first thing in the morning to supply technical support and tactical military strategies to conduct an assault of this nature. As always the General was worried about his daughter's safety but she assured him that she would not be involved in the action.

"No Dad not this time. All the action that I will be seeing will be from right here either in front of my computer or via the dedicated satellite link." "This was your idea?" "No actually my fiancée insisted." "Good man so we will see you in the morning." "We?" "Absolutely you know that I will be there but only in an advisory capacity. It's the Lt.'s job to handle the details of this operation." "No Dad it's my job to handle the details of this operation." Rosaland reminded him.

Dr. Reid smiled uneasily as she hung up the phone. For some odd reason she didn't have a good feeling about this. Her instincts led her to believe that her father knew something that he wasn't sharing with her and her first thoughts was to see if by some miracle or some act of God she could elicit the missing information from someone close to the general. Someone who might know exactly what he was hiding.

Nevertheless she continued to work on her satellite link up and the other surveillance equipment to make sure that everything would be in order. All of a sudden an idea hit her. She would call Sonia Blackwell. She didn't know how willing Sonia would be to talk to her but she did know that if anybody would know Sonia certainly would be that body.

forty-nine

Rosaland decided to put in a call to the infamous Ms. Blackwell and arrange for a meeting. "Sonia this is Dr. Reid from O.N.S.I." "Hi I was wondering when you would call." "So you were expecting me to call?" "With all the activity that's going on in New York right now yes and I expected you to call sooner a lot sooner. What can I do for you?" "Do you have some time when can we meet? I really need some answers."

"I'll be in town tomorrow. I will be traveling with your father. I'm sure that we can break away at some point. Do you have a place in mind?" "Yes I know the perfect place. Tomorrow just follow my lead and I will make the necessary arrangements."

"Sounds good to me I'll see you then." Rosaland knew that she would have to carefully devise a plan to meet Sonia alone. She would never be able to fool her father about her intentions so she was going to have to create a diversion. Also she was changing her mind about her participation in this bust; she had no intentions of being stuck behind her computer or in front of the satellite when the deal went down.

She wanted to be part of the action after all this was her case. She had been instrumental in all the developments that the N.Y.P.D. had so far so why should she be left out? Rosaland had no intentions whatsoever of hearing about this second hand; she was going to be there. She just had to figure out how and in what capacity.

Also Rosaland knew that Bobby would not support her on this one. He had already made his position quite clear. Not only to her but to the rest of the force as well. So she would need to find another ally. Someone that would help her execute her plan. She calmly walked into the Lt's office.

"Arthur do you have a minute? You need to see the surveillance layout and how it hooks into the satellite." Both Arthur and Bobby followed her back to her office where she demonstrated the satellite hookup and explained the layout. "Now the only other information that I need is the weapons check and their capabilities so that I can tie that in to my computer. That will help us to formulate the accuracy of our position."

"It will also help me to calculate our strengths and weaknesses in the event that something goes wrong I can create a contingency plan." The Lt. and the detective were both very impressed with the strategic situation that she had compiled.

Arthur was the first to speak. "I can give you the weapons information tomorrow after we meet with Lt. Jones and the rest of your O.N.S.I. team. They will be arriving first thing in the morning right?" "Yes" "I would like you to attend that meeting." "Oh I had no idea that I wouldn't be attending?" she responded flippantly "Of course I'll be there it's my team. And now that we are on the subject a simulation exercise might prove to be instrumental."

"It would provide a computer generated situation in which we can examine response time and weapons accuracy; also it will create a series of events that could possibly occur that we might not have anticipated. After the simulation we will know what works and what needs to be improved. We don't want to send our boys in holding only their Johnson's in their hands."

"I agree. When can you set up the exercise?" "After I meet with the insurgent team tomorrow and get some background information on the teams specialties, you know their areas of areas of expertise. That how we will know who can do what. Who is better at what? I can feed all this information into the computer and it will generate the best possible solutions. We can schedule the exercise after that."

Bobby listened attentively and marveled at the conclusions that she had come up with. He would never have thought to test the outcomes of this situation in such a manner. He smiled approvingly as she concluded her presentation. Bobby was relieved that she had taken her mind off of being a part of the action and focused on what she was the expert at and she was indeed the expert. She was very good at what she did.

"Well if there are no more questions gentlemen I'm going to have to call it a night I'm very tired." "Let me take you home" the detective volunteered "Bobby I need you a little longer there are a few more details we need to work out." The lt. responded. "I'll be alright."Dr. Reid insisted "No I'll get a uniform to drive you home it's very late and I need Detective Semione for a while longer."

"Excuse me Lt. let me speak to Dr. Reid in private for a moment." Bobby escorted Rosaland out of Arthur's office into the break room so they could talk privately. "Hey why don't you stay in Brooklyn tonight with Papa? Just until I finish up here then I'll take you home. It would make me feel much better than you going to Harlem so late." Bobby was still slightly shaken up by the murder of the co-ed.

"Thanks Baby but I'm exhausted. I want to take a nice hot bath and go to bed. I drove to work this morning so if you can walk me to my car I can get myself home." "O.k. but call me when you get in just so I will know that you are safe. Can you do that for me?" "Yes" "Will you do that for me?" "Yes" "Are you still mad at me?" "A little bit but we can talk about that later."

Bobby pulled her to him and held her tightly in his arms. Rosaland reached up and wrapped her arms around his neck as their lips met. She kissed him passionately leaving him breathless and wishing for more. "Baby I'm very tired. Please walk me to my car." Bobby made sure that she was safely inside her vehicle as he watched her head toward Harlem.

As Bobby was driving up Harlem River Drive he called Rosaland. She had paged him when she arrived home but he and Arthur was so caught up in completing their work that he hadn't had the time to return her call. The phone rang four times before she finally answered.

"Hey" he whispered when her heard her sleep filled voice over the phone. "Hey yourself" she whispered softly "Were you sleeping?" "Yes" "What are you wearing?" Bobby questioned her sexily; Rosaland smiled and responded "One of your shirts" "My shirt?" "Umm hum I wanted to be in your arms when I went to sleep." Bobby smiled as he headed towards the brownstone. She knew exactly what button to push when it came to him.

"Hold on Baby I've got a call coming in" Rosaland tried to hold on but before long she had drifted back to sleep with the phone in her hand. When Bobby returned to the line all he could hear was her faint breathing "Rosaland Baby are you there?" But this time he got no response "Baby?" She was sound asleep. Bobby hung up and continued enroute to Harlem. When he arrived he let himself in and followed the sound of the phone to her bedroom where he found her lost in sleep.

He removed the phone from her hand and placed it back on the receiver. At that moment she moved nestling her head deeper into her pillow. Bobby removed his jacket and his shirt and placed them on the chair beside the bed. He put his weapon along with his badge on the nightstand and then he leaned over to remove his shoes. Bobby sat at the head of the bed playing in her hair.

This was the first time that he actually watched her sleep. He carefully observed the angelic look on her face as she lay lost in her dreams. It was at that point that Bobby knew deep in his heart that he wanted her in a different way. Even though he had proposed to her several weeks ago it finally hit him how much he wanted her to be his wife. He couldn't believe that it had taken him so long to realize in his heart that the next time he made love to her he wanted to make love to his wife.

Bobby knew that he couldn't trust himself with her; he knew that her slightest touch could turn him to butter. He craved her sweet chocolate body and her moist warm honey pot so instead of climbing into bed and ravishing her he put her head on his lap and fell asleep holding her in that position rubbing his fingers through her hair.

fifty

When Rosaland awoke the next morning she could tell that Bobby had been there but he was no where to be found. After she finished her shower as she was getting dressed she noticed the small black box that was on the night table. "This is for your protection. Wear it with my love in mind" the note said.

She immediately recognized the handwriting and opened the box to discover that it contained a lovely silver cross embedded with diamonds. She smiled as she placed the cross on her neck. Rosaland loved all the gifts that Bobby was constantly showering her with. They all seemed to have their own special meaning and this cross was precious. It symbolized his commitment to their love.

Bobby knew what receiving a cross would mean to her and it was his pleasure to be the giver. Rosaland was so busy admiring the cross-that she had completely lost track of the time. She had to hurry and finish dressing so that she wouldn't be late for the meeting. She wanted to talk to Lt. Jones alone before they started; she had decided that she would confide in him in the hopes that he would help her with her plan.

Rosaland knew that Bobby didn't want her to be involved physically with this operation but for some reason she had too. She only hoped that Bill would understand her reasoning even if she didn't quite understand it herself. Also she would have the opportunity to talk to Sonia Blackwell this morning to find out what Sonia knew about this situation that she didn't. Her instincts told her that Sonia knew a lot more than what she was telling a whole lot more.

When Dr. Reid arrived at her office all the players were starting to fall into place. Just as she expected Lt. Jones was the first to arrive. She could set her clock by Bill; he was just that attentive especially when it came to her.

Detective Semione watched with a great deal of curiosity from the Lt.'s office as Dr. Reid seated Lt. Jones.

"I wonder what that is all about?" the detective commented to his Lt. "Probably some O.N.S.I. business you know how secretive they can be. The General has undoubtedly sent some last minute orders or change of plans. I'm sure they will bring us up to speed." Even though the detective was listening he wasn't buying it. No matter how fondly he thought of Bill he knew how Bill felt about Rosaland. That fact alone always clouded his judgment when it came to the two of them.

"Detective we have got work to do. You need to get your focus" Lt. Yancy demanded "If this man's presence bothers you so much and it's obvious that it does then you need to do something about it. This is neither the time nor the place and I need your undivided attention." "No boss it's not like that!" "Yes detective it is like that and you need to deal with it."

At that point Detective Semione altered his focus from the direction of Dr. Reid's office where she and Lt. Jones were engaged in deep conversation back to the business at hand. "Oh I'm definitely going to do something about it!" He thought to himself as he laid out the blueprints for the night club.

"Bill I need your help?" Dr. Reid said sexily once he was seated in her office. "What do you need?" He asked demonstrating a great deal of concern. "This conversation is strictly between you and me?" Once he agreed she continued "I don't want to be stuck in front of my computer during the bust. I want to be in on it." "What? What are you talking about? I was under the impression that you weren't going in? What changed in the last twenty-four hours?"

"My mind. I have worked too hard on this to be on the sidelines. I'm a major player in this game and I want to play." "The General will have my ass for this you know that don't you? Not to mention that hot headed Latino boyfriend of yours. Rosaland this is not a game. This can and probably will be extremely dangerous."

"If any one of us walks out of there alive we'll be damned lucky. Why would you want to subject yourself to that kind of danger when you don't have to? I don't understand you. Make me understand and then maybe I might consider helping you."

"Bill I have spent the last two years of my life tracking this man from country to country. I'm up early in the morning retrieving information on his whereabouts; I go to bed at night wondering what his next move is going to be and if I can stay ahead of him."

"I feed the information to the N.Y.P.D. I have top secret surveillance and intelligence clearance so that I can monitor his transmissions or what we think are his transmissions and trace his foreign bank accounts which I haven't been able to pinpoint yet."

"I feel closer to this man than I do to my own father. I have lived with him so much these last two years who better than me should be in on this raid? Who has as much at stake as I do? If we have finally got this man cornered then I really need to be there. I don't want second hand information."

Lt. Jones listened sincerely to her arguments. He did from a military standpoint understand her point of view; as with any good hunter if you have stalked your prey you have to be there for the kill. "I have to think about this. You have got to let me think about this. There are too many extenuating circumstances for me to make a snap decision just like that. Your father and my ass are among the most important ones."

"Give me a while to think about this. I need to weigh the pros and the cons. I'll give you my answer by the end of the day. Oh by the way Rosaland why me?" "Because" she said enticingly "I need your help." Bill looked at her and it took every ounce of control in his body not to grab her and kiss her. Instead he walked out of her office shaking his head. "That went real well" she commented sarcastically to herself as she prepared for the meeting.

Sonia Blackwell had just arrived when Dr. Reid emerged from her office. She noticed that Lt. Jones seemed to be settled and she also noticed that Detective Semione seemed to be a little disturbed when she stepped into the conference room and called the meeting to order.

"If everyone is here we can begin. Does anyone want coffee before we get started? We might be here for a while." as Dr. Reid walked over to pour her coffee she could feel both Bobby and Bill starring at her body. She deliberately wore a skirt that was just a little to short along with her most seductive pair of black sheers with the seam up the back. She knew the effect her legs would have on Bobby but she wasn't so sure if they would work on Bill. Much to her delight they worked on both.

Detective Semione's eyes followed her across the room. Looking first at her well shaped legs in the black sheers back to her well rounded ass in the little tight skirt and then directly into the eyes of Lt. Jones who was starring at her ass the same way. Both the men made eye contact with each other and then they both looked away.

It was at that point that Bill decided he would help her and as for Bobby he had a revelation of his own. It was at that point that he decided that he would marry her soon. Dr. Reid watched as everyone became situated. She then took her place at the head of the table and started her meeting.

"Lt. Jones what do you think would be our best strategic approach to entering the nightclub?" Lt. Jones had prepared a presentation just for this occasion. He delivered his information with a great deal of accuracy and precision. "It would be to our advantage to hit him hard and strong in one single sweep."

"We are not going to have another opportunity to strike and once we hit we are putting ourselves in position for retaliation. If we don't capture him you can bet your sweet ass that he is going to hit us back hard. With Carlos Calderon since we don't know where he is getting his information, or who is supplying his intelligence, he might hit anyone of us either as a group or individually."

"I'm sure he knows by now whom he is up against. Especially since we keep coming. We know for sure that the O.N.S.I. is on his list of things to do. We just don't what or how he intends to do us. I would suggest that before we make any major move that we have a strong surveillence system in place and I understand that Dr. Reid is taking care of that."

The Lt. glanced in her direction as he spoke and she answered him with a nod of confirmation. "It's important that we know exactly what we are getting into and where it leads. The surveillance will supply us with that information." At this point Dr. Reid chimed in; "It might be helpful if we could send an undercover team in beforehand. Just to get a look at the layout. Even though we have the blueprints its one thing to have the diagram on paper and it's another thing to have first hand knowledge of the facility."

Lt. Yancy what do feel about that line of thinking?" "It makes sense. We would rather be safe than sorry even though we recently had two under covers in the club. Detective Semione what can you share with us that we might not already know?" "First" the detective replied "We have reason to believe that the mirror behind the bar is a two way conductor. We have information that leads us to conclude that Carlos can see everything that goes on from that point. He can see everyone that comes and goes. We know that the bartender wears a hearing device and that he communicates regularly with Carlos or whoever is in charge during the course of the night."

"It's obvious that he is talking to someone so if we are planning to capture Mr. Calderon we need to find another point of entry. If we come through the front he is definitely going to know that we are there. There also seems to be a great deal of activity or traffic that goes on. You know a lot of people in and out, but because it's a club nobody seems to be paying any particular attention to it. My partner noticed it and she pointed it out the last time we were there."

Dr. Reid looked at the detective suspiciously but she never said a word. "I believe that there is something else going on from that location but we don't have any evidence to back that up." Dr. Reid had to regain her composure before she spoke "Lt. Yancy I have a proposal. I would like to send another team in tonight. I would like to use O.N.S.I. agents. Lt. Jones is a new face so he could go in completely undetected. Ms. Blackwell here is our best source of information and even though she hasn't confirmed this I believe that she has people already in place. Am I wrong about that Sonia?"

"No actually you are very perceptive. I do have people there. The General has had people there for a while." "How hard would it be for you to go in and look around for us?" "Not hard" "Would you be interested in a night on the town compliments of the O.N.S.I.?" "It sounds interesting. What do you want me to do?" "Sonia I want you to do what you do best. Find out what is going on inside the club."

"If you are sending in O.N.S.I. We need to be there too." Lt. Yancy interjected. "I want Detective Semione to go with them as backup." "Detective semione is too high profile. He will be recognized immediately and he has been there too many times. That's why I want to use O.N.S.I. They are new faces. They could blend right in."

"Dr. Reid your proposal sounds workable but if you are sending in O.N.S.I. then I'm sending in N.Y.P.D. This is a joint operation and we need to be there. If you think that Detective Semione is too high profile then I guess we need to do something about that."

"We have ways and he is definitely the best man for the job. I'm sending him in with your team. He and Lt. Jones can work together on this one." "O.k. then that's set. We can continue this meeting in the morning. Are there any questions, comments or concerns?"

Dr. Reid looked around the room to see who had what to say. "Nothing. Everyone knows what they need to do? O.k. we'll pick this up again tomorrow. Ms. Blackwell I need to speak to you". The meeting had lasted for hours and Dr. Reid had a headache. She didn't know if it was from the fact that she hadn't eaten, or whether it was from the fact that Bobby had said "she" and deep down inside she knew who she was.

Dr. Reid walked back to her office and sat quietly starring out the window. "That was a great meeting" Lt. Jones stuck his head in her office "I am very impressed. I will help you. You can count on me even though this will mean my ass; I've got your back." Rosaland smiled "Thanks Bill I owe you one."

Dr. Reid walked back into the conference room where the Lt., Detective Semione, Lt. Jones and Sonia Blackwell were engrossed in deep conversation. Bobby was leaning over Sonia going over the details of their assignment. "Lt. Yancy I wasn't trying to leave the N.Y.P.D. out I was just concerned that Detective Semione's presence would arouse suspicion. Especially since he had just been there not to long ago."

Bobby looked up into Rosaland's eyes and he knew that something was wrong. Her eyes told him the whole story but he couldn't for the life of him figure it out. "Sonia when you are finished here I really need to talk to you." Dr. Reid went back into her office and thought about her next move.

She knew Bobby was holding back on her and she was upset. She would have to act unaffected because she was going in on the raid and that was directly against his wishes. "A penny for your thoughts" Bobby said softly as he entered her office. Rosaland turned around in her chair and smiled at him but she never said a word.

"Would you care to join me for lunch? I would like to talk to you." "Actually bobby I want to have lunch with Sonia, I need to talk to her. It's very important." "O.k. I'll see you for dinner and I don't want any excuses. If you have got something to say to me I want to hear it. I know you Baby and I know that something is wrong. You're not going to put me off so get ready to talk to me."

"O.k. so what are you going to do for lunch?" "Since you turned me down I guess I'll have lunch with your boyfriend." "You've got a lot of nerve Bobby. A lot of nerve." Bobby walked back in to her office and closed the door. "What are you talking about? What's on your mind? What's bothering you? Nobody is going to lunch until we get this straight."

"Whom did you partner with on your last undercover assignment?" "I worked with Rousseau, why?" "How come you didn't tell me?" "What's to tell? Is that what's wrong with you?" "Yes" "Rosaland don't do this. Not now it's not worth it. You know that in this division you partner with who you are assigned to and that's how that is. We have had this conversation before. I'm not going to keep having this same conversation with you. I'll see you for dinner and I hope by that time that you will be in a better frame of mind."

Bobby left her office knowing that he had deliberately misled her. If she ever found out or even suspected what had happened between he and Rousseau that night their relationship would be over. Bobby knew that she would never be able to forgive him.

When Rosaland thought about it she realized how foolish she had acted and she felt bad. Bobby was right they always came to a stalemate when it came to Diana and besides Bobby would never cheat on her; little did she know that he already had.

fifty-one

As Bobby ate his lunch he contemplated whether he should try to explain to Rosaland what had happened that night. He had been wrestling with this issue since it happened and it would be nice to finally get it off his chest. He was very uncomfortable with this dilemma and he didn't like knowing that there was something between them.

Bobby knew that no matter what he came up with this was definitely a no win situation and they both would lose in the long run. Even though Rosaland had a great sense of fairness she would never understand or accept this behavior from him. He couldn't tell her. No matter what this had to remain his secret.

"Excuse me is this seat taken?" Bobby recognized her voice immediately as he turned to find Rosaland standing behind him. "I'm sorry" she said as she took the vacant seat next to him. "I thought you were having lunch with my boyfriend" she smiled trying to be sarcastic. She reached behind her back and produced the rose she had been holding. "Peace offering" she said as she handed him the rose. Bobby was quite taken back by her gesture and leaned over the table to kiss her lips. "I thought you were having lunch with Ms. Blackwell" "I can talk to her later this is more important." "I'm glad you're here I want to talk to you about us."

"What about us?" "What are we doing? And when are we going to do this? We can go to city hall right now if that's what you want. Is that what you want?" "No" "Well then talk to me. Tell me what you want or have you even thought about it." "Bobby I think about it all the time. I want something nice and intimate. Something unique and special. Something rare and exquisite aren't those your words?" Bobby grabbed Rosaland's hand and placed it on his lips.

Rosaland gently rubbed her hand on his cheek and leaned over to kiss him. The two of them lingered there briefly gazing into each other's eyes. "So you have thought about it?" Bobby said softly "Yes" she replied demurely "I think about it everyday. I want it to be just right; I want it to reflect our love."

"Excuse me miss are you ready to order? Do you need a menu?" "No I'll have a salad and some iced tea" Rosaland waited for the waitress to leave before she continued her conversation "Bobby what do you want?" "I just want you to be my wife. I don't care how that happens. I just want it to happen soon. It's now or never Baby so whatever we decide to do let's do it right. I want to make my grandfather proud."

"So I see that you have been thinking about this too." "Of course I have. I've been thinking about it ever since I bought the ring. Actually before I bought the ring and to be honest I'm tired of this distance I feel between your father and me. I see how he and Arthur are with each other and we all work to closely together for our relationship not to be harmonious."

"We should have done this a long time ago. We both deserve it." "Bobby you amaze me and you are right we do deserve it." Bobby slipped his hand under the table and was rubbing her inner thighs carefully maneuvering around her weapon as he spoke. "It's time Baby" "Uum" Rosaland moaned in a voice so low that only Bobby could hear her as she experienced the detective's hands between her legs.

"O.k. I'll start the arrangements." "We had better get back to work before we get in trouble." "Work has never stopped you before." She smiled longingly. Bobby left the money for the bill on the table as he escorted Rosaland back upstairs to the precinct.

Dr. Reid arrived back at her office to find Sonia Blackwell waiting. "I'm sorry Sonia to make you wait but I had some personal business to attend to. I hope you haven't been waiting long."

"No actually I just arrived. I had lunch with Lt. Yancy and Lt. Jones. We were expecting Detective Semione to join us but I guess he had other plans." "Sonia I didn't mean to put you on the spot earlier but I need to know how do you feel about tonight? I know it has been some time since you have been in the field and I want you to feel comfortable. Are you alright with this?"

"I must admit this is different but it might prove to challenging. The hardest part about what we do is acting natural. In this field you are always somebody else. It might be refreshing just to be myself." "So you are alright with this?" "Yes I'm fine." "Come take a ride with me. There is someone that I would like to introduce you to." The two ladies made their way out of the precinct and Sonia headed to her car that was waiting by the curb.

Dr. Reid steered her in another direction. "I want to talk to you privately. We'll take my car." Dr. Reid led her through the parking lot and noticed that Bobby's car was easily accessible so she borrowed it. Once the ladies were on the road Dr. Reid continued "Sonia how long have you been working for my Father?" "It's been about ten years now." "Have you always worked in this capacity?" "More or less. I've been the government's ears for a long time. I was happy when they assigned me to work with the General. You know in this field you see and hear a lot of things that you really don't want to know."

"Tell me about Carlos Calderon. The real story." "What do you mean?" "Sonia two years ago I was given a dossier and a psychological profile about a man that operates so far above the law that he is practically untouchable. Every time we get close he gets ghost."

"It has become obvious that someone is feeding him information. Selling him information. Giving him information. He knows ever move we make how? He successfully infiltrated the O.N.S.I. and that's damn near impossible but he did it."

"He shouldn't even know that we exist but he does. All I want to know is what is really going on? I feel like I'm chasing a ghost. He appears and then he disappears just like that. I know that there is a lot more to this story I just feel so stupid that it has taken me two years to figure it out."

"Carlos Calderon is the biggest drug lord in the world. This man has his hands in everything from arms, to pharmaceuticals, to international finance, to biotechnology to the damn corner store. Everything. He is powerful, he is charismatic and he needs to be stopped. He is expanding his empire as well as his influence to other nations."

"You have no idea how many times his name has come up in connection to international arms deals with terrorist and other covert organizations that are a threat to our national security. Carlos is a bad ass boy. He's a real bad boy, but we have reason to believe that we have discovered his weak spot."

"He has a weak spot? And want might that be?" "You?" Rosaland was totally shocked. "Me?" She questioned in utter disbelief. "Yes you!" "But he has never even met me." Dr. Reid was flabbergasted. "We have reason to believe that he has. That is what your father has been holding back. That's why he wants you out of this game. Besides the fact that it is becoming too dangerous. You didn't hear this from me. I could lose my job for this but apparently Carlos seems to be quite smitten with you."

None of this made any sense. How could a man that she has never met, a man that knows nothing about her, have emotional feelings for her? Dr. Reid was at a lost for words. "What makes my father think that this is true?" "His instincts. Actually several months ago we were able to intercept a brief portion of a conversation. In this conversation there seemed to be a mention of your name and how lovely Carlos thinks that you are."

"That's it. That's nothing. How did you get smitten from that?" "Well there was more. The General was alarmed that this man would even know you by name and that he would be discussing you in this manner. That's when he pushed the panic button and called out all of his reserves."

"In what manner?" "The conversation was of a sexual nature. Do you need me to spell it out for you? Trust me on this; it was graphic enough for us to know that this man has a great deal of feelings for you." "Who knows this?" "Me, your father and now you."

Dr. Reid's mind was racing trying to figure this out. She thought back on the last two years of her life as she drove to the Bronx, trying to remember anything that would connect her to Carlos Calderon.

She remembered the perils that they had faced in Bolivia. She remembered the death and destruction at the Waldport but for the life of her she could not remember ever being in the presence of this man. This information would haunt her as she tried desperately to put the pieces together in her mind.

Sonia observed at that point that they had driven to a very desolate area in the Bronx. There was nothing but old abandoned warehouses that were all boarded up and looked ready for demolition. Dr. Reid pulled up to the back of the last of these buildings and blew her horn.

Immediately the door was opened and she drove in as it shut behind her. The car was transported down to the ground floor where upon arrival they were instantly transformed into a world of high tech weaponry and the latest computer technology and satellite intelligence systems. When Sonia stepped out of the car she was amazed by the sophistication of their surroundings. It was as though she was at the home office of the N.S.A.

The computers were buzzing and processing information at an incredible rate. The mainframes were all linked into a highly digitized network that was not only connected to the pentagon but to the office of the President of the United States. "This is my playground." Dr. Reid said smugly.

"This is the real headquarters of the Office of National Security Information. This is where I come to play." A very distinguished gentleman Dr. Koffi Ekouevi greeted Dr. Reid and her guest. Dr. Ekouevi graduated from Harvard University with a PhD in telecommunications network systems. When it came to intelligence and weapons Dr. Ekouevi was the man.

Sonia was instantly attracted to Dr. Ekouevi a very handsome quite muscular black man who sported a bald head. "Dr. Reid how nice of you to visit us. Is this Ms. Blackwell?" "Hello Dr. Ekouevi it's nice to see you as always and yes this is Sonia Blackwell." Dr. Ekouevi extended his hand and when Sonia placed her hand in his he kissed it softly.

Ms. Blackwell I have heard a lot about you." "I hope that it was all good." "It was all interesting but Dr. Reid neglected to tell me how beautiful you are. Shall we get started?" Sonia looked bewildered.

"Please follow me." "You're in goods hands Sonia Dr. Ekouevi is our weapons expert among other things. I'll see you in a couple of hours." Dr. Reid decided that she would workout while Dr. Ekouevi worked with Ms. Blackwell. Besides she had a lot of things on her mind that she needed to sort out and this new information about Carlos was indeed mind boggling.

However she knew now more than ever that she had to be in on the bust. There was no way that she would be able to remain on the sidelines. She wanted to know exactly who he was and what he knew about her. The one thing that she did know for sure was that she would need another team. It was more important now than ever that she have Intel and surveillance on the inner workings of the Club Oasis. Dr. Ekouevi would know exactly what equipment she would need to secure her information.

Dr. Reid watched from the observation deck as Dr. Ekouevi and Sonia Blackwell became familiar with each other. She noticed that there seemed to be a great deal of chemistry between them but they both strictly adhered to the business at hand.

Dr. Reid needed to talk to Rachael; she was the only one she knew that she could trust with this newly discovered information. Dr. Reid placed a call to her father. "Dad I need a favor. This is concerning the operation at the Club Oasis. "What do you need?" "I need another team. A rookie team some fresh new faces." "And what are you going to do with them?" "I want them to gather intelligence at the club."

"You already have a team assigned to do that. Why do you want two?" "I'm following a hunch." "Is there more to that or am I suppose to guess." "I just want to gather some information that only I know I have. There is still a leak and I want to plug it up. I will be very surprised if Bobby and the other detectives find anything when they hit that club."

Carlos will probably have it clean by the time we get there. This will give me the opportunity that I need to gain access to the club layout. All I want is a complete diagnostic of the interior." "And you need rookies to do this for you?" "Yes" "Why?" "I'm following my instincts" "You've been hanging out with Detective Semione too long!" "Yes Dad and that's a good thing. Bobby's instincts are sharp and he always follows them."

"Ok where and when?" "Have them at the Hemslet Palace by 4:00 this afternoon. I'll meet them between 4:30 and 5:00 with further instructions. I need two couples and have them registered under the name John and Joann

Swann." "Is there anything else?" "That's all for now. Dad this is strictly off the record and between you and me."

"Get back to me with whatever you come up with. I'll be waiting for your call." "Thanks Dad I'll talk to you later." For the next two hours Dr. Reid put herself through a rigorous and grueling workout trying to clear her mind and prepare her body for the upcoming event.

Dr. Reid was waiting in Dr. Ekouevi's office when he finished with Sonia. Sonia was very impressed with Dr. Ekouevi's knowledge and expertise in weaponry. He had found just the right side arm for her. One that she felt extremely comfortable with. It had been years since Sonia carried a weapon.

"Dr. Ekouevi I need some special surveillance equipment for tonight. Can you help me?" "What do you need?" "I need something that is small and compact that can give me a complete layout of any facility. I need to be able to discover any hidden passages or doorways or stairways that might be disguised. In other words I need to be able to see through ways or behind mirrors or through floors. Is that asking for the impossible?"

"Absolutely. What are you trying to accomplish? As if I didn't know." "Before I send in the O.N.S.I. team I want to know every nook and cranny of that establishment. I don't want my agents to encounter any surprises no trap doors no revolving walls nothing."

"Carlos Calderon is a very unscrupulous gentleman who we know is out to destroy us. I have already lost enough O.N.S.I. agents one of whom I shot myself and I don't intend to lose another agent because of this man. So can you help me?"

"Yes Dr. Reid I believe I have just the equipment that you are looking for. Actually I have wanted to try this equipment out for a while so now is my chance. It looks like we may be able to kill two birds with one stone. I need to be able to fit this equipment to your agents so where and when?" Dr. Ekouevi always rose to the occasion.

"Today at 5:00 at the Hemslet Palace. I'll meet you in the lobby and we'll go from there. Dr. Ekouevi this is strictly between you and me no one else needs to know. I'm plugging up the wholes in this organization; can I count on your support?" "Yes, I'll be there does anybody else know about this?"

"My Father, me and now you and that is as far as it should go. Do you understand?" "Yes." "Thank you. How did it go with Ms. Blackwell?" "She's a very interesting woman but it went just fine. I'm sure she will be comfortable with her choice." "Good then we're all set?" "Yes I'll see you at five." "You can send Ms. Blackwell to my office as soon as she is ready; I have a few more phone calls to make."

Dr. Reid shook Dr. Ekouevi's hand as she headed back to her office to wait for Sonia Blackwell. Dr. Reid was pleased that she had befriended Sonia. She always seemed to have her hands right on the pulse of the city. That quality was becoming invaluable in her quest to capture Carlos Calderon. She only hoped that she had made a wise decision and she knew that only time would tell.

The General made all the necessary arrangements and when Dr. Reid arrived at the Hemslet Palace she found her team waiting in their room just as she had instructed. Dr. Ekouevi was waiting in the bar watching for her to signal so that he could follow her lead.

Dr. Reid strolled casually into the bar and motioned that he should proceed to the elevator. They both entered the elevator deliberately not acknowledging each other. Dr. Reid exited the elevator on the fourth floor and Dr. Ekouevi rode to the sixth floor before he made his exit. He found the stairwell and walked down to find Dr. Reid standing by the door.

Dr. Reid slipped her key into the lock to find her four junior operatives deep in conversation. Her entrance startled them as their conversation came to an end. Dr. Ekouevi dressed in all black remained posted by the door holding his briefcase securely in his hand. There was an air of uncertainty in the room as Dr. Reid approached the group sitting on the sofa. "One of you should have some paperwork for me?" she said pleasantly as she waited for one of the four to respond.

"And just who are you?" said one of the cocky young agents as he stood up from where he was seated on the sofa. "I am the same person that will fire you all of you if I don't have the appropriate paper work in my hands in two seconds." She smiled sweetly. From that point on they knew that she was not to be played with and he handed her the papers immediately.

"For future reference you should never question a superior not in this line of work" Dr. Reid stated as she opened the envelope and read the contents. "So let's see who we have here. Scott, Maria, Jillian and last but not least Louis, the one with the smart mouth." Louis looked down at the ground as she made this last remark.

"According to your instructor you all come highly recommended. That's good to know." Dr. Reid continued to read their profiles and was very impressed with their credentials. Once she was satisfied with their documentation she walked over and handed the profiles to Dr. Ekouevi who put them away in his briefcase. "Have you all ever worked as a team before?" "Only in simulation" Jillian spoke up. "Simulation is good; it presents you with real life situations."

"Are you all comfortable with each other? For this assignment you are going to need to partner up. In partnering it is of the utmost importance that you know how that other person thinks and works so that you will know what to expect in the case of an unplanned circumstance."

"We have worked in teams of two before; this is the first time that we have been combined into a team of four." Maria answered in a humble tone of voice. "O.k. that will work. For this assignment you need to partner with the person you feel the most comfortable with. You will be together for the rest of the evening and you will appear to be two couples out for a night on the town. You are to have no intimate contact with anyone other than your team members."

"We are sending you to a nightclub to gather surveillance information. This is an easy assignment and you all should have some fun. We are providing a budget so that you all can enjoy yourselves. We want you to eat drink dance play games and appear to be in love. We want to know about the bar the mirror behind the bar the restaurant the game room the bathrooms and all entrances and exits and any other areas that have public access. You are not, I repeat not to enter into any areas that are marked private. No locked doors or any areas that are off limits to the general public." "We have no intentions of bringing any attention to what we are doing there."

"So let me understand all you want us to do is go to this club and party?" Louis questioned. "That's exactly right just party and have a good time be thorough cover every area of the club that has public access. The surveillance equipment will do all the work. Are there any questions?"

Dr. Reid looked around the room into the faces of her junior agents. They all seemed to be confused about what they were being assigned. Dr Reid spoke up "This is very simple just go in as two couples enjoying a night out. Have dinner some drinks dance play games but stick only to your group members. Don't get me wrong you can speak to people but that's about it. You are not on a date you are working."

"It is your job to show affection to your partner the way you would if this was your girlfriend or boyfriend. Just make sure that you gather enough surveillance in every room especially the bar the mirror behind the bar and all the other areas that I mentioned before. If I have to repeat this another time then maybe I should reassign you to elementary school. Is this clear?"

"Yes it's clear." This was the first time Scott spoke. "Good now team up chose your partner." After the two teams were formed Dr. Ekouevi sprang into action. He carefully removed a host of equipment from his briefcase and placed them on the table in front of them. He chose Scott and Jillian to be fitted with Intel. Dr. Ekouevi spoke with a heavy French accent but his English was very easily understood.

"Jillian these earrings are very sensitive and must be handled with care. Don't play them just let them dangle from your ears. You can't take them off.

They are made out of a very lightweight alloy so they shouldn't cause you any discomfort. You don't have to act any differently than you normally would because of them. When you walk into the room the earrings will do the rest. The pendant is just a decoy; it looks more realistic if you have a matching set."

Dr. Ekouevi fitted Jillian with the earrings and pendant. Dr. Ekouevi's manner was kind and gentle and he was extremely soft spoken. Jillian felt very much at ease as he placed the earrings in her ear. He flashed a smooth smile as he completed her fitting.

"Scott we have two ways we can go either cell phone or pager or both. Most of you young professionals walk around with all these gadgets attached to your belts. The cell phone has a wider range than the pager but it would look odd if you had one and not the other so just to be on the safe side let's use them both."

"Scott this is not a phone so you can't use it like a phone if you need to make a call you have to go to a payphone." "Let's make that a little clearer Scott" Dr. Reid chimed in "No phone calls until you leave the club." Scott nodded "I understand." Dr. Ekouevi handed Dr. Reid a white envelop which she in turn handed to Louis. "Here is your budget. You have eight hundred dollars for the evening enjoy."

"You are giving us almost a thousand dollars for a night on the town?" "Louis it is very important that you all fit in and that you don't draw any attention to yourselves. This is enough money for dinner drinks and games. Just get my information. Oh by the way I will be there. You all need to ignore my presence. In other words if you happen to see me you didn't see me. Don't speak or act as though you know me because I am working too."

"Please understand that your team needs to report back to this room at exactly 3:30 a.m. We will have someone here to collect the equipment. Don't even think about being late." "You have told us everything except where we are going?" Louis blurted out. "That might be nice to know?" Dr. Reid laughed "You all are going to the Club Oasis on First Ave. Have a good time."

Dr. Reid looked in Dr. Ekouevi's direction and motioned that they should go. After making sure that there were no more questions comments or concerns the two of them departed. Dr. Reid headed back to the N.Y.P.D. to return Bobby's car and then she headed home to Harlem.

Rosaland was nervous as she dressed for the evening. She couldn't get the information that Sonia shared with her this afternoon out of her head. She was very curious about Carlos's supposed feelings for her actually she was intrigued but if this was in fact correct she decided to use this newly acquired information to her advantage.

If he were there maybe her presence would draw him out into the open. She had no idea that she had met him on several occasions or that he had held her in his arms. She scoured through her closet not having the foggiest notion what she would wear but she knew that she needed to be alluring and seductive if she was going to entice him out and into her world.

She found the perfect little black dress that was barely there and decided to couple it with her signature black stockings with the seams up the back. As she placed the dress carefully over her head it fit her figure like a glove and exposed her back down to her slim waist. Her dress was short tight and very revealing. Bobby would be very irate if he thought for one minute that she had dressed this way for any man other than him. But she rationalized by saying to herself that she had a job to do.

Rosaland was becoming the real life grown up spy. So much so that it was beginning to frighten her. She was treading in dangerous territory and playing with Carlos was playing with fire. She concluded her ensemble with her oversized black linen jacket and she was off.

When Rosaland arrived at the club the street was lined with patrons waiting to be admitted. The atmosphere outside the club was lively as the line moved slowly toward the door. Rosaland looked around to see if there could possibly be another way that she could gain entry. Also she thought how obvious she must look dressed in the manner that she was entering a nightclub unescorted.

Rosaland stood back and waited for an opportunity to present itself before she could make a move. At last she spotted a beautiful young lady standing in the line alone this was perfect. Rosaland walked over to the young woman and asked her politely "Excuse me are you standing in line alone?" "Yes I am" the young woman smiled "Do you mind if I go in with you. Maybe we can sit together. My sister was supposed to meet me hour an hour ago and I really don't want to walk in by myself."

"Oh that's fine. This will work out for both of us; I really didn't want to go in by myself either." The two ladies chatted superficially as they waited their turn in line. Under normal circumstances Rosaland would never have stood in line but because of the nature of her assignment this was very apropos.

Once they were inside the club Rosaland flipped the waiter a fifty and he found a nice table for them in his section. "I feel like we are old friends. What's your name?" "Mishawn Styles and you?" "Rosaland Reid. It's nice to meet you Mishawn Styles." "Just what brings you out tonight?" Mishawn asked an already distracted Rosaland.

"Oh just looking!" Rosaland motioned for the waiter "Mishawn would you like a drink?" "Yes" "What would you like?" "Hennessey on the rocks"

"You are a girl after my own heart. I knew there was a reason that I liked you."

The ladies laughed as the waiter approached and Rosaland ordered their drinks. When the waiter returned Rosaland noticed Scott standing by the bar. She watched as he returned to his seat to find the other members of his party having a good time. As Rosaland sipped her drink she allowed her eyes to journey around the room in search of her team. Mishawn interrupted "Rosaland what line of work are you in?"

"Computers and you?" "I'm the executive assistant for a large insurance agency." "Do you like your job?" "It can be a real stressor sometimes." "What jobs aren't? My job stresses me out a lot." "Well let's drink to two stressed out sisters." The two ladies offered a toast to each other and took another sip of their drink.

It was at this point that Rosaland discovered Bill standing by the dance floor. She knew that if Bill was this close that Bobby must be somewhere near but he was in character this evening so she would have to wait until he approached her if in fact he did.

"Excuse me Mishawn I see an old friend." Rosaland removed the oversized blazer before she made her way across the room to where Lt. Jones was standing. Lt. Jones was extremely impressed as he watched her walk in his direction. Mishawn followed Rosaland across the room with her eyes to see who this old friend was. She was surprised to find such an attractive man. For some reason Mishawn thought that Rosaland might know a lot of attractive men so she was very glad to have made her acquaintance.

As Rosaland approached Lt. Jones she was intercepted by Matthew. "Just where do you think you are going missy?" Her brother smiled as he hugged her. "Hey there sweetheart" Rosaland smiled back holding her brother tightly in her arms. "What brings you here?" "Partying darling as you can see this is a target rich environment." They both laughed "Matthew you live your life between your legs." "Oh that hurts" Matthew escorted his sister to the bar and ordered drinks.

Rosaland was very happy to see her brother. It had been a while since they had been out together; even though she was working this could be fun. "What are you doing here without the shadow?" "Oh he's in the house. He's here somewhere."

"So that must mean that you are working other than that he would be right by your side especially with you being dressed this way. What are you up to? And I did notice Lt. Jones lurking in the background so whatever it is it must be something big."

Rosaland placed two fingers over Matthew's lips and with that gesture all his suspicions were confirmed. Bobby was watching Rosaland from the corner by the jukebox. He was very much aware of her presence and was waiting until the right moment to approach her. He watched her laugh and joke with her brother and he definitely noticed how much she wasn't wearing.

Mishawn was paying careful attention to Rosaland's movements as well even though she didn't know for sure she guessed that she was up to something. "Matthew I have a lovely young lady that I would like you to meet" Rosaland said as they finished their first drink "I just met her this evening but I think that you might like her."

"Where is she?" Rosaland grabbed her brother's hand and led him to the table where Mishawn was still sitting. "I'm sorry Mishawn but I have someone that I would like to introduce you to. This is my brother Matthew."

Mishawn was immediately taken by this fine specimen of a man. "Hello I'm Mishawn." "Hi Mishawn I'm Matthew." "Well why I don't leave the two of you alone so that you can get to know each other. I'll be back in a minute." "Take your time" Matthew suggested and Rosaland was off. She needed to make sure that everything was proceeding according to plan.

Rosaland spent as much time by the bar that she could. If Carlos were here then one of his henchmen would surely alert him of her presence. Bobby observed how deliberately she paraded herself in front of the two way mirror and he found himself wondering exactly what she was up to. The atmosphere in the club was beginning to heat up. The crowd was lively and the music was good.

The dance floor was packed with sweaty gyrating bodies moving melodiously in time with the pulsating beats. With the constant influx of people it was hard for Lt. Jones or Detective Semione to watch for any unusual activity. It was hard for Bobby to watch anything. He couldn't take his eyes off of Rosaland.

She had him completely mesmerized. Bobby hated these assignments because it gave Rosaland complete liberty to be as off the hook as she wanted to be and there was nothing that he could do about it at least not here.

Just as Bobby decided to move his position from the jukebox he noticed a group of well-dressed Japanese business men enter the club. Their presence was very much out of character for the rest of the club goers and then they disappeared behind the bar one by one. So now Bobby knew for sure that there was another entrance that they had previously overlooked.

Bobby remained in place to see what else he could observe from his spot. Lt. Jones had also noticed the traffic and made several mental notes concerning the newly arrived visitors. This evening was turning out to be very productive.

"Hey boss you need to look down here. Your girlfriend is in the house" Carlos immediately came to the mirror once he received this message from his bartender. Looking down into the crowd, he spotted her instantly. "Who's with her?" "She seems to be alone" "She is never alone. Watch her and tell me who she talks to." "O.k."

Carlos watched her quietly for several more minutes. He was delighted at how sexy Rosaland looked this evening. Carlos paid careful attention to how her black dress hugged her body in all the right places and he was particularly excited by the plunging back. It was as though she were deliberately teasing him placing herself in front of him only to pull back at the last minute.

Her long black hair hung sexily below her shoulders and flowed luxuriously as she moved. What was it about this woman that he could feel her in every bone of his body? Bobby felt her the same way deep within his soul. Her mere presence sent sparks of electricity up and down his spine. Matthew and Mishawn spotted Rosaland as they emerged from the dance floor.

fifty-two

"That was the longest minute" Mishawn said sarcastically. Rosaland laughed "You know how that goes. So I guess you two had a good time?" "Yes we did and thanks Sis" "Thanks for what?" "Thanks for introducing me to such a wonderful lady. She is really special." "My pleasure sweetie." Mishawn could tell from their exchange that the two of them were very close.

"By the way where's the incredible hulk? I' haven't seen him all night." Rosaland shrugged and she hoped that Matthew would drop the subject. "Who is the incredible hulk?" Mishawn questioned innocently. "You see that ring on her finger it comes with a man just as big and since he is nowhere to be found then I guess it will be my responsibility to make sure that you get home. Tell me when you are ready; we both have to work tomorrow." "O.k. give me a few minutes. I'll be ready soon."

Carlos had come back to the mirror and was watching as she engaged in conversation with her brother and his new found friend. "That's her brother" Carlos reported to the bartender "I knew that she wouldn't be alone. I have to attend to our friends. Watch them for the rest of the evening." "O.k. you got it".

Matthew and Mishawn headed back to the dance floor and Rosaland made her final round of the club. She knew that Bobby was there and she had hoped that he would have made his presence known to her. She was tired and she wanted to go home. Tomorrow would be another day and she would know just how successful they had been.

When Matthew and Mishawn emerged from the dance floor the three of them left the club. Both Bobby and Bill were happy that Matthew had happened along and that he had taken her home. The rest of the evening was relatively uneventful but the two of them remained until the early morning when the club closed.

After Matthew dropped Mishawn to her car and made sure that she was safely inside he escorted his sister to his vehicle. As he drove up Harlem River Drive he asked her point blankly "What the hell was going on tonight? And where was Bobby? I can't believe that he would let you be in that club all alone."

"Matthew Bobby was there trust me. I know that he had his eye on me all night I could feel it. But we were working and we both had to do what we had to do. We are going to take that club down so I would suggest for the next week that you don't need to be anywhere in the general vicinity. Tonight was a typical operation we were watching the traffic flow and we were gathering surveillance information."

"We believe that there is lot more going on there than meets the eye and it is not a safe place for you or any of your friends to be for a while. Do you understand what I'm telling you? Stay away from the Club Oasis! Find someplace else to party." "O.k. Sis I'm cool I just needed to know. I knew it had to be something out of the ordinary for Bobby not to be close at hand."

It was about four o'clock a.m. when Matthew dropped Rosaland off at the brownstone. As she undressed for bed she wondered if she would see Bobby this morning. Lately they had both been on such tight schedules that they had no time for each other. They always seem to be coming or going or locked away in some meeting for hours.

Rosaland couldn't remember the last time they had slept together or the last time they had made love. She missed him and wanted nothing more than to be in his arms right about now.

She closed her eyes and tried to envision the last time he was buried deep within her body. She recalled the sublime pleasure that Bobby always afforded her. Rosaland ran her hands over her wanton body and before long she was fast asleep.

Lt. Jones and Detective Semione proceeded to the N.Y.P.D. after they departed from the Club Oasis. Detective Semione couldn't wait to get out of his body makeup. That was the one thing that he dreaded about being in character all the makeup. He always felt extremely uncomfortable and the extra layers weighed him down and it took so long to take off. It would be another hour before he could get home and he really needed to see his girl.

The image of her nude body was embedded deep in his thoughts and he wanted to smell her hair. Bobby couldn't remember that last time they had slept together or the last time that they had made love. He knew that if he couldn't remember than it had been too long and he definitely needed to do something about that.

Bobby sat at his desk quietly for about twenty minutes jotting down the details of his observations. He and Lt. Jones would compare notes tomorrow but for now all he wanted was to go home and to hold her. "I'm out of here" Bobby announced as he made his way down the steps to the parking lot. Once inside his vehicle the exhausted detective made his way uptown to Harlem.

When Bobby arrived in front of the brownstone he noticed that there was a light on the second floor. She was safely at home. Bobby gently opened the door and left his shoes at the bottom of the steps. He crept up the stairs to the bedroom where Rosaland was sound asleep. Bobby could tell by the condition of the room that she must have been feeling the affects of the alcohol. Her clothes were scattered about forming a line to the bed.

Bobby decided not to disturb her just being here with her was satisfaction in and of itself. Besides he wanted to wash the remnants from the makeup off of his body. Bobby undressed silently and stepped into the shower. The warm water felt good as it flowed over his lean muscular physique.

Bobby grabbed for the shampoo and washed the crusted makeup from his hair. He immediately recognized the smell as he lathered up to remove the debris. The only ingredient missing from this shower was her. When Bobby finished he went back into the bedroom to find her still lost in sleep.

Bobby reached into his underwear drawer slid into his boxer briefs and went downstairs to the den. He had taken the bottle of the body lotion that Rosaland always had on hand to the den with him and leisurely applied the lotion to his still moist skin.

Bobby fixed himself a drink and then went to the stereo unit to find some music that would help him to wind down. "So Carlos Calderon really did have something going on" Bobby thought to himself as he sipped his drink.

The smooth sounds of Carlos Santana filled the room as Bobby relaxed and put his feet up. He couldn't remember the last time that he had relaxed at home with her even though she was upstairs sleeping they were still together.

Bobby closed his eyes and let his mind drift into the music. Rosaland was slowly becoming conscious of the Latin American rhythms that were creeping into her bedroom. As she slowly opened her eyes she could see that the bathroom light was on she knew that Bobby was home.

He had a habit of always leaving that light on. Rosaland's head was spinning from the effects of the Hennessey but she managed to pull herself together and get into the shower.

She let the warm water run leisurely over her head and down her shapely torso as she washed the smell of smoke out of her hair. Rosaland lathered up her body delicately. She wanted to be fresh and clean and soft when she presented herself to Bobby. As she stepped out of the shower she noticed that the faint sounds of the music was growing louder.

Bobby really seemed to be enjoying himself downstairs. After applying his favorite body lotion she fumbled through her lingerie drawer to find several pieces that she had never worn some of them still had the tags on them. Rosaland selected a stretch lace baby doll with a sexy off the shoulder shape delicate bell sleeves and matching panties.

The derriere skimming length was perfect for what she had in mind. She applied Bobby's favorite fragrance to her pulse points between her cleavage and between her legs and then she joined him downstairs in the den.

Rosaland found Bobby in a nice relaxed frame of mind with his feet up. He was lost in his own world as he sat with his eyes closed listening to the soulful rhythms of Carlos Santana. Bobby held his drink in one hand as he ruffled through his still slightly damp hair with the other.

Rosaland stood at the bottom of the stairs gazing at him for a while before she sat next to him and placed her head on his shoulder. Bobby pulled her close and placed a kiss on her forehead. He was surprised that he hadn't noticed her presence before this but he was pleased that she was here with him now.

Bobby hugged her close and placed another kiss on her head "do you want a drink Baby" Bobby whispered as he changed his position so that he could be even closer to her sexily clad body. "No baby I've had enough. I just want to be close to you." Rosaland replied starring directly into his eyes.

Rosaland leaned her body closer to her baby and kissed him tenderly "I missed you this evening" she murmured as Bobby inserted his tongue down her throat. Rosaland responded by wrapping her arms tightly around his neck and pressing her luscious ample breast into his chest. She ran her hands through his hair as she placed solid kisses on his lips.

Bobby pulled Rosaland on to his lap and held her around her waist. He slid the black lace baby doll completely off her shoulders allowing her breasts full liberty. He gently caressed the ample mounds as he kissed her passionately up and down her neck.

"Ohh Bobby" Rosaland moaned in a low guttural tone of voice. "I've missed you" Rosaland ground her pelvis into his signaling that she wanted more. Bobby was thoroughly absorbed into possessing her body. He removed his hard throbbing manhood in its excited state from his boxers and rubbed it sensuously back and forth between her legs.

Bobby grabbed the top of her panties and ripped them from her torso letting the delicate lace fall to the floor. Rosaland fingered his huge erection and placed it firmly between her legs and deliberately let Bobby enter her wet craving cavern. Bobby moaned loudly as he pushed himself deep inside. Bobby could feel how wet warm and receptive she was as he pumped his hard muscle into place.

Rosaland quivered with desire as she rode up and down on his stalwart penis. Rosaland laid her head on Bobby's shoulder as she encouraged him to invade her body. Bobby held her hips in place as he applied his manly thrusts gaining total penetration of her inner most being. He buried his head between her breasts as he mouthed her hard nipples delicately biting them in her most sensitive places.

"You like that?" Bobby murmured softly not waiting for her to reply. Rosaland pressed her body down to meet his and soon they were locked together in their passionate embrace. Rosaland moaned and sighed as Bobby pleasured her. Bobby pumped steadily in and out unmindful of the stretching she was experiencing.

Rosaland took him wholly with each lunge she wanted all of him and she needed him to completely fill her with his lust. Rosaland held her breath as their passion heated to the boiling point. Both of their bodies completely absorbed in desire. Rosaland wrapped her arms and her legs firmly around Bobby's lean body. In this position it was easy for Bobby to flip her onto her back. As her body hit the sofa Bobby pushed himself into the furthest recesses of her sweet love spot. He rode her deliciously in and out, back and forth totally filling her with his hot desire.

Rosaland screamed "Ohh Baby!" as Bobby pressed his powerful strokes deep within her. Bobby continued his lecherous onslaught on her precious privacy; he reached down to remove the wet lace that was clinging to her body. Now he had her beautiful hot chocolate completely exposed to his attentions.

"That's better" he whimpered in a low sexy voice. Bobby pressed his sweaty chest close to hers crushing her breasts as he administered his luscious advances. Bobby kissed her delicately as the sweat from his forehead fell in drops onto her open mouth. Rosaland reached up to wipe some of the sweat from his brow as they moaned and groaned together in unbridled lust.

Bobby had her just where he wanted her wet and wide open. This was the point where Bobby totally dominated her applying his strokes rapidly and ferociously in a passionate attempt to afford her the utmost pleasure possible. "I love you" he grunted as his strokes increased.

Bobby loved her and he wanted her to feel it. He wanted her to know how he longed for her when they were apart. He wanted her to know how much he thought about her during the times when he couldn't get his hands on her. And most of all Bobby wanted her to understand beyond a shadow of a doubt that she belonged to him. Body and Soul.

Bobby pressed his full massive length into her body with each excruciating thrust. Rosaland closed her eyes and held on tightly, her pouting mouthy lips murmuring "I love you Bobby. I love you" as the tears began to form in her eyes. "I love you too Baby" Bobby responded barely audible in her ear as her body bounced up and down.

"Who do you belong to?" Bobby commanded as he felt her body start to shake and quiver under his powerful blows. "Who do you belong to?" Bobby repeated his command a little bolder as he feed her lust his fire. "You Oohh Bobby. You Bobby!!" She cried emotionally as her body exploded with the impact of an orgasmic volcano.

Bobby fought hard to hold back his own explosion. He wasn't quite finished with her. He always wanted more. He could never seem to get enough of her. Bobby plummeted into her wet hot love box hard and furious treating her body to immense gratification. Bobby watched her face contort in a lustful gaze as he plunged deeper and deeper in a passionate frenzy.

Rosaland clung to him digging her nails into his strong back. Bobby consistently fed her his girth and his length causing her to scream and cry out loud. Bobby raised his body so that it fit neatly into hers as he continued to pound relentlessly between her legs.

In this new position Bobby achieved the greatest penetration possible. Rosaland's strong body had been transformed into putty under his arduous embraces. She had never known a time when Bobby was so insistent. Bobby prolonged the pleasure that he was deriving from being buried so tightly within her.

He palmed her ample ass with both of his artful hands and pressed his groin deep into her inviting pelvic area. Bobby exploded with the fury of a ball of lightening. His explosion was so intense that he sent her over the top again and the two lovers shivered uncontrollably in each other's arms. "Oh Bobby!" Rosaland screamed erotically at the top her voice as the tears streamed down her face.

Rosaland lay in Bobby's arms crying shaking and gasping for air. She could feel his seed spout forth from his enormous manhood and inundate her womb which provided her with ultimate pleasure. It would take Bobby several minutes before he had gathered enough resolve to calm her down and allow her to catch her breath.

Bobby held her writhing form close to his shaking sweating body as he applied gentle kisses to her lips while they waited for sleep to overtake them.

fifty-three

When Rosaland awoke the next morning she was nestled snuggly in her bed and Bobby was asleep next to her. As she sat up she noticed that he had his arms wound tightly around her waist. Her movements caused him to stir and then he opened his eyes.

"Hey Sleepyhead" she said pleasantly as she moved in to kiss him. "Where are you going?" He asked her still half asleep. "Some of us work for a living" she said in a laughing manner as she relaxed next to him. "Why don't you ride in with me today?" Bobby said convincingly. "I don't have to report in until noon." "Baby I need to be in now" "You're the boss. Do your boss thing. You can report in whenever you want. Spend the morning with me."

"What a lovely invitation that sounds very nice." Rosaland placed her head on his chest and closed her eyes. Bobby squeezed his arms tightly around her neck. He was happy that she had accepted his offer without any hesitation. Rosaland fell back to sleep instantly. Bobby held her in his arms stroking her hair and kissing the top of her head and before long he too was fast asleep.

It was three hours later when the lovebirds opened their eyes and of course now they were running late. "Come on Baby we are going to be late!" Rosaland warned as they both jumped into the shower. "I wish we had more time" Bobby commented as he watched the warm water cascade down her perfect figure.

"We have all the time in the world just none right now." She smiled "You know Rosaland you can be so smart sometimes." Rosaland laughed as they cleansed their bodies and exited the shower. "I was going to make my special eggs ranchero for breakfast." Bobby said as they dressed in a hurry.

"Bobby look at my hair. What am I going to do about my hair?"

"Your hair looks great like that way; you should wear it like that more often." "You have got to be kidding?" Rosaland snapped. "No I'm serious I like your hair like that. You should wear it like that more often." Rosaland looked doubtfully at Bobby as she grabbed a large bottle of baby oil and poured a generous amount in her hands and applied it to her wet hair.

"At least when it dries it will be curly." She thought to herself. Bobby and Rosaland frantically rushed around the bedroom trying to find something to wear. Bobby watched as Rosaland hurriedly slipped into her underwear and smiled to himself. That was one of the things that he loved about her how beautiful she looked in her underwear.

"What are you smiling about?" She asked "I'll tell you later when we have more time." "Come on Bobby we are already late!" "I'm ready you need to get ready." Rosaland looked over to find that Bobby was ready and waiting on her.

She grabbed a nice tailored shirtdress from her closet and threw it on. She slid her feet into a pair of patent leather pumps that she had left standing at the foot of her bed and they both scurried towards the door.

As they drove down Harlem River Drive Bobby commented again on her hair. "Your hair really does look nice like that." Rosaland smiled at him "Thanks" she responded as they proceeded to the precinct. "When do you think we will have this Calderon situation wrapped up?" Bobby questioned her totally changing the subject.

"I don't know but I hope that it is soon. I need to know what you all discovered last night and I also have some other information that might be helpful as well. But I won't know anything for sure until I meet with both teams."

"I want you to promise me something." Bobby looked serious. "What?" "As soon as this mess blows over you and I are going to take some time off to get married. Rosaland this is ridiculous that we can't find a day to get married. You planned Rachael's wedding in two weeks and you can't find fifteen minutes for us. I don't know whether to be upset or insulted."

"Come on Bobby that's not fair. You know that I am doing everything I can right now; you can't blame me for this war on drugs. I'm only trying to do the best I can with what I have to work with. But I will promise you that as soon as this is over we will both sit down and plan our wedding together."

"Baby let's just go away and do this." Bobby coerced. "Bobby I'm not getting married without my family and neither are you. Your grandfather is all you have left and whatever we do he needs to be included. Bobby I can't believe that you are being so selfish."

"Selfish. How am I being selfish? We should have done this a long time ago." "O.k. I'll make a deal. We can take a week. We can spend the early part of the week together and we can use the weekend for our wedding. We can find someplace close so all our family members can be there. That's the best that I can do. Do we have a deal?"

Bobby laughed what was he ever going to do with her? "Yes beautiful we have a deal." He laughed shaking his head. "We can check the Internet for the ideal location." "What about New Orleans? I hear that's a nice place for a wedding?" "We can check it out. What about up the coast Connecticut? Cape Cod? Martha's Vineyard?" "That's a possibility too. It would be easy to get the family there" "O.k. let's do it."

They finally agreed on something. Bobby was pulling up in front of the station. "Why don't I get out here?"Rosaland was so used to their routine. "No let's go in together." Rosaland smiled broadly "Yeah" Bobby nodded in agreement "Yeah".

"Detective Semione I'm so glad that you could join us today!" Lt Yancy said sarcastically as Bobby entered his office. "We were wondering when you might grace us with your presence." "I'm sorry boss I got a little hung up this morning." Lt. Yancy looked across the hall to see a vibrant Dr. Reid enter her office. "That wouldn't have anything to do with my sister-in-law now would it?" Bobby smiled and never said a word.

"We need to get started; we've got a shitload of work to do. Lt. Jones and Ms. Blackwell have been here for hours." Lt. Yancy walked across the hall to Dr. Reid's office. "Dr. Reid you have a messenger waiting for you. He has been here since 9:00 a.m. He says he has orders not to talk to anyone but you."

"Send him in" "Are you Dr. Reid?" "I am" "I have a package for you. You need to sign here." Dr. Reid put her John Hancock on the form and the messenger handed her the package. "Dr. Reid we need you in this meeting" "Lt. you have to start without me. I have some pertinent information that I need to review. I'll be in as soon as I look over this material."

When the Lt. left her office Dr. Reid closed her blinds and fed the video into her machine. As she watched the footage she was absolutely amazed at what the junior team had uncovered. She watched in awe as the video revealed everything that they needed to know.

Dr. Ekouevi was a genius. His surveillance equipment had worked perfectly. She would make a note to give him a raise. She had her evidence in black and white. Every entrance every exit the exact length of the basement the entrance behind the mirror the two offices one on the second floor and another on the third floor and what do we have here?

A drug processing center right under their noses. "Yes!" They all heard her shout from behind closed doors. Bobby knew that she could be loud. "Looks like somebody got some good news" he commented to his Lt. "Well let's wait to see what it is" Lt. Yancy responded calmly.

"Dad this information is invaluable. I need to get this to you right away." "Calm down sweetie and tell me what you've got." "No Dad you have to see this for yourself. You need to be here. How long will it take you to get here?""This information is that important?" "Yes Dad" "Then I'm on my way. I'll see you in an hour." "Dad do me another favor." "What is it this time?" "I need you to pull Sonia out but she can't know that I am requesting it." "Why?" "I'll tell you later but I am going to need to work her again. So she can't know that I want her out. Make up some urgent assignment that needs her immediate attention and get her out of here please Dad."

"O.k. I'll page her right now." "Thanks Dad I'll see you when you get here." Dr. Reid continued to view the video tape both with surprise and amazement. This information had definitely made her case. The O.N.S.I. was in position to close the Club Oasis permanently. This tape had finally confirmed all their suspicions. If they struck swiftly they might be able to catch the notorious Mr. Calderon with his hands in the cookie jar.

"I'm sorry gentlemen for the delay where is Ms. Blackwell?" "She was called away to Washington." Lt. Jones spoke up. "But she was just here" "the General's office called her just a few minutes ago and she left. She said to tell you that she would get back to you and that she apologizes for any inconvenience that her abrupt departure might have caused the operation."

"O.k. we need to move on. Why don't you all bring me up to speed on last night's operation while we wait for the General?" "The General is coming?" "Yes he is on the way as we speak." "Well why we don't just wait until the General arrives and we can do this all at one time." Lt. Yancy suggested. "That sounds good to me; I know for sure that he would want to hear all the details. He'll be here in about an hour."

Detective could I talk to you for a moment in my office?" "Sure what's up?" "This will only take a minute." Detective Semione followed Dr. Reid into her office and she shut the door. "Bobby we have a little time before my Dad gets here we could surf the web for a suitable location."

"I thought that this was something important" Bobby looked pleasantly surprised. "This is important Bobby and we have the time right now let's do this. I swear I don't want to hear your grumbling and complaining if you don't take the time to do this with me now."

"Rosaland what has got you so excited? Calm down sweetie we can do it now." Bobby sat down at the computer with Rosaland as she started their search. "Let's see what are we looking for fancy hideaway? Bed and breakfast? Retreat? What?

"Let's try bed and breakfast; I like the sound of that." "Bed and breakfast it is" Rosaland clicked that information on the Internet and waited for the listings to upload. "Band B in Connecticut" to be more specific. Several more listings appeared Rosaland clicked the first selection and while waiting for the web site to download she leaned over and kissed Bobby tenderly.

When their lips parted she gazed softly into his eyes. Rosaland turned her attention back to the Internet but Bobby continued to stare lovingly then he started to run his fingers through her overly curly hair "I really do like your hair."

Lt. Yancy knocked at the door of Dr. Reid's office after observing them from a distance. When the Lt. gained entrance he knew that he had interrupted a private moment. "Detective Semione I need you in the other room." "O.k. just let me have one minute." Bobby responded still starring intently into the computer screen. "What's going on in here?" Dr. Reid looked at Arthur starry eyed "Arthur we are getting married."

"It's about time; I know that your sister will be happy to hear that. But you have to handle this later on your own time. Right now I need Detective Semione in the other room."

Bobby got up and followed the Lt. out of her office. Lt. Yancy reached back and shook his hand "Congratulations Bobby good man." Arthur immediately put his detective back to work. There was still crime in the city that had nothing to do with Carlos Calderon.

The unit was in its usual uproar. There was always plenty of action at the one five. Truly there was never a dull moment. In both the professional arena and the personal area there was always something going on? The buzz in the office was constant, as people came and people went under all kinds of circumstances.

Lt. Jones noticed that Dr. Reid was alone in her office and he went in. "Hey I saw you last night. You looked great. Why do you keep doing this to me?" He asked mercifully. "Bill what am I doing to you?" "Never mind you distract me. I came to see what you wanted. What do you want me to do about the situation that we talked about yesterday?"

"Are you coordinating the SWAT team?" "I could why?" "I want to be on it" Rosaland was being extremely aggressive. "Rosaland are you out of your mind? I'm not putting you on the SWAT team. No way No way!" "Why not?" She pouted sexily.

"Why not? Are you out of your mind? Training for one. Do I need to say anymore?" "Bill the SWAT team goes in first. I need that advantage. I need to be able to be first on the scene. I'm prepared to do this and I am a federal officer. You could do it! You could put me in there." She insisted.

"I don't know Rosaland that a little too aggressive." "What's too aggressive Bill? We have a job to do and that job at this time is to stop Carlos. I need to be first on the scene." "The only way that I will do this is if you train with them."

"Bill we are not going to have time for training. When we strike we hit that's it." "I don't know. I just don't know." "Bill you know that I can do this. Let me do this. I am a graduate of the academy. Bill I am an officer of the law and I can handle my weapon." She was pleading at this point. "Let me think about this?" "No Bill you have to decide now. You should really help me with this. This is O.N.S.I. jurisdiction I need to be first on the scene."

"I'll have to go in with you. That's the only way that I will do it." "That's fine Bill that's fine. Do we have an understanding?" "Yes I'll get back to you on this." Rosaland strolled across the desk and kissed him delicately. "Thanks."

Bill nodded as he left her office. Lt. Jones knew that he would be facing big trouble maybe even court martial if anything went wrong. The General was his commanding officer and this was his daughter. Why was he in the middle of this? He shook his head to himself.

The General arrived exactly in an hour. It was always amazing how he could be on the scene so fast. "I know when I called you, you were in Washington Dad. How did you get here so fast?" "I wasn't in Washington. I was actually on my way to New York when you called. That's how I got here so fast. Now what is this urgent information that you have?"

"Wait until you see this. I believe that you will be very happy". "Oh by the way Rosaland I'm very happy to see you." "Thanks Dad I'm sorry." Rosaland kissed and gave her Father a warm hug. "Lt. Jones is in the conference room why don't you have a seat with him while I round up the rest of the crew."

Dr. Reid escorted her Father into the conference room and made sure that he was comfortable. Rosaland knocked on Lt. Yancy's door "Lt. the General has just arrived. I have him waiting in the conference room. Can you call Detective Semione?" "We'll be right there" the Lt. walked over to Detective Semione's desk "Bobby we need you now. Danny take over for a while."

Bobby followed Lt. Yancy into the conference room. Dr. Reid closed the door behind her as the five of them discussed the events of the previous evening. "Well what happened last night?" It was the General that finally broke the silence.

"Every thing was pretty routine but we did notice that there was an enormous amount of traffic in and out other than the usual club goers." Lt.

Jones started "Also the club was visited by a group of well dressed Japanese business men." "They all disappeared behind the bar." Detective semione added.

"Behind the bar?" The Lt. questioned "Did you really see them go behind the bar?" "Yes we both noticed it. I believe we can pinpoint the exact location. There is definitely an entrance there. That's all we were unable to uncover." "Detective that's more than what we had."

"I've got more" Dr. Reid announced proudly. "I've got a complete surveillance profile on the club. We have accurate information on all the entrances and exits as well as what's behind the mirror and what's on the third floor and the surprise in the basement!" Rosaland was boastful.

The entire team looked shocked as she continued "I sent in a surveillance unit last night with the aid of my father. Their mission was to gather useful intelligence. Two of the members were fitted with special equipment. We have videotape of every thing that we need to know Lt. if you please."

Dr. Reid handed the tape to Lt. Yancy. Detective Semione was still starring at her. She hadn't said a word about this to him. They had spent the entire morning together and she never opened her mouth. Lt. Yancy turned down the lights as he fed the tape into the V.C.R.

"Listen up gentlemen. This is what we have. We have exits at both the north and the south walls" Dr. Reid pointed out. "They are not visible to the unsuspecting eye. We have entrances at twelve o'clock and three o'clock on the east and west walls. Look at what's behind the bar. First let me start by saying that the mirror is indeed two way and there are two floors behind it."

"On the second floor as you can see these are the executive offices. Here is the computer equipment extremely state of the art technology if I must say so myself."

"You can tell by the grey areas that this is electronics." She pointed out. "Here is the security system for the club. It comes with both audio and video capabilities." Dr. Reid traced the lines from the second floor throughout the club. The bar, the dance floor and the restaurant."

"This is the audio feed for the club. The office can hear and see everything that goes on in that place. Here we have another entrance from the second floor to the third floor. This area seems to be living quarters. Here is a bedroom, kitchen area, bathroom, den and more computers"

"Looking from the outside there certainly doesn't appear to be this much space but this place is huge. I want you all to notice how sophisticated the alarm system is. State of the art. The slightest disturbance and it goes off silently. The intruder would never know that it has been tripped."

"This type of system will get you caught every time. And last but not least gentlemen what have we here? It reminds me of a drug processing center. There is approximately 19,000 square feet of narcotics being processed probably on a daily basis. Bingo we got him!" Dr. Reid looked directly into Detective Semiones eyes and smiled. She then turned her gaze towards her father. The General was at a lost for words. She told him that this was important and she was right.

"This is incredible. How did you pull this off?" Her father was amazed and extremely pleased. Every time the General feels the need to remove her from danger; she always comes up with another job well done.

Lt. Yancy poured over the material astonished as to how thorough her presentation had been. Detective Semione looked over the Lt.'s shoulder as he pointed out areas that had gone undiscovered for months. Dr. Reid was quiet as the rest of her crew digested and discussed this new information. The General pulled her to the side.

"Why did you want me to pull Sonia out? I've been puzzled since you made that request." "Last night I observed Sonia in a situation that I wasn't sure of. I have nothing on her just a hunch but I feel like she knows more than she is telling both of us about Carlos Calderon. Dad I have no proof and I could be wrong but I couldn't chance revealing this information to anyone other than the people in this room right now."

"Rosaland I've known Sonia for years. She's clean." "I didn't say that she wasn't Dad. I never said that. I just need some more answers that all." "And where do you expect to get these answers?" The General asked demonstrating a great deal of concern. "From Sonia of course." Rosaland replied.

"Now that everybody has had a chance to review this information do you have any observations or suggestions as to how we might proceed?" Dr. Reid looked to Detective Semione for a response. "First things first when is this going down?" "The sooner the better. Lt. Yancy what do you have to say about that."

"Definitely the sooner the better. Two days tops. Any longer than that and our position will be challenged." "Lt. Jones two days is the window. What can the O.N.S.I. do with that?" "Two days is fine. I'll be coordinating the swat team so that should give them plenty of time to prepare. We need more time with this video. I need to bring them all up to speed. We don't have any time; so all players must be thoroughly informed. We can't leave anything to chance."

"Tomorrow I need to brief them. Also I want Detective Semione down with this. He needs to go in with us. Detective how do you feel about that?" "Sounds good to me Lt. who are we using for back up?" "Schmidt and Rousseau, Easley Martinez and Cole and Sanchez from Brooklyn south." "Lt. are you going in?" "You bet your ass. I'm going in with SWAT." Dr. Reid didn't like how this was developing but she couldn't say anything she had to go with team consensus.

The General made special note of how well they worked together as a team. They all participated in the decision making and they all listened to each other. Detective Semione moved in close to Dr. Reid as they all reviewed the videotape over and over again. Lt. Yancy worked out the route for the N.Y.P.D and he needed to call in another favor to get the detectives from Brooklyn south in on this.

The team worked the rest of the day and through the night. The phone lines were buzzing with the constant influx of information. It was well after midnight before they decided to call it quits. Dr. Reid looked around. She was always involved with the same group of men; her pack and her father was always at the helm.

General Prescott A. Reid had orchestrated their lives for as long as she could remember. Rosaland loved her father she admired him and she always wanted his approval. Whenever it came to her Dad she always wanted to do it right.

The General coordinated the rest of the O.N.S.I. forces in Washington via satellite link and put them on the alert. The General wanted to spend some quiet time with his daughter. He hadn't seen her in a while and he wanted just to talk to her. He had promised himself that he wouldn't push her personal situation with Detective Semione.

The general liked Bobby. He knew that he was a good man. "Rosaland I have to wrap it up here. I am scheduled to be in Washington tonight." "Dad you need to be available to me tomorrow I am going to need your help. This is a pretty big order and you guys want it to go on a platter delivered right to your door."

"That's right sweetie with a bow. Just call me. Rosaland how are you getting home?" "Bobby" "Why don't you let me take you home? Better still let's go have a drink just the two of us." "I would love to Dad; just let me finish up here." "I'll be downstairs in the car. I need some air."

Once the General left the conference room Dr. Reid spoke up. "You guys were great today. Thanks for backing my play. Lt. What do you make of the Japanese?" "Too early to tell. I don't have enough information to form an opinion. What do you think?" "Well it indicates to me that Mr. Calderon and company are expanding globally or at least may be contemplating moving towards that arena."

"That's a good possibility. It's definitely something to think about. "What are those two talking about?" Dr. Reid questioned as she pointed in the direction of Bobby and Bill "I would hate to disturb them." She smiled as she walked over to deliberately interrupt. "Excuse me I'm sorry to interrupt but I just wanted to say good night. It looks like you two are going to be here for a while."

"Yeah we will be here for a minute." Lt. Jones replied "Alright. I'm gone" Rosaland looked directly at Bobby. "Give me a minute Bill." "How are you getting home?" "My dad actually we are going to have a drink." "I'll catch you at home." Dr. Reid blew a kiss in his direction as she left the precinct.

"Man where did she get all this damned information? She just goes off and she does shit. She never asks and she doesn't tell me anything anymore. I hear about shit when every body else does…" Bobby was upset and Bill knew it.

"..Shit. She can at least say something. She never says anything she just does it. I don't know where she gets her information but that girl always comes up with some shit. And she is always right. She is so fucking dangerous and she doesn't even know it. She is just a Daddy's girl following orders." Bobby was pissed!!!

Bobby was shaking his head as he vented his concerns. Bobby didn't know why he was upset, he just was. She should have told him what was going on. She is always so secretive when it comes to the O.N.S.I and or her father. Bill was caught between a rock and a hard place.

"Man how could I have gotten myself in this situation" Bill thought to himself as he listened to Bobby. Bill knew that if Bobby was this angry over her not telling him about the surveillance information, he would hit the ceiling if he knew about the SWAT team. Bill thought about the prospect of telling him but he couldn't betray her in that manner. She had personally asked for his help. She knows what she wants to do and how she wants to do it. This was turning out to be a real mess. What the hell was he going to do?

fifty-four

The Harvard Club was always delighted to host the General and his family under any circumstance. The General's table was ready when they arrived and as soon as they were seated their drinks were served. The General looked at his daughter as they sipped their drinks. He was amazed as to how much she looked like her mother.

Rosaland and her Father sat in silence as they both finished their drink. Rosaland was tired and it was nice just to be with her Dad. The General motioned for the second round and again they were served immediately.

"So how's it going?" "Fine" Rosaland smiled as she waited for her Father to proceed. "Why are you smiling?" "I'm just waiting for you to say what's on your mind Dad. I know that it is something."

"When is the last time that you have seen your sister?" "Rachael and I were together a couple of weeks ago. I've been so busy lately that I haven't had anytime to spend with her. Arthur's been on the same schedule so I know she knows what is going on."

"Why don't we call her right now?" The General pressed Rachael's number into his cell. "Hello Dad?" "Yes" "Hi where are you?" "I'm out with your sister." "Arthur told me that you were in town today. You know he is still at the station. What the hell is going on over there? He is never home."

"Why don't you come and join us? My driver can be there in 30 minutes." "O.k. I'll get ready. It will be nice to get out for a while." The General smiled and then he called his son. "Matthew this is your father" "Yes sir" "Are you at the hospital?" "Actually Dad I was just about to leave." "Good then you can join us at the Harvard Club." "I'll be right there. I'm signing out in twenty minutes. I'll see you then."

Only the General could call all three of his children at 1:00a.m. in the morning and they all respond. It would be nice to be together as a family.

"This will give us some time to talk before your brother and your sister get here. Rosaland I am very proud of you. You have done a great job. I can't tell you how pleased I have been with your efforts. You do good work kid."

The general toasted his daughter. "Thanks dad" she smiled gratefully. "This is really hard work. It is so demanding. I have no life. I can't even find the time to get married Dad." "You can always find time to get married" "We can't. I'll just be glad when this is all over." The General noticed that his daughter was pouting.

"It will be over soon. I was just going to ask you about Bobby, how is he doing? How are you two doing?" "Well Dad we want to get married and we don't have any time. We are planning a weekend event. We started looking this morning. No yesterday morning, it's already another day."

"Do you see what I'm talking about? There is no time. That was a perfect example. I see him less and less; we just see each other like two ships passing in the night. It's a good thing that I work with him or I wouldn't see him at all. Its not that he is never home I am never home. I know what Rachael is going through Arthur is never at home; he is always at work with me."

Last night I was out all night, Bobby was out all night, Arthur was out all night working. They are still at work." "That's the nature of the job especially when there is a desired out come. We have to do what we do best and that takes time." "Did you and Mom have the same problem?"

"That's what comes with this job. Its constant motion and very unpredictable. Your mother was very much like you she was always busy. Especially after all of you were born but she made time for me. My own special time. Just the two of us. I see her in you so much."

It was a rare occasion when the General spoke about her mother this way. Rosaland knew how much he missed her even now after all these years. "Your mother would be proud of you just as proud as I am." Rosaland smiled at her Dad and relaxed back in her chair with her drink.

The General noticed at that point how much Rosaland had grown in these last two years. She was an extremely knowledgeable and confident woman. Rosaland and her Father were lost in conversation when Rachael arrived. "What is going on over at that zoo you call work?" Rachael said with a smile as she kissed her sister. "My husband is never home!" "At least you have a husband I can't find time to marry mine."

"That's because you should have married him a long time ago." "Who asked you anyway Rachael?" "I'm your sister since when do you have to ask? I'm just going to tell you and you know I'm right." "Please give this girl some wine or something." The two of them laughed like they were teenagers.

"You know Rosaland I'm really mad at you. I haven't seen you in at least two weeks. The only reason that you might have a chance is that I haven't seen my own husband in about the same time frame so I know that its work related. Just what the hell is going on anyway?"

"We are finally closing in on the Calderon cartel. Hopefully by this time next week this will be all over." "You know Arthur is so closed mouthed about all of this." "It's crazy Rachael but it's almost over." The waiter handed Rachael her wine as she continued "He and Bobby are either out all night or on the phone all day. They have been like this for months."

"Rachael this is a crucial time for both the O.N.S.I. and the N.Y.P.D. This is an intense operation. We are all so jumpy maybe to the point of being paranoid. I know that I can trust this team; it's a really good team. If we are successful we are going to create some major ramifications with this one. Big ripples."

For the first time Rosaland looked worried and scared. Her Father and her sister both could see it in her face and hear it in her voice. The General detected something else in his daughter's tone; he could feel her excitement. She liked this game. Rosaland was more like her mother than she would ever know.

"Rosaland I have never known you to be this nervous about anything" Rachael was concerned. "This is a really touchy situation Rae and its all my responsibility." Rosaland sipped from her drink. "It's just so important that I do this right." "You are doing just fine; don't fall apart on me now." The General warned. "I'm fine Dad" Rosaland reassured him.

Matthew was following the waiter through the door as they finished their conversation. As Matthew walked toward his family he was smiling very happy to see all of them. Last night was the first time that he had a chance to take some well-deserved relaxation time. "It's my favorite girls!" Matthew announced as he kissed his sisters. Both Rosaland and Rachael got up from their seats to hug their younger brother.

He held each one of them in a deep hug that lasted for a while. Matthew kissed rosaland and Rachael several times before he walked over to his Father and hugged him as well. "Hey Dad! What's up?" "Hello son and how are you?" "I'm doing well sir." "Outstanding young man outstanding." The general motioned for Matthew to sit next to him.

The waiter was standing ready to take Matthew's drink order and to serve a fresh round to the rest of the family. "I'll have Hennessey heated please. As a matter of fact we will all have Hennessey heated, except for one white wine." "Yes sir" the waiter was gone to attend to his orders.

"Dad how's everything in Washington?" "Washington will always be the same son nothing ever changes. Even though it would be nice if certain individuals whom I won't name but who are all present here tonight would visit their father more. When is the last time that either one of you have been home?"

"Dad we love you and we promise that we will all come soon." Rosaland was always the first to butter him up. "Well you had better." The General was always delighted to spend time with his children. No matter how grown up they all thought they were or how complicated their lives seem to be they were just his children and he loved them.

The waiter returned at this point and served his guest. "To my brother Dr. Matthew Reid" rosaland lifted her glass and Rachael corrected her "To our brother" and they all sipped. "To what do I owe this?" Matthew questioned. "We just love you" Matthew smiled and drank. "Rachael how's married life?" "I wouldn't know my husband is never home." "Rachael you married a cop, a detective lieutenant to be more precise surely you didn't think that you would actually see him."

"Both of you ladies have a thing for officers of the law." Matthew laughed. "It's all her fault" Rachael pointed her finger at her sister. "My fault how is it all my fault?" "You introduced us" "Oh blame me for everything" they all laughed. "Matthew how's Mishawn?" "She is lovely" "Who is mishawn?" Rachael looked puzzled "Rosaland introduced us last night."

"There you go again?" "No Rachael she's not in law enforcement." "So where did you meet her?" "Actually I met her last night at the club. She is a really wonderful person. We sat together I really like her." "So do I" Matthew smiled. "I forgot to get her card last night; I don't know how to get in touch with her." "I have her number; I'll give it to you." "Good I would like to talk to her she is really a smart girl."

"I don't like the sound of this?" "What" "She's a really smart girl. You only say things like that when you are thinking about some other type of relationship." "Other than her just being my girl" "Oh she's your girlfriend now?" "Well not yet but she could be" "Well just let me know when I can call her."

They all laughed again. "Matt what do you think Rosaland is going to do?" "Rachael I do not trust Rosaland. Who knows what's on her mind? That's why Bobby is always mad at her. He never knows what she will do next." "Did he tell you that?"Rosaland responded very much on the defensive. "No Rosaland I'm just kidding. Really I'm just kidding. He has never said anything to me about that. But you must be guilty."

"Matt you are not right." "Stay away from my girl then. We can have at least one happy marriage in this family" "Matt that was cold" Rachael pouted "We are happy when we see each other." "Just kidding Rae."

The General chimed in. He couldn't hold back any longer. "This is a perfect example of what I was saying earlier" "What Dad?" "The reason why you all should come home more often." "Why Dad?" "Because you all are nuts!" They all burst into laughter.

As Bobby and Arthur left the station Arthur informed him "Bobby the General is at the Harvard Club with the family. I'm heading over there to pick up my wife. Care to join me?" "I need to go to Brooklyn and check on my grandfather. I haven't spent any time with him lately. I need to make sure that he is eating right. This might be the only time I have. Are you going to be there for a while?"

"I'll probably be there for a short time but I can wait until you get there. I'm not in any hurry?" "I have to play this one by ear don't wait. I'll hit you on your cell to let you know if I can make it." "Later" Arthur was out.

Bobby had been worried about his grandfather the last couple of days. He wanted to spend some quality time with him. They hadn't talked about Abuelita in a while and Bobby wondered how Papa was adjusting to the change in life without her.

Bobby hated when his schedule became so time consuming. It left him no time for anything else. Bobby had a myriad of thoughts flashing through his head as he drove towards home in Brooklyn. He had definitely decided that in a couple of weeks he would take some time off to sort out his priorities and put his life back into some resemblance of order.

Spending time with Papa would be at the top of his list. When Bobby arrived in front of the restaurant he was surprised to see that it was already closed for the evening. Bobby looked at his watch and noticed that it was not quite 2:00a.m. They usually closed the restaurant around 2:30a.m. His first instinct was to draw his weapon and find out what was going on.

Bobby entered the house through his bedroom door that was at the top of the steps off the deck and quietly looked around for anything out of the ordinary. He carefully descended the stairs that led to the interior of the house and noticed that nothing was out of place. Bobby placed his gun back into its holster and strolled into the living room looking for some sort of disturbance. The house checked out. There was nothing wrong.

Bobby went downstairs into the kitchen to discover Papa but he was not alone. Bobby was happy and very surprised to find Esmeralda seated at the table with his Grandfather. They were having coffee and talking. "Esmeralda I am so happy to see you. What brings you here?" Bobby questioned her as he placed a powerful hug around her neck.

"Your grandfather invited me to have dinner with him this evening but the restaurant was so crowded that I had to lend him a helping hand. We have just now finished eating." "Well what ever it was it sure smells good. How did you get here?" "The General's man brought me here and he will pick me up when I am ready to go back. I am staying with Ms. Rachael tonight."

"Bobby are you hungry?" Papa asked, "I'm tired and hungry. I had a real hard day today. I'll just grab something from the frig." "Don't worry Mr. Bobby I have something for you." Esmeralda walked over to the oven and removed a covered dish that she had set aside for him. It was still warm and Bobby sat down at the counter in back of them to eat.

"No Roberto come join us please." Papa pleaded as Bobby moved to the table where they were sitting. "This is good Esmeralda. This is really good." Bobby ate quietly as he listened to their conversation. "It is so nice to be able to speak in my native language" Esmeralda confided in Spanish. Papa answered her in Spanish as well telling her that they always speak Spanish in their home and in the restaurant."Esmeralda how did you meet the General?" Bobby was very interested in her past. If she was going to be spending any time at all with his Grandfather there were things that he wanted to know; also Bobby knew that Esmeralda could provide the missing links of Rosaland's history that she never talked about.

"Actually Mr. Bobby it was Ms. Anna that I first met. It was she who saved my life. I will never forget her and I owe a great debt to her family for keeping me in the United States all these years. I have been with the General and his family for more than fifty years."

"I came to them when I was sixteen years old. I was a young girl alone in a strange country. My auntie brought me from Equador illegally and in transportation we became separated. I was in the back of the truck when I saw my auntie being moved to another bus. I tried to run to catch up with her but I couldn't get out of the truck. There were so many people packed in front of me I couldn't get to her and then she was gone. I was left all on my own."

"I huddled close to another woman that was of an age that she could have been my mother. I didn't want anyone to know that I had no protection, no familia. I stayed very close to her day in and day out and I never said a word. When we arrived in Belize she placed an American dollar in my hand."

"It was crumpled and folded into a thousand pieces. She must have been saving it for years. She gave it to me. Then she kissed me on my cheek. I stood there fighting back the tears. I was so scared. I had no idea of what to do or which way to go and of course I couldn't speak the language."

"Somehow I got placed in this group of young teenage girls that were being shipped off to a remote destination in close proximity to a military base. There was a man Mr. Luis Ramirez that had a house for young girls. Mr. Ramirez would use the girls to sexually service himself and the men stationed at the military base."

"Mr. Ramirez also owned the only general store on the military base." Bobby listened intently as Esmeralda revealed her past openly and honestly.

"Mr. Ramirez was a very mean man. He quite often would beat and sexually abuse the girls. He always talked to them in a demeaning manner in an effort to destroy any self esteem that they might have. To keep them low."

"He constantly screamed and belittled the girls in public to keep them submissive to his demands on their bodies. When we arrived at the ranch that first night it was made very clear exactly what was expected of us."

Esmeralda shook her head to make sure that Bobby and Papa knew what she meant. Bobby knew all to well what she meant. He still had a series of unsolved murders of young girls who had been sexually assaulted and dumped naked in the streets."

Bobby was very interested in the history of this powerful family that he had become an intricate part of. Esmeralda continued "Ms. Anna and her husband were stationed on the base. She always came into the general store to shop for her groceries. Mr. Ramirez had outside connections. He often carried items that were difficult to find. He carried several American items as well. That made his store popular with the officers and the enlisted men and of course their wives."

"I had escaped Mr. Ramirez's abuse to this point but my time was coming soon. There was just a few of us left who hadn't been raped by him. On this particular day I was attending the general store when Ms. Anna walked in. She was the prettiest little woman I had ever seen. The girls look just like her. Ms. Rosaland acts just like her."

"She was confident and rich. And she had a great command of the Spanish language. She carried herself in a very regal manner very kind and very caring."

"On this particular day Mr. Ramirez was threatening to beat me for not cleaning the store to his satisfaction. He was calling me such names as stupid and ugly and he was cursing me really badly. Mr. Ramirez was not accustomed to African Americans knowing the language. So he never thought to curve his tongue in their presence."

"Ms. Anna asked him was I his daughter after hearing him degrading me in a most humiliating manner. When he replied no then she very sternly told him that he had no right to talk to me in such a vicious tone and especially not in front of customers. Mr. Ramirez was stunned by her forcefulness and the fact that she knew what he had said."

"She proceeded to tell him that in the future he needs to be more conscious of how he conducts his business or it might be bad for him. The General entered the store but he wasn't a general then. He was a tall striking figure of a man in his military uniform and his presence emulated a great deal of power and respect."

"Mr. Ramirez knew for sure that he was about to have some trouble because he had no right to speak to another man's wife without showing respect. But Ms. Anna handled the situation. She introduced her husband to the owner of the store who was then forced into an impossible situation."

"The General thanked him for treating his wife with kindness and respect. Mr. Ramirez owed Ms. Anna. After she gathered her groceries she told Mr. Ramirez that all she would request in return was his promise to treat me kindly. That was it. That was all she said. Before she left the store she smiled at me and informed Mr. Ramirez that she would do her shopping once a week on a Tuesday and that her husband would always come to escort her home."

"From that day on Mr. Ramirez never screamed at me or touched me. As a matter of fact whenever Ms. Anna did her shopping Mr. Ramirez always made a point of making sure that she knew that I was safe."

"Wow what a story" Bobby was impressed with Ms. Anna's fortitude. "Esmeralda how did you get to America?" "Ms. Anna brought me with her when she discovered that she was pregnant. I was such a young girl and I hadn't noticed at all until the day she came to say goodbye. She told me that she was going home to America to have her baby; she didn't want to give birth so far away from her mother. I immediately burst in tears."

"I just couldn't stop crying. I grabbed her around her waist and held on to her tightly. Ms. Anna started crying as well as she held me in her arms. After a moment she regained her composure and then she went into the office with Mr. Ramirez. They were there for a while but when she came out of the office she told me that if I wanted to go with her I could. She literally bought me from him."

"Mr. Ramirez agreed to this. I was never so happy. I ran to pack the small amount of clothing that I had and I ran back praying that she would still be there. She was waiting for me with her husband. Ms. Anna taught me how to read and speak English and they gave me a fine home. She made sure that I went to school and she always kept my chores small so that I could learn. She was such a good woman; I was so sad the day she died." "How did she die? Bobby was very curious. "A plane crash took her." Esmeralda remembered tearfully.

"Everybody was in shock and the General was so hurt and lost without her. The General held us together as a family. He continued to allow me to go to school; in return I cared for the children. We had the twins. They were about six and Matthew the baby was four. I don't think that either of them understood that their mother was dead until much later on."

Papa and Bobby were both intrigued with this tale from the past. This information provided them both with a broader perspective of the General and his family. "Rosaland never talks about her mother that much." "She probably doesn't remember her that much Mr. Bobby. She was six years old that was twenty-one years ago."

"I know that Ms. Rosaland always has fresh flowers in the house especially the bathrooms because her mother taught her that." "She does Esmeralda all the time. She never forgets about the flowers no matter how busy she gets I've noticed that."

"When ever she comes to Washington, she always spends time in the rose garden. I believe she tries to stay as connected to her mother as she can. I know they all do. They were all such young babies. Too young to lose their mother so tragically."

"I watch them all now. They are all grown up and they live their separate lives. Ms. Rachael is married. She is a lawyer. Ms. Rosaland is deeply in love. She is a doctor. Mr. Matthew such a handsome man so much like his father and he is a doctor. Ms. Anna would be proud of her children. She would be especially proud of her husband for holding his family together and not allowing his children to grow up unloved."

"Did Ms. Anna work Esmeralda, do you know? What did she do for a living?" "Yes she did work. She was a very important woman. She was the American Ambassador to Belize." "She was the want?" Bobby was at a loss for words. "Yes. She was the ambassador. Both she and the General were stationed in Belize and they were both working for the government. Like I said Mr. Bobby she was a very important woman."

"That explains how she got you from Ramirez. The poor bastard was probably scared to death of the both of them the General and his wife. How could he say no?" "Rameriz was a terrible man. The things he did to those young girls. Ms. Anna saved my life she got me away from him."

"Has the General always been so strict?" "Yes, always especially with his girls. He always made sure they had the best but he wouldn't allow them to feel privileged or spoiled. He always made them keep their feet on the ground remember where they came from and they always worked hard. All the kids had jobs and they worked for their money."

"The boys didn't stand a chance with the twins. Their father was so protective. The boys always came around and when they did they were all too scared to try anything." "Shit I'm still scared!" Bobby laughed as he thought to himself. Especially since I have taken certain liberties with the general's daughter."

"Mr. Bobby Ms. Rosaland loves you so very much. I've never seen her take to a man the way she has to you. The night you got shot I thought she was going to lose it. Actually she did lose it. She cried for hours until I found you. There is no need for you to be scared of her father trust me." Esmeralda was laughing. "If he was going to do something he would have done it a long time ago!"

"Yes I know but that doesn't negate the fact. Listen I've got to go to bed. We have an early day tomorrow and I have already been up much too long. Esmeralda it was indeed a pleasure to spend this evening with you and Papa." The more Bobby learned about the Reid family the more intrigued he became.

"Do either of you need anything before I leave?" "No Roberto we are just fine. Thank you." "Esmeralda do you have a way home?" "Yes Mr. Bobby. The General will send a car for me. I'll be fine." "Goodnight and don't stay up to late" Bobby smiled lovingly at his Grandfather as he climbed the stairs that led to his bed.

fifty-five

When Bobby emerged from the shower all he could think about was Esmeralda's story. She had shed so much light on the Reid background. He had no idea that Rosaland's mother was a dignitary. He had no idea that she worked for the government. As Bobby closed his eyes all he could see was Rosaland's beautiful brown body. Bobby was experiencing a real problem when it came to sleeping without her. He hated it. He missed her warm tender body lying next to his; he missed that purr she makes when she is just about to fall asleep. Bobby could hear her sighs of ecstasy in his head as he drifted off to sleep.

The N.Y.P.D. was buzzing when bobby arrived the next morning. All the detectives had been called in for a briefing on the upcoming events. Detective Semione arrived early and sat in the back as usual. He watched quietly as the rest of the unit filed in and took their seats. Diana was one of the last detectives to enter the room."

"Detective Semione noticed immediately how beautiful she looked. She was radiant and glowing as she took her seat. Bobby couldn't take his eyes off of her. There was something about her. A glow. He caught himself starring and turned his attention to the window."

"The room was filled with chatter as the detectives speculated on what the rotation would be. Lt. Yancy finally closed the door behind him and that signaled the beginning. Detective Semione looked around for Dr. Reid. He couldn't comprehend her absence. Where was she?

Bobby thought for a moment. "If she wasn't here then she was somewhere else doing something else. Now all he had to do was figure out what?" Detective Semione's train of thought was interrupted by the Lt. as he laid out the details of the upcoming seizure.

"We have a full blown drug distribution center right here in New York. This area is approximately 19, 000 square feet of space and is housed in one of New York's most popular night clubs. Our job is to gather evidence and to shut it down. This effort will be in joint cooperation with the O.N.S.I. the N.Y.P.D. and the D.E.A."

"Our unit will be backed up by SWAT and O.N.S.I. Special Forces. This is going to be a dangerous operation and we would like to keep the body count low. You have permission to use whatever force necessary to secure this facility. You need to work in teams of two or three and if possible try to make sure that no officer is ever alone. I know that is going to be difficult but just watch your backs."

"We believe this club to be owned and operated by Carlos Calderon and the Calderon Cartel. It is an important facility to his international operations. Our surveillance informs us that this might be one of his biggest east coast operations so it will be heavily guarded and secured. There will be plenty of gunfire, count on it."

The Calderon Cartel is equipped with tech nines, magnums and a various assortment of assault weaponry and those are the ones that we know. His organization is very well funded so you can imagine what we don't know."

"The SWAT team will be first on the scene after they gain entrance the detectives will go in next in teams of two or three and I hope that is well understood. Because if it's not God help the fuck up. The O.N.S.I. Special Forces will go next and the D.E.A. will bring up the rear."

"I know what you are thinking so let me answer you now; each organization involved is responsible for briefing their unit. That's why it's just us here. But rest assured we all have the same agenda and we are on the same team."

"The Calderon Cartel is the enemy. This operation will take place at approximately 9:00 p.m. tomorrow night. We are prepared to strike and we are hitting hard. Everybody needs to be in full body armor if you expect to make it out in one piece. Are there any questions?"

Lt. Yancy looked around into the faces of his detectives. He could see that they were all studying the layout that he had on the overhead. There was an uneasy silence that fell across the room when the Calderon Cartel was named. "Who gathered this Intel? Who ran the surveillance? And how do we know that it is accurate?" Detective Schmidt spoke up.

"The Intel was gathered last night and it is the most comprehensive Intel we have to date. The surveillance was set up yesterday afternoon. It has clearly defined all our parameters and our objectives. It's all right there. The O.N.S.I. under the direction of Dr. Reid gathered the information. I believe we can trust the accuracy. We can certainly trust the validity. We will use the standard search and seizure protocol done right by the book."

"No variations on this one. Straight by the book. Any more questions?" Lt. Yancy looked for more questions. The detectives had already formed their teams as they went over the diagrams. "Diana you look really beautiful today. Glad to see that you are feeling so well." Bobby whispered in her ear as they studied the Intel. He couldn't believe that this lame conversation was all that he could come up with. Diana turned and half smiled at the detective. "So if there are no more questions then I suggest you all get to 96th street for your training. Everybody now!"

The detectives filed out of the room and headed up town for a grueling one-day training exercise. Detectives Semione and Schmidt would work together on this one. Bobby could always trust Danny's instincts and he knew how he worked.

They would already have enough elements of the unknown to deal with; he needed to know his partner. Bobby was at least grateful that he didn't have to worry about Rosaland tomorrow night. His head would be focused on the task at hand and not worried about saving her life. There was some consolation in that.

Dr. Reid reported to SWAT first thing that morning. She had promised Lt. Jones that she would and she was there. Lt. Jones ran a tight ship and he was precise. He led the SWAT team through a series of drills that would enhance their abilities in the field.

Lt. Jones ran several simulation exercises in which each member of the team was responsible for the safety of their unit. In this division it was important that each marksman hit his target the first time; there was no room for second place.

"You've only got one shot. That is all that will stand between you and coming out alive." Lt. Jones introduced several position exercises that heightened their sense of awareness about the surroundings they could expect to encounter in the club. They knew that the cartel would be in force guarding the distribution center. The SWAT team would be the first on the scene so they would be direct targets in this scenario.

As Lt. Jones carefully watched Dr. Reid go through her training he again found himself wondering how he had let her talk him in to this. Rosaland had become very precise and very accurate in her abilities as a shooter. Lt. Jones was surprised at her adaptability under fire.

Rosaland wasn't playing and she could definitely hold her own. She knew her weapon and her body was in good physical condition. She moved with the precision of a well oiled machine. She rolled into position and discharged her weapon in the direction of the enemy. Rosaland was so caught up in her training routine that she neglected to notice that Lt. Yancy had arrived from the one five. Arthur disappeared into the locker room and when he emerged he was in full training gear. He positioned himself and at the next command he fell right into action.

Arthur was a veteran at this game and he knew very well how to survive. Rosaland liked working with Arthur he always brought a sense of experience to his work. Arthur was a very enthusiastic player as well as a deadly shot. At some point in this simulation they were going to encounter each other; she only hoped that he wouldn't tell Bobby.

The two lieutenants carefully executed the drills in sequence with the other members of the SWAT team as they all blended into one unit. Lt. Jones was very pleased with the productivity of the drill and the level of awareness that the unit had of their objective but their timing was off. Lt. Jones had to work the unit harder on their precision and timing exercises.

He shouted out his commands as he ordered the unit to move across the room. He wanted them to penetrate the perimeter as early as possible. They had to be fast in order to gain the advantage in a short period of time. Lt. Jones bellowed out his orders as the unit responded with their bodies. "We'll be here all night!" He hissed aloud as he choreographed their accuracy and their precision with their weapons.

"That's looking better" he screamed "But it's not good enough! You need to move out and you need to have better timing with your weapons! Do you want to come home alive? Not one of you is going to make it home! Now stop bullshitting and let's get to work!" Lt. Jones started the drill procedure all over again.

He watched closely as the team responded with the accuracy and the precision that he required. Everyone on the SWAT team knew their places and they moved expediently to penetrate the premises in a timely manner.

Lt. Jones grilled them extensively over and over as they performed the drills to his satisfaction. "Today's training could mean your life tomorrow. You need to stay close to the ground under extreme gunfire and immediately take cover don't leave your ass out." The unit listened intently to the Lt. as they rolled and took cover drawing their weapons on the count of three.

The next exercise was conducted in pairs. Both teams a and teams b had the experience and the training for this type of pairing and this exercise would pit the best against the best. Rosaland was indeed honored to be among the best of the best. She executed the maneuvers with the skill and accuracy of a seasoned officer. She had been spending a great deal of time with Dr. Ekouevi at his facility in the Bronx and it was paying off.

She presented a firmer more agile personification as she performed the drills with a high level of confidence. She wanted her team members to know that they could count on her when their lives were on the line.

The sweat ran profusely over Bobby's golden caramel colored muscular physique as the N.Y.P.D. pursued a very rigorous style of positioning exercises. The detectives had the jurisdiction on the drug facility and they all knew from experience that wherever there is a large quantity of drugs there would also be plenty of weapons and even more people who knew how to use them. They were not in any position to leave anything to chance.

The detectives worked efficiently with the N.Y.P.D. training division as they prepared for the events scheduled to take place tomorrow. The trainers for the division took no pity on the detectives when they were called for a op. It was their job to whip them into shape and to make sure that no body left until that job was completed. They had no concern for time or money when it came to preparing their officers for battle.

They were fighting the war on drugs and they were playing to win. The detective unit was sharp and coordinated as they worked on their timing and their precision. The SWAT teams' duties would be to secure the premises, but the detectives would be responsible for any gunplay that ensued and they would also be responsible for the capture of any one involved from the club staff to their hired guns. Anyone moving once they gained entry into the club.

The detectives were seasoned and they all had a variety of experiences that they brought to the training ops. The detectives knew that no matter what you thought you were facing in a seizure situation that it would always be worse and they ran through the training exercises with this in mind. The entire unit pushed themselves to the max as they prepared for their encounter with the infamous Carlos Calderon and his ruthless cartel.

Detective Semione was nervous about this one. He didn't like the atmosphere surrounding this seizure. The N.Y.P.D. had three units training in three different places for one seizure. And the fact that the D.E.A. was bringing up the rear bothered him as well. For the D.E.A. to take a third position meant that the drugs were not the focus of this operation. So what else was going on here that had escaped the rest of the team? Detective Semione pushed his muscular body to the limits as he executed the maneuvers with the skill of the seasoned professional that he was.

Bobby, Diana and Danny rolled and dived across the floor drawing their weapons on the count of three. These were the same simulation drills that all the teams were running. They had to be uniform in their approach; the ultimate result desired was the capture of Mr. Calderon and the end of the Calderon cartel.

Both of the units worked to their full capacity: Lt. Jones uptown with SWAT and the detectives of the N.Y.P.D. downtown with their training division pushing themselves beyond their limits as they competed for accuracy and precision. The sweat rolled off of their exhausted bodies as the teams endeavored to be in their best prime physical shape.

Lt. Jones led the SWAT unit along with his distinguished guests Arthur and Rosaland through a series of strenuous firearm proficiency drills. This drill left most of the unit dead due to slow reaction time. Lt. Jones drilled the unit over and over until their response time had increased dramatically. He refused to let them rest until they did it right. Bill's military training was in command of this situation and he executed the training seminar with that experience and that discipline.

He was relentless in his quest for perfection from all the trainees participating in this operation. Bill would make sure that no one left until they all did it right. Tomorrow night their lives would be on the line. Bill's persistence today could be the very reason they made it out alive and they all knew it. The team worked diligently to meet the demands of Lt. Jones as he barked out his orders for the drill.

"Well I guess we will be here all night! Now move! Let's get this done right! Move, take aim, fire! Now move out, damn it!" Lt. Jones clapped his hands to help supply the timing that he wanted for the exercise. The SWAT team moved in complete synchronization to his rhythm. Arthur kept his eye on Rosaland whenever he had the chance. He watched as she completed her exercises and she watched as he completed his.

Rosaland admired Arthur's skills and his ability to remain calm under pressure. Arthur was surprised and delighted to discover that Rosaland performed so well under pressure. The last time Rosaland and Arthur had worked together on assignment was in Bolivia. Arthur was pleased to see the growth and the maturity in her technique and her ability to handle her weapon.

As Rosaland finished up the last series of instructions Lt. Jones called a break. He was starting to see the sluggishness in their bodies that occurred due to lack of nourishment. Lt. Jones had a good eye; the unit needed their bodies replenished and well nourished for the afternoon training exercise on the obstacle course. This would prove to be the most ambitious training operation that any of the members of SWAT had ever undergone.

fifty-six

Lt. Jones's entire unit collapsed as he excused the team for lunch. Rosaland fell into a breathless perspiring heap on to the floor. Her perspiration covered her body and rolled down her forehead into her eyes. Her hair was soaking wet and her body was exhausted. She lay there for a few minutes trying to catch her breath before she took her shower. She had to get out of these wet clothes.

After Rosaland sat up she pulled her uniform top over her head exposing her wet skin to the cool air that was circulating in the room. As she sat there in her sports bra her perspiration drenching her breast she noticed that Bill was standing in the door laughing and shaking his head. Arthur walked over to his sister-in-law and extended his hand to pull her up off the ground. "Come on let's get some lunch" Arthur smiled as they walked toward to locker rooms." I didn't expect to see you here?" He looked puzzling down at her as she wiped the perspiration from her face.

"This is a better position for the O.N.S.I." she replied when she finally caught her breath. "I see even if it kills you!" Arthur responded casually as they reached the locker rooms. "I'm not the only one. At one point everybody in the room was dead!" Arthur laughed "Yes and that included me. I'll see you in a minute."

Bill was waiting by the door when Rosaland and Arthur emerged. "I have the car waiting" He said pleasantly as he escorted them through the door. "I have a nice place that we can go for lunch" Once they were in motion Bill turned to Arthur "What are the detectives doing today?" "They are with the N.Y.P.D.. training division for the morning and they are hitting the obstacle course this afternoon."

"That sounds good Arthur; all three of the units will be on the course so we can coordinate the efforts. That's good. Arthur tomorrow morning we need to go downtown and repeat today's exercise. This way your detectives can be well versed in what we are doing. Our entire inside team will have received the same training. That lowers the risk factor not much but enough to notice."

"I was hoping we could arrange an exchange like that. "Detective Semione has the lead on this one so I'm sure that the detectives will be pleased. "Good looking out." "Rosaland where are you with the surveillance?" "I have my experts in place; we are doing equipment checks tomorrow afternoon. They are testing the audio portion this morning. We will be listening from now on. Tomorrow we will have visual. I know that's cutting it kind of short but we already have the complete layout."

"Rosaland this obstacle course is an ass kicker I'm telling you now so be prepared." "I'm ready?" "You looked pretty good out there today. You surprised me for some reason and I don't know why I didn't expect you to be that good. I'm sorry."

"Thanks Bill that means a lot." "I agree with him. You did look pretty good. I like your weapon control; you did a really good job with that. It showed a great deal of growth in your development." Arthur added to the conversation. "This is looking good."

Detective Semione and his unit dressed for the afternoon activities. It had been a long time since he hit the obstacle course so he was looking forward to the workout. This was definitely something that he needed to do more often so today was a good day to start.

Detective Schmidt was also looking forward to the obstacle course. He liked the workout. It was rigorous and it required his total concentration. It challenged his discipline. "Bobby are you up for this?" Danny asked as they headed for the van that was waiting in back of the precinct to transport the unit safely and quietly to the course. "Yeah let's do this. You know we need to do this more often." They both nodded.

"I didn't know you guys from N.Y.P.D. worked so hard. I thought you were a bunch of pretty rich boys just playing detective. I take my hat off to you." Detective Cole said teasingly. "And what about us?" Detective Easley chimed in "What are we?"

"Extremely lovely ladies whom I have the pleasure of working with" Wesley smiled at Yvonne. "Good recovery detective let me shake your hand for that one." Danny said looking directly into Diana's eyes. "Oh yes you must give the ladies their respect."

Bobby smiled to himself. How often had he had that conversation with Rosaland about her job? Bobby knew what to expect from her. He knew that she would be on the obstacle course and deep down he also knew that there would be no way that she wouldn't be in on the seizure despite his very vocal protest.

Bobby was not only prepared for what he needed to do he was also prepared for what he would have to do for her. He thought about the last time he talked to Matthew and he realized that what Matt had said was right. It was his job to protect her no matter what and he would do it.

The obstacle course was located in a remote and desolate area of the Bronx. When the van pulled up there were several other vans already in the parking lot. The detectives could see the other units lining up and they hastily proceeded to fall in place one by one on the course.

The players were clearly identified by their brightly colored uniforms that bear the initials of the agencies involved. The unit commanders wore the uniform of their team. The ATF (alcohol tobacco and firearms) unit was the last to arrive. That was the missing link. Detective Semione had been right again with his instincts; he knew there was more. The presence of the firearms unit confirmed his suspicions. They were also expecting to find weapons. And by the size of the unit they expected to discover a large amount of weapons. The picture was becoming clearer to Bobby as he paid careful attention to his surroundings. This whole operation seemed to be growing out of proportion.

It was at that point that Bobby realized that this operation had been of sizable proportions from the beginning which explained all the secrecy. Detective Semione looked over the crowd to see if he could spot her shape somewhere among the multicolored masses but to no avail. As the commander of the ATF unit approached the podium the exercises officially began. This was Bobby's last chance to spot what direction she might be in.

He looked up to catch Arthur's attention. As they made eye contact Bobby followed Arthur's head movement that pointed him in the direction that he was seeking. All he wanted to know was where she was. That information would have to hold him until later.

Rosaland was also trying desperately to spot Bobby before they began. She glanced in the vicinity of the podium to catch Arthur starring in her direction. She followed his line of sight which led her to where Bobby was standing watching over her. He wanted her to know that he was there. They both made a quiet mental note of each other's position and then they both went to work.

The obstacle course was a long and complicated exercise. It presented many surprises as the levels of difficulty increased. Rosaland was struggling and it was hot. This was proving to be more physically challenging than she had anticipated. She pushed her body to its ultimate limits as she rolled and jumped and fell through the vigorous complexities of the course.

She and Arthur had started out in close proximity but as the time passed she soon lost sight of him. Bobby moved with skill and expertise through the vigorous complexities of the course. As far as Bobby was concerned the more difficult the better. He liked to push his physical limits that's why he made such a priority of staying in shape.

The sweat poured from his forehead as he rolled and fell into place. Bobby excelled at this type of exercise; it put him in a familiar environment. Bobby liked to stay close to the ground when he worked. From his perspective this position gave him a better sense of control of the situation.

Danny was a rugged outdoors man himself. He loved to climb and scale walls and be involved in heights. Danny moved from wall to roof top with the agility of a cat. His job in New York City didn't allow him much time to really enjoy his outdoor skills as much as he would like. An afternoon on the obstacle course was just what the doctor ordered.

Bobby and Danny ran the course energetically and enthusiastically. Both of the detectives trying to increase their previously established time records. The competitive atmosphere that surrounded the running of the obstacle course served as an incentive for the team as they strove for perfection in their placement. There was no way that the N.Y.P.D. would let the Brooklyn south detectives have any bragging rights.

The two divisions fought it out to the bitter end. Bobby and Danny were both determined not to let their opponents over take them. Wesley and Justin fought for the honor of their precinct but to no avail. In the end Bobby had earned the maximum score for both accuracy and speed and Danny placed a close second. Wesley held third place and Justin staggered in at fourth. The conclusion of the exercise was the traditional three-mile run and the exhausted and disgruntled participants were dismissed to either revel in their glory or languish in their defeat.

Bobby decided to wait for Rosaland not knowing exactly how long it would take her to complete her run. Bobby was proud of the fact that she had hung in there and was managing to complete the course and he wanted her to know how he felt.

Arthur noticing that all his detectives had gotten dressed ordered them all back to the precinct. "We have work to do so grab some dinner and report back to the house in an hour. We will be burning the midnight oil. There are still several details that need to be worked out. The van is out front; all that is missing is your bodies in it."

Sanchez and Cole I've got you for the duration so you need to go with them." The Lt. watched as his unit filled the van and he then decided to join them. It would be easier for him to go with his team back to their house. The Lt. wanted to go over the surveillance tapes again with his unit to make sure that they were familiar with the layout; he wanted them to know it like the back of their hands before tomorrow night. The clock was ticking and the time was running out.

When they arrived at the precinct Bobby, Diana and Danny found a nice restaurant close to the house for dinner. The restaurant was small but the ambiance was charming. It was soft and busy, quiet in an exciting sort of way the perfect place for a late night dinner.

The three detectives were very tired and they still had the whole night ahead of them. As Bobby relaxed in his chair he wondered why he had never discovered this place before. It was nice and he felt comfortable here. Bobby made a mental note to himself that he would come back when he had some time to really enjoy this atmosphere. It was Danny who broke the silence.

"That was rough today; I am definitely out of shape. I really need to start going to the course at least once a week." "I'm with you" Bobby responded off handily. "Diana you looked pretty good out there today." "I've been working out a lot lately; I didn't know it would come in handy so soon." "So what do you think we'll be up against tomorrow?" Bobby looked both of the detectives straight in the eye.

"It's hard to tell" Danny answered "but I'm sure that this won't be easy. There is no way that we are going to just waltz in without a fight." "Bobby you should be giving us some heads up. You live with the boss." Bobby started laughing "I didn't even know she had the video surveillance or that she had sent in her own team of under covers."

Bobby sipped his coffee as his thoughts returned to her. "When it comes to the O.N.S.I. she does things her own way. She might discuss it with the General but she never discusses it with me. I'm not O.N.S.I. and she doesn't tell me any of their business. She is so secretive when it comes to that organization."

"Bobby it sounds to me like you are losing your touch." Diana couldn't resist taking that pot shot. "No it sounds to me like Bobby has met his match." Danny said flippantly fully understanding how deep Bobby's feelings for Rosaland ran. "Look you two don't we have work to do? It's about time that we got to it." That was Bobby's way of changing the subject. Diana and Danny smiled at each other as they continued to eat their dinner.

Rosaland lowered her aching body into the Jacuzzi with the hope that the jets could help to ease the pain. Her discomfort was so intense that no matter what she did she couldn't manage to get comfortable and her body cried out in agony as the hot water swirled around her. Tears of anguish swept down her face as she persevered the distress embedded within her shapely form.

Rosaland could be her own worse enemy sometimes. No one told her that she had to attempt the obstacle course and now her body was paying for it. Rosaland finally able to relax wondered what was she going to do tomorrow; there was still another day to train and she needed to coordinate the surveillance.

Dr. Ekouevi's would run the whole operation from O.N.S.I. Headquarters so at least she wouldn't have to worry about that. Her first priority at this very moment was to be able to move. She needed to find a masseuse. If she couldn't get one tonight then she would definitely have to locate one by tomorrow morning. As she thought about the rigorous schedule that she would be facing due to the upcoming events she had to take care of her body now.

When the water cooled down she climbed out of the tub and called Rachael. Rachael had a Bulgarian woman that came in from time to time and now was a good time to call her. "Hey Rachael" Rosaland said in a faint voice "What's going on sweetie? Rosaland what's wrong?" Her sister was obviously alarmed. "Nothing that a good massage can't cure. Will you call your girl for me?"

"Sure you sound completely out of it. What happened today? I called you several times; you were out of your office all day." "We had an all day training exercise uptown and we finished it off with an afternoon on the police obstacle course." "What! Rosaland I swear sometimes you amaze me. Why on God's green earth would you spend the afternoon on the obstacle course? You are not a cop. What do you need that type of training for?"

"Rachael tomorrow night we are shutting down a real bad man. There is no way that I am going into any situation without the proper training. I do want to come home."

"I know about the operation. Arthur spoke to Judge Black this morning before breakfast about the search warrants. I had no idea that you were involved. Since Arthur was securing the warrants I just assumed that this was N.Y.P.D."

"Rachael this is strictly O.N.S.I. The N.Y.P.D. is there as our guest. This is the culmination of two and a half years of work." "What do you need Sarah for?" "We finished with a three mile run and my body is sore. I can barely move. I know this is last minute but I really need her tonight. I'm not going to have any time tomorrow. Well I'm not going to be able to move tomorrow so my time is going to be irrelevant. I'm not going to be able to do my job.

"Oh God Rosaland. I wish you had a different job! It's bad enough that my husband's life is always on the line but here lately so is yours! You are always in the middle of something dangerous. I wish Dad would have never given you this job. Didn't he know how dangerous this was going to turn out for you? You have a PhD; you can do anything. Why do you have to be involved in this?"

"It's my job. Are you going to call Sarah or do I have to listen to this for the rest of the night?" "I'll call her. I'll send her right over. You sound like you are dying." "I am Rachael. I'm in bad shape!" "I'll call her sweetie. I'll make sure that she comes; as a matter of fact I'll bring her over."

Arthur won't be home for hours so that means that Bobby won't be home either. I'll take care of you tonight. Besides I need your help with something. I'll see you in a minute." Rosaland loved her sister. If there was one person she could always count on. She could always count on Rachael.

fifty-seven

When Rachael arrived she found her sister sitting in her bedroom window box working on her laptop. Rosaland was so preoccupied studying the spreadsheet that she didn't notice Rachael's presence until she was in the bedroom. Rachael had Sarah to wait downstairs while she sought out the condition of her sister.

"So Ms. I'm going to work out with the N.Y.P.D. How are you?" Rosaland looked up into the face of her sister while the tears streamed down her cheeks. "Thanks Rachael for coming to my rescue and I worked out with SWAT." Rosaland tried to smile at her sister as she hugged her tightly. Rachael could feel the tightness in her body. "Sarah is downstairs and we are paying her by the hour so where do you want her to set up?"

"Ouch Rae that hurts. Can we do it here? Honestly I don't think I can make it downstairs." Rosaland said wiping the tears from her face. "You are in bad shape. Ok you get yourself ready and I'll go get her." Rosaland nodded as Rachael went downstairs to retrieve Sarah.

"Hey baby where are you?" Arthur asked Rachael "I've been calling our house for at least an hour. I thought you would be home." "I'm in Harlem at Rosaland's. She is in pretty bad shape tonight." "What's wrong?" Arthur was very concerned. "Oh nothing a little TLC can't cure." "What's going on up there?" Arthur asked again in a demanding tone of voice. "Calm down sweetie. There is nothing wrong and we are both all right. She had a rough day and she needed some help. Honestly baby we are fine."

"Ok since that's all you are giving me we will talk about this later. I'll be home in a couple of hours. Will you be there or do I have to come and get you?" "No I'll be there. I'll see you when you get home. I love you" and with that Rachael hung up the phone.

Arthur had his back to the door so he didn't realize that Bobby was standing behind him. "What's going on boss?" Bobby asked sensing that something was wrong. "Nothing just checking in with Rachael. She's up in Harlem with Rosaland. They're fine." "Are you sure?" "Yes" Arthur was a little worried but he knew to trust Rachael. If she said everything was fine it was. Besides he couldn't take the chance of distracting Bobby. Not when they still had so much work to do.

Bobby excused himself for a moment and called to find out what the hell was going on. "Hi Baby what are you doing?" "Bobby this is Rachael." "Hi Rachael let me speak to Rosaland." "Bobby she's a little tied up at the moment. Can she call you back?" "Tied up doing what?" "She is having a massage and she can't get to the phone right now. Bobby she will call you back as soon as she is finished."

"All right just tell her that I'll be there in a couple of hours. "Everything is fine Bobby I'll tell her. Do you still want her to call you back?" "No as long as everything is alright I'll see her when I get there. Just tell her that I called." "Will do." Rachael smiled as she hung up the phone. She knew that Bobby was going to call. Actually she expected both Arthur and Bobby to come busting in the door with guns blazing.

She was happy she was able to diffuse what could have been a volatile situation. They were all so paranoid lately and so prone to over reaction. Rachael would be glad to see the end of this case. Maybe she could get her husband back and all four of them could resume their lives. Rachael looked in on Rosaland and noticed that Sarah seemed to be offering her some relief. Rachael could hear her sister moan as Sarah massaged the knots and the soreness out of her muscles.

"Ms. Rachael will you please fill the tub with some nice warm water and some bath salts?" Sarah instructed. Rachael nodded and went into the bathroom. "Ms. Rosaland after I finish I want you to just soak in the tub. It will make your body feel better." Once Rosaland was relaxing in the tub Rachael decided that it was time that she headed home. She wanted to be there when Arthur got off and she didn't want to be in Harlem when Bobby got home. She knew that the two of them would want that time alone.

"Rachael look in my wallet and pay Sarah. Give her a really nice tip. She did a great job. I just might make it." "Are you alright?" "Yes I'm fine." "Ok then I'm out. I have to drop Sarah off." Rachael walked over to the tub and placed a kiss on her sister's forehead. "Thanks Rachael. I'll call you in the morning." "Oh by the way Bobby called. He said he would be here in a couple of hours." And with that Rachael was out the door.

When Bobby arrived home he found the brownstone nice and quiet. He expected to walk in and hear Rosaland and Rachael laughing about something. Whenever the two of them were together after work they always found something or someone to laugh and joke about. That was one of the things that he loved about their relationship. They always found time for laughter.

Rosaland was in an extremely quiet mood as she sat gazing out of the window lost in thought. Bobby noticed the way her robe hung sexily off of her naked shoulder. He walked over and sat down behind her and then he placed a soft kiss on her shoulder and her neck. "Hey beautiful" he whispered as he gently wrapped his arms around her. Rosaland snuggled back in his arms and closed her eyes. "You looked really good out there today" "No Bobby I almost died out there today. My body was so sore when I came home that I couldn't move."

"Rachael told me that you were having a massage. How do you feel now?" "Much better. I'm just tired and sore but I'll live." "You seem awfully quiet." "I'm just thinking about things." "About what things?" "Us, the job, tomorrow, things." "This sounds serious let me get comfortable and we can talk about it." Rosaland turned her head to look at him straight in his eyes. She nodded her head in affirmation and then she turned her gaze back to the window.

"I'll be right back" Bobby said as he removed his jacket and threw it over the chair. He went downstairs to make them both a drink and when he returned he slipped into the shower. Rosaland sipped her drink slowly while she waited for Bobby to finish.

The warm water felt wonderful as it ran down his strong physique. Bobby stood motionless as the water inundated his body from head to toe. His muscles were tight from all the physical exertion of the day and the water was soothing. It felt good to relax while the jets from the shower head gently massaged his magnificent physique.

Bobby was conscious of the amount of time that he was spending in the shower because he knew that Rosaland wanted to talk to him. He wanted to talk to her as well. He was proud of the way she handled herself today and it was important to him that he let her know. Of course he still wouldn't agree with her decision to be a part of the SWAT team but he had to give her the respect that she deserved for making sure that she was as prepared for the bust as she could be.

She worked hard out there today and that hard work had gained her the respect from her coworkers as well as her team members. They knew that they could count on her if the going got rough and it indeed was going to be rough. Let there be no doubt about it.

As Bobby was leaving the station this evening he overheard the SWAT coordinator talking to Arthur about "That O.N.S.I. girl who held her own."

Her presence had made quite a statement today within the law enforcement community and it also called attention to the outstanding capabilities of the O.N.S.I.

When Bobby emerged from the shower he was happy to find that she hadn't fallen asleep but was relaxing peacefully in the same location that he had left her in. She was still gazing serenely out of the window lost in thought. Bobby noticed that her glass was empty so he assumed that she was feeling better.

Bobby walked over and stood next to her as he continued to dry his body with the large lush bath sheet. Bobby wrapped the towel around his waist as he sat down next to her. He looked over her shoulder to see what had her so interested. "Would you like another drink?" He asked softly as he kissed her exposed shoulders. "Uum" she sighed as she nodded yes to his question. Bobby kissed her one last time before he went downstairs to refresh their drinks.

While he was gone she slipped into a black silk sleep sheath with thin spaghetti straps and she applied two drops of his favorite perfume to her pulse points. When Bobby returned he was pleased with what he saw. He handed her a new drink and taking her hand led her to the bed. While she was making herself comfortable Bobby slipped into a pair of boxer briefs and joined on her on the bed.

"Now what's on your mind?" He mentioned as he sipped his drink. "What has you so lost in thought? Are you worried about tomorrow?" "Yes Bobby I am." "Do you want to talk about it?" "Yes I do. I'm really nervous about this Bobby and honestly I'm very scared."

"That's understandable baby. This is some serious shit that's about to happen. I think everybody is nervous about this one so you are not alone. This is a big ass operation. I can't remember the last time we had an operation with this type of joint cooperation. I'm really impressed that you were able to get this type of consideration and you or should I say the O.N.S.I. has jurisdiction."

"I still can't figure out how you managed that one. That really says a lot for the O.N.S.I. I think it's fair that you know everybody's watching you. You raised some eyebrows today." "Really?" "Oh yes" "Interesting?" Rosaland sat in silence for a moment then she continued "Bobby I want to talk to you about the O.N.S.I." "That's funny that you would mention that. You never want to talk to me about the O.N.S.I. What about the O.N.S.I.?

"Bobby don't be so sarcastic. Why is that so funny?" "It's a long story sweetie" "well I've got the time." "Rosaland lighten up. It's not that serious." In all the time that they had been together Bobby didn't remember ever seeing her like this. Whatever was on her mind was obviously bothering her. "I'm sorry honey. What about the O.N.S.I.? "After this whole Calderon fiasco is over" she paused and took a deep breathe "I would like for you to join it."

Rosaland looked at Bobby as her hair hung sexily in front of her eyes. "What?" "I've been thinking about this for a long time." "I'm listening" "I know that you have years vested in the N.Y.P.D. but I would like you to consider coming to work with me." Rosaland winced and gritted her teeth knowing that Bobby would never considered working with her like that.

"The O.N.S.I. is moving out of the N.Y.P.D. after this operation. We have a new facility to house our organization and our company is expanding. My father has secured a generous amount of funding from some private conglomerates and the agency will be taking on a broader responsibility in anti- terrorist activities as well as narcotics trafficking and arms dealing."

"What! Bobby almost choked on his drink. "What the hell are you talking about?" That violent reaction that she was expecting earlier was starting to come out "Yes. We've got the manifesto." "What damn manifesto?" "We have a government manifesto; we are definitely expanding our jurisdiction into the global arena."

Bobby lay there completely amazed. It was like he mentioned earlier to Danny and Diana. She never tells him a damn thing. "Global jurisdiction. Nobody has global jurisdiction. What about the fucking Geneva Convention?" "We do. We have global jurisdiction and the Geneva Convention only applies in times of war. We are fighting the war on drugs and international arms dealing and we have global jurisdiction for our operations."

"We also have international cooperation from other organizations that are involved with fighting this same battle. Baby I have been putting this deal together from day one. It has taken me two years, no two and one half years to get the proper facility. Now that I have the facility. I need the staff. I need the manpower. That's why it is so important that we shut down this Calderon character so we can move on to other groups that are rapidly growing in power before he connects to them."

"Believe me there is a new arms dealer or dope smuggler emerging every two minutes on the international scene and they are entering the market fully prepared to play hardball. That's why the O.N.S.I. has to be fully prepared to stop them. I can't do this without you and I have to do this or should I say the O.N.S.I. has to do this and we can't do this without you. We need your help and besides it's a great job."

"Rosaland have you lost your mind? I don't even know who I'm talking too." At this point Bobby was walking around the room shaking his head in total astonishment. "You know you just can't give this shit up can you? What about us? What happened to us? Two weeks ago you damn near chewed my head off because I didn't have any time to plan a wedding. This is two weeks later and now you are talking about global terrorism. Maybe Diana was right; apparently I am losing my touch."

"What has Diana got to do with this? Is that why you won't even consider coming to work with me? Because of Diana?" "Whoa time out!" Bobby made the time out sign with his hands. "What are you talking about? Don't get off the subject! We are not arguing over Diana. Not this time. We are talking about arms dealing and dope smuggling and global jurisdiction which is completely absurd. I'm a detective Rosaland. I work the streets of New York. I travel down these mean streets everyday trying to make life a little safer if I can. I don't play in this global arena that you seem to be so fond of. I'm sure your boy Bill will play along. He appears to be inclined to do anything you ask him."

"What the hell do you mean by that?" She shot a feisty look in his direction. "Rosaland you know exactly what the fuck I mean. There was no way you could just waltz your ass into a SWAT training session without somebody pulling some strings on your behalf. And I know that your boyfriend Bill pulled those strings. What the hell were you doing there anyway? You promised me that you weren't going in. I should kick his ass because he knew that I would never have approved of that move. But you know what I'm going to let you and your boyfriend do your thing with this international bullshit."

"Bobby where are you going?" "You know Rosaland it's late and we both need some sleep. We have a big day ahead of us tomorrow. I'm going home to check on Papa and then I'm going to bed. You need to get your priorities straight. I'm not asking you to choose between your job and me; I'm telling you to choose me period. Bottom line. If you can't deal with that then maybe we both have been wasting our time."

"Bobby how did we get here?" "That's a good question? You tell me." "Bobby please don't leave. We can talk about this in the morning." "Papa and Abuelita were married for fifty years before her death and never one time did they go to bed mad or angry with each other. I'll call you in the morning to see if you would like to have breakfast." Bobby grabbed his badge and his gun from the nightstand and he was out the door. "Well that went well" she thought to herself before she burst into tears.

Rosaland tossed and turned all night and Bobby didn't get a wink of sleep. What was he going to do with her? Maybe he shouldn't have come down on her so hard. No he wasn't going to allow her to keep putting them off. Bobby had decided that no matter how much it hurt he was moving on.

It was obvious to him that they were growing in the opposite direction of each other. She was ready to make her transition into the global arena and he was happy right where he was. He wasn't going to hold her back and he wasn't sure that he wanted to go where she was headed. Bobby knew that if she had taken the responsibility of the expansion of the O.N.S.I. that she would honor her commitment especially since her father was involved.

He couldn't compete with that. And what was becoming more apparent to him was he didn't want to compete with it. Bobby loved Rosaland more than anything but this relationship was not working. After tonight he was out.

"Roberto you are up early this morning. Didn't you get any sleep?" "Good morning Papa. We have some urgent business at the station today and I'm just trying to get prepared." Papa noticed immediately that Bobby was distracted; he knew that something was wrong. "Roberto what is the matter?" "Nothing Papa. I'll be fine" "When a man sounds like this it must be his woman."

Bobby looked at his grandfather with respect. He had a great deal of wisdom. "Yes Papa it is my woman. She is so hard headed and it is not working out." "You have to make it work. A good marriage takes a lot of time and even more work." "Yes but we are not married and that is the problem. She doesn't want marriage Papa she wants to save the world." "Well Roberto if you love her you have to help her." "Papa I do love her. I love her more than life but I can't do it. It has to be her decision."

Papa could see the pain in Bobby's face and he knew that it only presented an image of what he must be feeling in his heart. "Roberto you can't go to work like this." "I have to; it's too late to turn back now. I have to go Papa. I'll see you later." Bobby kissed his grandfather on the forehead and he was down the steps and out of the door.

fifty-eight

Rosaland waited patiently for Bobby to call her but he never did. She really needed to talk to him. She called his cell phone but he didn't have it on. When she called Brooklyn papa answered the phone. "Good morning Papa I need to talk to Bobby. is he there?" "Good morning Rosaland. How is your family?" Rosaland broke down in tears "Papa is he there?"

"No he already left for work. He said he had some urgent business. Are you alright?" "No. I'm not. I need to talk to Bobby," she sobbed out loud. "Where is he?" "I don't know sweetie. He already left for work." "I'm sorry Papa. Thank you" Rosaland hung up the phone. She knew that Bobby was not at work it was too early but just to make sure she called the one five. "I'm sorry Dr. Reid but none of the detectives have checked in yet." The desk sergeant spoke. "Their shift hasn't started. Do you want to leave a message for Detective Semione? I'll make sure he gets it."

"Yes thank-you. Have him to call me as soon as he gets in." Rosaland jumped in her car and headed downtown. She would just have to find him. As she frantically drove down Harlem River Drive she tried to think of where he might be this early in the morning. The tears ran profusely down her face as she desperately sought his whereabouts. This was like searching for a needle in a haystack. She had no idea where to begin.

Bobby was the best detective in the unit and she knew from experience that if he didn't want to be found she would not find him. On the other hand she needed to pull herself together because there was still a great deal of work to be done before tonight. She had two hours before she needed to report uptown and she was determined to track him down no matter what she had to do. She tried his cell phone but it was still turned off. She paged him from her cell phone but he never called back.

"Are you eating alone this morning?" The waitress asked as she poured his coffee. "Yes pretty much." "Do you know what want?" "Just coffee for now." Bobby looked down at his belt to check the number that had his pager vibrating. He knew that it was Rosaland but he didn't respond. This was going to be a lot harder than he anticipated; simply not calling her back was driving him crazy. Bobby knew her and he knew that if he didn't at least respond before he got to work that there would be a scene and he didn't want that. Not today there was too much at stake.

"Yes Baby what's up?" Rosaland finally relaxed when she heard his voice. "Bobby where are you? I've been paging you all morning." "I know I got them. What's up?" "Where are you?" "I'm having breakfast" "Where? Bobby can I meet you?" "Yes I'm at the Second Street diner." "I'm very close I'll be there in about ten minutes." Bobby thought about leaving he really didn't want to talk to her but he knew that if he wasn't there when she arrived the rest of the day would be shot to hell.

Rosaland took the time to fix her face before she entered the restaurant. She didn't want to appear as though she was not in some sort of control of her emotions, but any time it came to Bobby she fell apart. He was the one area of her life that she had absolutely no control over.

Rosaland looked around hoping that Bobby would be easy to find but the diner was crowded with the early morning breakfast crowd. When the waitress approached Rosaland said in a polite voice "Excuse me I'm looking for ..." "He's in the back..." "Thank you" Rosaland walked toward the back of the diner and there Bobby sat drinking his coffee.

"Good morning Baby can I sit down?" "Please" Bobby could tell that she had been crying. "I thought you were going to call me this morning?" Bobby looked her deep in the eyes "Rosaland we need to get something straight. Today is not a good day for us to be in conflict. We need to put this issue behind us at least for right now. Do you agree with that?" "Yes" "So can we conduct business as usual until later when we have the time to discuss this?" "Yes" "Because I need to go. I have some things that I need to do."

Rosaland was a bit confused. If she didn't know any better she could have sworn that Bobby just blew her off. "Ok" "Rosaland I promise we will talk later. You need to pull yourself together. You have a lot of people that are counting on you for leadership and support. Tonight is the real thing. It's not a drill and it's not a computer generated scenario. The bullets are real and their targets are real and you will be one of them. Hopefully we can get in and do what we need to do without the lost of a life but don't count on it."

"Somebody is not going to come home tonight. somebody is going to lose a loved one tonight and it's our job to be at our best for all those involved. All the agencies have worked on this to long for our personal relationship to throw things off. We both have to be on point. I don't want to go in distracted and I also don't want to go in worried about you."

Bobby stopped talking for a moment as the waitress refilled his coffee and poured Rosaland a fresh cup. Bobby didn't want anybody accidentally overhearing any part of his or her conversation. This was a private matter and he wanted to keep it that way.

"I'm sorry that I overreacted last night. I could have handled that a bit better but then again I didn't expect my future wife to be talking about arms dealing and dope smuggling. I might be a little naïve but for some reason I thought we would discuss our future or possibly make love or just spend the evening together in each others arms." That's when she realized just how upset he really was.

"Bobby I have always been able to be honest with you…" "Rosaland you don't tell me anything if holding back information is your idea of honesty we have a serious problem." "I tell you everything that I can tell you…" "Rosaland did you hear what you just said? That you can tell me? That's our problem." "Bobby you don't discuss N.Y.P.D. business with me and you never have! That's not fair that you feel that I should discuss O.N.S.I. business with you."

"That's because you are always there. You know more about N.Y.P.D. business than I do" he screamed. Bobby had to admit that she had a valid point. "I'm sorry too I'm sorry that I didn't know you have been feeling this way. I apologize." Bobby couldn't hold back any longer. He knew that she was on the verge of tears. Bobby leaned in close and kissed her gently on her quivering lips. "Fix your face" he smiled as the tears began to well up in her eyes.

Rosaland was surprised; she didn't know what was happening. Bobby was not one for public displays of affection. He kissed her to calm her down this time with more meaning. Rosaland responded immediately to his touch as she placed her hand in back of his head to pull him closer. "I love you Bobby." She whispered fighting desperately to hold back her tears.

Bobby acknowledged her sentiment by standing up and taking her into his arms and kissing her passionately and longingly. He pulled her body close to his and held onto her tightly. They both lingered in each other's arms for a brief moment totally ignoring the stares they were receiving from the customers. "Let's get out of here" Bobby said in a low undertone as he placed the money for the coffee and the tip on the table. When they were outside the restaurant Bobby wiped the tears from her eyes.

"Are you alright?" "I am now" "Baby you have to pull yourself together. I need to know that you are going to be alright." "Bobby I'm fine" "Well I might be a bit more inclined to believe you if you weren't standing here with tears running down your face." "I know but I am o.k." "Where are you working today or can you tell me that?" "You know Bobby you are such a fucking smartass. That's not funny. I'm working uptown again but I'm coordinating the surveillance. I won't be in the field until tonight."

"Ok just remember to cover your ass. It's such a nice ass." "And a lonely ass. I missed you last night." "And you are going to be a single ass if you don't start acting right." Bobby quipped as they walked toward her car. "Oh by the way you look really nice today." "What am I going to do with you?" Rosaland asked him playfully "Marry me and have my babies." Bobby winked as she pulled off and sped uptown.

Lt. Yancy had secured all the necessary search warrants and he was in the process of going over the diagram of the club layout when Bobby arrived. "Detective you are late" Arthur screamed as Bobby entered the conference room and sat down. "Sorry boss something came up" "Actually we just started you're lucky. Here is a copy of the layout please follow along.

"This is an updated copy of the club layout. Thanks to the O.N.S.I. surveillance we have all the entrances and exits that lead to the three levels. The SWAT team will go in first to secure the perimeter. They will detain anything that is moving. We are up next; as soon as the facility is secured. We go in. You have the authority to use whatever force is necessary to get your job done. If you are fired upon you have the authority to return fire."

"We know that there is a drug processing center on the bottom level; Let me give you a heads up on that. Dr. Reid shared that information with us and only us. The D.E.A. doesn't even know. They won't know until after we have shut it down. That gives us jurisdiction. All the D.E.A. can do after that is the actual confiscation of any narcotics or narcotics processing paraphernalia that we find on the premises. She did us a solid on that one."

Diana and Danny looked at Bobby who was studying the diagram. "Detectives Semione, Schmidt, Rousseau, Cole, and Sanchez will immediately secure that level. Be ready for anything. This situation is extremely volatile. Work in teams, stay with your partner and cover your backs."

"Detectives Easley, Baker and Lyle will secure the club and all personnel on the second floor. The O.N.S.I. Special Forces will have jurisdiction over the records, files and any other pertinent information found on that level. Dr. Reid included everybody in her plan. If this operation is successful it could lead to many major arrests and the possible apprehension of Carlos Calderon who belongs exclusively to the O.N.S.I.

"Make sure that you are properly identified. We don't want anyone to be a victim of friendly fire. We are hitting them hard and fast in one quick strike. There won't be time for a second chance. Are there any questions?

I want everybody in body armor and ready for a weapons check in fifteen minutes."

"Lt. where will you be?" "I'm going in with SWAT and the O.N.S.I. Special Forces." "Detective Semione I need to speak to you. The rest of you are dismissed." The Lt. waited patiently for his detectives to leave the room before he spoke to Bobby. "I know how you are about her and I know that you don't really want her there. I know that you can't watch out for her and do your job properly. So I made a promise to Rachael that I would look out for her sister. That's why I'm going in with SWAT and the O.N.S.I. Special Forces. This has nothing to do with you Bobby but I need you to handle that drug processing center and I need your mind clear."

"That's good looking out because I know that she is nervous about this one. I just want her safe." "You know Bobby she always looks out for you" "What are you talking about?" "The drug center we made a deal" "What kind of deal?" "She wants you to get credit for the bust that's why she didn't tell the D.E.A." "Oh man don't tell me that. I went off on her last night about the fact that she never tells me anything and now you are telling me this." "Just keep your head clear and do a good job Bobby. I'll make sure that she stays safe. Now you need to go get into your armor."

Dr. Reid worked with Dr. Ekouevi the whole day. They continuously ran the surveillance to make sure that they caught every angle of the intended target. They scoured the perimeters as well as the interior for anything that they might have possibly missed. Dr. Reid loved working with Dr. Ekouevi because he was so thorough. He never missed anything and if there was something new to be added he was the most innovative with his thoughts and ideas. The most important aspect of their friendship was the amount of trust that they shared between them.

Dr. Reid knew without a shadow of a doubt that she could count on him. She was looking forward to expanding his operations and utilizing his talents to their fullest extent. "I need to report to SWAT. Is there anything else we need to go over before I leave?" "No we are fine. We've got everything covered. You just need to be careful." "I will and I won't be alone. The O.N.S.I. Special Forces will back me up."

"You need to make sure that we have enough space for any confiscated materials and put a skeleton team in place to categorize the evidence." "You got it. One last thing are you comfortable with your weapon?" "Yes. If there is nothing more hopefully I'll see you and the surveillance tapes in the morning."

"You'll be here. I have made sure of that. Dr. Ekouevi said in his heavy French accent. The hour was rapidly approaching for the final confrontation. Dr. Reid was nervous as she donned her body armor. She thought about

Bobby as she strapped her weapon to the inside of her thigh and holstered her other one to her shoulder.

Dr. Ekouevi had designed this holster just for her. It was lightweight and it allowed the utmost in maneuverability. It fit nice and snuggly on her shoulder. If you didn't know that she was packing, it would be very easy to overlook. That could give her the competitive advantage if she were in a situation that called for fresh tactics.

Lt. Jones was calling all his operatives in from the locker room. It was time for them to do a complete weapons check before they hit the club. "We are hitting them hard and fast in one quick strike. There won't be time for a second chance. All the agencies are coordinated and they know at what phase of the operation that they are scheduled to strike. Keep your eyes open and your head down. Cover your ass and watch your back. Work in teams of two and be ready for anything. Let's go!"

fifty-nine

The combined forces of the N.Y.P.D, the O.N.S.I. and the D.E.A. converged on the Club Oasis at about 5:00 p.m. They had a window of two hours before the club was scheduled to open to the public. According to the surveillance this would be the time when all the traffic not related to the normal operations of the club would be taking place. The SWAT team positioned themselves at the front entrance and all other peripheral entrances and waited for Lt. Jones to give the signal. Lt. Jones waited for the rest of the units to fall into place and then he gave the order to move.

The SWAT team used the battering ram to bust down the front door. Immediately they swarmed the club like cockroaches. The team penetrated the interior of the first floor and stopped any motion from the employees that were scrambling here and there to hide or try to escape. The SWAT team held their position as they pinned down anything that moved.

Detective Semione and his team entered next and immediately advanced to the lower level. Detective Semione had discovered what would turn out to be the largest narcotics seizure on the east coast. The processing center was approximately 19,000 square feet of space all of which was being utilized for the manufacture and the distribution of cocaine.

"N.Y.P.D. Freeze!" The detective shouted. This is when all hell broke loose. The detectives were greeted with a hail of gunfire from semi automatic assault weapons. Detective Semione and his team had to take cover as they returned fire in the direction from which it was coming. The Special Forces of the O.N.S.I. upon hearing the rapid blaze of gun fire coming from below immediately ran to the lower level to support to the detectives.

Lt. Jones commanded his forces to take cover and try to squelch the perpetrators. Every member of the processing team was armed to the nines and responded successively to protect their freshly processed batch of illegal drugs. The sounds of the gunfire were so loud and so frequent that it appeared it would go on for ever.

Lt. Jones took cover and made a quick observation of the situation. There were several large containers of chemicals scattered around and he knew that if they were hit with gunfire that an explosion would soon follow; an explosion that none of them would survive.

It was at this point the Lt. Jones decided to switch tactics. The bullets flew around his head as he tried to make his way further into the interior. Detective Semione also noticed the large amount of stored chemicals. In order for the team to be able to survive he needed to open the space up. He remembered from the diagram that there were exits on both sides of the lower level. He used his walkie talkie to communicate with SWAT to open up the lower level.

"We have a huge supply of chemicals down here that are going to explode. We need you to open up our perimeters now! Get these doors open!" The SWAT team's reaction was instantaneous just as the outer perimeters were opened; the detectives were hit with another round of fierce gunfire.

Opening up the perimeters allowed an influx of the Calderon Cartel. They were coming out of the woodwork. Like ants, they were everywhere; the sounds of m-16's filled the room. "Oh shit!" Detective Semione cried as the cartel members protected their territory. The air was filled with the sounds of gunfire whizzing by and their window was closing.

Detective Semoine rolled into the middle of the floor and fired a series of quick rapid shots. The Cartel members started to drop like flies. Detectives Schmidt, Cole and Sanchez followed his lead and took out several more. They were starting to even the odds.

Detective Schmidt signaled that there were two more behind them and he and his partner rolled across each other aimed and fired. Both men hitting their intended targets. As Detective Semoine looked up he noticed that Detective Rousseau was crouched in the corner sweating profusely and throwing up. She had enough presence of mind to stay close to the floor but she was obviously weak and in need of some air. Detective Semione knew that he needed to get her out of there before she got shot.

Bobby circled around the back and grabbed her. She looked frightened and pale but she offered no resistance. "Diana are you alright?" He whispered being very careful not to give up their location with his voice. Diana shook her head to answer in the negative. She was not all right and in another moment Diana had fainted and sank to the floor in a heap.

Detective Semione grabbed her up in his arms and ran to the nearest exit where he placed her limp body outside the door. He looked around to see if they had been discovered aiming his weapon at the entrance in expectation of a cartel member.

He remained in this position long enough to make sure that the coast was clear before he pulled her to safety. "Officer down!" He screamed into the walkie talkie while he waited for a SWAT member to come to their rescue. When the officer approached he ordered "Take care of her and get her out of here!" Detective Semione then proceeded back inside to rejoin his team as they continued to be engaged in battle with the cartel.

The window of opportunity was closing and the Cartel seemed to be holding their own. "I've had about enough of this shit!" Detective Semione screamed to his unit and that signaled an onslaught from the N.Y.P.D. that was second to none. The remaining detectives rallied a defense that left dead cartels members all over the floor.

In a matter of minutes the gunfire ceased and all was quiet. Detective Semione signaled for detectives Cole and Sanchez to recon and within minutes the remaining Cartel members were captured. Lt. Jones led the O.N.S.I. Special Forces deeper into the interior of the lower level where more gunfire was heard.

The N.Y.P.D. held their positions and waited for Lt. Jones to communicate his position. "Situation secured" Lt. Jones reported as he escorted the arrested members of the cartel into the holding area.

After Rosaland's talk with Sonia Blackwell a couple of weeks ago her curiosity had been stimulated. Who was this man that was so allegedly intrigued by her? To her knowledge she had never meet the infamous Carlos Calderon and it would be ironic that she should have to meet him when she was arresting him but that was what she was here for and now it was her turn to do her job.

Dr. Reid motioned to Lt. Yancy as she headed up the stairs with her gun drawn. This was another one of the small details she had intentionally forgotten to leave out of the diagram. Carlos had a residential area on the third floor and this is where she expected to find him.

Her informant assured her that he would be in New York. That was why she scheduled the raid for today. She only hoped that the information was accurate. The acoustics on the third floor was the advantage that she needed; the third floor was sound proof. If he was there and if he was busy with a woman then he would have seen or heard nothing.

He had no idea that his club was being taken down. Dr. Ekouevi had the video feed focused on the third floor residential area. He fed Dr. Reid the information in full detail as she climbed the steps. Lt. Jones had divided the O.N.S.I. Special Forces and half of them accompanied her as back up.

"Mr. Calderon is occupied at this time with a beautiful woman. Well I'll be damned!" Dr. Reid stopped momentarily "What's going on?" "You are not going to believe this?" "Believe what? What the hell is going on?" "Mr. Calderon is being entertained by one Sonia Blackwell."

"What! I knew it! I knew there was something about her and to think I actually trusted her." "She has him quite occupied at the moment. If you are going to strike the time is now!" "Is he armed?" "Hardly" "Can we take him?" "Very easily" "Is anyone else in the room?" "Just the two of them" "What the hell are they doing?" Dr. Ekouevi laughed "Do you really need to ask? Let's just say you've caught him with his pants down."

Dr. Reid motioned to her team to surround the door. "Give him a minute don't be so cruel." "Dr. Ekouevi I'm ready" "Ok now!" Special Forces burst into the room. O.N.S.I. agents with their guns drawn and pointed at his head immediately surrounded Carlos. "Carlos Calderon you are under arrest for the intended manufacture and distribution of a controlled substance."

Carlos jumped up and tried to grab his gun. Sonia swung around and scooped up the weapon and pointed it at Dr. Reid. "You are not taking him!" She screamed "Drop the weapon!" "No Sonia you drop the weapon!" Lt. Yancy shouted as he moved in with his weapon aimed straight for Sonia's head. "Drop the weapon! Don't make me shoot!"

The O.N.S.I. Special Forces wrestled Carlos to the ground as they applied the handcuffs." "Take her too!" Dr. Reid shouted as Special Forces handcuffed Sonia as well. Dr. Reid refused to look at Sonia during these events. Actually she couldn't take her eyes off of Carlos. She was still trying to remember where she had met him or how he knew her but for the life of her she couldn't place him.

The more she starred at him the more uncomfortable she became. His body was very familiar to her. His height, his weight, his color, his strong muscular physique. It was as if she knew him well. "Get them both dressed and get them out of here. And no matter what you do don't forget to read him his rights!"

Dr. Reid ordered never once taking her eyes off of him. Carlos noticed that she seemed to be intrigued and smiled smugly to himself. His thick long black hair hung well below his shoulders and his heavily bearded face hid his true features but nothing could disguise his sexy hazel eyes. They were deep and defiant and right now they were full of rage.

"Excuse me but I know my rights. You can't enter my place without a search warrant." "You want a search warrant?" Lt. Yancy screamed as he stuffed the warrant down Carlos's throat. It was at that point that she noticed his left arm. There was the same birth mark that Bobby had on his left arm. The C crescent surrounded by the circle. It was in the exact same location.

Rosaland had run her fingers over that birthmark so many times that she could describe it with her eyes closed.

Whenever she touched it Bobby would always react. It was as though it was his power center. She pulled Carlos's hair away from his face looking deep into his eyes. Carlos starred back at her as she gently fingered his birthmark. "Where did you get this?" She asked softly trying not to be so obvious. "It my birthright. The Crest of Calderon. My father gave it to me at birth." Carlos whispered knowing that he had her undivided attention.

Dr. Reid jerked her hand back from his arm as if it she had been had burned. "Please get this man dressed and take him out of here!" "Dr. Ekouevi did you get all that?" "Every minute" "Good I'll need that tape first thing in the morning. Why don't you send in the surveillance team so that they can start labeling this evidence?"

"Will do" "Oh let them know that they might be here for a while so make sure that all search warrants cover us until we are finished. We have come too far to fuck this up now." "They are on the way."

Dr. Reid was trying her best to remain calm but she had been completely unnerved by this particular series of events. "Rosaland are you all right?" "Thanks to you Arthur I am fine. What's going on downstairs?" "Everything is under control." "Where is the D.E.A.?" "They should be on the scene momentarily."

"Good take Sonia downtown and hold her until I get there" "What do you want to do with Mr. Calderon?" "Place him in Lt. Jones's custody for now. The O.N.S.I. will be responsible for his transportation and make sure that he doesn't talk to any of his men."

As both Carlos and Sonia were escorted out Dr. Reid physically collapsed on the floor. It was finally over. The O.N.S.I. had Carlos Calderon and his east coast operations had been shut down. Dr. Reid pulled out her cell phone "Dad we got him!"

"Who was the first on the scene?" Special Agent Drax lead investigator for the D.E.A. asked once his team was in place. "Detective Roberto Semione of the N.Y.P.D. coordinated this section of the operation." Lt. Yancy answered proudly. "Where is the detective?" "That him over there" Lt. Jones pointed him out. "And who are you?"

"Lt. William Jones of the O.N.S.I. Special Forces." "Special Forces? Pleased to meet you we've been hearing good things about the O.N.S.I. Isn't that the new government agency headed by General Reid? Is this the same one?" "Yes and no. Actually the O.N.S.I. is headed by Dr. Rosaland Reid. I believe that she is upstairs her unit just took down Carlos Calderon!"

"Calderon we have been after him for years." "You and everybody else in law enforcement." Lt. Jones replied. Special Agent Drax walked over to where

Detective Semione was talking to his team about the bust in an attempt to coordinate the confiscations. "Bobby Semione I'm Special Agent Drax of the D.E.A." Bobby shook his hand.

"Ok detective do you want to tell me what you got here?" Detective Semione escorted Agent Drax around the facility pointing out the various machinery and the high volumes of chemical solutions and processed narcotics that they had confiscated.

"How did you know this was here?" The agent was a little suspicious. "We had no idea upon entering that we would find anything of this nature. We were able to obtain our warrants on the fact that we could trace a homicide victim to this facility moments before her death. In our sweep of the place we found this processing and distribution center."

"Let me understand this detective your unit had no idea that there were drugs on the premises." "No" "Well this is the largest confiscation to hit the east coast in quite some time. Well done gentlemen." Special Agent Drax called out to the D.E.A. agents "Let's get this stuff tagged and out of here. Everything goes even the crumbs on the floor. We've finally nailed this sucker."

sixty

The media was swarming all over the place. They had heard about the bust on the police ban and every news agency in New York was on the scene. The report of the capture of Carlos Calderon and the Calderon Cartel was front page news and probably all over the world by now. Everyone was desperately trying to determine who was responsible for this spectacular event.

"Rosaland the media is in an uproar they all want to interview you" Arthur was insistent. He was so proud of his sister in law. "Alright I'll talk to them but first there is one thing that I have to do. Can you get me out of here without anybody seeing me?" "I'll try" "Where did you take Sonia?" "She's at the N.Y.P.D. just like you ordered."

"Well I need to get there as soon as I can." "Who knows that she is there?" "Nobody other than myself." "Well we are going to have to keep it that way. If Carlos finds out that she helped us he will have her killed. She went out on the limb for us today and we have to assure her safety."

"Whoa slow down. Sonia was in on this?" "Yes Arthur Sonia was my informant. That's how I knew that Carlos would be here today. Sonia set this whole thing in motion." "So that was all an act?" "Yes we had to play it that way so Carlos wouldn't suspect her involvement. We would have never caught him if she hadn't gotten him into bed."

"I didn't want to use her like that but she insisted. She felt that it was the only situation that would work and seem natural she was right." "Well you can't go now there is too much media attention. She's safe and we can keep her under wraps until this frenzy dies down."

"My Father is flying in from Washington. Sonia is going back to D.C.with him. How did Bobby do?" "Now you know Bobby he did just fine. He did exactly what he was supposed to do. He shut him down."

"How many people did we lose?" "I'm not sure of the exact body count yet. I'll let you know but we got more of them than they got of us." "Good" Rosaland hugged her brother in law tight. "I'm glad we made it out of this alive." "So am I sweetie. So am I."

As Dr. Reid walked out of the club she was bombarded with reporters all wanting to know how she did it. "Dr. Reid what can you tell us about the capture of Carlos Calderon?" "No comment" she replied as she tried to push through the crowd.

"Dr. Reid what is your connection to General Prescott Reid?" Another reporter asked her. "He is my father." "Was he instrumental in this operation?" "No comment." "Dr. Reid what is your connection to the N.Y.P.D.?" "I work there." "Dr. Reid is it true that you are the head of the O.N.S.I.?" "Yes that is for now." "For now what do you mean by that for now?" "No comment."

Detective Semione who was standing about twenty feet from her could see that she was becoming irritated by the throng of buzzing reporters and came to her rescue. He pushed passed the reporters to grab her arm and lead her away. "Detective Semione what is your connection to Dr. Reid?" "We work together."

The cameras were flashing as the media took endless pictures of the couple as they tried to make their way through the crowd and into the police van that was waiting by the curb. "Dr. Reid can you share some information with us?" "The O.N.S.I. will be prepared to make a formal statement tomorrow. We have scheduled a press conference in the morning and at that time we will answer questions."

"Dr. Reid isn't it true that you and Detective Semione are involved?" "Yes we are." At that point flashbulbs were going off like fireflies. The cameras were everywhere covering all angles as the two stepped into the van and it pulled away from the curb. Rosaland was so happy to see Bobby. She fell into his arms not caring who was watching them. Bobby planted deep long kisses on her lips and held her tightly as they made their way towards the precinct.

After they released from their embrace all the detectives cheered. They were all smiling and slapping high fives with the other members of their teams. "Good job!" Arthur shouted. That was some great team work. I'm going to make damn sure that you all receive commendations for this operation."

"Well Lt. don't leave yourself out you did a great job as well." Bobby held Rosaland in his arms on the ride back. She placed her head on his shoulders and closed her eyes thinking about the Crest of Calderon that both Bobby and Carlos wore on their left arm and wondering what was their connection.

"This is my birthright" those words just kept echoing in her ears. Rosaland was very familiar with the Crest of Calderon because her fiancée wore it proudly. Bobby had the same crest and shield on his left arm. Carlos demonstrated a great deal of honor when he spoke about the crest. Bobby on the other hand knew nothing of it's origins it was simply a birthmark to him.

Rosaland had questioned him about it on several occasions but he didn't know anything to tell her except that he liked it. "This makes me stand out. Nobody else has a birthmark so distinct. I'm sure it has some significance" she remembered him saying once. "I like it."

Now she knew that there was someone else with a birthmark so distinct she had just seen it. Rosaland's body started to shake uncontrollably; she was suddenly overcome with an acute sense of anxiety. Bobby immediately noticed that she had started to quiver. He looked down to make sure that she was all right and then he pulled her close to him on the seat and tightened his grip around her.

Bobby looked around to take a head count of the remaining detectives. This was one of those rare circumstances where the number of causalities was low. The person that he had been worried about from the beginning was sitting next to him and as soon as they were back at the station he would call the hospital to check on Diana.

Rosaland decided that after checking on Sonia to make sure that she was safe and to thank her personally for her help and meeting with her dad who should be arriving shortly she would go uptown tonight. She wanted to do some research.

This episode was going to trouble her until she got some answers. When all of the detectives had piled out of the vehicle Bobby pulled Rosaland to the side. "Are you alright?" He was very concerned. "Yes baby I'm fine." "Are you going to be alright for the rest of the evening?" "Yes why?" "We are going to be here for a while. We have to finish up our paperwork." "It sounds like that could take all night."

"It might you can never tell." "I'm sure that I can find something to do." Rosaland smiled "The General will be here and he and I will be debriefing Sonia. That might take some time." "So where is your family going to eat later? As soon as I finish up here I'll join you." "I don't know I'll call you from wherever we end up. If it's really late we'll be at the Harvard Club. They always accommodate the General."

By this time they had reached their offices. The first thing that Dr. Reid did was to seek out Sonia. "Sonia are you alright?" Dr. Reid grabbed Sonia and held her. She could feel her body trembling from the earlier events. "I hope that nobody knows that I am here. Where are you holding Mr. Calderon?"

"Lt. Jones has him in custody uptown. We had to stash him somewhere away from everybody. The General is on his way to escort you home. Sonia what you did today was very brave. You really put yourself in harm's way." "It's all part of the job." "Yes but not too many people would have been so willing to do that part of the job."

"We've been tracking Mr. Calderon for a long time this is as close as anyone has gotten. That was our window of opportunity Thank god it worked out." "We would never have been able to get the surveillance if it hadn't been for your quick thinking the agency owes you." "Just get me the hell out of here!" "We can definitely do that!" The General's powerful voice responded. Dr. Reid looked toward the direction of the voice and ran to hug her father. "We got him Dad." She said softly. "We finally got him."

The general hugged his daughter close and kissed her gently on the top of her head. "Outstanding job well done." "Where is he?" "Lt. Jones has him. We are holding him uptown until we find a safe place to put him. If we put him in with anybody else we are going to have trouble. Mr. Calderon has a extremely charismatic sense of persuasion and I would like to have a chance to talk to him."

"You can't talk to him as a matter of fact I want you to stay away from him. Lt. Jones can interrogate him." The general spoke in a firm tone. His daughter knew that he meant what he said. "Don't go any where around him. This man is a drug dealer and an arms trader. What could you possibly want to talk to him about? You have done a great job. The O.N.S.I. has done a great job. Let the government take it from here."

Rosaland stepped back to look directly into her fathers eyes; she knew that he was serious. But she had to talk to Carlos. She really needed to know about that crest. The General knew his daughter and he knew that she wasn't listening. "Lt. Jones" the General talked into his phone. "Don't let anyone near the prisoner. I am in the process of making arrangements for his transportation. Talk to me only on this one."

"Yes sir" Lt. Jones answered as the General hung up the phone. "Rosaland let's get Ms. Blackwell out of here and back to safe territory." "Ok Dad. Are you staying in New York tonight?" "No it would be wise for us to leave now. I'll come back in a couple of day. We can get together then. Call your sister and make sure that she has all the necessary paperwork in order. It's going to a busy day tomorrow. There will probably be a complete media circus outside the courthouse."

"Rachael will be prepared Dad don't worry. I need to get out of this gear. Again Sonia thanks." The General left the building down the back staircase with Sonia Blackwell and headed straight for Washington.

Once Dr. Reid was dressed she went back to her office to work on her computer. She noticed that the detective squad was working diligently on their paperwork. Detective Semione disliked typing this was the only part of his job that he absolutely hated.

Dr. Reid watched from her desk as he hacked out his report. She knew that at this speed he would be all night. This was the perfect time for her to leave. Dr. Reid slipped quietly out of the door and made her way to the elevator undetected.

As she drove uptown she contemplated how she was going to convince Bill to let her talk to Carlos. She had heard her father issue his orders to his Lt. whom she knew from experience would follow them to the letter. She decided that her best approach would be to play ignorant of the fact and to hope that Bill would believe her. After all it was she who had captured the notorious Mr. Calderon. He was her prisoner and that gave her the right to question him.

When she arrived in the Bronx Dr .Ekouevi greeted her. "I didn't think I would see you so soon." He commented once she had gained entrance into their secret complex. "Dr. Ekouevi I need your help again. I want you to find out everything you can on the Calderon family."

"What do you want to know?" "As much as you can find on the family history." "That might some time." "Take as much time as you need but I would like a complete dossier as soon as possible. How's our prisoner tonight?"

"Mad, angry, upset and threatening to kill everybody that had anything to do with this operation." "So he is in a good mood" "If you want to call it that." "Where is he?" "Upstairs with Captain America." "Can I see him?" "Officially he is your prisoner I don't see why not? But I wouldn't recommend it he's too violent. He has been cursing in Spanish since he arrived. I wouldn't mess with him tonight. Wait until tomorrow."

"When are they moving him?" "Not until tomorrow night we just got the orders from the Big Dog himself. They are shipping him off to Washington after the N.Y.P.D. interrogates him about the murder of that last girl. You remember the one they found in Harlem on your doorstep. Your boyfriend seems to think he did it or that he knows something about it."

"Well if Bobby thinks that he did it he probably did. Bobby has really good instincts. I'll put my money on him every time." "It's nice to know that you are so objective about this."

"Dr. Ekouevi I am being completely objective about this. I've been working in the N.Y.P.D. for almost three years and they have a pretty good conviction record. If they believe that he is involved he probably is. That's all I'm saying. So you think I should wait until tomorrow?"

"I do." "Will you start on my request?" "I will after I finish viewing the surveillance from today's operation." "Thank you Dr. Good night. I'll see you in the morning." As Rosaland drove back towards the precinct she called Bobby. She was surprised to find out that he had already left.

He told her that he would be working all night maybe he left because she had left. He was probably in Brooklyn with Papa. He would call her later so she decided to go home and call it a day.

Bobby was waiting in the reception area when Diana emerged. She was extremely surprised to see him there. "They told me that someone was waiting for me would that someone be you?" "That would be me." "What are you doing here?" "I was worried so I came to check on you for myself. I've never seen you lose it like that. Are you alright?"

"Yes Bobby I'm fine. The doctors said the fumes from the chemicals overcame me and that's what made me pass out." "It took this long for him to tell you that?" "Yes you know doctors. They had to do every test in the world. This shit always takes time." "Do you need a ride home?" "Yes I do considering that I was brought here in the ambulance. Are you offering?"

"Yes I am." "Are you accepting?" "Thanks Bobby I still feel queasy. I would really like a ride home." "Are you done here?" Diana nodded "Yes let's go."

As Bobby and Diana drove toward her house she asked him directly "So Bobby how is it being with her?" "What?" "How is it being with her?" "I guess I deserved that?" "Yes you did. We have never really talked about this and I think I deserve to know what happened with us? You owe me that and I should be very upset that it has taken almost three years before we have had a chance to talk about it."

"I love her Diana. She means the world to me. It's good being with her." "Well that's very obvious I'm just trying to figure out when did all this happen? Were you cheating on me with her?" "No" "So how did the two of you get together?" "It just happened." Bobby thought a while and then he confessed. "No Diana that's a lie. It didn't just happen. I went after her hook line and sinker. From the first time I saw her I was attracted to her and I wrestled with it for a long time."

"When I stopped seeing you I wasn't seeing anyone. I was taking some time just like I told you. About six months later I started seeing her. But by the time that happened I was already very much in love with her. I'm sorry Diana. I never meant to hurt you."

As Diana listened to Bobby the tears flowed freely down her face. She couldn't believe that she still loved him so much but she did. She couldn't get him out of her system; no matter how hard she tried.

"So Bobby why are you here?" "Because I care about you as a friend." "Well I don't need you to care about me!" She sobbed. As Bobby pulled up in front of Diana's apartment she ran from the car in tears. When Diana was safely inside her apartment she collapsed on her bed. She was very upset and she was very pregnant.

Diana remembered that night vividly in her mind. Bobby had been powerful and possessive and in the end he saved her life. A pregnancy was something that you couldn't hide. There was no such thing as being a little pregnant either you were or you weren't and Diana definitely was.

Diana was experiencing a great deal of mixed emotions. On the one hand she loved Bobby. She loved Bobby with all her heart and soul but on the other hand Bobby was in love with someone else. Someone he intended to marry. This had the potential of becoming an extremely volatile situation and somebody was going to get hurt. Maybe everybody involved.

sixty-one

"The dynamic duo" was the caption that appeared on the front page of the New York Times. The article featured a picture of Detective semione and Dr. Reid as they talked to the media. The story about the capture of the infamous Carlos Calderon had world wide impact. All the media agencies were clamoring for a piece of the pie.

The N.Y.P.D. was in a buzz when Dr. Reid and Detective Semione reported to work the next day. There were pictures of the two of them plastered across every newspaper in the world and all the copies had been laid neatly on her desk. She and her team of detectives were the flavor of the month. The phones had been ringing off the hook with request from reporters and producers from all the news magazines for personal interviews.

The uniform officers and the rest of the station personnel sent up a round of applause and cheers when they reached the front desk as they made their way to the elevators. The O.N.S.I. had scheduled a press conference for the early afternoon as Dr. Reid had promised to address the issue of shutting down the Calderon cartel's east side distribution ring and to answer as many questions as she could about the O.N.S.I. and their role in the war on drugs.

This sting would carry international implications and all the agencies that had been involved were lining up for jurisdiction. "What a mess" Bobby whispered in her ear as they made their way upstairs. "I'm sure this is just the beginning" she answered as the elevator door closed in front of them.

Bobby used this time to kiss her tenderly before they started work. "Remind me to tell you that I love you" he smiled at her "before we get too busy" "Well?" she gazed sexily into his eyes waiting for his response. "I love you" "I love you too" she smiled as she placed a delicate kiss on his lips. Just then the door opened and all the detectives from the one five stood at the entrance clapping as the two of them emerged.

Dr. Reid smiled brightly as she walked into her office. Her eyes immediately focused on the stack of newspapers strewn all over her desk and the endless mound of pink slips that indicated how many people were waiting for her to return their calls.

She could see that this was going to be a long day. There was so much paper work that needed to be done after a major operation that Dr. Reid didn't know where to begin. Her fax machine was overflowing with documents marked urgent and every one of her phone lines was blinking.

"Dr. Reid before you get started I need to meet with you in my office." Arthur said in a gentle but commanding voice "Lt. I've got this press conference scheduled and I need to get prepared. Can this wait?" "It will only take a minute but it's very important."

"O.k. I'll be right in." When Dr. Reid arrived in the Lt.'s office she noticed several strangers among the detectives. They all had on dark suits and they all looked official. "This is Dr. Rosaland Reid. She is the director of the O.N.S.I." The Lt.'s introduction was brief and to the point. "Dr. Reid this is Special Agent Troy from the D.E.A." "We've met" she nodded.

"Dr. Reid we have some questions about the drugs." Dr. Reid looked at Detective Semione as she took her seat. "Yes?" "Dr. Reid in your investigation of Carlos Calderon did you have reason to suspect that there would be drugs on the premises?" "No I wasn't aware of the drugs until after Detective Semione made the bust. He discussed it with me after they were confiscated. Why? What is going on here?" She was starting to catch on.

"We are simply trying to determine whose drugs they are??" "What do you mean whose drugs they are? They belong to the Calderon cartel." "No what I mean is who gets the credit for their discovery." "Detective Semione made the bust and the N.Y.P.D. gets the credit after all they were discovered in their jurisdiction."

"And you had no previous knowledge that they might be there?" "No the O.N.S.I. has been tracking Mr. Calderon for years on matters of national security. The N.Y.P.D. went in on murder charges isn't that correct?" "Yes Dr. Reid that's correct." Lt.Yancy responded "So it appears to me that the N.Y.P.D.. is responsible for the discovery of the drugs. But I'm sure in terms of the confiscation that something can be arranged. After all we are all on the same team or at least I thought we were."

"We are Dr. Reid but this is a major amount of dope and quite frankly we don't feel comfortable leaving this enormous amount of drugs here on these premises." "As long as Detective Semione and his unit receives the proper credit for their work I don't really think it matters who takes possession of the drugs provided that they are properly cataloged, tagged and labeled."

"So your organization had no prior knowledge of their presence?" "No" "And you never discussed this with your boyfriend beforehand?" "I beg your pardon? No I did not and I resent the implication. Exactly what are you trying to say? Are you questioning my authority? My integrity? Perhaps you need to talk with General Reid concerning this matter." Rosaland went off.

"Thank you Dr. Reid for your time and I apologize if I offended you in any way. Again let me congratulate you and your team on a job well done." The rest of the suits stood up and clapped.

"Thank you is there anything else? Because if not I have a lot of work to do. It was nice meeting you again Agent Troy. And oh by the way Detective Semione is not my boyfriend he is my fiancé there is a big difference." She smiled as she casually left the room. All Bobby could do was smile and shake his head she was unbelievable.

"O.k. Lt." Agent troy announced my guys will cataloged the drugs and give you a receipt." "I hope you don't mind if we help seeing that we are all on the same team. Detectives semione and Schmidt why don't you give these guys a hand?" "Whatever you say Lt. You're the boss. This way guys." Detective Semione said as he led the agents down to the evidence room.

"Bobby" one of the agents asked once they were working on the evidence "Is that really your fiancé?" Bobby smiled "Every inch of her."

"Dad the D.E.A. is here. They have some concerns about the validity of the bust." "What kind of concerns?" The General puzzled. "I don't know maybe you need to speak with them to find out." "Alright I will. Who is the agent in charge?" "Special Agent Troy?" "How's everything else?"

"This place is like a media circus. We have a press conference scheduled for this afternoon and the phones are ringing off the hook but other than that its business as usual."

"Good get back to me if you need anything. Again sweetie job well done. Outstanding!" "What about Carlos Dad? What plans do you have in store for him?" "Lt. Jones will be transporting him to Washington from his safe house in the Bronx in about an hour and we plan to keep a lid on him once we get him here to D.C.. He has a lot of questions to answer and believe me they better be good answers. I mean some damn good answers" as the General hung up the phone Rosaland detected a great deal on anger in her father's voice.

The General's first priority was to call his friend George the director of the D.E.A. to find out exactly what was going on. The General had become familiar with George during his service on the National Security Council.

"George we seem to have a problem with one of your agents an Agent Troy. I believe his name is. Not only is he questioning my daughter's authority he seems to be questioning her integrity as well. What are you going to do about that?"

"Pres I'm sure there has been some mistake but no matter what the circumstance I'll take care of it. Is there anything else that I can do for you?" "No not at the moment." "O.k. let me make the appropriate calls and I'll get back to you." "Thanks George for your promptness in this matter."

The General was on to the next item on his agenda. It seemed like a matter of seconds before Agent Troy's phone was ringing. "Troy what the hell is going on down there? I just received a call from General Prescott Reid about you questioning the authority of the head of the O.N.S.I..? What's that all about? Whatever it is I suggest that you clean it up immediately if not sooner do you catch my drift?" "Yes sir I'll attend to it right away."

Agent Troy was dumfounded at the speed in which this situation had reached the attention of his superiors. It hadn't even been an hour and he was already on the hot seat with the head of the D.E.A.

"Detective Semione could you take over here? I have to go upstairs for a few minutes." Bobby nodded yes as he watched the Special Agent disappear up the steps. "I wonder what put that fire under him." Bobby said to Danny as Troy rushed up the steps.

"He fucked up somewhere" Danny quipped as they continued to label the evidence. "Bobby how long are we going to be down here? Can't the uniforms take it from here?" "The Lt. wanted us to help so we are helping." "Yes but I would rather be solving crimes arresting bad guys busting drug dealers you know real detective work."

"Yes I know what you mean I have a stack of files on my desk that I need to get busy with. But you know a bust of this magnitude could lead to a promotion or at least an accommodation so let's just finish up and then we can get back to the real stuff. Besides I don't trust these guys. I'm not leaving them down here alone until all this evidence is cataloged." "I'm with you" "We need to speed this operation up fellows" Bobby shouted "Some of us have real jobs to do" "Keep your pants on detective we all have real jobs to do and this is part of it." "Just speed it up smartass."

Dr. Reid worked feverishly preparing for the press conference and she wasn't in the mood for any interruptions. She had so much material to cover and her time was running out. She had to make sure that she didn't leave any of the agencies involved out and that everyone received credit for a job well done.

Her phone was still ringing off the hook and it was all beginning to become a bit overwhelming. "Dr. Reid may I have a word with you?"

Rosaland looked up from her computer to find Agent Troy standing in front of her desk. "What is it now Agent Troy? I am very busy." "I would just like to apologize for any misunderstanding that might have been communicated earlier."

"Was there a misunderstanding? It seemed perfectly clear to me what was being implied. I understood precisely what you meant." "You are not going to make this easy for me are you?" "I'm sorry Agent Troy make what easy for you?" "I'm offering you my sincere apologies not only for myself but on behalf of the D.E.A. as well."

"Is this an official apology Agent?" "Yes" "Well then I would like it in writing." "Yes ma'am." As Agent Troy left her office Rosaland thought to herself "What a jerk!" As she continued to work on her presentation.

Rosaland looked at her watch and realized that she had less than an hour before Showtime. "Lt. is everything ready for the press?" She asked Arthur as she made her way into his office "Is there anything that I have overlooked?" She questioned as she handed him her report.

"Rosaland calm down you'll be just fine. Give me a minute to look over your report." Rosaland left Arthur's office and went into the ladies room to fix her face. Diana was in the mirror when she walked in and Rosaland noticed that the detective seemed to be picking up a little weight especially in her face but she really didn't have the time or the inclination to investigate any further.

"How are you feeling detective?" She asked out of consideration. "I'll be fine thanks for asking." Diana responded half heartily. There was still a great deal of tension between the two of them "It's good to see you back." Rosaland nodded and left the bathroom. Arthur could see how nervous she was when she re-entered his office.

"Dr. Reid this is a great report if you just follow your format you'll be just fine. You know I was thinking maybe we should send a representative from the department one of the detectives in case the press has some questions about the drugs. How does that sound to you?"

"That's a good idea Lt. that would be the ideal image to present to the public. Whom do you have in mind?" "The press has labeled the two of you the dynamic duo it would seem appropriate the Detective Semione should accompany you. Let me pull him up from downstairs."

"Oh that would be perfect. That's just what the D.E.A. needs to see me and my boyfriend in front of the camera." "No what the public and the media are going to see are the two people who were responsible for the capture of an international fugitive. This will show the joint cooperation of our department and your agency. Yes let me get Bobby up here now."

The Lt. called the detective on his cell phone "Bobby I need you upstairs ASAP." When Bobby arrived he passed Diana in the hall. "Bobby are you busy I need to talk to you." "The lt. wants to see me can we talk later?" "Sure look me up when you have some time." "O.k." Diana headed for the street as Bobby entered the Lt's office.

"Lt. what's up?" The detective questioned. "Detective we have a slight change of plans" Bobby looked at Rosaland and waited for the Lt. to continue "I would like you to accompany Dr. Reid to the press conference this afternoon as a representative of the department. She is going to need someone there who can answer any questions that the media might impose about the drugs found on the premises and since you are receiving credit for the bust you are the perfect man for the job. Any questions?"

"Was this your idea?" The detective asked his fiancé. "No detective it was my idea." His boss responded "After all you are the dynamic duo. Let's give the media what they want for a change and let them run with it." "You're the boss" the detective added.

Diana watched from her office as the three of them conferred on their strategy and she took note as to how closely Bobby and Rosaland worked together and also how happy they seemed to be doing it.

There was a natural chemistry between them that even Diana couldn't deny. Her gaze followed as Bobby entered his office to grab his jacket before escorting Dr. Reid downstairs to where the press conference was scheduled to begin in about five minutes.

"Are you nervous?" Bobby asked Rosaland as they entered the elevator. "Yes extremely I have never done a press conference before. It would be easier if I knew what to expect." "Sweetie you will be just fine just follow the media's lead and don't let them paint you into a corner answer the questions as directly as possible and don't volunteer any information that they don't ask for not unless you can use the information to your advantage."

Rosaland listened intently as Bobby tried to guide her through the process. Rosaland trusted Bobby. They were so good together she felt very comfortable with his guidance and his presence. They really were a dynamic duo a match made in heaven.

Rosaland was surprised when Rachael walked in even though she was very happy to see her. "Rae what are you doing here?" Her sister asked as she hugged her tightly. "Arthur called me and told me how nervous you were about this so I thought I would come by to lend some moral support. I see the incredible hulk is here." Rachael motioned with her head in Bobby's direction. "I should have known that he would be by your side."

"Actually this was your husband's idea. But I must admit it was one of his better ideas." They both started laughing. Rachael loved to watch her sister work. She had such a dangerous job and she handled it so well. Rachael admired her bravery.

At that point Bobby walked over to where the sisters were standing engaged in conversation. "Hello Rachael" Bobby hugged her "is the DA's office involved in these proceedings today?" "Not yet I'm here as moral support for my sister" "Good looking out" Bobby turned his attention to Rosaland "Are you ready beautiful" he smiled "It's Showtime"

Dr. Reid climbed the steps and took her place behind the podium in front of the cameras. Detective Semione entered after her and took his place to the rear of the stage. He stood quietly in place as Dr. Reid began her speech. Bobby's presence was reassuring as she addressed the public and the members of the press.

She spoke confidently as she outlined the necessary details of their operation. After concluding her speech she introduced Detective Semione and brought him to the forefront. Bobby was commanding in his presentation. It was as though he had been doing this forever. He was a natural as his charm mesmerized the audience to the point that he had the media eating out of his hands.

Bobby opened the floor for questions in his own charismatic manner and answered the questions brought to the table concerning the drugs that were found on the scene and how deeply this would affect the war on drugs here in the United States.

As Arthur and the rest of the N.Y.P.D. watched the simulcast they applauded Bobby's professionalism and the methods of diplomacy he utilized to feed the press. He left the media laughing with a joke about the dynamic duo as he turned the podium back over to Dr. Reid.

The normal protocol for a situation such as this would have been for the Detective to take his place at the rear of the stage but Bobby used this opportunity to remain standing by her side as she concluded the conference. Bobby grabbed her hand and led her from the podium with the media clamoring for more. Rachael was extremely impressed with the manner in which the O.N.S.I. and the N.Y.P.D. handled the press conference.

sixty-two

Carlos Calderon was impressed as well. He watched them from the safe house in the Bronx and it was at that point that he swore his revenge. He would definitely stop them some kind of way. His expert team of lawyers were already working diligently to find some legal loophole to have him released.

The fact that the O.N.S.I. was holding him without officially charging him with a crime was the basis of their argument but they had to prove it. The O.N.S.I. if discovered would be charged with violating several international treaties with his detention but no one in his cartel knew where he was. The press conference had confirmed the fact that he was in custody and that drugs had been seized from his nightclub which was enough to hold him for 48 hours.

Lt. Jones had been placed in charge of the interrogations but Carlos was hard as nails and he refused to give up any information and under no circumstance was he willing to cut a deal. Deals were not in his nature; he didn't negotiate with anyone because he was the king. All he had to do was snap his fingers and the world opened up like an oyster on his behalf and for his pleasure.

He was counting the hours before his lawyers would have him free and then both the N.Y.P.D. and the O.N.S.I. would have all hell to pay. The more Lt. Jones applied verbal pressure to the disgruntled drug lord the calmer Carlos became. "Where is that famous temper that I have heard so much about?" Bill shouted as he tried unsuccessfully to push his buttons. "I should have known you guys are all talk and no action."

Carlos jumped up from his chair and landed a powerful blow straight to the Lt.'s head knocking him off his feet. Bill reacted by rushing Carlos and tackling him to the floor. The two men struggled as Bill applied a series of blows to Carlos's face busting his lip. As the blood poured from his mouth Carlos quickly reversed this position as he grabbed Bill in a headlock. Bill broke the lock and applied another series of blows to Carlos's body sending him sprawling across the room as bill rushed towards him Carlos hit him with a backhand blow which knocked bill to the floor. Carlos jumped on him and snapped his neck.

"You want to see my temper!" Carlos screamed. "I'll show all of you my temper!" Carlos grabbed the gun from the Lt's holster and shot the two O.N.S.I. guards that Bill had posted outside the door. Carlos politely walked out of the safe house and once outside it was easy for him to disappear into the crowded streets of the Bronx. After all vanishing was one of the things that Carlos did best.

It would be hours before this event would be discovered and by that time it would be too late for Carlos would be safely back on Calderon Island.

"Rosaland that was great!" Rachael hugged her sister after the conference "and to think you were so nervous for no reason. Bobby you are the man. Gimme some rock!" Rachael held up her fist. I see now why she loves you so much. The two of you are phenomenal together. Remind me to keep you on my team."

"So it was o.k.?" Rosaland asked sincerely. "Come on Sis it was better than o.k. it was great. You both did an excellent job. Why don't you guys meet me after work? Drinks are on me!" Rachael looked at her watch "Hey I need to get back to the office. I'm sure my phone will be ringing off the hook. I'm glad that I'm not prosecuting this case."

"I wish you were prosecuting this case that way we would be sure to get a conviction." Bobby said as Rachael rushed back to work. "You will get the conviction no matter what. Tell Arthur that I will call him later." Rachael shouted as she jumped into a cab.

When Detective Semione and Dr. Reid got back upstairs the office was in an uproar and the phones were ringing off the hook. The squad room was busy before the conference and now it was in a state of total hysteria. Some of the members of the press had made it past the uniforms and were desperately trying to interview any detective that had anything to do with the bust.

This story was hot and the media was going to ride it as long as they could. The professionalism exhibited by Detective Semione put the fine members of the N.Y.P.D. in a good light and he had cemented a good media relationship. The rest of the day was spent on the enormous amount of paperwork that accompanied an operation of this magnitude. By quitting time everyone was happy to call it a day.

After work Detective Semione had other things on his mind. Before Rachael and Arthur arrived Bobby would use this time to pin Rosaland down to a date. "So" Bobby said nonchantly as they sipped on their drinks "When are we going to tie the knot?" Rosaland smiled and replied, "I'm already ahead of you. That's what I was working on this afternoon. I think I have found the perfect location. I should have a confirmation by tomorrow."

"Oh yeah?" "Yes" Rosaland leaned over the table and kissed him tenderly. "You two need to get a room." Arthur said jokingly as he and Rachael joined them. "The dynamic duo is at it again." "Baby how are we ever going to live this down?" "I don't know once the media gives you a label it sticks like glue." They all laughed. "So why don't we just make it official? Mr. and Mrs. Dynamic duo" "Sounds good to me." Bobby reached under the table and put his hand under her skirt. Rosaland looked at him and smiled shaking her head.

Bobby motioned to the waiter and ordered them another round. "Bobby drinks are on me" Rachael reminded him. "You can get the next round" he smiled "I would like to propose a toast to the O.N.S.I." the four of them lifted their glasses. "Thanks Baby" Rosaland leaned over and kissed Bobby again. "I love you. You know Bobby you always get so emotional after a major operation." She laughed "That's because I'm happy that we survived. Come on let's dance."

Bobby pulled her up from the table and on to the dance floor. All Bobby wanted to do was feel her body close to his. What he really wanted was to be alone with her and show her how much he loved her. As Bobby held her in his arms it suddenly dawned on him how long it had been. He missed the feel of her hot breath on his ears. "You are the sexiest woman in the world." Bobby whispered in her ear as he held her tightly in his arms.

Rosaland wrapped her arms around his neck and nuzzled her head into his chest as they moved slowly around the floor. It was so nice being in his arms it felt so safe and so comfortable. Rosaland could stay there forever. Rosaland placed her hands behind Bobby's head and directed his lips towards hers. She kissed him deeply and passionately as he ran his hands down her sensuous curves. Bobby pressed his body closer to hers as they encircled the dance floor."Hey you two the music has stopped" Rachael said softly as she and Arthur left the floor and walked back to their table hand in hand. Rosaland and Bobby joined them as they all quietly sipped their drinks.

"Bobby this is a nice place. I really like the atmosphere. How did you find it?" Arthur commented. "Actually quite by accident. Danny and I came here for dinner one night after the training session. I liked it so much that I made a note to come back with my favorite girl." He looked at Rosaland and winked "I thought that she might like too."

"I do Baby It has a very intimate atmosphere very private." Rosaland concluded as she rubbed his leg under the table. "Is anybody ready for another drink?" Rachael interjected "After all this is a celebration." Racheal motioned for the waiter and after he served the table another round of drinks she proposed a toast.

"I would like to propose a toast to my very brave sister" Rachael said as she lifted her glass "Honestly I don't know how you do the job you do but I'm very proud of you for doing it."

"Here here!" both Bobby and Arthur chimed in as they all lifted their glasses. Bobby leaned over and whispered into Rosaland's ear. If a picture is worth a thousand words the expression on her face said it all. Smiling she leaned close to him and place her lips tenderly on his. "I would like that" she murmured softly as their lips parted.

"And now I would like to propose a toast "to love" Rosaland looked at Bobby passionately as she sensuously sipped from her glass. "I'll drink to that" Arthur added as he pulled his wife close and placed his arm lovingly around her shoulders. Rachael reached over and kissed Arthur first on his cheek and then feverishly on his lips.

Bobby pulled Rosaland from the table and hit the dance floor. The Latin American rhythms were slowly beginning to fill the room with the sounds of salsa. Bobby loosened his tie and gyrated seductively to the throbbing beats.

Rosaland followed his lead as he circled her body and grabbed her from the back pressing her close to him. Suddenly the floor was filled with lusty writhing bodies dancing to the hypnotic pulsating vibrations of the music. There was pure sensuality in the air as the couples lost all their inhibitions to the spell-binding melodies.

Rosaland loved dancing with Bobby. His presence was so commanding and oh so seductive and his body exuded emotion. Rosaland closed her eyes as she wiggled in front of him raising her skirt to expose her lovely legs. Bobby placed both of his hands on her hips and ran his palms over her well-shaped ass as she rotated her hips in a circular motion down the front of his lean bronze torso.

Dancing with Bobby this way always left her body so wanton and her inner recesses so wet and combined with the effects of the alcohol in her system Rosaland was on fire. Rosaland being unmindful of her surroundings unconsciously started to unbutton her blouse. It was then that the music began to die down and the crowd on the dance floor began to disperse.

Bobby led Rosaland back to the table and waited for Arthur and Rachael to reappear. Bobby seized the moment to take her in his arms and kissed her passionately filling her mouth with his tongue.

Rosaland responded breathlessly to his tender embrace as she wrapped her arms tightly around his neck and pressed her body close to his excited manhood. "I love you" she whimpered holding him securely in her arms.

"Let's go home" Bobby suggested. Rosaland nodded her consent. When Arthur and Rachael made it back to their table Bobby announced "We're out of here".

"Thanks Rachael Arthur we had a wonderful time." Rosaland said as she kissed her sister. Bobby shook Arthur's hand "I'll see you tomorrow boss" Bobby motioned for the waiter and handed him a $100 dollar bill. "This should take care of everything." The waiter smiled and thanked Bobby for his generosity. Bobby escorted Rosaland out into the brisk night air as they strolled hand in hand to their car.

"We're going to Brooklyn tonight baby" Bobby told her once he started the car. "It's closer" Rosaland sat back to enjoy the ride. "So tell me about this place you found?" "It's a nice quiet bed and breakfast in Connecticut. I think that you will like it. They seem to be accommodating. I will know for sure tomorrow."

As Bobby headed the car for the bridge he placed his hands under her skirt and rubbed her inner thighs. Rosaland sighed at the feel of his fingers next to her bare skin. "Where is your gun?" Bobby questioned her. "I took it off in the bathroom. It's in my purse." "Baby what did I tell you about that? You never know when you might need it. Rosaland please keep your gun on you." "Well I know I don't need it now." She asserted as she opened her legs wider.

"So when are we doing this?" "Next weekend it that soon enough?" "It's only been three years baby girl. Your father hates me because I'm sexing his precious daughter and everybody knows it. You need to make an honest man out of me." "I'll do my best." She laughed as Bobby parked the car behind the restaurant.

"Ssh!" Bobby cautioned her as they made their way up the back steps "Papa is probably sleep and he hasn't been doing so well lately. I'm very concerned about his health." Rosaland removed her shoes once they entered the building and left them by the door. "Go upstairs and make yourself comfortable while I go get us something to eat. There's a bag on my dresser it's for you."

Rosaland loved gifts and excitedly hurried to the bedroom to see what he had bought for her. Bobby had a real sensitive side to his nature that she admired. He never tried to hide his feelings for her or about her; as a matter of fact he wore them on his sleeve. Despite his hard macho exterior when he was with her he was butter in her hands.

As Rosaland opened the package she was surprised at its contents. Bobby always seemed to find the most amazing gifts for her. His taste was exquisite.

Rosaland quickly undressed and placed the gold silk gown over her head. It hung sexily off one shoulder as it molded to her voluptuous curves and both of the sides featured a mesh of delicate lace that exposed her skin.

On the left side there was a deep split that exposed all of her leg up to her lovely thigh. Rosaland went in the bathroom to muse her hair; she wanted it messy and all over her head. She liked wild hair especially at times like this.

She checked the bag again only to discover that it did not contain any panties. She laughed Bobby was so nasty. She slid her feet into the gold mesh sandals her right ankle adorned with the black pearl anklet as she posted herself at the head of his bed waiting for him to return.

When Bobby walked into the room he smiled. "Is this what you had in mind?" She inquired invitingly. "No actually you look a lot better than what I had in mind. Are you hungry?" "Yes but not for food." Rosaland looked at him longingly as he approached the bed. Bobby placed the tray on the chest of drawers and slowly began to remove his shirt; he unbuckled his belt and let his pants fall to the floor as he stepped out of them.

Rosaland watched as his strong, muscular bronze colored body came into focus. She was awestruck by his Latin American magnificence.

"You look delicious in that gown why don't you model it for me?" Rosaland left her post on the bed and paraded in front of him strutting enticingly back and forth showing off not only the new silk garment but her luxurious figure as well.

Bobby reached for her and ran his hand up her leg to her waiting love canal and then he pulled her on to the bed. He planted deep kisses on her lips and along her neck. Rosaland moaned as Bobby held her body tight pressing his massive frame firmly on top of hers. She relaxed as he kissed her breast lightly and then she felt the warmth of his palms as they ran across her large erect nipples.

Rosaland ran her fingertips over his sleek physique as she delighted in his affections. Bobby delicately sucked her buxom breast sending electric shocks through her body. "Ohh" she sighed as he sucked expertly on her sensitive fleshy mounds. "You're overdressed" he muttered in a low tone. Rosaland shifted her body slightly as Bobby pulled the gown over her head.

"Now that's much better" he said sedately allowing her to revel in the freedom of her nakedness. Bobby lost no time in taking possession of her sweetness. He plunged his excited massive manhood deep into her inner sanctum. Rosaland moaned loudly at their initial contact as he pumped himself into place. "Ooh Bobby!" She purred as he pumped his massive length into the love of his life.

"I love you bobby," she whined as he filled her with his wanton desire. Bobby thrust his agile body in and out of her moist wet cavern affording her the ultimate of pleasure. Rosaland pumped her body up to meet Bobby's manly thrust as the two of them climbed the heights of ecstasy together.

"Oh you feel good" Bobby whispered as he feverishly continued his assault on his beautiful chocolate drop. Rosaland opened herself up to him as Bobby aggressively loved her body. Rosaland clung desperately to him as he pleased her riding that wave of unbridled lust that he inspired every time he touched her. Bobby stroked her deeply plunging thrusting and pumping furiously into her tight wet privacy. She wrapped her legs securely around his waist as he rode her completely.

"Ooh Bobby Bobby!" She screamed loudly as he buried himself to the hilt feeding her his length. "Ohh you like that baby you like that?" Bobby moaned as his quenched her appetite. "Bobby Bobby" she cried out as she started to shake and sob uncontrollably. Bobby knew what her tears meant; he knew that they signaled her ultimate release.

"Come on baby. Come with Daddy" Bobby screamed as he could no longer contain himself. Bobby's Latin American essence took over that essence that she loved so deeply. He plunged unmercifully into her both of them totally out of control lost in the passion of their love. Rosaland was the first to fly as her powerful orgasm swept over her body. Her tears ran in abundance down her lust distorted face as Bobby filled her cavern with his seed. They both cried out in pleasure as the sounds of their explosion filled the room.

sixty-three

The N.Y.P.D was in an uproar when Detective Semione and Dr. Reid arrived for work the next morning. "What's going on?" The Detective asked as a uniform officer brushed by them. "You need to see the Lt." he responded as he left the building. The news of Carlos Calderon's escape and Lt. Jones's death had reached everyone but the two of them.

Dr. Reid looked around at all the turmoil as she made her way into her office. Her fax machine was overflowing and all of her telephone lines were lit up.

She hurried over to the machine and grabbed the first sheet from a stack of many. As she read the paper she froze in horror. She couldn't believe her eyes. She looked around for Detective Semione who was in with his Lt. She carefully observed as Bobby grabbed his head in sorrow and disbelief.

At that moment her secured line rang and she knew immediately that it was the General. "Rosaland I need you in Washington a.s.a.p. I have sent a special helicopter for you and it should be arriving at any minute." "Dad what the hell happened?" She questioned her father. "Not now just get your ass on that chopper and get here as quick as you can." With that her father hung up the phone.

She ran to Arthur's office with a look of pure panic in her eyes. "Bobby I've got to go. I'll talk to you later; I'll call you from D.C." "Where are you going?" "My Father wants me in D.C. right away. He has sent a helicopter for me. It's probably upstairs right now. Bobby Bill is dead!" She screamed with tears streaming down her face "I know I'm sorry to hear that. He was a good man."

They were both very remorseful about Lt. Jones's death but there was no time to show it. The Detective left the office to accompany her up the stairs to the helipad. "Oh shit" she screamed when they reached the roof. "I left my laptop on my desk." "Wait here I'll get it." The detective said "Wait here!" As Bobby looked around he could see the chopper in the distance. Bobby decided to wait with her until the chopper was on the ground and then he would go for her computer.

As the chopper approached he turned to go down the steps. It was at that precise moment that all hell broke loose. The force of the explosion rocked the N.Y.P.D. to its very foundation.

Rosaland's body flew up in the air and hit the building with a devastating momentum leaving her body bruised, bleeding, torn and unconscious on the roof.

Bobby was blown down the steps by the impact of the blast and his body tumbled to the next landing where he laid unconscious.

The one five was shocked to its very core. The blast from the chopper set off a series of explosions leaving the lobby leveled and the building completely destroyed. The aftershock from the blast was felt for miles as telephone lines and other forms of communications went blank. As Arthur pulled himself up from the rubble he observed the devastation of his house.

There were countless bodies piled on top of each other and at this point it was hard to tell who was dead and who was alive. Danny managed to make his way to Arthur's office his head bleeding profusely from a gash he received from the force of the explosion.

"What the hell happened?" He shouted as he sifted through the demolished office. "Detective I need you to get me a complete count of the casualties!" The Lt. commanded as he attempted to regained some sort of control.

Bobby who had been slightly stunned by the explosion was slowly coming back to reality and in an instant he remembered that Rosaland was on the roof. Bobby's head was spinning as he ran up what remained of the steps. He stood in the smoke filled air trying to gain some visibility so that he could locate her. It was at that point that Bobby discovered her lying unconscious against what remained of the wall.

Bobby was panic stricken as he sifted through the debris and rushed over to check her condition. Rosaland was bruised and blood was gushing from the corners of her mouth. Her clothes appeared as if they had been torn from her body and her face and hair was severely charred. Bobby bent over to check her pulse to see if there were any signs of life. Her pulse was faint and weak; she was barely alive and hardly breathing.

Bobby snatched her limp lifeless form from the ground and holding her securely ran down the steps. Bobby took the steps two at a time until he was on the ground level. The streets of New York were in a state of bedlam and were jammed with screaming sirens and ambulances and what remained of the N.Y.P.D's mobile patrol cars unit.

The uniformed officers and the rest of the station personnel were being evacuated as they ran bleeding and injured from the remnants of the building. Detective Schmidt and Lt. Yancy were still inside trying to round up what remained of their staff.

The emergency medical technicians were scurrying back and forth between the dazed and the wounded trying to save as many lives as possible. Bobby after observing the chaos which was transpiring on the streets in front of the station or what remained of it decided on another course of action. He knew that she needed help and she needed help immediately if not sooner.

At any moment he knew that he could lose her. The emergency workers and the fire department were bringing bodies out by the handfuls. Time was of the essence as Bobby ran determinately up First Avenue holding her securely in his arms. He ran with the speed of lightening his only motivation was her life. He literally had her life in his hands and he was going to do everything within his power to save it.

N.Y.U. Medical was just up ahead and he knew that Matthew would be on duty. When Bobby entered the medical center the doctors had already been alerted to the disaster. "Get Dr. Reid" he shouted as he placed her on the grynie. Matthew came running to meet the detective.

"She was on the roof when the chopper exploded" Bobby explained screaming "She has been unconscious ever since." Matthew grabbed his sister's grynie and rushed her into the emergency room.

"Miles call my father!" He shouted to his coworker as he rushed his sister into surgery. "And then take care of the detective!" The emergency room was being filled with the injured victims. They had wounded policemen and personnel everywhere. Matthew worked diligently on his sister trying desperately to save her life.

As Dr. Miles Martin was attending to Bobby's injuries exhaustion completely overcame him and Bobby passed out on the table. Rachael was the first to arrive at the hospital. She was looking for her husband. She had tried to reach Arthur by phone but the lines were down. The grid surrounding the N.Y.P.D. had been completely barricaded off and even with her clearance she was not able to get through.

Rachael was frantic; she had no idea of the status of her sister or her husband. She was in tears as she sought to get some answers. "I'm trying to locate my brother Dr. Matthew Reid?" Rachael inquired at the reception desk. "Dr. Reid is in surgery Ms. Reid" "No I'm Mrs. Yancy. I'm looking for my husband Lt. Arthur Yancy. Has he been admitted?" "No ma'am. No one by that name has been admitted."

"Thank-you" that information put Rachael's mind at ease at least for the moment. Rachael tried to dial Arthur again on his cell phone and again she received no answer. Then she thought to call her sister. Rosaland was supposed to be at home this morning. She told Rachael that she would be going in late.

Rachael sincerely hoped with all her heart that this one time she actually did what she said that she would. When Rachael received no answer she became hysterical.

In her heart she knew that Rosaland was in that building and Arthur was too. She rushed back to the information desk with tears running down her face. "Please help me!" Rachael begged "Please tell me if a Dr. Reid has been admitted."

"Yes she has." The admitting nurse confirmed. "She is in surgery. And we have no information on her condition. A Detective Semione brought her in." Rachael immediately began to shake uncontrollably as she burst into tears.

Bobby had regained consciousness and came stumbling out of the hospital room where the doctor had left him after repairing a couple of busted ribs. He had her blood on his shirt and a bandage on his head. His shirt was shredded and torn his ribs were busted but thank God he was alive.

Bobby walked over to the desk to inquire about her condition and he was told that she was still in surgery. Bobby was groggily pacing back and forth when he discovered Rachael sitting in the waiting room alone crying. Bobby stumbled over to comfort her.

"Bobby what happened?" Her words came choking out between her tears. "I'm sorry Rachael Rosaland was on the roof when the building exploded." "She was what! Rachael was in total shock. "How is she?" She demanded "We don't know?" "Where's Arthur?" "I don't know that either?" "Bobby look at you? Are you alright?" "I'm fine. My head is killing me but I'll make it. Have you called your Father?" "Yes he's on his way."

Bobby sat down next to Rachael and held her hand while they waited together for any news." Rachael and Bobby waited for what seemed liked hours before Arthur arrived. Rachael spotted her husband as he ran toward her and she flung herself into his arms. Arthur held her tight and tried his best to comfort her. All Rachael could do was hold on tight she never wanted to let him go.

Bobby remained in his seat groggy, lethargic, shaken and still waiting for some news good or bad. Rachael filled Arthur in on the details as she regained her composure. "I'm sorry baby I would have been here or I should have been here earlier except that the P.D. is in such a shamble. I lost a lot of good men and women today. Whoever did this knew exactly where and how to hit us."

"How's Rosaland? I just found out that she was here." Arthur consoled his wife as he placed gentle kisses on her lips. "Don't worry baby your sister is a fighter she'll be alright." "Bobby's here and he's pretty shaken up. I know that he is hurt Arthur but he won't admit it." Rachael motioned to where Bobby was waiting alone.

All Bobby could do was to think about Rosaland and how incredible she was last night and how much he loved her. Bobby was a man of strong convictions and he would get the monster that was responsible for this even if it took the rest of his life. Bobby painfully lay back in his chair wishing, hoping, and praying for the best.

"How you doing Bobby?" Arthur asked as he sat down next to him. Bobby didn't respond. "We took quite a hit. We have a lot of dead officers friends of ours and a lot of wounded officers that I pray to god will make it."

As Bobby turned to look at his boss he could see the pain that his Lt. was experiencing. Arthur carried a lot of hurt in his eyes and he was deeply troubled about the tragic event and the devastation of his precinct.

Bobby on the other hand was experiencing a time warp. Time had stopped for him; his only concern was Rosaland. Even though Arthur was there Bobby really hadn't heard a word that he had said. All he could think about was the sight of her as she lay unconscious against that brick wall. He knew that she was hurt and he in turn was hurting. The hours passed slowly. It was as though time was dripping minute by minute as Bobby waited patiently.

It was at this point that Matthew emerged from the operating room. He walked directly over to where a distraught Bobby was sitting. "I'm sorry Bobby we did all we could do but we couldn't save the baby." Matthew noticed immediately the look of shock on Bobby's face. "The baby?" He repeated as he stumbled back into his chair. His eyes filled with tears as he repeated for a third time "The baby?" Bobby looking at Matthew in complete wonder and amazement.

"Rosaland is in serious condition she is hemorrhaging severely. The next 24 hours are critical" Matthew continued "She will need to be monitored constantly. She has lost a lot of blood. And she suffered a severe blow to her head as well as to her abdomen from the force of the blast. We managed to control the bleeding but at this point only time will tell."

"Can I see her?" Bobby asked trying to get his emotions under control the tears still rolling down his face. "Just for a minute Bobby I need to go and talk to the rest of the family. The information about the baby stays between us."

Matthew escorted Bobby into her room. As Bobby walked over to her bed he noticed how small and totally helpless she looked. Her face and hands were bandaged and she had tubes attached to her body everywhere. All Bobby could do was stand there and stare at her as the pain in his chest increased. His heart was broke and it hurt like hell.

How could he lose her like this? "I'm sorry sir you have to leave" the nurse said as she placed a plastic insulation tent around her bed "Dr.'s orders" Bobby looked up and nodded as se stepped aside so that they could do their job.

Bobby had never felt so vulnerable or so defenseless. There was nothing that he could do for her. No matter how much he had tried to protect her all his efforts had been in vain. She was lying less than 25 feet from him in critical condition and only time would tell.

sixty-four

Bobby's head and heart was still reeling from the news of the baby that she had been carrying. How come she hadn't told him? Did she even know? When was she going to tell him? Was she going to tell him? There were a thousand questions that needed to be answered but none of that seemed important now the only thing that mattered to him was her survival.

Matthew told him that the next 24 hours would be critical so for the next 24 hours he would remain as close to her as possible. Bobby watched her from the other side of the door a situation that he was definitely unfamiliar with when it came to her but under the circumstances he would respect the rules.

Bobby found himself at a complete lost; this was the first time in all his years as a detective that he didn't know what to do. Bobby's mind flashed back to the first time he saw her that day at the academy. Then he remembered the first time he made love to her that night in Harlem the night that changed his life.

That was the night he realized just how much he loved her and Rosaland in return had honored him with her body. Her most precious possession and for the first time he knew that she loved him as well. These next 24 hours were going to be pure hell but somehow he would make it. He had to make it not for himself but for her.

"Bobby you need to eat something" Rachael said softly as she handed him a sandwich and a cup of coffee. Bobby turned his attention away for a moment. "I can't eat. Not now maybe later." "Bobby you have been here all day you really need to eat." "I can't Rachael. I can't leave her I'll be fine thanks for the coffee."

Rachael could feel his pain and she wanted to help him. But no matter how much she insisted he would not leave. Rachael went back to the waiting room and took her seat. Arthur had left the hospital hours ago. He still had the problems of his precinct to deal with. He had F.B.I. and C.I.A. agents coming out of the woodwork as well as army intelligence.

They were all trying to piece together what had happened and who was responsible for this act of violence? Or if it was an act of terrorism? It would take months before they would be back on their feet and he had to establish a new base of operations somewhere soon; he needed to reach out to another station or agency to find accommodations.

The General had been at the hospital with the rest of his family and after learning of his daughter's condition decided to go downtown with his son- in-law to see if he could be of some help. There was nothing that anyone could do here but wait.

"Bobby the phone is for you" Rachael said as she handed him her cell phone. "Yeah?" "Bobby what's going on down there? Has there been any change in Rosaland's condition?" "No things are pretty much the same. What's going on up there?" "It's a complete mess Bobby. It's going to take months before we can sort this out. We are still pulling bodies out of the rubble. I know this is not the time but I can really use your help."

"I can't leave her boss not now." "Rachael is there Bobby. If there is any change she'll call us or Matthew will call us. Right now there is nothing that you can do." "I can be here. What if she wakes up and I'm not here what then?" Arthur was at a lost for words. He knew how Bobby felt but he needed his help as well as every other able-bodied officer he had available.

"O.k. Bobby I understand your position and if I were in your shoes I would probably do the same thing just keep me informed." "Thanks boss." Bobby handed the phone back to Rachael.

"Arthur do you have any idea as to who is responsible at this point?" "No Baby not a clue and right now all of our intelligence is down so it might take awhile before we know anything. I need Rosaland I need Bobby. Oh Rachael this is a mess! I'll call you if anything breaks."

Arthur hung up the phone. Rachael walked over to Bobby and placed her arms around him "I know right now that this is hard to believe but we'll make it through."

Bobby kissed his sister-in- law lightly on her forehead. "Thanks Rachael" he said kindly as they waited together. The rest of the night passed in a quiet repose while uptown Arthur was desperately trying to put the pieces back together; he had a temporary location and a skeleton crew and he had everyone working through the night to help make some sense of this situation.

The General put some of the resources of the O.N.S.I. at Arthur's disposal in an effort to help make the transition a little easier but nothing would take away the hurt or the lost. The General was checking in with Rachael every 15 minutes but still Matthew had no change in his sister's condition to report.

Arthur could really use Bobby's help right about now; they needed him to help pull this thing back together. Both Arthur and the General knew that there was nothing they could do to get Bobby to leave the hospital. But they had to try to appeal to something in him they needed his help.

Bobby was also torn. He knew that he had a duty to the N.Y.P.D. and he also knew that Arthur was depending on him to help the unit get through this. He knew that he needed to get downtown so he could help survey the damage and he was worried about Diana. He only hoped that she had escaped injury or death.

Bobby felt a twinge of guilt for thinking about another woman at a time like this but they did have a past and a history. She was his friend as well as his ex-lover and he cared. But as always in Bobby's heart Rosaland was his first concern and he wouldn't leave until he knew that she was all right.

The time passed slowly as Bobby waited for some word on her condition; the waiting was like being in hell it was long and tortuous. Bobby walked back to her room and starred at her through the glass all he could think about was the sound of her laughter and the smart alec remarks she made when she was being facetious and how she always wrapped her legs around him when they made love. "The baby. The baby." was still ringing in his ears.

How could he make it without her? She was such a vital part of his life his very existence she was his girl and he loved her. He would give anything to trade places with her.

The hours dragged on and before he knew it, it was the next day. Rachael decided at that point she would make another plea on Arthur's behalf. Rachael knew that Arthur needed his best detective on the case and there was no way that he was going to get through this without Bobby.

"Bobby Arthur has been calling me every twenty minutes. He really needs your help downtown. I promise you that I will call you if anything happens." "Rachael don't you understand why I can't leave her? You of all people should understand."

"Bobby I do understand. Believe me I do. But my husband is dealing with a crisis downtown and he needs your help now. There is nothing that you can do here. We just have to wait but you can be so beneficial downtown with your unit. Bobby they need your help."

"I'm here and I will stay here forever if that's what it takes." "The N.Y.P.D. is involved in a situation that time is of the essence and you are a vital part of that essence. I know that this is hard for you but from what I understand the body count is stacking up and you would definitely do more good there than here. But ultimately it's your decision; I just know how much Arthur depends on your instincts."

Bobby looked at Rachael and for the first time he realized just how much she looked like her sister. It's so funny but even though they were twins he never noticed how identical they really were. Rachael handed Bobby her phone "Yeah boss. What's going on down there?" "A fucking mess! Bobby you know that the first 24 hours are the only 24 hours" "I'm headed down. Rachael will keep me posted. I don't know how much good I'll be I've been up all night."

"What ever you can do Bobby. I really need your help." "I'm on my way." "Rachael promise me" Bobby said as he turned to her "if anything changes you will call me right away?" "Bobby I will. You know that I will. You can trust me. I know how hard this is for you."

Rachael gave Bobby a kiss on the cheek as she escorted him to the elevator. Rachael's heart went out to him. She could really feel his pain and she knew that he didn't want to leave.

It was at that point that Rachael's mind flashed back to when Arthur had been shot in Bolivia and how tormented she had been waiting and praying for his recovery. It would in her opinion be better for Bobby if he could stay busy waiting is always such hell.

When Bobby arrived downtown he was shocked at the total devastation that had transpired. The N.Y.P.D. was just a shell a fragment of what it had been for years. He knew that the body count would be high; there was too much damage for it to be any other way. He had been so involved in his own personal situation that he had neglected to take into account the true scope of the damage that his unit had experienced.

The rescue squad was still digging bodies out of the rubble; the body bags were stacking up. Detective Semione stood in front of what remained of the building in total disbelief. Whoever was responsible for this act of cowardice knew exactly when and how to hit them. It had to have been an inside job; the damage was just too extensive for it to have been a random act of violence.

"Detective Semione I'm glad you decided to join us. We could really use some help around here" Bobby looked back to see his partner slowly walking toward him. "How's Rosaland Bobby? Man I am so sorry that she got hurt." Danny grabbed Bobby and held him tightly "but I'm very happy that you didn't. It's good to see you."

"Rosaland's down. She is hurt real bad. she's still in critical condition. Has anybody figured out what went down?" "Not yet. We're still trying to get an accurate body count. At this point we don't know who was in the building and with all of our phone lines down we don't have the ability to take our calls. The Lt's cell phone has been ringing off the hook so right now that's the only resource we have available."

"Where is the boss?" Danny pointed in the direction of where he had last seen the Lt. "He's somewhere around here. I know that he will be glad to see you." "We need to set up a temporary facility who's working on that?" "You are" the Lt. said with a great deal of authority. "Find me some space. Get me an office set up somewhere. Anywhere a.s.a.p. I need to know how many of my officers are still alive and I needed that information yesterday.

Call Brooklyn south and get me some off duties and some uniforms up here. The F.B.I. has been up my ass all night but this is one investigation that I'm not going to let them take over. This is my house and it is still my watch."

Detective Semione understood perfectly well what the Lt. meant despite his own personal feelings it was his watch too and if they were going to solve this situation and establish responsibility the N.Y. P. D. had to be re-organized. The unit needed an active communications network; they had already been down too long.

"Danny come with me" Bobby motioned. "First things first. Let's find some shelter. My baby's got some secret hideout uptown in the Bronx. She thinks that I don't know about it. But I know that they have a state of the art communications network and I know that they also have the manpower to help us out. Let's just see if I can remember where it's at."

"How do you know this Bobby?" "Even though she never tells me anything I know more about her operations than she realizes. She's a cool customer when it comes to the O.N.S.I.; very closed mouth and extremely secretive."

"So sometimes I have to be a detective if I want to know anything. That is what I do. So I followed her. Plus I know that the O.N.S.I. has a new facility. She has been talking about it for months. They are moving out of the N.Y.P.D.

"I thought you said that she never talks about the O.N.S.I." "I know about the facility because she has been recruiting starting with me." Danny was at a loss for words. "We had a big fight right before the Calderon operation about me joining the O.N.S.I. I actually came down on her pretty hard but none of that seems important now."

"Bobby you have been following your girlfriend?" Danny repeated "Yeah for a couple of months now." "Seems a little obsessive wouldn't you agree?" "Not really not if I want to know what she is up too?" "What she's up too? There seems to be a serious lack of trust in your relationship." "No I trust her completely it's her job that I have problems with."

"So who were you following her or her job?" Bobby looked at Danny and laughed "A little bit of both I suppose." As Bobby drove towards the Bronx he remembered precisely where the abandoned building was. What he didn't know was how to get in. "Bobby what are you doing? Where the hell is this?" "One of her many secrets." Bobby murmured to half to himself "Now let's see exactly how this works."

Bobby pulled his car close to the door and then he stepped out to ring the bell. In a matter of minutes the elevator opened and he pulled his car inside. Danny sat in amazement as the elevator closed behind them and transported the car up to level one of the O.N.S.I.

"Bobby you have got to be fucking kidding me man. What the hell is this? Mission impossible?" "Something like that? Hey this is not my shit but we need some help and this is where we can get it." Dr. Ekouevi was waiting on the lower level when Bobby arrived. He didn't appear to be particularly shocked by the Detective's presence even though he was somewhat puzzled that he had penetrated their headquarters so easily.

Bobby and Danny both stepped out of the vehicle. Danny stood down as Bobby approached Dr. Ekouevi "I'm Bobby Semione. Dr. Reid is my fiancé. This is my partner Detective Danny Schmidt." "I know who you are. The General called and said that I should be expecting you. How is she doing?" "We don't know but she is receiving the best of care. It's too early to tell."

"How do you know about this place?" Dr. Ekouevi asked point blankly "I know let's just leave it at that." "What do you need?" "We really need your help. I know you know about the bombing and right now our infrastructure is null and void. We need a communications network set up so we can reorganize our staff and we need a temporary facility so we can get back to business. We need your resources"

"Detective do you all have any idea who is responsible for this?" "No and without communications we will never be able to find out. "My fiancé is lying in the hospital in serious condition and without the proper facilities there is nothing that I can do for her to help catch the perpetrator. The first 24 hours are critical and our time is running out Lt. Jones is dead and Rosaland might be next. Please help me."

Dr. Ekouevi was way ahead of the detective. He knew that he would probably come to him; he just didn't realize that Bobby knew as much about their location as he did.

"Detective I have already set up a facility for you. It's close to your station house on 3rd ave. Here is the address." Dr. Ekouevi handed Bobby a piece of paper containing the address and a set of keys. Also you will find that we have established several phone lines and a chalkboard which are already up and operating. I took the liberty of putting in a direct line to the O.N.S.I.

just in case. I know how Dr. Reid operates; I have worked with her long enough."

"Long enough for what?" The detective questioned suspiciously. "Long enough to know that she would want me to make sure that you have all of our resources at your disposal. Also here is a list of the personnel we have and their files. They are all cleared and you can trust them."

"Right now you only have phone lines and a couple of computers but in the morning I will set up some more sophisticated equipment that will enable you to gather some Intel." Dr Ekouevi replied in his heavy thick French accent.

Danny was in a state of complete disbelief. He had no idea that Rosaland was so connected or that her organization was so covert. "Thank-you" Bobby said as he extended his hand to Dr. Ekouevi who was happy to be able to be of help.

"I'll see you both in the morning. You gentlemen know the way out." Dr. Ekouevi nodded as he watched the two detectives leave and made a mental note that he would change the entrance code tomorrow.

sixty five

Once they were on the street Danny said "I know now why you follow her. That scene was out of a James Bond movie this shit is unbelievable." Bobby looked at his partner and never said a word.

Bobby called his Lt. on the cell phone "Yancy" "Hey boss we are all set up" "What do you mean set up?" "We are back in business; we have a temporary facility on 3rd Ave close to our house equipped with several phone lines and a couple of computers."

"You're kidding?" Arthur was surprised. "No I have the keys and I'm on my way down to check it out. Also tomorrow we will be in a position to gather some Intel." "I'm not even going to ask how you got that set up so quickly good job detective. Give me a call after you check out the facility. We need to move our staff in immediately if not sooner."

"Also Lt. I have a list of names and the files of some additional personnel courtesy of the O.N.S.I." "I said I wasn't going to ask but then again I already knew. Any word on Rosaland?" "I'm just about to give Rachael a call right now." "O.k. detective I'll see you soon." The Lt. was off the phone and on to the next situation.

"Rachel any news yet?" "No Bobby everything is still the same. Matthew just left her and he has nothing to report. She is still listed in critical condition but she seems to be holding her own." "O.k. I'll be back in about an hour probably closer to two but if anything new arises..." "Bobby I will call you." "Thanks Rachael"

"O.k. partner let's go and check out this place." Bobby nodded at Danny as they sped downtown toward 3rd Ave. After a long silence Danny asked "Bobby how are you holding up?" "Just barely" "When was the last time you got some sleep?" "The last time I was with my girl. I slept like a baby that night. I miss her."

"Bobby she's going to make it." Bobby nodded confidently "I know." It was then that Bobby realized that he still had on the same clothes. He was still wearing her blood on his shirt. "Danny I need to go change. It will only take a minute."

"Go ahead partner do what you need to do I'm cool." Bobby changed course and proceeded to Brooklyn where surprisingly Papa was waiting for him in the restaurant. With all that had been going on Bobby had neglected to call his grandfather. Bobby noticed immediately that Papa was in a very disturbed state. "Roberto where have you been? Why haven't you called? I've been trying to reach you Roberto all the phone lines at your precinct are down. What is going on in New York? It has been all over the news for the last two days; a bomb hit the one five? Rosaland is in the hospital? This is not good Roberto. This is not good!"

Papa hugged his grandson to his heart; Bobby could feel his Grandfather's body trembling. "Don't worry Papa everything will be alright. We will find out who is behind this we just need some time. Come on Papa sit down." Bobby sat his Grandfather down at one of the tables and fixed him a drink. "What about Rosaland Roberto how is she?" Papa asked after he regained his composure.

"She was hurt Papa. She's at N.Y.U. Medical; we are waiting for some word on her condition" "Why are you not with her?" "Her family is with her." "You are her family." "I know Papa we are her family. Right now I need to change. I have to get back to work. Arthur needs my help the unit needs my help beside right now there is nothing that I can do for her" "You can be there" "I am there" Bobby said as he touched his heart." And she will always be here." Papa nodded as Bobby ran up the steps to shower. "Danny grab something to eat the kitchen is open."

Bobby relaxed as the warm water engulfed his bruised body; his ribs were still very sore. He had been so caught up in the events of these last couples of days that he had totally neglected himself. It felt good to let the water flow all over his body but his longing for her was building. No matter how hard he tried to control his urges he couldn't stop thinking about Rosaland and the last time he made love to her.

She was always so passionate and so willing in his arms. Bobby brushed the water out of his eyes as he pushed his hair off of his forehead while the tears ran down his face. This was the first time that he had to himself since her injury to allow his real feelings to show. Bobby took his time getting dressed as he carefully sorted through his wardrobe trying to find the pieces that she had bought for him; she was always buying him something.

At last he found what he was looking for. This was her favorite suit. He fumbled through his closets until he found the shirt and tie to match. As

Bobby looked at his reflection in the mirror he was pleased with the results and he knew that she would be pleased as well. He had lost some time coming home but he was glad that he had.

It had given him the opportunity to bond with his Grandfather and that brief moment had given him some renewed strength. "Bobby Diana called for you this morning. She said that she was worried that she hadn't seen or heard from you." Danny looked at bobby curiously and was a little surprised that his partner appeared to be so relieved with what his Grandfather had said.

"I have been a little worried about her too. I'm glad that she is alright. Papa I really need to get back to work it's my responsibility to get this unit back on its feet." "Please be careful Roberto and watch your back." Bobby kissed his Grandfather on his forehead as he and Danny headed back to Manhattan.

"So what's going on between you and Diana?" Danny asked after a while. "What do you mean?" "It's a pretty simple question?" "Nothing. If I didn't know any better I might think that you are interested." "I might be. Do you have any problems with that?" "No should I?" "No you shouldn't. I was hoping that you would say that."

Bobby smiled at his partner. "That was a long time ago. We have both moved on with our lives." "I'm glad we got that straight." Danny commented seriously.

"O.k. this is 3rd Ave. What was that address?" "It should be around here somewhere let's pull over we can walk the rest of the way." "Good idea" Bobby replied as he pulled the car to the curb. "This is kind of a swanky area" Danny mentioned as the two detectives walked along the avenue. "Well it's courtesy of the O.N.S.I. You know they have deep pockets. Here it is."

Bobby pulled the keys from his pocket and opened the door. It was just as Dr. Ekouevi had said. There was a complete office equipped with desks, phone lines and computers. It was very spacious and could easily accommodate what was left of the unit. "Yeah Boss we are here on 3rd. It's perfect. It's all set up and ready to go. The address is 1375. You should send the team on over we can be up in a couple of hours."

"Excellent you'll have a crew in about twenty minutes. I just talked to Rachael; there is no news yet. Detective I want you to stay there and supervise this operation but I need detective Schmidt back here with me." "Danny Lt. Yancy wants you back at the house. You can take my car. I'll pick it up later."

Danny nodded as Bobby tossed him the keys. "I'm going to call the O.N.S.I. They might as well put in the Intel; we can do this all in one shot."

Bobby continued "Carry on detective I'll see you in a minute." The Lt. hung up the phone and started to call his officers.

"Rousseau I want you to report to 1375 3rd ave. It's our new home. Have you heard from Easley?" "No I've been trying to call her all night." "O.k. you get over there now." Diana left as soon as she was off the phone.

"This is Lt. Yancy from the N.Y.P.D.; let me have the desk sergeant. "Sergeant Rooker" "Rooker this is Lt. Yancy N.Y.P.D." "How's it going up there?" "We need some help. I need you to call upstairs to the detective unit and get me as many dicks as you can spare. I need everybody on or off duty. Also I would like to specifically request Cole and Sanchez."

"You got it Lt. we'll send you as many officers as we can lay our hands on." They need to report to 1375 3rd ave. That's our new home for now. I have a detective on the scene, he'll fill them in."

Detective semione was on the line with the o.n.s.i. "Dr. Ekouevi this facility is perfect. The N.Y.P.D. extends our sincere appreciation for the timeliness of your department. Would it at all be possible for your team to install the Intel today?"

"We need some time detective." "We need the Intel Dr." "Is there anyway we can work this out?" "We'll do the best we can. I can be there in lets say half an hour." "Great I'll see you when you get here. Let's get this show on the road."

Detective Rousseau was the first to arrive. She had no idea that Detective Semione would already be on the scene. Diana was so happy to see Bobby alive that she ran into his arms. Her sudden burst of affection threw him off guard nonetheless he was happy to see her alive as well.

"Bobby the precinct is a disaster! We have dead bodies all over the place. The rescue team is still uncovering bodies and I believe that my partner might be one of them."

"Easley?" "Yes she was scheduled to work that shift and I haven't heard from her. I've called everywhere that she might be and I can't find her. She hasn't reported in and for some reason I've got a real bad feeling about this."

"That's why we need to get our communications established. We need to know for sure what the body count is. We need our staff accounted for. We will never know if we don't do this now."

"Bobby I heard about Rosaland. How is she?" "We don't know?" "I know you don't believe me but I'm truly sorry. I hope that she is going to be alright." "She's hurt pretty bad." For some reason at that moment Bobby thought about the baby and a strange look came over his face.

"Bobby what's the matter?" "Nothing" "You can talk to me Bobby. What's the matter?" Bobby shrugged it off "Diana let's just get this done." "O.k. what do you want me to do?" She said after realizing that whatever it was he definitely was not going to share it with her. "Get on the phone and get the word out where we are located and call the media and initiate an emergency hot line so that the officers can start calling in." "I'm on it."

Detective Rousseau took a seat and began to work. Dr. Ekouevi was the next to arrive with his O.N.S.I. staff. "Detective Semione these are the team members that I told you about. They are here for as long as you need them." "Thank-you Dr." Bobby said as he shook his hand. "I need them to man the phones. Detective Rousseau is working on the hot line so the phones should start ringing soon. While they are doing that we can be working on installing the Intel."

"Let's do it." Dr. Ekouevi said as he rolled up his sleeves and got down to work. By the time that the Lt. arrived the temporary unit was in a buzz with everyone working on re-establishing their command. "O.k. guys we should have an accurate body count by the end of the day also help is on the way. Brooklyn south is lending a hand as well our friends from the Bronx. We should have enough manpower so let's find out who is responsible for this."

Lt. Yancy was totally in command of his unit as they worked side-by-side pulling the one five back together. "Lt. the bomb squad just called in. They're sending a man over looks like they found the wiring signature of the exploding devise. They would like to show it to you before they send it to the F.B.I. lab." Detective Semione reported.

"Good looks like we are finally making some headway. Rousseau how many officers have reported in?" "Check the board Lt. there are starting to call." "Any word from Easley yet?" "No sir she hasn't reported yet." "Who hasn't reported yet?" Detective Rousseau recognized the voice of detective Wesley Cole.

"I'm sorry Wes but we haven't heard from Yvonne. We are hoping that she will see the hotline and call in." "She was working the early shift. I know for a fact that she was in the building. I dropped her off that morning myself." Wes was trying desperately to hide the emotion in his voice but he knew she was in that building.

"Well let's give her some more time." Detective Rousseau said as she nervously went back to work. "Where do you want us Lt.?" Justin Sanchez asked. "I need you Cole, Schmidt and Semione working the streets. We still have a city to protect and the last time I looked the crime rate was on the rise." "Diana she is not going to call." Detective Cole whispered "She was in the building."

Bobby looked in Diana's direction and noticed how shaken up she was. He knew that not only were they partners they were also good friends. This tragedy had left its mark on the whole department. Everyone in the unit was hurting and most of them were hurting in a bad way. Bobby was determined that no matter what he would get to the bottom of this.

Lt. Yancy walked over to Bobby and pulled him to the side "Bobby you need to get over to the hospital. Rachael just called there has been a development in Rosaland's condition. Go now and call me later." Bobby didn't like the seriousness in Arthur's voice. He had been around long enough to know that whatever it was it couldn't be good. He looked at his Lt. and was out the door.

When Bobby arrived at the hospital he found Rachael in tears. His heart fell to his knees and his legs became shaky. The detective felt as though he was a condemned man walking to his death. "What's going on?" He asked trying very hard to remain strong. "Where's Matthew?" "He is still in with Rosaland." The General responded "He'll be right out."

Just as Bobby turned to head toward Rosaland's room Matthew emerged visibly shaken. He looked Bobby straight in his eyes and his expression was not encouraging. Bobby didn't know what to do or to think, but in his heart he knew that this was not good.

"Matthew what is going on? How is she? Talk to me man; don't leave me hanging like this!" Matthew pulled Bobby to the side "Bobby Rosaland has slipped into a coma." Bobby staggered back and fell against the wall. He put his hands up to his head in disbelief as the tears poured from his eyes. "When?" He managed to mumble the words. "Sometimes during the night. Bobby I have been watching since she arrived. She slipped right through my fingers."

Matthew was in tears as he explained the situation as best he could. "She is still with us and she can still recover from this. The recovery rate on this kind of a injury is high. The statistics show that we currently have about a 70-30 recovery rate; most of those that recover have full memory and they lead normal productive lives."

"There is so much research currently being conducted in this area. Extensive studies are being facilitated at the universities in this area but as of right now Bobby we just don't know when." "I knew that I shouldn't have left her!" Bobby sobbed.

"Your leaving had nothing to do with it. She suffered a serious blow to the head Bobby and the trauma of the impact is what caused her to slip away. There wasn't anything that could have been done. We just have to wait. Under these circumstances all we can do is pray and hope that she recovers."

"We have her on life support and we will be feeding her intravenously. That's all we can do. I'm sorry Bobby but that's all we can do for now." "I need to see her" Bobby said as he entered her room. Bobby couldn't believe his eyes. She looked like she was sleeping peacefully. Bobby walked over to her bed and kissed her as he fought back his tears.

He buried his face in her hair and then he burst loudly into tears. The General came into the room after Bobby had been there for a while to escort the distraught detective out. "Bobby I'm so sorry son." The General took Bobby in his arms and held on to him tightly. This is the first time in the three years of their relationship that the General had embraced him.

"I know you love her Bobby. I've always known that you loved her. It's just that you didn't do it my way. That is the reason that I have been so distant. I always wanted the best for my children. All of my children. Especially my daughters.

"I've always placed them on a pedestal and that's where I wanted them to stay untouched by the world. But you touched her and she fell hard. Like she was hit with a ton of bricks. I guess I wasn't ready for that."

"We can get through this son but we are going to have to work together. Fortunately we haven't lost her yet. Bobby there is still hope. She can come back to us. I know her Bobby. She will come back to us." The General looked deeply into Bobby's eyes and they both could see the hurt that the other was experiencing. This was a hard pill for the two men in her life to swallow.

"I need to talk to her." Bobby requested as he sat down next to her on the bed. "Rosaland if you can hear me and for some reason I know that you can I'm so sorry that I wasn't able to protect you this time. We have been through so much together. Too much for it to end like this. Please know that I love you and I will always love you till death do us part even though we never made it that far."

"I'm going to find the person responsible for this baby and I'm going to kick his ass. I give you my word on this. Now you have to give me your word that you will come back to me."

"I need you Baby real bad and I want you back in my life. Hell I don't have a life without you no I don't want a life without you. So you just get some rest now and I'll be back tomorrow and the next day and the next day and however many days it takes until I can take you home."

Bobby leaned over and kissed her deeply "Please Baby wake up!" He whispered as he kissed her on her forehead "Please come home to me. I'm so sorry about the baby."

Bobby was so shaken up that he had to leave the room. The General watched the detective through the door of his daughter's room. He knew that Bobby loved her; After all he had defied any and every attempt the General had made to interfere with his relationship. But it wasn't until this very moment that he realized how much.

He could see the depth of his emotion all in his face. Bobby really didn't know what he was going to do. For the first time in his 33 years he felt completely lost. Bobby drove around for what must have been hours before he headed back to 3rd ave.

For some reason he didn't want to be bothered with law enforcement or the N.Y.P.D. He had other things on his mind or one other thing on his mind, her. He needed some time to sort through things. He had lost so much today and he was feeling the pain.

He desperately wanted her back but for the first time in a long time he had to face the possibility that maybe she wouldn't come back. Or if she did what if she wasn't the same? There were a thousand questions that flashed through his mind and they all needed to be answered. What the hell was he going to do? And most importantly how was he going to carry on? Right now he just didn't know. The sound of his cell phone snapped him out of his haze.

"Bobby where the hell are you?" It was Arthur on the other end "We need you back here." "Yeah Lt. I'm sorry. I'm on my way." "Listen I'm sorry about Rosaland. I just got off the phone with Rachael; she's really broken up. The whole family is broken up. I can only imagine how you must feel. If you are not up to this I understand." "No I'm not up to it but then again I don't have anything else to do and sitting around feeling sorry for myself won't get me anywhere. I'll be there in a minute."

The Lt. admired Bobby's attitude. "Come on in Bobby we have work to do." It took all the courage that Bobby could summon from deep within his soul for him to continue on but he had a job to do. People's lives were in his hands and he had a duty to protect and serve.

There was so much going on inside of Bobby's head at this moment. Not to mention the pain that he was experiencing in his heart. When Bobby arrived back on 3rd ave. The house was in movement. The familiar buzz of the building was the first thing that caught his attention. Everyone was busy reorganizing his or her unit.

Detective Rousseau and Detective Cole were both very emotional over the news of the death of Yvonne. She had been on duty at that time. Detective Cole knew that she was he had dropped her off. Detective Rousseau was extremely distraught over the death of her partner who was also her best friend. The body count was rapidly mounting. The Detectives of the one five wondered how many more of their friends and coworkers would end up on that list.

As Bobby watched Diana and Wes grieving over the loss of Yvonne, and as his eyes glanced around the makeshift office it was at that very moment that the reality of what had happened to his unit hit the detective. It suddenly dawned on him why Papa had been so worried and so upset; he had barely escaped death, Rosaland was severely injured and many of his friends and colleagues were still missing in action.

Detective Semione's heart went out to Diana. He knew the pain she must be feeling. How much it must hurt to lose her friend. Unconsciously Bobby picked up the phone and called the hospital "Yes may I have the I.C.U." As he waited to get connected he noticed the expression on Wesley's face. It was one of sadness and loss and pain.

"Dr. Reid please…" Bobby continued to hold "tell him it's Bobby" "Bobby" Matthew answered "How is it going down there?" "Hectic we are operating with a skeleton crew and the crime in the streets is escalating. It's like every criminal in the world is on the war path. How's my girl? Matthew I want some good news this time."

"She's still the same Bobby. I promise when there is a change in her condition you will be the first to know. You have my word on that." "Thanks" he sighed half heartily "I guess I'll get back to the grind." Bobby's eyes met Diana's as he hung up the phone.

"Are you alright?" He asked softly. "No Bobby I'm not. I can't believe this. Yvonne took my shift that day because I had to go…" Diana couldn't hold back her tears. "This should have never happened" she sobbed angrily "Yvonne should have never been there." "Diana you can't take this so personal. This had nothing to do with you." "Yes Bobby this has everything to do with me. She wouldn't have been here at that time if it wasn't for me."

"Diana she was here. No matter what the circumstance surrounding why or how. None of us had any idea of the danger that was awaiting us that day. I'm sure whoever planted the bomb didn't care who was here; they wanted to kill us all. I'm sorry about Yvonne. I'm really sorry."

Bobby pulled Diana into his arms to offer her some support and to comfort her. The tears ran profusely from her eyes as her body quivered in his grasp. "Its o.k." Bobby whispered. "Sometimes it's good to cry."

It took a moment for Diana to regain her composure. Lt. Yancy and Detective Schmidt walked in at that point. The Lt. was very curious as to what was going on. Danny looked at Bobby who was very much into taking care of Diana. "Thanks Bobby. Let me go in the bathroom to fix my face I'll be fine."

When Diana excused herself Lt. Yancy was the first to question the Detective as to what was going on. "What's going on with Rousseau?" "For some reason she seems to be blaming herself for Easley's death. She feels responsible for her being there that day." "Why?" "I don't know but she is taking it pretty hard." Danny walked over and was listening intently as Bobby tried to explain to his Lt. what Diana had shared with him.

“There is no need for her to blame herself. She certainly isn’t at fault here. Maybe I’ll talk to her later.” This was Danny’s opportunity. As soon as Diana emerged from the ladies room he stepped in. “Diana” he smiled lightly. “Would you care to go out for a bite to eat? You have to be hungry.” “I wouldn’t be good company right now but thanks for asking.” “I can be a good shoulder to cry on. Try me you might just like me.”

Danny could sense Diana’s hesitation “besides it’s no fun eating alone especially when you are upset. “Come on; come have a bite to eat with me.” “What about after work? That might work better for me.” “After work it is. Just let me know when you are ready.”

Diana smiled and nodded her head. Danny had been trying to catch Diana’s eye for sometime now but she was always so preoccupied with her own personal situation that she never seemed to notice how he watched her as they worked or how he looked at her when he knew that she wasn’t paying any attention. Diana was sexy and alluring and Danny hated to see how she pined after Bobby even though she would never admit it. Tonight would be his chance to set the record straight. She was a beautiful and vibrant woman and he would show her how much he appreciated her charm and her company.

sixty-six

"Detective Semione" Bobby turned his attention from the phone to a squeaky but familiar voice. "Detective Semione do you remember me?" The woman asked as he turned his attention towards her "Of course. How is your daughter? I appreciated all the help you gave me concerning my grandmother." "She's fine detective thanks for asking." "So how are things going for you? What brings you here?" Bobby asked not knowing what kind of answer to expect.

"I think I know who did this?" "I beg your pardon who did what?" Detective Semione invited her to have a seat in the makeshift office very interested in what she had to say. "You know who did what?" "This? Who destroyed your precinct? I believe it was the same man that was involved with your grandmother." Bobby was stunned at this revelation and he was extremely interested in this information as well. He listened as the woman went on.

"I didn't exactly tell you everything when you were investigating your grandmother's murder. I was afraid for my life and the life of my child. But I did see the man who did the actual shooting detective and he is a man that looks a great deal like you. Only he has a heavy beard and very long black hair. That's why I wasn't so sure that I could trust you. The resemblance between the two of you is very remarkable. This is why I never said anything before. But I saw him again last week and I recognized him immediately. Thank God he did not see me."

"So why do you think he had anything to do with our situation?" Detective Semione asked point blankly trying to follow her logic. "Because of whom he was talking to. He was talking to a very bad man. A man known in our neighborhood as "El Incendios. He has a reputation for being a very bad man."

"El Incendios? The fireman? Do you think you could give a description of this man to one of our officers so we could get a composite sketch of what the man you saw looks like?" Even though she still seemed to exhibit a great deal of fear the woman nodded in agreement to the detective's request.

"This El Incendios? Could you supply an address or an associate anybody who you think might know him?" "Detective I m really afraid of these people. If they have any idea that I am here they will kill my daughter and me. I have told you all that I know." "Its o.k. could you wait here for a minute? Could I get you anything? Coffee? Something to eat?"

"No I'm alright but I need to leave soon detective. I left my kid with a neighbor." "This won't take long." Bobby was trying to remain as calm as possible. "Hey boss you need to hear this. We have a witness!! I have someone here who could possibly provide us with some information on the bombing. Maybe even a positive i.d."

The Lt. looked at the detective with a great deal of disbelief. "She can give us a description. We need a sketch artist down here as soon as we can get our hands on one. If you can't find us one you need to make us one. Also she knows of a possible associate of this man somebody from her neighborhood."

"Bobby is this person reliable?" "Yes she has helped us out before. It's worth taken a listen; we don't have any other leads." The Lt. picked up the phone and placed a call to Brooklyn south. If any precinct would cooperate it would be them. "This is Lt. Yancy from the one five. We need a sketch artist. How soon could you get someone over here?" "We could have somebody there in about thirty minute's Lt." "You need to make it 15 minutes and we appreciate your help." "You got it."

"Bobby where is this person?" "She is sitting at the table." "Is that her?" The lt. questioned his detective. "That's her. Her name is Heidi Martinez. She did me a real solid with the investigation of my grandmother. I trust her and she came here on her own accord so I believe that she seriously wants to help. Besides she seems to be the one person who can connect these two events."

"O.k. well we can start by taking her statement and by that time the sketch artist should be here so she can give us the composite. Do you really trust her detective?" "I do." "Well let's hope that she can help us out."

"Heidi this is Lt. Yancy. He runs this unit. Would you mind repeating to him what you told me? He needs to know everything Heidi; you don't have to hold anything back. Everything you say will be held in the strictest of confidence."

"As soon as you finish with your statement if you can give us a description of the man that you saw I'll take you home." Bobby said in a soothing tone of voice. Heidi nodded at Detective Semione to show him that she appreciated his interest in her safety and she proceeded to repeat her story to Lt. Yancy.

As she told of the events that lead her to the N.Y.P.D. the sketch artist came in. "Did somebody call for a sketch artist?" Harrison Alexander shouted as he entered the office. Harrison was a long time friend of Arthur's and it had been years since the last time they had come into contact with each other.

"Harrison Alexander" the Lt. said in an excited voice extending his hand "it's good to see you. I should have known they would send you." "Lt. How long has it been? I heard that you got married. What have we got going on here?" "We have a witness and we need a profile. She is a little shy so I want you on your best behavior."

Harrison nodded in agreement as he prepared to take the information. "Heidi this is Harrison. He works with the N.Y.P.D." the Lt. explained calmly "Just relax, take your time and give him all the details that you can remember. I want you to tell him anything that comes to your mind about this mans facial characteristics. It's important that you pay careful attention to anything that might be odd or that might be distinguishing about his face. Any marks or scars, how his eyes are set, his eyebrows anything that might be helpful. Do you understand?" "Yes Lt. I will do my best." The Lt smiled as he and Bobby stood back and listened as Heidi painted Harrison a thorough picture of the suspect.

When the composite sketch was complete both Arthur and Bobby were shocked at the final results. Heidi said that the man looked exactly like Bobby only he had a beard and long hair and that was precisely what the finished product looked like.

The resemblance was uncanny. It was as though they could have been brothers; actually they could have been twins. "I need to hold onto this for a minute" Arthur remarked "before I put it into circulation. Bobby can you get me a copy of any material that the O.N.S.I might have on Carlos Calderon, a picture from his arrests anything."

"Also you need to take her home so you can get back. It looks like we will be pulling an all nighter; we have a lot of work to do. I'm sending out a different unit to canvass the neighborhood. I want to find this "El Incendios" this fireman but I want to do it from the street. I don't want him to know that we had any help on this at all."

"It will be better for everyone involved if we play it like that do you agree?" Detective Semione could feel where his boss was coming from and he liked the play. "I'm with you." "Good then get your witness home safely and let's get busy. Also let her know that if anything comes out of this we will definitely take care of her. You know in terms of a reward."

The Lt. watched as the detective escorted Heidi from the office. "Thanks Harrison, as always for a job well done. Good work. Now we can at least put a face to this disaster." This was the first break that they had caught on this case and Arthur hoped that it would pan out.

As always he felt personally responsible for the officers and all the other administrative staff that he had lost in the explosion. He would make this investigation his first and only priority. He felt that he owed at least that much to their families. "Boss if we are going to be burning the midnight oil I need to stop in at the hospital. I have to see Rosaland. I need to check on her."

"I understand detective. Take some time but get back as soon as you can. If this is our guy then we have a great deal of work to do before tomorrow. I want to get his face on the wire as soon as possible. He already had a three-day head start on us. I want to get this man."

Detective Semione nodded as he accompanied Heidi out of the 3rd ave. facility. "Thanks for coming in." He said as he walked her to his car "We really appreciate all your help. Also if this pans out the Lt. wants you know that there might be some reward." "I didn't do this for a reward detective." "I know it's o.k. but if there is any reward you are certainly entitled to it. Where do you want me to drop you off?"

"I'm staying with my cousin uptown in Spanish Harlem and my daughter is with her playmate the little girl next door." "So this "El Incendios" where will we find him? Uptown or in Brooklyn?" "He will be in Brooklyn." "Can you tell me anything else about him?" "Yes he is always surrounded by men. He never goes anywhere alone."

"That's definitely worth knowing anything else." "Detective I just know that he is a very bad man. He is dangerous." Bobby drove towards the West Side Highway. All he could think about was how they were going to zero in on this guy. He definitely didn't want anything to happen to Heidi.

"Heidi why don't you let us put you in protective custody until this is over. Even though "El Incendios" would never know that you had anything to do with this. I would feel much better knowing that you are out of this." Hide thought about his preposition. "No detective we'll be alright. We are going to stay uptown." "Are you sure?" "Yes I really don't want to be in protective custody ever again. It's so confining and my daughter can't play or do anything." Bobby knew that protective custody was confining but he was concerned for her safety. He knew from experience that anything could happen and he just didn't want to be responsible.

Detective Semione had decided that he would pick up her daughter and hide them both for a while. The canvass of the area would start soon and he didn't want her anywhere that she could be easily found. "Heidi I'm placing you in protective custody for now. I know you don't want to do it but it's for your own safety."

Heidi looked at the detective in shock. Why would he do that? She had just confided in him now why would he turn against her so harshly? The detective had a job to do and Bobby knew of the danger. He always followed his instincts. That was that Latin American machismo that he was so famous for. He always took control especially with women.

Despite all her protest Heidi knew that she was fighting a losing battle. As they drove Detective Semione tried to console her "This won't be a long process. I can assure you that we will be moving on this very soon. But I can't take a chance with your life Heidi. So you are going to have work with me on this."

Heidi was quiet for the remainder of the trip but deep down inside she knew that the detective was right. Now Bobby's next concern is where was he going to stash her? He didn't have the time or the normal resources of the department so he had to think fast.

The only place that came to mind was with Papa. He knew that she would be safe there. "Heidi what would you say if I set you up with a job?" Again Heidi was shocked. "What kind of job?" She inquired innocently. "I was thinking that maybe you could help my grandfather in the restaurant for a couple of months. It's decent pay, free meals and we could use the help. At least this way I can give you some compensation. How does that sound?"

"It sounds good to me." "So will you do it?" "Yes. When do I start?" "Why don't you grab your daughter, throw some things in a bag and I'll take you to Brooklyn now." While Heidi was getting herself together Bobby placed another call to Arthur. "Hey boss this is going to take a little longer than I thought. I'm going to place our witness in protective custody for the time being."

"That's a good idea where are you going to put her?" "Well I was thinking about taking her to Brooklyn" "I'm listening detective" "She can stay with my grandfather for the time." "Do you think that's a good idea?" "I don't know about good but it's the only one that I could come up with." "How's is your grandfather going to feel about that?" "He'll be happy to have the company. But just in case something goes down I need to know that she is safe."

"We're uptown now and we will be heading for the bridge in another minute or two. I still need to go by the hospital and then I'll be back." "O.k. do what you have to do." "Here let me help you with that" the detective offered as he placed Heidi's overnight bag in the car. They drove quickly and quietly to Brooklyn.

Papa was extremely surprised to see Bobby and his guest but he was happy nevertheless. He cherished his grandson and he was worried about him as well. Papa knew what strain Bobby was under operating without Rosaland. He knew the depth of the emotion that his grandson carried in his heart for this woman.

"So who do we have here?" Papa inquired as Bobby escorted Heidi and her daughter inside. "Papa this is Heidi and her daughter Brianna. They are going to be staying with us for a while. Heidi has agreed to help us out in the restaurant for a couple of months."

Bobby explained the situation to his grandfather. "That is of course if it is alright with you?" "Of course Roberto whatever you think is best. It would be nice to have some help during the day." "O.k. Papa I need to leave them here for now. Please look after them until I get back."

Bobby gave his grandfather a reassuring look as he rushed out of the door. Papa nodded and Bobby knew that everything would be all right. Bobby lost no time making his way to the hospital. The General and Rachael were still sitting in the waiting area when he arrived. Bobby could tell immediately there was no change in her condition from the expression of worry that the General wore on his face.

"Sir" Bobby greeted him extending his hand. "Detective" the General acknowledged his presence giving him a firm handshake. "I'm sorry son there hasn't been any change." Bobby nodded indicating that he knew that would be the case. "I just really need to see her" Bobby said as he made his way towards her room.

"Bobby" Matthew greeted him warmly. "Hey Doc I need to see my baby. I just want a few minutes alone with her." "Bobby I won't even let the General in the room. I need the air to stay as sterile as possible. I'm trying to make sure that her burns heal properly." "I need to see her Matt. You have to let me in just for a few minutes."

"Bobby this is a clean room. You are going to have to go through decontamination if you go in there other than that I can't let you in." "Show me the way." Matthew could tell by the determination in Bobby's voice that he had to let him in. There was no way that he was going to accept anything less than that.

"Bobby you have to suit up in these scrubs and you need a mask. I have to keep the air germ free." Bobby nodded as he changed into the scrubs. "The General is going to have my ass for this but I know what's going on." "Matt it hurts so bad without her." Matthew led Bobby to her room.

"You've got ten minutes Bobby and I'm pushing it allowing that much time." "Thanks Matt I owe you one." "No you don't" Matthew replied as he left the room. She looked so helpless lying there with her face and hands all bandaged but just to be near her was good enough for now.

"Don't worry Baby we'll be alright. We'll get through this. Just come back to me. I love you and I need you and I miss you so much." He said softly trying very hard to fight back his tears. Bobby realized at that moment how in a matter of a second your life could be completely changed.

Just three days ago they were making love and planning their future and now there was nothing but uncertainty. The one thing that Bobby knew for sure was that by any means necessary he would kill the bastard that was responsible for this. "Bobby I can't let you stay any longer." Matthew's voice interrupted his train of thought. "O.k. I need to get back to work anyway."

This was the first time in a long time that Bobby didn't have control and he didn't like it. He didn't like it at all. After he changed he walked out to where the General and Rachael were still seated. Both of them could tell that he was extremely shaken up.

Both the General and Rachael wanted Bobby to know that they were all family and he could reach out if he needed their support. "Any leads son?" The General questioned him after allowing him to regain his composure.

"Yes as a matter of fact we got our first big tip tonight. We are following up on it now. It comes from a reliable source an eye witness so hopefully it will pan out." "Will you keep me informed as to your progress?" "Without a doubt sir." "If you need any help Bobby you can call me." "I will. Thanks for the help you have already given us. The O.N.S.I. put us back in business."

"That was nothing. We've got our feelers out as well. If anything comes up that is helpful you'll be the first to know." "Thank you sir. I appreciate the kindness." "Bobby just keep me in the loop. We will work this thing together."

"I've got to get back to work but if anything comes up I'll call." The General nodded as they departed. "I'll see you Rachael" Bobby said as he kissed her lightly on the cheek. "Call me" "I will".

sixty-seven

The next twenty-four hours would be intense. Lt. Yancy and his remaining detectives would use the information supplied by Heidi to lay out the foundation to capture El Incendios. This operation would have to proceed in a quiet and hasty manner because time was of the essence and there were so many eyes and ears inside the defunct N.Y.P.D.

Lt. Yancy had surmised that the attack on the P.D. had to have been an inside job but he didn't have a drop of evidence to support his theory. The only detectives in his unit he knew that he could trust for sure were Semione, Schmidt and of course Rousseau but to this point he hadn't shared his suspicions with either of them.

"Bobby got a minute? I want to talk to you." "Sure boss" the curious detective replied detecting from the Lt.'s tone of voice that something was amiss. "What do you make of this whole thing?" Arthur asked "I don't like it" "Your gut Bobby, what are you gut feelings about this situation?"

"It seems a little too compact; there is no latitude here. Too neat." "Do you think it could possibly have been an inside job?" "I wouldn't rule it out. Why? What are you getting at? Talk to me boss. My girl is laying in a coma. Somebody is responsible and if you feel that this was an inside job I want to know. Talk to me."

"I feel the same way you do; this job was a bit too neat. I think some of the information came from someone in this unit. Why don't we talk about this later after work?" "Sounds good to me I could certainly use a drink or two." "O.k. then we will save this conversation for later." Bobby nodded as the Lt. started his briefing.

"We need to move fast on this one. We have a limited amount of time and resources and a whole city to turn inside out. We have an eye witness that can put our guy in the vicinity around the time of the bombing and we have a face." The Lt. passed the sketch among his team.

"I haven't put this on the wire yet because I want to get a head start. I want Bobby and Danny to canvass and I want Rousseau, Cole, and Sanchez to back them up. Whatever it takes. We are not backing down on this one; I really want to get this guy." "So what's the move?" Danny asked.

As the Lt. looked around the room he was comforted in the fact that the remaining detectives were reliable and he knew from past experience that he could count on their loyalty. "We have to move fast before this situation gets any further out of hand than it already is. This is unacceptable; no way is anybody going to get away with this. Not today, not here, and not on my watch."

"We need to pick up this "El Incendios" without drawing any attention to what we are trying to do. I have run him through BCI and he has an old warrant that we can snatch him up on. I want Bobby and Danny undercover. Just stake him out for a while watch where he goes and what he does. I want to know whom he talks to, whom he sleeps with and what and where he eats."

"I want you to take him when you can catch him alone. If you have to wait days then we will wait for days. I don't what his guys to have any idea at all as to where he is at or who has him. Let's make him disappear. Poof" the Lt. popped his fingers. "Just like that."

Danny was so busy looking at Diana that the Lt. was wondering had he heard a word that he had said. "Schmidt what do you think about that?" "It sounds like a plan but if we are going undercover we are going to need some gear. If we go driving through the neighborhood they are going to make us and they will go underground. We need to be smooth and we need to hit quick."

"Bobby can you get us some help from the O.N.S.I.?" "Yes I just talked to the General at the hospital. He has promised us whatever help we need." "Get on the phone and get us some dicks. We need a whole team of investigative specialist. Some no nonsense get to the task at hand dicks." Bobby got on the phone; he knew that Dr. Ekouevi would cooperate.

Bobby set up a meeting with Dr. Ekouevi and the rest of his unit. This would be the perfect opportunity for them to strategize and develop a fool proof plan to catch this guy. The Lt. wanted some results; he wanted some arrests and some convictions on this one. He had had enough. Arthur had no intention of continuing to be blackmailed or held hostage by these lunatics.

They had destroyed his precinct and killed most of his officers. This was definitely war and the spoils go to the victor. The Lt. was pulling out all stops on this one and calling in an enormous amount of favors. He was going to stop these guys permanently. The image of Rachael's face was constantly appearing in his mind. All he could see was her tears streaming down her face. He remembered Diana's pain as she heard of the news of Yvonne. There was too much sorrow and too many tears for him not to do everything in within his power.

Arthur knew how Bobby must feel and how hard it must be for him right now. Bobby and Rosaland shared a deep emotional bond; one that went beyond eternity and everyone knew it. Arthur watched the detective carry out his duties and admired the manner in which Bobby conducted himself.

For Bobby he had another image. All he could see was Rosaland bandaged in the hospital. His heart was heavy and hurt and his body missed hers. His life seemed to be moving in slow motion as he watched the events come and go. Bobby knew that if he stopped moving he would completely fall apart and then he would be no good to anyone, especially Rosaland.

He could feel Arthur's determination and he knew that he had to help. He wanted these guys just as much as his boss probably even more and between the two of them he knew they would get him or them who ever was responsible. They would not stop until they did. This was a very intense time and emotions were running high. Everyone was on edge, not knowing what to expect next.

"Ok. let's go over this one more time. Bobby, you and Danny are in the neighborhood. Diana, Wes and Justin you are on back up. When is Dr. Ekouevi meeting with us?" "He said he would be here tomorrow morning."

"He needs to bring audio and visual surveillance equipment. Not only do we need film on these guys we also need sound. I want to see what they do and I want to hear what they say. Is that understood?"

This is the last time they will get away with this kind of an action." The detectives of the one five knew that once the Lt. made up his mind on anything that was how it was going to be. "That's enough for today guys. I'm going to the hospital to get my wife and I'm taking her home for a good night sleep. Bobby are you coming with me? I really want to talk to you."

"Yes I'll follow you to the hospital." "Dr. Ekouevi will be here in the morning so I would suggest that you all be here on time. Good night see you in the morning."

When the rest of the detectives left for the evening Arthur and Bobby headed uptown. Diana and Danny headed toward the Brooklyn Bridge for a nice quiet intimate dinner.

It had taken Danny three years to finally get her attention and tonight he didn't want to share her with anyone. Danny could sense that there was something on Diana's mind. He thought that maybe it was the death of her partner but whatever it was Danny planned to be there for her tonight.

"Bobby I'm taking Rachael home tonight. She really needs some sleep and I need some loving." "Shit I hear you. How do you want to handle this?" "Why don't you follow me to the little bar that is right around the corner from the hospital? We can have a few drinks." "Sounds good to me. I need a drink or two or three." Bobby smiled.

After Arthur and Bobby parked and were settled at the bar Arthur started into his conversation "Bobby how are you feeling? I've been meaning to talk to you and I know how hard this must be for you. " Arthur stated from a concerned point of view. "I was impressed with how you handled the situation with Heidi. I hope the information she provided works out. It was good of her to come in"

"Heidi has worked with us before. She helped me with Abuelita." Bobby said softly as he sipped his drink. After a moment or two of silence Bobby continued "Yes Arthur this is very hard for me. My whole world is on hold. I don't know if I'm coming or going but I know I can't stop."

"Bobby I can't pretend to know what you going through and I know that words will not lessen your pain but all I can say is that you need to hang in there and we will catch this son of a bitch. You can bet your ass on that."

Bobby nodded as Arthur finished his statement. "You are damned right we are going to get him. His ass is mine. But Arthur you have something else on your mind. You alluded to it earlier so why don't you just tell me what you know."

"Well Bobby I told you that I thought this was an inside job. My suspicions have been confirmed. We have uncovered certain communications that have been traced back to the one five. Someone has been selling our secrets to our friends in Colombia. Now if we can connect "El Incendios" with our friend from Colombia; a certain Mr. Carlos Calderon then we have a hit." "You know Bobby I know that Carlos was involved but we need proof. We have a paper trail on this end now all we have to do is to connect it on the other end and we've got him."

"Arthur this guy is so damn slippery. Who is helping him? Every time we get remotely close he slips through our fucking fingers like some kind of a damn magician." "The problem Bobby is that the man has so much money. He can and does buy anybody that can further his cause.

"How can you fight money? That is what we are up against. All you need is to find someone that has a financial problem and you've got your in. Who doesn't have financial problems these days? Everybody needs money. That is how he keeps one up on us." "That's why I'm worried he can get to anybody and apparently he got to somebody inside our house and now we are fucking out in the street." "And my baby is in a coma. I am going to kill him." so Arthur what's the move?"

"Tomorrow we get our surveillance equipment from the O.N.S.I. and then you and Danny sit on our only lead until we grab him up."

"Arthur" Bobby hung his head in sorrow. "I haven't had a chance to talk about this to anyone. We lost a baby." "What?" "Yes Rosaland was pregnant when she hit that wall. I didn't know it. She may not have n known it but apparently she was far enough along to miscarry. That was my first child. I've never even made a baby before or if I have nobody has told me." Bobby joked trying to lighten his mood.

"I'm still numb about it and I don't know what I can do. I don't know what to feel or where to place this pain but it hurts. What is going to be more painful is when I have to tell her. The reason we were late that day is because we went down to apply for our marriage license."

"Maybe that was why she was so willing to do it. I don't know." Bobby signaled for the bartender to pour the two of them another round. Arthur listened intently at a complete loss for words.

"Does Rachael know about this?" "No. Matthew promised me that it was between me and him. You know how strict the General is. That man would kill me if he had any idea that she was pregnant. He would have my head or should I say my balls. Shit he wants to kill me now because of our living situation." Bobby took a big swallow of his drink.

"You know I was joking with Rosaland that she needed to make an honest man out of me to get me off of her dad's fucking hit list. You see the way he looks at me. The General told me three years ago when he found out about us to marry her. That decision had to be between her and me and now that I am ready she's in the hospital. Life's a bitch."

"Bobby I'm sorry. I had no idea." Arthur was sympathetic. "Nobody knows how much my heart hurts. All I want is to be able to hold my girl and my baby and I can't do that. I need her to hold me and she can't. You need to take your wife home and hold unto her with both arms. If we get through this Arthur I am never going to let her go."

"Bobby you need to get some sleep." "What the hell is that? Some unknown commodity. No. I'll stay at the hospital tonight. I can catch some sleep in the lounge. Are you about ready?"

"Yes I told Rachael that I would pick her up." "Let's go. You can get your wife and I can sit with mine. Sounds like a plan to me." As Bobby finished his drink he laid some money on the bar and he and Arthur walked around the corner to the hospital.

"Hello Gorgeous" Arthur whispered to a very sleepy Rachael once they were in the waiting room. "I've come to take you home. Bobby will sit with Rosaland. You need some sleep." "Hi Baby. What time is it? I must have dozed off." Rachael smiled as she stood up and went quietly into Arthur's muscular arms.

"I've missed you" she murmured as she gently placed her lips on his. Arthur pulled his wife close to his body and held her tightly in his grasp. "Let's go home" he whispered as he gathered up her things from the chair that she had made her home for the last three days. Rachael was tired and she wanted to be with her husband.

It seemed as though it had been a life time since the two of them had been alone and at this point they were both overdue. "Baby I want to stay with Rosaland a little longer." "No Baby not tonight" Arthur said as he pulled her arm gently in the direction of the door. "Bobby is here and he wants to spend some time with her. I want to spend some time with you. Come on let's go home." Rachael nodded her consent as the two of them left the hospital.

Arthur was gentle and passionate with Rachael that night. Taking her into his arms as soon as they entered their apartment. Rachael responded ardently to her husband's attentions and relaxed in his embrace as she removed his shirt and tie. Arthur reached his hand under her blouse to remove her bra. He wanted to feel the warmth of her naked breasts pressed into his bare chest.

"Oh Rachael" he moaned as he pressed her close. "Arthur" Rachael murmured breathlessly as he slid her skirt over her hips and let it drop to the floor. Rachael reached down to remove Arthur's belt and he let his pants slip to the floor as well. They both stepped out of the puddle of clothes that lie at their feet and pulled each other closer in an intimate embrace.

Rachael felt so good in his arms. Her shapely body fit like a glove in his. She ran her hands over his muscular physique as she kissed her husband up and down his neck. "Ooh Baby" Rachael sighed as Arthur delicately removed her panties. He wanted his wife in the worst way. Arthur bent down and placed his hungry mouth on her fleshy breasts sending waves of electricity through her body.

Rachael reached down and placed her hand on his throbbing penis freeing him from the constraints of his underwear. She rubbed her fingers up and down his powerful shaft sending Arthur over the edge. Arthur picked Rachael up and carried her to the bedroom.

Arthur entered her body gently but forcefully. Rachael graciously accepted his manhood into her inner most parts as she writhed in the splendor that Arthur was affording her. "I love you Baby" Arthur moaned as he planted himself deeper into her hot love canal. Rachael opened her body so that she could accommodate his length as he thrust inside of her. The room became engulfed with the sound of their love as Arthur pumped himself deeper and deeper into her willing body.

"Ooh Arthur" Rachael whimpered as she placed her open mouth on his "Ooh I love you." The sound of Rachael's sexy voice in Arthur's ear just added fuel to his fire as he stabbed harder and harder into her privacy. Arthur loved his wife and it had been a long time since he had the chance to show her just how much.

He was completely engrossed in the feel of her velvety body as Rachael wrapped her legs tightly around his waist. "Arthur" Rachael said softly "You feel so good" "Is it good Baby?" "Yes Arthur always" Rachael whispered as Arthur relentlessly plunged deeper into her core. As the sweat poured off of their bodies Rachael began to quiver from the intensity of his thrusts.

Arthur could feel that she was rapidly approaching her climax and her excitement was bringing him to his. He wanted to hold back. He wanted to prolong her pleasure but the heat from her body took them both over the edge. Rachael cried out in unbridled lust as Arthur filled her love nest with his hot seed.

"Arthur I want a baby!" Rachael cried out softly as Arthur held her tightly in his arms. "So do I." He whispered tenderly while consoling her. Arthur kissed her passionately as they continued to make love for the rest of the night.

sixty-eight

The next two weeks would be intense. Bobby and Danny had all of their resources lined up and they had finally located the highly sought after "El Incendios". Dr. Ekouevi had installed the state of the art surveillance equipment that allowed them to gather information without being detected. They monitored him on a constant basis uncovering his favorite haunts and his best girl whom despite his fierce reputation he seemed to be very much in love with. "Love can bring the strongest man to his knees." Bobby commented as they listened to "El Incendios" making love.

"Yeah I know the feeling." Bobby looked at Danny curiously "What's going on with you?" Bobby questioned his partner. "Nothing that's the problem. I want to get closer to Diana but she is keeping me at bay. She won't let me in. It's like she has this secret and she's not telling anyone. Well she is not telling me that's for sure. Something is up with her but I'll be damned if I know what it is."

"You know when I'm with her she seems to enjoy my company but then there is always a point when I want to get closer where she goes inside and I completely lose her." Bobby listened to Danny as they watched "El Incendios" on the closed circuit screen. "What are you going to do?" Bobby asked "You know this is better than H.B.O."

"Man I don't know. She is making it so hard. I know she has some feelings for me other than our working relationship. I'm just going to let it go; if it happens then it will happen. Shit Bobby you know her better than me." "I can't get into this. Nothing personal. You have to do this on your own."

"Some partner you are turning out to be. I would help you if you needed it. I don't care about your past relationship with her. That is what I'm counting on. If you know her moods you should enlighten me. Help a brother out. You know how hard I am trying to get with this woman. Would you want someone to stand in the way of you and Rosaland? Hell no. You would have moved mountains to get with her and you did. I just want the same chance."

"You know what I had to go through to get with her. Diana hates me. She thinks I was cheating on her and I wasn't. Her father is still ready to kill me and if he knew the latest he would surely kick my ass. Trust me." "The latest? What's the latest?" "You don't even want to know." Bobby shook his head.

"Diana doesn't hate you. I can tell you that much. She believes you about the cheating because she says she knows the kind of man you are. What has her is that she just can't understand what happened. The two of you were so good together." Bobby starred at Danny in total disbelief.

"Rosaland happened. I didn't plan it and I couldn't have prayed for it. Rosaland was God's gift to me." Danny understood exactly what Bobby meant. He remembered Bobby's words to him that first day Rosaland walked into the N.Y.P.D. At this point their conversation was interrupted. "Our boy is on the move." Danny pulled the van out slowly so that he could follow "El Incendios" without being noticed.

Bobby was noticing the flow of the traffic and trying to devise a plan to catch "El Incendios" off guard. "Danny lay back a little." "I've got this partner; this is not my first date." "Just watch your speed dude." As the two of them followed him a little further Bobby observed "If we get close enough to pin him in at the next intersection we could grab him up so fast he wouldn't even know what hit him." "Let's do it. Let's get this son of a bitch."

As "El Incendios" reached the intersection Danny sped up and pulled the van across the flow of traffic to pin him in. Bobby jumped out of the vehicle and snatched to door open. The angle at which Danny parked left it impossible for "El Incendios" to make a move. They had him pinned in.

Bobby punched him hard in his face and slammed his head into the hood of the car as he grabbed him up in his collar and flung him to the ground to attach the cuffs. "What the hell!" El Incendios screamed in Spanish as the blood flowed freely from his mouth and his nose.

He struggled with the detective as he tried to throw him into the back of the van. Bobby used this opportunity to punch him in the stomach and to land two more powerful blows to his mouth. The detective instantly threw him in the back of the van as his partner sped away. "What the fuck!" The madman shouted "Who the hell are you?"

"El Incendios you are under arrest. You have the right to remain silent everything you say can and will be held against you in a court of law." Bobby scowled as he read him his rights. "Under arrest for what?" "Outstanding parking tickets. Now doesn't that beat all?" Bobby picked up his cell.

"Lt. We got him and we're bringing him in now." "Bobby take him uptown to the holding facility at the O.N.S.I. We don't have the room to interrogate him here. Also I want you to keep a low profile. We don't want anyone to know that we have him." "O.k. you need to call ahead to make the arrangements."

The Lt. was elated at the news. This was their first real arrest in conjunction with the bombing. Two weeks after they got their first real lead they had a suspect in custody. This would really look good to their superiors.

"Danny turn around. We have to take this piece of shit uptown." Danny made a hasty u-turn and headed the van towards the Bronx. "Bobby I thought you were going to kill him back there." Danny said looking at his partner. "I was." Bobby responded without showing any emotion. "Bobby we need him." "That's why he is still here."

Danny knew that tone and he also knew that when his partner used that tone the best thing to do was to let it pass. "Exactly what are we doing here?" Danny waited for Bobby to give him some sort of direction. "We have to take him in for interrogation." "Who is going to conduct it?" "In all likelihood I would say the Lt. After all this is his investigation."

"We need to drop him off and let Dr. Ekouevi hold him until the Lt. arrives." "Bobby are you sure you want to leave our prisoner with the O.N.S.I.?" "What are they going to do to him? Eat him?" "No but we did all the work and I don't want anybody getting the credit. If we leave him I'm going to stay with him until the Lt. arrives." "Fine I don't have a problem with that. He is our prisoner but somebody needs to be on third. We all can't be out of the house."

"Then you need to head home while I wait for the boss to arrive." Bobby was quiet as they drove to the remotely located headquarters of the O.N.S.I. Danny was a little alarmed by his partners silence but he knew that if Bobby had something up his sleeve he would reveal it shortly.

That was one thing about partnering with Semione for all these years. Danny had gotten to know him very well almost too well. Bobby's silence was eerie and Danny expected that at any moment his partner would explode.

"Danny I want to talk to this guy before the Lt. arrives." Bobby looked at Danny seriously and Danny knew that there would be no way that he could stop him. "Bobby listen to me. Don't lose your badge over this. He's is not worth it." Bobby smiled. "It's alright I've got this."

"Bobby I'm going to give you ten minutes." Bobby looked at Danny as if to say "What's up?" Danny didn't even hesitate "Look whenever it comes to Rosaland you loose your fucking head. Bobby we need to get all of them.

This man could lead us to Carlos. Yeah I said Carlos, because I'll put money on the fact that he is behind this." "Now before you go and lose your temper think about that." When Danny was finished he threw up his hands and backed off. Bobby was listening but he didn't hear a word that Danny said.

Bobby was angry. Hell he was mad. All he could think about was how his life had been completely altered. Bobby wasn't going to keep his head and Danny knew that. Danny knew that under any other circumstance he would have never let Bobby loose on "El Incendios". It would be another twenty minutes or so before they would arrive in the Bronx. Danny hoped that Bobby heard him but knowing Bobby he probably didn't.

sixty-nine

Dr. Ekouevi was expecting them when they arrived. He had a special security detail waiting in the event that they experienced some unexpected trouble. The first thing he noticed after transporting the prisoner from the van was the blood.

"What happened to him?" He questioned curiously looking from Bobby to Danny. "He tried to escape." "Well we will make sure that won't happen again." Dr. Ekouevi turned to the detail "Clean him up and put him in three." "Dr. Ekouevi I need ten minutes with this man." "O.k. you can talk to him when they clean him up." Bobby nodded and rested on the back wall.

He was tired; this whole pursuit was beginning to become endless. He wanted to get some valid information out of this guy. Bobby had enough of all the bullshit. He wanted to put this behind him; he wanted to file this case away.

"Detective you can see the prisoner now." Bobby nodded. "El Incendios" was seated and cuffed when Bobby walked in. They met eye-to-eye as the detective approached his suspect their gazes locked upon each other. There was an instant dislike that each held for the other. This wasn't going to be easy.

Bobby seated himself directly in front of "El Incendios." They continued to stare at each other in a deadly manner. There was an uneasy silence between them as they both checked each other out. Bobby relaxed in his chair as he continued in silence and then he did the strangest thing. He walked over and released "El Incendios" from his restraints.

"El Incendios" rubbed this wrist as they were freed. Bobby put the cuffs in his pocket and then he took his seat. "Let's talk. I think we have been silent long enough." "You can start by telling me why I am here?" "You are under arrest. That is why you are here." "For what? You have to tell me something better than some bullshit traffic warrants. Not the way you took me down. Now what is going on here?"

"You tell me what the hell is going on. Now this conversation seems to be flowing in the right direction." "El Incendios" continued to stare at the detective not saying a word. "Tell me a tale; you can make it up as go. I want to hear about a bomb. A bomb that was placed in the N.Y.P.D. about three or four weeks ago. Now would you happen to know anything about that?"

"What are you talking about?" "Tell me about a bomb or better yet you can tell me about the man that ordered the bomb. Either one I'm open." "I don't know what you are talking about." "That's not what I heard. I heard that not only do you know about it you were the one that actual built it. That's what I heard. That's the word on the street."

Bobby stood up coolly as he continued. "The story I hear is that you have made several bombs. That this was not the first but just one of many. Is any of this sounding familiar?" "El Incendios" was still quiet starring at the detective as he revealed more of what he knew. He began to become uncomfortable in his chair.

"We have a witness that can place you in the vicinity. Is any of this ringing a bell?" Bobby could see his discomfort was becoming more apparent. He knew that he was on the right track. "So it's like I said when we first started talking. Why don't you tell me what is going on?" Bobby gave him some time to consider if he was going to come clean.

The detective slid his gun from its holster and placed it in the table. He listened patiently for "El Incendios" to say something anything. "Don't make this hard man; you are going to tell me what I want to hear!" Bobby was in an uproar. At this point that El Incendios made his move. He jumped in a single bound over the table right at the detective.

He threw a punch in Bobby's direction and scrambled to get across the table to his gun. Bobby threw a punch that landed right in "El Incendios's" face sending him crashing to the ground. As Bobby approached El Incendios kicked the detective in the face sending him sprawling across the floor.

Bobby rebounded back with a series of blows that landed in El Incendios's chest and stomach. Bobby then leaped up and placed a powerful kick to his groin that left him sprawled out in the middle of the floor. Bobby grabbed his neck in a headlock and then he shouted in a loud voice "Are you going to tell me what I want to hear." The detective was squeezing his neck applying a huge amount of pressure as he waited for an answer. "El Incendios" delivered a shot to Bobby's rib cage that caused the detective to double over and loosen the headlock. "El incendios" used this time to his advantaged as he broke free from the detective's grip.

Bobby struggled to regain his position with his suspect as he slid his leg out to knock "El Incendios" back down to the ground. Bobby then applied a barrage of punches to "El Incendios's" face and stomach bringing him down once again to the floor.

The detective then grabbed "El Incendios's" head and started pounding it into the ground. Bobby slammed his head hard into the ground as he screamed "Tell me the fuck what I want to know!" Bobby held "El Incendios's" hair in his hands as he pulled his head up ready to slam it a final time into the concrete floor.

Both the detective and the suspect had blood dripping from the corners of their mouths as their conflict raged. "El Incendios" wasn't ready to give up any thing; no information, nothing. And the detective didn't have a problem in continuing to kick his ass. "Motherfucker I will beat this information out of you. Don't fucking play with me!" Bobby screamed as he landed another series of excruciating hard blows to El Incendios's" head.

"Don't play with me; tell me what I want to know!" Detective Semione demanded. "You are going to tell me what I want to know!" Bobby struggled with "El Incendios" as they rolled across the floor both of them trying to gain a serious advantage over the other one. Bobby elbowed him in the face as they continued to pound away at each other. Bobby finally gained the upper hand and grabbed El Incendios in a head lock. Bobby squeezed tightly on his neck as he calmly stated

"Now tell me about the bomb?" Bobby applied more pressure on El Incendios's pressure points and at this point he was tired of the confrontation. The detective applied more pressure with the intent of ending his misery. "O.k. maybe I do know something." He spat as he tried to catch his breathe.

"That's better. Now tell me what I want to know" Detective Semione pulled "El Incendios" to his feet and placed him in his seat "Now let's talk" the detective said as he wiped the blood from the corners of his mouth. "El incendios" had blood running from his head as well as his mouth and a couple of broken ribs. Even though he was ready to talk Bobby wasn't satisfied; he reached over and pounded a series of blows right to El Incendios's head. The fact that he had caught him so much off guard sent El Incendios sprawling to the ground.

Bobby then moved around to place his body directly over El Incendios as he slammed his foot into his head. Bobby steeped into El Incendios's head a few more times before he realized that he should stop. The detective reached down and picked his dazed bleeding body up from the concrete. Bobby then threw him back into the chair he had just knocked him out of. "I've had just about enough of this shit! Talk to me!"

Bobby picked his head up from the table and then slammed it down again. "Talk to me!" He said this time a bit calmer. "We can stay here all day with me kicking you ass which I will gladly do or you can talk." The detective felt a lot better and now he was ready to do business with this piece of shit.

"Ok." "El Incendios" screamed fearing the detective's next move. "O.k. maybe I do know something. Calm the fuck down we can talk." At this point the detective backed off. He placed his gun back into his holster and put the hand cuffs back on his suspect. He moved around to the other side of the table and sat down. Bobby gazed intently into "El Incendios's" eyes as he waited patiently for him to spill his guts.

"About three months ago I was approached by one of my boys from the hood about a job. In my line of business you ask little questions especially if it's a home boy. He had an order that he wanted me to fill. That's all I know. I wasn't told anything else."

"You took that ass whipping just to tell me that. I know you can do better than that." Bobby laughed. He would gladly beat this scum to death without getting a bit of information out of him. "El Incendios" didn't realize how close to death he really was at this time. The detective wasn't to be played with. Not now.

"I didn't say that was all that if know. I just said I wasn't told anything." "Well I'm waiting." "Yeah we had this meeting with this man, some big Colombian, in this real expensive nightclub. I could tell from his setup that he wasn't to be fucked with. He had guns everywhere. I felt nervous in this place. The security was tighter than a fucking condom."

"I thought that at any moment all hell was going to break lose. He was the person that gave me the specs. He never once told me what or where. He just gave me the order and I made the bombs."

"What was his name? And where is this nightclub?" "Man he will kill me!" "Shit I'll fucking kill you. Are you serious?" The detective pulled out his gun and placed the barrel to "El Incendios's" head. "I need a name" Bobby said calmly as he cocked the trigger. "You know I should kill you for just making the damned bomb."

"El Incendios" started to sweat as the detective pressed the gun harder into his temple. "He was introduced to me as Antonio Rivera but that wasn't his real name." "How do you know that?" "Because when they paid me they called him Mr. Calderon. They told me how grateful he was for a job well done and that I should expect to hear from him again."

"Who called him Mr. Calderon?" "The man that gave me the money." "Can you identify this Calderon?" "Maybe if I seen him again." "Well you are not going to get a chance to see him again so I need you to describe him to our sketch artist. Let's see if we can put a face to this man."

Bobby put his gun back into the holster and walked over to pick up the phone. "Can we get a sketch artist down here?" He asked as he continued to watch the wicked "El Incendios". Dr. Ekouevi had all types of resources at his disposal so in no time flat "El Incendios" was painting a portrait of Antonio Rivera also known as Carlos Calderon.

Dr. Ekouevi stood by silently as he listened to "El Incendios" describe the man that brokered the deal. He carefully painted an exact portrait down to the last detail. When the sketch artist was finished what he had in his hand was the face of Carlos Calderon; a face they had come across all to often in the last three years. "This is our man" the detective handed the composite to Dr. Ekouevi who looked over it without uttering a word.

"This man seems to be menacing us; we need to find out what his real intentions are. Obviously there is something that we are overlooking. He wants something other than what we are looking for. Now what is it? What is the constant here that we are missing?"

"He is laughing in our faces. As soon as we have him for one crime he turns around and commits another one right under our noses. But there is something else here that has his interest and it's not all these random crimes. He is using them as a diversion. He is going to do something else and that is going to be what he has intended to do all along."

Dr. Ekouevi was convinced within himself that he was right. He had tracked this behavioral pattern before and he knew the psychological profile very well. Carlos was a deadly adversary and worthy of all the attention and the resources that the O.N.S.I. could muster but he was playing with them. He had not yet gotten what he was after.

Dr. Ekouevi had another train of thought on this as well; whatever Carlos wanted, had to do with Bobby. There was definitely some connection here other than the fact that they looked so much alike. A resemblance that the detective failed to see.

The name Antonio Rivera left a bad taste in the detective's mouth. He knew of the attention that Mr. Rivera had tried to lavish on Rosaland; he couldn't believe that he had missed the play. He remembered the flowers, the phone calls, and that night at the Club Oasis when he was all over her.

Bobby was becoming inclined to agree with Dr. Ekouevi. Obviously there was something else at stake here. Some factor that they were all missing. But this game that Carlos was playing involved all of them."Dr. Ekouevi I want to get our boy here to write up his part in this whole thing. Make sure that his writing is nice and legible. We want the Lt. to be able to understand every word."

The detective snapped as he threw the pad in front of "El Incendios." "As talented as you are with your hands I know you can write. Now I want everything. Names, dates, details, amounts, contact numbers or any other method or means of communications. Be specific in what you write. I want it perfectly clear."

Bobby stated as he stared at his suspect with a look of utter disgust. "What do we have here?" Arthur asked as he entered the room. "He's just about to write. Bobby replied as he stood over "El Incendios." "Dr. Ekouevi will you keep an eye on the suspect. I need to talk to my detective." Dr Ekouevi nodded in the affirmative as the Lt. pulled his detective out of the room.

"What the hell happened to him?" The Lt. snapped. "He tried to resist arrest."Bobby replied completely unbelievable. "Do you think for one moment that I believe that?" "It's the truth. He tried to resist arrest and I had to subdue him. All strictly by the book."

"What is his part in all of this?" "He made and planted the bomb." "Really?" "Yes this is our bomber. We got him. He built the bomb and the man who ordered the bomb was none other than the famous Mr. Calderon or Antonio Rivera, which ever you prefer. He gave us a composite and he's writing it now. The whole story."

"Good job detective. Good work. Now as long as I don't have to worry about what physically happened to this man? I guess we can move on?" The Lt. looked at detective Semione instinctively and Bobby showed no concern for "El Incendios's" current condition. "He was resisting arrest." As the Lt. and the detective re-entered the room the Lt. was the first to speak. "Dr. Ekouevi the O.N.S.I. is going to have to keep this man on ice for a while. Especially since he gave Calderon up. The word travels fast in these circles."

Dr. Ekouevi nodded his head as he led "El Incendios" from the room. El Incendios broke away from Dr. Ekouevi's grasp for just a moment and spat in Bobby's direction "Punta!" Bobby just starred.

"Bobby what's on your mind? What are we going to do about this? What is the best way to handle this shit?" "I don't know right now but what I do know is that we need to squelch this shit. The next time we hit him; we have to make sure that we shut him the fuck down." Bobby was seeing red.

"This man has nine lives. He just keeps coming back. Too bad that he is on the wrong side of the law; we could use a man like this." Bobby said sarcastically as he shook his head. "Was that your professional opinion detective? Because it sounded rather personal to me."

"Of course it's personal. At this stage in the game how can it be anything else? This man has interfered with my life for the last time. It's bad enough that we have been chasing this character for three years. I can't even remember when he became the complete focus of our unit instead of the crime on the street that we used to be responsible for trying to solve. It's very personal at this point."

"Bobby I think we should look at Dr. Ekouevi's theory. It might hold some weight." "What do you mean?" "Obviously we are overlooking something; let's think about what else he might want. It 's reaching but at this point what do we have to lose?" "O.k. I'm listening." Bobby sat on the table and focused his full attention in the direction of his Lt.

"This man has money, power, and connections up the wazoo. What is a man like this looking for?" "A challenge maybe?" "Maybe not bad. Now where can we go with that?" "Some people keep on until they get caught. They like the challenge of pulling it off. It gives them a rush, a high. Maybe our boy falls into that category."

"So what would it take to stop him?" "We need to figure out what he wants and what is he going to do next, and be there to stop him. This guy is too smart to have all these crimes be random. I think they have some order and I think that they are all connected. I just can't figure out the common factor."

"What does all this have in common? We need his updated profile. Is there any way I can get my hands on that?" "I'm sure that the O.N.S.I. has the profile after all this is their man." "Oh really I could have sworn he was our man. As much as he stays in our face. Can Dr. Ekouevi get the profile?"

"We'll soon find out." The Lt. placed a call upstairs to Dr. Ekouevi's office. "Dr. Ekouevi we need an updated profile on Carlos Calderon. Can you supply us with one?" "Dr. Reid is the only one with access to those files." "Can you access her records?" "Not without her permission or her password. It's O.N.S.I. policy that the code is changed on a regular basis. So only she will know what the current access code is."

"There is no way you can override her system?" "Her codes are classified; she is the only one that has authorization. Even if we managed to gain access the files would still be classified and she has the code. We don't have them. Not updated."

"Well what can you give us?" "I'll see what I can access." "Rosaland is the only person that can access the system. Dr Ekouevi will give us what he can but she has the updated files." Bobby starred into space shaking his head. "You see what I mean Rosaland is down. That is fucking personal. We can't get any information from her. Nothing. We don't even know if she is going to make it. I'm sick of this motherfucker playing with my life!"

Bobby slammed his fist down on the table with a loud thud. Arthur could feel his anger and there was nothing that he could do but let the detective vent. He knew that Bobby was hurt and frustrated. They were all frustrated but Bobby's stakes were higher. His future was lying in the hands of the experts at N.Y.U. Medical. His life had been put into a state of limbo by one senseless act. An act of pure revenge.

Bobby contemplated his next move; he had to pull this thing together and try to make some sense of it. "Boss we need to fry "El Incendios." We need to make it a public event. Let the media in on it and let them go wild. He is the person who actual made and planted the bomb. We go after him, we gain public opinion." "Go on I'm listening." "We put this case in front of the public. We let them in on the proceedings; the public will take it from there. That will create enough distraction to make Carlos think we are no longer in pursuit of him for the bombing. If we put all of our resources on finding Mr. Calderon; maybe we can catch him off guard for once."

"We need more than just public opinion detective." "What more do we need? We have a solid case." "What we have to portray here is that El Incendios' knows more about the Calderon operation than he does. We have to portray him as a cartel member, an insider who has spilled the beans. The public will be more inclined to sway their opinion in our direction."

"The cartel will come after him if we do that." "The cartel is going to come after him no matter what; we both know that. That's why we have to play this smooth. We keep him under wraps until the last minute. That might be the move that Carlos makes; trying to get him away from us."

"He would do it." "Hell yes we know he would do it. That fucker wouldn't hesitate." Both Arthur and Bobby looked at each other; at this point they both knew their adversary very well. "We have to bring the O.N.S.I. in on this. We owe it to Rosaland. We can't take him down without her team. That wouldn't be right."

"Bobby this is going to be a bloodbath not unless we can stop it. He is going to come after whoever is involved. That's the N.Y.P.D. and the O.N.S.I. You can't commit her organization to this." "I can't! The hell I can't! I can and I'm going to. I just did!" "We are going to need all the resources of the O.N.S.I. if we are going to pull this one off."

"Yeah we need her files; her computer at the P.D. was destroyed. But if I know her I know that she has them backed up on her computer at home. I know they are there. I need to go and play around with it." Bobby was thinking out loud "You know she was asking for her laptop when this whole incident occurred. I know that she has those files backed up somewhere between those two computers."

"Dr. Ekouevi will give us whatever he has. We can start there. Why don't we take a run downtown and see what equipment has been recovered. Who knows we might just have some luck." "We need more than luck; at this point anything is better than nothing."

The Lt. called Detective Schmidt when they reached the car. "Danny I want you to meet me at the station. We need to know what if any equipment has been recovered. We are particularly interested in Dr. Reid's laptop or any thing that remains of her desktop. Put a priority on this. We are on our way."

"I'm on it." "We need to talk to the General boss. Your father-in- law." Bobby blurted out. "Our father-in- law. He will talk to you just as much as he will talk to me." Bobby knew that Arthur was right. He had just experienced a different side of the General. "Well we need to start with him. If anybody can get us into her files it would be him. I'm sure that's where the order originated to change the codes anyway."

"You're right." "Where is he?" "He left for D.C. this morning." "Well we need to go to D.C. the Lt. nodded as they drove downtown. When they arrived in front of the ruins of their station Danny was already on the scene. He had already made the contact with the emergency workers that were in the remains of the building.

Danny walked over to the car as both Bobby and Arthur emerged. "Tell me something good detective." Danny shook his head "Negative at this point they are still searching for bodies. No equipment." "O.k. we are going to Washington. We can take the Red Eye." "I need to go by the hospital first." Bobby interjected. "Let's go." "I'll follow you."

Rachael was reading when Arthur approached. She was so engrossed in her work that she didn't see him until he placed a kiss on her the top of her forehead. "Hey" she smiled. "What are you reading?" "I'm just trying to catch up on some of my cases." "So how's it going?" Arthur whispered hotly in her ear. Rachael stopped reading and leaned over and kissed her husband's lips. She kissed him deeply and tenderly and then she smiled as their lips parted.

"What are you doing here?" She whispered. "We are on our way to D.C. to talk to your father." "I see. When will you be back?" "Tonight this is official business. Call your father and tell him that we are coming."

Bobby was starring at Rosaland through the window. There was still no change in her condition even though her healing process was well under way. Bobby noticed that there were fewer bandages on both her face and her hands. That was some progress. She was still so helpless and fragile.

All Bobby wanted was for her to open her eyes. He wanted her to feel his presence and respond to him as only she could. He wanted to kiss her and hold her and make passionate love to her in that special way strengthening the bond that held them so close.

Bobby missed her and his heart was hurt. "I need her back." He said calmly to Matthew who was standing next to him. "Bobby we are doing all we can. We all need her back. At least she is stable. Whatever is going on inside her brain she is holding on?" "I need her back Matt. I really need her back." Bobby hadn't heard a word Matt said. He was lost in his own thoughts and his own desires.

Bobby was suddenly overcome with a great deal of sadness as his thoughts turned to the baby, their baby, a symbol of their love. This was so painful and it all happened in the blink of a moment. Bobby had to remain strong and every visit took more and more of his strength. "Bobby do you want to go in? If so you know the routine. I can give you about twenty minutes but that is really stretching it." Matthew said softly.

"Hey man. I'm trying. I'm doing everything that I know and something's that I don't know but i'm trying. I'm going to bring her back." "I know Matt I know. No I'm not going in. We have to go. I just needed to see her before I left." Bobby stood and talked to Matthew a few more minutes before he was finally ready to leave. Arthur and Danny were standing by the elevator while Bobby kissed Rachael goodbye.

seventy

"The next train leaves at 6:00p.m. if we hurry we can just make it." Danny said as he got off the phone. "Hey Bobby how are you doing?" "I'm holding on. Thanks for asking." "That's what partners are for no let me rephrase that, that's what friends are for." These men were friends. Their bond went beyond their jobs and one thing they all knew for sure is that they would never turn their backs on each other. The Red Eye was packed with commuters returning home from a day of work or play in the Big Apple. Arthur, Bobby, and Danny decided that they would sit in the bar car. They all needed a drink. It had been a long day. A lot of action had transpired and finally they had to face the General. The bar car was noisy, smoky, and crowded.

They waited patiently until a table became available and they sat down. In situations such as this Bobby always made sure to carefully survey his surroundings. He checked out everyone. The last thing he wanted was any sudden surprises. This situation felt a little uneasy but Bobby attributed it to the fact that the train was so packed.

"It's a little crowed in here" Bobby commented "Yeah it's kind of tight. I guess that just makes it all the more interesting." Danny echoed Bobby's sentiments. "You two behave" Arthur said humorously. "Bobby haven't you beat up enough people today? "I told you he was resisting arrest and I had to subdue him." "If Rachael was his lawyer she would blow you out of the water with that one." "I'm glad she is on our team." Bobby replied calmly. "Who do I have to sleep with to get a drink around here?" Danny called out looking to see if he would get any response. "It looks to me like you need to go stand at the bar like everyone else." Arthur stated and at this point they all started laughing.

It was a good laugh and a well needed one; they had all been so tense and on edge for weeks. It was an especially good moment for Bobby. He couldn't remember the last time he had a good laugh or felt at ease. "I'll get the drinks. What are you two having?" Bobby volunteered. "We are officially off duty." "Well since you put it that way I'll have a jack and coke." Danny answered "and I'll have Hennessey on the rocks" Arthur shouted as Bobby pushed his way through the crowd to the bar.

Bobby was so caught up in the moment that he didn't realize how much attention his presence was creating from the female contingency that occupied the bar car. "Are you alone?" One stunning blonde asked as she pushed up on him, deliberately brushing her breasts across his chest. The blonde was vivacious and lively as she surveyed the sexy detective's physique and decided to take a more direct approach; she definitely liked what she saw.

"My name is Gail Winters and i'm with the State Department." She smiled as she held out her hand. "Let me guess C.I.A. or F.B.I. .?" "Neither" "Everybody on this train is F.B.I. or C.I.A., Justice or State." "Not everyone." Bobby smiled politely as he juggled the drinks. "Are you alone?" Gail inquired. "No i'm with friends." "Where are you headed?" "We're going to Virginia." Bobby said as he turned back to the table.

"Nice ass" she smiled and winked as she walked away. Both Arthur and Danny were paying close attention to the exchange between the two. "So partner I see you still have it." Danny laughed "Don't go there" Bobby warned as he sat the drinks on the table. "What was that all about?" Arthur smiled as he sipped his drink. "Well we are about to find out she is heading right this way." Danny chimed in as he watched Gail make her move.

"Hi guys. Do you mind if I join you?" "No not at all." Danny responded "Please have a seat." Danny slid over and Gail sat in the vacant seat directly facing Bobby. "Hi i'm Gail" she smiled as she extended her hand. "I'm Bobby" "Umm Bobby?" "Arthur" "Hello Arthur." "Danny" "Hi Danny." "Out of all three of you handsome men I only see one wedding ring. Does that mean that two of you are available?"

"Well Gail you certainly get right to the point." Arthur commented. "I notice that I didn't get any answers." Gail looked directly into Bobby's eyes "Are you married?" "I'm engaged." "Damn are you happily engaged?" "Yes. Talk to this man" Bobby jokingly pointing to Danny.

"Sorry honey I'm taken too." "It figures oh well nice meeting you." Gail said as she switched away from the table. "Nice to meet you Gail from the state department." Bobby echoed once she was out of hearing range. "Women actually do that?" "She just did and she was certainly interested in you Bobby." "Don't go there" "Arthur what does this guy have that we don't have." "I don't know Danny but maybe we need to take some lessons." they all just laughed.

"I want another drink but I'm scared to get up." "I'll go this time maybe I can get lucky." "You just had your chance to get lucky." "Not when she's trying to get with you. Shit I want someone that's trying to get with me. You feel me?" Bobby nodded "I hear you. This is going to be interesting."

The bar car was packed with attractive females. All shapes, colors, and sizes. Laughing, drinking, smoking and checking out the men. "Man I am so glad that I am married. I wouldn't know what to do if I had to be in this meat market." Arthur looked at Bobby as he finished his drink. "It's a scary thought. I don't know what I would do if I lose my girl." "Bobby you are not going to lose her. She is strong and she is a fighter. She's going to make it through this and so are you." "That's what I keep telling myself but it has already been four weeks and she has had no signs of improvement."

"She is receiving the best of care. The best and she is healing. I know what is going on because I live with her sister. This is a part of every body's life. I hurt for you but you have to stay strong for her, and you and me. This is the toughest thing that I have been through. My wife is torn apart. I live with her crying, her pain and there is nothing that I can do about it. This is the woman you love. I know how you must feel. It's hard on us all Bobby. We all share your pain. Rosaland is going to make it. She is too determined not to."

"You guys look like you are at a funeral." Danny chimed in as he returned with the drinks. Bobby looked up at him and responded "We're alright." "I know. Have a drink. It's too many women in here. I know what or should I say who you are thinking about. She is going to make it Bobby. She will. I'm telling you she will. Bobby this toast is for you. If you men would lift your glasses".

As they complied Danny continued "To Rosaland." They all drank and Bobby smiled. Danny turned his attention back to the many wonderful women in the room. This was a target rich environment. He wasn't sure where he stood with Diana so he decided to check out the scene. There were so many beautiful women on the train; Danny decided to make himself available.

They had another two hours before they would reach D.C. Danny decided to use the time wisely. Gail Winters had also decided that she wasn't going to let the smooth detective off the hook so easily so she approached him again for the third time.

"Bobby even though you are engaged you can still have a drink with me or is that against the rules?" "No Gail have a seat." "I think I'm going to hang out with Danny by the bar" Arthur announced as he gave up his seat to the extremely flirtatious female. Obviously Gail was a girl that was used to having her own way and she wasn't going to let this absolutely gorgeous man ruin her record.

"So Bobby" Gail continued once she was seated "What is it that you do?" "N.Y.P.D. "You're a cop?" "An investigations specialist." "So you're a cop?" "I'm a cop." "Uum the plot thickens." She smiled enticingly as she crossed her legs.

"How long have you been in this line of work?" "About ten years and you?" "I've been at the State Department for about five years." "Gail you're a beautiful woman. Where is your man?" "He's out there somewhere. I just haven't met him yet. or maybe I have." She gazed dreamily into the detectives beautiful hazel eyes. Gail maneuvered her stocking feet so that she started running her foot up the leg of his pants. Bobby started smiling as he shook his head.

"What?" She questioned innocently "You haven't heard a word I said all night have you?" "Well you haven't said that much or should I say that you haven't said what I want to hear." "And what is that Gail? What do you want to hear?" "For starters how about dinner, a movie, some great sex." "I'm flattered Gail but I can't." "Who's going to know?" "I'll know." "You have never cheated?" She asked inquisitively. "No. When you have what you want Gail there is no need to cheat."

Bobby smiled confidently. "Sounds like i'm missing out." "You are if you are settling for anything less." "She's a lucky girl" Gail said sarcastically. "No I'm the lucky one and I'm smart enough to know that." "So there is no way that I can convince you?" "Wrong guy but keep looking you will find him." "So should I thank you for letting me down easy?" "No I didn't do you any favor. I'm just not interested."

"You know you seem like a nice guy. It's too bad that the nice ones are always taken." "Why don't you go and talk shit in my partner's ear. He's a nice guy and he is single." "You know Bobby it's too bad that I didn't meet you before you met her. Things really might have been different." Gail smiled and winked as she strode across the floor back to the bar.

Bobby laughed out loud as he thought to himself "No way." Both Danny and Arthur joined Bobby as he finished his drink. "We can't take you anywhere." They joked as though they shared some mutual secret. Bobby just shook his head and looked at his watch. "I need to get off this train before I get in trouble."

The General was waiting patiently for the trio to arrive. Rachael called ahead and the General was eager to be of help. He would do just about anything to put his family back together. He knew that the N.Y.P.D. was doing everything in their limited power but he also knew that they were missing a vital link and that link was Rosaland.

She held all the answers somewhere in her files, or on her computer, or in her head she had the answers. They just had to access them. The General had Esmeralda to prepare a meal for his visitors. He knew that after the train ride they would be hungry and he really wanted to know what they knew.

The General planned a nice casual evening. It had been a long time since he had any of his relatives in his home so even though this was business it was still his pleasure to have his son-in-laws spend the evening with him. They all missed Rosaland so much. Her presence was vital to the strength of the family. They had all been pulling together since the bombing but now a concentrated effort was in order.

The General was very much interested in what they had discovered and what he could add. Esmeralda paid close attention to Bobby as usual. She knew that Rosaland would expect her to take care of him so it was her pleasure to make sure that he was all right. After they finished dinner and everyone had time to relax the General called them into his study and closed the door.

This was between them and everything they said would remain in the room. It was time that they started to think outside the box; whatever they came up with would be held in the strictest of confidence. "We caught the bomber. We got him." Bobby started the conversation. "Oh really. When did this happen?" "We have been following him for weeks. We brought him down today. We have evidence that can connect him with none other than the Calderon Cartel."

The General sat back at his desk as he listened to the detective's report. "We're going to use him as bait to draw out Carlos." "How do you plan to do that?" Arthur picked up and continued "We are going to portray him as knowing more than he does. This will bring Carlos out of the woodwork to go after him and when Carlos goes after him we will go after Carlos." "That might be costly, very costly. Have you all thought about the consequences?"

"Yes. We are prepared for a bloodbath but hopefully we can avoid that." "How are you going to avoid that?" The general was extremely curious. This plan seemed to have a lot of holes but that is why they came to see him. He had the power and the resources to fill in all the empty spaces.

"So what do we know about the suspect?" "His name on the streets is El Incendios, and his specialty is building and planting bombs." "What is he, local talent?" "Pretty much. He has a reputation in the neighborhood, arson for hire, that sort of thing." "And how is he connected to the Calderon Cartel?" "He can identify Carlos Calderon as the man who ordered and paid for the bomb that leveled the P.D. We have a full confession."

"That's a start but please tell me that you have more." "We have more. El Incendios gave us a composite. He put a face to the name. What more do we need?" "A plan. A concrete way to stop this maniac once and for all. These Calderon's have been messing with my family too long and I definitely intend to put a stop to it. What is the O.N.S.I.'s role in all of this?"

"They have the resources." "General" Bobby came right to the point "Do you have access to Rosaland's computer? We need her files and we also need an updated profile on Calderon. Dr. Ekouevi told us that she has the only updated version. I know if she has one, you have one."

"We need to be able to track his movements to see if there is some pattern to his random behavior. We have shut down one of his east coast operations but apparently according to "El Incendios" he has another one and we need to find it and we need to shut it down."

"Where did you're man say it was?" "He didn't know but he said it was expensive." "You believe him?" "I believe he told us everything he knew." "What makes you so sure?" "Because Bobby beat the shit out of him. If he knew anything he told us." Danny added.

The General looked up at Bobby who was standing facing the window with his hands in his pockets. Bobby was lost in his thoughts about Rosaland. He was remembering the time they made love in the upstairs bedroom the day the Arthur and Rachael got married. He remembered how hot and how passionate she was that day. Everything in this house reminded him of her and of how much he missed her.

"I want her back." Bobby said half to himself and half to the other gentlemen in the room. "I miss her." The General knew of the pain that Bobby was feeling. There was not a day that had gone by since Anna's death that he hadn't thought about her and he still missed her after all these years. As the General began to access his files an idea hit him.

"You know who could give you the best and the most complete profile on Calderon? Sonia Blackwell. She knows more about him than anyone." "I thought you had her hid" "We do. But I have access. I can have her here tomorrow. She is our best bet. She is going to know things about Calderon that are not on this profile." The General handed the print out to Arthur who in turn handed it to Bobby.

"This is the last entry Rosaland made on Calderon. She entered it a couple of days before the accident." Bobby observed as he carefully read over the profile. "If we are going to talk to Sonia tomorrow, I had better call Rachael. We hadn't planned to stay overnight General; I told her that I would be home tonight. I don't feel comfortable being out of town with her sitting at the hospital like that. She seems so vulnerable."

"I can do something about that. I'll put some men at the hospital. They will be there within the hour." The General picked up the phone and placed a call. "Now I need to bring Ms. Blackwell back from the dead. Let's see how hard this is going to be."

The General had to think for a while about his plan. Meanwhile Bobby and Danny were still pouring over the profile trying to spot something that might give them some further insight into the character of Carlos Calderon.

"I know its here. I know how she thinks" Bobby kept saying over and over to himself as he read the profile. "Excuse me gentlemen" the General said as he left the room. Bobby looked at both Arthur and Danny and smiled "This is when he starts his mission impossible shit. That's where she gets it. The two of them are so fucking secretive. Watch when he comes back everything is going to be all set."

When the General emerged he confirmed Bobby's statement. "Ms. Blackwell will be here in the morning and here is some additional information on the Calderon operation, including his current financial status, or as far as we can ascertain." He handed the documents to Bobby "These are from Rosaland's computer. I had to search a minute through all her codes but this might be of some help."

Bobby knew his girl; he knew that she would have what he needed. She always does. "Arthur I need some time to go over this stuff." "Well you have until tomorrow morning. It would be nice to have some information before Sonia arrives. It would really level the playing field."

"Bobby it looks like we might be up tonight. I'll help you." "I know you are going to help me. Let's get to it. General we need some room to spread out. Where can we go?" "There is a bedroom at the top of the steps. I'm sure you remember where it is."

Bobby looked the General square in the eyes trying hard not to show his surprise "Yes sir I know right where it is. Danny lets go get on this." As they climbed the stairs Danny asked "What was that all about?" Bobby looked at Danny "You don't even want to know." "Yeah Bobby actually I do. What the hell was that about?" Bobby laughed as they entered the bedroom; "I made love to Rosaland in this room on Arthur and Rachael's wedding day. We thought it was a secret but I guess we were wrong."

"You're kidding?" "No i'm serious. She had been in D.C. the whole week of the wedding. I hadn't seen her so when I arrived we came up here. I was just thinking about that while I was standing at the window and he brings it up. General Prescott Reid, the man."

Bobby took off his jacket and laid his gun on the night table. He walked over to the bar poured them both a drink and handed it to Danny as he continued "The night I got shot after that Latin American fiasco I made love to Rosaland in this house. He knew about that too." Bobby sipped his drink as he rested his feet on the table.

"Man if Rosaland hadn't been in the room he probably would have shot me that morning. Danny when I woke that night she was there. Just watching me, holding me, waiting for me to come around, despite her father, she was there."

It hadn't hit Bobby until this very moment how important that was. It was her way of taking a stand. She had refused to leave him that night. No matter what. Bobby was reminiscencing about their past. This house held so many memories for them. It was hard for Bobby to just be there.

"We have to stop this lunatic" Bobby asserted as he poured over the completed profile that he had strewn all over the table. "Bobby exactly what are we looking for?" "I don't know Danny. I guess anything that sticks out or anything that catches your attention. I really don't know." "Bobby do you really think that we can make Carlos come after this guy? This "El Incendios" seems like such a small fish. Do you really think that Carlos thinks he is that important?"

"If we play it right according to this profile he is very egotistical, a real power player. So if he thinks that somebody else has the spotlight he will probably make a move just to show us who is in charge. That's when we can grab him up and hopefully keep him this time."

As Bobby read the profile he was impressed as to how much detail Rosaland had included "anti social, sexually deviant behavior, no remorse, intellectually superior, a product of a dysfunctional environment, extremely loyal with strong family ties."

"Bobby" Danny interrupted his train of thought. "My mind keeps going back to Dr. Ekouevi's theory. Maybe we are looking too hard. Maybe the thing that he wants is right in front of us and we just don't see it."

"Could be but this shit is giving me a headache. Let's see what Sonia comes up with tomorrow that might give us more insight. Because frankly right now i'm tired and I don't have the slightest idea what we are looking for. And none of this is going to help Rosaland!" Bobby screamed as he flung the stack of papers against the wall.

Danny could feel Bobby's frustration. "Calm down partner. We'll figure it out. We've cracked harder nuts than this before." Danny reached over and hit Bobby's fist. "Now pick up this shit so we can get back to work." The morning rolled around completely undetected by the detectives. Several times during the night both Bobby and Danny dozed off, until they finally decided to go to sleep.

"Sonia should be here any minute now" Bobby said as he tried to wake Danny. "Come on let's grab something to eat before she arrives." "Man I need to shower and I hope the hell we can get back to New York without going on that train." Bobby threw the towel at Danny's head and pointed to the bathroom.

"That way. I'm going down the hall." Bobby relaxed as the hot water ran deliciously over his muscular naked body. Bobby stood motionless as he indulged himself in the warmth of the water. It felt good and it had a genuine calming effect on his temperament. Bobby had been flying off the hook lately at the drop of a dime and it was time that he got himself back under control.

Danny was right. When it came to Rosaland Bobby's heart always took the lead. He couldn't help it. He loved her. She was in his blood and as he looked down at his excited manhood he realized that he wanted her in his bed as well.

Esmeralda greeted the detectives as they came down to breakfast. As always she took special care to prepare a breakfast that she knew Bobby would enjoy. Esmeralda was worried about him; he was always edgy these days and she knew that he was not eating right.

"Good morning Mr. Bobby" she greeted him with a cup of coffee "I have prepared a special breakfast for you and you better eat it." She smiled as she served him and his partner. "Good morning Mr. Danny." "Where is the General?" Bobby looked around. "He won't be joining you for breakfast this morning. He and the Lt. had to make a special errand."

"After breakfast you and the detective are to meet them in the study. Now eat!" "Bobby I think Esmeralda likes you." Danny joked as they ate their breakfast. Bobby smiled, "No she likes my Grandfather."

seventy-one

Sonia Blackwell was the first to arrive after breakfast. It had been a while since her last encounter with the N.Y.P.D. and she wasn't sure how she felt about being involved with them again. The O.N.S.I. was convinced that the N.Y.P.D. had been infiltrated and the General had compromised her safety by ordering her here.

The death of Lt. Jones had left a wide gap in the chain of command and Sonia knew that whatever he wanted with her or from her, he must have felt that it was important enough to breech his own security measures. Sonia had been in isolation for her protection, so she had no idea about Rosaland or the devastation of the N.Y.P.D.

Sonia was still the best source of information on Carlos and the Calderon cartel. Sonia was in a key position and had been monitoring the Cartel's movements for several years. She had continued to work hand in hand with Dr. Ekouevi on the surveillance, but they always ran into a stumbling block when it came to Carlos. They just couldn't put their hands on him or manage to locate his hideaway.

"Detectives Semione and Schmidt" she greeted them as they strode casually into the study. "Ms. Blackwell how nice to see you again." Danny commented as he shook her hand. "So Bobby, I see you are flying solo? Where's your better half?" She questioned innocently. Bobby looked very surprised that Sonia would ask such a question. "You haven't heard?" "No heard what?" "Rosaland is in the hospital." "Hospital for what? What the hell happened?"

"She was caught in the explosion that leveled the P.D. and she was one of the lucky ones. We have over 600 dead officers and a hundred more that are still missing." "What!" "You didn't know this?" "No Bobby i'm sorry.

This is the first I've heard of this." "So this is what this is all about?" Sonia murmured half under her breath.

"How is she?" "She has been in a coma for a month with no signs of recovery. She is in serious condition. We don't know." "Bobby i'm sorry. I really didn't know. Now I know why the General would move me out of isolation. This is beginning to make sense. Do you know who is responsible?"

"I like Carlos. We have a witness that can tie him to the bombing." "I don't know Bobby a bomb that is really not his style. He is more personal than that. Not unless he had someone else to plant it." "We have a signed confession and he gave us a composite. We know that Carlos financed for the operation." "Interesting?" "What?" "If this man has so much information on Carlos, why is he still alive?"

"Because we got to him first." "Maybe or maybe not. I need to go to work. Let's see what else we can come up with. Excuse me gentlemen I'll be back in a little while." Both Bobby and Danny looked at each other as Sonia rushed out of the door. "Where is she going in such a hurry?" Danny questioned his partner. They were both puzzled and surprised by her immediate departure.

"The one thing I hate about the O.N.S.I. is that everything is such a fucking secret. They have information on everything and everyone and it's always F.Y.I. I'm betting you that Sonia knows a lot more than she is telling us about this whole situation including Rosaland. Where could she have been that she wasn't informed about what we've been going through here?"

It has certainly been local and national news for the last several weeks?" "I don't know Bobby but she seemed genuinely surprised about Rosaland. Not unless she is just a damn good actress I would venture to say that she really didn't know." "Yes partner that is my point exactly. Where the hell has she been that she wouldn't know that? And what does she know that would make her rush out like a bat out of hell after the General went through all these security measures to get her here?"

"Something is going on. I believe Ms. Blackwell knows a lot more than she is telling us." "Bobby she hasn't told us anything yet." "Yeah I know. Now why is that? I've been living with this secret spy shit for three years Danny and believe me by now I know bullshit when I hear it and when I see it and this is bullshit."

Bobby was so busy venting that he hadn't noticed that Sonia had returned to the room. She as carrying what appeared to be a laptop. Danny watched as Sonia stood in back of his partner listening to his frustrations and setting up her equipment. "Bobby

I'm here for you" Sonia replied softly.

"There had to be a good reason why the General would pull me off of my current assignment and this is the best one that I can think of. Carlos may be responsible for the bombing. I'm just saying that generally that is not his style. He is more personal. Carlos likes his victims to know that he did it, he doesn't leave them guessing. He leaves his message very clear "Yes I did this. That is his signature."

Sonia was on the phone to O.N.S.I. Headquarters at this point. "Dr. Ekouevi I need the wiring signatures for the bomb that hit the N.Y.P.D. and any comparison information that you have on file with similar signatures. We really need to tie the Calderon cartel to this one. Can you help me?" Sonia smiled impishly as she listened to Dr. Ekouevi's reply to her last request. "Koffi you need to keep your mind on business." Sonia whispered as she entered the information he was providing into the computer.

"Now let's see how many hits we can generate." "Sonia when do you have to go back?" Dr. Ekouevi asked quietly as he fed her the information. "Not until tonight. Why?" "I'm coming to get you. There is some very sensitive information that I can share with you but it needs to be in person. I can't take a chance that this information will get out. Can you meet me?" "Probably. I'll see what I can arrange with the General. I'll get back to you on that." "Sounds good I'll see you then."

"Looks like we are in luck guys. Dr. Ekouevi has some information that he is willing to share with us. He says that it is of a very sensitive nature so it should be helpful." "Thanks Sonia" "I need to meet him. He didn't want to share the information over the phone. I need to coordinate a time with the General; does anybody know when he will be back?"

"We don't even know where he is?" "I guess we will just have to wait. What else can you guys share with me?" Bobby and Danny told her the story and the connection of "El Incendios" to the Calderon Cartel. She listened intently as they proceeded to fill her in on the details of the investigation and how they made him.

"Where is he now?" "We've got him under wraps" "You are using him for bait aren't you?" She commented more than she questioned. "We need to put this to rest." Sonia could hear the determination in Bobby's voice. "Ok. Is there anything else?" She looked both of the detectives in their eyes "Anything else?" "That's all we have" "That's a lot Bobby, a whole lot. As soon as the General gets back we can get to work. Now in the meantime where is Esmeralda? I am starving." Sonia left the study to make her way into the kitchen.

"Well Bobby do you feel better? I really think she is sincere in her desire to help us. She'll help us." Bobby nodded it was at this point that his cell phone went off "Semione" "Bobby this is Matthew." "Hey Matthew what's up?" "I need to talk to you. When can you get here?" "What's going on? Talk to me now what's up?"

"I need to talk to you in person. I need your permission to have the plastic surgeon start her work." "Matthew i'm in D.C. with your father. I can be in New York in four hours if I leave now." "Four hours. Can't my father arrange transportation for you? I don't think I can keep the doctor here for four hours."

"Your father isn't here. We are waiting for him. I'm leaving now." "Wait Bobby hold on…" Matthew put the detective on hold while he called his father on his private line. This was the line that only his children used to communicate with him. "Dad. I need you to arrange transportation for Bobby back to New York. Can you arrange that? I've finally located the specialist; the plastic surgeon and he needs to be here." "Yes tell him that some one will pick him up in about ten minutes. I need him back in D.C. as soon as possible; we have a lot of work to do."

"Bobby someone will pick you up in twenty minutes but the General says that he needs you back as soon as you are done here. You all have a lot of work to do." "Sounds good. I'm ready. How is she doing?" "She coming along but its still touch and go." Matthew wished from the bottom of his heart that he could tell Bobby that she had regained consciousness and that she would be alright. One day he would be able to tell him that but for now he had to take her healing one stage at a time.

"Well Matthew as soon as my ride arrives I'm out. I'll see you when I get there." Bobby turned to Danny "Partner I have to go to New York. That was Matthew and I need to be at the hospital. Something has come up with Rosaland." "Is everything alright?" "Things are pretty much the same" Bobby admitted sadly "but Matthew has finally got an appointment with this specialist and I need to be there. I will call you on my way back."

When Bobby arrived at the hospital Matthew and the doctor were waiting. "Bobby we are in here" Matthew motioned as Bobby entered the corridor. "First I need to see my girl I'll be there in a minute. Bobby entered Rosaland's room and was pleasantly surprised by the remarkable amount of healing that had already taken place.

Matthew had removed her bandages and Bobby could see for the first time in weeks her beautiful face. There was some scarring but under the circumstances she looked quite beautiful to him. He walked over to her bed and placed a kiss on her forehead. He stood there beside her bed quietly gazing down on her desperately hoping that she would open her eyes.

"Bobby the doctor is waiting Matthew came in to remind him "We need you in here." "She looks good" Bobby commented as they left her room. "Don't worry Bobby I'm here to take care of her and I will take good care of her. She is my sister." "I know." "Bobby this is Doctor Romaine Ward. Dr. Ward is a top plastic surgeon and she has agreed to consult with us on

Rosaland's case. Dr. Ward has a great deal of success with reconstructive surgery and skin grafts and she is the best person to perform the operation."

Bobby noticed immediately how young and how beautiful dr. Ward was. "It's a pleasure to meet you" Bobby extended his hand to gently shake hers. "Detective Semione I have heard a lot about you and let me say that I am extremely sorry about your wife."

"Thank you." "Dr. Reid asked me here to look at your wife's case but before he can turn over any records or information to me I need your written permission. It is important for insurance purposes that I have your permission other than that later on down the line we can run into some complications."

"Now just from the information that Dr. Reid was able to supply I can tell you that this is not a difficult procedure but it will be time consuming. To be effective it will have to be done in stages because healing occurs in stages. I have prepared a copy of my resume; I feel that it is very important that you know a little about my background. Now if you will sign these forms Dr. Reid can give me the patients X-rays and I can begin my research."

As Bobby read over the documents he was impressed with the Dr.'s credentials. "You seem to be so young to have accomplished so much." "I have worked very hard to be a leader in this field of medicine. Also this is a field that gives me the opportunity to help out my friends" she smiled as she looked at Matthew.

"Laser grafting is a new and very innovative technique that is currently being used extensively in Europe. It is a virtually painless procedure that can help to replace damaged or scarred tissue with new tissue. Dr. Reid if I could have her x-rays I can show you a computer generated image of what we can do."

Bobby watched Dr.Ward with a great deal of admiration as she ran through her program explaining to him every step of the way what she intended to do and why. "As you can see" she concluded "We can restore your wife's beauty with the laser grafting procedure without leaving any additional scarring to the areas that we are grafting the new skin from."

"This is all very interesting" Bobby commented "What has been your success rate with this kind of operation?" "The laser procedure has a highly proficient success rate but as with any surgery there is always a risk." Bobby carefully studied the graphic images on the computer. She was good.

"This is good. Thank you doctor for your help." Bobby stood up and shook her hand. "When can you get started?" "We can schedule her first surgery for tomorrow morning." "That sounds good. Matthew will you be there?" "No I'll be observing. This is not my area of expertise. Dr. Ward has my complete confidence." Matthew smiled at her. "She will handle all the aspects of this operation Bobby." Bobby nodded in agreement as he handed her the signed consent forms. "Let's just do it."

Bobby sat quietly on the edge of her bed starring into her face. She still looked so helpless. Matthew had removed most of her bandages and all Bobby could see was her. It had been a while since he had come and just spend some time with her. It was hard for Bobby to be so close to her without wanting to touch her or fill her with his desire. He leaned over and kissed her gently on her lips.

"I miss you" he whispered as their lips separated. Bobby wished that she would respond. He wanted so desperately to hear her call out his name. That was one reason that Bobby found so much comfort in his work he needed to stay busy. He couldn't afford to think about how much he wanted to make love to her. How much his body missed hers?

How good it always was between them. He wanted her so much so very much all the time. Just being at her bedside was so uncomfortable. Just thinking about her kept him in a constant state of arousal. Bobby's body hurt from his desire.

"Bobby we need to prepare Rosaland for her surgery tomorrow morning. We just need to run some test." "Ok" Bobby responded distantly "I need to go anyway. Where's Rachael?" "She is outside in the waiting area" "Ok. Matt take care of her" Matthew patted Bobby on his back as he left the room.

"We'll take good care of her. She is in good hands." As Bobby stepped outside the room he took a deep breath. He wanted her back. He really wanted her back bad. Bobby stood and watched through the window until they drew the curtains and then he turned to leave.

Bobby spotted Rachael in the waiting area just as she had been from day one. She was doing her work and staying with her sister. "Bobby" Rachael greeted him as he walked over to where she was seated. She stood up and gave Bobby a hug. "How have you been? You guys have been so busy. How are you holding up?" "I'm good well under the circumstances I'm good."

"This surgery is good news" Rachael smiled "It shows some improvement. I like Dr. Ward; she really seems to be on top of her game." "Yes she is sharp. I like her too. This is good." "Bobby why don't you have dinner with us? When you guys finish up what you are doing in D.C.? You haven't been over for a while. Why don't the three of us make it an evening?" "Rachael that sounds really good. I would love too. Does that offer include a home cooked meal?" "Absolutely I wouldn't have it any other way" "Then you have a date. It will be fun."

"Bobby we are family and we really want to see you." "I'll be there. Take care of my girl" Bobby said as he kissed Rachael on her cheek. "Take care Bobby" Rachael responded as he left the hospital.

Bobby was back in Washington two hours later. The General, Arthur and Danny were seated in the General's study around his desk when he entered. They were engaged in deep conversation as the detective approached. "Bobby how is Rosaland?" Danny asked before his partner could take his seat.

"It was good. Matthew has found this brilliant young plastic surgeon that has a new laser technology that she wants to do." "That sounds good Bobby" Arthur added. "She's a highly qualified specialist" the General interjected "She will do a good job."

"I know. That is not the question. I want rosaland out of this coma. I want that over. That is when I will feel really good about this whole thing when she is back strong and smiling. What's going on here? Bobby switched the subject. "Well we are trying to zero in on Mr. Calderon. We have some new information that will prove to be most interesting." The General continued "We can match the signatures and we can verify the connection to your guy. This "El Incendios" might be more important than we had originally thought."

"Really why is that?" "He seems to be connected to much bigger fish in the arms industry. Making bombs might be his past time activity, that is according to this latest report." The General placed the folder on the desk for the detective to pick up. Bobby laid the contents of the folder open on the desktop and all three of detectives carefully read its contents.

They immediately noticed the top secret classification that was stamped on the cover. Bobby looked at Arthur as they continued to read. The profile of "El Incendios" was extensive. He was connected to arms dealers in Eastern Europe, the Middle East, and Russia. There was some hint of activity from North Korea. The O.N.S.I. had him on their watch list. The N.Y.P.D. had him in custody.

"You guys did a great job with this one." The General applauded as they continued in amazement at the dept of the information that was contained in the folder. "How does this connect Calderon?" Bobby asked "I don't see any mention of him here at all."

"Yes detective read on you will. It's there; it's all there. Arthur I can assure you that your team of detectives will be promoted if you turn him over to us. This is excellent work. We have been trying to catch this man for years; he is one more link to Calderon. And with his obvious connections to the scum of the arms world he can lead us to others. This is classified information so this conversation can't leave this room."

Bobby remembered the look of venom that "El Incendios" had in his eyes. He would never forget the hatred he felt for that man. He wanted to kill him and now after reading his profile he wished he had. "El Incendios" was notorious. He was big talent. After finishing the profile Bobby clearly understood why the government wanted him. "So he is associated with Carlos on a arms deal. The son of a bitch. He did know him. Look at this shit; they are sitting side by side."

Bobby threw up his hands; "We would have never made him on these charges. He would have walked from our little bullshit and we have a very strong case a damn strong case." "Well we got him." Arthur interjected. He is our man. I'll turn him over. As long as my detectives get the credit for the collar you can have him."

"What about the information that Sonia is gathering. When will we have that?" "Ms. Blackwell is going to report back in the morning. In the meantime I have two other profiles on Carlos Calderon that I was able to access through his connections with the various other individuals that are in those pictures."

The General laid those two folders on the desk and they noticed once again the top secret classification. Bobby picked up one and passed it to Arthur. He and Danny read the other. "This is the most comprehensive information that we had been able to gather on Carlos Calderon in a while." the General began.

"We extracted this from Rosaland's computer. This is what she had been working on before the accident. She gathered all of this Intel through the O.N.S.I. surveillance team. She highlights not only his vast holdings, his connections to drugs, arms, biochemical involvement, money laundering etc. etc. etc. And the list goes on. She set up the surveillance that provided us with these pictures as well as the transcripts.

She had audio as well as visual. No one has ever been able to get that close to Calderon." "Maybe that's why he went after her." "Bobby he didn't go after her he came after all of us." Arthur reminded him "And that included you. Plus how would he know? This file is too comprehensive for him to have known. He would never have exposed so much detrimental information knowingly.

"He didn't know about this. This is not why he ordered the attack on the N.Y.P.D. It looks to me like Rosaland caught him with his pants down. Not literally but she has an airtight case of international involvement. She did a great job on this; the O.N.S.I. has to share some of the credit." "My sentiments exactly" the General added. "Anybody got a problem with that?"

Danny said matter of factly "This is good shit. Real good shit". "General why haven't we heard anything from Carlos about this? Why is he laying so quiet?" "That's a good question Bobby? All we can think is that he has gone underground. But he will re-surface. They all do and we'll be there. It's just a matter of where and when."

“Those are the two big w’s” Danny said calmly. “That’s why we need to keep this surveillance open. Currently this is our best source of information. He’ll slip up and when he does we will get him.”

“Gentlemen I would like to call the hospital and check on my daughter. So i’m going to call this session to a close. I think we have discussed quite a bit of information here this evening. I know Bobby must be exhausted. He has been back and forth all day. I have arranged an early dinner. You all can study the material in the den if you want to continue to work. My house is your house. By now you all should know your way around. We won’t be hearing from Ms. Blackwell until the morning.”

“Thank-you sir for sharing all this with us” Bobby shook the General’s hand. Bobby liked working with the General. He was always so commanding and yet so smooth. Bobby admired the way he was always in control calling all the shots. He could clearly see why he had earned all those stars.

“Bobby i’m going to call the hospital. Do you want to stay?” “Yes I would.” “We will just wait out in the den” Arthur said as he and Danny left the room. Danny continued to pour over the profiles. He was absolutely intrigued at the amount of information that Rosaland had managed to capture. He wondered how long she had been working on this.

“Lt this is incredible. She has detailed everything to the tee. It would have taken us forever to retrieve this amount of info. I like the O.N.S.I. I like how they work. They are real slick. So what are we going to do tonight?” Danny asked “I certainly hope we are not going to sit around here all night. This is D.C. Let’s see what we can get into.” “Sounds good to me. After dinner we can decide what spots to hit.”

seventy-two

Sonia smiled as Koffi opened her car door. It had been too long since she last had the occasion to be with him and her body ached for his attentions. Koffi gathered her in his arms and kissed her passionately on her open lips. Sonia wrapped her arms tightly around his neck as Koffi pulled her close to him. He held her tightly in his arms as he kissed her ardently up and down her neck.

Koffi slid his hands wantonly over her lush breast and down her ample figure as he filled her mouth with his tongue. Sonia melted in his embrace as she pressed her torso deep into his crotch in an inviting manner. "Oh I've missed you" he whispered to her with his heavy French accent. "I didn't know when I was going to see you again."

Sonia sobbed softly under her breath as she mouthily kissed Koffi as if they would have no tomorrow. Sonia moaned hungrily as Koffi engulfed her with his tender embrace. She felt so good in his arms. Koffi ran his lips up and down Sonia's neck and then he buried his head deep into the warm cleavage of her soft full breasts. Koffi kissed the fleshy mounds first one then the other causing Sonia to gasp out loud in ecstasy as his warm wet mouth made contact with her bare exposed breasts.

"I love you" he moaned as Koffi pulled back and led Sonia by the hand to his bedroom. It seems as though he had waited forever to be in this position with her and he wanted to take full advantage of it. He finally had her alone and all to himself. Neither one of them knew when this opportunity would present itself again. Koffi closed the door behind them and led Sonia to the bed where he slowly began to undress her intoxicating body.

Sonia's skin was soft and supple under his caresses as he deliberately stripped her luxurious form down to nothing. Sonia couldn't believe that after all this time she was finally again in his arms. Sonia watched from her throne in the middle of his bed as Koffi erotically removed his clothing piece by piece in front of her. He intentionally displayed his muscular physique for her approval.

Sonia eyed him mischievously as he revealed for her satisfaction his fully hard and erect manhood. Sonia watched with a growing feeling of anticipation as he joined her on the bed. Sonia's blonde hair hung sexily over her vanilla cream colored skin and her green eyes shone brightly from desire.

"You're so beautiful" Koffi breathed in her ear as he took Sonia in his arms and allowed his tongue to wander to the innermost recesses of her delicious body. Koffi kissed, nibbled and sucked. He licked on her most private possessions as he gently squeezed her fully formed breasts in his strong possessive fingers. She felt good in his arms and she tasted good in his mouth.

Koffi was dedicated to loving her completely. Tonight would be their special night. A night of love and romance. Sonia cried out as his probing tongue entered her love nest. She writhed in ecstasy under his expressions of love. She willingly opened herself up to him to accommodate his passions and to allow herself to float in the sea of sensual pleasure the he was lavishing on her wet love canal.

"Ooh Baby" she whispered as he plunged his hungry tongue deep into her willing receptacle. Sonia groaned ardently as Koffi continued to feed on her beautiful playground. Sonia was lost in the bliss of the moment as her body convulsed in orgasm. Sonia breathlessly cried out as Koffi licked and sucked her pleasure button into a state of total explosion.

The sound of her sighs filled the room as Koffi offered her the pure satisfaction of erotica. Koffi's desires to enter her were becoming more than he could bear. He needed to feel himself buried deep inside of her. He released her turbulent body so that he could mount her.

Sonia opened her legs wide to receive him waiting anxiously for his presence. Koffi's penetration was deep and demanding. He plunged his hot throbbing manhood solidly between her legs. Koffi moaned out loud at their contact. He pushed himself deeper with each powerful thrust as their bodies connected in the intimacy of sensual lovemaking.

Koffi buried his extreme length with each stroke as Sonia strongly thrust up to meet his need. Sonia was in heaven as she rode his crest. Koffi was powerful and deliberate as he opened her body completely with each of his wanton pulsations. Their connection was magical. Sonia cried out in pure ecstasy as Koffi pounded furiously into her tight constricting privacy.

She held him captive within her body with each of his manly strokes. Koffi was mesmerized by how good she felt wrapped around him. Her warm sensitive body engulfed him like a tight warm glove as he rode her like a stallion. Sonia bucked and whimpered as Koffi filled her every desire.

Koffi drove and strode and pumped himself deeper and deeper as Sonia wrapped her legs around his torso as he pleased her. Sonia trembled and spasmed as she pressed her body as far into his as she could. Koffi pummeled out of control deeper and deeper until the tears starting flowing emotionally down her face.

Sonia's body was on fire and she was hot and volcanic. Koffi was the force of nature that could put out the flames. Both their bodies burned in passion and in lust as they filled the air with the smells of love. Koffi pressed his generous length continuously until he could feel Sonia erupt underneath him; this was his signal to pound her relentlessly until they exploded body and soul in unison.

Sonia's passionate screams filled the room as she called Koffi's name over and over at the top of her voice. The two lovers swam in a sea of carnal bliss as they surfed the waves of fleshly pleasure. "I love you" they both whispered repeatedly to each other weakly as they fell into an exhausted heap of sweaty, lusty repose.

Bobby, Danny and Arthur had decided to check out the locals in D.C. It would be a change of pace for all of them and besides they needed to relax. They had all been working a lot harder than any of them realized. Bobby was driven to bring this madness to a halt. He wanted his life back, his love back to the way it used to be. No he wanted it better than it used to be and in his opinion it couldn't get any better.

The General recommended a nice jazz club that he thought they would find to their liking. "I know a nice place in Arlington. A beautiful Mexican woman owns it. The place is called Lucy's and she usually has a nice jazz band on the weekends. I think you all might enjoy the atmosphere."

"What is the element like?" Bobby asked. "It's a nightclub Bobby. You know how that goes." "Well it sounds nice. Let's check it out." Arthur and Danny both agreed that they needed to release some energy and a visit to Lucy's might be what the doctor ordered.

"O.k." Danny joked as they climbed into the car "Let's get the rules straight now. Both of you are married men so that leaves all the single honeys to me." Arthur and Bobby laughed "Are you sure you can handle that?" Bobby teased "That's a tall order. All the honeys?" "Yes. That is all the honeys that don't fall out over you." "Me? I'm out of it. Not only am I married as you say I'm also fucking depressed. Who in their right mind would want to be around me?"

Arthur and Danny both laughed out loud. "So now you are depressed?" Arthur echoed. "Yes. Can't you tell I have been depressed for months?" Danny, Arthur and even Bobby fell out laughing.

The General was right about the atmosphere at Lucy's. It was a nice place that seemed to cater to an older more sophisticated crowd. Upon arrival the owner Lucia Castaneda whom the General had taken the time to call in advance greeted the gentlemen warmly. "I have a table already prepared for you." She said as she escorted them to their seats.

"We have a nice Latin American jazz band scheduled to play this evening. Their first set will start in about thirty minutes so that should give you guys enough time to get something to eat." Lucy motioned to the waitress "Take good care of these gentlemen; they are special guest of the house."

The pretty young waitress acknowledged her bosses request as she prepared to take their order. "What can I get you guys? "She smiled as she placed the menu in front of them. "Could you give us a couple of minutes?" Danny asked. "Sure just signal me when you are ready." Danny watched the pretty girl as she walked away from the table. "I like this place." he said "It feels good."

"Yeah yeah. You liked that young girl's ass" Bobby quipped "You couldn't take your eyes off of her." "Occupational hazard. I check out everything. Just like the three guys that just entered. They look like trouble. I'm checking them out too."

Bobby turned around slightly to look in their general direction. "Looks like you might be right about them. Let's see how they play it." "Hey" Arthur interjected "We are not here for this. This is not our jurisdiction. Do you all remember that word? We are not in New York and this is not our territory. We are here to relax and have a good time so why don't we just do that?"

"I'm with you boss." Bobby said looking back over his shoulder as the three gentlemen took their seats. "So what are we having?" Arthur asked. "What about that lovely leggy blonde at the end of the bar. I can start there." "Danny you think between your legs." "Yeah I do." "So what's up with you and Diana? I thought the two of you were making progress."

"I don't know what's going on with Diana. One moment she wants me close the next she is pushing me away." "You know Diana is transferring out of the unit." Arthur added. Both Bobby and Danny were stunned. "Why?" Bobby asked. "Personal reasons. She has already received a new assignment." "Really?" "Yeah she is out of there." "Where is she going?" "Narcotics. There was a spot that opened for a detective and she took it."

Bobby looked at Danny "What's all that about?" "Bobby I don't know. This is the first I've heard of this. I told you she runs hot and cold with me. One minute she's close the next she is as far away as she can get. Whatever she has going on; she's keeping it a secret. She won't confide in me. Easley was probably the one person who she talked to and Easley is dead. I have no idea what to make of this. I wish Diana would give me a chance. I could really love her."

Danny said regretfully. "There is no need to cry over spilled milk. You can always get some more." "It sounds like you are giving up." "No I'm giving her some space. When she wants to talk she will know where to find me. But in the meantime excuse me gentlemen."

Danny walked over to talk to the blonde at the end of the bar. "That's interesting. Why would Diana want to leave the unit?" Bobby looked at Arthur. "I don't know. She requested a transfer and she got it. She has a good record of service so it wasn't a problem getting her reassigned." Bobby motioned for the waitress "Arthur what are you drinking?" When the waitress approached the table Bobby ordered his drink and Arthur ordered his.

Danny was comfortable at the bar. "Look at him. He is in there already. Mr. Lover lover." "Give him a break Bobby. Danny's one of the good guys." "I know. Danny has been my partner for years. I'm just surprised that he and Diana didn't hit it off." "Why?" "Because I know how much he cares about her." "So why don't you talk to her." "Maybe I will."

As Bobby sipped on his drink he found the news about Diana to be quite disturbing. What was going on with her? What secret could she have that would cause her to leave the one five? What was going on in her life? What were her personal reasons for leaving a unit that she had been in for years? Especially since the General was about to recommend promotions for all of them.

Bobby was completely puzzled. He sipped his drink as he thought about Diana. Yvonne's death had touched her deeply. She hadn't seemed the same since; withdrawn, distant and alone. Bobby knew the feeling of losing someone close. It was painful. Bobby missed his dear Abuelita so much even after all this time. Diana must have been feeling that same sense of loss. Losing a partner was hard. It was the one experience no officer of the law wanted to face.

"Bobby what are you thinking about?" Arthur interrupted his thought. "Diana. I would really like to know what all the mystery is. Why would she leave the unit this way? It just bothers me. That doesn't seem like her especially after all the work she put in re establishing the unit after the bombing."

"You are still looking out for her do you realize that?" Bobby threw up his hands and shook his head. "It's not like that anymore." Arthur sipped his drink. "Arthur, Diana and I have a history. Everybody knows that. It's not going to go away. We happened and we happened for a number of years." "How did we get on this?"

"Rosaland has never liked my past relationship with Diana. She feels that we are still too close; maybe she's right to a certain extent. It is definitely a really tender issue with her. Generally when we have a problem it is usually centered on that."

"Isn't that to be expected especially under the circumstances?" "Yes and all of us working under the same roof didn't help. It only complicated matters." "Well Bobby all that is in the past." Arthur said solemnly. "Now let's just pray for Rosaland's recovery. I would like my wife back too!" "I'll drink to that." Bobby raised his class.

"I'm going back to New York in the morning. I'm going to be there when they start her surgery." "Bobby we need you here. We are just about to crack this thing." "Arthur she needs me there. No I need to be there with her." Bobby stated looking Arthur directly in his eyes. Arthur knew that there was no need to argue. When Bobby was like this nobody could stand in his way. His mind was made up and he would follow it.

The hot encumbering rhythms of Latin America filled the room in a melodic manner. The smooth flow of the piano sounded clean and crisp as the acoustic guitar blended in. Suddenly the tempo changed and the room became engulfed with dancing bodies. "This in more like it." Bobby said as he sipped his drink and tapped his feet to the sounds of the music.

Bobby motioned for the waitress to bring another round as he and his brother in law settled back to enjoy the rhythms of the night. The music was sweet and soothing to his ears. Bobby loved music and he really enjoyed Latin American jazz. Tonight he might actually have a chance to relax and let his guard down. As Bobby glanced across the table he noticed that Arthur was swaying and bobbing his head to the beat.

They both nodded their approval as the waitress returned with their drinks. Danny was still very much engrossed in conversation with the pretty blonde but he was also keeping a constant eye on the three men who had entered the bar earlier. Danny knew the criminal element when he saw it and these three were definitely of the criminal type.

"What about your friends?" She whispered in response to something that Danny was whispering in her ear. "What about them?" He smiled "They are grown men. What do they have to do with this?" "It's just that you are with them." Danny looked puzzled. "Am I missing something here? Do we look like we are attached at the hip? Help me out." "I would love to." She smiled in response to his question. Danny smiled.

Bobby sat back and loosened his tie. His thoughts kept returning to Rosaland and how much he wished she were here. Bobby missed dancing with her. He loved the way she tossed her hair as her sexy body shimmied to the music. When he closed his eyes he could see her smiling and dancing in front of him. If he thought long and hard enough he could faintly smell her hair. Bobby loved the smell of her hair.

Nothing could replace the feeling of being with her. Bobby opened his eyes and focused in on the lively couples on the dance floor. He watched as their bodies intertwined with each other. Touching, gyrating and pulsating in time to the music. He smiled sexily as he moved his body to the groove and enjoyed the scene.

Arthur noticed that Bobby was relaxing. This was good. He appeared to be releasing some of his tension. It would be nice to see him back to his old self. Someone else was noticing Bobby as well. Actually there were two someone's. Two beautiful someone's who had their eyes on both Arthur and Bobby all evening. The ladies used this moment to make their move. "Would you like to dance?" The buxom honey colored Mexican beauty asked directly starring into Bobby's face.

Bobby was caught completely off guard because he hadn't noticed her approaching their table. "My sister would like to dance with your friend as well." She smiled sweetly as she extended her hand. "Arthur what do you say? Are we going to leave these lovely ladies hanging?" "Definitely not." Arthur answered as they got up and headed to the dance floor.

"There they go." Danny laughed as he watched his partners take to the floor. He wondered how long it would take before they would start to enjoy themselves. Bobby was beginning to feel the affects of the liquor as he was led to the dance floor. He gently held her hand as he pulled her close to his sexy physique. It felt nice to have a woman in his arms. The senorita was amazed at the strength that his body possessed.

As Bobby guided her around the floor she was completely taken by his elegance and his charm. When Bobby wrapped his powerful arms around her slim waist she became mesmerized, as their bodies flowed to the cool sounds of the crisp Latin jazz.

"Where has he been all my life?" She thought to herself as she relaxed in his arms and placed her head lightly on his chest. Bobby had to be careful not to slide his hands along her curves as they glided seductively across the floor; he didn't want to create any false impressions.

Bobby's thoughts at this time turned back to Rosaland. He couldn't remember the last time he danced with her or held her in his arms so closely. Bobby's body ached for her tender touch. All of a sudden Bobby's thoughts were interrupted by the sound of gun fire.

He immediately shouted "Get down!" as he reached for his gun. Both Arthur and Danny responded in the same manner as they motioned for the inhabitants of the club to get down so they could see from which direction the shots were being fired.

"Stay down!" Bobby shouted as he noticed a group of women desperately trying to escape. Bobby looked around and observed Danny moving in close to him. "What the hell is going on here?" Bobby questioned looking Danny square in the eyes. "The shots are coming from the direction of the bar." "Shit is this a holdup?" "I'm not sure but I know this has something to do with those three banditos that came in earlier."

Arthur was motioning trying to get Bobby's attention. Once Bobby looked over in his direction Arthur's eyes keyed in on what was happening. Bobby followed along Arthur's direction and noticed two men at the bar emptying the register and another man stationed by the door as the lookout. Lucy was trembling while the man held his gun to her head as she carefully placed the money in a brown paper bag.

"First they are going to hit the register and then they will hit the crowd." Bobby whispered. "Not unless we stop them first." Danny echoed. "Well partner whatever we decide to do the time is now." Danny nodded. Arthur signaled Bobby with his eyes as Bobby moved in. Bobby had to get that gun away from Lucy's head before he could do anything. A sudden or unexpected move could mean her death.

Bobby took careful aim and fired. His bullet landed right between the perpetrators eyes knocking him off his feet. Danny scrambled to the bar and knocked the other perp down with a sharp blow to his head from his elbow. The man landed in the center of the bar completely knocked out as his weapon fell from his hand.

Arthur rushed to the door and subdued the third suspect by placing his gun to the back of his head. This caught the perp totally off guard. "Give it up or lose your life. The choice is yours." Arthur threatened point blankly. Lucy screamed as the would be robber fell to the floor his gun falling out of his hand. She cowered down behind the bar shaking and crying not knowing what was going on.

Bobby ran up to the bar and kicked the gun from reach. He looked around to see if anyone of his partners had been hurt in the altercation. "Danny!" "Yo!" "Boss!" "I'm good" "Let's put this thing to rest. Lucy call the police now!" Bobby issued his orders as he waited for the shaking distraught woman to pick up the phone. In no time flat the sounds of sirens engulfed the air.

"Show your badges!" Arthur screamed as the D.C. cops rushed into the bar. "N.Y.P.D.!" Arthur shouted as a dozen officers entered the nightclub with their guns drawn. "N.Y.P.D.!" He shouted again motioning for Bobby and Danny to hold their positions. The armed officers pulled back and lowered their weapons. "N.Y.P.D.!" Arthur shouted again as he showed his badge.

"Lt. Arthur Yancy, N.Y.P.D. and these are my detectives Semione and Schmidt." "Lt. what are you doing here?" "We were just out for a night on the town when these guys tried to rob the place. The one behind the bar had a gun to the owner's head. That's why we had to take him out. It was a clean shoot. You can find the other two pieces of crap over here."

"Stupid Motherfuckers!" the D.C. officers laughed as he hustled them to their fee. "How are you going to rob a place full of cops? Detectives no less?" "We need to get an ambulance for the owner; she appears to be really shaken up." Bobby commented as he helped Lucy to her feet. "It's a good thing that you were here" she sobbed. "Thank You." "It's O.k." Bobby comforted her. "Just tell the officers what happened. Are you up to it?" "I'll be fine." "Are you sure?" "Yes I'm sure. Remind me to thank the General for sending the three of you here tonight." "You have a nice place here. We had a good time." Bobby comforted her. At this point the D.C. detectives arrived.

"Well well. Arthur Yancy what brings you down here?" Arthur was surprised to see his old friend Lt. Elijah Smith. "Eli!" he smiled as he shook his hand. "Is this where you have been?" "Yes I've been in D.C. for about five years now." "Has it been that long?" "Yeah maybe a little longer. What happened here?" "Armed robbery, assault with a deadly weapon, take your pick."

Bobby and Danny were calmly talking to the other officers filling them in on the events of the evening. Arthur and Eli continued to talk as the coroner removed the body from the nightclub. "Arthur how long are you here for?" Eli asked as he finished up the inquiry. "We are here on business. I'll be here tomorrow."

"Do you have some time that we can catch up? I understand you got married to some big wig lawyer. The D.A. of New York. I'll tell you Arthur you were always lucky. Here take my number and give me a call with your schedule and I'll see what time I can meet you. Where are you staying?"

"In Alexandria." "That's not too far. Just call me and we'll make some arrangements. It's good to see you. Oh by the way nice job. These three idiots fit the description of the group that has been randomly hitting nightclubs all over D.C."

Eli escorted Arthur and his detectives out of the club. They all stood outside in the cool night air and talked casually. All Bobby could think was that he was definitely going to New York in the morning. He had just shot a man and even though that was a part of his job. he just couldn't escape the feeling that, it very easily could have been him.

He needed to be with Rosaland he sincerely wanted to taste her wine. He would just go and sit with her after her surgery. Bobby had the need to be close.

"I don't know about the rest of you but I need a drink." Danny stated point blankly. "I'm going back in." "I think I might join you partner, the night is still early." Bobby and Danny turned to re-enter the club. "Arthur are you joining us?" "I'll be in a minute. I want to talk to my cat for a moment. We go way back."

The two of them nodded as they closed the door behind them. Once back inside Danny and Bobby headed straight for the bar. The patrons that remained seemed to be trying to get back into the groove. The altercation had basically emptied the bar and the atmosphere was somber. The band played softy in the background trying to rekindle the excitement.

"Are you alright?" Danny asked his partner as he sipped his drink. "Yeah you know how that goes. You never get used to it." "There is nothing like a robbery to kill the mood." Danny joked. "You know you are sick. There is definitely a problem." Bobby laughed.

Danny shrugged his shoulders. "Come on. Let's sit down." As the gentlemen walked to a nearby table the band started to get back into the groove. The piano rang clear as the percussions started to chime and the rhythms filled the air. "I like this band. They remind me of the Latin Kings" Bobby said calmly as he started to pat his feet to the music.

"After this set I'm ready to call it a night. I need to get back to New York. Rosaland is scheduled for surgery tomorrow morning and I would really like to be there." "I'm with you partner. I've had enough excitement for one night." Just as Danny finished his statement the pretty blonde that he had been talking to earlier walked over. As she approached the table Danny added "maybe not." Bobby shook his head. "Danny you think between your legs." "Yeah you might be right." Danny smiled as she sat down next to him.

"Hi" she said looking at Bobby. "I'm Brenda remember me?" She looked directly at Danny. "You didn't tell me that you are a cop." "You didn't ask." "So does that offer still stand?" She asked deliciously "Absolutely." Danny grinned. As she leaned over and whispered into Danny's ear she passed him a small piece of paper. "I'll see you in about thirty minutes?" She whispered as she got up to leave. "Nice meeting you" she winked at Bobby as she switched off.

Bobby looked at Danny inquisitively "Are you sure you can handle that?" "I don't know but I'm damn sure going to try." Danny smiled as he finished his drink. "I'll see you in the morning" "No you won't." "That's right well then I'll see you when I see you." Arthur was surprised when Danny walked out of the club alone. "What's up?" He asked as Danny approached. "I've got something to take care of; I'll see you in the morning." "O.k. what's up with Bobby?" "He's alright." "Good see you in the morning." Danny held a taxi and sat back as he handed the driver the note.

seventy-three

The train ride back to New York was quiet. Bobby relaxed in his seat as the Red Eye made its way into Manhattan. He wanted to make sure that he was there in time to see her before they started her procedure. Bobby was always hopeful of the moment when she would open her eyes. Nothing would please him more. If there were no delays he noted as he looked at his watch he would have just enough time to shower and get to the hospital.

Bobby felt a great deal of optimism about this whole thing. If Matthew had employed the best laser surgeon in the business then maybe he had some hope that Rosaland would regain her consciousness soon. Bobby admired the loyalty and the dedication that her family demonstrated towards her recovery. Neither Matthew nor Rachael had left her side since the accident. They had allowed him to do what he needed to do without the guilt of not being there.

Matthew knew that if anyone could stop this madman if would be Bobby. The General, on the other hand knew that if he didn't stay busy he would be consumed by the overwhelming feeling of responsibility that he shouldered. Why his Baby? His precious twin girl? It was eating him alive and he knew that he had to remain in control if their family were to survive this and remain a strong unit.

Bobby had a consuming desire to see his Grandfather. He definitely intended to spend more time with Papa as soon as he put this thing to rest. As Bobby closed his eyes he found himself thinking about the people that he cared about. Those precious few individuals that were extremely close to him. He had been so busy lately and there were several people whom he felt that he wanted reach out to.

Bobby found himself thinking about Diana. He definitely wanted to know what was going on in her life. Why was there so much mystery surrounding her leaving the job? Bobby's curiosity about Diana lingered. He decided that he would sit with Rosaland today. That would allow Rachael and Arthur the opportunity to spend some well-deserved time alone. Bobby was looking forward to being able to spend some time alone with her as well. It would be a great comfort for him to just be near her. Her presence might afford him some sense of stability. With all the traveling back and forth from Washington to New York and the shooting he was feeling a little disoriented.

Bobby wanted to go home; he needed to go home. It would be nice to sleep in his own bed. Once the train had arrived at Grand Central Station Bobby had just enough time to grab a cab and head off to Brooklyn. The restaurant was quiet and dark when Bobby entered. He made his way through the familiar darkness as he climbed the back steps that led to his bedroom. His first instinct was the check in on Papa.

Bobby found his Grandfather sleeping peacefully. Next he checked the bedroom that was occupied by Heidi and her daughter Brianna; they were sleeping restfully as well. Bobby closed his bedroom door behind him as he started to strip down. It felt good to get out of those clothes. Bobby let his clothes fall in a heap on the floor as he started his shower. Bobby stood in the bathroom gazing into the mirror. He needed to shave, he could use a haircut and a little sleep would definitely be appreciated. The bathroom was slowly starting to fill up with the steam from the shower.

The hot water felt good on his body. Bobby relaxed in the shower as he immersed himself under the pulse of the jets. As he closed his eyes all he could think about was Rosaland's wet, delightful chocolate body snuggled up next to his under the water. In his mind he could feel her pressing her wet figure in his arms, kissing him softly as he slid his hands up and down her sensuous curves.

Bobby smiled as he lathered up his golden muscular torso. He loved the fact that the mere thought of her could generate so much excitement. Bobby's passion for her was becoming more intense as the time went on. Whenever he thought of her he found himself in a constant state of arousal. Bobby had it bad for this woman and he loved every minute of it. Bobby was suddenly shocked back into reality as he realized how much time he had spent in the shower.

He really needed to get to the hospital. Bobby finished up his shower and proceeded to get dressed. He had just enough time to grab a quick cup of coffee before bolting out of the door. Matthew was surprised to see Bobby so early. He knew that he would be there but he wasn't sure what time. "Bobby?"

Rachael looked both shocked and pleased "Hi" "Hi Rachael I came to make you a deal." Rachael looked at Bobby curiously "What kind of a deal?" She asked innocently really puzzled by his presence.

"Why don't you head on home? I'll take care of Rosaland today. You take care of Arthur. He really needs you." Rachael smiled at Bobby realizing what he had just said. She really needed to spend some time alone with Arthur. They were overdue. "Deal" she added hesitantly "But I'll be back." "Take your time. I've got the whole day. I've got this."

Bobby winked "Go on." "O.k. are you sure? What if you have some emergency or something?" "I'll handle it." Bobby said as he helped Rachael with her coat. "Who will stay with Rosaland in the event?" Rachael protested. "Go!" Bobby commanded her in his smooth manner. Rachael smiled as she headed out of the door to the elevator.

"Bobby we are just about to get started. Dr. Ward is here. Do you want to get dressed or are you going to watch from the observation deck? It's up to you." "Will I be in the way if I dress?" "No it's up to you but if I may make a suggestion?" "Of course" "If I were an observer I'd watch from the deck." "Why is that?" "You will get a better view and in general it's just a better place to be. The operating room is always so cold and we need to keep the atmosphere as sterile as possible. After the surgery you can sit in recovery with her." "O.k. then that is what I will do. Which way?"

After Matthew got Bobby situated in the observation room Dr. Ward began her work. Bobby was amazed at the precision in which the young Dr.Ward performed her procedure. The advances in technology that she was utilizing were incredible. The miracles of modern medicine and the correct applications could produce phenomenal results.

Bobby watched with a great deal of amazement at the skill of the operating team. It was like a scene out of a science fiction movie. He observed how the laser cut deep into her skin seemingly without destroying the active skin tissues. The way Dr. Ward manipulated the damaged skin and replaced it with fresh skin was ingenious. Dr. Ward worked fast and efficiently and before long the whole procedure was complete.

When Bobby looked at the clock he was surprised that two hours had gone by. He was so engrossed with the merits of modern science and the expertise of Dr. Ward that he had totally lost sight of the time. Bobby couldn't believe what he had just witnessed. He sat in amazement as he watched the team convert Rosaland's face back into the beauty that she had always been. Bobby was suddenly overcome with the desire to be near her. He left the observation deck and was standing at the door of the operating room when Dr. Ward emerged.

She was cool, confident and extremely pleased with her work. She knew that the operation had gone well and with time she knew that her patient would heal. This was a long procedure but she felt very certain of a successful outcome. Bobby liked her style. Dr. Ward stood looking through the window of the O.R. observing her team and then she turned her attention to the waiting detective.

"Bobby the procedure went well. It went very well. For the next few weeks we have to monitor her progress and pay careful attention to the healing of the grafts. This is the stage that if not carefully monitored infection could set in. So we will be diligent in that area. Other than that your wife should have a full recovery in terms of the laser surgery."

"How long will it be before I can see her?" "Once you go through decontamination you can stay with her. You have to wear your mask. We have to maintain a sterile environment." "Dr. is there any chance that this surgery could help to bring her out of her coma?"

"I would really like to be able to answer that question with a positive response but we don't have any data that points in that direction. The human body is such a complex machine; any small change in one area directly affects change in another area. Anything is possible, especially when we are dealing with the subconscious."

She smiled graciously lingering intentionally to see if Bobby had any more questions. "Bobby let me point something out to you." Dr. Ward turned back to the O.R. "You see those?" she pointed "Those are deionized electrodes. What they do is supply a gentile level of electricity to the skin to aid in the proper healing. They are a constant source of stimulation. We have no evidence to prove my theory but I believe that electro sensitive pulse could be helpful in the area of coma research. We have no data to support this. It's just my instincts."

"I make my living relying on my instincts. When it is all said and done my instincts are about the only thing I really do trust. I trust my instincts as well as the instincts of others. They are usually right or can lead you in the right direction."

"That is a very interesting perspective Bobby. Very intuitive. I know that this is a good technique; we have just never had that many opportunities to utilize it. I was elated when Dr. Reid contacted me and explained his sister's condition. It was perfect; I didn't know that anyone else had any interest in this area of my work. I have a great deal of confidence in this research."

"How long will those be in place?" "We don't know. That's what we will be monitoring. We have a state of the art system Bobby. You can be sure that we carefully note all the data. This is a very innovative technique and we are very thorough in our analysis of the information to support our results. We have all hopes of this becoming a standardized procedure in coma recovery."

Bobby was very optimistic. After his conversation with the doctor he felt good. "Electrodes" that was interesting. Bobby had never thought about this. It made sense electricity, stimulation it could work. Bobby watched as they wheeled Rosaland into recovery.

He walked over to the door as they situated her in the bed then he entered. Bobby sat down quietly next to her bed and rejoiced in the fact that she was still with him. When Rachael arrived home she expected Arthur to call. She knew that he was still in Washington but she thought that at any moment he would walk through the door.

Rachael stripped down as she started her bath. Rachael found her scented candles and placed them around the bathroom; a nice relaxing bath would soothe her. Rachael closed her eyes and found herself dreaming of Arthur; it would be nice to be able to spend more time with him. Rachael would be so happy when their lives returned to normal; she missed him desperately.

Rachael wanted to feel Arthur's arms around her. His lips gently kissing her and his hard muscular body deep inside of hers. It had been such a long time since they had the pleasure of enjoying each other. Rachael's body relaxed as the jets swirled the hot water around her sensuous figure. Arthur had convinced the General to give him a ride back to New York in the chopper. They could land at the top of the Chrysler building and Arthur could be home in about an hour.

He really wanted to be alone with his wife. All he could do was think about her soft tender body pressed tightly next to his. Just as Rachael stepped out of the tub the phone rang. "Hello" she answered "Rachael, hi Baby" Arthur said softly. "Arthur, where are you?" She questioned him innocently. "I'm airborne Baby, en route. I'll be in New York in about an hour. I was just making sure that you were there. I'll call you when I land."

Rachael was ecstatic when she hung up the phone. Her husband was on his way. The mere thought of Arthur excited her beyond words; her body began to tingle and became wet in anticipation. An hour would give her just enough time to prepare for their afternoon rendezvous. Rachael smiled to herself as she applied her finest body oil. She wanted everything to be perfect for the two of them today. It had been so long since she had the opportunity to please her man.

Rachael was delighted at the prospect as she carefully selected just the right shear black teddy for the occasion. She decided that she would do something wild and exciting with her hair. Or better yet she would just let it flow naturally over her shoulders and down her back. But she would do something exotic with her makeup.

Rachael smiled to herself. She was actually planning a seduction and she was going to make sure that it would be a memorable one. Rosaland would be very proud of her. Rachael missed talking about sex with her sister. She loved the way they giggled as they swapped stories of their sexual exploits with their men. Those are the things that only a sister could share and she wanted that back.

She wanted her back. She needed her back. Rachael took her time as she prepared her sensuous body for an afternoon of pleasure. Rachael was lounging suggestively on the couch when Arthur arrived.

She smiled seductively as he entered the living room. Arthur was speechless at her beauty "Oh My God "he thought to himself as he approached her magnificently displayed figure. Arthur dropped his jacket and his shoes as he came closer to his heart's desire.

He was loosening his tie when he sat on the couch and kissed her passionately. Arthur let his tie drop to the floor as he grabbed her in his arms in a deep sultry embrace. Rachael relaxed in his embrace as she opened her moist wet lips to apply luscious kisses to his hungry mouth. Arthur looked Rachael deep in her eyes as he ran his probing fingers delicately over her tender body.

Rachael gasps softly in his ear as she felt her husband's firm fingers touch her in her most private place. Arthur pushed Rachael flat on the couch as he nibbled erotically on her full firm breasts. Rachael sighed loudly as she felt his wet lips on her warm flesh. "Oh Arthur oh I miss you…" she moaned as he continued to kiss her breasts wantonly.

Rachael's body felt so warm and exciting. Arthur let his hands roam freely along her exquisite curves touching her with a great deal of love and emotion. He missed her too. Of course he did. She was the dearest thing in his life. Rachael began to unbutton his shirt wanting very much to feel his naked chest against hers. "Let's do this the right way." Arthur whispered in her ear as he stood up. He began to strip down in full view of his anticipating wife. Rachael smiled as she watched her husband shed his garments and reveal his generous bloated manhood.

Rachael was mesmerized by his magnificence. Rachael's hands roamed over his hard muscular body as Arthur slipped her teddy smoothly down her willing form to let it land quietly on the floor. And now the tender moment begins.

Arthur fell gently into Rachael's waiting arms. Arthur kissed her deeply as he speared his excited manhood firmly inside her waiting love pot.

Rachael and Arthur both moaned at the electricity that their bodies generated as he filled her wet cavern with his presence. Rachael wrapped her arms tightly around Arthur's neck as he found his way home. Arthur continued to pound himself firmly into place feeding Rachael's voracious sexual appetite.

Rachael graciously accepted Arthur's dominance in her inner recesses as he filled her body with sublime pleasure. Rachael groaned and sighed as their bodies gyrated in sexual harmony. Arthur buried his length deep within her with each powerful stroke. He pressed and thrust and pumped his wife into complete ecstasy.

Arthur was totally enthralled with her hypnotic appeal. Rachael moved her hips in time with his masculine strokes as she held him captive inside her volcanic canal. She pumped her hot body into him as she sought her release. "Oh you feel so good" Arthur moaned over and over as he maneuvered her body for deeper penetration.

Rachael cried out in pleasure as she felt Arthur's further entrance into her lusty honey pot. The room around them turned into a magical sea of erotic delight as they experienced the bliss of loving each other. "Oh Rachael" Arthur whispered ardently as he held her velvety flesh close to him.

Arthur plunged energetically in and out of her writhing triangle as they rode the tidal wave of delectation, neither of them wanted this moment to end. Rachael gasped for air as Arthur continued his piercing strokes. Suddenly Arthur's energy soared as he shifted his position and began to ride her like the true Mandingo stallion that he was.

Rachael screamed, panted and moaned out of enriched fulfillment as she dug her nails into the rippled muscles in his back. Arthur was in awe of the tightness he was experiencing being buried to the hilt inside of his sweet wife. It felt so good. "I love you Rachael" Arthur grunted in between his down strokes as Rachael bucked her body up to engulf him.

Arthur and Rachael became one as their sweat covered bodies continued to seek the ultimate satisfaction of their sensual union. "Ooh Arthur. Arthur" Rachael screamed as she felt her explosion approaching. "Rachael. Ooh Baby!" Arthur shouted loudly as his powerful orgasm overtook them both. Rachael molded her body to his as they rode the crest of supreme desire.

Arthur collapsed exhausted on top of Rachael's sweet sweat covered breasts. Rachael wrapped her arms around him holding him close, lost in his love. Arthur lovingly kissed her face, her lips and her cheeks and forehead repeatedly, as he whispered "I love you" in his most gentle voice. Rachael smiled as she kissed the sweat from his eyes and relaxed in the warmth of their afterglow.

Bobby sat patiently by her side as he watched her progress. They had been in recovery for hours. He wondered if Arthur had made it home all right or if he had made it home at all. He expected at any moment that either

Arthur or Rachael would call to check on Rosaland's progress. He was totally surprised when he saw both Arthur and Rachael walking in.

"Bobby we have to go. The General has uncovered some crucial information and we need to be in Washington by this evening. He is preparing a briefing and he says that this is the break that we have been waiting for. Dr. Ekouevi and Sonia Blackwell have come up with something but he didn't want to talk about it over the phone."

"What's going on?" Bobby questioned as Arthur tried to fill him in as best as possible. "The O.N.S.I. has hit pay dirt on the Calderon cartel. If all goes right this could be the end of this nerve racking bastard!" Arthur looked at Rachael who was absolutely glowing. "I want my life back and I want to put this piece of shit away. I know you do too!"

"Its o.k. Bobby if you need to go. I'll stay here. I'll call you if anything changes." Bobby was really quite torn; deep in his heart he didn't want to leave. He wanted to spend the day watching over her and being in her presence. "Bobby we have to go!" Arthur urged. Bobby nodded as he reluctantly pulled himself up from where he was sitting.

Rachael grabbed Arthur and kissed him feverishly. They remained caught up in their embrace for a moment. "I'll see you when I get back." Arthur affirmed. Rachael nodded as she watched the two of them leave the hospital. Rachael quietly sat down by her sister's bed and held her hand totally was lost in her thoughts about her afternoon rendezvous with Arthur.

"What the hell is going on?" Bobby asked as they got into the car. "How are we getting back to D.C. at this hour?" "57th street heliport. The General will have the chopper waiting." "Where is Danny?" "He's still in D.C. I'm sure he's at the General's by now." "This must be some hot shit?" "It might be what we have been looking for. I don't know but he said it was urgent."

"When did he call you?" "Right in the middle..." Bobby smiled "Sorry" "It was all good." Arthur smiled as he sped towards the 57th Street Bridge. As promised the chopper was waiting and ready for take off as soon as they arrived.

Bobby noticed that Arthur was showing a great deal of excitement as they strapped in for the ride "You think this might actually be something?" Bobby questioned him sincerely. "Let's hope so" Arthur replied as he sat back for the ride to Washington. "We'll see when we get there."

Bobby noticed that Arthur was playing with his wedding ring and smiling. Bobby knew what that smile meant. His mind drifted back to the last time he actually felt Rosaland's warm body next to his. He starred into the distance as he remembered how passionately she called out his name. Bobby caught himself; he knew that under no circumstance could he remain this distracted. But all he could hear was her sweet voice in his ear.

Bobby hated helicopters. They were so noisy. Bobby was relieved when they finally landed. He and Arthur were immediately escorted to a waiting car and whisked away to the General's estate. Bobby was surprised to find Dr. Ekouevi standing in the study. "This must be important." Bobby commented to Danny as he observed that the O.N.S.I. Special Forces were out in mass. Sonia Blackwell was briefing the General on her latest discovery when the three of them walked into the room.

"We've been waiting for you." the General motioned them in before closing the door. "You are not going to like this but we seem to have uncovered what was really behind the bombing. It seems our friend Mr. Calderon hit the mercantile gold exchange at the exact time he leveled the P.D. The vaults of the exchange are located under the tunnels that lead to the financial district."

The General was pointing at the various locations on a large overhead that he had set up for this meeting. Bobby and Arthur listened curiously as he continued. "This is the heart of the financial district. This is where he leveled the P.D. With the collapse of the infrastructure he moved his team in dressed like O.E.M. and the vaults are empty. Over 750 billion in gold bullion and another 500 billion in bearer bonds with the attached bearer coupons gone."

"All Eurodollars. At the same time another team hit the national armory. They use the same mode of entry dressed liked O.E.M. and the weapons are gone. The inventory of the missing items Mr. Calderon now has stinger 220 and laser guided missile technology at his disposal all military issue."

"All this was done in the wake of the massive cleanup that occurred with the N.Y.P.D. The station was used as a tactical weapon while the cartel carried out their original objective. And with the disruption in the satellite transmission we are just now uncovering this mess." The General was furious.

"Do you know how much of a head start this man has on us? We are just now discovering the scope of this operation and he has probably already sold the weapons on the open market to the highest bidder. These weapons could fall into the hands of any rogue nation. This is bad! This is really bad! The Senate Committee on Arms is in a tizzy. They are having a shit fit up there on the hill."

"When the shit hits the fan on this one all of our asses are going to fry. There is just no way we will ever be able to keep a lid on this one. No way in hell. To pull of a crime of this magnitude takes brains, brawn and some powerful connections." "This might be an ignorant question..." Bobby interjected "But how do we know its Calderon?"

"The bomb squad was able to identify the signature of the explosive device. It's the same explosive used in the N.Y.P.D. bombing. It's the same signature." "Well we know who is responsible for that. And we can follow the money. We know who paid him to do it. That definitely sounds like Calderon to me."

"Oh there's more." "More?" "Yes Bobby. A lot more. Sonia has gotten wind of a secret meeting with the heads of the Calderon Cartel and the head of the Japanese Yakuza. You don't want to mess with the Japanese Yakuza. They can be a deadly force to contend with. And we understand that the topic to be discussed at this meeting is weapons."

The General looked at Bobby as he continued "That gives us some hope that maybe the weapons are still in the wind which means they might be recoverable. But our intelligence hasn't been able to track a time or a location." "Who else is in on this?" "In about 72 hours we are going to have F.B.I., A.T.F. and the office of the treasury breathing down our backs. This is definitely going to get ugly."

"This is already ugly" Sonia commented "We just received these." Sonia loaded the disk she had just downloaded from the General's computer. "These are the members of the Japanese Yakuza" she said as she flashed the first picture. Sonia then proceeded to brief them on each one of the members, their backgrounds, their political connections, their criminal records and their total net worth.

Bobby and Arthur were both amazed at how deep this whole situation was becoming. The amount of information the O.N.S.I. had accessed on the Japanese Yakuza was impressive.

Sonia knew every pertinent piece of information on every one of them. She traced their history from the elders, the original founders, to their current day criminal activities. They were indeed deadly and driven by a code of honor based on the religion of the ancients and they had their hands in everything.

"All I can say gentlemen" Sonia concluded "Is we definitely don't want these two groups to become business partners. A partnership of this caliber can and will only mean trouble." A hush fell over the room as they all tried to comprehend the mass amounts of information that had just been disclosed.

Bobby was the first to speak "Tell us about the weapons. I take it that is why Dr. Ekouevi is here." Bobby looked in Dr. Ekouevi's direction who nodded in the affirmative. "According to the inventory only assault weaponry was taken but according to the actual warehouse inventory list that was provided to us from the A.T.F. there was some other real serious shit taken. Top secret prototypes, laser projection missiles, aluminum coated magnums, which you all know can go completely undetected through any security system or check point."

"Several cases of maximum assault 250's, and as you all know that weapon is so powerful that the government only made a limited number. The technology on that prototype is brand new. Nobody had it but us. And the key word here is had, past tense. When these hit the streets the counterfeit/black market is going to be off the hook. Everybody and their grandmother will have one of these guns."

"They snatched air to target projectile weapons and the list goes on and on. Calderon not only has hand guns, he has a fucking air arsenal as well. Everything you need for the perfect ground strike and all for sale. We are still updating this list. Who knows what else he has managed to get his hands on. We are all going to be wearing a big fuck you. The Japanese Yakuza are already heavily armed. Trust me on this one. We can't afford to let this kind of weaponry fall into their hands if they don't already have it."

The General who had been sitting quietly stood up "We have a more serious problem. The cartel has the sdp35. It is a portable nuclear weapon, top secret technology. We were in the process of transporting it but we had to house it in the armory for reasons of national security. The package was in transit when the shipment was hijacked. They took the train while it was sitting on the tracks due to the congestion created by the N.Y.P.D. disaster."

"It was actually loaded and out of the armory on a heavily armed detail transport when it was hit." "Can it get any worse?" Arthur shook his head. "That's about as bad as it gets." The General answered. "This is incredible. Are you sure this is everything?" Danny spoke up. "This is the scope of our investigation. We have given you everything we know and now you know what we know."

The General walked around to take his seat. The atmosphere was somber; as they weighed the gravity of the situation an eerie chill crept over the room. "General what resources do we have at our disposal? And exactly what will be the extent of our involvement?" Arthur inquired. "The O.N.S.I. has the lead on this one. That should answer your question about the resources. Your involvement well that's another issue. We need your help, and the help of all the people who owe you one. We need to tie your investigation into ours so we can make this a joint effort. No other organization knows as much as your unit."

"Bobby and Danny were able to track down "El Incendios" and to tie him and the bombs to Calderon. You all have the resources on the streets. It's like I said before in about 72 hours we are definitely going to have company. A lot of company and the more of a head start we have on them the more we will be able to maintain control over this whole hornet's nest."

"So who backs up whom?" Danny asked. "For the next 72 hours its N.Y.P.D. and O.N.S.I. Special Forces." "What's the plan?" Bobby asked. "The first thing we need to do is to confirm this meeting. Time, date and location." Sonia added. "The next thing we need to do is stop this transaction." "We need to get those weapons back under wraps." Dr. Ekouevi emphasized.

"This is going to require force; this is going to get rough. Calderon is not going to just let us waltz in and confiscate his shit." Bobby reminded them "We are going to need some real fire power on this one." "That's why you have the O.N.S.I. Special Forces. These guys are the best of the best, the elite. They don't fuck around."

The Calderon Cartel is becoming too big for their britches. We have to stop them. We must. This has gone way beyond national security. This is going to have global implications if we don't squash it." The General was at the war table and he was carefully selecting his troops. "Arthur we need to re-establish the O.N.S.I. inside your precinct.

"We can't help you there. That was Rosaland's area. She's the only one that knows what she does." "I understand that but we need to reconnect you to COM STAT., we need that information flow." "What ever you need to do." "We need to do that right away. Dr. Ekouevi can you take care of that?" The Dr. nodded. "Make that a priority."

"Sonia I need you back on Intel. I need that information ASAP." Sonia immediately went to work. "Bobby, Danny and Arthur I need you to go over your complete file on Calderon with Special Forces. You need to fill them in on what you have and they will give you everything that we have. I want a total information exchange here. No holding back from either side."

The detectives agreed to cooperate fully. "I'll be assigning a communications analyst to track the COM STAT transmissions and Dr. Ekouevi will do the actual decoding." "Bobby I need to talk to you privately" the General motioned Bobby to his side. "I want you to stay for dinner. This is really important."

"Ok" Bobby agreed. He was very curious to find out what the General wanted. It had a been a while since the two of them had a heart to heart, maybe it was time. Other than that Bobby couldn't figure out for the life of him what could be so important. The General continued to delegate, placing everyone in a position to do what he or she does best. The General outlined his tactical plans as his team sprang into action.

"How's my daughter?" The General started his conversation as they sipped their after dinner drinks. "She came through the surgery just fine. It was fascinating watching what they can do. Dr.Ward definitely knows her stuff. Now all we can do is wait. We are back to the waiting game."

"How are you doing?" "It's hard and it's getting harder." By this time Bobby had gotten to know the General very well and he knew that this conversation was leading up to something. Bobby looked the General directly in his eyes "What is this all about? I know this is about more than how Rosaland is doing? Because I know that you know how the procedure went."

"Bobby I just want you to think about something." "Think about what?" "Think about temporarily replacing Rosaland at the O.N.S.I." "What?" "Bobby we need somebody to run that operation until she returns. We are at a serious stand still without the O.N.S.I. functioning in the N.Y.P.D. We really need that information system in place."

"Yes but what does that have to do with me? I'm not an information specialist; I'm a detective. An investigations specialist. I fight crime for a living." "That's why you would be the perfect replacement; you know what's going on not only in the precinct but also on the streets."

"Rosaland does her work from a computer. I don't have enough knowledge in that field to hold a position like that. Besides I would feel very uncomfortable assuming a role that I know that I am not qualified for." "Bobby that is why I asked you to think about it. I really need you with me on this one. As soon as Rosaland is well enough to resume her responsibilities she is back at the helm. Until then we are in deep shit without the O.N.S.I.

"General I know with your wealth of resources you can find someone within your organization to temporarily fill that position. Someone with the right background who could do a good job for you until she returns." "Yes Bobby I can. I need someone that I can trust with top security information as well as with specific codes."

"General I will help you as much as I can, anytime I can, but you are gong to have to get someone else. I can't leave Arthur holding his dick. The department is already understaffed. We are pulling officers in from every precinct trying to cover our shifts, catch some criminals and stop some crime. And now with this new wave of Calderon bullshit we will be working twenty-four seven. I just don't see how I can do this."

"Bobby grab your drink and walk with me. I want to show you something." Bobby picked up his drink and followed the General back into his study where he promptly closed the door behind them. Bobby started smiling.

"General if you are asking me to do this because you think Rosaland talks to me about her work, she doesn't. She never has. Granted she might give me the heads up on things that happen within the unit that might affect outcomes. But she never tells me anything. She just makes it happen."

"Bobby that is exactly the bond that I need. That is absolute trust and that is what the O.N.S.I. is all about, absolute trust. Why do you think I hand chose Rosaland for this job? Because of that trust."

"Yes but she is highly trained for her position. That is why she does such a good job. You are asking me to do something that I don't know anything about. How can I do a good job being that unprepared?" "Bobby we can train you" "Yes but how long will that take?" Bobby shook his head "More time than we have right now."

"General I know you have some secret spies somewhere that you can put into place until she returns. I can be more beneficial doing what I do best and that is stopping this motherfucker in his tracks. Now I can definitely do that." The General was convinced now more than ever that Bobby should be O.N.S.I. He was definitely the right man for the job now all he had to do was convince him.

"Bobby come with me" the General motioned. Bobby compiled and followed the General into another room off the study. The General did the most unusual thing. He pushed a button that was hidden in the corner of his lounging chair. Suddenly the wall began to open revealing a set of hidden steps that lead to a lower level.

Bobby followed the General down the steps to discover the most extensive underground surveillance network. Bobby looked around in total amazement even though at this stage of the game he didn't know why he was still amazed or surprised by anything that the General did or any resources that the General had at his disposal.

Yet he was still impressed. "You talk about fighting crime for a living well Bobby that is what I have been doing practically my whole life, fighting crime. We have a new wave of crime to fight now on an international level." The General confided in Bobby as they walked and talked. "What is all of this?" Bobby asked.

"This is what keeps me connected with the rest of the world. Information is a commodity Bobby and it is a product that is in high demand. I have information transmitted from all over the world; right here to this very location. It's all in the air you just have to catch it. This is what gives me my edge. The O.N.S.I. analyses the material and then prioritizes it as to its importance."

"Some of it is coded, some of it is classified and some of it is bullshit. We look at each and every piece of it. It comes here first and then it goes to the various government agencies." The General sipped his drink while Bobby just listened.

"Fighting crime let me tell you? I have information on arms deals; there is a plethora of illegal weapons available to anybody that has the money. And money everybody has money or can get it. That makes our job harder, much harder."

"I have information on major narcotics operations. I have information on illegal banking and money laundering schemes; you name it. I can tell you about unorthodox international currency trading operations. Not the mention the computer crimes."

"We constantly have to watch for hackers trying to steal information or illegally gain access to top security systems and files. Information that they will sell to the highest bidder. That is crime, and that level of criminal activity affects everybody. It's my job to stop it on all fronts."

Bobby knew that the General was a powerful man but it was not until this very moment that he realized just how powerful this man actually was. This whole scene was incredible. Bobby had to stop and think if he was still in the real world. The General was comfortable in the mist of all this. It was his element. He was so natural. Bobby understood now why Rosaland was so motivated. It was in her blood. She got it from her father.

"Bobby" the General continued "When Rosaland recovers she is out. No more. She is out of all this action adventure bullshit. I have a nice cushy office job waiting for her. It's a very high profile position and it is nice and safe." "I don't know sir but for some reason I don't think it's going to be that easy. Rosaland's involvement in all this drives me crazy. But she is dedicated to it."

"Bobby she will remain O.N.S.I." "That's what I was afraid of. She will still be in this shit only in a more powerful position. How is that safe?" The General noticed the expression on Bobby's face and it finally hit him as to the depth of love that this man felt for his daughter.

"Bobby it's the safest environment that I can put her in. She will work out of a heavily guarded facility and she will have all the resources of the O.N.S.I. Special Forces at her disposal. She'll be safe." Bobby listened as he finished his drink. "We'll see. I hope she decides to marry me, have a couple of kids, and teach at one of the universities. I would be happy with that. I don't want her in this at all. This work is always going to be dangerous. General why are you showing me all this?"

"Because I know why you are reluctant about the O.N.S.I. and I wanted you to see just how deep this worm hole goes. This is an extensive highly efficient organization and I want you to become a part of it. An important part of it. I want you to think about it."

The General lead the way back up the steps and closed off the room. Bobby went to the bar and poured him and the General another drink. Bobby sat quietly trying to absorb the events of the afternoon; after all he had been bombarded with a head full of new information. He sipped his drink and starred into the room, not really focusing on anything, just really lost in thought.

"Bobby dinner is ready" the General broke his concentration. "I can see why she loves you so much." He said as he left the room. Bobby smiled.

seventy-four

After dinner Bobby was ready to go back to New York. He wanted to go by the hospital for the rest of the evening. He knew that after today he and Arthur's time would be non-existent. "General, do you think I could get a ride back to the city?" "Yes I thought you might want a ride. I have arranged your transportation; they are ready when you are."

"Thank-you sir" Bobby extended his hand. "I'm hoping to hear from you soon Bobby." The General nodded as he shook his hand. "You will" Bobby said as he left. He had a lot to think about and he wanted to be near Rosaland while he did it.

Both Rachael and Arthur were surprised when Bobby walked in.

"I thought you would be in Washington for the rest of the night" Arthur said as Bobby approached. "We finished early so I decided to come back. How is she?" "She's the same Bobby" Rachael said softly. "I'll stay with her tonight. Why don't the two of you catch a movie?" "No Bobby why don't you go get some sleep? You look exhausted." "Rachael I'm fine. Why don't you and your husband go do some husband and wife stuff?" Rachael looked at Arthur and then agreed.

"We'll see you in the morning" Rachael kissed her brother-in law on the cheek. As Rachael gathered up her things Arthur talked quietly with Bobby. "I'll see at about 11:00." "Have a good night" Bobby called as they left arm in arm.

About an hour later Dr. Ward entered the room. "Detective?" She questioned "When did you get here?" "I've been here for about an hour. What are you still doing here?" "I want to monitor her. I'm going to watch her for the next 24 hours." "Are you expecting any changes?" "No it's still too early to expect any change but I have special interest in this case so I'll be giving her a lot of my time and attention."

Dr. Ward checked the microprobes and then she left the two of them alone. Bobby looked down at his beautiful fallen angel and prayed with all his heart that she would open her eyes. The night passed with Bobby in deep thought about the General's offer.

When Bobby reported to work that next morning the whole department was in an uproar. Everything was being moved or replaced and the makeshift station was in a state of chaos. Bobby noticed that Dr. Ekouevi was installing the new computer system that would connect the N.Y.P.D. back to the O.N.S.I.

The General's orders were already being carried out. Arthur was shouting commands as his station was being dismantled by the O.N.S.I. technical team under the direction of Dr. Ekouevi. Dr. Ekouevi acknowledged the detective as he entered and headed for his small office.

"Bobby we have to get on this right away" Arthur called him into his office. "Danny is down the hall. Grab him and get over to this address. Multiple homicides the neighbors called it in after hearing the shots. It might be drug related. Check it out." Bobby walked back to get Danny.

"Danny we've got to roll." "Good morning to you too. Where the hell have you been?" Bobby smiled. "Let's go" the two detectives were out the door as Bobby explained the call. "The Lt. thinks this might be drug related so keep your eyes open." Danny nodded as he checked his weapon.

"How's Rosaland?" He asked as they proceeded towards the address. "She's still the same. She'll have light bandages on her face and hands for about a month. Her Dr. feels that her skin will heal without any scars. That's good. As for the coma well nobody knows. We'll see what this new technology is about. I stayed at the hospital with her last night."

"Bobby you need a break." "I'll take a break when this situation breaks. What I need is to make love to my woman." "They have enough black and whites here." Danny pointed out as they pulled up in front of the address. "Let's go see what's up" Bobby said as the exited the car. "What happened here?" Bobby asked the first uniform officer he approached.

"It's ugly detective" he said as he held the police barrier so that they could pass. "Second floor" another uniform added as they climbed the steps. When they entered the apartment, they noticed at least six covered bodies. "What happened?" "Looks like somebody went on a rampage; we have bodies all over the place. There are six in this room and four in the next room."

"Who are these people?" Bobby and Danny both put on their gloves as they started to investigate. "You guys need to back up and wait for the photographer. I don't want this scene contaminated." Bobby shouted. "I need forensics. Where the hell are they?" "We're right here." "I want clean samples of everything and dust everywhere in these two rooms. I want clear prints.

Do we have a weapon?" "No detective no weapons." "Well they were shot with something. I want two uniforms to canvass the area. Check the alleys, abandoned buildings, dumpsters and the roof to see what you can turn up."

"How did the shooter get away? Where did he go?" "Check every apartment, the basement and every hole in this building. Find me something." "Yes detective. We're on it." "Bobby this looks like a professional hit to me." Danny commented. "What makes you say that?" "The angle of the bullets and the precision of the wounds. Look these shots were fired at point blank range. Up close right to the head."

"Who lives here? Where is the landlord?" "That's him over there in the corner." Bobby turned his attention towards the sleazy character that was standing very nonchalantly in the corner. "Who lives here?" Bobby asked him directly. "This apartment was leased to Sylvia and Eduardo Lavado. They have been living in this apartment for about two years. They are good tenants."

"What constitutes a good tenant?" "They pay their rent on time." "How have they been paying?" "By check" "Well obviously Sylvia is not here. Where does she work?" "I don't know." "Put an apb out on Sylvia Lavado. We need to find her and we need a copy of one of her rent checks." The landlord agreed to cooperate and was dismissed.

"I'll be sending someone over to talk to you tomorrow. Please be available and have the information." "Bobby this is a fucking mess. Get rid of the rest of these motherfuckers so I can tell you what really happened." Bobby looked at his partner and he could see from Danny's face that he wasn't going to like what he was about to hear.

"I need some id on these people. Which one is Eduardo Lavado? Get me some id on these people right away!" Bobby screamed. "Danny hold your thoughts for a moment until I can put some names to these bodies." "Not a problem partner." Danny said as he continued digging for clues. "Bobby we have two shooters" "Yeah?" "Look we have two different sets of shell casings" Danny held up the evidence with a pencil.

"Two separate casings and from the looks of things somebody got caught off guard." "Danny do you recognize any of these people?" "No" "New talent?" "Could be" "Now who are they and where did they come from?" "The bigger question partner is why they are dead?"

"Let's see what we have here" Bobby said as they entered the other room. "Are there any women among the victims?" "No all male victims. All Latin American. My guess is Colombian?" "Why Colombian?" "The tattoos. They all have them." "Do you know for this sure? Tell me about the tattoo."

"This tattoo is no secret detective; it belongs to the Colombian cartel. Standard issue." "We have a room full of dead Colombians. No ids, no weapons? This is fucked up." "Oh Yeah, this shit is going to get real ugly."

"Detective" Bobby turned in the direction of the voice "Let me show you this" Bobby followed the officer. "It looks like this is where they came in." He pointed to a foot print on the sink. "Get this print" Bobby ordered the tech "Be careful this may be our best lead." "So who came in and who left? Someone else has just joined the party."

"Bobby" Danny called to him "Listen this entrance explains the whole scene. That's why we have bodies in two different rooms. This was an ambush. They got hit from within from the back. That is how everybody got caught off guard. The Colombians were first and then the rest of the house." "Yes and what did they take?"

"Why do you think they took anything?" "It must have been something here? What would make them kill everybody? This place has been wiped clean. It's too clean and something's missing." "We need to get some id on the bodies in the first room. One thing for sure they are definitely not Americans."

"Yeah, I want somebody to check this vent. Find me somebody to go in there or get me a video feed. Send some wire up there and get me a visual. Find out where this exit leads to and send in forensics." Bobby ordered. Bobby and Danny walked around the crime scene a few more times to see if they saw anything that they might have previously overlooked.

"Partner who is missing from this party?" Bobby asked Danny curiously "We'll know as soon as we find out the identities of our friends in the front room." Danny responded "In the meantime we need to run this by the O.N.S.I. just to see what they might know."

"We probably won't be able to get any information until tomorrow anyway so why don't we just wait until we hear what the uniforms come up with from the canvass. You know Danny there is always somebody out there who saw something."

Danny nodded in agreement. "The trick is to find that somebody that is willing to tell us." "Detective we have another footprint." The officer pointed out. This one is leading towards the back room." "Mark it off" Bobby instructed the officer. "This is kind of sloppy. Why would they leave so many footprints?" "Well I don't think they did it intentionally, it's called a leaky faucet."

Danny said pointing to the old fixtures and this is probably our best break." As Bobby and Danny crouched down to study the barely noticeable footprint the one thing that they both paid particular attention to was the size. It was rather small almost child like. Bobby carefully scrutinized the tiny print.

"Danny from the size of this print this is either a child or we are looking for a race of people with extremely small feet." Bobby and Danny looked at each other. "Get forensics over here!" Bobby shouted. "Yes we are right here." "I need a rush on these prints!" Bobby pointed carefully to the areas he wanted covered.

"We are almost finished here detective. We'll put a rush order on this." "Good. Good work now let's see who these belong to." "Bobby are you thinking what I'm thinking?" "Probably but let's wait to see what forensics comes up with." "Bobby we need to canvass this area ourselves."

"It's too hot right now. If anybody saw anything they are fucking scared to death and they are not going to talk to us. No we'll wait we can canvass tomorrow. We might get a better response. Let's give them some time to think about it."

The two detectives finished up their preliminary investigation of the crime scene and walked outside. The size of the crowd was rapidly increasing as the word of what had happened quickly spread through the streets. As Bobby surveyed the anxious and curious looks on the faces in the crowd he knew that someone in this crowd knew exactly what had happened or who was responsible. Now all he had to do was wait to see who would come forward.

Debora Brockinghaus Vertikoff owned a small herb shop close to the apartment building. Actually she was located right in back of the building and quite often she witnessed the comings and goings of its inhabitants. She thought it particularly strange that no one had come knocking on her door about this.

She would just wait and see who would finally figure out that she might have some information concerning this multiple murder. As she stood in front of her building with the rest of the crowd she noticed for the first time the tall handsome detective. She observed his sexy nature as he talked casually to the uniformed officers.

Debora's eyes followed his tall commanding figure as he moved carefully to avoid any confrontation with the crowd. She watched as he summons the rest of the officers to his side and listened intently to any thing they had to report. It was obvious to Debora that he was in charge and if she would talk to anybody about what she had seen it would be him.

She would wait to see when he would ring her bell. Debora moved to the front of the crowd hoping that the detective would notice her. "Who is that?" Debora asked pointing to Bobby. "That's Detective Semione." The officer replied "Why do you ask?" The officer was curious "Do you have something to tell us?" "No I was just wondering who he is."

The officer looked at her suspiciously. Debora watched with a great deal of interest as the sexy detective handled the crowd. It was at this point that she decided he would be the only person that she would talk to. Debora noticed the officer that she had just questioned talking to the detective. Bobby instinctively started walking toward the attractive cocoa colored brunette.

"Hello. My name is Detective Semione. The officer told me that you might possibly know something about this?" "Hi detective" she extended her hand. "Where did he get that from?" she asked. "I don't know. You tell me. Do you know anything about this?" "Anything about what?" Bobby smiled; he could see that she was holding back.

"Do you live around here?" "Yes I live in the building next door." "Have you lived around here for a long time?" "Yes about three years." "Do you think I could have your name?" He asked "Just in case I might need to talk you in the future?" Debora smiled she thought he would never ask. Bobby pulled out his pad and wrote down her information. After he finished he reached in his pocket and handed her his card.

"If you think of something that might be helpful give me a call." "If I think of anything detective I just might do that." Bobby stayed to chat with her for a couple of minutes before he went back to talk to Danny. "I think she knows something" Bobby said as he watched her disappear in the crowd.

"Who is she?" "She lives in the building next door. She grows and sells herbs." "How are we going to play this?" "Let's wait and see if she comes in on her own. If not we need to send one of the female officers over to talk to her."

"I don't know Bobby but for some reason I don't think a female officer will be able to get as much information out of her as you might be able too."

"Don't start" Bobby warned Danny. Danny threw up his hands "It's just an observation." "Well then maybe you need to go talk to her. She knows something I can tell that for sure." "Are we just about done here partner?" Bobby questioned "Because we need to move. We need to run this whole thing by the Lt."

Arthur was busy fielding all the phone calls. He had his boss on his back and the Captain wanted some answers. "Arthur what the hell is going on down there?" The captain screamed "I'm getting calls from everyone; the Mayor is on my back because the Governor is on his so quite naturally that means I have to be on yours! Now what the hell is happening?"

"We are on top of it." "What are you doing?" "We just got the call; my detectives are out in the field. We'll have some answers as soon as they return." "Arthur this is going to be a shit storm. The higher ups are already screaming." He was relieved when Bobby and Danny returned. He motioned them into his office as he continued to dodge the anger and the insistence of his superiors.

"Let me get back to you. My detectives just walked in." Arthur was happy to hang up the phone. "What the hell is going on out there?" Arthur demanded. "I just got my ass chewed up and spit out."

"We've got a real mess down there Lt. ten dead bodies and four are definitely Colombian. We are waiting for forensics to give us the id on the other six. It looks like it was ambush. Somebody came through the bathroom vent and they left two identifiable footprints. We're checking those out now. We might have a witness. A Debora Brockinghaus Vertikoff. She's a vendor who lives in the building next door."

"So when are you talking to this woman?" "I talked to her briefly. I could tell that she knew more than she was saying. I have her name and address; we were hoping that she might come in on her own. Everybody was real closed mouthed." "We have ten dead bodies and nobody heard anything?"

"This was definitely a professional job. They probably used silencer and they hit them really quickly. There would have been no other way for them to kill everyone unless it quick and fast." "So who do we like for the missing party?" "We don't know. It's hard to tell but one thing I found to be interesting. We got bodies everywhere and the place was wiped clean. It was too clean. I'm trying to figure out what's missing? Money, drugs or weapons? It's one of the three. Why else would you kill everyone?"

"You guys need to get to work on this one. I need some answers. I want you to start with forensics. Get me some definites. Check out those prints and interview this woman she might be our only lead." Bobby and Danny nodded and went back to work. "We need to go over to the morgue and check on our D.O.A's. The coroner may be able to tell us something by now." Danny interjected.

"Ok I want you to hit the morgue and then the witness in that order. Keep me informed on this one." Arthur concluded as he went back to work. "Find out about the shots the neighbors claimed they heard. Because if a silencers was used somebody is lying to us." Arthur's phone was ringing off the hook as he motioned the two detectives out of his office.

As they headed towards the morgue the detectives pondered the situation. "This is ugly" Bobby commented "Aren't they all?" Danny replied "Yeah they all are and they are getting worse." "Who is missing from this picture Bobby? It is obviously something here that we are completely overlooking." The car was silent as the two drove hastily in the direction of the morgue.

"Danny do you ever get the feeling that we are running in circles?" "What do you mean?" "After we check the morgue then we should go talk to Dr. Ekouevi. Find out what he knows about this and then the witness. We'll have more to go on. I'll bet you any amount of money that the Colombians are probably connected to Calderon. And if they are in any way related Dr. Ekouevi will know."

"Bobby so what is up with this witness?" "I don't know. She's holding back. I know that for sure. We'll talk to her. But she is the last stop. Afterwards I need to go to the hospital." "Have you heard anything more?" "That's what I'm going to find out."

The detectives found the coroner hard at work when they arrived. "So what do we have here?" Bobby asked as he and Danny took position on either side of the table. "Well detective this person was shot point blank in the head with a 44 magnum" the coroner said as he handed Danny the container with the bullet fragments he had removed from the corpse.

"Tell us something that we don't know. Like whom this person is or was or better yet where is this person from." "Judging by the bone structure of the face I would guess Russian, probably Georgian." the coroner continued "Danny what would put Colombians with Russians?" "Narcotics?" "Do these guys have any tattoos?" "Yes as a matter of fact they do." The coroner replied as he turned up the sheet to reveal a log on the skin of the deceased."

"Danny find out about this." "I'm on it. I need pictures." "Here you go detective." the coroner's assistant handed Danny a file and a camera. "These are all the pictures we have so far." "Thanks." Danny nodded. "Bobby I need to take these to the lab. I can do the research from there."

"Let's run those through the O.N.S.I. Dr. Ekouevi might even have this on record already. We can go to the lab if he comes up empty." "O.k. you keep working on this and talk only to me." "O.k. detective you got it." The coroner nodded as he went back to work.

"Colombians and Russians. I don't even like the sound of that." Bobby looked at Danny as they left the morgue. "Not to mention whoever is missing. Let's hope Dr. Ekouevi has some answers." "Ekouevi always knows something." "Yeah I'd better call Arthur. He is probably shitting bricks by now." Danny laughed.

"Lt. we have a positive i.d. on our victims. They are Russian." "What!" Arthur screamed "For a minute there I thought you said Russians." "That's exactly what I said." Bobby waited for his boss to respond "Is it Russian mafia?" "We are checking that out right now. They all have the same insignia so I'm guessing Russian mafia maybe. I'll know shortly. I'll get back." Bobby hung up.

Danny was looking over the photos as Bobby ended his conversation with the Lt. "I haven't seen this one before." Danny commented as he carefully studied the design. "It's certainly different." Danny had a great deal of expertise in the area of tattoos and body art; Bobby listened intently as Danny explained what the symbols could possibly mean.

By this time the two were pulling up to the entrance of the O.N.S.I. Headquarters. By now they both knew the routine so once they were secure inside Bobby and Danny immediately approached Dr. Ekouevi. "Dr. Ekouevi" Bobby started "Please tell me you know something about all of this."

"Well I just got the update on the situation. This is what we have Russians, Colombians and maybe the Japanese." "The Japanese?" Danny echoed "Yes it seems the Japanese are players. How they are connected to Mr. Calderon is another story." "Dr. Ekouevi I have some pictures." Danny offered them up. "I'm not familiar with this insignia; do you think I could use the lab to do some research?" "This way detective."

Dr Ekouevi led Danny into the computer room. It was filled with all the latest in state of the art technology. The detective immediately went to work; this sort of thing fascinated him. This was an insignia that he was unfamiliar with so he was extremely interested in what he would find.

"Bobby I'm going to need a minute with this." Danny warned as he started his research. "How long?" Bobby questioned. "At least a couple of hours. Maybe more maybe less depending on how this plays out." Bobby contemplated what he would do while Danny worked in the lab.

"O.k. I'll head down and talk to this witness. This will back the Lou off both of our asses." "Yeah do that and hook up with me later. If she knows anything hopefully we can tie all this together." Bobby nodded as he walked out. "I'll get back to you." Bobby jumped in the car and closed the elevator. Once he was on street level he sped off immediately.

Bobby radioed in to the station "Put me through to the Lt." He said to the dispatcher. Bobby waited for his call to go through. Finally he heard the Lt.'s voice. "Arthur I'm on my way downtown to talk to this witness." "Good Bobby. Find out what she might know. Where's Danny?" "I left him in the lab with Ekouevi; he needs a couple of hours to follow up on a lead."

"O.k. keep me informed." Arthur commanded as he hung up the phone. Bobby was having mixed feelings as he drove uptown; part of him wanted to go to the hospital and the other part was very intrigued by this new witness. There was something familiar about her but Bobby couldn't put his finger on it. He really felt uncomfortable with the thought of interviewing her without his partner or another officer present.

Bobby radioed the house again; "This is Semione; put me through to the Lt." He ordered. "Go ahead detective." "Lt. Is Cole on duty?" "Yes" "Why don't you have him to meet me?" "You need back-up?" "I'd rather be safe than sorry." "Ok. Don't go in until he arrives." "Roger that."

"Cole" Arthur shouted "You need to meet Semione at this address now. Don't make a move until he arrives. The two of you need to go in together." Cole shook his head as he headed out the door. Arthur smiled to himself; he had never known Bobby to be intimidated by the presence of a female.

In the meantime Danny worked diligently on the insignia all afternoon. "Why does Bobby always get to interview the pretty ones?' he smiled to himself as his partner headed uptown. "I could sure use his help on this one." "Danny how are you coming with that tat?" Bobby asked as he checked in on his cell phone. "Any luck?" "Nothing so far" Danny responded "Why? What's going on?" "Cole is going to meet me to talk to this witness; I'm not trying to lose my job over this one." "Well Bobby if that were the case I could have come with you." Danny replied "No I need you there trying to break that code. Get back to me with some results."

Danny worked feverishly trying to identify the origins of the insignia. "Who does this kind of work?' he asked himself "And what the hell does this mean?" He questioned out loud as he fed the computer what he thought would be an identifying or common characteristics. But with all his input he was still coming up blank.

Danny questioned himself over and over "Was this regional? Was it gang related? Or is it a family crests? It could signify a member of the international triad or it could simply be a jail house tat. But whatever it was and whatever it meant each member was wearing it so he knew that this was definitely something organized; something with life long family roots and something that had a great deal of significance.

There was still something he was missing. Something he just couldn't put his finger on. Danny studied the insignia looking for some detail that perhaps he overlooked that could possibly provide him with a clue to the origin or the meaning. In the meantime his thoughts shifted back to his partner. "I hope Bobby is having better luck." Danny thought to himself.

seventy-five

Detective Cole was waiting in the car in front of the building when Bobby arrived. He had gotten this assignment over the phone from the Lt. and he needed to be brought up to speed. "What is the situation?" He asked Bobby once they were finally together. "We are here to interview a witness." "What's her name?" "Her name is Debora Brockinghaus Vertikoff. She is a dancer and she lives on the top floor. It's possible that she can help us identify the shooters on the Manhattan murders. When I talked to her this morning I could tell that she knew more than what she was letting on."

"She might have seen or heard something. At this point we don't have any leads so any thing she can tell us is more than what we have." "Why do you need me here?" "Back-up. You know what they say two heads are better than one."

"Since when do you need backup to interview a woman? What is really going on here?" "I guess we will find out once we talk to her." Bobby quipped sarcastically. "You know what I mean" Wesley replied. "Let's just talk to her and get this over." Bobby defended his impatience. "Bobby I have been working with you off and on for years now and the one thing that I know is you have never had a problem interviewing a witness. Now what is really going on here?" "I just think this witness is holding back. We might have to run the good cop bad cop so that is why I need you here."

Bobby explained as they made their way to the door. After viewing the directory Bobby finally rang the buzzer. "N.Y.P.D. ma'am. Can we talk to you?" Bobby spoke directly into the intercom "Who?" A faint voice replied. "N.Y.P.D. we would like to talk to you about this morning." "O.k. come on up. Top floor."

Once inside Bobby noticed immediately what a nice building this was. The lobby was done in art deco and there was an artsy vibe or air that lent a certain character to the place. "This must be an artist's haven. Rosaland would love this building." Bobby thought to himself as they entered the elevator. For some reason he couldn't stop thinking about her today. She was heavy on his mind and in his heart. Maybe he was feeling guilty because for the last couple of months he had spent no time at all at the hospital with her. Rachael had really been holding down the fort so that he could work.

Everything seemed to be connected to Calderon one way or the other and it was up to Bobby to sort out this mess. He hoped that Rosaland would understand but he knew that she wouldn't. After today he would have to formulate a new schedule. One that would allow her some time.

"I wondered when you would be knocking at my door detective." Debora said sexily as she stood in front of the elevator. She couldn't help herself as she starred lustfully at the tall good looking detective. "My my, what a delicious piece of man candy." Debora thought to herself deliberately not taking her roving eyes off of Bobby.

Both Bobby and Wesley were completely taken back by Debora's beautiful well shaped body as she stood in front of the elevator in her skin tight dance leotard. She had a towel wrapped around her neck and beads of sweat pouring off of her brow. "What can I do for you?" She asked in a breathy voice. "Wow" Wesley thought as he carefully surveyed her voluptuous curves.

"I see now why Bobby didn't want to be alone with her." he continued his train of thought smiling to himself. "Good cop bad cop my ass!" Wesley noticed the exchange of glances between the two of them. Debora obviously flirting and Bobby deliberately ignoring her coquettish advances.

"Detective Semione, we met briefly this morning and this is detective Cole. We would like to ask you some questions about the murders that happened one street over." Bobby said getting right down to business. "Murders? What makes you think I know anything about those murders?" Debora objected.

"Well that is what we are here to find out." The handsome detective chimed in. "How many people were murdered?" She asked showing a little bit more interest. "Gentlemen do you want to talk here in the hall or do you want to come inside?" Debora questioned as she walked towards her apartment. Both Bobby and Wesley followed her with their eyes simultaneously looking at the wiggle of her well-shaped ass and then at each other. Bobby shook his head; this one could get him into deep trouble.

Once inside the apartment Bobby noticed the artsy décor. He liked the vibe; it was nice, simple and down to earth. "Do you mind if I finish my workout while we talk?" Debora asked as she closed the door and went back to stretching her body. "No not at all" Bobby answered. "Nice place"

Bobby continued "how long have you been a dancer?" "About thirteen years" "Thirteen years. You don't look much older than that yourself."

Debora smiled. "I started dancing when I was about twelve detectives and believe me I'm much older than that." She looked invitingly at the sexy hunk. "I'm sure you two didn't come here to talk about my dancing career." "We came to talk about what you saw." Bobby threw that out at her. Debora stopped and looked up at the detective. "How do you know I saw anything?" she exclaimed

"Well did you?" He barked back totally taking control of the conversation. "What can you tell us about this morning?" Wesley added trying to bring the conversation back to focus. Deborah got up and walked over to her window box. "You know this is my absolute favorite place out of all this space. Every night about the same time I end up here. I like sitting here because no one can see me."

"Why it is so important that no one sees you?" Bobby inquired "because I' m usually naked. I sit here after I finish my workout and my shower and let my body air dry in the breeze." Bobby looked up at Wesley as Debora continued.

Wesley could feel the sexual tension building between the two of them and decided that it was time to diffuse it. "Look Ms. Brockinghaus Vertikoff this is very important. If you saw anything we really need to know. We have ten dead bodies in the morgue and not a clue."

"O.k. my company is in performance all this week so I have been up late every night this week. A couple of days ago I noticed some activity. It seemed as though someone or some ones were running across the roof. It all happened so fast I didn't really pay attention. I thought I was hallucinating or just tired."

"Last night it happened again. This time I paid particular attention hoping that who ever it was they wouldn't see me. It was about four or five men all dressed in black moving at light speed across the roof and down the side of the building. They all had these rope like devises they used to shimmy down the wall."

"So you are saying they jumped off the roof?" "No detective nothing so exotic. They simply walked down the wall. Their ropes were attached by this thing. The top looked like a spider and they slid down the ropes. They walked the walls down to the street. You know the device I'm talking about; mountain climbers use them. You know something out of a James Bond movie."

Debora was becoming more excited trying to get the detectives to picture in their minds the device she was talking about. Wesley was writing all this down in his notes as she continued to describe the series of events. I waited a while and then I walked over to see if they were hanging around or if they were gone. They were gone but one of them did leave a rope. I stashed it in the corner."

Debora walked over and pointed to the cattling hook that she had in the corner. "Did you see what they looked like?" Bobby questioned her more intensely. "No they were wearing hoods or masks but their faces were definitely covered. They were dressed in black from head to toe and they moved incredibly fast. In a matter of seconds it was all over."

"Did you touch this?" Wesley asked as he handled the rope with his gloved hands. "Yes. I pulled it down and left it there." "Well we need to get this to forensics and see what they find. In the meantime Ms. Brockinghaus Vertikoff because you did touch it, we are going to need you to come down to the station and give us a set of prints."

"A set of my prints for what? I'm not the criminal here. I didn't murder anybody and I'm not going down to your station. I don't have time for that!" She screamed. "Calm down Ms. Brockinghaus Vertikoff. It only takes a few minutes. You can do it on your lunch but this is how we can eliminate you and concentrate on the real perps. If you touched it your prints will be on it and right now it is our only piece of solid evidence."

Bobby explained trying to calm her down. "Will you be there?" She asked innocently. "Yes as a matter of fact if you like I will walk you through it." "O.k. when do you want to do this?" "The sooner the better. Time is of the essence here. These are some pretty nasty bad guys; they left a lot of dead bodies." Bobby smiled sexily. Debora immediately became wet between her legs.

"Detectives if you would be willing to wait while I get dressed we could do this now." Debora said thoughtfully feeling a new sense of cooperation. "We wouldn't want to interrupt your workout." Wesley quipped sarcastically. "Really it's no problem." Debora replied as she headed towards her bedroom. "You would be willing to do that for us?" Bobby questioned. "Yes I want to help." She called back. "O.k. we'll wait."

Wesley looked at Bobby and nodded "very smooth partner." "We have to move on this now. Let's just hope Danny is having luck with that insignia. If we can tie the two together we will know how to proceed. Right now all we know is that we have a network of killers on the loose that we don't know a thing about."

Bobby looked around the penthouse as they waited. "This is a really nice place." He commented. "Rosaland would like this." "How is Rosaland Bobby? Any signs of improvement?" "No she is still in a coma. It's been six months and nothing. All we can do is hope and pray. We have been so busy lately that I haven't spent the adequate amount of time with her. Thank God for her family or I would be ass out. I really miss her. You know everything is starting to remind me of her."

"Who is that detective?" Debora asked as she emerged fully dressed and ready to go. "It's personal are you ready?" "Yes" "Let's go." "Do you know how long this will take?" Debora asked once they were in the elevator. "Two hours tops" Bobby replied. Once downstairs Bobby remembered that he and Wes had arrived in different cars. He was so used to working and riding with Danny. Now what was he going to do? Who was going to transport her? It was very obvious that Debora was going to ride with him and he really didn't trust himself to be alone with her, not even for a minute.

It had been a while since a woman other than Rosaland had this kind of effect on him and he definitely had no intention of getting in trouble. "Ms. Brockinghaus Vertikoff why don't you ride with Detective Cole. I have a stop to make before we hit the station." "Wes take Ms. Brockinghaus Vertikoff in and get her set up. I'll be there in about 15 minutes. I have a stop to make."

Debora was surprised at the change in Bobby's behavior but she went along with it. The detective walked the witness to the car and waited until they pulled off. Once alone in his car Bobby felt guilty for his interest in this other woman. What was surprising was that it wasn't all sexual. He found her to be unique. She had a great body and very intelligent conversation plus she was pretty. A very vulnerable combination for a man in his situation.

It had been six months since Bobby felt warm flesh pressed against his or the touch of soft tender lips or the fragrant smell of her hair. Bobby desperately needed to hold his girl. After sitting for a while and contemplating Bobby started the car and found himself heading towards to hospital.

Rachael was very surprised to see him. "Bobby! What are you doing here at this time of the day? Is everything alright?" "Yes Rachael everything is fine; I just needed to be here that's all." "I know how busy you all have been. How's the case coming?"

"It's just getting more and more complicated. Rachael listen I'm sorry about my time…" Rachael put her fingertips to Bobby's lips. "Don't Bobby. It's o.k. that's what family is for; we can lean on each other in times of need. Don't you know that I know if you could live here you would? You can't be in two places at the same time and I would rather have you out there trying to solve this crime than just sitting around doing nothing and I know rosaland would."

"Rachael I love her so much it hurts." Bobby added "I know." Rachael whispered as she gave Bobby a well-deserved hug. "A hug always makes things better. Besides I have gotten so much work done in the last six months from here. Not bad for a makeshift office huh?"

Rachael said trying to lighten the air. "So when is the last time you slept in your own bed?" Bobby asked. "While I'm so busy chasing bad guys what is that doing for your marriage?" Rachael looked at Bobby sheepishly, a little taken back by his concern. "When is the last time you spent a romantic evening with your husband? Or better still when is the last time you spent a quiet evening taking care of yourself?"

Bobby pulled out his cell "Boss why don't you come and pick up your wife?" "I beg your pardon?" Arthur replied. "I'm going to stay at the hospital tonight with Rosaland. Why don't you come and pick up Rachael?" "Bobby we are swamped here." "Sometimes Arthur we have to remember what is important."

"I'm out of here; tell Rachael I'm on my way. I'll pick her up downstairs." "Rachael get your things together. Your husband is picking you up downstairs. He is on his way." Rachael walked over and kissed Bobby. "Thanks Bobby" "No thank you. Now get ready." "It's been so long since I've been home I don't know what to take." "Don't take anything other than yourself. No work. Now get out of here. Your husband should be downstairs right about now." Bobby said looking at his watch. Rachael smiled as she ran toward the elevator.

Bobby walked over to the window and starred inside. Rosaland was lying there with tubes and attachments everywhere. She looked so fragile, so helpless and so vulnerable.

"Detective I'm surprised to see you this early." Bobby turned around to look into the eyes of Dr. Ward. "Dr. Ward. It's good to see you. How is my girl?" "Her condition remains the same detective." "How long is she going to be like this?" "It's hard to tell. It's already been six months. It could be a year or she could wake up tomorrow. We just don't know. But she is in good hands. I can guarantee you that. Actually I'm going in to remove the bandages and the electrodes. After I'm finished why don't you just talk to her?"

"Will she be able to hear me?" "We have scientific evidence that says she can. Many of our coma patients remember bed side conversations that occurred while they were under. It couldn't hurt." Bobby nodded. "I believe that. Can I come in while you remove the electrodes?" "No detective we have to maintain a sterile environment. This won't take long. On second thought this might take some time but you can come in after I'm finished." Bobby waited while the Dr. attended to his sweetie.

"God Rosaland I wish you would open your eyes" he thought to himself as he watched the Dr. remove the bandages. "This separation is killing me and I'm probably going to end up in trouble." Bobby stood with his body pressed into the glass. He felt guilty for all the time he hadn't been here. He felt troubled by his thoughts of indiscretion and he was truly heartbroken to see her like this. He could feel the need for her all through his body. Bobby ached for her touch, her taste and her feel. He wanted nothing more than to plant himself deep inside her very being and remain there until he heard her scream out his name in ecstasy.

It had been such a long time since her heard her scream or moan or beg for more. Bobby was working himself into a sexual frenzy just thinking about her absence. "God I miss you" he said out loud as he watched Dr. Ward carry out her work.

Once she was finished Dr. Ward motioned Bobby to come in. "Do I need to put on a mask?" "No you are alright. I'll be out of your way in a minute. She looks great." Dr. Ward smiled as she observed her patient. "Her face and hands have healed remarkably well. They will probably be extremely sensitive to touch but other than that she's good." "What do you mean sensitive to touch?" "Well once she wakes up she will probably experience a great deal of pain in certain areas. That's common when you receive an injury of this nature."

"Other than that?" Bobby questioned. "Other than that she should heal just fine. This is why I love this treatment; its new age medicine and it works. Not to mention that it's mine." "I'm sure that is why you come so highly recommended." Bobby added.

Dr. Ward smiled "Flattery will get you everywhere detective." They both laughed as she left the room. Bobby sat at the head of Rosaland's bed running his fingers through her hair. He remembered what Dr. Ward said about the pain so he tried to be extremely tender. He bent over to gently kiss her lips hoping for some response but there was none. Then he remembered that this could only hurt her if she was awake.

From what he could tell she was far from it so he kissed her again this time more passionately. Again there was no response. Bobby decided that it might not be such a bad idea to try to talk to her. After all what could it hurt? There was no one there except the two of them so why not give it a shot. At this point he would do just about anything to have her back in his arms.

"Hey Baby" he started. "You should know how much this sucks and how mad I am that we are in this situation. Well Rosaland this is fucked up and I am mad as hell. When I am mad like this, you are the only one that understands. Everyone else thinks that I am off the hook or out of control but you know that I am going to kill this motherfucker."

"For six months I have been running around trying to track down the son of a bitch that did this to you and I don't have a fucking clue. In the meantime life is going on for everyone around us and we are lost in a time warp." Bobby shook his head as he continued. "I want you so bad it hurts and there is nothing I can do about it. Nothing we can do about it except wait for time to have mercy on us."

Bobby sat at the head of Rosaland's bed running his fingers thru her hair as he continued. "Wow Babe we have been through so much since we have been together and thru it all we have managed to survive. Let's make it through this too. I'm not ready to not be with you. I can't even image not being with you. It's too scary a thought or even worse it's too scary a reality."

Bobby leaned over and kissed her again. "I haven't been this scared since that night at the Tito Puente concert. Do you remember that night? You were about to kick my ass to the curb. I had no idea what I had done but you were sure mad as hell at me. My whole life was in your hands that night."

"It had been about three weeks since I had seen you. I had no idea that you were going to be at that concert. You left my ass high and dry. You just disappeared. No phone calls, no e-mails, nothing. I never expected to see you that night and then there you were. A vision. A Goddess in red surrounded by a bar full of men. I lost it. I couldn't believe that you would try to play me like that. As though there was nothing going on between us. As though nothing had ever happened."

"I was your little secret. I have never been anybodies secret." Bobby said sarcastically. "You were hurting and you hurt me. I had never been hurt by a woman before not like that. I tried to talk to Rachael but she wasn't divulging any information. I called your Father and he was completely closed mouthed. The only person in your family that seemed to have any compassion for me at all was Matt."

"Even thought he didn't tell me of your whereabouts at least he listened which was more than I got from anybody else. "I told you the first night we made love that you belonged to me and it was obvious to me at that point that you didn't believe me. When I say that believe it."

"You know I actually went up to Harlem to find you. I flashed my badge, I checked your house and I talked to your neighbors who all seemed to know that you where in Washington, everybody knew but me. Boy did I feel like a fool. I'm supposed to be your man and I had no idea that I was the brunt of your joke."

"That is when I discovered that you have a mean streak, a dark side. You had done that deliberately. I couldn't believe that you wouldn't talk to me. I guess I had that coming. Even though I'm still not so sure about that. Had I been in your shoes or seeing it from your eyes I might have done the same. No I would never have handled the situation that way and I wished you hadn't either."

"You know I often wonder had I not run into you that night, what would have happened to us?" Bobby started laughing. "Who am I kidding? The way you dropped me. If I hadn't run into you that night there wouldn't be any us. Lack of communications kills a relationship every time."

Rosaland was just lying there unresponsive, but she was listening and she could hear him. "That night changed my life. I knew that if I let you leave that concert without me. It would never be the same between us. I knew that we would go back to being coworkers and following the rules. I couldn't have that. I was so much in love with you then and now that love has grown even more. I still can't believe we ended up in Harlem Park on top of the Saab."

"One of my better moments I must admit. I was amazed that after treating me so cold you were so warm, tender, and generous." "That's when I realized just how much your heart must have hurt. You were just as much in love as I was, probably more. That was the night that saved our love and saved my life."

"After that life with you became a whirlwind. I never knew what to expect from you. The sky was the limit. Who would have believed that your family or should I say you owned a luxury yacht docked in the middle of Manhattan?"

"Or that you would have me chasing dangerous powerful drug lords through Central America barely escaping with my life? Or that you would violate every rule you were taught and make love to me in the wilds of Bolivia or in your father's house on more than one occasion."

"It all seems so long ago and I want that back Rosaland. "Open your eyes!" Bobby demanded "Please open your eyes." Bobby waited before he continued. "Oh man Rosaland I will never forget that magical weekend we spent on the yacht. That night was outrageous. That was our first time on a waterbed and that was the first time you cooked for me. I had no idea that you were a gourmet chef who specialized in "soul food". I love native dishes. That was one of the best home cooked meals I had ever eaten."

"I couldn't believe that one night turned into a weekend. I almost lost my shield on that one. Not to mention that by the time we got back everyone in the N.Y.P.D. knew about us. I'm still amazed as to how that got out but it did. It had to be old man Pritchard. I remember when I arrived for our date; he was so curious and so protective, almost antagonistic. He told on us."

"I had no idea you would turn out to be so freaky. I'm glad we sailed up the coast. I would have never been able to explain the screams to Mr. Pritchard. I would have never been able to face him again; at least not until the wedding which would have happened by now."

"Between him and your father my shit was in hot water. Actually when I think about it the only thing I knew for sure up to that point was that I was totally crazy about you and every time my thoughts turned to you my dick got hard, really hard."

"That was the night I recognized how much you thought about me. You knew everything that I liked or wanted or fantasized about. You were totally in my head as though you had studied me. At work you were always so professional and distant. I wanted you to love me and that night you gave me my indicator."

"You definitely fulfilled my every waking desire. Our love affair has been one incredible ride. So powerful and so exhilarating. I don't want it to end. Maybe the affair part but not the love part." Bobby smiled at her as he spoke. "Baby I promise if you give me some time I'll get much better at this." Bobby leaned over to kiss her again.

seventy six

Bobby walked away from the bed and headed over to the window. He stood calmly gazing out with his hands in his pockets as he watched the magic of the city unfold beneath him. It was starting to get dark and the streets were beginning to come alive.

Bobby watched as the people began to flood onto the sidewalks from the various office buildings. From her hospital room high atop the city he noticed the lights from the enormous amount of traffic as it cascaded down the F.D.R.

Bobby missed sharing the wonders of Manhattan with Rosaland. She was enchanting in the evening. That is when she really came alive. She was so perfect for him; she understood everything about him except his need to fraternize. That sexy smile he always flashed, the seductive swagger in his walk, the risqué tone he took with members of the opposite sex, always demanding, always in control.

All of these charming characteristics are what made him Bobby. Little did Rosaland realize when they first met that this would be the problem that would plague their relationship for years to come. There would always be some woman lurking in the background ready to take her place in his bed.

Bobby continued to talk to Rosaland for what appeared to be hours. He hoped that something he said would trigger something inside of her consciousness and bring her back to him. As Bobby talked he was invigorated by all the good times they had shared as well as the bad. They had been through a hell of a lot in the last three years and the good definitely outweighed the bad.

Three years. Where had the time gone? Time had gone by so fast only to be at a complete stand still right now. Bobby made a promise to himself right then and there; if she recovered he would marry her as soon as possible. He would never make this mistake again. Bobby knew that no one would ever love her as much as he did.

"Baby if there was anyway I could change places with you I would in a heart beat. This is killing me. Rosaland please open your eyes. Come home to me." Bobby was practically begging only to be answered by her stillness.

The night was wearing on and Bobby never felt as close to his love as he did now. Even if she never heard a word he said just being here with her was a very precious moment. He had no idea when he would be able to do this again, so he would enjoy the time. At this point time was all he had.

"You know Baby the first thing I want to do when I get you home, well actually the second thing?" Bobby turned away from the window to look in her direction. "I want to go dancing. It has been too long since we have been out on the town. Just the two of us. I remember that small club in Bolivia. It was dangerous, hot, dirty, crowded and the air was smoky and stale, but you were the most sensual woman I had ever been with in my life."

"The way you moved. It's like your body was on fire. I had never felt you so hot and so sizzling. I can still envision the sweat as it poured over your brow, down your neck, and between your breasts as we danced. I felt like taking you right there on the dance floor. I can still feel your wet body pulsating against mine as you moved sexily to the music."

I remember the touch of your lips as you opened my shirt and kissed my chest. I thought I was going to explode. But you kept on, rubbing, touching, and grinding your hot hips deep into mine. I thought you were going to undress me right in the middle of the floor. That would have been fine by me."

"It was the hardest thing in the world to keep my Johnson in my pants. I couldn't keep my hands off of you and you couldn't keep your body off of me." Bobby closed his eyes as he revisited his memory. That was the night I discovered Dr. Rosaland Reid, Cyprian love goddess. Central America really brought out the passion in you that night. I loved it. You were absolutely incredible."

"I loved seeing that side of you. It was definitely an eye opener. One that I will never forget. Now that I think about it, we did a lot of firsts that night." At this point Bobby was smiling completely to himself lost in his memories.

Bobby had been at the hospital for hours. Dr. Ward was surprised to see that he was still there but she did notice that he was very much involved in conversation. She was pleased that he had taken her advice. He made himself completely comfortable in Rosaland's room. He had discarded his jacket, shirt, and tie. His gun and holster were hidden under the nightstand and he stood in his socks as he continued his trip down memory lane.

The night lights of the city proved interesting as he focused on the images of the people that scurried below him. They reminded him of ants all running in different directions with no clear destination in mind. Bobby was so lost in his own thoughts that he never saw Rosaland's finger twitch.

He stood with his back to her as he watched the people below him. This time Rosaland's finger moved as though a shock wave had gone through her hand. But Bobby still didn't notice. When he finally turned back to her the movement had stopped.

Rosaland found herself trapped at the bottom of a black hole; an endless chasm that seemed to go on forever. She lingered lost in the dark unable to move towards the light. Her body was just floating in a state of limbo, a void; as she listened intensely to Bobby pour his heart out. She could certainly hear every word her man was saying loud and clear, but she couldn't respond.

She had no idea where she was, how long she had been here and why she couldn't make it back. Bobby's voice surrounded her spirit in its entirety, and seemed to provide some comfort in her efforts to reconnect to him. She would use the direction of his voice as her guide, as a vehicle to transport her back to reality.

As Rosaland looked around in an attempt to recognize her surroundings she noticed that a tunnel seemed to be forming at the base of the hole. Frantically she tried to move in its direction as she noticed how the eye began to enlarge. Maybe her body could fit through the needle before it began to dissipate. But there was something holding her back.

Rosaland watched as the light at the end of the tunnel grew brighter and she knew that if she were ever going to leave from this place now would be the time. She struggled with every bit of energy she could muster to break free and move towards the light, move towards the familiar sound of his voice.

She could hear Bobby's words resounding in her ears. She could hear him pleading for her to come home, come back to him and she could sense the longing in his voice. She desperately wanted to accommodate his desires. Bobby asked out loud "Rosaland can you hear me at all?" as he turned to look in her direction.

She was still unresponsive. "I guess you can't" he commented as he continued to talk. Rosaland wanted to shout from the top of her lungs "Yes Baby I can hear you!" as she struggled against the darkness. She pulled and strove to break free of the obstacles that were holding her hostage in the dark. Soon she could feel her spirit begin to levitate to meet the light which was engulfing her comatose body.

The light felt calming and soothing and for some reason Rosaland knew that she could trust it. Her resistance was slowly being torn away as she relaxed and let the warmth overtake her. The sound of Bobby's voice seemed to be propelling her in his direction. The brilliance of the light began to overwhelm her and she began to move her head from side to side trying to evade the glow.

For the first time in months Rosaland could see herself looming over her unconscious body. Her spirit hovered as she realized that she was outside of her self-watching these events unfold. Rosaland was beginning to put together the pieces of what was really happening. She asked herself why she was lurking above the room and whom was that helpless creature laying in the bed?

After a bit of observation Rosaland discovered that the helpless creature was she! That is why she couldn't get back. She had no idea what had transpired and why she was separated from her body. She watched as Bobby talked to her but she was still unable to answer. Her spirit began to move towards her body. She needed to put an end to this separation. It all seemed to be very painful. At this point Rosaland felt herself slide back into her body. What an experience!

Suddenly Rosaland moved her head again and again Bobby didn't notice. Then he heard her voice as she moaned. "Ohh" she breathe gently, barely audible. But Bobby heard her! He looked in her direction and noticed immediately that her head was in a different position.

Bobby rushed over to the head of the bed and waited for another indicator. That is when he noticed her finger move. At this point the tears welled up in his eyes and began to roll down his face. "Come on Baby" Bobby demanded "Come back! Come home! Open your eyes!

Bobby could see the struggle on her face as she tried to open her eyes. Then he heard her again. "Bobby?" She moaned out his name. "Bobby?" She repeated as he drew nearer and then she let out a shrill blood curdling scream. "My face! My face!" She screamed loudly as the tears began to roll down her cheeks. Rosaland was experiencing excruciating pain in her face and hands. All remnants of the laser surgery she had undergone six months ago.

This was her first initial reaction to the procedure. "Bobby! My face! My hands! " she cried out" They hurt like hell!" All Bobby could do was smile through tear filled eyes and look at her. Rosaland had yet to open her eyes. She couldn't. The pain was overwhelming. She was extremely disoriented as she tried desperately to open her eyes.

"Bobby! Bobby!" she repeated his name over and over as she attempted to open her eyes. "Come on Rosaland! Please open your eyes! At this point Bobby was pleading. "Open your eyes! Rosaland open your eyes!"

Rosaland reached up and wildly snatched the electrodes from her forehead and hands. What ever this was on her body was she wanted them off. They were very intrusive and they seemed to be the cause of all the pain. At this point she was an emotional mess crying and fighting to regain her consciousness.

Suddenly it happened. For the first time in six months Rosaland opened her eyes to the world. Bobby was staring down at her as she became coherent. His was the first face she had seen since the explosion. "Hey Baby welcome home…" he whispered softly as he bent over gently to kiss her lips.

"Bobby my face? What happened to my face? My hands? They hurt like hell." Rosaland cried out as she tried to sit up. "You're o.k. Your face is fine and your hands are healing." Bobby said as he kissed her lips again gently pushing her back on the bed. "How long have I been here?" She mumbled through her trembling tear filled voice. "Too long" Bobby responded between kisses. "Much too long."

"Bobby" Rosaland murmured breathlessly as he increased the intensity of his advances. "Baby hold me. Please hold me close…" she begged. "Let's call the Dr." Bobby insisted as he tried to break away from their embrace.

"No not yet…" Rosaland responded to him with a fever of her own as she pulled his body close to hers. Rosaland was on fire. Her body was burning with pent up sexual desire. She was hot and steamy and all she wanted was Bobby next to her. Touching her, kissing her and loving her. "Bobby please!" Rosaland begged as she pulled his strong body on top of hers. "Please Bobby…" she pleaded as she held on tight basking in his kisses. Her hands were in extreme pain.

She could feel his need, his urgency and it seemed to coincide with hers. Before long Bobby had stripped Rosaland of her gown as he allowed his hands to roam freely over her delicate naked contour. Bobby could feel the heat exuding from her body. Rosaland moaned and groaned as she felt the delightfulness of his touch. They were lost in their senses as they explored each other for the first time in months.

It was hard for Rosaland because of the pain in her hands so Bobby stripped her down. "Ohh Bobby I love you" she whispered as she felt the last vestige of her gown slip from her shoulders. Soon she felt the hardness of his chest and body pressing into the suppleness of her breasts. All she could do was moan and succumb to his will.

Bobby was hypnotic and Rosaland was mesmerized. She was his narcotic and he was completely addicted. "Oh Baby I have missed you" Bobby moaned as he mounted and speared his massive length deep into her. Rosaland responded with a loud scream as she felt his engorged member enter her sore tender privacy. The tears were flowing freely between them as they strove to complete their junction.

"Bobby" she sighed sexually in his ear as he ground his swiveling hips into her pulsating inner sanctum."Ohh Bobby" she whimpered as Bobby buried his weapon deeper. His force was powerful and almost unbearable; after all it had been so long. Rosaland was experiencing a great deal of pain but was willing to bare all to be with her man.

"Ohh Bobby I'm so hot. My body is on fire…" Rosaland panted seductively almost out of control. Rosaland shifted her body and held on tight wrapping her legs securely around his thrusting pelvic area. Bobby was lost in the feel of her. All he wanted to do was to love her, please her and wrap her securely in his arms. Bobby grabbed her ass pulling and holding her snuggly into him. She was the perfect fit. Rosaland screamed out at the depth of the penetration she was experiencing.

Bobby strove to supply her with the satisfaction she so desperately desired. "Ohh" they both moaned simultaneously as they further engaged in the art of their lustful combat. Rosaland surrendered her wet tight honey pot to his exotic dance of gratification with each thrust. "Ohh Bobby Bobby…" Rosaland cried out as Bobby slid his tongue deep into her mouth sucking delectable kisses from her pouting quivering lips.

Rosaland positioned herself to receive more of his massive swollen length as Bobby kept his delicious rhythm steady and pleasing. Bobby was hot, hard and horny and he made sure that Rosaland was completely impaled to the full steam of his manhood. The more he fed her the more she wanted.

Bobby kissed her full mouth nibbled her ear lobes and fondled her swelling breasts as he ran his rough masculine hands along her slim naked curves. Soon nothing could be heard except the luscious moans and delightful groans of the passionate playmates as their bodies bucked and bounced in salacious harmony. Bobby was formidable in his style and his affections. He wanted nothing more than to hear her scream out his name in ecstasy as only she could.

God he had missed her and now was his chance to show her how much. Bobby loved the way her velvety chocolate mocha chino skin mixed with his smooth golden butterscotch complexion. He liked watching as their bodies blended in total bliss.

It was his job to make her happy and Bobby took this responsibility very seriously. "Ohh Rosaland…" he moaned as he adjusted her supple form in his arms. Bobby picked up her legs and pumped deeper and deeper filling her inner cavern with pure delight. "Ohh Baby…" Bobby whined over and over again as he lavished her with his love. He could feel her very essence as he totally captured her body and soul.

Bobby and Rosaland were so caught up in their moment that they lost all sense of time. After all it had been months since the last time they had the pleasure. Rosaland held on tight as the night went fleeing by. Both she and Bobby floated in their sensual cocoon clinging wantonly to each other. Rosaland screamed out as the power of her orgasm overtook her. In the dawn of the early morning twilight Bobby deposited life inside her satiated body for the second time.

At this point Rosaland was completely hysterical as Bobby took her breath away. The tears were flowing down her face and she could not stop shaking. She was experiencing pain everywhere and all she could think about was how good she felt.

Bobby held on to her emotionally distressed body trying to calm her but to no avail. Her body bucked and convulsed and exploded under his titillation. Rosaland was screaming so loud Bobby was surprised that hospital security wasn't on the scene. "Baby…" Bobby whispered. "Baby somebody is going to hear us…" he said as he motioned her to be quiet with his fingers.

At this junction Rosaland remembered where they were and nodded in agreement her eyes filled with tears of enjoyment. Bobby held Rosaland close as she tried to catch her breathe. He gathered her exhausted physique close in his arms and as the early morning light entered the room the two lovers fell into a restful sleep.

Rachael waited for Arthur for what must have been all of ten minutes. "I'm sorry Baby" Arthur said as he pulled up in front of the hospital "the traffic is horrendous. It's backed up all the way to the bridge. There must have been some sort of accident."

At this point Rachael had gotten into the car and was kissing her husband's lips. "Hello to you too!" She said smiling, kissing her husband on his cheek and forehead as she adjusted her seat belt "So what brought this change of scene on?" Arthur asked as they headed uptown. "Bobby decided to stay with Rosaland at the hospital and he insisted that I come home and be with you" she answered excitedly. "You know I really feel sorry the guy. He seems to be so lost without her." "Not lost enough to marry her when he had the chance." Rachael retorted. "Now look you almost sound bitter. Don't be like that" Arthur replied.

"Arthur I have watched my sister, my only sister whittle away to almost nothing for the past six months. I know how much she loves this man. She would have married him by now." "Are you sure about that? Because from what I understand it was Rosaland who didn't want to settle down." "Who told you that?" Rachael inquired. "An inside source. I know your family has a real thing about marriage. Don't tell me that your Father is still upset."

Rachael eyeballed Arthur "Yes despite what we are going through as a family, he is still upset with those two. Not just with Bobby, with Rosaland too. He feels she has no respect for his rules." "Does she?" Arthur questioned.

"You'd better believe it." Arthur reached over and kissed his beautiful wife again. "We aren't going to fight over Rosaland and Bobby." Arthur looked at Rachael sternly. "Not tonight."

Rachael understood "You're right. We are not going to fight tonight." Rachael leaned over and took Arthur's hand. She held it gently as they made their way through the traffic home. Rachael sat quiet for a moment mindful of Arthur's warning and then she continued. "It's just that I hate seeing my sister like this." Rachael cooed. Her head resting on Arthur's arm. Arthur smiled as Rachael finished her statement. "It's so unfair. She is so vibrant and so full of life and we never know if she is going to recover from one day to the next. I can't take it. I just want her back; it's just that we are so happy and so fortunate to have each other, I want the same for her."

Rachael was shaking her head "I don't mean to sound so ungrateful." "Its o.k. Baby. Everyone is under a lot of pressure right now but you have to remain positive Rachael. Positive thinking, faith and prayer are about all we have right now."

Arthur hated when Rachael was so sad. He knew how close Rachael was to Rosaland and he would do just about anything to cheer her up. He loved when she smiled. These last six months had been hard on everyone. Rachael was extremely affected. Rosaland was her other half, her confidant, her personal financier and her sexual advisor. After all they came in pairs and life didn't work well without her.

"Don't worry Rachael" Arthur finally added as they pulled up in front of the building. "If anything comes up I'm sure Bobby will call. Let's just enjoy tonight. Rachael you have got to remember that Rosaland being in this condition is not Bobby's fault. He didn't have a damn thing to do with it. A few more inches to the right and they both would be laid up, if not dead."

"I know" Rachael conceded. "It's just that I want him to do the right thing by her that's all. It's been three years. That's a long time." "He will do the right thing by her. You know Bobby he always does the right thing by her. But what can he do now Rachael except wait?"

He can marry her when she recovers" Rachael sarcastically threw that in. "You know you should mind your own business..." Arthur corrected her "Worry about your own marriage." Arthur tapped her on her well-formed ass.

Rachael smiled as they headed upstairs. Once inside the apartment Arthur was on her. As soon as the door closed behind them Arthur had Rachael in his arms planting lascivious kisses on her wet inviting mouth. His force caught her off guard as he pressed his strong muscular body into her lithe well shapen form.

Rachael relaxed in his powerful embrace and returned his affections positioning her rotating triangle in front of his heated piston. "Ohh Rachael" Arthur moaned happy to finally be alone with his wife. "God Rachael" Arthur murmured again as he gently started to unbutton her blouse. Soon Arthur had Rachael's full heaving breasts exposed to the delicate touch of his lips. He kissed her fleshy nipples hungrily, savoring her sweetness as he removed her bra and let it fall gently to the floor.

Arthur come and get naked with me in the Jacuzzi" Rachael teased as she grabbed Arthur's hands and led him into the bathroom." I would love a nice hot bath and we haven't done this in a while." She said as she bent over the tub to start the water. Arthur was standing behind her holding on to her waist as he waited for the tub to fill. Rachael slipped out of her skirt as she let it fall over her shoes. She then began to light the candles that surrounded the tub.

"Baby why don't you make yourself comfortable and get us something to drink while I finish up here." Arthur immediately followed his wife's lead and stripped down to his undies. He then left the bathroom only to return some minutes later with a silver tray full of exotic goodies for the two of them to enjoy.

"It's a little bit early in the evening to start drinking but what the hell." Arthur announced as he reentered the bathroom. "Arthur forget tradition. We are celebrating. How often do we get an evening to ourselves?" Arthur looked around to notice the candles burning seductively. Rachael had lowered the shades creating a very erotic setting. He could also smell the faint aroma of vanilla, which he knew to be Rachael's favorite. The atmosphere was set. The evening was on. He would be sure to thank Bobby in the morning.

Rachael pulled her hair up as she settled into the warm water. Arthur waited until she was comfortable before he handed her the glass. "Umm" Rachael said as she tasted the champagne. "It's nice and cold." Rachael sipped her drink and closed her eyes totally relaxing her body. Soon she felt Arthur position himself in the tub right in back of her. He slid gently into the warm jets of bubbling water rubbing his tall masculine body close to hers as he too got comfortable.

Arthur kissed Rachael on the back of her neck while they enjoyed their drinks. Rachael was relaxed. Her head resting lightly on Arthur's chest. "This is nice" Arthur commented as he started to nibble on Rachael's ear lobes. He kissed the long of her neck and then he buried his tongue down her throat. Arthur turned his attention completely to his wife. He held her passionately in his arms allowing his hands to slide over her wet enticing body.

Rachael gave in to his kisses as she turned her body to face his. She maneuvered herself into a sitting position on his lap pressing her heaving fleshy breasts amorously into his chest. The water began to splash around them as they became active. Rachael wrapped her arms around her husband's neck as they shared a magic moment. She kissed him tenderly and lovingly savoring his embrace.

Arthur began kissing her wet breasts again this time taking her full luscious breasts and nipples in his mouth one at a time. Arthur kissed and sucked and licked her fleshy mounds as they gyrated back and forth in the water. He let his hands slide over her voluptuous figure and down the small of her back all the time eating away at the nape of her neck. Rachael was so hot she was boiling over. Arthur had definitely lit her fuse. She looked longingly at her husband as her hands sought out the hot huge head of his enormous manhood.

Arthur's body was on fire as well. His erection stood stiff and strong in the warm soothing water. Rachael played with his excited member using her hands to rub the gigantic hard on erotically back and forth. Arthur was taken back; he loved when she touched his naked exposed flesh. He loved it even more when she put it to her lips. And she loved it too. She loved sucking her husband's pole. That was the one lesson she had learned from her sister, how to please her man in that way.

Rachael ducked her head under the water as she took Arthur in her mouth. Arthur moaned loudly as his body started to shake upon contact. Rachael relaxed her lips and swallowed even more of Arthur's tasty appendage moving her head up and down under the water. "Ohh Rachael" Arthur moaned thoroughly basking in the sensations his wife was affording him.

Rachael lifted her head to catch her breath and she went down again, this time taking more and more of his enormous length in her mouth and throat. Rachael emerged smiling from the water. She was feeling a bit frisky and it was Arthur's lucky day. She closed her eyes as the water cascaded down her forehead and into her face.

Arthur wiped the water from her eyes and planted another series of deep heart felt kisses on her mouth. Rachael responded accordingly. She was feeling racy as she anchored herself on Arthur's lap. This time she wanted the more solid affair that only her husband could give her. Rachael wiggled her torso into position and accepted Arthur into her body. She sighed out in pleasure as he filled her aching cavity with his hardness.

Rachael cried out in pleasure while Arthur held her securely in place as he stuffed more and more of his pulsating crusader deep within her. Rachael panted as the water splashed under their vacillating movements. She rode Arthur long and hard and she enjoyed every minute of it.

"Is this the way you like it?" Arthur uttered in his husky baritone voice as he increased his rhythm. "Yes Arthur. Yes" she squealed passionately as she rotated her hips and fell instantly into the beat of their lovemaking. "It's so good!!" Rachael screamed out throwing her head back and letting Arthur completely overpower her. Arthur increased the intensity of his movements poking, pushing and pumping her relentlessly.

Rachael's body was warm and satisfying. Arthur couldn't remember the last time he had the pleasure so he would enjoy her now. It was indeed his obligation to please her and he was very grateful for the job. Arthur gathered his wife in his arms to further demonstrate his affections.

Arthur had Rachael boxed in the Jacuzzi. He manipulated her into a tight little space where he continued to invade her tight little space. Rachael's body bounced up and down as Arthur pounded her to his full stem. Rachael sighed, screamed and groaned as Arthur filled her with delight.

Soon the bathroom as well as the rest of the house was filled with the sounds of lustful lovemaking and splashing water. The couple abandoned all time and space as they bathe in the sea of orgasmic bliss. The atmosphere was heavenly as they shared their love so tenderly. "I want a baby! Arthur please give me a baby!" Rachael cried out as her orgasm hit sending her over the top. "I'll do my best!" Arthur promised as they fell back into the splashing water.

seventy-seven

The next morning the hospital was in an uproar. The word was out. Dr. Reid had awakened from her coma. She woke up sometime during the night. Dr. Ward was elated. Her patient had finally recovered. Now she had the actual evidence that proved her theories. Her controversial/experimental treatment worked and she would forever be grateful to Matt for having faith and confidence in her abilities.

Rosaland awoke to the sound of orders being barked from left to right. Her hospital room had turned into emergency central and was full of doctors, nurses, technicians and orderlies all deeply involved in her recovery. Bobby had gotten up earlier that morning so not to be discovered in her bed. He would never forget last night.

He stood strong and proud, happy for her return to reality. After her examination he would get on the phone and notify the rest of her family. For now they would share this experience. Bobby had a lot to talk to her about and he wanted to be the first to break the news. He knew that she would take the lost of their baby hard and he wanted to bc the one to tell her.

He also needed to see her reaction; he needed this for his own state of mind. There were still so many unanswered questions. Why hadn't she told him of the pregnancy? What was the big secret? Why the big secret? He needed answers that only she could supply.

Bobby knew that her family would never forgive him if he didn't notify them immediately. "General" Bobby spoke into the cell phone. "Rosaland has recovered!" He stated calmly. "What!" The general replied. "Rosaland has recovered. She regained consciousness this morning. The Dr. is with her now." "Bobby what are you saying?" The general questioned him with glee. "Rosaland is awake; she is with her dr. right now." "Can I speak to her?" "They are a little busy at the moment but she is up and she is conscious."

"Good Bobby. Good. I'll be there as soon as I can." The General hung up the phone and shouted for joy.

Arthur and Rachael were just turning over when the phone rang. Rachael jumped at the sound fearing the worst. It would be her luck that Rosaland would take a turn for the worst the one night she had a chance to get away. "Hello" she answered hesitantly "Rachael?" "Bobby?" "Rachael we've got some good news." Rachael promptly sat up in the bed shaking Arthur from his sleep. "What Bobby? What is going on?" "It's Rosaland. She has regained consciousness." "She what?" Rachael repeated as she shook Arthur vigorously. "Arthur Rosaland is conscious. She's up! This is Bobby on the phone." Arthur sat up as Rachael continued her conversation. "She is with the Dr. now. I already spoke to your Father and I'm sure Matt has gotten the word through hospital channels."

Rachael jumped out of bed and ran into the bathroom. She threw some cold water on her face as she listened to Bobby describe the scene. "It's a mad house over here. The doctors have scheduled her for a series of test. She will probably be sore as a pin cushion by the time they finish poking at her."

"Bobby I'm getting dressed. I'll be right over." "Take your time. She'll be here. Have some breakfast first Rachael. We will probably be here all day." "O.k. Bobby are you sure that she is alright?" "Yes. She is alert and I must admit she looks pretty damn good from here." "O.k. we are on our way."

By this time the word had definitely gotten to Matt. He came running into the room fresh out of surgery. His gown was soiled and it appeared that he had been up all night or at least most of the night. The first thing he noticed was his sister sitting up in the bed. Dr. Ward was checking her eyes, her pulse and listening to a very vibrant heart beat. "What an outcome. Everything seems fine so far." She flashed an excited smiled at her patient. "Please allow me to introduce myself. I am Dr. Romaine Ward and I have been your doctor for the last five months. Your brother Matt and I went to medical school together and he called me in to consult on your case. I specialize in alternative creative reconstructive laser surgery or ACRLS."

Dr. Ward had moved around the bed and was now checking the electrodes that had been ripped from Rosaland's forehead. "What happened to these?" She looked curiously at Rosaland who pretended not to hear her. "What are those for?" Rosaland asked her point blankly, her eyes following the good doctor around the room.

Dr. Ward was checking the readings from the complicated equipment and the electrodes that had been attached to her face and head for the last six months when the doctor noticed that the time had stopped sometimes in the early morning. "Dr. Reid do you remember anything?" "Yes, I seem to remember everything. Bobby told me that I have been here for six months. Is that true?"

"Yes according to your chart that is exactly correct. Do you remember anything about the accident?" "Yes I remember the roof exploding; I remember trying to shield my face from the heat. I remember seeing Bobby being blown back down the steps. Everything after that is a blank."

"That is very good; most coma patients have very little memory after such a traumatic experience. Excellent. What else do you remember?" "I remember trying to get back to Bobby. I remember I was in a black hole or tunnel and something was holding me down, I tried to struggle to break loose and the next thing I remember is waking up here in the hospital."

Bobby sat on the side of the bed as the doctor conducted her interview. Rosaland reached over and touched his hand as she talked. Her hands were still very tender so he avoided holding them. He gently placed her hand on top of his.

"Dr. Ward what is alternative creative reconstructive laser surgery exactly?" Rosaland questioned. She was very interested in the young innovative surgeon.

"ACRLS is a technique for reconstructive surgery that I developed for coma patients. Usually when a patient is in a coma normal or traditional surgery is prohibited. This technique allows the patients reconstruction to be completed while the patient is in a comatose state. The electrodes feed energy to the skin to encourage the healing of the tissue. It's a relatively painless procedure even though I have heard the after affects can be very excruciating."

"So that was the pain that I felt?" Rosaland said as she looked at Bobby. "When did you feel pain?" The Dr. asked trying to get to the missing hours from the time she woke up until the time she called the nurses station. "It was this morning; I felt it when I first woke up." "Do you know what time that was?" Dr. Ward continued to dig. "No I don't remember. I didn't look at the clock."

"But you did feel pain?" "Yes I did." Dr. Ward made notes on Rosaland's chart as they spoke. "Where?" "Both my hands and my face." "How long did it last?" "When I first woke up it hit me and after that it died down. It lasted all of five or ten minute's maybe, maybe a little longer." "Can I say five minutes, would that be accurate?" "More like ten."

"Dr. Reid I need to schedule you for an internal examination. Are you up for it?" "Internal examination? Why?" "We just want to make sure that you are healing properly. It's part of your treatment. I'll set up the appointment with ob/gyn."

"Ob/gyn?" Rosaland looked puzzled at Bobby. Bobby knew that now was the time. He needed to tell her about the baby. "Is this interview about over or can anyone interrupt?" Matt said in his normal jovial tone. He was smiling from ear to ear as he approached her bed. "Hi Big Sis!!" He shouted out as he wrapped his arms tightly around her neck. Matt held Rosaland securely in his arms planting kisses softly on the top of her head. "Welcome home" he whispered in her ear. "Welcome home sweetie."

Rosaland let the tears flow gently down her face as she held onto her younger brother. She wrapped her arms around him as tight as she could bare and they simply held each other in this position for a while. Bobby was happy to see this pleasant exchange between brother and sister. That was one of the things he loved about being a part of this tribe the closeness that they shared.

After all Bobby didn't have any siblings. He was the only child or so he was raised to believe. Bobby and Matt's eyes met and Bobby noticed that Matt was crying. "Matt I need to talk to Rosaland before they take her downstairs to ob/gyn." Bobby nudged him gently. Matt looked up and the expression on Bobby's face said it all.

"O.k. I'll be back. I need to make my rounds." "And change your clothes" Rosaland threw in "You look a mess." she said as she smiled brightly in her little brother's direction. "The boss is back" Matt quipped as he made his way out of the room.

Bobby sat next to Rosaland on the bed. It was the first time this morning that they were alone. He knew that dr. Ward would be back soon so he wanted to clear the air. He didn't know exactly how to start the conversation so rosaland picked up on his cue. "Bobby why am I going to see the ob/gyn? Do you think the Dr. knows about last night?" "No baby. Well she might, she's a smart cookie and she knows that we didn't account for a few hours but that's not why you are seeing the gyn." Rosaland sat up starring directly into Bobby's eyes. "Why am I seeing the gyn? Was I damaged in the explosion? What!"

"Rosaland I don't know how to tell you this so I'm going to jump right in." "Ok." It was at that moment that Rosaland realized something was wrong. Bobby was fumbling around with his words and that was not his style. "Bobby what's the matter?" She asked as she rubbed her hands over his face. Bobby took her hand from his face and kissed it gently.

"Baby I don't know how to tell you this. We lost our baby." "We what!" Rosaland shouted as her body began to shake nervously. "What Baby? What are you talking about? What are you saying?" She shook her head in disbelief as the tears began to roll down her face. "What Baby? What are you talking about? We weren't having a baby!" She screamed. But she could tell by the saddened look on Bobby's face that they were.

Rosaland immediately broke in to uncontrollable tears. Bobby knew then the reason why she hadn't told him. She didn't know. His questions had been answered; he had no doubt in his mind. Bobby tried to scoop her up in his arms but she pulled away. "Bobby we weren't having a baby, were we?" The look on her face saying it all.

"Yes we were. The force from the explosion caused the fetus to abort." "Fetus to abort? What are you talking about?" Rosaland was totally out of control by now. She was crying hysterically and shaking profusely. Bobby tried to console her; he had no idea that she would take the news so hard. "No, no, no!!" She cried out "How could that be? How could that happen? How come I didn't know?"

At this point Bobby had her wrapped in his arms with her head on his shoulder. He could feel her weaken body shaking excessively and her heart pounding profusely "bobby I didn't know. I swear I didn't know." She kept repeating over and over as the tears flowed abundantly. "Oh Baby, it's alright…" Bobby said again trying to console her. "It's alright. It's alright. The most important thing is that you are alive. I thought I was going to lose you. We can always make another Baby but there is only one of you."

"Can we Bobby? Can we make another baby?" Rosaland looked up at Bobby to notice the tears as they rolled down his face. Her heart broke instantly. She could see the pain that he was experiencing and she found herself wondering who had been there for him? Whose shoulder did he have to cry on? Who did he have to talk too? Rosaland reached up and pulled Bobby to her.

"I'm so sorry…" she uttered holding him tight. Bobby rubbed his hand over her abdomen as they both cried together. When Dr. Ward re-entered the room she could see that they were very involved and needed some privacy. She could see that both Bobby and Rosaland were completely broken up and in need of some more quality time alone.

"Dr. Reid we will be moving you downstairs in just a minute. Detective you can wait here for her. This won't take too long." "No I want him to come with me." Rosaland pleaded "No Baby. Its better if I wait here and besides somebody needs to direct this traffic. Arthur and Rachael are on their way and your Father will be here soon. You're in good hands."

"Rosaland how are you feeling?" Dr. Martin asked. "Actually miles I feel pretty crappy." "Are you experiencing pain?" "Yes a great deal." Dr. Martin pressed his hand firmly on Rosaland's abdomen and she winced. She was very tender in that area. She initially attributed the pain to Bobby's size and length and their early morning liaison but now she knew the true origins of her discomfort.

"What happened?" She asked her doctor. "According to your last examination we discovered a twelve week gestation." "Twelve weeks. That's three months. How come I wasn't notified?" "You were called on 11/19." "That's the same day as the explosion" Rosaland thought back thru time. "How come I didn't know? I was still having my period. What about the symptoms? How come I wasn't experiencing anything?"

"I'm sure that you were. You just probably didn't recognize what was happening. That happens sometimes. Some women have their menstrual well into their pregnancies. You must be one of them." "Isn't that unusual? Am I alright?" "You seem to be fine. I will know more after the test results come back."

"Can I still have children?" "Yes. Your chart shows a healthy uterus which is a blessing after the force of the blast. There is no reason why you can't conceive again. You're fine in that area." "Bobby thinks I knew and didn't tell him." "How do you know that?" "I could see it in his face." "Why would he think that? The detective has been very worried about you; I'm sure that is what you saw." "I know Bobby."

"Rosaland I have to do an internal examination and I need a urine sample." Dr. Martin told his patient. "What do you need urine for?" Rosaland asked a little nervous. "Pregnancy test. It's standard procedure. I'm sure you are fine." Dr. Martin noticed the discomfort in her face as he examined her internally. He was surprised that she was still so tender in this area.

"Does that hurt?" He asked his patient very concerned. "Yes. Actually it does." "A little, a lot, what?" "It's bearable. I'll be alright." "You shouldn't be feeling this much discomfort. I need to watch that. The body heals at its own rate." Dr. Martin made a note on Rosaland's chart. "We'll see how you are feeling tomorrow?" "Tomorrow? Can't I go home today?" "No it's too soon. We'll watch you for 24 hours and if everything comes back positive we will release you in the morning."

"In the morning? I have been here for six months. I want to go home!!" "We'll monitor you progress tonight and release you in the morning. Hospital procedure." Dr. Martin smiled. "It's nice to have you back."

Bobby noticed how long it was taking Rosaland with the examination and he became worried. He sincerely hoped that she was all right. He remembered last night and prayed unconsciously that he hadn't caused any more damage than she had already sustained. They needed each other so desperately. Bobby waited patiently outside as Dr. Martin finished.

Once Rosaland was given a clean bill of health Bobby escorted her back to her room. Which at this point was full of activity? Dr. Ward had pinpointed the exact time that Rosaland recovered. It was as she had suspected. There was a two-hour lapse. As she watched Rosaland and Bobby interact she knew exactly where the two hours had gone.

When Rachael entered the room the tears were already rolling down her face. She expected to see her sister lying there and was both happy and disappointed to see an empty bed. But her disappointment didn't last too long. A minute later a smiling, beaming Rosaland was wheeled into the room. Rachael watched as Bobby attended to her ever so tenderly. It was nice to see them back together.

Once Rosaland was safely tucked back in bed Rachael rushed over and threw her arms around her sister's neck. "Oh Rosaland welcome back!!!!" Rachael cried uncontrollably as the two sisters held each other so tightly. All Rosaland could do was cry and hold on. Her hands still experiencing a great deal of pain.

This was truly one of the happiest moments in her life. Just to be reunited with her family. "How do you feel?" Rachael whispered "I'm o.k. I'm still a little sore; but Dr. Martin says that's normal." Rosaland looked around at Bobby. "Bobby I want to talk to Rachael. Do you mind?" "Of course not. I'll wait with Arthur and Matt. It's Ok. I know it's been a long time. You two need some time alone." Bobby smiled kissed Rosaland on the forehead and left the room.

"Rachael you are positively glowing!" Rosaland commented as the two sisters settled in for their discussion. "How can you tell through all these tears?" Rachael replied smiling from ear to ear. "Well you are not crying now and you look simply beautiful. You got some last night!" Rosaland teased. "Is it that obvious?" "Yes" "Rosaland it has been such a long time since I had the pleasure of my husband. It felt so good." "Tell me about it!" Rosaland muttered half under her breath.

Rachael looked her sister right in the eyes "You guys didn't?" "We did for almost two hours" "Rosaland you just had a miscarriage, well not just but six months ago. Should you be doing that?" "Too late. Rachael who else knows about the baby?" "Everybody including Dad. I thought he was going to kill Bobby when he found out. He hit the ceiling. He was so mad. His perfect daughter had been ruined. The more you fuck up with Bobby the better I look."

Rosaland sat and listened as her sister filled her in on what had been going on with the family in the last six months. "Rachael how did Dad find out?" "The same way we all found out. The day of the explosion. Rosaland after he got over the initial shock of the accident he was so mad at Bobby! Oh My God! All he kept saying was how could he be so irresponsible with you. He blamed the whole pregnancy on him."

"Rosaland you know how Dad is. He does not believe in sex before marriage. Not for his girls. That is just how he is. You know if you try the cow why buy the milk?" Both of the sisters repeated at the same time mocking and imitating their father's voice. Rosaland was laughing nervously. She still had yet to face her father. "He is going to kill me." Rosaland said showing a great deal of concern.

"Dad knows about me and Bobby. He has known for a long time. I sure hate to disappoint him but I love Bobby and I don't care if we ever get married just as long as we stay together. You know the funny thing Rae, on the day of the accident the reason we were late is because we went to apply for our marriage license.

"It's probably sitting in the mail somewhere. Shit it has probably expired by now. That was six months ago. I can't believe that I have been here for six months." "We have all been here for six months. All of us. It's as though time stopped. Last night was the first time I have slept in my own bed in God knows when. But to see you now means that it was all worth it."

Rachael reached over again and hugged her sister. At this point they were both becoming extremely emotional and Rosaland wanted to shift the conversation back to Bobby. "At first we were alternating." Rachael continued "Making sure that someone was here with you around the clock. Then as Bobby and Arthur got busy chasing the bandito that caused this disaster I volunteered to stay. I literally turned this wing into the D.A.'s office and I have been here ever since. I must admit though I have gotten a lot of work done right from this location. There was no way that I was going to leave you alone not even for a minute."

Is Dad still mad at Bobby?" "I don't know?" "Well how has he been treating him?" "I don't know? I have been here with you. " "Has he been giving him the cold shoulder?" "Ice would be a better description."

"This was not Bobby's fault and I won't let Dad place the blame on him!" Rosaland yelled angrily almost in tears "Rosaland you need to talk to your Father. You of all people know how he is." "Doesn't he care that I lost my baby? Does it really matter that we aren't married. Since when does it take marriage to create a life?"

"When your Father's name is General Prescott Arthur Reid and you know it. So you can pout and moan and groan all you want but you know how he is and you know how he feels. He has never made it a secret." "You know sweetie I am so sorry about the baby."

"I'm not going to try and pretend that I know what you are feeling because I don't. Knowing you and how you feel about Bobby I know that you must be hurting." Actually I'm sure that both of you are hurting."

"Bobby is in a much better place than I am." "That's because he has had six months to deal with the loss. Give yourself some time to heal and you will be all right. You have a lot of people who love you and who support you. We'll make it through this."

"Rachael I want to go home. I don't want to wait." "Rosaland the earliest you can be released is tomorrow morning and with all this media frenzy we are probably going to have to sneak you out." "I want to go home today; I want to go home now!" Rosaland pouted.

Bobby peeked his head in the room to see how the girls were doing. They were still deeply involved in their conversation. Rosaland motioned for him to come in. "Your Father is here. He wants to talk to us." Rosaland looked at Rachael with anticipation. That is exactly what she was trying to avoid.

She didn't want to talk to the General right now. Not about the pregnancy or her intimate relationship with the detective. But she knew her father to be a no nonsense man and she also knew that whether or not she wanted to talk she was going to have too.

"Hey Sweetie" the General said as he rushed into the room. "How's my girl? It is so good to see you awake." He smiled as he walked over to kiss his daughter. He held her closely as he placed kisses on her face and forehead. "Hi Dad" Rosaland replied holding her Father ever so close to her heart. Rachael could tell that no matter what Rosaland was already off the hook.

"That's my girl" the General asked softly "Are you alright?" "I'm fine now Dad." Rosaland purred as she rested in her father's arms. The General kissed the top of her head lovingly rubbing his hands through her hair. "I'm sorry about the baby." He added gently and Rosaland immediately broke into tears.

After watching the tender exchange between Father and daughter Rachael got up and left the room. Bobby sat down next to his beloved on the bed and waited patiently for the axe to fall. Rachael was smilingly shaking her head as she walked out of the room; she knew that nothing was going to happen. Rosaland could get away with anything. The General would fuss and raise hell but that was about all.

Bobby started the conversation. "General I know you are upset about the situation between your daughter and me. I want you to know sir that I love her and I will do anything for her. She is my life." Bobby's word's were so sincere and so heart felt that the General reached over grabbed Bobby and gave him a hug.

"I didn't come here to cast blame; I came to see my baby girl. Whatever you two do is between you; I have learned that by now. Just don't hurt her or disgrace her that's all I ask." "You have my word sir." Bobby extended his hand and the General accepted it. "Bobby you are a good man." Rosaland was beaming from head to toe right about now very happy to see the two men in her life on one accord.

seventy-eight

"Now we have to work on a plan to get you out of here." The General said "The media is in a feeding frenzy. Everybody wants a statement from the injured survivor." "Am I the only survivor?" "No but you are the director of the O.N.S.I. and you have been in a coma or vegetative state for the last six months. Definitely newsworthy. I can just see the headlines now."

"Rachael we have a problem to solve" the General barked at his daughter as she re-entered the room. "We have to get your sister out of here and we have to do it as quickly and as quietly as possible." "O.k. Dad but how?" Rachael looked confused. "We need a master plan, the media can be hell and frankly I don't think Rosaland is up to it."

"General sir what can I do to help?" Bobby offered. "You have to get her pass all those vulgar reporters Bobby and as soon as they see you they are going to zero in on her." "O.k. so what do you propose?" "I know" Rachael chimed in as though a light bulb had just gone off inside of her head. "We should schedule a press conference. You and I Dad. While we are giving a status report on Rosaland's recovery Bobby you can sneak her right out the front door and have her home in time for dinner."

"Sounds too simple" Bobby added "It just might work." "Bobby all we are trying to do is to create a distraction so you can get her home. From this day on there is going to be so much media attention on the two of you, you are going to relish this time." "Believe me Rachael I know. They are still waiting over at the P.D. for any word. Trust me I know."

Rachael scheduled the press conference for 10:00 a.m. the next morning. She and the General were proud to share the news of their miracle with the public. Rachael hoped that all would go well. She hoped news of the miscarriage hadn't leaked out but with this group of vultures you never knew.

If they said anything that would hurt or disparage her sister's reputation it would be on. There would be heads to roll and as the District Attorney of New York State she would make sure that it happened.

Rosaland had been home for about 2 months. She was slowly but surely making her way back to the real world. Harlem had never looked so beautiful. She was undergoing therapy to make sure that all her motor and coordination skills were functioning and also she was trying to deal with the psychological effects of her "miscarriage."

It was hard for her at times and then at other times it was bearable. She blamed Carlos for all of her pain. She grieved her lost with Bobby at her side as they focused on their future. The bond between them was stronger than ever as was their love.

So many times at night Bobby would grab her and hold on to her making sure that she was there before he made tender passionate love to her. He wanted nothing more than to protect her from all harm. Rosaland was extremely fortunate because her memory was intact. She did remember everything before and after the blast. She had little facial scarring left from the laser surgery and her hands were healing according to schedule. The discoloration in her skin was fading and she was just starting to feel whole again.

Rosaland knew that it was time for her to report back to the O.N.S.I. She was ready to re join the fight against Carlos Calderon. There was no way that he would get away with this. He had left over half of the N.Y.P.D. dead and those statistics almost included her. Dr. Reid had a special network installed that would allow her to constantly monitor the movements of the infamous Mr. Calderon. If he appeared anywhere on or close to Manhattan Island she would snag him. That was how extensive she had cast her net.

She was out for revenge. Dr. Reid had committed the full resources of her organization to the capture and demise of Mr. Calderon and his cartel. She talked to Dr. Ekouevi ordering him to monitor any and all transmissions on or from the Calderon cartel.

"When is the last time we have heard from our friend?" She waited patiently for an answer. "Not in a while. Not since the explosion." "What is keeping him so quiet?" "We don't know." Her reasoning was that he had gone back underground waiting for the most opportune moment to resurrect from the dead. She was watching, and waiting and definitely holding a grudge.

"I can't believe we haven't heard a peep from our boy in the last 7-8 months. What is he waiting for?" She asked Dr. Ekouevi during one of their more confidential conversations. After the devastation he caused I'm not surprised that we haven't heard from him. We probably won't hear anything for a long time to come." "You think so. Carlos is too brazen to just lie down and play dead. Besides he likes to toy with us too much. I'm sure that he will surface. If for no other reason than to just taunt us."

"Well when he does we will know it. All the surveillance we have focused on him, if he farts we can tell you how bad it smells." "I can not believe that we lost this many officers and friends. What the hell did he use?" "A nice c-4 cocktail." Dr. Reid was looking over the photos that had been waiting on her desk for the last six months.

"You mean to tell me that Carlos Calderon had the roof of the N.Y.P.D. wired with c-4? How? How the hell did he get inside our house without us noticing? How could he get that close to us and still remain undetected?" Dr. Reid bombarded Dr. Ekouevi with a thousand questions and she wanted answers to all of them. "I thought we were the professionals."

"It's obvious he had some help. This appears to be an inside job to me. We had the P.D on a complete lock down and the next day the whole building was gone." "I know this Dr. Ekouevi and my question is still the same. How? Who is helping him? How could he infiltrate our network and waltz right into our organization? Our front doors? Right under our noses?" "Dr. Reid we are talking about Carlos Calderon here. Mr. Deep pockets himself and this is New York City. If you've got the right money you can buy anything or anybody anytime."

"Dr. Ekouevi we need to check out the current N.Y.P.D. personnel. I want background checks on everyone from the janitor to the chief. From Arthur to Bobby and anybody in between and that includes me. Run everybody the agency has ever hired through B.C.I. and if that comes up a blank use Interpol. I need some answers." Rosaland was getting stronger and taking control.

"Somebody is helping this man and I want to know who and for how long. We need to clearly define our perimeters and just how much our operations have been compromised. If he had help six months ago he still has inside help and I want a name!!" "Rosaland do you really want me to check out everyone the N.Y.P.D. has ever hired?" Dr. Ekouevi questioned seriously.

"You're damn right I do and I want you to do it now." "Do you know how long that is going to take?" "Well it will take much longer if you don't get to it." "You know that is going to make a lot of people mad including your boyfriend." "Well sometimes you have to do what you have to do and this is one of those times. Had we done this earlier we may have been able to save a lot of lives. Not to mention our infrastructure." She thought out loud.

"Besides we are not investigating them but we are going to find out everything we can about the people that are around them." "The new facility is holding up well. It's definitely not big enough but for now it will have to do." "Of course it will have to do. It's all they have. Dr. Ekouevi do you realize how much money the O.N.S.I. dropped just moving into that facility? Not to mention the mainframe that we installed. I almost had to kill my Dad to get it. Now everything is gone."

Dr. Reid was completely outraged as she rubbed her hands over her stomach. She couldn't take her eyes off of the photos and the massive devastation. What once had been a building was now a giant crater in the ground.

"Hey Sexy" Bobby called out once he reached home. He was expecting to find Rosaland in the living room relaxing listening to her favorite music or in the kitchen preparing one of her fine meals. But alas, she was neither place. He knew then where to find her as he entered her study; there she was pasted in front of her computer.

"Hey Sexy" Bobby repeated as he walked over and kissed her luscious pouting lips. When Rosaland turned around to acknowledge his presence it was then that he noticed the tears running down her face. Bobby looked around checking out the room. The first thing he noticed was the pictures from the P.D. that were strewn all over her desk in a state of disarray. "What are you doing? Are you alright?" Bobby whispered in her ear rubbing her shoulders. "Oh Bobby this is terrible. Why would anyone want to do such a thing?"

"Your guess is as good as mine. Revenge, payback, mean spirited, who knows. But one thing I know for sure is that we are going to get him." "Where are we in our investigation?" She quizzed him. Bobby noticed how expertly Rosaland slid that in. "What have you been doing all day?" Bobby repeated. He needed to hear her say "I've been working."

Dr. Ekouevi entered the study. "Hey detective. How's it going?" Bobby nodded "So you have been working with my girl all day?" Bobby was on a fishing expedition. "Yes we have been at it all day and I'm just about to be out of here." Dr. Ekouevi nodded to his boss. He knew when to take his clues and that was certainly one of them. Plus he had a lot of work to do.

Bobby smiled to himself and shook his head. Once she got on this it was going to be hell stopping her. Rosaland got up and gave Dr. Ekouevi a hug "I'll see you in the morning bright and early." She said putting emphasis on bright and early. "How bright? And how early?" The good doctor asked. "Make sure that you are here by nine." "We'll do. O.k. you two have a good evening." Dr. Ekouevi shook Bobby's hand and was out the door.

"What's for dinner?" Bobby looked famished. "What time is it? I have been so caught up with this case I lost track of time. Oh sweetie I didn't cook anything." Rosaland felt guilty as she looked at the clock. "It's o.k. I was waiting but would you care to go out this evening?" Rosaland smiled "I would love too." "O.k. so finish up here and get dressed." "Where are we going?" "I'll think of somewhere nice even though you did forget my dinner." Bobby said sarcastically.

"Rosaland do I have to remind you that this is official N.Y.P.D. business?" "No you don't. I know that at a time like this both agencies need to join forces." Bobby knew what was coming and to be quite honest he wasn't ready. He didn't want her to go back to work. Not so soon. He knew that she would literally turn into a madwoman with this obsession with Calderon.

"Baby why don't you wear this one?" Bobby selected one of her sexiest black dresses. "This one is too dressy. What about this one?" She protested holding up another. "I like this one." He said firmly. "O.k. where are we going?" "It's a surprise." "Good I like surprises."

While Rosaland slid into her underwear fresh from the shower she noticed Bobby on the phone. "Please make sure that my table is ready. This is a very special night for us. It's the first time we have been out since the explosion. This is what I want…" Rosaland could hear Bobby barking orders but she couldn't hear the specifics.

"I wonder where he's taking me." Rosaland thought to herself as she continued to get dressed. "Come on baby hurry up. We are going to be late" Bobby screamed once he was ready. When Rosaland entered the room Bobby's heart stopped and his knees went weak. She was absolutely gorgeous. It had been a while since Bobby had seen her look so radiant. "You look beautiful" he whispered sexily in her ear. "So do you" Rosaland replied as she snuggled close to his hot hard body. "Don't start something you can't finish" Bobby teased. "Oh I can finish it" Rosaland snickered as they left the brownstone. Bobby reached into his shirt pocket and noticed that he had forgotten something. "I'll be right back."

Once they were on the road Rosaland asked him again "Where are we going?" "You'll see" he grinned. It was then that she recognized the exit as they headed on to the Brooklyn Queens Expressway. Rosaland started smiling. It had been a while since she had been to the restaurant in Brooklyn. It would be nice to see Papa. She settled back and enjoyed the ride holding tightly on to Bobby's hand.

That evening the restaurant was enchanting. Papa had gone above and beyond preparing for his grandson. Bobby had requested a special occasion and Papa was there to make it so. All the tables had fresh crisp linen, a lovely floral arrangement and a lit scented candle to add to the ambiance.

Papa had installed a jukebox some months ago and the air was filled with the sounds of sensual Latin American rhythms. The regular dinner crowd had been served and now the restaurant was empty. She couldn't believe that the two of them had the whole restaurant all to themselves.

Rosaland was glowing as they were seated. "Good evening Rosaland. Welcome home!" Papa spoke as he gave her a big hug and kiss. "It is so nice to have you back." "Oh Papa. It is so nice to be back. The restaurant looks great." "We have certainly missed you around here." Papa looked in Bobby's direction. "Roberto has been lost without you."

Bobby was behind the bar mixing up a batch of Rosaland's favorite drink. In the last three years she had changed her choice of drink three maybe four times. Now she was on chocolate martinis. "A toast!" Bobby announced as he walked back to the table. "Papa please join us." Papa picked up his glass and they all drank to life, love and family.

"Bobby how did you manage all of this?" Rosaland asked as she sipped her drink. "Nothing is too good for my girl. With the right cooperation its amazing what you can get done." Bobby winked as their lips met in a gentle kiss. "Come dance with me!" Bobby pulled her towards the dance floor. "I would love too" Rosaland graciously accepted as she fell gently into his powerful grasp.

Bobby held her lithe form tight pulling her close to his commanding physique. "It's been such a long time since we have been dancing" Bobby whispered voraciously in her ear as he nibbled hungrily at her lobes and the luscious nape of her neck. "Ohh Bobby" Rosaland moaned lustfully as their bodies became lost in the sensual sway of the exotic melodies.

After dinner and a few more drinks Bobby decided it was time to get down to business. "Baby, when are you planning to go back to work?" "Oh Bobby. Do we have to talk about this now? I'm having such a wonderful time and I don't want to argue. Not tonight." "It's now or never. it's up to you."

"Well I'm unofficially back to work." "Unofficially, what does that mean?" "I'm not sure. But I have to be honest with you. I am investigating the bombing. I am trying to ascertain the facts. I will be looking into it and all of this is off the record." "Well would you do me a favor before you officially go back on the record?" "Sure Baby anything." Rosaland purred.

Bobby was preparing to get down on his knees. He was a bit nervous and he felt a little out of place but he had to do this. Bobby stood up and then dropped to one knee. Rosaland's mouth opened a little in surprise as a stupefied grin came over her face. Bobby looked up at her and smiled. "I believe we have been down this road before. Let's see this time if we can make this happen. Rosaland will you marry me?"

Bobby reached in his shirt pocket pulled out her engagement ring and slipped it back on her finger. It seemed as though an eternity had passed since he first popped the question. He had the ring cleaned and polished in her absence and the diamond shone brilliantly. Her hands were still a little sore but the ring fit comfortably.

"Yes! Bobby. Oh yes!" She replied as the tears filled her eyes. Rosaland wrapped her arms around Bobby's neck as he whirled her around the room. "Yes!" She shouted over and over again in a state of euphoria placing tiny loving kisses all over his face.

"Papa we are finally going to get married!!" Bobby shouted to his grandfather across the restaurant. "Rosaland is finally going to let me make an honest woman out of her." Rosaland smiled and shouted with glee. Papa came out of the kitchen holding a bottle of the restaurant's finest champagne.

"Well it's about time you two!" He shouted while he filled the glasses with the ice cold bubbly. "Come let's toast!!" Papa responded raising his glass in the air "To my grandson Roberto and his lovely fiancé Rosaland. May God bless this union!" "I'll drink to that!"Bobby remarked and Rosaland echoed "Here, Here!!" The three of them hugged each other in happiness.

"Rosaland I want a date!" Bobby demanded loudly in front of Papa. "And I have a witness." Bobby looked sternly in her direction. "Give me a date!" "Bobby tomorrow. We can set the date tomorrow." The drinks and all the excitement was going to her head. "Rosaland I want a date tonight. Promise me that we will tie the knot before you officially go back to work." "I promise Bobby. I give you my word." "O.k. call your family and make the announcement; I want them off my case." Bobby kidded.

Later that evening as Bobby and Rosaland lay talking in bed; Rosaland asked Bobby again "Where did you find the time to do this? It was so incredible." Rosaland was looking at the blinding stone on her finger. "Well Baby to be honest, when I saw you and Dr. Ekouevi I knew that if I didn't get a commitment now, I would never get a commitment."

"Bobby that's not true." "Rosaland you have been home for months and you haven't even mentioned marriage. Get the calendar and give me a date." As Bobby thought about it he continued. "You know I want to do something special. I want our ceremony to have a special meaning. I almost lost you once and I want to thank God for giving me a second chance."

Bobby's train of thought intrigued Rosaland. "Special meaning so what's on your mind detective?" She asked waiting for Bobby to share his innermost thoughts.

"Lately I have been thinking about Abuelita. She has visited me twice since your accident." Rosaland was quiet as she listened to Bobby tell his tales. "This is the second dream I have had about her in the last six months and I feel that she is trying to tell me something." "What?" "I don't know and normally I wouldn't believe in this sort of thing but this feeling is too strong to ignore. I can't kick it."

"What feeling?" "I would like her to be a part of our ceremony. I would like to honor her and Papa by getting married in her native church." "What?"

Rosaland was at a loss for words. She had never seen Bobby so sentimental. "Her native church? Bobby where might that be?" "The Church of the Holy Spirit. Iglesia del Espirito Santo de Belize."

Rosaland's mouth flew open in complete surprise. "You want to get married in Belize?" "Yes in my grandmother's presence. This would mean so much to her and to me." "Does Papa know about this?" "No not yet. I couldn't tell him until I knew what you would say; after all you are the bride." "Wow. How romantic. I would love to get married in Belize. How can we arrange that from here? Somebody would need to be there…" In Rosaland's mind she was already there.

"My mother took us to Belize once. When we were little kids shortly before her death. It's a lovely island. We were in the Cayo District. That is where we learned to speak Spanish. My mother used to love it there. It was one of her best-kept secrets. I remember this one church we always went to. We were there for a couple of months and we visited this church everyday. It sat in the middle of the city. It was as though God just dropped it there. It was an old white church with the most incredible stain glass windows. I remember how peaceful the rectory felt. I used to love to sit there and look at the windows."

"I can't believe this" Bobby said completely amazed. "That's the same church. That's Abuelita's church. It sits right in the middle of La Plaza Calderon or as the gringos say Calderon Square."

"This is phenomenal. Out of all the countries and churches in Central America; you have been to La Plaza Calderon. Either this is a freaky coincidence or it a definite sign that this is meant to be. Either way I'm hooked. So what do you say?"

Rosaland always felt so defenseless when Bobby gave her that special look. "I would love to marry you in Belize Bobby. I would be honored. It would have special meaning for my family as well. My mother, may she rest in peace really loved it there." Bobby got up and walked over to the stereo. He sorted through his collection before he remembered where he had put his latest acquisition.

"I bought something for you today." He mentioned as he changed the CD. "I hope you like it." Bobby vocalized creating a sensual atmosphere in an already sexy room. He glanced over at her half nude body as she languished generously on the bed.

"You know Rosaland ever since you were released from the hospital I feel so guilty when I am with you like this. I guess your Father has finally gotten to me." He then proceeded to light the scented candles as he removed his shirt. "Its o.k. sweetie. He gets to everybody." Instantly the sultry sounds of the soulful Anita Baker filled the room. "Nice" Rosaland murmured as she held out her arms in open invitation.

"O.k. Baby give me a date." Bobby demanded tenderly as he ran his hands along her curvaceous figure while applying sweet kisses to her moist succulent lips. "Ohh Bobby" she gasps deliciously as he dropped his pants. Rosaland loved to watch Bobby undress. His body was so strong, so powerful and so muscular. One hundred percent man; a real hard body.

"Give me a date" Bobby whispered again his desire bubbling over. "Make an honest man out of me." He teased as he found himself on top of her. Rosaland's body was trembling in anticipation. Bobby loved the feel of her skin next to his. He also loved her sweet chocolate covering. Her body was so soft and so smooth and yet so strong. He could lay in her arms forever.

"Turn over" Bobby instructed as he began to explore her delightful offerings. "Ohh Bobby..." She squealed as he started using his tongue like a deadly weapon in her hot heaving cave. "You like that?" Bobby moaned in between his luscious slurps. "Yes Bobby!" "You like that?" "Yes Bobby" Rosaland was on the verge of tears. "I know what you need." He insisted as he prepared her for his ultimate invasion.

"Feel this" he said lustfully as he placed her delicate hand on his massive intruder. It was hot in its head. Rosaland could feel the electrifying heat that arose from his hard throbbing girthy shaft. Bobby was breathing hard and his heart was racing. He knew that it was nothing more than the incredible charms of his chocolate enchantress that left him so breathless.

Rosaland clutched and grasp at him with both hands digging her nails into his flesh. Her nails raked across his ears and back. Bobby knew that it was time to take her. Rosaland's body trembled spasmodically. She became unhinged for seconds at a time then whimpered and caught her breath before feeling another surge of passion during which she would grab him tightly, literally crushing herself against him. "Ohh Baby uhhh you take my breath away!" Bobby moaned as the lights went out and they both gave in to sweet surrender.

seventy-nine

"Rachael can you believe it?" Rosaland was screaming excitedly in the phone to her sister. "We are getting married in Belize!!" Rachael was at a loss for words "In Belize? How exciting? How beautiful? Why Belize?" Rachael inquired trying to make some sense out of this whole thing. She had never heard Rosaland so excited.

"This is all Bobby's idea. Abuelita was born in Belize and Bobby wants to get married in her native church. Iglesia Del Espirito Santo. "Why does that sound so familiar to me? Rosaland how are we going to plan a wedding in Belize? Did you tell Dad?" Rachael always shot a million questions.

"I guess either we go there or we can do it over the internet. I don't know but we need to get started. All the basics we can do right here. And yes I spoke to Dad and he is just as excited as I am." "Dad is excited about going to Belize?" "Not exactly. He doesn't know the Belize part yet. I thought I would ease that on him. But he does know about the wedding." "Rosaland you know Dad does not like Central America. You know he has a thing about going there. How are you going to justify that?"

"Rachael this is my wedding. Bobby wants to get married in his grandmother's church. Dad will just have to bite the bullet on this one." "Rosaland you obviously have lost your mind. Dad is not going to bite the bullet on this. Are you serious?" "Rachael just work with me. I can handle Dad." "Rosaland we lost our mother on a flight from Central America and now you expect Dad to just trot right on down to Belize because you say so?"

"No Rachael not because I say so. I'm getting married and he has to be there. You said it yourself he has been treating Bobby like shit for the last six months and now it's time to stop. Dad wants us to get married so we are getting married. Why does it matter where it is?" "Rosaland you know when it comes to Bobby you really lose your mind. Is the dick that good?" "Oh yeah. Even better." They both burst into laughter.

"O.k. sweetie. Let's start with the guess list and after that we have to find an airline that will give us a group rate on flights. We need to include all of this information when we send out the invitations." Rachael was busy writing down her list of things to do when the phone rang. "Rachael let me talk to your sister!" the General barked. Rachael handed Rosaland the phone. She could tell by the sound of her Father's voice that this wasn't going to be pleasant.

"Rosaland what's this I hear about Belize?" The General asked in a fatherly tone. "Hi Dad. How are you today?' she replied trying to diffuse the situation. "Bobby wants to be married in Belize." "Why Belize?" "His Grandmother was married there and he wants to honor her memory." "Under international law a marriage there is only legally binding there. It will not be recognized in the United States. But of course your sister should have told you that."

Rosaland looked at Rachael who was busy jotting down some notes of her own. "Oh by the way Rosaland, a marriage in Belize is not legally binding in the U.S." Rachael recanted not realizing that her father was saying the same thing on the other end of the line. "You and Bobby will have to marry here first; a simple civil ceremony and then you can have the religious ceremony in Belize in order to be legal." Rachael smiled as she continued writing.

Then all hell broke loose. "Rosaland you know I have certain feelings about Central America and you know why. I lost my wife, your mother there. How could you agree to this?" Her Dad hissed. "Dad I'm sorry. I wasn't thinking. I was just so taken away with the idea of such an exotic setting for my wedding. I thought that Mom would like it."

Rosaland's last statement completely disarmed the General. It left him at a lost for words. The General's tone totally changed. "Do you know how hard it is going to be to arrange security for you down there? And your guest list, who's on this list? And how many people do you think will really fly to Belize for a wedding?"

"I know this is going to take a lot of work to pull this off. Dad it's what I want. Bobby and I are finally getting married." "Ok, Ok. I'll make some calls, send out some scouts and arrange for a security detail. Work out your particulars and get back to me. I need details every step of the way and I'll do what I can do."

"I love you Dad." "Yeah, yeah. I have heard that before." The General shook his head and hung up the phone. "I swear Rosaland; you can get away with anything with Dad." Rachael commented jealously as the girls went to work on the wedding preparations.

The next three weeks were a madhouse as Rosaland and Rachael rushed around Manhattan trying to coordinate her big event. There was the dress, which she had to have designed, the invitations that had to been hand addressed and a thousand more details that had to be perfect.

She remembered how much planning and time that had gone into Rachael's wedding and now she was in the situation of trying to prepare her own wedding on the same scale in half the time. The pressure was mounting and the time was flying by.

Bobby was in just as much turmoil as he and Papa made numerous calls back and forth to the country trying to coordinate the honeymoon. Bobby had a special surprise planned for his bride and he wasn't going to tell her until the actual day of the event. He was also working hand in hand with the General to make sure that security was tight and that the family would be safe.

Papa used all his connections to make sure that Bobby would be accommodated. It had been many years since he had been to Belize and this wedding was just as exciting for him as it was for his grandson. It would be nice to be back in the old country again.

Abuelita would be so proud of the both of them. But there was something troubling Papa. There was a conversation that he and Bobby needed to have and he didn't quite know how to bring it up. Abuelita had begged Papa before her untimely death to tell Bobby the secret of his past. She had always felt that he deserved to know who he was and where he came from. Papa felt deep in his heart with all the transition going on that now was the time.

"Roberto come and have some wine with me." Papa requested after they were alone. Bobby knew his grandfather and he knew that whenever he made a request for wine that there was something on his mind.

"What is troubling you Papa? What is on your mind? Talk to me." Bobby inquired escorting Papa to the deck. "Let's sit outside and talk. It's a nice evening and it has been a while since we spent some real time together." Papa nodded and followed his grandson upstairs and out to the deck.

Bobby placed the bottle of wine and the two glasses on the table and took a seat. "Now what's on your mind? Talk to me. Let me help." Bobby encouraged his Grandfather to share his thoughts. Papa took a sip of the wine and Bobby noticed that his hands were trembling. What could have his Grandfather so shaken up? Bobby wondered as he sipped his wine and waited for him to speak.

"Bobby I am so proud of you." Papa started out. "It's amazing how time flies." He laughed. "I remember when you were knee high to a grasshopper and now look at you. The lead detective with the N.Y.P.D. who is about to be married. Where did the time go?" Bobby continued to wait to see where this was going.

"Your Grandmother would be proud too. You know she really loved Rosaland. She always felt that you made a good choice with her. At first she wasn't so sure, the different ethnic backgrounds and all, but when she saw how much the two of you loved each other. She was certain that you made the right decision." Bobby listened as his Grandfather stalled for time.

"There has been something that I have wanted to talk to you about for years. Your grandmother wanted me to tell you this several years ago way before her death. She wanted you to hear this from the both of us. But the time never seemed right."

"And the time is right now?" Bobby raised his eyebrow. "I've put this off too long." Bobby could see that his Grandfather was visibly shaken and now his curiosity was bubbling over. "Put what off too long?" Bobby asked about ready to explode. "What Papa. What is it?" "It's about your birth. Your heritage." Now Papa had Bobby's full attention.

"My birth? What are you talking about?" Bobby was completely puzzled. "I was born in Brooklyn?" Bobby chirped. "No Bobby you were raised in Brooklyn?" Now Bobby was really interested. "What are you talking about Papa? Spit it out." The investigator in him totally taking control.

"Roberto please don't be upset with us. But everything we did we did it out of love for you. We should have told you how you came to us a long time ago." "How I came to you?" At this point Bobby decided to just listen. No more comments. He could see that this was really very hard for his Grandfather.

"The isle of Calderon is located in Central America somewhere close to Guatemala. It borders Belize and Guatemala. The exact location is unknown. There has always been some myth that surrounds its actual existence. It's some sort of mystery. We believe that is where you were born."

Bobby listened intently as his Grandfather proceeded. "We believe that because of the stones that we found attached to your clothing when we got you? The isle is famous for the mining of a precious gemstone known throughout the world as the stone of Calderon. Your grandmother use to wear one on her ring finger. Do you remember it? She got that stone from you. I had it made into a ring for her."

"On your arm you wear a royal crest. Yes Bobby that is a family crest. It is the officially crest of the royal family of the Island of Calderon. It is only worn by the rightful heirs to the throne and the Calderon fortune. And that is you and your brother. I know that all your life you have been wondering about your "birthmark."

We had the crest traced many years ago. We used an investigator from the old country. The one that had originally worked for your father. Apparently your Father had been looking for you since your birth. That is when we discovered your tragic past and who you really were."

Bobby sat silently as he listened to Papa reveal this unbelievable tale of destiny. "It took us a while before we believed what the investigator had told us. He was a really old man and we thought that maybe his memory was not so good but we knew that his words were true."

"The story had been out for years on the island about the missing Calderon heir. The identical twin son that had been smuggled out of the country to save his life. That son was you. You are an urban legend." At this point Bobby interrupted. He could no longer sustain his silence. "You know my father? You know who my real father is?" Bobby was shouting at his poor defenseless grandfather. "Yes Roberto. I have known for years."

Papa hung his head in shame. "And it has taken you thirty six years to tell me? Papa do you know the whole story?" "Yes Bobby" "Then you have to tell me. You have to tell me everything. I have waited to know this all my life." "Bobby please don't be angry with me, with us. We loved you and we wanted to keep you safe. You were the only Grandchild that we had. You came to us so late in life. Long after we had given up all hope of ever having a child of our own to love and care for. I couldn't take you away from Abuelita once you were here. It would have broken her heart. It would have killed her."

"Please try to understand." Papa was pleading with his Grandson. "Its o.k. Papa just talk to me. Please tell me everything." Papa's old form was shaking profusely. Bobby had never seen him so nervous or look so aged. Bobby walked over and gave him a gentle hug. One that let Papa know that no matter what they discussed today Bobby would always love him and care for him. No matter what they were still family.

As Papa sat there he could feel the spirit of his dear sweet Abuelita fill the room. "Tell him" the voice whispered innocently in the air. "He is a grown man now it will be all right. He will understand." Papa took comfort as the breeze flowed gently through the room. Bobby could feel the cold air as it circulated around Papa. He knew that there was something special going on in the room but he did not dare to guess what.

Papa waited for Bobby to take his seat. "I need a drink" Bobby declared as he placed the bottle on the table in front of them. "Continue" he ordered his Grandfather as he poured both of them a fresh glass of wine.

"Bobby Abuelita was over fifty years old when we got you. That was one of the reasons it was so hard for us to let you go. My brother Manuel was your mother's great uncle. Your mother was a young servant girl named Elana who worked for Jorge Calderon. Mr. Calderon had a real liking for her."

"He watched her for many years as she grew and matured. That is why he kept her in the house so he could make sure that no other man touched her. Your mother was very young and beautiful; a girl full of life and Jorge took total advantage of all of her charms. At first she worked in the house along with the other women and then later when he felt she was ready he had her transferred to the fields. He placed her in the fields so he could have complete access to her. He ravaged her everyday after that."

"They had a passionate love affair. Rumors started to circulate around the island about the young little peasant girl who had stole the great Mr. Calderon's heart. After she became pregnant he built her a house on the outskirts of his hacienda so that he could watch her and also so that he could be present at the birth."

"Mrs. Calderon, Jorge's wife was very much aware of the carrying on's of her husband and she became very hateful and jealous of the relationship shared between her husband and this dirty little field whore." She swore to get revenge on the young slut who now shared her husband's bed. No disrespect to Elana.

"When Mrs. Calderon found out that Elana (your mother's name was Elana) was pregnant she became enraged. Papa was old and he was repeating himself. There was no way that she could allow this girl to be the mother to the heir of the throne. She had tried for many years but she could not have children of her own."

"She thought that Jorge would replace her. Divorce her but he never did. He allowed her to remain the lady of the house but his attentions strayed elsewhere in other directions. Once Jorge became involved with Elana he refused to touch his wife. He never touched her again. Mrs. Calderon could not live with this so she took deadly revenge."

"She hired a band of renegades to kill Elana and the unborn baby when the time was right. She knew that she would have to be cunning and shrewd if she were going to get away with it. She knew that Jorge would take revenge on the person or persons responsible for the death of his lover and his seed. But Mrs. Calderon was so blinded by jealousy and envy that it did not matter."

"She was intent of their destruction. She wanted her husband's affections back and she was willing to commit murder to do it." The story goes that Calderon was completely taken with Elana. Once he had her house built he moved her mother in with her so she could take care of her while she was with child. He visited with them often making sure that the two of them had a comfortable life and what they needed. He truly did love her. He gave her everything in his power except his hand in marriage."

"Elana sent a messenger to the hacienda the night before to give Jorge the news of the impending birth. When he arrived the next evening it was just in time to see the first son slide down the birth canal and then the second. It was twin boys. Jorge was elated. He had waited all these years and now he had fathered a set of twin boys. The true heirs to the Calderon fortune."

"Jorge stayed with his new family for the next two weeks bragging and lording over his offspring. When Mrs. Calderon got the news of the twins poor Elana's fate was sealed." "It was Calderon himself who performed the crest ceremony. A tradition that had been passed along from generation to generation of Calderon's all the rightful heirs."

"Jorge had struggled for so many years with the thought that this may never happen that his lineage would end. Jorge was already an older man and he knew that his child producing years were lost. His lovely Elana. His young, fresh, sweet Elana had made him the father of twin sons. Carlos and Roberto Calderon. He would be forever in her debt."

Papa looked at Bobby who was touching the crest on his arm as the tears rolled down his face. "How do you know all of this?"Bobby asked. "The investigator. He wrote it all up before he died. It's all documented. Times, dates, places, a copy of your birth certificate etc. We had it verified. It's authentic."

"How did you get it?" "We paid for it." "So Jorge Calderon is my father and Carlos Calderon is my twin brother?" "Yes as incredible as it all sounds. It's the truth." "The man that I have been tracking for the last how many years? The man that blew up the hotel in Bolivia? The man that bombed the N.Y.P.D. killed my baby and almost killed my girl is my twin brother?" Papa was in a state of disbelief. This was the first he heard about the baby.

Bobby was in a state of shock as he asked these questions out loud. He was experiencing a plethora of emotions. Everything from shock to outrage to hurt to anger. He sat down and took another hefty drink. "What happened to my mother?" He looked firmly in Papa's tear clouded eyes. "It's all in the report Bobby; you can read it when you are ready." "No please continue; tell me I'm ready."

"About three months later Mrs. Calderon found out that Jorge had to leave the island on business. He had been spending every waking moment with Elana and her sons since the birth. Everyone on the island knew about you boys. As a matter of fact Jorge was planning a big celebration to show you both off to the world. Rumor was that Elana was pregnant again. Mrs. Calderon knew that Jorge would be gone for about three days and this would give her the time to set the renegades on Elana and her boys."

"As luck would have it Jorge had cut short his business and was making his way back to Elana. That night as he approached he could hear men laughing and shouting. He also heard the shrill screams of a woman. The screams came from so far off in the distance that he didn't pay much attention to them until he got closer to the house and he could hear a baby crying."

"He immediately recognized the sound of his son's voice. He didn't know which one it was but he knew the voice belonged to one of them. As the baby's cries became louder and louder Jorge was frozen with the terrible thoughts as to what could have happened. He immediately drew out his guns and jumped from the car.

His men scattered as they surrounded the house. All Jorge could hear was the sound of his baby crying. He followed the voice to find a burly bearded man holding his son. Jorge snuck up on the man from behind and placed the barrel of his gun into his temple." "Where is my family?" Jorge demanded as the man went white. His whole body was trembling in fear as Jorge pulled back the trigger. "Where is my family?" Jorge demanded again as he removed his son from the arms of this bandit.

"Mr. Calderon you had better come look at this..." one of his men said as he led Jorge into the bedroom where Elana lay half naked, strangled, raped and murdered. She had been beaten profusely around the face and head and her clothes had been torn from here body. Her legs had been pried open and there was a trail of blood from her private area."

"He could see the bruises on her arms, her back and her stomach and the finger marks on her neck. Her mother was in the other room on the floor. Raped and murdered in the same manner. Jorge screamed out in pain when he saw his beloved. He cried out in agony as he sat beside her on the bloody bed."

"Who would do such a terrible thing as this to my family?" He yelled frantically as he hit the bandit with his gun in the face. "Couldn't you see that she was with child again?" The scared man hit the floor hard blood gushing profusely from his mouth. They were never supposed to get caught.

"Where is my other son?" He shouted "Where is my son?" At this point Jorge had lost all rational thinking. He was out of control with grief. He had placed the baby in the arms of one of his generals as he began to beat the bandit unmercifully.

Jorge was in a rage. He did everything in his power to cause the desperados the most excruciating pain ever. They would definitely be punished. Not only would they suffer but their families would suffer as well. "Where is my other son?" He screamed as he kicked the life out of the man. "Where is my son?" At this point Jorge stopped his brutal beating of this intruder. "By the time I get finished with you, you will wish that you were dead. Who sent you here? Which one of my enemies sent you to destroy my family? Where is my son?"

Jorge picked the half dead man up and tied him to a stake. He ordered his generals to fill a caldron full of water and let it start to boil. The whole time he was sharpening a large butcher knife that was used for the dismembering of cows. "By the time I am finished with you, you will be dying to tell me what you know."

Calderon screamed, this time with much more venom than before. "Who would pay you to do such a thing? Don't you know who I am? I am Jorge Calderon!! How dare you invade my land!! My family!! And my island like this!!"

Jorge had gone mad with grief as he proceeded to skin the man alive. "Now tell me who paid you?" As the man refused to answer Jorge took another slice out of his skin.

"Mr. Calderon we caught another one." Jorge's general reported as he threw another bloody pummeled man into the middle of the floor. "Where is my son?" Jorge demanded in a vicious tone as he shot the other renegade in the knee. "I have had quite enough of this. You will talk." He shouted loudly as he shot him again in the arm. "Where is my son?"

"Por favor!! Mr. Calderon. No mas!!!" The man begged for his life "We had no idea that this was your residence or in any way connected to you!! The lady who paid us never told us about you. She told us to kill the girl and the children. She never mentioned you!!"

"So you invade my home, rape and murder my woman and steal my children?" Calderon asked in a complete tirade but it was much too late for regrets. Elana and her mother were dead and one of the twin boys was missing. The die had been cast."

"That night was the most brutal event that had ever taken place on the island. The crusade was so bloody and so vicious that it was burned into the island's tumultuous history along with Elana her mother and all of her memories. Jorge searched long and hard that night trying to find any trace of his missing baby boy. He called for a massive island wide manhunt.

The troops scoured the land back and forth but there was no baby to be found. Frustrated and full of sorrow after burying Elana and her mother Jorge set the whole area on fire and watched with tearful eyes as it burned to the ground."

For the next twelve months Jorge sought out all the relatives and friends of the two bandits and viciously murdered them. He murdered women and children; he wiped out every living relations, whole towns and villages, anything or anybody that had a connection with the death of Elana and her son.

He never forgot what the dying man had said about the woman. That thought haunted him for years to come. Who was this woman? Even though deep down he knew the answer he just couldn't bring himself to face it. But the most important task was to find the woman that set this up. Somebody knew who she was and somebody was going to tell him."

"Did he ever find out who set them up?" "Yes it was his wife." "What ever happened to her?" "She mysteriously disappeared. Never to be seen or heard from again."

"Bobby Jorge continued looking for you until his death. That is when all the inquires stopped." "When did my father die?" "He died in 1967 in a plane crash." "I was nine years old." Bobby picked up his glass and poured another powerful shot of liquor down his throat.

"Papa I still don't understand. How did I get separated from Carlos?" "Your mother was trying to get both of you out of the house. She was young and she was scared. She grabbed some jewels and ran to the window screaming for help. She was trying to dress two baby boys and herself. Manuel heard her screaming and came to help her."

"By the time she handed you out of the window the bandits were upon her and snatched her back in with Carlos still in her arms. That was the last time that Manuel saw her. He remembered her begging and pleading for the life of her son and then he heard some shots and he started to run for safety."

"As a matter of fact he took a bullet in the arm as he escaped into the woods with you." "Manuel had been critically wounded but he made it as far as Guatemala with you. He called me from there and told me that he was sending a package to America and that I should guard it with my life.

"I promised him that I would meet him in New York. He had to deliver you because he couldn't put a small baby on a ship alone so he braved the journey to bring you here." "When the ship arrived Manuel was dead and the authorities handed you over to me and we have had you ever since. Bobby was amazed. What an incredible story. Who would believe such a tale? Who would believe that he is a Calderon? A true Calderon?"

Bobby sat in the kitchen with the bottle dangling from his hands. He was certainly on his way to a major bender. He ran his finger over his crest. His power center. That's what he had called it all these years and now he knew why. He was a Calderon. All he could think about was Rosaland and how was she going to take all of this?"

He knew that he had to tell her but how and when was another story. Was she ready for this? She had just recovered from a major set back caused directly by Carlos Calderon. How is she going to react knowing that he is Bobby's brother? His identical twin brother? So many questions and so little answers. Bobby didn't know which way to go.

Bobby sat as still as a drunken statue while Papa finished up the story. He was in a complete state of shock and disbelief. "Papa you wait three weeks before I am going to get married to tell me this?" Bobby was outraged as he put his fist through the wall. Papa was quiet.

At this juncture the phone rang; Bobby in his drunken stupor picked it up. "Hello?" "Bobby?" "Yes, hello?" "Baby, where are you?" "I'm here. Where should I be?" "Are you serious? You should be picking me up from midtown?" "Oh Shit, Baby I completely forgot. Papa is filling me in on some life shattering events. He chose tonight of all nights to tell me about my past. Can you make it home and I will pick you up tomorrow?"

"Sure. Are you alright?" Rosaland was really starting to worry. "I guess I am alright. Ask my Papa." Bobby looked at Papa who looked away. "Bobby what is going on? Have you been drinking? Are you drunk?" "The answer is yes to both questions. Yes I have been drinking and yes I am drunk."

"I'm coming over" Rosaland insisted. "No not tonight. I have some things to work out. This is not going to be a good time. I'll see you tomorrow." And with that last comment Bobby hung up the phone.

eighty

Rosaland was confused; she didn't at all like the sarcastic tone she detected in Bobby's voice. What was his grandfather telling him about his past? What past? And the fact that he was drunk was also disturbing to her. What was he doing drunk when he was supposed to be picking her up? How could he just leave her in midtown? This was not at all like Bobby. She was going to Brooklyn to find out what was going on. Rosaland called back hoping that a different Bobby would answer the phone.

"Bobby?" "Yes Baby?" "Bobby what the hell is going on?" "Some unfinished business between me and my Grandfather." "Should I be worried?" "Why are you worried? This has nothing to do with you?" "O.k. I'm coming over so we can talk. "No Baby not tonight. Why don't you go to your sisters?" "I have a home; I can go to my own house. If you don't want to see me just say you don't want to see me. Don't tell me where to go." "O.k. I don't want to see you." Bobby slammed down the phone again. Rosaland was stunned. She had never heard Bobby so rude.

He had never been that ill tempered with her before. But he had made it perfectly clear that he did not want to see her tonight and she wouldn't press the issue. Her feelings were already hurt so she decided to let it be. She wouldn't give him another opportunity to hurt her some more. One of them might say something that they would later regret and it was three weeks before the wedding. All she knew was that what ever he and his grandfather was discussing certainly had him in a foul mood and all she hoped was that it did not affect her wedding.

Rosaland strolled along 57th street lost in her thoughts of Bobby. She wondered what could be so important but she decided not to give it another thought. Whatever it was they would work it out tomorrow. She would give him the benefit of the doubt even though he had hung up on her twice.

57th street was a unique shopping district because it housed so much. The street was lined with bridal shops, bridal boutiques and baby stores. Funny how they made that connection. Rosaland had some time to kill so she decided to go window shopping while she waited for Rachael. There was always some last minute something that she could pick up and she didn't want to forget anything. She browsed leisurely checking out shoes, purses, gloves and other accessories for her special day.

Out of the corner of her eye Rosaland thought she recognized the woman who had just brushed past her. She looked around to notice a head full of black curly hair. Rosaland thought the woman reminded her of detective Diana Rousseau but this woman was nine months pregnant. It looked as though she was ready to give birth any day now.

Rosaland looked in her general direction and then shrugged it off. No one had told her that Diana was pregnant; as a matter of fact the last she heard Diana had transferred from the N.Y.P.D. right after the explosion. The last report the squad had was that she was still having problems dealing with the death of her partner.

That was why she left the unit; this woman couldn't possibly be her. Detective Rousseau was no longer living in New York. Rosaland back tracked to make sure that her eyes were not playing tricks on her. She glanced through the window but her vision was blurred. She couldn't tell if it was Diana or not and she definitely wasn't going to expose herself and go in.

The woman looked liked Diana but Rosaland couldn't tell for sure. Woe be it for her to start a rumor that wasn't true. Diana pregnant? The first person Rosaland thought about was Bobby. That was Diana's one true love. If Bobby had been messing around while she was in the hospital she would know. Somebody would have told her by now.

Somebody always knows and somebody always tells. But what if it was Diana. What would she say? They had never been the best of friends so Rosaland decided that it was in her best interest to leave it alone. Rosaland walked a few more blocks and then decided to go see for herself.

Her curiosity had gotten the better of her so she walked backed to the baby store and prepared to confront the woman whom she thought to be Diana. When she entered she noticed that the baby store was empty. "Can I help you?" The sales person called out from behind the curtains. "Well actually I was looking for someone. Your last customer was her name Diana Rousseau?"

"Who wants to know?" "An old friend. We used to work together." Rosaland smiled "She didn't give me her name. The other woman was the customer." The saleswoman replied "but her friend called her Kim." "Kim?" "Yes the one having the baby her name is Kim. Is that your friend?"

"No I thought she was someone else. Thanks" Rosaland replied briefly as she left the store. "Well that certainly wasn't Diana" Rosaland thought to herself relieved. "Poor Bobby I blame him for everything." She laughed as she shook her head feeling a bit foolish.

It had been three days since Rosaland heard from Bobby. She was really beginning to worry that something was going terribly wrong. The clock was ticking and they were scheduled to leave for Belize in less than two weeks. Now was not the time for him to pull a disappearing act. Whatever business he needed to clear up between he and his Grandfather now was the time to get it done.

Bobby didn't know how he was going to explain this to Rosaland. But he knew that he needed to tell her and he wanted to share this with her now. He was a Calderon!! A direct heir to the Calderon fortune and a direct descendant from the Calderon lineage. This whole situation had Bobby's head so messed up. Exactly how was Rosaland supposed to process this?"

How could she marry a man that was a direct descendant from the sworn enemy of her father? The General had a vendetta against Jorge Calderon. A hatred that had lasted through two decades and now his daughter was going to marry his son? The son of his sworn enemy? Bobby knew that once the General found out the secret of his past that he would never allow that to happen. Their marriage would never take place under these circumstances.

"Baby I really need to talk to you" Bobby pleaded with Rosaland over the phone. "Bobby I haven't seen or heard from you in three days. What the hell is going on?" She snapped sharply back into the phone. "Do you want to talk to me and find out or are you going to make this hard?" Bobby was trying to keep his cool and not lose his patience with her but sometimes Rosaland could be so headstrong and so difficult. "Make what hard?" She retorted "Are you trying to break up with me?" Bobby knew that she would go there.

"Rosaland can't you just accept the fact that I need to talk to you and it is extremely important?" "Yes Bobby but I'm scared. You have been acting strange lately and there is something going on. I'm not sure that I like it. Actually I feel threatened and unsure and I don't like that at all."

"It's going to be alright? We are going to be alright but we desperately need to talk." "All I want to know is that we are getting married. Are we getting married Bobby?" "Yes" "Then everything is alright?" "Everything between us is alright." "Where do you want me to meet you?" Rosaland asked. "I'll see you tonight. Wait up for me." Bobby hesitated.

"Oh I actually get to see you tonight? How did I get to be so lucky?" She said sarcastically "Keep it up and you will be walking down the aisle alone. How's that for lucky?" Rosaland was quiet. She knew for some reason that he was serious. "That's better. I'll see you tonight."

Rosaland waited for hours for Bobby to arrive. She called his cell phone frequently only to receive no answer. At this point she was frantic. She had no idea what was going on and she was not happy. There was a nagging feeling in the pit of her stomach so she decided to take a ride to Brooklyn. She had waited long enough and now she needed to find him and find out what the hell was going on.

When Rosaland arrived she was surprised to find that the restaurant was closed. That was not a good sign. The lights were out and the door was locked. The place was completely dark. She was really starting to get nervous as she walked around to the back of the building.

She felt relieved when she noticed that the lights were on in the kitchen. She looked around to find Papa sitting quietly in the corner. He was gazing out into space as though he was totally preoccupied. So preoccupied that he did not hear her knocking on the door. "Papa" Rosaland shouted as she knocked harder trying to get his attention. "Papa, Papa" she screamed while she continued to bang on the door. At last she got his attention. It must have taken 15 or 20 minutes for Papa to finally open the door.

"Papa is everything alright? Where is your head? Why is your brain in the clouds? What is going on? Where is Bobby?" Rosaland yelled at the elderly gentleman. "Calm down Rosaland. Catch your breath. What are you doing here?" Papa asked trying to settle her down. "Where is Bobby?" She demanded. "What the hell has been going on around here? Why is the restaurant closed? Why is this place so dark? And where the hell is Bobby?" At this point she was screaming and on the verge of tears. Bobby could hear all the commotion that was going on downstairs in the kitchen and he recognized her voice. He knew that it would only be a matter of time before she showed up.

He knew better than to stand her up but everything was spinning out of control. He stumbled down the stairs half dressed in a drunken stupor. "Baby" Bobby threw out his arms "What are you doing here?" He asked flippantly in his intoxicated state. "What am I doing here? Why are you still here? You should be uptown talking to me. Bobby are you drunk?" Rosaland was furious. "Somebody is going to tell me what the hell is going on around here!! Bobby have you been drinking for three days? The last time I talked to you, you were drunk or on the verge of getting drunk. "Look at you!" She shouted "You look a mess. When is the last time you had any sleep?"

Rosaland couldn't believe that this. Whatever it was was going on so close to their wedding. What had sent Bobby over the edge? In all the years she had known him she had never seen him like this. This was not like him. Not like him at all. Bobby stumbled over to her and fell into her arms throwing her completely off balance. Rosaland tried to catch him; they both stumbled as she guided him to a chair.

"Sit down Baby" she said softly trying desperately to regain her control. She could smell the liquor on his breath. The one thing that she did not want to do was to fight with him before she knew what was up. Once she had him secured in the chair she started a fresh pot of hot coffee. "Let's get you sobered up and then maybe we can talk." Bobby sat there starring at her as she walked around half watching him and half looking for the coffee. Bobby was a little more stable now as he tried to pull it together. Rosaland stood across the room and watched silently as the coffee began to brew.

She walked over to her inebriated boyfriend and placed his head on her chest. She held him there gently afraid to ask him any more questions. She wanted to know but in his current state of mind he was extremely vulnerable. "I'm not who you think I am?" Bobby murmured under his breath his head housed in between her breasts.

"What Bobby I didn't hear you?" "I'm not who you think I am!" He repeated. "I'm not who I think I am!" He surrendered inevitably. Bobby was beginning to ramble; so Rosaland began to work on sobering him up. She poured him a hot cup of black coffee and sat there quietly as he drank it. She waited for a moment and then she poured him another.

"Drink up" she ordered while she watched him ingest the new cup. After the second cup Bobby was starting to respond. Once he finished his third cup he knew that he had to talk to her. Once she had given him the fourth cup Rosaland sat down at the table directly facing him. She looked him straight in his eyes and demanded "Talk to me Bobby. Please."

She had used the magic word and she definitely deserved to know what was going on. Bobby was still silent and his head was spinning so she began. "Bobby" she said gently as she held both of his hands. "Tell me what's happening to us." She spoke slowly and deliberately trying to get him to open up. "You have been on a three day drinking spree. You haven't been to work and you haven't been with me."

"Nobody from the squad has heard from you in days. The restaurant is closed. Papa looks as though a knife has been driven through his heart. What or who are you hiding from?"

Bobby looked at his loving partner. He knew that now was the time to come clean. If anyone could or should understand it was her. "Baby I'm sorry. I should have been more considerate but that is a little hard to do when you are having your life stripped away from you."

"What are you talking about? Who is stripping your life away?" Bobby put his head down on the table. "Baby please talk to me" Rosaland pleaded. "My grandfather decided that it was time that I knew who I really am."

"What do you mean? Who you really are?" "Who I really am? Where I come from? My background? My parents? My heritage? My lineage? And all that sort of thing." She could hear the bitterness in his voice. Rosaland didn't like the sound of this while she waited for him to continue. Bobby decided to just hit her with it. "My name is Roberto Francisco Calderon. I am the illegitimate son of Elana and Jorge Calderon. Carlos Calderon is my twin brother."

"What?" She screamed as she stumbled back. If Rosaland hadn't already been sitting down she would have collapsed from this news. "Are you serious?" She inquired but she could tell from the look on his face that he was dead serious. "But how can that be?" She stuttered "What are you talking about?" She was completely dazed and dumbfounded. "It's a long story. It's a long tragic story" he corrected himself. "And it is one that I find hard to believe. But I have the proof. I wear the proof everyday and deep down inside of me I know that it is true."

Bobby pointed to the crest on his arm. "The Crest of Calderon." All of a sudden Rosaland's body was covered with goose bumps. She remembered where she had seen that crest before. Carlos had one on his arm! In the exact same spot. She had seen it the day the O.N.S.I. captured him. She knew then what it was and that it was the same as the one that Bobby wore but she had never said a word.

"My father branded both me and my brother with his seal because we were born out of wedlock. He wanted us to know our rightful place in the world. My mother was a young servant girl who was raped and murdered shortly after we were born. Jorge Calderon's wife who was very jealous of their union set her up. We are the rightful heirs to the throne of Calderon."

"This is incredible..." Rosaland uttered as Bobby continued with his saga. Rosaland was shaking by the time Bobby finished his tale. All she could do was look at him in disbelief. "How do you know that all of this is true Bobby?" "It's all documented; Papa has had the file for years." "Where did he get a file? Who composed a file?" "He paid for it. Somehow the original investigator found us and Papa bought him off." "Why didn't he return you to your parents or your island when he found out?" "My parents? They were both dead. Actually my Father died when I was nine. So Papa and Abuelita kept me here with them. They are the only relatives that I had ever known."

"A Calderon. Wow" Rosaland repeated remembering the first time that she heard that name. "Bobby we have been chasing this man for years. We have him connected to drug dealing, arms dealing, rape and murder and that's just what we know. What are we going to do?" Bobby could hear the strain in her voice. This was all too overwhelming.

"Well I know that if your Father finds out the wedding is off." "Off!" Rosaland panicked. "What are you talking about off? The wedding can't be off. It's too late. There will be no way to cancel at this late date." "My father has made all the arrangement for security. Papa has made all the arrangements for the ceremony and the reception and we have already spent a fortune..."

"Calm down sweetie, take a deep breath. I didn't say that the wedding was off. I said that if your father finds out about this before we get married then the wedding would be off. There is no way that he will willingly let you become a Calderon."

Rosaland was in distress. She felt that her whole future was being stripped away right before her eyes. At this point the tears started falling out of control. Rosaland's body began to convulse as she welled up in pain. Bobby jumped up and grabbed her. "Bobby please. Don't do this to me. Don't do this to me." She sobbed uncontrollably. Bobby held her tightly as he tried to console her. "It's alright Baby." He said softly kissing her hair. "It's alright." "How is this alright?" She whined. "It's going to be alright." He promised. "Come on and pull yourself together honey. We can figure this out. Rosaland you have to be honest with me? Do you still love me?"

"Of course I do!" "Even after what I just told you?" "Bobby I love you. I will always love you! None of this matters to me as long as we are together." "Are you sure? Because one day when the truth comes out you might have to go against your Father for me. Can you do that?"

"My Father is a very rational man. When and if that time comes I'm sure the three of us we can work it out." Bobby took notice on how expertly she dodged the question. That night took a lot of understanding and a lot of love. Rosaland and Bobby talked for hours about his new found identity and what it meant to him.

This was one of the most incredible evenings they had ever shared as a couple. Now Bobby's curiosity was ignited. He would find out everything he could about his past. Now he wanted more than ever to be back in Belize. His wedding would have a special meaning. He was going to be married to the woman he loved in his homeland.

"When are we going to tell your Father?" Bobby asked. "We have to tell him. Rosaland. After all he has to know. He is the one who has given the orders to take down the Calderon cartel. How is he ever going to trust me again if I hold this back?

"We can tell him after the honeymoon." Rosaland joked "By that time it will be too late for him to do anything." "It won't be too late for him to shoot me." Bobby's eyebrows went up. "Yes it will. He will see how happy we are and we will be home free." Rosaland sounded so naive.

"If you say so." Bobby motioned for her to join him on the bed. "I'm sorry at the way I handled this whole thing." Bobby confessed as he snuggled close to her. "I'm really starting to pay for this bender." He complained as he grabbed his head.

"You certainly had me scared to death; I didn't know what was going on. All I could think was the worst. Are you all right? Damn Bobby that's a lot to have dropped on you all at once. Are you sure that you are alright?"

She ran her hands softly over his burly unshaven face. "I'm getting there. This is a hard pill to swallow. Papa thinks that I hate him and I don't. I can't blame them for loving me. My whole world has been turned upside down. Baby at this point you are the only thing that is real. The rest is all lies and confusion. My whole life has been one big lie."

"No Bobby you can't look at this like that. Your life has not been a lie. Maybe your name but definitely not your life. All the major accomplishments and achievements you did them. You have worked hard for your place in this world. Making sure that you didn't succumb to the street gangs or the wise guys, finishing college, joining the police force, getting through the academy, making lead detective, meeting me, nobody did that for you. You did that for yourself."

"You have brought down a lot of bad guys Bobby. You have put a lot of scumbags away. You have done a lot of good on these mean streets. You have saved a lot of lives. Don't underestimate your contributions. Baby you have earned the right to be proud of whom you are. You have so many good qualities, so many unique attributes that make you who you are. How can you doubt that? Bobby for Christ sake your father was the king of Central America. How could you not be proud of that?"

"Now if we can just figure out how to tell your Father. Rosaland really I don't want this to blow up in my face. I want to come clean with the General. This is very important. I have to handle this situation correctly with him. I can not afford to lose his trust." "We will work on the General" she winked as she started to undress.

eighty-one

The weather in Belize City was blistering. The climate was lush, tropical and extremely sensuous. Belize City was connected by the western highway to Belmopan and Santa Elena/ san Ignacio and then the Bengue Viejo Del Carmen where the wedding was to be held. They were situated right on the border of Mexico City and Guatemala. All the principal towns and villages were linked by roads that led to Belize City.

"Oh Rachael have you ever seen such a lovely place?" Rosaland shouted once they landed on the island. "Bobby look!" Rosaland pointed out several beautiful attractions from the window of the plane. Rosaland could breathe the excitement in the air. Rosaland, Rachael and Bobby went down a week early to make sure that all the arrangements were set for their upcoming nuptials. This was going to be a spectacular event. Bobby and Papa had gotten over their differences and were coordinating all the last minute preparations between phone calls.

Papa was so happy that Bobby had forgiven him. With the weight of this secret off his shoulders it set his heart at ease. He was happy that he had told him; now Abuelita could rest in peace. Rosaland was beginning to feel a bit squeamish about being so far away from home. She felt safe with Bobby but she would be much happier when her Father and the rest of the O.N.S.I. security team arrived.

The General still had no knowledge that his daughter was about to take the name of his sworn enemy and Rosaland had no idea of what Bobby had planned for their ceremony. She didn't know what name he was going to take but whatever his decision she would stand by him.

Rosaland was elated when she walked into the church. It was magnificent in all of its original splendor. Rosaland marveled at the natural wood veneers and the beautiful stain-glass windows. They were so large extending to the ceiling and the craftsmanship was extraordinary. As the sun passed through the translucent panes, the glass shone like sparkling diamonds causing the figures to appear to come to life. This was certainly a sacred place. What a perfect setting for her wedding.

"Oh my God this place is so beautiful. It's so holy. It's just as I remember only better." she commented quietly as they explored the vestry. "Do you like this church?" Bobby asked his bride to be. "I do." She said as she looked around. "Do you remember this church Rachael?" Rosaland asked looking for some sign of recognition from her sister.

"Yes I do. It is so beautiful, so ornate. Look at the natural wood in the pews, and the altar. It's as though this place was stopped in time. It's just like it was 20 years ago. Wow." "I still can't believe that this is happening." Rosaland looked at Bobby.

It's ironic just how much this union meant to her especially since she and Bobby had been carrying on such a torrid sexual affair for the past three years. This was the one time that her Father was wrong; Bobby was going to marry the cow even though he had been sampling the milk for years.

"Well it won't take much for us to decorate this place." Rachael commented after they finished their inspection. "All we need are the candles, the isle runners and the flowers and we are set. Everything else is here." It was at this moment that the priest arrived. "Are you the Semione party?" He asked Bobby as he extended his hand.

"Yes Father. I am Roberto. You can call me Bobby and this is my fiancé' Rosaland and her sister Rachael." "My name is Father Anthony. Well Bobby have we met before? You look very familiar. Is this your native island? You look like someone who might have been born here or around here."

"No Father. I have never been here before. I was born in Brooklyn." "Perhaps I know your father. I have been the Parrish priest here for many years." "No I don't think so." Bobby was beginning to feel a little uneasy. "Well it's certainly a pleasure to meet you now. Even though this is an extremely unusual circumstance. Not too many Americans book a church here in Belize for a wedding."

"Well this church holds a certain sentimental value for us." Rosaland smiled. "You must be the bride; you are such a beautiful woman. We are so happy to have you here; we will make your wedding special. It will be the most beautiful day." The priest promised as he shook her hand.

"Now if the three of you could step into my office we have some paperwork to fill out." The trio followed the priest into the back of the rectory. After the preliminary paperwork had been completed and all the questions had been asked and answered to his satisfaction Father Anthony conducted a tour of the facility carefully detailing the turbulent history of the church.

It was there in the archives that a picture of a young very prominent Jorge Calderon caught his eye. "Who is this?" Bobby asked pointing to the old worn photograph. "Oh that is a picture of our patron saint Mr. Jorge Calderon. "He was the savior of our village. Many years ago a band of renegades set loose on our island torturing and raping our women and killing our children. The renegades waited until all the men were out of the village so the women and children were unprotected. It was a horrible massacre."

"Mr. Calderon stopped the slaughter and restored the island. He donated millions of dollars to the families and the villages that had been victimized. And that of course was before his untimely death." "How did he die?" Bobby wanted to see if the information was the same. "He died in a plane crash. He was searching for his lost son."

Bobby starred long and hard at the photo and there was no denying the resemblance. He looked exactly like the image that was embedded in the paper. He had the same stature and build as the gentleman in the picture and the same serious look on his face. To Bobby it was almost like looking in a mirror. The genealogy was right, but the timing was all wrong.

Rosaland watched the expression on Bobby's face as Father Anthony finished his story. She thought she caught a glimpse of a tear in the corner of his eye. She wanted to comfort him she could feel his pain. "Rachael why don't we leave these two alone?" Rosaland suggested as she dragged her sister from the archives. Rachael was suspicious but she followed her lead. "Rosaland what is going on?" Rachael whispered. Rosaland gave her the hush sign. "Why is Bobby so emotional over that man in that old picture?" Rachael insisted.

"Rachael you have to promise me to keep this a secret?" Rachael was intrigued. "I'm asking you Rachael please under no circumstance can you tell this to dad. Please promise me?" At this point Rachael was about to burst. She was dying to know what the big secret was. "Of course, of course you have my word. Your secret is safe with me. Now what the hell is going on?" All of a sudden it didn't feel like such a good idea to be in Belize.

Rachael listened intently as Rosaland told her the awe-inspiring tale. She sat quietly and listened solemnly to all the sorted details. This was truly unbelievable."Why does the name Jorge Calderon ring a bell?" Rachael wondered out loud more to herself than to her sister. "He is the father of the notorious Carlos Calderon heir apparent to Central America."

"Oh my God!" Rachael screamed the light bulb finally going off. "Bobby and Carlos are related?" "They are brothers' Rachael. Identical twin brothers. Same mother and same father. Bobby is a Calderon. The missing heir to the Calderon Empire." Rachael sat in a state of suspended animation before she finally spoke. "He is also the missing link to the Calderon cartel." Rachael reminded her sister. "The same cartel that Dad has been trying to destroy for years."

Once in Belize Bobby started his own secret investigation. After talking to Father Anthony his mission was clear. He had the feeling that the Father knew a lot more about his past than he was revealing so he felt that this was as good a place as any to start.

Bobby had to be extremely careful and this could get very dangerous. He was a stranger on the island and strangers that looked like him did not ask questions in a place like this. Not the kind of questions that he needed to ask. All of their lives could be in jeopardy if his secret got out. He didn't know how to start and there was no one that he could trust not even the good priest.

He had to make positively sure that he did not disclose his identity even though his looks were a dead give away. Bobby had no idea if anyone was still searching for him but he definitely did not want to alert Carlos Calderon of his presence or that he knew their history; their blood connection.

He needed to find out everything he could about the neighboring isle of Calderon, its rightful descendants and what was his place in this intricate puzzle. He also needed to know as much about his rich and powerful father as he could. But most importantly his instincts dictated that he had to get Rosaland back to the America.

He had to keep her out of this web of deceit. He would never forgive himself if something happened to her. This investigation was personal and had nothing to do with her.

There were answers that he needed to make his life whole again. If there were men after him then they would come after her. Suddenly it didn't feel safe for her anymore. There was no telling where this adventure might take him and she needed to be out of the line of fire. This had all become so complicated.

General Prescott A. Reid hit the island like gangbusters. It had been a long time since he had visited this part of the world and his guard was up. He still housed a certain uneasy feeling about Central America. It felt as though he were haunted by the ghost of his past in this country.

The General had his top O.N.S.I. Security Force and the president's secret service agents stationed along all of the major highways leading into Belize City. The island was in an uproar with all the traffic that was bustling in and out. The talk was all around town of the upcoming American wedding. It had been a while since Belize City had seen this much action.

The local authorities and the towns' people had all been notified and were offering their full support and cooperation for the three-day event. In a matter of two days this town was going to host everyone from the head of the Chinese royal family to the president of the United States and many prominent members from the national security arena.

The guest list was long and impressive; a virtual who's who from the intelligence world and the affair was limited to family and close friends. The general had been working day and night since he arrived training his operatives and the local "policia" to be ready for anything. He also recruited a team of insurgents from the hills just to keep an eye on things.

He had the whole island working hand in hand coordinating the new surveillance techniques and methodologies that he would be implementing. The General's intelligence post was state of the art. His command center was established in the old vestibule in the back of the church and staffed with intelligence officers on twenty-four hour shifts.

The activity was feverish and he found it hard to work with over half of his security detail in the wedding party. Father Anthony was happy to accommodate him and his team especially after meeting Bobby; he felt that the General's presence might be warranted.

The General had heavily armed guards placed in every nook and cranny of this foreign environment to ensure the safety of his daughter and her guests. He had every aspect of their stay monitored through international Interpol for security purposes. The General was determined to see that nothing was going to go wrong.

The bridal party started to arrive earlier that same week. There were numerous activities planned for their three-day extravaganza. The excitement was mounting as the lovelies became familiar with their exotic playground.

Bobby and his boys were just as engrossed trying to get small things like lustful bachelor's parties out of the way.

It was extremely hard trying to arrange the sensual fiasco without Rosaland's knowledge. Joke she knew every detail. Everyone on the island told everyone else. The word was out. It was amazing how quickly "word of mouth" spreads. Everyone in the bridal party was having a wonderful time; eating, drinking and basking in the sun as they prepared for the upcoming ceremony.

The bridal party's route had been carefully mapped out to and from the church. The reception was going to be held at the Hacienda de Mystic the most exclusive resort on the island and the one that was in the closest proximity to the church. Also it was the only establishment that featured a marble stair case. A must for the wedding photos.

It was rumored that the Hacienda was owned and operated by the Calderon cartel but that had never been confirmed. Drug lords often used small towns like this as fronts to launder their money. Papa found the owner and his wife very hospitable and was pleased to do business with them. He never suspected any impropriety on their part. The couple had run this resort for years and demonstrated a great deal of pride in their events. Most of the wedding receptions in the town were hosted at the Hacienda, but none of the festivities of the past had ever been this elaborate or this secure.

The General tried to keep everything under his locus of control. It was his duty to provide for his daughter and her guests on her special day and he was going to deliver. He had all of the housing specs to all of the hotels that were providing shelter to the Americans and he knew their entrance and exit protocol by heart so nothing could go wrong.

The night before the wedding Rachael came in to talk to her sister. They had been so busy partying all week that it seemed as though they could never find a minute alone. Rachael was dividing her attention back and forth between Arthur and Rosaland and Rosaland was trying to make sure that Bobby didn't succumb to the hookers at the bachelor party.

She was calling him every 15 minutes to ask "What are you doing?" Rosaland was lying on the bed relaxing in her underwear and mud mask with the phone in her hand when Rachael knocked on the door. Rosaland had her hair tied up and a head full of rollers.

"Hi sweetie can I come in?" Rachael asked as she entered the room handing her sister a glass of champagne mimosa. "Of course you can" Rosaland replied "What are you still doing up?" "Well you know the guys are at the bachelor party" Rachael pouted "and I can't sleep."

"Come in here you" Rosaland said laughingly as she threw a pillow at her sister. Rachael ducked and collapsed on the bed. "Rachael isn't this the most romantic place?" Rosaland asked as she kicked her legs in the air. "Yes it is. It is lovely here. I can see now why Mom loved this place so much. Rosaland how can you sleep in those things?"

"Who's sleeping? My hair is so thick that I thought I would give Doris a head start. At least by tomorrow it should be dry. I want everything to be perfect." "I know how you feel; I remember I felt that exact same way on my wedding day and everything was perfect. Just like it will be for you tomorrow."

Rachael leaned over to kiss her sister's crusty face. "Yeech!" She exclaimed "I hope you don't let Bobby see you in that mess!" "Calm down Bobby is so busy partying I'm sure that I won't see him until tomorrow. Its bad luck for the groom to see the bride the night before the wedding." Rosaland pouted. "Well I'm going to inspect first thing in the morning!" Rachael added as they both burst into laughter.

When Rosaland awoke that morning she had a special feeling. Her wedding day had finally arrived. She was excited beyond all control as she sat up in her bed. Today she would become Mrs. Roberto Semione or Mrs.

Roberto Calderon an event that had been three almost four years in the making.

"Oh my how times flies" She thought to herself as she reminisced back to the first time Bobby made love to her. She couldn't believe how much this day meant to her as the tears began to well up in her eyes. She missed her Mother and wished that she could be here today.

She walked out onto the balcony to allow the early morning sunlight to caress her body. This might be the only moment that she would have to herself so she planned to take advantage of the solitude. She stood basking in the warmth of the sun while overlooking the shoreline and the brilliance of the crystal clear blue water that flooded the coast. The angle at which the rays reflected off the blue prism made the water resemble shimmering liquid diamonds, glistening in the sunlight.

The ceremony was scheduled to begin at sunset. There were still so many preparations to be done and so little time left in which to do them. Rosaland was worried about her flowers. The General had promised to have them on time but they had yet to arrive. He had them picked fresh from Anna's garden and turned into bold gold floral designs for his daughter's special day.

Rosaland's stomach was feeling queasy and she had a slight case of nausea. She attributed her early morning condition to the drinking from last night and didn't give it a second thought. She prayed that by this afternoon she would feel better. She decided to lie back down for another hour or so hoping that this nauseous feeling would pass. At about 10:00a.m. the phone rang. Bobby was surprised to find her still sleeping. He thought that by now she would have been up for hours. He had been up for hours.

"Good morning" she whispered sleepily into the phone. "Good morning beautiful. Are you up?" "Hi Bobby" Rosaland said turning over in the bed. "I can't believe you aren't up yet? I missed you at breakfast. Are you alright?" "I'm fine. Just feeling a little hung over that's all." "I thought that I was the one that should be hung over." He joked.

"I didn't have that much to drink but champagne can have that kind of effect. I'm fine." "Well you had better be. Today is the big day! It's now or never." "You sound just as excited as I am." Rosaland teased. "I am and just as happy" Bobby confessed. "Let's get it on."

Rachael entered the room shortly after Rosaland finished bathing. "I want to spend some time with you before things get hectic" Rachael stated placing the large black velvet box she was carrying on the table. "Good morning" Rosaland smiled as she motioned her into the room.

Rosaland was relaxing with her feet up rubbing her stomach. Rachael could see in her face that she wasn't feeling well. "Rosaland are you alright?"

She inquired "a classic case of pre-wedding jitters that's all." Rosaland replied and shrugged it off.

"Well sweetie this day has certainly taken a while to get here." Rachael smiled lovingly as she kissed her sister "but it has finally arrived. I know that Mom is smiling down on you. She would be so proud. Bobby is a fine man not to mention good looking. You and he have been through a lot to get to this day."

"I don't know of any other couple who could have survived all the obstacles that the two of you have faced." Rachael hugged her sister tight to her heart while she held her hand. "Here" she gestured wiping the tears from her eyes "It's your turn to wear these" Rachael said handing her sister the family jewels. "Mom would want you to wear them."

Rosaland graciously accepted the box and sat down to gaze at the jewelry inside. Both of the sisters were silent for a long time while they bowed their heads in prayer and thoughts of their mother. At that instant there was a knock on the door. Rachael opened it to be handed a large white box containing the most beautiful and exotic golden floral creations.

"They made it on time!" Rachael shouted out hysterically "Thank-you Mom!" She said looking up towards the sky. Rosaland was a little bewildered by Rachael's outburst. "Dad had a little trouble matching your color scheme. He didn't have enough gold roses in the garden and of course you didn't have a second choice.

"He was frantic" she explained "He had to go to at least a dozen florists but look!"Racheal exclaimed "He made it happen!" Rachael put the box down on the counter to examine its contents. "Perfect" Rosaland admired the bouquets. "I love my Father!!" She shouted at the top of her voice.

By this time the day was in full swing. Doris and her team set up her makeshift salon and began to transform the entire bridal party into the belles of the ball. Rosaland and Rachael sat and laughed as they were manicured and pedicured.

Rachael decided to tell her about all the trouble she and her Dad had finding the flowers "You and your gold." She said as she rolled her eyes in her sister's direction. "You always have to be difficult." "Not difficult Rachael, different." Rosaland asserted as she winked her eye.

After the sisters were serviced the rest of the bridesmaids joined in. Instantly the noisy room was filled with the shouts of five half naked women as they talked, laughed, joked and splashed water at the bride. "Not the hair!" Rosaland shouted as she tried to shield her hair from the moisture. Soon the entire bridal party was engaged in a playful water battle.

Rosaland had chosen an exquisite strapless spectacular. The gown was made of gold organza. It featured an intricate design of cascading gold leaves and flowers resembling ivory along the bust line and the hemline which was both detailed in a deeper shade of pure gold. The organza skirt was full and luxurious with a cathedral length train. The bunched waist accentuated Rosaland's shapely figure and featured golden roses at the closing. The ultimate in femininity.

It was the perfect balance of the latest trend from Paris and a classic design. Rosaland paired it with a cathedral length veil that was spun from the purest of sheer golden fibers. The veil was soft, fluid and it flowed gently over her shoulders and beyond the ground.

The jewels in the tiara that set high atop her head matched the elegant gold setting of her mother's necklace, earrings and bracelet to the tee. It couldn't have been coordinated better; it was as though each piece was made for the other.

Rosaland had chosen a deeper shade of metallic gold for Rachael. The gown was made of golden embroidery with a sheer beige tulle lining and a small train. The dress was extremely sexy and fit Rachael's body like a glove drawing attention to her fleshy cleavage and her voluptuous curves. Rachael would never have chosen a gown so revealing for a wedding in a church but Rosaland insisted and Rachael gave in.

Rosaland also insisted that Rachael wear a gold tiara similar to hers from her own private collection with hanging diamond and gold earrings. The diamonds in the choker matched the stones in the earrings to perfection. Rachael never liked borrowing her sister's expensive jewelry but for today she would make an exception.

Rosaland and Rachael were both running around like chickens with their heads cut off when the General poked his head into the room. He was amazed and delighted as he looked for the first time upon his two golden girls. "You both look so beautiful" he said as he placed his hand over his heart. The girls smiled as they welcomed their Father into the room.

"Dad you look awesome" Rosaland shouted out unable to control her emotions. The General was in full dress regalia complete with shining brass accessories, white gloves and a freshly polished side arm. He stood tall and majestic. The epitome of an officer and a gentleman.

"At first I wasn't so sure about the gold" the General admitted to his girls "but seeing you both now you couldn't have made a better selection. You look gorgeous. So elegant both of you. I don't know who's prettier the bride or the bride's maid. Bobby is certainly in for a surprise. Simultaneously both girls kissed their Father on both sides of his cheeks.

"I'm losing my last daughter today" He said quietly hanging his head. "You will never lose me Dad." Rosaland responded with a kiss to the cheek "Or me either" Rachael confirmed with another kiss to the other cheek.

"Rosaland if only Anna were here to see you today." The General sighed feeling the vacant void that had been in his heart ever since her death. At moments like these he really missed her. "She is here Dad. She is here in spirit and she is in our hearts like she is everyday."

The bride slid on her gloves and picked up her lovely golden bouquet as she checked out her image in front of the full length mirror for the final inspection. She dotted on her perfume. Rosaland could hear the music starting downstairs. "It's Showtime!!!" the General announced as he escorted his twin daughters out of the door one on each arm.

Rosaland couldn't believe how nervous she felt. She thought that today would be a walk in the park. They had both waited so long. Her stomach was in knots as she ascended the stairs. Her dream was finally coming true. She felt as though she was the luckiest woman in the world.

eighty-two

Bobby stood masterful as he waited for the ceremony to begin handsomely adorned in Armani from head to toe. The cut on the black satin tux was impeccable and fit his body flawlessly. It was as though it had been hand crafted. The gold in his ascot and vest matched Rosaland's gown to perfection. A gold rose that the General personally pinned on his new son in law accented the tux.

Once the guest had been seated and the wedding party was in attendance the processional began. The bridesmaids were draped in soft shimmering gold; glistening from head to foot escorted by a dashing detail of Armani clad gentlemen all dressed in white and adorned in gold.

Papa and Esmeralda had each been seated on their respective sides of the church. Papa standing proud for Bobby and Esmeralda elated that Rosaland had included her in the ceremony. She too was dressed in light gold. Esmeralda had cared for all three of the children since Anna's death and was touched that they thought of her as Mom.

It had been hard trying to fill the vacancy left by their mother but Esmeralda always did her best to show them love and to give them care. Today she felt that love being returned abundantly. Bobby waited anxiously at the mid point of the alter for his bride to appear; he too was a bit nervous. His single days were over and now it was time to make her his wife. He was truly sorry that it had taken this long.

The organist piped up the processional as the maid of honor marched into the room escorted by her stylish husband. Arthur and Rachael were always such a dashing couple; they really looked good together especially today. Rachael had also been feeling a little lightheaded that morning before the ceremony but she attributed it to the excitement of the day and didn't give it a second thought.

Arthur had never seen Rachael look so beautiful, so alluring or so enticing. He was completely taken by her utter femininity. She was a vision a goddess in metallic gold as she moved gracefully down the aisle in tune with the music. Arthur loved when Rachael dressed sexy and seductive. She was so conservative otherwise.

He loved experiencing this softer side of her. This would truly be a day to remember.

Bobby waited patiently for his bride to enter as Father Anthony and his alter boys began preparations for the candle lighting ceremony. The alter boys moved in an energetic fashion lighting the candles at the pews and then back to the front of the church. There was a great deal of excitement in the air as the guest waited in anticipation for the arrival of the bride. Finally the doors of the church opened and the General stood arm in arm with his lovely daughter resplendent in gold organza.

Bobby's heart skipped a beat as he gazed for the first time upon his lovely bride. Rosaland was breath taking. She was absolutely beaming. She waited for the wedding march the traditional "here comes the bride" to begin as she exuberantly started her march down the aisle.

The guests were awestruck as the cavalier general and the gold and white procession poured into the church. Once the General had escorted the blushing bride half way down the aisle Bobby moved into place next to his girl as they walked the final stretch arm in arm.

Bobby smiled as his father in law turned her hand over to him. "I'll take it from here." He said proudly. Bobby's heart was so touched by her loveliness that he planted a deep passionate kiss on her lips in the presence of God and the entire church; taking her breath away. She was totally captivated by his ardor and his enthusiasm. The roar of the crowd filled the sanctuary as their lips parted. Rosaland smiled as she wiped the lipstick from his mouth.

Bobby hated lipstick and he usually avoided it like the plague. But today she could get away with anything. This was a once in a lifetime affair. Rosaland's eyes started to well up with tears as they moved into position in front of Father Anthony.

Harrison Alexander was the photo journalist assigned to cover the wedding for the New York Times. Harrison started his career at the N.Y.P.D. as a sketch artist and he knew the couple relatively well. Bobby liked working with him. Harrison had eventually graduated into investigative reporting at Bobby's urging.

Harrison had quite a nose for a good story and Bobby thought that he had a very professional eye. Bobby commissioned him to create a personal photographic memento of Rosaland and for Rosaland on this blessed day.

Bobby had followed Harrison's work and he knew that he could capture her in all of her innocence and all of her passion. Bobby wanted photo's that highlighted her beauty. He wanted candid shots that showed her true expressions and that put emphasis on her true emotions. What she was really experiencing. He wanted something different than the usual wedding albums. He wanted Harrison to capture their moment in film. At the precise second that the couple's lips parted Harrison stepped out from his seat and snapped off a series of shots capturing true loves expressions in time.

Harrison knew that in order to fulfill Bobby's wishes and in order to create the type of album that he envisioned he would need to be sharp, stay alert and follow the bride closely for the rest of the event. And thus "The Private Moments" collection was born. Harrison would forever be in Bobby's debt.

Once the bride and the groom became stationary. They turned to each other. The alter boys lowered the house lights and began lighting the candles. They moved expertly through the pews and back to the alter. Instantaneously the cathedral was filled with the warm iridescent glow of the sparkling flames and the faint charming scent of French Vanilla.

As soon as all of the oohs and ahh's died down calm fell over the chapel. Bobby stood quietly contemplating, holding her hands and starring deeply into her eyes. He then openly apologized in full view of the entire church "Baby I should have done this a long time ago. Please forgive me." Rosaland fought desperately to hold back her tears.

Father Anthony conducted the ceremony in a sacred and timely manner. It was just as they had rehearsed. "Marriage is a sacred institution..."the Good Father started as he invited the congregation to join the couple in prayer before they exchanged their own vows.

"Rosaland I have loved you from the first moment I saw you so many years ago. You touched my heart and my life has never been the same" Bobby confessed "We have had our share of good times and bad times. We been through hell these last six months but we made it."

"We are here now together with our families and friends. Those who have stuck by us as a testimonial to our strength and our power as a couple and our love for each other. I am so honored to share the rest of my life with you"

"Do you Roberto Francis take this woman Rosaland Ann for your lawfully wedded wife?" Father Anthony intervened. "I do". "Bobby I love you. Before I met you I was afraid to open myself to anyone but your love changed all of that. You have touched my soul in a way that I never thought possible."

"I am so fortunate to be loved by you. I would be honored to share the rest of my life with you." "Do you Rosaland Ann take this man Roberto Francis for your lawfully wedded husband?" Father Anthony interjected "I do." After that emotional exchange of vows Father Anthony called for the rings.

"The wedding ring is an outward symbol of the inner bond…" he quoted as the couple prepared for their final exchange. Rosaland was astonished when Bobby placed the band on her finger. It was not at all what she had been expecting. Some jewelry speaks louder than words and this was one of those occasions.

Bobby had taken the time to have her band made. She was delighted with the meticulous cut and the color of the stones. The yellow gold setting showcased the 12 princess cut baguettes to harness the ultimate power and the beauty of the light contained within them. The weight of the band impressed her. It was heavy and it had a good feel. It was the perfect match for the 4-carat diamond that she had proudly sported for the last three close to four years.

The inscription inside the band read "Baby I can't do enough…"That was the title of the song they first danced to. It was Bobby's request. She couldn't believe that he remembered. Rosaland would never forget that night. Bobby allowed Rosaland to read the inscription before placing it on her finger. "With this ring I thee wed…" Bobby repeated after Father Anthony as he winked securely at his honey. At this point the battle that Rosaland was desperately fighting to hold back her tears was lost. Harrison snapped another picture as the tears rolled down her face.

Now it was Bobby's turn to receive his band. Rosaland had a surprise in store for him as well. She reached down and pulled the heavy band of gold from the pillow. She smiled as she read the inscription to him. It was still their secret." To Mr. C from Mrs. C. eternally yours." She smiled. She placed the band on his finger. It was made of the same superior yellow gold filigree with 4 superbly cut round diamonds. It was a bit much for the macho detective but it was a perfect match to her own.

When Bobby heard his inscription all he could do was smile and look at her in total amazement. Rosaland winked back at him blew him a wispy kiss and repeated "With this ring I thee wed…"At this point Bobby and Rosaland acknowledged their undying love and pledged eternal faithfulness to each other with a heart felt hug. This part was not in the script. "You look good enough to eat." Bobby whispered softly in her ear. "Promise" she answered back.

The organist blessed them with a most beautiful rendition of "You and I" a classical love song made popular by Mr. Stevie Wonder. Bobby knew her love for rhythm and blues and thought this song to be so appropriate for their ceremony. He had chosen it carefully. There was not a dry eye in the house at the conclusion.

After lighting the unity candle and having another silent moment in prayer the organist offered her second rendition; a soulful version of "Just Because" a popular wedding song recorded by the incomparable Anita Baker. "When I think about how much I'm loving you…"

Her voice filled the air. This song had particular meaning to Rosaland because it explained in words just how she felt about her man. She loved him just because. "You may kiss your bride" Father Anthony announced as Bobby took Rosaland affectionately and longingly in his arms.

The church was in an uproar as they cheered, clapped and whistled at the intensity of the kiss. Passion filled the sultry air that night in the cathedral as Bobby's hands roamed sexily down her body. "Get a room!" Matt shouted as the church exploded in laughter. "With the power vested in me I now pronounce you husband and wife and present to the world Mr. and Mrs. Roberto Semione!"

Father Anthony motioned for the couple to turn and face their guests. They were finally married and the crowd went wild with cheers and applause!!!

eighty-three

The Hacienda De Mystic was the most majestic building in Belize City. It had a very palatial façade and it stood alone high above the city looking down on the inhabitants of this beautiful island. It was the oldest commercial establishment in Belize and it was rumored that the hotel had belonged to the Calderon family for many years.

The story goes that the resort was built to serve as the vacation home for the Calderon cartel. The infamous Jorge Calderon used to entertain his mysterious African American mistress within these walls. It is alleged that Jorge carried on a secret love affair with the wife of a powerful American for many years.

All the elite members of the murderous cartel and their families knew of the forbidden liaison and were welcomed guests at the Hacienda year round. Of course everything and everyone that happened here was kept here especially the affair. If anyone talked about it or even alluded to it they somehow seemed to disappear.

Papa used his contacts in Belize City to arrange for this prestigious location. He had no idea of the rumors or the history that was connected to this notorious place; he knew only that the Hacienda was the finest and probably the safest establishment on the island.

Papa just wanted to add to Bobby's joy. He felt in his heart he had already done enough damage. He should have never held out on Bobby so long. Ultimately he only hoped that his Grandson would someday understand and forgive him.

The General's task force thoroughly investigated the location and they found it to be immaculate. All the surveillance reports came back clean and there were no pending or outstanding threats, debts or investigations connected to the gracious facility.

The General had his NSA team generate a list of all the hacienda employees. They ran complete background checks through BCI and international Interpol. They all came back clean. Almost too clean. There was no clear or present danger to the guests or the events scheduled to be hosted at the Hacienda. There was also no mention of the Calderon cartel on the original charter or deed or their rumored connection to the Hacienda De Mystic.

Rosaland and Bobby kissed all the way to the reception. From the time they entered their limo they were locked in love's mad embrace. Bobby could not believe how incredible she looked and felt and he couldn't wait to take her in his arms. Rosaland responded with the same fever.

She was hot for him that evening and she couldn't wait to feel him buried deep within her body. In all their years together she had never seen him look so commanding, so confident and so at ease. He looked really good. A delicious piece of eye candy.

The newly weds clung to each other sharing yielding kisses until the limo pulled into the circular driveway surrounding the Hacienda De Mystic. Once the couple was escorted inside they were both amazed at the luxury and the elegance of the interior. Designed in the Spanish colonial tradition it was a blend between the old and the new.

Rosaland and Bobby stood awestruck as they glanced around the lobby. The Hacienda featured an enclosed patio that contained a luxurious garden with a magnificent marble fountain. Rosaland stood in complete amazement.

The foyer was a marble menagerie. A fine collection of marble imported from all over Spain and put on exhibit here. The lobby was a remnant of an era past. A decade of wealth and decadence and power that now eluded this particular part of the island. It was as though time stood still.

An elaborate crystal and gold encrusted chandelier hung from the ceiling directly above the reception area. The ornate marble desk was inlayed with polished brass and gold railing. There was an intricate heart shaped mirror at the front desk trimmed in gauche gold edging surrounded by flourishing ivory.

The lobby contained four large circular bay windows with the window sills edged in the same powerful gold inlay. From the windows you could see the orchids dripping from the trees. The piece de resistance, the finishing touch was the looming marble staircase that filled the center of the room. It was an enormous display of old world beauty, art and craftsmanship.

It was beautifully situated so that it would catch the eye of every guest that entered within. "Wow" Rosaland exclaimed as she was taken in by the natural beauty of this enchanting setting. "Wow. How did Papa ever find such a place like this?" She whispered to Bobby in pure amazement as she continued to look around focusing in on the lovely marble staircase. "This place is incredible!" She uttered.

"Mr. and Mrs. Semione?" Jose Ortega the events coordinator greeted them. "Yes" Bobby answered holding Rosaland's hand tightly and extending his other hand to shake with Mr. Ortega. "Let me be the first to welcome you to the Hacienda De Mystic. It is our pleasure to serve such distinguished visitors from America. We have issued an "especial seguridad para el Presidente." Mr. Ortega suddenly lowered his voice. "We have worked secretly with your security team and I can assure you that everything is the best we can offer. Your guests have been seated and are waiting for your arrival."

He motioned to the couple "This way please and oh by the way Mrs. Semione you look absolutely beautiful. You fit right in here. It's as though this room was made for you. Mr. Semione you are a lucky man." Jose smiled as he led them to the reception area.

Rosaland was intrigued as they passed the staircase. It was the most elaborate fixture she had ever seen in her life. It stood tall and majestic in the middle of the grand foyer. It lent the feel of old world Havana back in the days of its opulence and grandeur.

The architect that constructed this was extremely talented. A true visionary. "You like the staircase Mrs. Semione? Jose noticed her fascination. "Oh yes it is beautiful. I have never seen one so beautiful." "You must go and stand on the balcony. It offers the most marvelous view of our humble city." "Yes I will as soon as we have a minute." She assured him.

Once the bride and the groom arrived the festivities started. Everyone clapped and cheered as the pair entered the room. The bridal party was aglow and the first course of the meal was being served. Rosaland noticed how heavily guarded the room was as they made their way to the Diaz.

There were secret service agents crawling out of the woodwork plus the General had added his own team of special agents the wolverines just to make sure that nothing went wrong. After all his daughter was hosting the President of the United States along with his top aides and advisors so he knew that security would be tight. Her own team was in place with Dr. Ekouevi taking the lead.

She and her husband were both so honored that the President chose to stay and participate in the party even if it was a special favor to her father. At the reception Rosaland couldn't take her eyes off of Bobby. She was so smitten like a little pussy in love.

She kept remembering his apology. His true confessions of love at the alter and she thought to herself she should have done this a long time ago.

Why would she put him off so long? But none of that mattered now; from this day on they would be united as one.

Harrison Alexander was lurking in the distance snapping endless rolls of film round after round trying to capture the magic moments, the secret glances and the wordless conversations that the two were sharing heart to heart.

The island setting was sultry and the mood was provocative. All the requisites of the grand and beautiful were here; gigantic mountains, a valley of poetic softness, lakes, volcanoes and a waterfall that marked a silver line down its sides.

Rosaland found the night air intoxicating with raw sensuality. She was beside herself with uncontrollable lust. Her body was on fire and couldn't keep her hands off of her Latin American hunk.

Every time the guests touched their forks to their glasses; Bobby lavished luscious kisses on her sweet lips. There was magic in the air as the guests danced the night away rejoicing both in the beauty of the island and the couple uniting in joy.

As the night rolled on the crowd became intimate. Once Bobby and Rosaland had gotten all the traditional wedding formalities over the party took on a life of its own. Escalating to another level. A more adult level.

The soulful Latin American rhythms filled the room and passion and desire filled the air as bodies bounced and gyrated to the mesmerizing beats. At this point Papa interrupted Rosaland and Bobby from the dance floor and whisk her away from the festivities. Asking her to join him to catch a breathe of fresh air.

Once they were alone Papa pulled her to the side for a chat." I've been waiting to talk to you all day." He started in humbly reaching into his pocket and nervously producing a piece of jewelry with the most precious amber colored stone. It was a unique blend of amber and a beautiful aquamarine; definitely rare.

Papa smiled as he looked for the last time upon the lovely heirloom. "Abuelita wanted you to have this" he said placing the ring on Rosaland's finger. "It's a family treasure; it's from Bobby's mother or father probably both. It was only stones when we got them Abuelita had it made into a ring. She wore it all the time."

"I remember seeing it on her finger the first time I met her." Rosaland interjected. "The stones were hidden; they were stuffed in his clothes when we got him. He had about twenty or thirty of them in this old blue velvet pouch that was pinned to his underclothes." Papa felt relieved. He finally had the chance to clear his conscience. The truth was out.

Papa handed Rosaland the pouch. It was in the original condition. She could see how the years had worn on the faded velvet fabric; she also noticed immediately the Calderon crest that was embedded in the material.

It was the exact same insignia crest or seal that Bobby wore proudly on his arm. It was also the same crest that Carlos arrogantly displayed on his upper arm as well. The connection had been confirmed. Bobby referred to it as his "power center."

Rosaland looked down at her finger only to gasp at its loveliness. "We were amazed when we discovered them." Papa continued "they were the only clue that we had to connect our grandson to his past. Who he was and where he came from." Rosaland looked at the stone immediately sensing the familiarity. "I know this stone." she said half out loud and half to herself as she looked at Papa with curiosity.

"I know this stone" she repeated as she held it next to her necklace. "It's the same stone that is in my mother's jewelry. It's the same stones that are in my mother's necklace!" She was both shocked and amazed.

"Papa I can't accept this." she tried to take the ring off and give it back but Papa stopped her placing his hand on hers in a gesture that said no. "No it's alright. This is for you. Abuelita told me to give this to Bobby's wife and I believe that person is you."

He smiled softly. "What is this stone?" She finally asked when her voice was clear and she could speak. "It's called the Stone of Calderon" he replied before he walked away. Rosaland was overwhelmed; this was the first time this evening that she was sincerely at a loss for words. The tears slowly filled her eyes and began to flow down her face. At this point in the evening her makeup was ruined.

She hugged Papa to her breasts holding him close and then kissed him on his cheek. Afterwards she thanked him for the thoughtfulness of Abuelita. "This is her way of letting us know that she is here with us today." Papa nodded to Rosaland who was in total agreement. "So is my mom. She is definitely here with us today." Rosaland commented to herself looking up at the sky.

After Papa left her she sat down in the garden and starred at the ring. It was rare, expensive and profoundly beautiful. It felt as though it had been made expressly for her. It fit her finger perfectly. A feeling that Rosaland found to be a little unsettling.

As a matter of fact she tried to shake off the goose bumps that appeared on her arms as she felt the eerie cold breeze that passed through the trees. She marveled at the coincidence of the stones being of a similar cut and similar color. "The stone of Calderon" she repeated over and over to herself. How had her mother come into possession of such a unique gem? They were obviously indigenous to this region so where did she get them? And how did she get so many? There were a thousand questions that went through her mind as she sat pondering trying to fit the missing pieces of the puzzle into place.

Rosaland went to search for Bobby. She found him standing on the magnificent marble staircase in the lobby with his head in the clouds. He was starring intensely out onto the balcony lost in thought. Bobby was so caught up in his mind that he didn't hear her approach. Rosaland climbed the steps quietly and stood silently by his side waiting to capture his attention.

"A penny for your thougths"she whispered seductively in his ear. Bobby turned abruptly and grabbed Rosaland taking her strongly in his arms. He planted a soul-stirring kiss on her lips. The kiss was deep, lusty and passionate as their lips locked in an electrifying embrace. A deliberate attempt to excite her libido, to make her blood boil. It was a love thirsty scene right out of a movie. A classic love story.

Harrison Alexander spotted the couple from the court yard below and instantly ran to capture the moment. He snapped rolls and rolls of shots immortalizing this exceptional scene. As a true test to his talents he moved into the perfect position to capture the staircase, the couple and the enduring looks of love that emanated between the two.

"May I please have this dance?" Bobby asked provocatively holding his new wife in his arms. "We don't have any music Rosaland giggled as she snuggled close to accept his invitation. "We can make our own." Bobby winked as their lips locked again.

The balmy night air was intoxicating as Bobby applied tiny steamy kisses to the nape of her neck. Rosaland shivered as she felt his hands remove her necklace and start for the zipper on her gown. "Nice dress" Bobby whispered as he slowly pulled the zipper down teasing her as he continued to apply small titillating kisses down her back.

Rosaland's body gyrated in response to his movements and her signals indicated that she had desirable intentions of her own. The view from their balcony was exquisite. The lake was a surface shining like a sheet of molten silver enclosed by rocks and mountains of every form, some barren and some covered with lush greenery. Down the borders of the lake and apparently inaccessible by land stood the Hacienda De Mystic, situated between two huge volcanoes.

Further down was another volcano and farther still was another, loftier than all of the others, with its summit buried in the clouds. There were fleecy clouds of vapor rising from the bottom, moving up the mountains and the sides of the volcanoes.

At the foot there was a rich plain running down the water, and on the opposite side another immense perpendicular mountain side. In the middle of the plain, buried in foliage and a thick forest of fruit and flower trees, stood the Iglesia de Espirito de Santo Belize, with the spire of the church barely visible. The horizon appeared steep and perpendicular and the view of the mountain-walls was sublime.

The plain formed a triangle with its base on the lake; the two mountain ranges converged to a point and formed a path through a tropical garden. The climate was completely different here and productions that would not grow anywhere else in Central America flourished.

The land was lush with the fragrant scent of pineapples, oranges and lemons. The best fruits of Central America that grew in profusion at the foot of the lake. The sensuous atmosphere was floral, tropical and luxuriant. It would have been magnificent to see a tropical storm, to hear the thunder roll among the mountains and to see the lightening flash down the lake. Bobby thought to himself.

Bobby stood in back of Rosaland grinding as he slowly undressed her. "Nice touch" he mentioned as his eager fingers fumbled at the rose shaped fasteners that cinched the waist of her gown. Rosaland turned to face him as he nibbled salaciously on her earlobes. Once Bobby released the last clasp her gown floated whimsically to the ground.

Bobby carefully guided her feet out so that she wouldn't trip or fall over the very expensive rumpled garment. "Well we finally did it!" He smiled as he slid his tongue deep into her throat. Rosaland opened her mouth as her body started to shiver while Bobby's groin pressed deliciously into hers. Rosaland was lost in his magic as his arms encircled her waist pulling her close. She feverishly responded with an urgency of her own as she wrapped her arms tightly around his strong muscular physique.

"Oh my God Baby. You feel so good" she moaned as she relished the taste of his savory kisses. She could feel his thick meaty flesh spring to life. The shaft growing larger and harder under her amorous titillations. Bobby ran his fingers up and down her curves caressing her shapely tender ass in the palms of his hands. "Oh Baby" he moaned as his body became satiated with lust. Bobby gyrated harder against her as he began applying small nibbles to her neck while his tongue licked down to her heaving breasts.

"Ohh Bobby" she exhaled breathlessly as she allowed her husband to continue his exploration of her most tantalizing attributes. Soon they were caught up in their rapture, their bodies rhythmically in sync with each other as they stood exposed in the shining light of the moon. Bobby picked Rosaland up and carried her over the threshold into the bedroom. He placed her wanton body in the middle of the red satin sheets as he continued to apply sweet breath taking kisses to her full pouting lips.

Rosaland cooed in ecstasy as their two writhing bodies clung to each other. Rosaland clad only in her gold teddy, wedding garter and her crystal sandals while Bobby was still fully dressed with his shirt open.

Bobby wanted nothing more than to rip the shiny garment from her shapely body and take her right then and there but at this point the couple separated. Bobby planned to do this right. He calmly walked over to the night table and popped the cork on the cold bottle of champagne that had been waiting for them after the reception.

"I would like to propose a toast" the groom said proudly to his bride as he poured the cold bubbly into their personally engraved crystal glasses which happened to be a special gift from her father. Rosaland smiled as she accepted her glass. "Wait one minute" she requested as she leaped from the bed and ran to the balcony to retrieve her dress. "Wouldn't want anything to happen to this" she said as she draped the gown over the headrest of the couch. "It cost too much. Now that's better. Where were we?"

"We were just about to drink a toast. Come join me." Bobby motioned for her to come and sit on his lap. "To us Mr. and Mrs. Roberto Calderon" Bobby lifted his eyebrows and his glass "May we always be this happy." "We will Mr. Calderon" Rosaland echoed.

Bobby and Rosaland tipped glasses and then kissed each other. Afterwards they intertwined their arms in a lovers embrace and drank emptying their glasses. Now Bobby was ready to get down to business. "How do you like your new name?" Bobby asked as he began to strip away his clothing.

Rosaland began to recite one of her favorite poems as she watched her sexy husband undress. "Give me your name" she started "Give me your name and I will whisper it into the forest..." she continued as Bobby dropped his pants. "Whisper is right" Bobby joked "Because once your Father finds out we are both dead meat."

"Give me your name and I will spell it out in the sands..." Rosaland continued dreamily as she sipped her champagne.

At this point Bobby was lying next to her on the red satin sheets. "Oh this bed feels good" Bobby commented as he lay back trying to get comfortable. He reached over and put his arm around his new bride. Rosaland curled up next to him smiling happily.

Due to the amount of time they had to prepare for the wedding and the travel to Belize, it had been a while since the two of them had been together. They were both desperately in need of each other. Bobby was whispering enticing words into Rosaland's ear. Words of invitation erotically explaining how he felt about her. How much of a woman she was to him and how much he loved her. His hands started moving along her curves as he pressed his fingers into her inner thighs and moving higher along the sensitive passage to her vibrant honey pot.

He covered her mouth with his again while his hands moved right up to her teddy as he slowly removed it from her delicate body. All that she was left wearing was her garter engraved with both their initials mid way up her thigh from their ceremony.

Rosaland pulled him close and rubbed her beautiful naked body up and down against him. Bobby pressed in and moved his fingers around in her hot wet privacy. Rosaland squirmed and moaned into his mouth as Bobby allowed his tongue to slide down her luscious lips, the delicate nape of her neck, her full voluptuous breasts and the flat of her stomach until he reached his favorite spot. A place that had only been visited by him.

Soon she felt his quivering mouth enter her heaving cavern. Bobby was using his tongue like a deadly weapon deep inside of her delicious orifice. With his other hand he gently massaged her tender fleshy breasts. Rosaland squealed softly. Her nipples tingled and sprouted tautly between his fingers. Her quivering body burned all over as he caressed her in her most private place. Bobby ran his hands up and down her sides reveling in the feel of her silky soft skin.

Rosaland's body was wonderfully smooth. Bobby loved the exotic contrast of her mocha chocolate to his creamy caramel. It was an exciting combination that always left him wanting more. He ran his hands down to the wide full curves of her hips as he continued his salacious assault upon her inner sanctum. Rosaland screamed out in ecstasy as bobby ate her like the tender delicacy that she was.

She cried out in extreme pleasure and delight as his powerful attentions brought her to her first orgasm of the night. The night was just beginning for the newly weds. Rosaland's body was still writhing from the sensual ardor of Bobby's tongue when he entered her creamy wet temple.

His passion was burning high as he slammed his weapon of mass destruction deep into her wanton cave. They both cried out in pleasure from the feel and the force of his insertion as they made their initial connection. "Ohh Bobby I love you" Rosaland whispered barely audible over and over in his ear as he started his lascivious pumping rhythm completing their union. Bobby moaned as he applied sweet kisses to her quivering lips while his motion increased. "Ohh Baby" Bobby moaned as he committed himself to supplying her with pure pleasure. Bobby touched her heart and her soul as she opened up to his loving.

"You like that?" He whispered in his sultry sexy voice as he pushed in harder causing her to tremble with excitement. "Oh Yes. Yes I do" she cried out as her excitement mounted. She had never felt him so wanton or so demanding.

Bobby felt a passionate surge of desire as he touched his lips to her breasts. Rosaland could feel him all through her volcanic delirious body. She exalted in his raw sensuality and he rejoiced in her compliant feminine mystique. The two lovers strove to fulfill their desire as they embraced the night.

Rosaland couldn't remember the last time she felt so happy, so safe and so secure. It was amazing the weight that those two simple words carried. "I do." Now it all seemed so different. They seemed to be so much more connected. For the first time in years she really felt they were one. "Rachael was right" Rosaland thought as she lay comfortably in her husband's arms.

Bobby had his arms and his legs wrapped around her tightly as they bask in the afterglow of their lovemaking. "I love you" they whispered simultaneously while they exchanged steamy kisses their passion running high. "Mmmmm Baby" Bobby moaned.

"Come here and let me give you some more of this good Calderon loving." He smiled seductively as he reached for her. "Good Calderon loving" she repeated breathlessly. "I'll take some more of that" she sighed innocently. Rosaland was surprised that he used his name so proudly, so freely; as she cuddled as close to her man as she could get delicately touching his "power center" with the ball of her finger. Bobby's body convulsed at the feel of her soft probing fingers on his most sensitive spot. It was as if he had been struck by a bolt of pure lightening. The shivers went all through his being.

Rosaland wrapped her arms gently around Bobby's neck "Ohh Bobby. I am so happy" Rosaland cooed sexily as she nibbled on his ear. "I can't believe we finally made it." "Yeah. We have been through hell to get to this point. This road has been rough. Shit damn near impossible." Bobby's mind drifted back to reflect on all the pain and the hurt that they had experienced in the last three years.

"Lying here with you now. The way you look. How good you feel. How wonderful you smell. It was definitely worth the wait." Bobby murmured as his sweat covered physique snuggled closer to hers.

"I love you" she whispered as the tears gently filled her eyes. "And I you" he replied as their lips met in a succulent kiss. Bobby's blood raced; already he found his body tingling with pleasure. All of the worries and the complications of their lives were forgotten at least for now.

Rosaland shivered anxiously. Her deep breath made a purring sound that escaped throatily. She exhaled deeply as she looked up at him and smiled. This was a most tender smile. A smile that brought pure delight to his soul. Bobby's thick meaty manhood was throbbing wildly. Bobby ran his hands along her curvaceous figure as he prepared for his final assault. He slipped his hands under the twin globes of her beautiful ass wiggling her into position.

Rosaland graciously opened her legs in anticipation of her craving cavern being filled to the full thick stem. Pleasure shot all through her at once as Bobby buried his meat deeply to the hilt. Rosaland twisted and shuddered as Bobby drove his powerful hot stinger through her as fast and as hard as he could. Deep inside of her. Both of them panted and groaned their whole bodies shivering with lewd steaming lust.

Bobby plunged back and forth, in and out, again and again, harder and harder, in and out, and in and out. The pleasure burned through Rosaland's body like a lightening rod and she lost all control. All she could do was squirm and scream as Bobby's hard enormous erection claimed her inner honey pot for its own.

Rosaland's eyes closed tight as she would writhe to another wave of incredible passion. "Ohh Bobby" Rosaland moaned over and over again as Bobby strove to satisfy her yearning.

Bobby was amazed at how tight and wet she was. It added steam to his already inextinguishable fire. He plunged and thrust and pumped in exalted ecstasy. His body was on fire and she was burning out of control. Each time his weapon stabbed her waves of sensuous pleasure shot all through her.

Rosaland's nails dug hungrily into his back as he rode her furiously, deliberately and passionately. They grabbed at each other as they continued to engage in their lustful combat. His hands scratched her flesh just as she was doing to him. The night was filled with the sounds of moans and cries of passion.

Bobby made no apologies for his tenacity. He drove his stinger to the full stem with each lunge. Bobby pushed as fast and as hard as he could, deep inside then pulling back fast, screwing around and around, driving in, smacking against the back of her hot, inviting privacy.

Both of them panted and groaned. Their whole bodies shivering with steamy desire. Bobby was making love to her as though it would be the last time. He could never get enough of her and tonight was no different. They clung to each other as if there would be no tomorrow. Rosaland wrapped her long sexy legs around Bobby's thrusting torso, increasing the flow of her own pleasure and allowing him complete penetration of her inner most being.

"Ohh Bobby" Rosaland cried out over and over again. "Ohh Bobby, Bobby!" She uttered breathlessly totally engulfed in his ardor. Still Bobby plunged back and forth, in and out, pushing and pumping while sucking delicious kisses from her quivering lips.

"Is that how you like it?" He moaned as the sweat from his brow fell gently in her face. Rosaland was so caught up in his lust that she could only nod in agreement as her body bounced up and down to his salacious rhythm adding to the intensity of her erotic peak. Bobby's lower half convulsed in the grip of his rising climax. Rosaland meanwhile was already far along in her orgasm.

She writhed and groaned shaking her body one way and her head another. Bobby's gigantic bloated pulsating member plunged harder and harder back and forth with the force and intensity of a bucking stallion. He was hot, she was hot, and the night was incredible as the newly weds consummated their blessed union.

They lay quietly together for a moment their exhausted bodies covered in sweat. Rosaland's head lay against Bobby's as she panted in his ear. He twisted her head slightly and pressed his lips and tongue against the back of her neck. She sighed pleasurably.

"I love you Rosaland and I always will" Bobby said to his wife as they held each other tight. "Bobby look the sun is coming up. Have we been making love all night?" Bobby smiled and pulled her close. "Get ready for round three. We've got all weekend." He whispered seductively in her ear. Rosaland laughed as she nestled her head in his strong muscular chest.

Carlos Calderon and his henchmen had been circling the Hacienda for hours just waiting for the opportune moment to make their move. He would finally teach his meddling brother a lesson. One that Bobby and his new wife would never forget. Carlos smiled deviously as he hatched the final chapter in his well-conceived plan. Both Bobby and Rosaland would pay dearly for all the trouble they had caused him over these last years.

Carlos couldn't believe that Bobby and Rosaland had fallen so easily into his hands. He couldn't have planned it better. Who knew that they would choose Belize for their wedding and the Hacienda for the honeymoon? Bobby's sentimental side would be his downfall. Now all Carlos had to do was watch and wait. Biding his time would be interesting.

His security team had confirmed that the couple planned to be in Belize for the next week so he had all week to gloat and to contemplate his next move. He would teach them to respect him and if they didn't he would destroy them.

Rosaland had been feeling a little queasy by weeks end, but she didn't pay it much attention. She and Bobby had consumed a lot of champagne over the short time period they had been at the Hacienda so she simply thought that was the reason for the uneasiness. She should have paid more attention to her symptoms. She should have listened to her body but she was so caught up in love that she overlooked it.

"Baby come look at this" Bobby motioned for Rosaland to step out on the terrace. "It looks like a thunder storm is heading our way." Bobby pointed to the cloud formations overhead as the two of them stood in the cool breeze "Bobby do we want to be here for a thunder storm?"

Rosaland asked showing a little concern for the approaching bad weather. How bad will it get? "It depends. Sometimes the storms are relatively mild but if it becomes electrical then we are in trouble." "Why?" "Because generally the electrical storms knock out all the power and sometimes it can take days before we can regain service."

"I don't know about the Hacienda. It should sustain the storm but you can never tell and I definitely would not want to be stuck here without any services or any lights."

At this point the rain was gently starting to fall and the night was darkening. Bobby grabbed his wife and kissed her passionately. "What say we leave in the morning?" He coaxed. "Ok." she murmured as she surrendered to his kisses. "As long as I can take you with me."

She wrinkled her nose at him. "You are never going to get rid of me" Bobby teased. "We are in this for the long haul. You and me together forever." It was at this point that they heard the first lethal clap of thunder as they immediately ducked inside their room.

Once inside the rain started to beat down harder. Rosaland called her pilot to arrange for their departure in the morning. She noticed as she talked that the lightening was becoming more frequent and sounding much louder. Bobby comforted her with a drink and his warm body on the bed. "Everything is set; we can leave first thing in the morning." "Sounds good" Bobby agreed.

"Maybe we can take a few days off when we get back to Manhattan" he continued looking at her and smiling sinisterly. Rubbing himself between his legs. "Bobby I swear. You are so nasty. Don't you think about anything else?"

"No not when I'm with you. I can make love to you morning, noon and night and twice on Sunday." They both laughed hysterically as they playfully rolled around on the bed with Rosaland finally ending up on top.

Rosaland's big breast heaved as she rubbed her wet crotch into his. The big piece of meat swayed from side to side as it began growing longer and thicker, its head rising up. She reached down and ran her hand along the hardening shaft. Bobby's body and his hot shaft were already starting to throb.

Bobby was extremely well endowed and Rosaland loved every inch of him. She craved him intensively all the time. "Ummm" she murmured as she continued to play with his enlarging manhood. Her delicate fingers supplying Bobby with pure pleasure. Then she did something out of the ordinary.

She lowered her head and allowed Bobby to fill her mouth with his girth. Bobby moaned loudly as he felt her wet moist mouth around the head. Rosaland exhaled and swallowed more and more of the meaty serpent down her throat. "Ohh Baby" Bobby screamed totally overcome by her luscious sucking sensations. She bobbed her head up and down taking more of the magnificent swollen shaft into her mouth. At this point Bobby was in a supreme state of sexual bliss as he pushed more and more of his enormous head down her throat.

Rosaland gagged and then swallowed as she continued her splendid assault. "I love this woman" Bobby screamed out as he lay back excitedly on the bed and relished in her lusty carnal attentions thrusting forcefully and steadily in and out of her delicious mouth and face.

Rosaland pulled Bobby slow and steady into her craving mouth providing him with the ultimate of oral pleasure. Rosaland altered her body so she was now planted securely in between his legs running her wet tongue between his hairy heavy balls totally offering him complete access to her lascivious tongue and mouth.

Rosaland sucked vigorously until she had taken as much of his swollen head and shaft in her mouth as she could swallow. She sucked him lovingly and energetically, in and out, down to the stem and then back to his full head, expertly applying the ultimate in carnal pleasure.

She enjoyed the way he felt and tasted in her mouth as she gobbled up more taking him deep in her throat to his fully engorged stem. Bobby was completely taken by her lewd sexually aggressive behavior while he reveled in the lecherous moment as he repeatedly grunted and groaned out her name.

"Ohh Baby, Ohh Baby" he grunted out of control "Rosaland, Rosaland!" He screamed as she continued her ongoing assault. She wanted to please him. To pleasure him and to give him a night that he would never forget. She buried her head in his groin pulling and sucking his gigantic hardness deep in her throat like a vacuum.

Bobby had her face stuffed with his rod of rock solid hardness as he continuously fucked in and out of her mouth. All he could see was her head forcefully bobbing back and forth and a look of exalted torture mixed with pure ecstasy on her face. Rosaland wanted to please Bobby. She strove to open her love up to him and she wanted him to feel the depth of her devotion and desire. It had taken what seemed like an eternity for them to get here. To finally be united as man and wife and she relished it. The night was theirs and she was certainly going to enjoy it.

Rosaland could feel Bobby's body starting to shake and quiver. He groaned out loudly as he shifted his position and slowly began to pull out. Rosaland gobbled up more of the tremendous hardened joint in her mouth holding him tightly as Bobby tried to dislodge it and slide it from her throat. He could rapidly feel his explosion approaching and he definitely did not want to finish in her mouth. Not tonight. Tonight he wanted to feel her soul. To revel in her essence and to explode his powerful seed deep into her wet cavern.

Rosaland allowed Bobby to dislodge himself from her face completely only to guide his hot head straight to her luscious privacy. Rosaland held the hard hefty weapon firmly in her grasp as she placed the massive instrument of pleasure at the entrance of her moist cave. Rosaland moaned out loud again as she slid his hugeness into place, taking much of him deep into her slit and belly on the first thrust. She continued to ride him long and hard. Opening up, riding him so completely that she could take him to the hilt. Right down to his fully engorged stem.

"Ooh Bobby" she sighed sexily as they began their pulsating rhythm. Their bodies violently pounding into each other. "I like it when you are brave" Bobby murmured in her ear as he pounded up her with more intensity. Bobby grabbed her delicate waist and rammed her hard directing her movements as he slammed into her. Forcing her to open wider than she had ever been before.

Rosaland held on as if her life depending on it, as she strove to achieve fulfillment. The two of them vigorously engaged as their bodies thrashed about seeking the ultimate in satisfaction. "Ooh Baby I love you" Bobby grunted as he buried himself deeper and deeper causing Rosaland to scream louder as she pushed harder.

Bobby opened her legs wider as he forced more and more of his huge weapon between them. Soon the room was filled with the moans, groans and grunts of carnal combat as the newly weds lustfully clung to each other. Rosaland was on fire. She jumped and bounced up and down on the enormity of his hard rammer.

She moaned and groaned and screamed at the top of her voice as her husband pleasured her and filled her sweat covered body with his desire. Bobby had never felt her so hot or so wanton and he had felt her plenty of times.

Tonight was definitely something special, something unique and something phenomenal as the two of them shared their unbridled passion. They had never been so happy or so fulfilled or so much in love as they relaxed into a sexually induced stupor holding on to each other possessively. Both Bobby and Rosaland could hear the gentle rain as it beat lightly against the window and eventually the two lovers fell into an exhausted sleep.

Later that night Rosaland was awakened by the shattering sound of lightening as it clapped loudly in the distance. The room was filled with a cool chilling breeze. Rosaland walked over to close the open portal and she then jumped back into bed cuddling close to Bobby and settling back into a sound sleep.

The newly weds were up early the next morning partially disturbed by the violent rainstorm that occurred the night before and partially because of their consuming desire for each other. Bobby and Rosaland stood lovingly on the terrace as they looked out over the lush forest that completely surrounded the Hacienda.

"It is so peaceful here" Rosaland said softly as she rested her head on Bobby's strong chest. He held her securely in his arms close to his heart as they stood in silent contemplation. "Bobby this is so wonderful. So private, so secluded. It's better than a dream come true." Bobby nodded in agreement.

"It is nice" he smiled "And the best part is being with you "mi espousa" Bobby locked his arms around her as their lips met in a passionate embrace. "Whoever thought that married life would be so good." he said playfully as the two of them laughed.

The early morning sun was just starting to make its orbit to the top of the sky. It left in its path a golden rainbow that traversed the clouds. The seven colors that it displayed were bright and bold and beautiful in the early morning serenity; each color softly and gently blending into the next.

What a lovely way to start the day Rosaland thought as Bobby slid her gown up over her head leaving her exposed to his tender caress. He pulled her warm chocolata figure aggressively towards him kind of throwing her off balance. Rosaland fell shamelessly and helplessly into his inviting arms.

Bobby loved her smooth mochacina color. She was truly his African American Princess. How could he have been so lucky? He asked himself that question over and over through the years. But whatever the answer, he was happy that it was he. He had been in love with Rosaland for what seemed to be his whole life.

He couldn't even bring himself to think how life was before her. Did he even have a life before her? It all seemed so long ago, ancient history. He was sure that Diana would probably hurt him if she knew the depth of his true feelings, but that was truly how it was for him.

Rosaland was his shit. She was it for him and he loved her that deeply: there would never be anyone else so close to his heart. She was his all. He would never love another, the way he loved her.

Bobby and his lovely wife were thoroughly engrossed in their lovemaking on the balcony when the rain started to fall. At first Rosaland noticed the light mist that fell gently on her heaving breasts and then came the hard larger drops. Bobby tried to no avail to shield her naked body from the pounding of the droplets covering her as much as possible with his strong, muscular physique. Soon he grabbed her up and they both rain for the shelter and the comfort of their room.

Once inside they stood by the window and watched as the winds increased and the trees swayed violently. "This is not looking too good" Bobby uttered in her ear. "We certainly wouldn't want to get caught up in this." He mentioned.

He was planted by the glass door and watched with a great deal of concern as the weather became stormy. The sky blackened as the storm clouds rolled into place blocking the sun. Suddenly their beautiful sunny sky had transformed into a dark cloudy resemblance of itself.

Rosaland reached across the bed grabbed her robe and gently wrapped it around her naked body. The room was a bit breezy. "Baby how about some breakfast? I'll go downstairs and see what I can scrape up." Rosaland nodded as Bobby left the room.

This would be a good time to shower she thought to herself as she went into the bathroom. "Who knows if we will have any hot water after this storm" she thought out loud as she turned on the shower and let the steam fill the room.

Bobby had been all over her that morning and would probably be feeling amorous for the rest of the day, the rest of the week. She smiled to herself. He was so predictably nasty. Now would be a good time to freshen up before he came back upstairs.

Rosaland relaxed leisurely as the warm water ran down her curvaceous form. She carefully prepared herself for a third dose of Bobby's good loving which she knew without a doubt would be either before or after they ate. She took her time as she dressed herself in a sexy, revealing little number. Fully exposing her heavy cleavage which she knew Bobby would like. As she opened the door to leave the bathroom Rosaland felt a powerful, painful blow to her head. First one, then another sending her body sprawling to the floor, knocking her unconscious.

Bobby entered the bedroom singing with a tray of fresh fruits, breakfast rolls and juice. As soon as he stepped into the room he felt the heavy handle of a blunt object come crashing down on the back of his skull. His crumpled body hit the floor hard with a thud.

When Bobby came to his hands and feet were tied and bound. His mouth was taped and he found himself strapped into a chair. As he tried to adjust his eyes he looked over to find Rosaland laid out on the bed in the same condition. Her mouth was taped shut, her hands and feet were bound tight and Carlos Calderon was posted at the head of her bed.

He sat watching her as she lay there squirming on the bed, kicking her tied legs and wrestling with the restraints on her wrists. Rosaland and

Bobby had ruined his east coast distribution center. They had taken down his Bolivian operation and they had caused a great deal of damage to his international operations in both Central and South America. He had lost millions in unrecoverable revenues and now it was time for some payback.

"Well my brother" Carlos spat revengefully as he noticed that Bobby was regaining consciousness. "Detective so we meet again." Bobby was shaking his head trying to open his eyes so he could see exactly what the fuck was going on. He was dazed from the force of the blow as the blood trickled down the side his face. His heart was pounding excessively as he struggled in the chair.

Bobby's eyes were adjusting as he looked around the room trying to figure the way out of what was going on. He saw five heavily armed men, two posted at the door, one by the window and two by either side of the bed. He knew that if he could get his restraints free he could take them all out. He would have to move fast or he and his wife would surely die.

"Ah Bobby" Carlos mocked "Don't you think your wife should dress a little more appropriately for guests?" He sneered referring to the extremely revealing lingerie she was wearing. Bobby could faintly hear Rosaland's muffled screams in the background. He wondered just how long they had been unconscious. The weather had become violent with lightening rolling and crashing in the far distance as the storm loomed.

Bobby looked up again to find Carlos taunting Rosaland by rubbing the barrel of his 44 magnum against her left temple and mockingly pulling the trigger. He was teasing her, punishing her and frightening her with the fear of death. He placed the gun at her head and then made the firing sound "bang" he whispered sadistically in her ear as he tauntingly moved the weapon to this other hand. He then pointed the barrel at her other temple and repeated the motion over and over again.

Rosaland's body was trembling in fear as the frightened tears rolled abundantly down her face. She still had not figured out what was happening? Her head was in incredible pain. But she knew without a doubt who this was and that they both were in grave danger.

At this point Carlos was in complete control. He smiled insidiously as he stepped off the bed and walked over to confront his brother face to face.

"Ah my beloved brother Roberto? Does it shock you to know that you are a Calderon? A true Calderon? One borne from Jorge and Elana?" "Yes my brother I know all about you. I know everything. Even things that your lovely wife doesn't know. I know."

Carlos snatched the tape viciously from Bobby's mouth allowing him to speak. "Carlos have you lost your fucking mind? How dare you touch my wife!!?" Bobby was screaming at the top of his lungs. "You motherfucker.

Don't you hurt her?" "Brother you are in no position to give orders, the only reason you are still alive is because I didn't kill you. Remember that! And FYI I am going to touch her. I am going to touch her everywhere know that" Carlos responded calmly. Almost too calmly.

"You fucking cowardice piece of shit. What kind of man would treat a woman like that? You think that makes you brave. You think that makes you a man? It makes you a fucking pussy!!" Bobby shouted trying to throw Carlos off guard.

Carlos was infuriated at the name calling as he punched Bobby hard in the mouth instantly causing his lip to split, swell up and bleed. Carlos moved in closer and kicked Bobby hard in his midsection.

Bobby doubled over in pain as Carlos kicked him again and again ferociously stomping Bobby into the floor. Bobby's face was bruised and bloody; his eyes were puffy and swollen shut as Carlos stepped back and backhanded his twin brother leaving him in dire pain.

Bobby moved his head feebly trying to shake off the blows as he mumbled. "What has she got to do with this? This is between you and me my brother" Bobby spat back as the blood rolled down his lips.

"Oh she has plenty to do with this" Carlos laughed offhandedly as he walked over to the bed and ripped the bandage from her mouth. Carlos leaned over and viciously planted his tongue down her throat as she jerked her aching head away and gagged in utter disgust.

At this point Rosaland was fully conscious even though her head was pounding severely; she was listening intensely to every word that was being said. "I have a little present for you Mrs. Semione. Something that I think you will find quite interesting." He said cruelly as he pulled the video tape from the table next to the bed where he had been sitting.

"I've had my hands on this for a while and now I feel that this would be a good time to share seeing that we are family and all." Bobby had been looking around trying to determine how he was going to get them out of here. He didn't know what Carlos had in mind but whatever it was he knew that he wasn't going to like it. Bobby noticed a knife that was stuck in an apple close to his feet; it must have fallen off the tray he had brought up from the kitchen.

If he made a move for it one of Carlos's goons would see him. He needed to create a distraction. The one thing that Bobby knew for definite sure was that only one of them was going to leave this room alive. "Ah, the wonders of modern technology" Carlos said flippantly as he inserted the video tape into the player. "Mrs. Semione I want you to pay special attention to this classic that was recorded just for you. When I made this little piece of documented history I definitely had you in mind." He said sarcastically.

Carlos had Rosaland's complete attention. She couldn't imagine what this could be. Bobby was relieved that Carlos had shifted the focus in the room; unwillingly Carlos had created the distraction that would give him the time he needed to escape his bondage. He watched the watchdogs through his swollen eyes as he slowly slid the apple over to his feet carefully concealing the knife with his shoe.

All of a sudden the room was filled with the sound of lusty fucking as the video came to life. Rosaland looked over at the TV to see Bobby's muscular body buried deeply between the legs of Diana. Rosaland immediately looked at Bobby as the hot tears streamed down her face.

"Ohh Bobby!" Diana was repeating loudly over and over again as Bobby plunged to the hilt and fulfilled her lust. Bobby was riding her long and hard, in and out, to the full stem. All Rosaland could hear was Bobby's moaning and Diana's screaming.

Rosaland couldn't take her eyes off of the video as she felt her body starting to go numb. All she could feel was the unbearable amount of pain in her chest. Her body was shaking and aching from the hurt that had consumed her. Her eyes screamed cried out loudly "No, no, no!" again and again. All that could be heard were her hurtful muffled sobs.

When Carlos looked on the bed to see just how crushed she was he smiled. His mission was complete. No matter what happened from this point on they would never be the same. He had made sure of that. He was going to ruin both of their lives the same way they had ruin his. Revenge is a bitch!! And Carlos was having his.

Bobby would never forget the hurt in Rosaland's face as the video played out. He struggled to free himself while the rest of the room was caught up in the moment. Bobby burst into action taking out the man by the door first with the knife.

He then made his way over to the window spinning the goon around so that he took the bullets that were meant for him. Before they knew what had hit them the second man was down.

Bobby grabbed the gun and the man using his body as a shield as he fired point blank into the chest of the third and fourth invader. Turning sharply he shot the fifth bad guy directly in the face and then he steadily aimed his gun at Carlos who still had his gun pressed deeply into Rosaland's head.

"I'll kill her!!" He shouted waiting for Bobby to back down "I'll blow this bitches head off!" He warned again. "Baby are you alright?" Bobby screamed but Rosaland couldn't utter a word. "Shake your head if you are alright" he demanded but Rosaland couldn't move. She was frozen with fear and pain. She just laid there with a 44 pressed into her head.

"Put the gun down or I will blow this bitch away!" Carlos shouted as he pulled back the trigger still pressing the barrel firmly into her temple. "One shot my brother and her brains splatter all over the wall." Carlos said pressing the gun harder into her trembling temple. Bobby knew that he wasn't bluffing. He knew that he was very serious.

At this point Bobby keeping his eyes on Carlos lowered his gun only after seeing the look of terror in Rosaland's eyes. She was petrified; frozen in horror and hurt. All she could feel was the pain of her breaking heart. Nothing else made any sense.

"So you are the missing Calderon my Father spent his whole life searching for!" Carlos argued. "He looked for you high and wide every day in every way. I spent my whole life before his death going in and out of airports and the back alleys of Europe on a never ending journey searching for you." Carlos sneered.

"My Father died on a plane looking for you. He looked so much for you that he forgot about me. His own living breathing son." Carlos had lowered the pistol from Rosaland's shaking head and angrily pointed the gun in Bobby's direction firing twice point blank, hitting Bobby directly in the chest.

Bobby squeezed off a round before he hit the floor that landed in Carlos's shoulder. Rosaland tried to jump up and she tried to scream at the top of her voice. Louder than she had ever screamed before. The salt from her tears burned a path down her face while she desperately tried to reach her fallen husband lying lifeless on the floor.

All she could visualize was Bobby's chest bursting into blood as the bullets penetrated his flesh. Carlos held her fighting, kicking body back harshly trying to restrain her even though his arm was bleeding profusely. The next thing Rosaland felt was the smack of the cold steel barrel smashing into the side of her head as the room went black.

Three weeks later Bobby woke up in a desolate hospital room in Belize. The room was dark and dreary and very much outdated. He was drugged, dazed and his face was extremely bruised from his bout with his infamous brother Carlos.

He had twin IV's running from what seemed in his mind everywhere. His chest was bleeding and bandaged and his ribs were broken. As he looked out at the early morning sky he noticed that it was still raining.

Bobby struggled with his meager surroundings trying to discern exactly where he was and what was more important where was his wife? The lethargic detective tried to sit up but his body was much to sore to accommodate his wishes. The pain was still surging through his chest as the antibiotics flowed through his veins to prevent infection.

"Where is my wife?" He mumbled as the young nurse moved in to check his vitals. Bobby weakly grabbed her arm as he demanded in his harshest Spanish "Where is my wife?" The young nurse shook her head in the negative not knowing and completely not understanding what it was that he wanted. "Where is my wife?" Bobby screamed angrily as the young nurse ran frightened from the room.

Upon watching the nervous girl running hastily out of the room Matthew entered. "Ah Bobby, glad to see you back among the living. It was touch and go for a while." He moved efficiently around the bed focusing his pen light checking Bobby's eyes. Very happy to see that his new brother-in-law had survived.

"Matt. Where is Rosaland?" Bobby questioned hysterically. Frantically ready to jump out of bed and to rip the IV's from his arm. Matt knew that it would be of no use to try to smooth his brother-in law over or to break the news gently not when it came to his girl, so matt let loose.

"Bobby we don't know where Rosaland is? When we got to the Hacienda you were lying in a pool of blood close to death and Rosaland was gone." Bobby sat straight up in the bed "What do you mean gone. Is she dead?" He questioned defensively trying to put two and two together.

Matt shook his head sorrowfully "Gone Bobby vanished, kidnapped, taken missing without a trace? We don't know if she is dead?" He cried softly as he hung his head.

Bobby jerked his body and sat up starring out of the window in disbelief as the hot tears ran down his face…

THE END

Printed in the United States
49129LVS00003B/52-126